10-43

SET THIS HOUSE ON FIRE

SET
THIS HOUSE
ON FIRE

WILLIAM STYRON

Random House
New York

That of that providence of God, that studies the life of every weed, and worme, and ant, and spider, and toad, and viper, there should never, never any beame flow out upon me; that that God, who looked upon me, when I was nothing, and called me when I was not, as though I had been, out of the womb and depth of darknesse, will not looke upon me now, when, though a miserable, and a banished, and a damned creature, yet I am his creature still, and contribute something to his glory, even in my damnation; that that God, who hath often looked upon me in my foulest unclean-nesse, and when I had shut out the eye of the day, the Sunne, and the eye of the night, the Taper, and the eyes of all the world, with cur-taines and windowes and doores, did yet see me, and see me in mercy, by making me see that he saw me, and sometimes brought me to a present remorse, and (for that time) to a forbearing of that sinne, should so turne himselfe from me, to his glorious Saints and Angels, as that no Saint nor Angel, nor Christ Jesus himselfe, should ever pray him to looke towards me, never remember him, that such a soule there is; that that God, who hath so often said to my soule, *Quare morieris?* Why wilt thou die? and so often sworne to my soule, *Vivit Dominus,* As the Lord liveth, I would not have thee dye, but live, will nether let me dye, nor let me live, but dye an everlasting life, and live an everlasting death; that that God, who, when he could not get into me, by standing, and knocking, by his ordinary meanes of entring, by his Word, his mercies, hath applied his judgements, and shaked the house, this body, with agues and palsies, and set this house on fire, with fevers and calentures, and frighted the Master of the house, my soule, with horrors, and heavy apprehensions, and so made an entrance into me; That that God should frustrate all his owne purposes and practises upon me, and leave me, and cast me away, as though I had cost him nothing, that this God at last, should let this soule goe away, as a smoake, as a vapour, as a bubble, and that then this soule cannot be a smoake, a vapour, nor a bubble, but must lie in darknesse, as long as the Lord of light is light it selfe, and never sparke of that light reach to my soul; What Tophet is not Paradise, what Brimstone is not Amber, what gnashing is not a comfort, what gnawing of the worme is not a tickling, what torment is not a marriage bed to this damnation, to be secluded eternally, eternally, eternally from the sight of God?

JOHN DONNE, Dean of St. Paul's,

"To the Earle of Carlile, and his Company, at Sion"

PART ONE

I

Sambuco.

Of the drive from Salerno to Sambuco, Nagel's *Italy* has this to say: "The road is hewn nearly the whole way in the cliffs of the coast. An evervaried panorama unfolds before our eyes, with continual views of an azure sea, imposing cliffs, and deep gorges. We leave Salerno by Via Independenza. The road turns toward the sea, looking down on *Marina di Vietri*. On regaining the coast we enjoy a glorious view of Salerno, Marina di Vietri, the two rocks (*Due Fratelli*) and Raito. Beyond a side turning we enjoy a sudden view of the colourful village of *Cetara* (4½ m.). We return to the sea and then make a retour round the grim ravine of Erchie, approaching the sea again at Cape Tomolo. Passing through a defile with high rocky walls, we come in sight of

Minori and Atrani with *Sambuco* high above them. The road diverges beyond Atrani and ascends the Dragone Valley."

About Sambuco itself Nagel's is characteristically lyric: "(1033 ft.) a little town of unusual appearance in an extremely beautiful landscape; the contrast between its lonely situation and its seductive setting, between the ruin of its ancient palaces and the gaiety of its gardens, is very impressive. Built in the 9th cent. under the rule of Amalfi, Sambuco enjoyed great prosperity in the 13th cent."

Sambuco, indeed, is no longer prosperous, although because of its geographical position it is undoubtedly better off than most Italian villages. Aloof upon its precipice, remote and beautifully difficult of access, it is a model of invulnerability and it is certainly one of the few towns in Italy which remain untouched by recent bombs and invasions. Had Sambuco ever lain upon a strategic route to anywhere it might not have been so lucky and at one time or another might have found itself, like Monte Cassino, crushed in ugly devastation. But the affairs of war have left the place intact, almost unnoticed, so that its homes and churches and courtyards, corroded as they may be by poverty, seem when compared to other towns of the region to be proudly, even unfairly, preserved, like someone fit and sturdy among a group of maimed, wasted veterans. Possibly it was just this remoteness, this unacquaintance with war and with the miserable acts of violence which are its natural aftermath, that made the events of that recent summer seem to everyone so awesome and shocking.

Lest from the above I be accused at the outset of sounding too portentous, I will say that these events were a murder and a rape which ended, too, in death, along with a series of other incidents not so violent yet grim and distressing. They took place, or at least had their origins, at the Palazzo d'Affitto (". . . a curious group of Arab-Norman structures rendered specially picturesque and evocative by the luxurious vegetation by which they are framed. The garden-terrace commands a wonderful panorama.") and they involved more than a few of the townspeople and at least three Americans. One of these Americans, Mason Flagg, is now dead. Another, Cass Kinsolving, is alive and flourishing, and if this story has a hero it is he, I suppose, who fits the part. It is certainly not myself.

My name is Peter Leverett. I am white, Protestant, Anglo-Saxon, Virginia-bred, just past thirty, in good health, tolerable enough looking though possessing no romantic glint or cast, given to orderly habits, more than commonly inquisitive, and strongly sexed—though this is a conceit peculiar to all normal young men. I have lived and worked for the past few years in New York. It is with neither pride nor distress that I confess that—in the idiom of our time—I am something of a square. By profession I am a lawyer. I am ambitious enough to wish to succeed at my trade, but I am no go-getter and, being constitutionally unable to scrabble and connive, I suspect that I shall remain at that decent, mediocre level of attainment common to all my ancestors, on both branches of the tree. This is not, on the one hand, cynicism, nor is it, on the other, self-abasement. I am a realist, and I wish to tell you on good authority that the law—even in my drab province, where only torts, wills, and contracts are at stake—demands as much simple deviousness, as much shouldering-aside of good friends, as any other business. No, I am not up to it. I am stuck, so to speak, with my destiny and I am making the pleasant best of it. While maybe not as satisfying as the role of the composer I once had an idea I might try to play, it is more than several times as lucrative; besides, in America no one listens to composers, while the law, in a way that is at once subtle and majestic and fascinating, still works its own music upon the minds of men. Or at least I hope to think so.

A few years ago, when I came back from Italy and Sambuco and took a job in a New York firm (somewhat second-rate, I must admit, and not on Wall Street yet laggardly nearby, which caused our office wits to suggest the slogan "Walk a block and save")— several years ago I found myself in a really rather bad state. The death of a friend—especially under the circumstances that befell Mason Flagg, even more especially when one has been on the scene, witnessed the blood and the tumult and the shambles—is not something that can be shaken off easily at all. And this applies even when, as in my case, I had thought myself alienated from Mason and all that he stood for. I will come to Mason's ending presently, and it will be described, I hope, in all its necessary truth; for the moment let me say only that it left me quite desperately stunned.

During that time I had incessant dreams of treachery and betrayal—dreams that lingered all day long. One of them especially I remember; like most fierce nightmares it had the habit of coming back again and again. In this one I was in a house somewhere, trying to sleep; it was dead of night, wintry and storming. Suddenly I heard a noise at the window, a sinister sound, distinct from the tumult of the rain and the wind. I looked outside and saw a shadow

—the figure of someone who moved, an indefinite shape, a prowler whose dark form slunk toward me menacingly. Panicky, I reached for the telephone, to call the friend who lived nearby (my best, last, dearest friend; nightmares deal in superlatives and magnitudes); *he,* somehow, I knew, was the only one dear enough, close enough, to help me. But there was no answer to all my frantic ringing. Then, putting the phone down, I heard a *tap-tap-tap*ping at the window and turned to see—bared with the malignity of a fiend behind the streaming glass—the baleful, murderous face of that selfsame friend. . . .

Who had betrayed me? Whom had I betrayed? I did not know, but I was sure that it all had something to do with Sambuco. And although I felt little grief over Mason's end—I want to make that clear right now—I still felt low, miserably low over what had happened in that Italian town. Now, looking back on it, I can see that maybe it was only because my most unhappy suspicion was this: that though I was in no way the cause of Mason's death, I might have been in a position to prevent it.

Nature of course has a way of dealing with even our most heartless despondencies. Gradually, so imperceptibly that I was hardly aware that it was happening, my memories began to blur and dim, and it was not too long before I was feeling almost normal. After a few months I even became engaged. Her name was Annette, and she was beautiful and rich, besides.

Yet if my gloom had pretty much disappeared, my wonder and curiosity had not. I knew that what was left of Mason, many months before, had been sent back from the Italy he loathed, and now rested—if even a dead Mason could be said to be at rest— somewhere in American soil. Rye, New York, I believe, but it doesn't matter. I knew that the Italian girl he had been accused of raping and beating had also died (I had seen her for several seconds that night, and she had been beautiful in a complete and stunning way, which I think accounted for much of my later distress). And I knew that the case—the *tragedia,* the Naples papers had called it—was closed, there being little aftermath for snoops and gossips and the simply curious to feed upon when the two principals were so firmly and decisively dead. Even the New York papers had given the story small play, I discovered—and this in spite of the Flagg name with its more or less glamorous attachments—possibly because Sambuco was, after all, a faraway place, but more likely because no one remained to expose his shame and guilt to the vulturous limelight. So, save for the exceptional fact that I had been in Sambuco at the time, in many ways I knew no more about the horrifying mess than the lowliest straphanger.

Except that I *did* know something, and this was what continued to bother me, and long after the time of those funereal blues I have just described. I did know something, and if that something was not much, if it was more in the nature of a strong suspicion than anything else, then it only served to keep my puzzlement and curiosity alive for a year or more. Even this curiosity would doubtless have passed from my mind had it not been for a cartoon I saw one Sunday in the New York *Times*. . . .

Anyone who has ever lived alone in a New York apartment knows or remembers the special quality of a Sunday. The slow, late awakening in the midst of a city suddenly and preposterously still, the coffee cups and the mountainous tons of newspapers, the sense of indolence and boredom, and the back yards, sunlit, where slit-eyed cats undulate along fences and pigeons wheel about, and a church bell lets fall its chimes upon the quiet, hopelessly and sadly. It is a time of real torpor, but a time too of a vague yet unfaltering itch and uneasiness—over what I have never been able to figure out, unless because in this most public of cities one's privacy is momentarily enforced and those old questions *What am I doing? Where am I going?* are insistent in a way they could never be on a Monday. The particular Sunday of which I am speaking was in the late spring of the year, a bad time for introspection. My girl was visiting her parents up in Pound Ridge, my friends were either away or indisposed, and I had buttoned up my collar in preparation for a lonely walk in Washington Square, when in the most idle fashion possible I picked up the editorial section of the *Times*. Perhaps again that early afternoon I had been thinking of Sambuco, stirring up old sorrows and regrets, and several futile recriminations. I am not sure, but I do know that when I saw the cartoon, and the signature, unmistakable, beneath it—C. *Kinsolving* —my heart leaped and I was wrenched backward in time toward Sambuco—hurried through memory, weightless, like a leaf. The whole thing poured over me again, but without the horror this time, without the sweats. I did not go out that afternoon. I studied the cartoon—it had been reprinted from a newspaper in Charleston, South Carolina. I studied the cartoon and the signature, and I paced up and down, making my gums sore with cigarette after cigarette, gazing out into the quiet Sabbath gardens (pretty soon there will be no more gardens in the Village) at the pigeons and

7

the beer drinkers in sport shirts and the prowling cats. At last when dusk began to fall and the chink of supper dishes sounded across the way, I sat down and wrote Cass a letter. It was midnight when I was finished. I had not eaten and I was utterly worn out. Shortly after one o'clock I went out to the White Tower on Greenwich Avenue and had a couple of hamburgers. On the way back I mailed the letter, which was less a letter than a document and which I addressed to Cass in care of the paper in Charleston.

The reply was a long time in coming. A month went by, then several weeks more, and I was on the verge of screwing up the nerve to write another letter when, sometime in July, I received an answer:

Dear Peter,

Naturally I remember you & was delighted to hear from you again. You were right, I dont guess there are many C. Kinsolvings. Glad you liked my cartoon & consider it fortunate that you ran across it in the Times if for no other reason than it prompted you to get in touch with me & write such a good letter. Im right proud of that cartoon which I think, despite my contempt for politics in general, took a good swat at D.C. hypocrisy. In regard to your question, these cartoons are gravy and not my actual metier, since I work half days at a cigar factory here in C'ton, & also teach a painting class though things go a bit slack both ways toward the end of Summer. However I dont look down on cartooning, who knows but whether its the American Art Form (not kidding), anyway consider myself in a direct line of descent from Daumier and Rowlandson & besides I get 35 bucks a piece & sometimes more, which as they say is not sparrow food. Also Poppy has a job sort of book keeping at the Navy yard & we have a very good coloured woman for the kids when theyre not at school so though maybe we are not eating as high off the hog as that other eminent Carolinian, B. Baruch, we are doing alright. Also, am painting in all my spare time & all that paralyzing death of the soul you must have seen is pretty much gone.

Peter, always wanted to thank you for what you did in Sambuco for Poppy & all. She told me everything you did & now I should apologize, using the weak excuse that I didnt know how to contact you in N.Y.C. But this would be a lie, so will only say now thanks again & trust you to understand.

Also, I can understand very well your interest in M. & your desire to know more of the situation down there in Sambuco. Myself I find it most difficult to talk or even think about M. & what went on, much less write about it. Yet its funny you know, just as you say youre in the dark about what happened in Sambuco, so from time to time I keep wondering who M. was, I mean really WAS & what was eating him & how he ended up the way he did. I dont guess anybody will figure that out & suspect that its all for the best any way you look at it. You are right in "surmising" that I had a rough time down there. I guess I drew pretty close to what is commonly described as the brink, but I seem to be O.K. now. Have not incidentally had a drop of beer, even, in going on to 2 years. It makes Sophocles much easier to read, and am now beginning to work my way straight through Shakespeare, making up at this advanced age for the deprivations of the U.S. public school system.

Anytime youre down this way, Peter, let me know. We live near the Battery in a 200-year-old house which doesnt rent for much & theres plenty room for a guest. Poppy remembers you with affection, also the kids.

Molti auguri
Cass

I have never had much faith in that "Any time you're down this way"—having used it several times myself in sticky situations when the true sentiment behind the phrase was all too apparent. It is polite and it is friendly, but it certainly does not plead or exhort. It is not the same as "It would be nice to see you again," and it is as far removed from "Please come see me, I miss you" as simple civility is from love. There was some quality in this letter of Cass', though, that made me believe that he would not take unkindly to a visit from me—actually, as regarding Mason, that he might even be as eager to see me as I was him. I had three weeks' vacation due me in September. The first of these weeks I had planned to spend with my girl Annette (there is something foregone and conclusive about that word fiancée) in the White Mountains. The other two I had left aside for a visit with my parents down in Virginia: they were both old and ailing and, while we have never really been as close as some families, something weary and sorrowful in their letters made me long to see them again. What I proposed to do, then—and this I wrote Cass right away—was to discommode him to the extent of spending a week end with him in Charleston, flying down from Norfolk sometime during the visit with my parents. I would not expect to stay at his house, despite the implied invitation. Would such and such a week end be all right? Would he get me a room in a hotel? It should in no way have surprised me, I suppose, but it did: I got no answer from Cass at all.

The time spent in New Hampshire with my dazzling Annette was a total and sweeping catastrophe. I will deal with it only to the extent of saying that it rained, that we lasted two days, and that when we left our mountain cabin in a downpour we were unbe-trothed. There were no sexual difficulties. We were just not meant for each other, we decided. Both of us put up a brave front about it all, but a love affair, like some prodigy of plastic surgery, is flesh laid on to living flesh and to break it up is to tear off great hunks and parts of yourself. I went down to Virginia feeling mournful, grim, indescribably bereft.

Of my sojourn in Virginia, however, there is a little bit more to say. Nothing in America remains fixed for long, but my old home town, Port Warwick, had grown vaster and more streamlined and clownish-looking than I thought a decent southern town could ever become. To be sure, it had always been a shipbuilding city and a seaport (visualize Tampa, Pensacola, or the rusty waterfront of Galveston; if you've never seen these, Perth Amboy will do), and in official propaganda it had never been listed as one of the orna-ments of the commonwealth, but as a boy I had known its gentle seaside charm, and had smelled the ocean wind, and had lolled un-derneath giant magnolias and had watched streaked and dingy freighters putting out to sea and, in short, had shaken loose for my-self the town's own peculiar romance. Now the magnolias had been hacked down to make room for a highway along the shore; there were noisy shopping plazas everywhere, blue with exhaust and rimmed with supermarkets; television roosted upon acre after acre of split-level rooftops and, almost worst of all, the ferryboats to Norfolk, those low-slung smoke-belching tubs which had always possessed their own incomparable dumpy glamour, were gone, re-placed by a Yankee-built vehicular tunnel which poked its foul white snout two miles beneath the mud of Hampton Roads. Hectic and hustling, throbbing with prosperity, filled with nomads and the rootless and the uprooted (*"Upstarts,"* my father said. "Son, you're watching the decline of the West."), the town seemed at once as strange to me yet as sharply familiar as some place on the order of Bridgeport or Yonkers. And, unhelmed, touched with anxiety, smitten with a sense of dislocation I have rarely felt so achingly before or since, I knew I could not stay there long; the fact is, I almost left on the same day I arrived, when, that evening, hunting in vague panic for a familiar scene, I wandered down to the river in the soft September dusk and instead of the broad, grassy field I had known so well (the "Casino" it had been called, shadowy at twilight with rustling sycamores, where there was a bandstand and a river view of the wide warm old James, mirroring stars: here we played baseball in the fading light and here, too, shirt-sleeved Negroes hawked peanuts and deviled crabs, until at last the tootling of clarinets faded and died, and all shut down, and lovers walked beneath the trees to the sound of sycamore balls plopping earthward in the stillness and the whistle of a freighter seaward-borne in the dark) I found a snarling Greyhound bus station and a curious squat lozenge-shaped building, greenly tiled, whose occupants numbered among them a chiropodist, a lay analyst and—of all things to tell about the fading South—an office full of public-relations counselors, or consultants.

But this is too familiar to go on about at length. In America our landmarks and our boundaries merge, shift, and change quicker than we can tell: one day we feel rooted, and the carpet of our experience is a familiar thing upon which we securely stand. Then, as if by some conjuring trick, it is all yanked out from beneath us, and when we come down we alight upon—what? The same old street, to be sure. But where it once had the solid resounding sound of Bankhead Magruder Avenue—dear to all those who remember that soldier who stalemated McClellan—now it is called Buena Vista Terrace ("It's the California influence," my father complained, "it's going to get us all in the end."); an all-engulfing billboard across the way (the zoning laws have collapsed; we used to swing on grapevines there, in the ferny mornings) tells us to "Listen to Jack Avery, the Tidewater's Favorite Disk Jockey," and though we are obscurely moved by intimations of growth, of advancement, we feel hollow and downcast. Nor is our nostalgia misplaced. Only fools lament change in itself, but in this "pillaged town," as my father called it, there was many a fool who on his deathbed would protest his innocence of total rape. " 'Bring back the greenery, bring back the leaves!' That's what they're going to holler," my father said. "That's what they're going to holler when the light dims. And all they're going to get is this here Avery."

It must have been on the afternoon of my fourth or fifth day in Port Warwick that my father, retired now from the shipyard, took me for a long ride around town in his car. We traveled all the old avenues, many of them strange to me now (the largest and most venerable trees seem to be the first victims of a municipal renascence: not only the magnolias but the oaks and elms had fallen, in a process of rebuilding that made way for, among other things, the first Bauhaus-inspired Pentecostal Holiness church in Dixie), and we had beer and pigs' knuckles behind the flyspecked glass of Jake Eisenman's grill, which alone amid the Laundromats and Serv-ur-Selfs and Howard Johnsons resisted change, resisted neon and plastic and chrome, resisted sanitation and a new clientele (the old young gang was still at it, sallow-faced and now balding amid the pool cues and the verdigris-tinged spittoons, still yacking about poontang and pussy, white and dark, though now also about that contortionist legal maneuver, the pride of Byrd-land, called inter*po*sition, which would surely keep the niggers in their place), and afterwards, a touch beery and afloat in the bright September heat, we made a brief circuit of the harbor and drove slowly alongside the blue and spectacular bay. It was a clear day, slightly hazed far out where gray gigantic cruisers and tankers rode at anchor, but salt-smelling, transparent and magical, white with sparkling gulls. We went past a beach where muddy-legged boys were out digging clams, and children played on the sand within reach of plump bandannaed mothers, suntan-oiled and glistening like seals. A motorboat, soundless upon the far reaches of the water, cleft the tide between twin silver parabolas of spray. For a brief instant pleasurably lost, I felt caught up in a reverie of years long past— flapping sails and smell of tar and clamshells cool and gritty in the hand—which changeless childhood seascape, even here, even now, seemed to elude and deny the marauding clutch of progress. A stoplight halted us, precipitately: it was the old man's spine-chilling knack always to slam on the brakes thus, with no margin for error and at the last moment of truth.

And as we stopped there, he said: "Son, you've been mighty down in the mouth since you've been home. What's the matter? Woman trouble?"

What could I tell him? Yes and no; it was woman trouble, but it was some other trouble more profound and unsettling which was at the root of *that,* and, having told no one else about Sambuco, I could not force myself to speak to him about it, either. I murmured something about the humidity.

Then (psychic weatherman) he said: "I know. I know, Peter. These are miserable times." The light changed and we heaved forth with a lurch. "They are miserable times. Empty times. Mediocre times. You can almost sniff the rot in the air. And what is more, they are going to get worse. Do you know that? Read Carlyle. Read Gibbon. Get times like these when men go whoring off after false gods, and the fourth or fifth best is best, and newness and slickness and thrills are all—and what do you come to at last? Moral and spiritual anarchy, that's what. Then political anarchy. Then what? Dictatorship! We've already *got one* in this state," he added, and spat out the name of that proconsul of the commonwealth whose works had kept him in a state of tense outrage for thirty years.

Rare and prodigious man, my father. Had he been born in the North I think he might very well have been an old-style radical. As it was—a good Episcopalian, whose circumstances had located him within the purlieus of the most stiff-necked parish this side of Canterbury—he had managed to work out a shaky compromise between his honest piety, on the one hand, and his enlarged human views, on the other, and the resulting tension had helped to make him the only true liberal I think I have ever known. To be one of this breed in New York is childishly simple; to be one in the South surpasses all ordinary guts. He had thirsted for understanding, for wisdom, in the same way that others yearn for money or prestige, and I think that at last he had found a large measure of both. He was one of the few men in Port Warwick who had ever read a book. Age had bowed and shrunken him a bit, but not life, and he had grown larger and larger in my eyes. I have never known a more decent man, and if during these later years he became here and there cranky or sententious or overtalkative, I could understand it, knowing that the hypocrisy and meanness at which he raged had become too much even for a man of his size. "Son, life is a search for justice," this old draftsman told me once, betraying not a flicker of self-consciousness at the immeasurable phrase. I know now that he never found it, but perhaps that matters less than that he moved through dooms of love, through griefs of joy, in his lonely seeking.

"I guess I've near about become a pariah in this town, Peter," he went on (we had been in second gear for two blocks and I had to nudge him to change it); "I guess I run off at the mouth too much, but I've been trying to tell these people the truth for going on to forty years now. And what happens? *Here's* what happens. Along comes this ignorant general with a baby-faced smile, who *acquires* religion and reads cowboy stories, and they vote him into office. When who was it that got them their nice houses and got them their Buicks in the first place? It wasn't any general. It was Franklin Roosevelt, *that's* who it was, whose principles and desire for a better way of life they repudiate as soon as five stars and a big grin comes along, promising them that they'll be all right, they'll never have to relinquish those gadgets and gimcracks they're tied to like an umbilical cord, and they can remain fat cats forever, getting softer and more silly and stupider as the years pile up. And to top it all, that isn't enough for them. They want everything. So on the state level they'll still vote in year after year this millionaire apple farmer who guarantees them good roads and miserable schools and above all that the nigro will never get an even break. Ahh!" he said, grim lips set as he shook his head. "Sometimes I think the Stoics were right, maybe. A good way out is to cut your throat, if you've got to."

I paid attention, turning my eyes from the bay. There was something restorative, clean—during an era of surfeit and silence —in hearing this renegade old man at the top of his wrath.

"No, I just won't talk to them any more," he said conclusively. "Nossir, they've heard the last word from Alfred Leverett, and they can go to hell in a Cadillac for all I care. I'm through with them all!" He grew red as a lobster, and he belched thunderously, and I feared for his heart.

For a while we drove in silence. Billowing white storm clouds loomed up on the far horizon, high up over the Eastern Shore, and a spindrift gray beard of rain swirled beneath them, unloosed in smoky tatters upon the sea. A white sail tilted far out, almost flattened upon the water, came erect slowly and gracefully as the cat's paw passed, corrugating the blue. And now the car, a 1948 Hudson Hornet tottering toward senescence, had begun to set up a threatful cricketing noise somewhere deep within its vitals (I had noticed it faintly the day before), but my father, brooding still like some Jeremiah reduced to the very ash of impotence and gloom, squinted into the setting sun and paid no heed to the racket. He was a vestryman of the church. His shoulders were stooped. He wore bifocals and his nose was skinny and beaked. I saw his lips struggle and form a soundless syllable. Then just a fledgling, tentative whisper it became: *scum.*

"Sometimes I think this is just a nation of children," he said, "of childish little minds. Now that Supreme Court didn't have no more right to do what it did than I would have in telling an A-rab or a Chinaman how to run his life. It was a dumb poor thing they did, the way they did it anyway. And everyone's going to suffer and suffer because of it. But these people down here—they don't realize that the nigro has *got* to get his just payment, for all those years of bondage. Look out there, son." He waved toward the sparkling water. "That's where they came in, in the year 1619. Right out there. It was one of the saddest days in the history of man, and I mean black *or* white. We're still paying for that day, and we'll be paying for it from here right on out. And there'll be blood shed, and tears." He mopped his brow. I turned my eyes eastward. A cloud passed across the day, then all was clear again, and for an instant I thought I could see those Dutch galleons, with their black bound cargo, lumbering up toward the muddy James.

"Watch out!" I cried. He had come close to running us into a ditch. Gusts of hot dust flooded through the car, and the bird calls beneath the hood became abruptly more chaotic and sick.

"What this country needs," he went on, regaining command, "what this great land of ours needs is something to happen to it. Something ferocious and tragic, like what happened to Jericho or the cities of the plain—something terrible I mean, son, so that when the people have been through hellfire and the crucible, and have suffered agony enough and grief, they'll be men again, human beings, not a bunch of smug contented hogs rooting at the trough. Ciphers without mind or soul or heart. Soap peddlers! No, I mean it, son, these are miserable times and I've seen all of them. We've sold our birthright, and old Tom Jefferson is spinning in his grave. We've sold out, right down to the garters, and you know what we've sold out for? A bunch of chromium junk from Detroit put together with chewing gum and spit!" Flushing and sweating, he jammed at the floor board with his foot. "Listen to the noisy junk, will you? Absolute unregenerate shameless piece of junk." He stamped at the floor board again. "What do you imagine's wrong with it?" he said in a querulous tone.

"Sounds like you might need new rings," I said, mustering a fake *expertise*.

"Nossir," he said, "we've got to start from scratch again, build from the ground floor up. What has happened to this country would shame the Roman Empire at its lowest ebb. The founding fathers had noble dreams, you know, and for a while I guess they were almost fulfilled. Except maybe for the nigro, the common man found freedom in a way he never knew or dreamed of—freedom, and a full belly, and a right to pursue his own way of happiness. I guess it was the largest and noblest dream ever dreamed by man. But somewhere along the line something turned sour. Godalmighty!" he exclaimed, leaning forward, ear cocked. "Something turned sour. The common man he had his belly stuffed, but what was he? He wasn't God's noble creature no more, he was just plain common. He hadn't grown in dignity or wisdom. All he had grown in was his gut and his pocketbook. He forswore his Creator, paying this kind of nasty mealy-mouthed lip service every Sunday to the true God while worshiping with all his heart nothing but the almighty dollar. He plundered a whole continent of its resources

15

and wildlife and beauty. The wisdom of all the ages, all the precious teachings of his ancestors, they were lost upon him. He spat on his nigro brother and wore out his eyes looking at TV and fornicated with his best friend's wife at the country club. He had all these here wonder drugs to prolong his life, and what happened? At the age of seventy he was an empty husk, saddled with a lot of ill-gotten lucre and a pile of guilt, terrified of death and laying down there on the sand at Miami Beach pitying himself. A *husk,* son! I know what I'm talking about! And do you know what? Come Judgment Day . . . come Judgment, the good Lord's going to take one look at this empty husk, and He's going to say, 'How do *you* lay claim to salvation, My friend?' Then He's going to heave him out the back door and He's going to holler after him: 'That's what you get, friend, for selling out to Mammon! That's what you get for trading your soul for a sawbuck, and forswearing My love!" His sad and sagging jowls were quivering with wrath, and tears of indignation swam at the corners of his eyes. I consoled him with a pat on the arm and cautioned him to take it easy; and then, at a filling station adjacent to a new housing development, I made him turn in, and we rattled to a stop with an aviary shrilling and chirping.

It was not the rings, it was the oil—the old man had let it run dry. And, "Can't run no car without oil, Mr. Leverett," said the garageman, with a knowing wink at me, as my father got out and as I eased back in the seat, stung with memory at these surroundings. My father's words had left me jaded and depressed. I felt unaccountably weary and worn out—old before my time—and I had a sudden sharp pang of total estrangement, as if my identity had slipped away, leaving me without knowledge of who I was and where I had been and where I was ever going. The mood lingered, filling me with lassitude, weariness, discontent. Later than I had thought now, the hour had grown dusky and faded and the pale rind of a new moon floated high up over the bay, above Norfolk and the blinking lights of beacons and great ships moored in the outbound tide. I heard tugboat whistles and now, behind me, the dull rumble and fuss of the swollen town which once long ago, even at this hour of homeward-going, was all serenity and stillness. And as I sat there, watching my father chat with the garageman ("Cousins?" he was saying in that kindly old passionate voice. "You from Nansemond too? Why, that would make the two of us cousins indeed!") it occurred to me in a sudden burst of recollection just where it was that we had come. Because here, long before

these acres of salt marsh had been reclaimed, before the coming of
the gypsum-white treeless boulevards and the ranch houses and
the children-crowded green suburban lawns, right here, several
fathoms beneath the foundations of this Esso Servicenter, I had
once been up to my knees in the cool sand-gray salt water, hunting for crawfish, and right here at the age of twelve I had almost
drowned.

On this very spot I had gone down, down in a cataclysm of bubbles trailing frantic handfuls of seaweed, and shot floundering to
surface way out on the tidal creek, spouting water like a whale and
strangling with sudden tumultuous love for my fleeting life, until a
colored crab fisherman, poised in his boat like some black merciful
and sweating Christ above the deep, hauled me in by the hair. I
got a beating, and for days I leaked water from my ears; my father
repaid the fisherman with a country ham and five silver dollars—
which even to reward a savior in those depression years was more
than he could afford—but though I was warned thereafter to stay
away from the place I sneaked back here, alone, during the summer days. For now everything about the place—the creek and the
scuttling crawfish, salt swamp and sunlight and flashing gulls, and
the streetcar trestle astride the reeds and the chiming uproar of the
trolley as it swayed through the marsh, rattled across the trestle and
was gone in a shower of popping sparks, its electric singsong monotone receding as if into infinity or time itself and leaving
all behind with a quality of noontime and seaside and an insect-
strumming drowsy yellow solitude—all of these seemed to be informed by a sense of mysteriousness and brevity. Like that moment when a long-familiar scrap of music is suddenly heard as if
with new ears, and crashes in upon you no longer a simple tune or
melody but a pure and wordless overflowing of the heart, so this
scene for me had more lights and darks than I had ever imagined,
and titanic new dimensions, and I stole up upon it with trembling
and fascination. Here there had been taken away from me that
child's notion that I would live forever; here I had learned the
fragility not so much as of my own as of all being, and for that
reason if it seemed a cruel scary place it also possessed a new and
fathomable beauty. So, packing a secret lunch, I went back there
day after day. Lying on my belly in the reeds I would poke the
crawfish with a stick, and watch them scuttle away, and brood
and dream in the hot sun. The streetcar would come with a metal-
lic whir and jangling, and recede into the stillness of noon. The
gulls would flash against the sky. In their boats the black fisher-

men, far out, would call for the wind in hymning voices and suddenly all would be still. And in that stillness, with the yellow new world spread out before my eyes, gorged upon mayonnaise and soda pop, I shivered with the knowledge of mortality.

Yet here on the identical spot, years later, I thought that nothing could be victim of such obliteration. My great-grandchildren's cleverest archaeology will strive in vain to unlock that sun-swept marsh, that stream, those crawfish, that singing trolley car. Everything was gone. Not just altered or changed or modified, not just a place whose outlines may have shifted and blurred (new growth here, no growth there, a new-fledged willow, a deepened cove) but were still recognizable, dependable, fixed—my marsh had vanished, a puff into thin air, and nothing of it remained. How many tons of earth, sand, rock, rubble, rubbish, and plain old Port Warwick garbage had gone into this stupendous unmaking would be hard to say; the job had been thorough and complete. Beneath it all, one seascape, entombed forever. Around us now in eccentric loopings, upon terraced lawns row on row, a horde of diminutive houses called (why?) Glendora Manor squatted in the twilight. Tail-finned cars larger than the dwellings themselves cruised ponderously through the tiny streets, scattering cocker spaniels, and coming to rest alongside lawns where sprinklers whirled, and motorized lawnmowers towed their masters through the greenly churning dusk, and globes on pillars glittered like silver basketballs. The trees, so far, were small but they appeared to be trying. And here, I calculated, drop a plumb line straight down from the Esso Extra pump and you'd hit the spot where I sank beneath the foaming brine.

So much for my childhood. In times of stress and threat, I've heard it said, in times of terror and alarms, of silence and clinging, people tend to hold on to the past, even to imitate it: taking on old fashions and humming old songs, seeking out historic scenes and reliving old ancestral wars, in an effort to forget both the lackluster present and a future too weird and horrible to ponder. Perhaps one of the reasons we Americans are so exceptionally nervous and driven is that our past is effaced almost before it is made present; in our search for old avatars to contemplate we find only ghosts, whispers, shadows: almost nothing remains for us to feel or see, or to absorb our longing. That evening I was touched to the heart: by my father's old sweetness and decency and rage, but also by whatever it was within me—within life itself, it seemed so intense—that I knew to be irretrievably lost. Estranged from myself and from my time, dwelling neither in the destroyed past nor in the fantastic and incomprehensible present, I knew that I must find the answer to at least several things before taking hold of myself and getting on with the job. "You mean Miss Minnie Morehouse, from Whaleyville?" my father was saying, in that slurred Tidewater accent which I too had had once, and lost. "Why, of *co'se* I was. I was there indeed. And put flowers on her grave!"

For a moment I believe I must have shut my eyes, then opened them again, thinking that somehow by such a ritual I might come miraculously to, amid the reeds once more, surveying the place where life had left me dumb-struck, shorn of illusions and innocence. But here in the changing present all was shadow: I saw nothing, heard nothing, except in my own mind again, where gulls flashed overhead and that trolley car swayed, chiming, as if through the light of centuries, and like a phantom. . . .

That evening I sent a wire to Cass Kinsolving in Charleston, telling him I would be coming down the next day. I had rarely done so rash a thing before, and I knew I had to take a chance on his good will. But without knowing about Cass I could never learn about what happened in Sambuco—about Mason, and my part in the matter.

Two years before, I had never laid eyes on Cass. Our meeting was not terribly auspicious, you might say—although even then he seemed to be an unusual sort—and he might have passed right on out of my life had I not, only a few hours later that same day, gotten myself situated on the periphery of those events of which he was the dead center. I would like to describe that meeting, and the circumstances which led up to it, if only so you will be able to understand why I went to Sambuco in the first place, thereby getting myself mixed up in the whole wretched business.

When Mason Flagg wrote me in Rome, inviting me down to Sambuco for a visit, I felt that nothing fitted in better with my plans. I had been in Europe for four years—and in Rome for three—and I had come to the point where I sensed that my roots, such as they were, must be replanted in native soil or shrivel away completely. So it was that Mason's invitation nicely coincided with the "last look around" I planned to take before going back to America.

How I got to Europe, and what I was doing there, is a brief and easy matter to explain. I had not been in the war (the one before

Korea), having gotten a really horrible education under Navy auspices at a college in Illinois, from which I emerged with an ensign's commission just two days after the bomb fell on Hiroshima. I went on to get a law degree and for a short time I worked in New York. Then, feeling somewhat cheated of travel and excitement, I decided to go to Europe—a traditional move, after all, for shiftless youths with murky horizons. I got a job in the legal division of a large government relief agency and for a while I was located in Paris, where I thought I might extend a democratic hand to the war-racked and the downtrodden, and where I ended up hearing the complaints of alienated bureaucrats, fellow employees from Louisville and Des Moines. My office had a fabulous view of the Place de la Concorde, and I occupied myself with itineraries and bills of lading which were works of art.

After a year I was transferred to Rome, and an even finer office facing on the ruined green sweep of the Circo Massimo: here in almost all seasons there was a carnival which livened up my days with braying horns and the crazed music of calliopes. I liked Rome, even though my routine—attending to the woes of the Agency employees—seemed just about the same: there is something in the Italian climate that makes the average American clerk, so remote from the mechanisms of progress, even more peevish and discontented; and the commissary milkshakes—because of the quality of the milk—were not nearly so good as in Paris, although toward the end of my stay I learned that they began getting fresh shipments by air from Dutch dairies. But the job paid well enough (embarrassingly so, compared to my Italian office-mates, who appeared to work twice as hard for half the pay) and I bought a spruce little Austin sports convertible to carry me up and down the long slope to my home on the Gianicolo hill. I had an apartment there in a run-down building and an old rheumatic woman named Enrica who cooked suppers for me and filled my evenings with her tireless lament. I had a phonograph, too, a scratchy machine left me by a former American tenant, along with what seemed to be all the works of Wagner, Liszt, and Tchaikovsky ever recorded. The view from my terrace was luxurious, especially during summer twilights when I'd sit there playing a Liszt concerto, drinking commissary whiskey and watching the whole city spilled out beneath me in a luminous frieze of rust and gold. I had two or three girls during that time—a girl named Ginevra, and then one named Anna Maria, and toward the end, perhaps as some augury of the end of my expatriation, a junior from Smith

College with wonderful black eyes—and usually there would be two of us there listening to the villainous music, perfectly content, while the setting sun touched the ramparts of the Forum with one last glint of perilous light, and the shadow of my hill, marching eastward, rolled up the city in darkness.

In all, it was a fine three years. I traveled all around and saw the sights and, possibly because I felt so happily enriched, regarded myself as somewhat superior to my friends at the Agency, whose limits of adventure in Italy were defined (outside of a flying trip to Capri each summer) by their apartments in the suburbs and by the bar downstairs in the Hotel Flora, where the martinis were dry and chill and made of the best English gin. I had, it is true, donated little enough to Italy but Italy had rewarded me in the simple fact of its warm and extravagant being, and since it is more blessed to give than to receive I felt that this, at least, might have made the Italians happy, where my grotesque attempts at "aid" and "relief" had not. At any rate, toward the end of my third year I decided to go back to America. Splendid as the city is, it is impossible to become Chief Justice of the United States Supreme Court in Rome. I had by that time saved a little money, and a number of ornate letters I had written had produced several tentative offers of jobs in New York. I might have departed Italy as blithe as a sparrow and with no regrets—except for Sambuco and the invitation I received from Mason Flagg.

The letter came on a day in early July, only a week or so after I had quit my job. I knew Mason had been in Sambuco ever since the spring. In May I had received a gossipy letter from him—the first in years—saying that he had gotten my address from a mutual New York friend, that he was now established in Italy for "a long spell of writing," and that he would like to have me come down. It was a letter, however, which for reasons I think will be made evident later, I chose at the time to ignore. This other invitation weakened me, though; I felt foot-loose and adventurous, with no ties at all, and I had my eye cocked for new vistas. The note was breezy but specific—"stay as long as you like"—and typical of Mason, who was never one to understate the scope of his operations: "We are living in the goddamdest palace you ever saw." I had never been to Sambuco, but Mason—with his picture of sun and sea, plus what sounded like a battalion of servants ("$50 a month for the lot and they stand around and out-yassuh any coon the old man ever had in Virginia")—made it all seem lazy enough and I decided, rather than wait around in Rome, to drive down

21

there the next day. I sent Mason a wire that I was coming. Sambuco is six hours by car from Rome; an hour from Naples. I had already reserved passage back to America from Naples, and so it was a convenient and fairly easy matter to switch my sailing to a date a week or so later. Not so the matter of my auto registration (it had expired), nor that of the car itself, which I had already made arrangements to sell through the Automobil Club Italiano, and which, if I was ever to swim in that cool blue sea far down the slope from Sambuco, I knew I had to hold on to. So my last afternoon in Rome—one I had expected to while away in mild nostalgia at some flower-rimmed café—was spent with a functionary at the auto club: a demonic, moon-faced woman, with sweat describing great blue hoops beneath her arms, who swore that at this late hour to think that I could in any way change the course of events was a sort of criminal dream. *"Questa non è l'America, signore,"* she wheezed darkly, *"qui siamo in Italia."* The registration had expired, and that was that. So much the same for the car—committed irrevocably. Documents were brought out to support this point, and a huge code book and a group of dossiers; but I had learned in Italy that the more emphatic an official "No," the greater one's chances for success. And so toward evening, sweltering, I came away with my renewal and with the wretched title to the car—in the only country in the world where such a victory can leave one feeling hopelessly beaten.

I drove home in twilight, happy to have my car back and to know that I could get rid of it in Naples before I sailed, after all. But I felt hot and exhausted; the woman had cowed me, and I fell into a sort of despondent reverie, driving at a cripple's pace toward home, past heat-worn and silent Romans, through avenues of withering, downcast trees. In St. Peter's Square there was not a soul in sight, save two humid, hurrying nuns, and over the great cupola the very air seemed to churn and billow with the dreadful incandescence of the day. "Oh it's hot—*God!*" I heard someone cry as I dawdled up the hill, but the city for once seemed oddly still —even the motorscooters had ceased their racket—all as if awaiting breathless, in one strangled hush, some latter-day holocaust.

Later, when darkness fell, it cooled off a bit and I was able to finish my packing. The house was a shambles—which was all right—because now, pictures down, chairs upturned, trunks and boxes everywhere, the place seemed stripped of any sentimental associations, and I was not disposed to snoop around for any. My Smith girl had left days before, spirited aloft on the first westbound plane

by her mother—an angular example of Detroit Gothic—who had
sensible plans for her daughter at Grosse Pointe. This was all right,
too, I suppose; the core of our romance—love in the Eternal City
—seemed long since to have become worn down by time and
familiarity, and she had begun to cadge jars of peanut butter from
friends at the Embassy, and spent long homesick hours going to
American movies. And they were practices to which, too late, I
realized I had been giving dull approval. But that evening I was
far from happy, or even contented, and I didn't know what to
blame. Possibly, though, it *was* only the apartment, unclad now in
that almost mystically inspired ugliness which Mussolini brought to
the works of his era: a room of plywood, chrome, leatherette, and
water stains, one sixty-watt bulb pulsing spiritlessly over all, and
from the phonograph, the *Pathétique*—a faint, blurred convulsion.
I was depressed to learn that I could have lived for so long in such
an eyesore, but still saddened that this one seemed to be giving me
up with the identical unconcern with which it had received me,
three years before.

Anyway, it was getting late when I finished packing—almost
nine o'clock—and old Enrica had my last meal on the table. She
was a study in bereavement as she served me my meal, snuffling
over the platter, wailing phrases in unfathomable Sicilian, and
gazing at me from the kitchen with furtive, stricken eyes. No employer, she boohooed, fingering her sparse mustache, had been so
kind, so *gentile,* and alas, she'd have to go back to Messina, because to work now for anyone else in Rome would be intolerable.
She kept mumbling over the stove, gloomily rattling pots and pans.
It helped make the meal a dismal one; the ravioli, on the table
since eight, was like plaster, the wine bilious, syrupy, body-warm.
But below the terrace the city spread itself out in a million flickering eyes of light. I could see the Colosseum, aglow in the phospho-
rescence of floodlamps, and a ruined assembly of stark white
shafts where the Forum lay. Far past these, two oscillating points of
red and green, an airplane, mounted the looming dark above the
Alban Hills. Over the south and east, where I was going, hung a
flashy crowd of Roman constellations, and a fire-trail of neon
where the outskirts of the city rambled up the hills into sightless
gloom and made Rome look suddenly more immense than any city
in the world. And for a moment—though perhaps it was just the
wine—I felt that Rome, too late, was finally intelligible to me, offering me at my departure no reproach at all, but only a tolerant,
valedictory, and many-eyed wink, in its vast immortal patience

with the barbarians of the earth, of which I was only the most recent. But the moment passed, I drank too much wine in a reckless effort to feel happier, and in an hour or so Enrica bade good-by to me. *"Addio,"* she cried, *"buon viaggio.* Enrica will miss you, signore."* And she hobbled out into the night, weeping bogus tears that came not wholly from grief, for later I discovered that she had taken with her, among other things (a fountain pen, gold tie clasp, etc.), my Remington razor, which at least she could use.

After this and by eleven o'clock, stumbling about the cluttered depot my apartment had become, I felt so intimidated that I could hardly wait to get to Sambuco. Feverishly I decided to leave that night. I loaded up the Austin, stuck a pint of bourbon in the glove compartment, and took off down the hill, dogged by the gray suspicion, all the way, that I had left something behind. But my tennis balls were with me, my guitar, and passport, and the pornographic studies, carefully disguised as a Maioli-bound Petrarch, which Mason had asked me, in a postscript to his letter, to get him on the Via Sistina. All was in place, I racked my head futilely, and only when the Tiber hove into sight did I realize that what I was really leaving behind—with both affection and a very special sort of malice—was simply Rome. But after so long a stay I felt such a leave-taking was peremptory, rude. I drove then, for the last time, into the Piazza Santa Maria in Trastevere, and there I had a beer.

It was shadowy and quiet around my café. From the restaurants the American sojourners had departed, leaving the square to a gang of children, a beggar scratching at a violin, and young priests with programs homeward-bound from some concert across the river and out this late, I guessed, by special dispensation. There was also Ava Gardner, who from her tattered billboard cast a peeled glance of vacancy toward the fountain, where eons of ooze had wrought, in place of beauty, an admirably weathered composure. It was a fine fountain and I gazed at it for a long time. In the wings of the church behind, blue in shadows, slumberous pigeons clucked and rustled and all was quiet. For a while, sitting there, I tried to feel that the evening was momentous, but I was uninspired, my thoughts tepid and shallow. Vaguely I had the sense that I was at some decisive instant in my life, with the most exciting part of my youth behind me, but this thought left me unstirred. My mood was dangerously close to self-pity; I felt like someone sitting amid the bunting and splendor of his own farewell party, at which nobody at all turned up.

The beer was good; warm air blew over me with the smell of

coffee, then of flowers, and I had a fleeting unhappy paroxysm of goatish lust. Then like stiffened silver one chime broke from the campanile high above, the half-hour. A gang of boys came racing by, the square for an instant alive in a scamper of footsteps, a flurry of naked heels. A restaurant closed for the night with a roar of descending shutters, and from afar someone called out *"Tommasino!"*—a summery voice, dying in the alleyways, touched with heat and fatigue and sleep.

For a while after this the square was deserted. Once a cat loped across my gaze with a squint-eyed, piratical look and a suave grin. Bent on who knows what unholy mission, he cruised up over the fountain steps, a yellow blur, and plunged dauntlessly into the shadows. Then all was serene and decorous once more, the heavens clear, starry, the air aromatic with blossoms, the fountain leaking slow trickling notes of water, like memorandums. I sat until the bell struck again, when the waiter came near, insinuating with a yawn the lateness of the hour. I paid him and sat there for one final moment, inhaling the odor of flowers. Then I got up and took my last look at Rome: at fountains, pigeons, cats, and priests, a crowd of whom came by just as I arose, two licking at ice cream cones, two gossiping in Irish—*Me old mother gave me this*—two clutching at missals and breathing soft flutters of prayer—the cloaks of all trembling like banners of mourning, and disappearing, black against a blacker black, up the moonless slope of Gianicolo, toward some good cloister. . . .

Then, driving south across dark Campania, I felt a great sense of liberation, but I hadn't reckoned on the effect of yesterday's harassments. This came later; for an hour or so after leaving Rome I experienced a rowdy euphoria and a sudden love for the Italian night; for the remarkable stars above, for the towns silhouetted on the hilltops, for the wind—smelling of countryside, of earth, of manure and vegetation—which cooled me off and set the sleeves of my garments, piled up behind me, to chattering like pennants. I had the top down; I drove fast, because the highway was straight and empty, and I bawled out songs on the wind. My headlights kindled fire in long lanes of poplars, the underbellies of their leaves a treasure of rustling silver, and in sleeping villages with Latin-book names—Aprilia and Pontinia—as white and as hushed as sepulchers, with only the dogs abroad. Above me bright stars wheeled across the heavens, but south in the open country all was black as death, without houses or familiar outlines, and stretching out on all sides into infinite darkness. My expansive mood began to fade about here. For miles at a stretch I could see nothing at all on either side of me—no homes, no humans, no growing things—nothing save the encompassing night. I began to feel strictly alone, and except for the noise of the car to remind me otherwise, adrift in a boat, rudderless and without course upon a black and starlit ocean. Then abruptly I was in cliff country, ascending the flanks of gaunt, wounded hills where nothing grew and no one lived, a wilderness of dried-up riverbeds and parched ravines, the hangout of thieves. I turned on the radio, and found only chill comfort: a woman's voice announcing *"Un po' di allegria negli Spikes Jones";* then from far off in Monte Carlo a faint, windy snatch of Beethoven, which soon dimmed away, becoming silent altogether. The American Army station in Germany was signing off in a hubbub of noise, with a program called the Hillbilly Gasthaus. There was something in this liaison of tongues and in the harmony of guitars and banjos and fiddles, moaning among these forsaken hills, which gripped me with anxiety; but yellowish light shone ahead, I plummeted down toward the coast, and soon was in the town of Formia, where the warm sea was rolling in from Sardinia.

All of a sudden exhaustion smote me like a fist. I came to a dead halt.

For some reason I date the events at Sambuco—at least my participation in them—from this moment. Had I been able to sleep easily that night, I might very well have been spared my trouble of the next day. Without *that* misadventure, I most surely would have arrived at Sambuco as fresh as a buttercup: not haggard, shattered, and forlorn, my composure hopelessly unmoored, and cursed with a sort of skittish, haunted depletion of nerves from which I never quite recovered. But second thoughts are no good. At that point I was worn out—face numb, eyeballs aflame, legs and arms sore at every joint. All of the hotels were shut down for the night, or displayed no-vacancy signs. So I drove onto a jetty overlooking the harbor, there put the top up, and settled back for sleep. The mosquitoes wouldn't let me alone. Frequenters of resorts, big July mosquitoes wet and gross with a summer's licentiousness, they bore down upon me on the shore breeze, whining with excitement and mooning ceaselessly about my ears. After an hour's battle I gave up and closed the windows. The car was soon an oven, stifling and breathless, in which only barely dozing I dreamed the exhausting nightmares of half-sleep. Half a dozen times I was aroused to see a flock of stars go slipping over the hori-

26

zon, then I dropped back into clammy slumber, where odd smells invaded my dreams, breaths out of time past—low tide at home in Virginia, mud and seaweed, fish nets drying in the sun.

When finally I awoke I cocked one sore eye open in the full blast of morning light. Away off, I could hear people yelling and splashing in the waves; above, peering down at me through the windshield, were two rueful, bearded faces.

"*È morto?*" I heard one ask the other.

"*Un inglese. Soffocato.*"

When I stirred, the two old men retreated slowly off across the sand, with looks of deep mystery. It was past nine o'clock; I was drenched in sweat, with a violent headache, and my body had that jittery feeling which accompanies a hangover. I knew I should be on my way, and was—after coffee and a wilted bun in a beachside joint thronged with strident Romans in bathing suits, all of them swilling Coca-Cola.

Such is the power of certain calamities on the mind that, once freed of the initial shock, one is able to view with bright clarity all the events leading up to the actual blow. The tone, the mood, the character of whatever transpired before, takes on the gray hue, itself, of disaster and is embalmed in memory with an awful sense of predestination. It is in such a way that I remember the road out of Formia, through Naples and beyond. Leaving the sea, the highway became wide and straight again. But it was Saturday, market day, and the road was swarming with traffic—wagons and carts piled high with produce and fodder, towed by donkeys, all moving so leisurely as to appear like sinister, stationary objects in my path. The sun rose higher and higher over the dusty countryside. Its fire settled down upon the hills; close by stood fields of blighted corn and trees in windless, shriveling groves. Up from the highway the heat rose in greasy waves. And through these waves, roaring, balefully glittering, and often straight at me, came a devil's pageant of vehicles—motorscooters and buses loaded down with vacationers, and caravans of hurtling cars. There were huge trucks, too, carrying gasoline, whipping past me at seventy and leaving a trail of scalding blue vapor on the air. Near Capua, outside of Naples, there was an epidemic of sheep into which I almost skidded, and I had to poke a gingerly path among their sad, expressively wagging behinds. In spite of the sun I put the top down again to get the wind. I also remember turning on the radio again, this time for distraction. By the time I reached the outskirts of Naples the steering wheel was slippery with perspiration. To my disgust I found myself sniveling with tension and with fatigue and murmuring aloud words of courage.

But it was the Alfa Romeo on the Autostrada to Pompei that led to my downfall. I had passed through Naples by then, for a brief moment calm, thinking that with only an hour more to go Sambuco was in the bag. There was less traffic; it was nearly noon, lunchtime, when most Italians abandon the road to purposeful Anglo-Saxons. It seemed to have turned cooler—though no doubt I was deceived—and I relaxed for the first time, diverted by the outer suburbs of the city, where black smoke was billowing up from a thousand factory chimneys. The noise I heard behind me was abrupt and thunderous, a shocking din which partook both of a salvo of rockets and an airplane in take-off, and above this, pervading it all, a thin, ominous, hurrying whine, as of the approach of a flight of wasps or bees; my eyes sought the mirror, where I saw it bearing down on me in savage haste—the snout of a big black car. With a foretaste of doom and of the fading beauty of life I composed myself to accept a rear-end collision, and a tight, goosey, half-despairing, half-gluttonous feeling swept over me as I watched it become larger and larger, barreling remorselessly on. Five yards from my tail the car swerved, slowed, came abreast: I beheld a fat young Neapolitan, one hand limp and cocky on the wheel, his girl friend all but in his lap, both of them grinning like sharks. We drove side by side for a moment, perilously swaying; then he was off and away with a noise like a string of firecrackers, and with the central finger of one fist raised in ripe phallic tribute. I tore after him for a while, gave up the chase, and fell into aching oppressive woolgathering. My heart was full of murder. I was only dreaming of revenge, doing sixty, when, a little beyond Pompei, I smashed broadside into the motorscooter. . . .

Luciano di Lieto: a liquid, resourceful name, one fit for a trapeze artist, or a writer of sonnets, or an explorer of the Antilles, a name certainly deserving more in the way of talents than those of the person who bore it. By turns hod carrier, road worker, peddler of erotic trinkets at the local ruins, a pickpocket so inept as to earn from the police the nickname "Fessacchiotto"—the Stumblebum —the man di Lieto was a triumph of stunted endowments. One day at the age of twelve he poked a meddlesome hand around in the engine of an automobile, and was shorn of two fingers, clipped off neatly by the fan. A few years later, plunged into some adolescent daydream, he wandered in front of a Naples streetcar, breaking both legs and leaving one elbow impaired forever. Only months after this, barely out of his casts, experimenting with fireworks at a seaside *festa,* he bent his dark, crazy regard down upon the muzzle of a Roman candle, and blew out his right eye. When I slammed into him he was twenty-three and in the fever of early manhood. All of these facts were revealed to me before the ambulance came, and perhaps no more than an hour past that moment when di Lieto came roaring out of a side road on a sputtering Lambretta and into my path, legs akimbo, poised tautly forward like a jockey, hair wild and rampant over his blasted vision, mouth and jaws working with hoots of joy even as I braked frantically on squealing rubber and plowed into him. It seemed as if those joyful cries were one and a part of the collision itself, preceding it for a chilling second before I even saw him and going on and on after the moment of rackety impact, when I sent the motorscooter flying forty feet up the road and kept skidding helplessly on, watching the blur of gray denim overalls and tousled black hair, still hooting, bounce up over the front of the car. Clawing at space, he seemed to suspend there for a moment in mid-air, before gliding with white floundering legs and arms across the hood of the car toward me, shattering the windshield in an icy explosion of glass. Like a collapsed puppet dangling on strings, he floated away past me and was gone. I finally came to a stop on the other side of the road in a shower of flip-flopping tennis balls, the radio undone by the impact and alive with deafening crackles and peeps.

When I recovered, I brushed the glass from my lap and stole shakily out of the car. I found myself alone with di Lieto, who lay face-up in the road, blood trickling gently from nose and ears, and with a sort of lopsided, dreamy expression on his features, part agony, part a smile, as if in this mindless repose he were being borne yearningly, at last, through the floodgates of his destiny. I gazed down at him, numb with shock and horror. He was still breathing but rather tentatively; one eye socket was pink and sunken (I thought this my doing), and with a grisly feeling I glanced around me for the missing eye. For a long while, or so it seemed, no one was around and no one came: it was a country crossroad, high noon in the sultry summertime, with insects humming and the smell of weeds, and with hawks that looked like buzzards circling high over the blazing fields. For what felt like an endless time I kept trampling around the prostrate di Lieto, reeling with shock and heaving shudders of anguish.

What followed immediately afterward seemed to be only a grotesque fantasia of events lacking sequence or order, in which I am able to pick out mostly random impressions, as of scenes from a movie film dimly remembered. I do recall finally a car moving out of the horizon, a dusty rattletrap weaving leisurely, which I hailed, and then two Pompeian matrons, profoundly emancipated, fuddled with wine, in rustles and flounces of shiny black silk, who debarked unsteadily from the heap and blinked in the dazzling sunlight, uncomprehending. "What is this here?" they murmured, stooping over di Lieto, and then spied the blood, clutched their hands to their breasts, and commenced sending up boozy entreaties to the Pompeian Madonna. *"Santa Maria del Rosario! Povero ragazzo!"* What happened to him? they cried. One, with an incomprehension that added brutal fire to the hellishness of the moment, asked me if he had fallen from a tree; immediately they wanted to pour water on him, turn him over, move him. I tried to tell them he must not be touched; only when my voice had risen to a hoarse cracked shout did they stop their outcry and clatter back to town for help.

In the long space that followed I sensed the heights of Vesuvius looming oppressive at my back. I sat on the bumper of the car and gazed toward di Lieto, who kept pluckily breathing, twitching a little and awaiting our rescue: it came at last and in a deluge. Cars began to stop, and trucks and carts; as if summoned there by hungry intuition a small village full of people appeared at the spot, trooping from all four directions toward the crossroad, galloping in clouds of dust across the fields. It was as if in an instant the desolate scene had been transformed into one of bustling life, every soul for miles gathered to the place with the instinct of a flock of homing, weather-wise birds. I remember only sitting head in hands on the bumper while they milled about, bending over di Lieto, pressing their ears to his chest for the heartbeat and making solemn pronouncements. "It's just a concussion," one said. "No," said another, an old stripped-to-the-waist farmer with skin burnt brown as a mummy, "his spine is broken. That's why we mustn't move him. Look, see how he twitches in the legs. That's always the sign of a broken spine." The crowd shuffled, jabbered away in a spirit both grave and somehow enraptured; many had brought parts of their interrupted lunches; they stood there looking on contentedly, munching on bread and cheese and passing around bottles of wine. A man asked me gently how I felt and if I was hurt; someone else gave me a shot of brandy, which quickly set me to retching. "Fessacchiotto," I heard a glum voice say through the spinning blue as I heaved, "the Stumblebum finally caught it." Then I saw two motorcycle cops, helmeted like spacemen, brake to a stop at the crossroad. They shooed the crowd toward the ditches like a swarm of buzzing flies and forthwith set up camp, making lordly measurements of my skid marks, stalking around the car and unearthing all sorts of data.

"Please. You going these machine?" one said deferentially.

"I speak your language," I told him.

"*Allora, va bene.*" When the collision occurred, was the Lambretta approaching the highway from the right or from the left? He was a conscientious-looking man in wringing poplin, very polite, and he began jotting down information in a notebook the size of a ledger.

"He was coming from the left," I said, "which I think you'll be able to tell easily from the position of the Lambretta. I couldn't *help* hitting him. It's not my fault, anyway. In the meanwhile the man lies there dying. Would you be kind enough to tell me where the ambulance is?"

"*Nome?*" he asked genially, ignoring the question.

"Peter Charles Leverett," I said, spelling it out.

"*Nato dove e quando?*"

"In Port Warwick, Virginia, 14 April 1925."

"*Dove* Port Warwick, Virginia? *Inghilterra?*"

"The U.S.A." I said.

"*Ah, bene. Allora, vostro padre? Nome?*"

"Alfred Leverett."

"*Nato dove e quando?*"

"In Suffolk, Virginia, U.S.A. I don't know when, exactly. Make it 1886."

"*Vostra madre?*"

"Oh, for Christ sake," I said.

"*Che?*"

"Flora Margaret McKee. San Francisco, California, U.S.A. Put down 1900. Listen, could you tell me when the ambulance is coming if it is and, if not, whether it would be possible to put him in one of those cars or trucks and drive him to Naples? I think he's in a grave condition."

To try to get anything across to him was like casting notes in bottles upon the limitless deep. In his kindly, bland, unruffled fashion he kept scribbling in his ledger, examining my passport and papers while the fierce sun beat down on us and the crowd shuffled and stirred upon the margin of the crossroad like murmurous watchers at some heathen ritual. At its focus, flat on his back, asprawl in sacrificial repose, di Lieto lay with his tangled sweet look of liberation and racking ecstasy, eyes half-closed and dreaming, attracting flies. Speaking of California, the cop went on cheerfully, his wife's uncle lived there, or so he believed, in a place called Vilks Bari, where he earned a good living as a worker of mines. Was I aware of that place? And was it near Hollywood? Now in regard to the man in the road, he continued, trying to allay my distress, I would be in severe legal trouble indeed, as I no doubt already knew, had the Lambretta approached from the right instead of from the left, which, from the evidence at hand—the skid marks, the position of the victim and of the Lambretta itself —it no doubt had; as it was, I was free to go at any time, provided I could put my car into operation, provided too I supply him with my next address in Italy (a detail, since I most certainly would not have to go to court, the indications of blame being so overwhelmingly in my favor); as for the man himself, di Lieto— "Fessacchiotto"—he had been spoiling for such a disaster for ten years (had I not been told by someone already about this thieving simpleton—his fingers, his streetcar accident, his eye?) and he had no one but himself to reproach if he should die on the spot, though it is true he was not an evil man, and death is bitter, *in verità,* even for imbeciles.

"*Basta, Sergente!*" I said, almost sobbing. "*L'ambulanza!*"

Just then we turned our eyes toward one edge of the crossroad, where there was a sudden commotion. A rickety truck drew to a halt beneath a tree. Down from its sides clambered a mob of men and boys, led by a cruelly gnarled old hag who struggled like a wounded bird across the sunlit space of ground, fell at di Lieto's side, and there on her knees began to howl noisily and piteously.

"Luciano! Luciano!" she wailed. "Luciano-o-o! *Che t'hanno fatto? Povero figlio mio!* Luciano-o-o! Come back, my sweet, come back, come back! Again the monsters have tried to finish thee! Look up into mamma's eyes, Luciano. Just once, Luciano! Don't let the monsters finish thee, angel. Show mamma once again thy dear sweet eyes!"

"*È mezza matta,*" the sergeant whispered. "She's always been a little cuckoo. She's his grandmother but she brought him up as a son." He seemed awed by the show, and a little uneasy. "All those other people are his brothers."

Infected by this awful grief, the crowd became hushed, stood transfixed at the roadside. For a moment the woman knelt silently, fumbling with her chin. A curious breeze came up, instantly chilling, and a gritty whirlpool of dust and leaves churned past us, billowing up, blossoming, flushing out of the weeds a flock of starlings which exploded from the meadow full-tilt and in raucous outcry, windmilling around us on the dusty blast. In white tatters the old woman's hair came flying loose, her black shawl went adrift from her shoulders, and a piece of newspaper came tumbling end over end through the arena, where, alone now, she and her grandson seemed like actors storm-swept by some diminutive and marvelous tempest; then the wind died, the old woman recovered her shawl, and the birds fled chattering across the fields.

"*Luciano, angelo mio,*" she moaned softly, "*perchè non dici niente, perchè non mi guardi?* Speak, child. Look at mamma. Luciano, I see thy legs twitching. Rise up on them and walk, angel; don't lie here like this in the road . . ."

Suddenly she seemed to falter; kneeling there, she raised her eyes from di Lieto and gazed slowly around the crowd, examining each face with a sudden, haunted, tigerish, homicidal look which, even before it lit upon me, caused my insides to squirm in panic. In some way I felt the first breath of her fury before it actually struck: at that moment when in seersuckers and in tourist's espadrilles, sun-glassed, crew-cut, and with an aspect of northern barbarity like an autograph upon my face, I tried vainly to squeeze behind the sergeant—when she spied me, scrambled to her feet with unbelievable nimbleness, and charged across the road toward me in a black floundering onslaught of execration and doom.

"*Svedese! Farabutto!*" she yelled. "*You've* done this to my boy! *You* ran him down with your machine, you wicked monster! May you burn in *hell!*" A quick apologetic breath went upward from her lips—"*Dio mi perdoni!*"—but she bore relentlessly down, gathering new wind, new imprecations, lunged past the flustered sergeant, and thrust a palsied, castigating finger like a gnarled twiglet beneath my nose. "Swede!" she cried. "Evil man! I know you and your kind. Don't try to hide your face from me. Look at him!" she said, with a gesture for the crowd. "Look at the man! Look how he shivers and shakes with fear. Ha! Now he knows he can't hide his crime. Speeding through our town, running down innocent people with his machine!" She turned back to me, her whole face—sunken eyes, moles, wrinkled cheeks, wild white hair—all aquiver and ablaze with terrifying wrath. "I know your kind! It was one of your kind who ran down the wife of poor Luigi Lucatuorto in Portici four years ago last Easter. In the springtime of life, too, a strong handsome girl with a sick father and four hungry children to feed. A lovely girl, big, healthy, minding her own way, struck down like a dog by a monster. You know about this? Tell me! You know? Not one lira did she collect, either, though her collarbone was broken and her back weakened for life!" She paused, turning toward di Lieto, and began weeping again. "Look there. What are you going to do about *him* now? What are you going to do about Luciano? Bleeding there, dying. An innocent boy who never once in his life caused anyone a moment's trouble or harm." Wheeling to me, she renewed the assault in a black outburst of fury. "A young innocent boy, I tell you! All of his life suffering at the hands of monsters! Don't stand there looking like a big fool! What are you going to do about him? What are you going to do about Luciano?"

"I don't know, signora," I began, "I'm terribly sorry—"

"Shut your mouth, Swede monster!"

The sergeant put a gentle, placating hand on the woman's shoulder. *"Senta, nonna. Non è svedese. È americano."*

"Quiet, too, Bruno Ferragamo!" she cried. "I know you! They're all Swedes! They came here during the war, when Luciano was only a child. Remember those bombs? Do you have so short a memory? Remember how they came, raping and bombing and destroying? You remember as well as I, *Sergeant* Ferragamo," she sneered, "or you should, you Communist! How Luciano lay there in the road after the bombing, his poor legs broken beneath him and bleeding, all crumpled and torn there and crying his eyes out, with his poor arm beneath him, which he has never recovered from. Oh what a sad day!" For a brief moment her voice sank down, cracked and reminiscent. As we watched her and fidgeted, there was a trumpeting noise far down the road, and the dim sound of tires sizzling, as of some vehicle moving at great speed. "Oh what a dark day. With the bombardments and the smoke all around and the bricks toppling all around us. Oh what a terrible day. I remember how I was cooking when the first bombs came. I wouldn't get out. I wouldn't get out, I tell you. Though they begged me and pleaded with me. I wouldn't go. I stayed there cooking. And then the bombs. With the bricks falling all around and the smoke coming up and Anna Teresa there screaming. Oh what a day! Then I ran out into the road. There was Luciano lying there, the poor child all crumpled up and bleeding. His legs broken! His arm beneath him! Crying and moaning! Crying, '*Nonna, nonna,* I hurt! My legs hurt me so!' "

"Listen, signora," the sergeant put in gently, "it was a streetcar. . . . And I'm not a Communist," he said in an aside to me.

The old woman came alive from her reverie like someone startled out of sleep. "What streetcar? Shut up, Bruno Ferragamo! Shut your antichrist Communist mouth! I'll not have you policemen lying about Luciano and putting the poor innocent boy in jail! While you allow these monsters to run over innocent people in the road. Like this one here! Have you forgotten the bombs so soon? How they came up from Salerno shooting and sacking the towns and raping, when we were living in Torre del Greco. Have you forgotten so soon? Filthy cabbage-eaters! Drinkers of beer! Remember that one, the English one, who took poor Lucatuorto's wife in the ruins and ravened her there and left her there bleeding and dying, her with four hungry children to feed and a sick father to care for, he so sick and all. What has happened to your memory, *Sergeant* Ferragamo? Luciano, who has never hurt a soul in his life. Luciano, the tenderest of boys, the kindest, who once took a sparrow whose wing was broken—a sparrow, mind you—and nursed him till he was well and grown. Now you would leave Luciano to suffer at the hands of monsters like these!" She rose up on tiptoe, bristling with fury, and set both of her hands to shaking an inch from my chin. "You! Have you too forgotten the bombs? Have you too forgotten the oath I swore that day when I picked up poor Luciano from the road! 'As the Blessed Virgin stands as my witness in heaven,' I said, 'they shall suffer and be punished for their sins before God!' Bombing and sacking our home in Torre del Greco! Raping! Stealing! Taking poor Lucatuorto's wife in the ruins and ravening her, her with a sick father and four hungry children to feed! *Invasato! Mascalzone!* Wicked monster! Swede! May you burn in hell! God forgive me."

Then I found myself too shouting, abruptly and uproariously and on the verge of tears, my Italian deserting me, uttering strange sounds which I just dimly realized were in my native language: "I'm sorry, lady! I'm sorry! I'm sorry! But I didn't bomb your house! I didn't bomb your house!"

Down the road the trumpeting noise approached bellowing, grew louder and louder with the sound of some Gabriel's horn blowing flat ruptured notes of glory: the ambulance appeared in a rack of dust and gravel, trumpeting senselessly even as it halted at the crossroad, and as my voice rose hoarse and unhinged in vain encounter with the outrageous din. *I didn't bomb your house! I didn't bomb your house!* I kept trying to say, but found my lips struggling with broken wisps of air, sent flying on the wind by the shocking horn, which thundered on and on.

And then it was all over. The scene dissolved before me as if suddenly and mercifully drowned: the old woman, whisked away by her grandsons, gone; people, policemen, trucks, cars, all gone; the lot of them vanishing in hot stampede after the ambulance and the ravaged di Lieto—broken, dead or dying, I knew not what, but at last nobly borne to the sound of illustrious, tragic horns which rolled over the sunlit countryside, diminishing, intoning rich mingled notes of triumph and grief.

On the shore drive between Salerno and Amalfi, just before the road turns off for the long steep ascent to Sambuco, there is a large sign painted on a wall. It is written in bold letters of black on white; the words are in English—

BEHOLD ABOVE YOU
THE PALACIAL VILLA OF
EMILIO NARDUZZO
OF
WEST ENGLEWOOD, N.J., U.S.A.

—and one's eye, impelled by spontaneous obedience to this mandate and in swift search of some majestic dwelling place, roves skyward up and through the high hanging slope of vineyards and orange trees and blinding red poppies, to a ridge of land thrust up like a hatchet blade against the sky: there fixed in the rock is a structure the size and shape of an Esso station, sporting portholes for windows, painted an explosive blue, and flaunting at its proud turreted roof half a dozen American flags. Narduzzo's villa is not listed in Nagel's *Italy,* but it is in its own way one of the marvels of the coast. After the wondrous drive itself, with its raw green pinnacles and peaks, its cliffs coming down from dizzying heights into a tranquil cobalt sea, the effect of Narduzzo's villa could not be more upsetting or dissonant if one were to blunder around a turning into West Englewood itself.

I mention this because now in trying to recall the rest of that afternoon I am able to remember practically nothing, until the moment when I must have been shocked into something resembling consciousness by the sight of Narduzzo's house. Of my departure from the crossroad I do remember backing the car out of the ditch where it had landed and with a signpost prying away the fender, which had wrapped itself around one front tire in a crumpled embrace. I remember too the whole front end of the car: a ruin of splintered chrome, broken metal, headlights knocked wall-eyed, and in the middle of the mess, faintly silhouetted, the ghost of poor di Lieto, his rear end outlined unmistakably in the poised half-crouch of a jockey. And from somewhere underneath there still trickled thin streams of water and grease and oil. Yet although the car seemed to work and though I set out again, at ten miles an hour, the rest of the trip remains only a shadow in my mind of some dim but incomparable misery. It was the sign and villa which brought me to my senses. I stopped in the road with a jerk and in a billow of steam, my distress all suddenly devoured—as I turned my eyes away from the hideous star-spangled villa—by the beauty spread out before me.

By then it was midafternoon, but already above me the great peak on which Sambuco stood had obscured the westering sun, sending a vast blue shadow across the sea. Past the outermost limits of the shadow, where the light still shone, the water was as green as clover, but here toward shore it was a transparent blue, lakelike, upon which half a dozen little boats seemed not so much to float as to suspend, held up over the clear sandy bottom as if by invisible threads. Behind me in the lemon grove I could hear the faint sound of a girl's voice singing. A splash of oars came across the water, and radio music from below in some fishing town, a shadow-town which never knew twilight or evening, and was forever eclipsed by a somber half-darkness at three in the afternoon. For maybe a quarter of an hour I sat listening to the voice among the lemon trees, the sound of oars and the radio, and gazed south down the jagged, glittering coast toward Sicily, which I could not see but which I knew was there, two hundred miles away over the smoky horizon. I felt bitterly exhausted, and whenever I thought of di Lieto a wave of desolation swept over me, but the view soothed me for a while. Without surf or turbulence or breakers' roar, or the flash of winging gulls, it was a quieting seascape to look at, a sedative for weary nerves and bones.

I started up the car again and was about to make the turn-off on the road up to Sambuco, when I saw a girl standing there, her thumb out, hooking a ride.

Her children were with her; at least they looked like hers. They had been gathering flowers. As I came up to them and stopped, a trio of small rollicking cheers went up, my radiator smoked and fumed, and cornflowers, poppies, and wild roses sprouted all around me in the enveloping steam.

"Hello there!" the girl said. "I'll bet you're an American. My name's Poppy Kinsolving."

"I had an accident," I said. "The name's Leverett."

"What a funny-looking car!"

"I had an accident!" I repeated.

"Oh *dear!* Are you all right?"

The cloud of steam swarmed away on the air and Poppy's face appeared at the window beside me. Hardly larger than her little children, and so resembling all three that she seemed like their big sister, she propped her grubby hands on the door and gawked around the inside of the car.

"What a mess," she said.

"It was this accident," I went on to explain. "I was coming down the highway outside of Pompei and I hit this guy on a motorscooter and when I did all my baggage came—"

"Goodness, you'd think people would be a little more careful."

"I *know* it!" I said indignantly. "This guy was blind in one eye, mind you. His legs had been broken, his elbow smashed, two fingers gone—"

"Oh the poor man. The poor *man!*" she exclaimed, her eyes growing round with horror. "That's what I *mean.* I'd think you'd drive your car more carefully, Mr. Levenson. Every time I pick up the paper I read about some American hitting some Italian with his car. I think it's just a shame the way people drive around in these irresponsible American cars. Is he still alive? I'd think you'd—"

"Leverett," I put in. "The car's British, an Austin. Look, what I mean is the guy *already* had one eye out when I hit him. He came out onto the highway on his *blind side,* from the *left.* And when I—"

"Oh the poor man. The poor *man!* What's he doing now? Did someone take him to the hospital? Was there a priest there? I do hope he got the last rites."

"I might have been killed myself," I said feebly.

"I do hope he got the last rites. But he's not going to die, is he? Stop it, Nicky!" She swatted lightly at her youngest child, a towheaded little boy of about two, who had begun to whine and tug at her skirts. Kneeling down, she began to lecture him in a soft, gentle voice, while the other two children put their flowers on the road and took command of the car, clambering over the trunk and hood and prowling all around me as they chattered away, inspecting the wreckage and then my baggage. I kept looking at Poppy. For an instant, in spite of all my distress and what she had said to me, I felt my mind becoming hopelessly entangled with her sweet face, her huge blue eyes, her disordered sweat-damp hair. Sunshine streamed down on her through the leaves of lemon trees. She was dressed in something resembling a flour sack, although I could tell that it was indeed a dress. In the freckled light, with the faintest mist of perspiration on her brow, there was something charming and stubbornly childlike about her, though not altogether sexless, and for the moment—urchin or nymph or whatever—she was exasperating and unbelievable. "You see, Nicky," she was saying gravely, "grownups have important things to talk about and it's almost impossible for Mother to say anything if you're forever tugging at her nice clean skirt. Now there, darling, be quiet now and say hello to Mr. Levenson. Felicia! Timothy! Close up that suitcase!"

"I don't know if he's going to die or not," I said. "I've got to call Naples and find out. Is there a phone up at Sambuco?"

"There's one at the café, I think. And at the hotel. At the Bella Vista. Oh, do you know who's staying up there now? All these movie stars! They're making a movie up there. And down in Amalfi. There's Carleton Burns and Alice Adair and Alonzo Cripps—you know, the noted director—and there's Gloria Mangiamele, too. Burns is an old pill and so is Alice Adair but I love Mr. Cripps. I've talked to every one of them. That is, a little bit, anyway. Mason Flagg knows them all—at least he knew Mr. Cripps—and they're always drinking up in Mason's apartment and of course we can't avoid them, living downstairs and seeing so much of Mason and all. Are you a friend of Mason's?" She paused to regard me gravely, quizzically, and, I thought, with some suspicion.

"Well, I—"

"You don't look like one of Mason's friends."

"What do you mean by *that?*" I said.

"Oh nothing. That is, I mean, well—you look so *ordinary,* if you know what I mean."

"Thanks a lot," I said.

"Oh no," she said, flushing a little. "Really, I mean, you look very nice. Only his circle of acquaintance is just so glamorous, that's all. They're all connected with the movies, you see, and you—" She paused. A sudden look of consternation, of trouble, passed across her face. "Oh, I think that Mason Flagg's a terrible man!" she burst out. "He's just wicked and terrible. A wicked and terrible, phony creep!"

"How come?" I said. There was something painfully familiar about this speech. It had been four years since I had seen Mason; yet now, gloom piling up on gloom, it occurred to me that it had been the height of folly to hope that Mason had changed, after all. "What's old Mason up to now?"

"Well, I won't tell you, you're such a good friend of his and all —" Her nose wrinkled in disgust. "But if you could just see how he's *dominated* Cass and taken advantage of his condition and all, so that sometimes I'm just at my wit's end—"

"What do you mean?" I said, puzzled. "Who's Cass?"

But the trouble, a fleeting feather of a thing, had vanished, and she was back on the movie stars again. "I don't think Cass can stand any of them, except maybe Mr. Alonzo Cripps. Cass even thinks he's funny-looking, though. I can understand him not liking Carleton Burns. What a pill! And Mr. Alonzo Cripps is so sweet and *so* funny. He gave Nicky a box of *dolci* the other day. He's such a peach. And so brilliant as a director. But that Alice Adair! She's so prissy and stuck-up. I don't think she means to be, but she is just the same. Phooey on her, anyway . . ."

As she prattled on, a giddy feeling came over me. I shut my eyes tightly while she talked, misery and fatigue creeping through me in a slow malarial chill. I was suddenly conscious of the smell of lemons, far off a steady splash of oars above the chatterbox noise at my side. "Gloria Mangiamele is some potatoes, I'll tell you. You should see the way the boys' eyes light up when she walks through the piazza. Mr. Cripps says she makes more money than any movie star in the world, because of Italian taxes or something. Oh, I'll bet you're the man that Mason's been expecting! You'll meet all of them! Mr. Levenson, what's the matter? Wake up! Timothy, get out of Mr. Levenson's face!" My eyelids popped open, and I beheld two eyes as white and round as ping-pong balls, and a chocolate-smeared grin an inch before my nose. "What's your name?" Timothy said.

"To hell with it," I said, starting the motor. "You kids get the hell out of here."

"Oh, there's Cass!" I heard Poppy say. "Children, here come Daddy and Peggy. They caught up with us."

I halted, turning. Up the road hand in hand with another child came Cass Kinsolving, who was singing a song:

"Oh, we went to the animal fair,
All the birds and the beasts were there;
Carleton Burns was drunk by turns
And so was Alice Adair."

A poisonous black cigar protruded from his mouth even as he sang; with his free hand he clutched a half-empty bottle of wine, uncorked for use. Over his shoulder was slung a knapsack stuffed with what appeared to be wet bathing suits, and the sack was dripping. In dungaree pants and nondescript sport shirt, a smudged beret aslant over his forehead, he approached us with a free-wheeling, jaunty, nautical stride, still singing—

"Mangiamele with the luscious belly . . ."

—and nearing us now, seeing the mutilated car, ceased his song and stopped in his tracks with a slow, wondering, half-whispered *"Ho-ly* Jesus!"

"Mr. Levenson hit a man on a motorscooter," Poppy said.

"Wow!" Cass said. "He sure did!"

"And knocked out his eyes and broke his legs and cut off two fingers and they don't know if he's going to live or not."

"Wait a minute—" I began to mutter angrily. "And the name's *Leverett.*"

"Jesus. You poor guy," Cass said to me. It was the sympathy I had been waiting for and I turned to him gratefully, introducing myself as Mason's friend. He took a pull from the wine bottle and propped his hands on his hips, surveying the car with a bleak, mournful expression. Sunlight glinted in white disks from his spectacles, giving him an owlish look, and one peculiarly out of place in view of the rest of him, which conveyed at once a vigorous outdoor expression of strength, even of brawn. He was not tall but everywhere solidly muscled, and now as he leaned slightly forward with his look of intent and sensitive concern he appeared like some stevedore turned scholar, or perhaps the other way around. He was thirty or a little more, but lines that looked like marks of trial and labor were like small lacerations on his face. "You must have really cold-cocked him," he said. "You can see the poor bugger's ass-end still printed in your radiator. A bloody amazing intaglio. It's a wonder you can still get the car up these hills. What did you do to him?"

He nodded solemnly, sucked on his cigar, and gave satisfying little grunts of commiseration as I briefly told him what had happened. The littlest boy, Nicky, played nearby at the side of the road, but Poppy and the other children had climbed part way up the slope through the lemon grove. "Here's one!" "Here's another!" I heard them cry, in far-off chirrups of delight and discovery.

"You poor, thrice-crossed, luckless bastard," he murmured finally, when I had finished my recital. He spoke with such fellow-feeling and compassion that I wanted to embrace him on the spot.

"It's just unbelievable," I went on bitterly. "They don't license these jerks, you know. They let some half-wit with half his eyesight gone get on one of these machines, and that's *it,* buddy. None of them has any insurance and even if it's their fault you're up the creek if they've smashed up your car. God knows I'm sorry I laid him out like I did, I don't want him to suffer any more than his crazy old grandmother does, but after all I'm no millionaire and every time I think of this peasant smashing my front end like this—I'm not insured for that kind of damage and God knows what it'll cost me—every time I think of that it burns me up!"

What he said next was not precisely sanctimonious, but its touch of reasoned mercy did not at all harmonize with my resentment. I felt somewhat betrayed.

He stroked his neck and sighed. "Yes I know," he said, "it's mighty tough." Then after a pause he added: "I don't know. Those people down there on the plain, they're so lousy poor, I doubt any of them could afford a license, even if there were such a thing. All those songs about bella Napoli, bella campagna, say otherwise, but I don't think most of those people get a hell of a lot of fun out of life. I suppose a ride on a borrowed motorscooter is a big thing for some of them. They get all jazzed up and I guess something like this is bound to happen once in a while." Then as if suddenly aware of the thought running through my mind (*you bleeding-heart*) he said: "Well, I know that's one hell of a consoling thing to say to you now. Here, what you need is a slug of Sambuco *rosso.*"

But I turned down the wine bottle he held out toward me. "I've got to get up to Mason's," I said shortly. "I'm sorry I don't have room enough to take you all up."

Poppy, perched in the distance on the branch of a lemon tree, called down from the orchard above us. "Mr. Levenson! Mr. Levenson!"

"Yes?" I said.

"It's *Leverett,* Poppy, for God sake!" Cass shouted.

"What did you *say,* darling?"

"Leverett! Leverett! L-e-v-e-r-e-t-t!"

"Well, Mr. Leverett!" she cried. "When you see Rosemarie de Laframboise! Do you hear me, Mr. Leverett! When you see Rosemarie! You know, Mason's girl! When you see Rosemarie when you get up to Sambuco will you ask her something for me!"

Her shrill little voice grew dim; we could barely hear her.

"Do you understand me, Mr. Leverett!"

"No, Poppy, dammit!" Cass yelled. "We can't hear you. Come down!"

"Yasker alendus cheska!" And something else, in a remote caroling voice, that sounded like "Fullishagold!"

"What's she talking about?" I asked him. "Who's this Rosemarie? De Laframboise?"

His face broke apart in a funny wide smile, not quite lewd but in the same general area. "That's Mason's bimbo," he said. "You'll meet her."

"Rosemarie de Laframboise?"

Then all of a sudden I realized why the "we" left so unexplained in Mason's letter had never really puzzled me, since I had known all along that Mason, wherever he was and at whatever time, might be expected to be living with *some* woman, even one with a name like Rosemarie de Laframboise.

"Rose-marie de La-fram-boise," Cass said in careful, fruity syllables. "The works."

In the depths of exhaustion—at least in the depths of *my* exhaustion, I have found—there comes a moment when the spirit makes one last flight outward toward consciousness and reason, before breaking up into crazy splinters, or being extinguished by sleep. At this point all of the senses, worn raw by tiredness, are for an instant uncommonly tender and as receptive to the mildest stimulation as new skin over a recent wound. I suppose this explains why, as Cass spoke, a confusion of emotions swept through me—a sense of wild, glamorous beauty but of something ominous, too, way off in the distance, as if against my tingling eardrums there already beat a sound of catastrophe inaudible to normal ears. For at that moment the sun had sunk far down behind the hills, so that everything in the grove around us—vines, stone walls, and trees—had become shadowy and blue, touched by this early, peculiar dusk. The little boy played in the gutter beside us, thrashing at the stones with a branch and uttering tiny solemn squeaks. Far up the slope Poppy still warbled sweetly away in high tones, not only half-unheard but now half-unseen in the twilight, poised in ghostly suspension among the leaves of her lemon tree. Music drifted up from below, a splash came from across the water. And all about us swam a wanton late-summer odor of earth and lemons and flowers, which sent a sharp blade of nostalgia through me, and phantoms of loveliness to galloping in my mind, and filled me with a rich, sudden craving for something I could not name.

Then at some moment during this seizure I realized for the first time that Cass, though outwardly composed, was quite drunk, and that again he was talking, not so much to me as to this lowering, tranquil dusk, and was filling it with sunbursts of weird eloquence as he swung his wine bottle through the air. "Their faces," he was saying. "Their faces! My God, haven't you seen them? They're like something out of Goya in his most bilious, baneful, toxic mood. Goya! He would've ransomed his legs for a crack at them. One of them—that oldest one—is positively antediluvian. He's got the primal curse on him, if ever I've seen it. And the other one, the lush-head, what's his name—Burns. There's a prince for you! I'd have sacks full of gold if he were a Medici. He's got a slit-eyed Tuscan look, like one of Lorenzo's seedy, black-sheep cousins dragged into town for a whorehouse romp. He's the only man alive, I swear, with solid-green eyeballs. Check 'em, Leverett," he said with a tickled laugh, turning to me, "and see if that's not a twenty-four-carat fact. And the dame, too. Check her. My God, she's dazzling. But a spook. Yesterday in the sunlight I saw her turn—it was bright noon with this harsh, enormous brilliance all around—and I swear the death's-head was laid beneath her skin as plain as if it had been chiseled marble. Then I saw her eyes, and upon my word they evaporated away before me as if they had become dissolved like jelly by that selfsame midday sun—"

I heard Poppy's voice, close by us down the slope now, cross and annoyed: "Goodness, Cass Kinsolving, if you can't find anything to hate better than those movie stars, running on like that. Mr. Leverett is tired and upset and wants to go up the hill. I *told* you about drinking all that wine on a hot day like this—"

"Look, Leverett," Cass went on, "am I boring you? Do you want to see faces, real *faces*? Are you going to be here for a while?

Let me take you back to Tramonti sometime. There are faces there right out of the twelfth century. I'll show you a face so proud and tragic and full of mortal splendor that you'll think you had stumbled on Isaiah himself. More! Back there—"

"Hush!" I heard Poppy say, stamping her foot. "I don't know what's gotten into you lately, Cass Kinsolving. Why are you *acting* like this—"

"You know," he said, "there's an old witch back there makes ninety lire *a day,* hauling stakes for the vineyard on her back. Ninety lire! Fifteen cents! On her back! I want you to see her face. She's got a face like something out of Grünewald, with this agony, you see, twisted perpetually on her lips so mean and gray that it's like some living lamentation—"

"*Stop* it now!" Poppy shrilled. "You're such a *bore,* Cass, when you drink all that wine! And you're going to ruin your *ulcer!* Mr. Leverett, just ignore him. What I was asking you is this: will you please ask Rosemarie de Laframboise to lend us Francesca for the evening? Felicia has a cold and I want to put her *right* to bed and I want Francesca to help out."

"Yes—" I began, but as I spoke, my warm languid sense of beauty swept away from me, replaced by a sickening feeling like terror. *Oh God not again,* I thought, *not again.* Because I realized that that hurrying, ominous noise I had heard buzzing in my ears was not a trick; it was real and full of peril, and was now almost on top of us. Ear-racking explosions rent the dusk. "Watch out!" I yelled. "Out of the road!" But it was too late. A gray-green blur surmounted by two crouched figures—a black-haired man hugged close behind by a girl in fluttering red pants—the motorscooter was already among us with a roar, sending Cass and Poppy in startled leaps to the fenders of the car, and children flying like wind-blown scraps of paper in all directions. "You fool!" Cass cried, but again too late. The motorscooter shot on headlong past us, in full-throttled acceleration discharging flatulent backfires of smoke, the girl's shiny red hips cantering with equestrian, rhythmical bounces to the rocking machine as it vanished at the curve. As we turned then in alarm to the side of the road, Nicky was still pinwheeling around as if sideswiped or clipped, and then he sprawled out on his face in the gutter.

Poppy fled to his side. "Nicky! Nicky!" she screamed. "Look up at Mother!"

I knew I had seen this before; abruptly—and I am certain for the first time in my life—I believed in the existence of hell.

"Speak to me!" she wailed.

At once we heard a cheerful voice. "I'm all right, Mummy. I just fa' down."

Then over Poppy's hoarse little sobs of relief, I heard myself telling Cass: "See what I mean about these Italians? They're sick! They—"

Cass stopped me with an imperious signal, and a gesture with his wine bottle.

"Don't get yourself in a spasm, my friend," he said quietly. "That wasn't no Italian. That was one of the flicker creeps. I think he comes from Ioway."

II

"It was one bitch of a day," said Cass. "A bleeding monstrosity."

I agreed that it was. I had told him—in detail, for the first time —about my collision with di Lieto and all the rest. And from time to time he would mop his brow, sweating in the Carolina sun. Then recalling the way I looked, he had laughed in high uproarious knee-slapping laughter, so loud and long that I began to laugh too, possibly aware for the first time of the humor even in that straggling debut; and finally, when we had laughed ourselves out and our mirth chuckled itself down into a kind of ruminative quiet, he said: "I know it wasn't funny then. It wasn't funny at all. But Lord, boy, you should have seen yourself. You looked like a big scared bird."

"But did you—" I began, then halted, not knowing what else to say. Here we sat, as we had off and on for two days, in a skiff in the middle of the Ashley River, fishing for channel bass. And though he, who had most of the answers, had told me next to nothing, I had told him a lot—I who had nothing to tell. It was hot, and sand gnats skittered about our heads; in place of his beret, which somehow in my memory had seemed a stock cartoon headpiece of the American expatriate, he wore a floppy straw against the blazing noon. This and a pair of old Marine Corps dungarees bleached to the shade of dried grass comprised his angling costume. The heat had misted up his glasses, and he was barefooted. He chewed on a fat cigar, molasses-brown, half-smoked, and unlit.

"Toadfish," he said with a snort, yanking aboard a pop-eyed struggling fish, flapping and burping. "Nothing more miserable God ever made. Swallow a couple yards of line in two seconds. Swallow your hand if you'd let him." He threw the fish back, alive. "Don't come mooching around here again, toad," he said to the fish. "Rather hook a water moccasin," he went on, "almost anything. Look out there. See where the tide rips there? Spot. You got spot up your way, don't you? Drop a line in there and you'd be dragging fish in for six hours. Don't need no bait at all. Mighty poor sport indeed, though. One time last July I went out with Poppy and we could have gotten a bushel basket of spot in half an hour. They're all bones, though, just nothing but bones and only a mouthful." He rebaited his hook and cast out the line again, squinting against the light. The river shores were immensities of shade —water oak and cypress and cedar; the heat and the stillness were like a narcotic. "September's a good month for this kind of fishing," he said after a long spell of silence. "Look over there, over those trees there. Look at that sky. Did you ever see anything so *clean* and beautiful?" I had never heard the word "clean" spoken with such passion; it had the quality of an offertory or a prayer. He seemed to sense this and, as if to cover up, said: "Un-unh, it wasn't really funny, was it? The guy. Di Lieto, that his name? You say that he's still—what?—*out?*"

"Cold as stone," I said. "In a coma. At least he was that way six months ago. I get a letter from this hospital in Naples every now and then. A nun there, she writes me."

"Ah merciful Jesus," he whispered. "So that would make it— how long? *Two years* for the poor bugger. You think he'll ever pull out of it?"

"I don't know. Some people have been known to be out five, ten years—even more. I've talked to doctors—friends, you know —and they say it's entirely possible, but don't bank on it. I send a little money every now and then."

"So it's not your fault." He paused again, and now this swift and vagrant look of sorrow, which I was to notice so many times when I was with him, traveled across his face: it was just a flicker, no more, reflecting loss, regret, yet an infinity of remembered pain. Then it was gone as quickly as it had come, and his face was all repose again, and peace, and wrinkled forbearance and calm. "So it's not your fault," he said again. "But you suffer over it. You're bound to. You suffer over things like that and you can shake—believe me—you can shake at the whole universe like a madman, hollering for an answer, and all you'll get is this here little snicker. Which is God, or somebody, telling you to keep a stiff upper lip. *Dio buono!* There ain't—*Hooboy*, watch it! You got a bite!"

But the fish already had wriggled itself off my hook. "Prob'ly a crab," said Cass, "or an eel." He looked at the sky. "Must be around twelve-thirty," he murmured. "Poppy's just about getting lunch ready, I reckon."

"But what I could never understand," I said, getting back to the main topic, "what seemed to me so incredible was not so much what he did at first. Rape. That was right down Mason's alley, you know." I halted. "No, maybe not that kind of rape. I couldn't imagine him going that far. Sadism, you know. Killing and all the rest. But the rape itself was at least believable. What I just couldn't figure out was this—well, what must have been this remorse of his. The remorse and then what must have been the final courage or guts or something to finish himself off like that in one last act of atonement. You know, it takes—"

"Suicide?" Cass put in. He removed the cigar from his teeth and squinted at me, making a thin smile. "It does not take anything whatsoever, my friend. Maybe desperation. Guts is the last thing it takes." He gazed at me, not without humor, shrewd, tugging gently at his line. "It don't take courage, guts, or anything else. You're talking to a man that knows. Goddam gnats," he said, slapping.

He had said something like that only the day before; it puzzled me then as it puzzled me now, but again, as at that moment, he allowed me no time to ponder it: almost as if he felt he had let slip something he should not have said, he went on with a question, shoving Mason aside and interrogating *me:* "What happened to your car, anyway? It was a crazy fantastic mess. Did you ever get it fixed?"

"No," I said, "I didn't have time. Remember how—well, you know it wasn't more than a few hours after that when all hell broke loose. It was monstrous, you know. I arrive in that kind of state, shattered anyway. Then the next day Mason's dead. After that I didn't care. I sold it to Windgasser for junk. Just before I flew back to New York. I think he gave me a hundred dollars for it."

"You mean our old sweet *padron di casa* Fausto?" He chuckled. "Now wouldn't you just know. Swear to God, on doomsday that guy will be scalping tickets for the seats front and center, including his own. I'll bet he fixed that wreck up and made six hundred percent on the deal." He chuckled again and fell silent. Then after a bit he said: "Tell me this, boy. Just how drunk was I that day, down there on the road? I mean when we ran into each other." His gaze upon me was so solemn that I began to fidget.

I started to say something but he broke in: "I mean the reason I ask, you see, is because somewhere along the line there everything just plain blacked out for me. Everything. Then it was the wee hours and I was in the shower and you were trying to sober me up. Everything between is a complete bare-assed blank. I'm trying to pin down the time when everything blanked."

"I don't know," I said, straining once again for memory. "Hell, you didn't seem so drunk. Well, as I say, you did get wound up finally and started haranguing me about some of those movie stars, but I'll swear even then you didn't seem—"

"*Mamma mi'!*" he cried suddenly, in a cackle of laughter. "Those outrageous preening Hollywood puffheads! I'd almost forgotten about them. What the hell were they doing there? Oh yes— Jesus, it all comes back! That watered-down Humphrey Bogart type—what was his name again? Burns! And that dream-doll, Alice Adair, with the tiny little brain. And Cripps—yes, I remember him." He turned, grinning, lined crinkled face rosy with amusement. "You know, the more I think about it the happier I am that you came down here. I was so unmercifully drunk. And now here you are, like some private seeing-eye, taking me back through the blind spots. I mean it."

"That director," I said. "Cripps. He was on your side, you know. All the way."

"I know it," he said reflectively, scratching his chin. "I wish—"

But then again, as if with a sudden onslaught of private, hidden sorrow, his face shadowed over and he fell silent. "Blues," he said wistfully, after a while. "That's what we should be trying to catch. Bluefish as big as your thigh, up in North Carolina. There's a place called Oregon Inlet where they are as thick as fleas. And each one's mighty good sport, you know. One time when I was a kid me and my uncle went up there on a kind of week end, and got us a boat, and we hauled blues in until I swear my hands got scraped plumb raw—"

"But you know when I first saw you there on the road," I said with some persistence now, "one thing I remember almost the most was when Poppy said something to me. About, well—" I paused. "Correct me if I'm wrong. She was really upset, you see, and she said something about Mason I think *dominating* you. . . ."

As usual (and I should have foreseen it) it was as if I were a radio which he snapped off gently, courteously, but with absolute and final determination: about Mason he would utter scarcely a word. "Oh, I don't know," he said, "I don't know about that. It wasn't really as bad as it looked, you might say." His eyes went skyward. "Getting late, you know." And with that we pulled in our lines, Cass started the outboard, and we put-putted back to shore for lunch.

I had looked forward to a week end at most. Yet, risking my job by overextending my vacation (several telegrams went to New York later, proclaiming sudden illness), I stayed for more than two weeks. No doubt it was his native generosity, the mannerly long-suffering hospitality of a fellow southerner, which allowed Cass to put up with my barging in on him as I did—that, and perhaps the fact that I had, after all, done him one or two favors in Sambuco. But I was not asking for repayment. Generosity, hospitality, kindness—these were a part of his nature, and that we liked each other goes without saying; but the understanding and harmony that grew up between us and drew us together came from another source. I realized it soon: deep down and for reasons I couldn't fathom, he had his own private riddles to solve and untangle. And just as I thought that he could clear up my oppressive mysteries, so he saw in me the key to his own.

I had offered to stay at a hotel. Cass wouldn't have it. "We're not exactly waxing fat off capital gains," he said, "but we sure as hell can give you a sack." My share of the groceries, however, he allowed me to buy. I slept in a mildew-smelling attic high up under the eaves of the rambling, desperately run-down and creaking old house he had near the Battery, and each morning I awoke to the sound of his children stampeding below, and Poppy shrilling after them as she got them set for school; for a bachelor it was an oddly pleasant and familial sound, and I would lie there for a while, listening, until this noise diminished finally, mingling with the soft Negro chanting of flower peddlers on the cobbled lanes outside. Directly below, I could hear Cass clumping around in the room where he painted every morning. Around my window the scent of jasmine bloomed, mockingbirds caroled in the garden, and, propped on my elbow, wide awake now, I would look down on the leafy sun-speckled unblemished streets of one of the loveliest towns in the western world.

"It just plain *is*," said Cass. "Funny thing, you know, in Europe there sometimes, when everything got as low as it could get for me, and I was hating America so much that I couldn't even contain my hatred—why even then I'd get to thinking about Charleston. About how I'd like to go back there and live. It almost never was North Carolina, or the pinewoods up there in Columbus County where I was brought up. I didn't want to go back there and I sure as hell didn't want to go back to New York. It was Charleston I remembered, straight out of these memories I had when I was a boy. And here I am." He pointed across the wide harbor, radiant and gray-green and still as glass, then in an arc around the lower edge of the town where the old homes, deep in shade, in hollyhock and trumpet vine and bumblebees, had been defiled by no modish alteration, no capricious change. "You'll search a long way for that kind of purity," he said. "Look at that brickwork. Why, one of those houses is worth every cantilevered, picture-windowed doghouse in the state of New Jersey."

We fished and we swam. Swimming with Cass was a passion; he was like a porpoise, and gulping bubbles arose where he vanished for interminable moments. Often we rowed in Cass' skiff with the blond and bright-eyed children. But most of all we talked. Luck, as it turned out, was with us. The painting class he taught ("It's not like having shares in General Electric," he said, "but you'd be surprised at how well you can do, if you work at it.") had closed for the summer, his part-time job at the cigar factory had folded, and there was this interim space in which to take it easy. "I only took that job to get free cigars," he told me, "which I've got to have now that I'm off the booze. But it's absolutely disgusting, you know. These cigars, they're *homogenized*. Actually, that's what they do: they take good smoking tobacco and squeeze it up like they were making candy and feed it into a big machine and it all comes out about as tasty as a piece of stale chewing gum. Great big blooping hunks of dog hockey. Don't tell me these machines help mankind, boy. I ran one. I got so dreary-assed bored it near about soured me on cigars forever. Which would have been a tragedy. Most artists are oral, this head doctor told me once, and they've got to have *something* to chomp on."

We shared a love for music, which helped. He had put together a hi-fi set out of parts. He was on what he described as a Buxtehude "jag" and while I was there we must have heard *"Alles was ihr tut"* fifty times.

And there were outings almost daily to the leaky and half-collapsed fishing shack on the river—sometimes just the two of us alone, sometimes with Poppy, on Saturdays and Sundays *en famille,* conveyed there in a third-hand army-surplus jeep which Cass had bought for a hundred dollars, and in which the seven of us (eight including the colored girl, Dora) bounced together in a writhing nest of mashed toes, wails, and sticky laps. The cabin was in a grove of live oaks bluish and creepy with Spanish moss. And here on the bank or afloat on the river, half-hypnotized by the heat and stillness and the glimmering noons, we tried to make sense out of the recent past.

"What about Rosemarie?" I asked him one day. "That great blond bundle of Mason's. What about her?" Hazarding a foray into what I had come to feel was forbidden territory, I thought I might con him into talking about Mason by using that most oily of gambits—sex. "I don't mean to be naïve," I went on. "I know that something like her around the premises wasn't any guarantee that he wouldn't have his hands on every female in sight. But you'd think that she would have been enough for him. Even him. At least enough so that if the girl—Francesca, you know—if she had turned him down as she obviously had, he wouldn't have gone off his rocker like that." I paused. "It just doesn't add up," I went on. "I mean, I knew Mason. But what he did was—well, it was incredible. To be a—you know, a cocksman is one thing, but a rapist is another. I mean a real out-and-out sex fiend is not what Mason—"

"She was quite a bimbo, that Rosemarie," he said drowsily. "A real foursquare, fluid-drive humping machine. Godalmighty. What a man couldn't have done with—" His voice tapered off and for a while he was silent. "I don't know anything at all about Rosemarie," he said evasively. "Nothing." He propped his elbow on his knee and gazed at me with bright intensity. "That was the trouble, see? When I was in Europe I didn't know anything at all. I was *half* a person, trapped by terror, trapped by booze, trapped by self. I was a regular ambulating biological disaster, a bag full of corruption held together by one single poisonous thought—and that was to destroy myself in the most agonizing way there was." He got up from where he had been leaning against a tree, tense now, the humor and warmth dissipated, and began to pace the ground. I prepared myself. Occasionally he would do this: that gentle and easygoing thread would seem to snap within him, and he was abruptly all tension, recriminations, gloom. Even his diction changed. In the oddest way I was reminded of some red-necked Baptist preacher, garrulous and thick on the sidewalk with informal folksy good humor, who, ascending into the pulpit, turns into a tower of glitter-eyed fire and passion. And the strange thing was that, with Cass, it didn't seem incongruous at all. Now in a pair of discolored swimming trunks, skeins of fallen moss clinging to his wet burly legs, he paused, made a painful expression, and pounded the side of his head to get the water out of his ears. "A man cannot live without a focus," he said. "Without some kind of faith, if you want to call it that. I didn't have any more faith than a tomcat. Nothing. Nothing! How can I tell you about Mason or Rosemarie or anyone else? I was blind from booze two thirds of the time. Stone-blind in this condition I created for myself, in this sweaty hot and hopeless attempt to get out of life, be shut of it, find some kind of woolly and comforting darkness I could lie in without thought for myself or my children or anyone else. Look at these hands, these fingers! Look at 'em, boy! See how steady they are when I hold them out here? Not a twitch, not a tremble, see? With practice I could be like that doctor who could tie surgical knots in catgut with two fingers stuck inside a matchbox. I'm bragging, these hands are one of my most precious attributes. Yet there was a time when a glass of wine in my hands could be no more than half full, else it would all slosh out. There was a time when I would look down at these hands and they'd be shaking and twitching so much that I swear to God they seemed to belong to somebody else, some old man with the palsy, and I'd pray for them to stop shaking until I wept." He paused and nodded his head. "I don't want to tell you my old troubles," he said. "This isn't no groaners' bench."

"Don't stop," I said. "I'm listening."

He sat down beside me. "No, that wasn't it," he went on. "The booze, I mean. It went deeper than that. I was sick as a dog inside my soul, and for the life of me I couldn't figure out where that sickness came from. I told you the other day about—well, about how I was brought up, up there in Columbus County, dirt-poor and an orphan and all. For a long time I thought that was it. Orphanhood, pore shivering orphanhood! Or how I never got an education past second-year high school. Ignorance, pore down-trodden ignorance! I remember when I was in Paris there, trying to be a painter, and in Rome too, the chorus of this wonderful old hillbilly song used to come back to me." He paused. "Maybe I'll tell you about Paris sometime. I had the goddamdest thing happen to me there I ever had in my life. Anyway," he went on, "this here song was called 'The Dying Paper Boy,' and the chorus went: 'I never had the chance that other boys had, I never had no mom nor no dad.' *Nor* no dad," he repeated, with a short chuckle. "Christ on a bleeding toboggan! I used to sing that all the time. I had enough self-pity wallowing around inside me to float a whole raft. . . .

"Or the war," he continued, "that was a good thing to peg it on. The crushing horrors of combat in the grim Pacific. Ha! Or the fact that I'd married a Catholic and a Yankee to boot, who had tricked me and saddled me with a colicky brood of noisy tadpoles whose very presence would be a hindrance to a bank clerk or a shoe salesman or an art critic, much less someone who was a sensitive bunch of nerves like myself. Or, well—" He fell silent again but the shade of a grin lingered on his lips.

"O.K.," I said. "So—"

"So I traveled blindly down across that continent, full of booze and blind as a bat, abusing my family and abusing myself—teetering on an edge between life and death that wasn't much thicker than a hair, you might say, until I got to Sambuco. I thought I might pull out of it there for a while, but I was deluded. On that day you saw me I was blinder than I ever was before or since. That's why I can't tell you anything about anything. I was numb, *out,* stoned—and for the life of me I can't tell you what happened. Only—"

Poppy called from the cabin. "Cass! Peter! Your beans are going to get *co*-wuld!"

"Only what?" I said.

"Hold your horses, honey!" he shouted. "Only you can tell me something, maybe. Maybe you can."

"Tell you what?"

"Tell me about that day. Think hard. There are several things already that—"

"Cass!"

"O.*K!* On our bleeding way!"

And so I had to tell him my story first. . . .

I barely made it up the hill to Sambuco after leaving Cass and Poppy on the road. It was a murderous climb for my ravaged Austin. After half an hour or so, and a dozen engine-cooling halts along the way, I came in sight of Sambuco's archaic gate: here the car in final mutiny quivered and fulminated and drifted to a stop as the magnificent sea came into view a thousand feet below and as all the trappings of the barbaric valley I had climbed—crags and cliffs and lizard-skittering walls—slipped out of sight behind me. I could hardly believe that I had made it.

Through the archway I could see the piazza of the town, captured in a dazzling noose of sunlight, but the view of the sea from these heights was immediately so theatrical and romantic that it was a few moments before I realized that both town and square seemed oddly quiet and deserted. It was a stunning view. I stood there for a few seconds hypnotized, once again filled with momentary relief. On the high slope across the valley some wretched poor sheep were grazing, but so perilously and at such a slant that like cutouts pasted there by children, they looked vulnerable to the slightest gust of wind. Then with a sound akin to music and almost beautiful, a bus horn's two fat honking notes floated up from the valley; this and then a church bell far off behind me in the scrubby wilderness made me aware again of how unnaturally silent it was here at the entrance to the town. I trudged off through the dark mildewed archway in search of a telephone, troubled once more, and despairing, and conscious at my sleeve of the quick futile clutch of a hand, of the *carabiniere* in the shadows who whispered to me frantically, much too late: *"Signore, aspett'! C'è il* film!"

I must have only half-heard the cop. At any rate, it pains me still to describe what happened as I strode unheeding past his groping hands, out of the moldering archway, and into the glare of Sambuco's piazza. Submerged in my worries, I must have been so absorbed that I did not notice the fidget and buzz of industry around the café table I blundered into, where sat a man and a woman chattering busily. Here, suddenly and fuzzily bewildered, I tapped the shoulder of a scowling waiter hovering near, my lips

56

parted on the first breath of a question: *Cameriere, per favore, c'è un telefo . . .*

From behind me, I heard someone roar: "Cut! Cut! Jesus Christ, cut!"

I turned to find myself exposed to a battery of cameras and arc lights and reflectors, and now to the pop-eyed rage of a roly-poly little man in Bermuda shorts bearing down upon me, his lips curled around the butt of a cigar.

"Hey, *paesan'!*" he yelled. "Vamoose! Get the hell out of here! Umberto, tell this guy to get out of here! He just killed a hundred feet of film! Vamoose out of here, *paesan'!*"

I felt a multitude of eyes upon me—from the mob of townspeople I saw gathered behind ropes gazing on, from the movie folk clustered beneath the lights, especially from the two people at the table I had blundered into. One of them was Carleton Burns, who returned my gaze with his world-famous look of bored, functional disgust. No one laughed. It was like dwelling in an extremely bad dream. For a moment, in the same way that di Lieto's old grandmother had scared me, I felt the queasy visceral terror of a small boy caught at some lurid trespass, and I went weak, cold, and limp and I sensed the blood of pure humiliation knocking at my temples, but then suddenly something in me—perhaps it was the heat, or simply this final embarrassment, or the fact that now, after suffering such conquest all day at the hands of Italy, it was my own countryman, a waddling small blob of one but nevertheless a countryman, who was abusing me—anyway, something within me popped like a valve, and I began to boil over.

"Umberto!" he shouted at me, though not to me. "Tell that carbinary to keep these people away! Tell this guy to get the hell out of here. Vam—"

"Vamoose yourself, you miserable jerk!" I howled. "Don't *talk* to me like that! Do I look like an Italian? I've got as much right to this square as you do! Who do you think you are, ordering me around—" In the wilting heat minute orange globes of hysteria exploded before my eyes and I heard my voice bubble up and upward, precariously pitched and rabid but somehow, I knew, almighty, for as I kept shouting at the little man I saw him stop dead in his tracks, cigar butt wagging uncertainly like a semaphore, and with eyes bulging goiterously in indecision and I suspect disbelief. Of the two final things I remember saying, the first—"You can't push Italians around!"—seemed as I spoke unscientific and hollow, but a mawkish sense of triumph, the first of the day, swept over me as I yelled, "I'm a *tired, weary man!*" and on that note turned on my heels and stalked shuddering like a beleaguered and temperamental actor off what, it suddenly occurred to me, was a set.

I might have walked out of the square, down the mountainside and back to Rome, so sore and consuming was my bitterness, had I not at that instant run into Mason Flagg. He was standing at the archway; he had seen it all, and appeared to be beside himself with joy. In a sport shirt baroque with silver flowers, a white ski cap raked sideways across his skull, he was hooting with laughter; as I approached him his laughter slackened to a silent, convulsed chuckle and one shoulder went up briefly in that high-strung twitch I had forgotten, but which I might have recognized him by, at any angle and from any distance, whether in Sambuco or Paris or Peru.

"Old Petesy," he said, giggling, pumping my hand, "let's flap off on a wild one to Goochville."

It was a private reference to our days in prep school. I remembered that it had always been his custom—whenever we met after a long time—to greet me in some such fashion and I generally answered in kind, with schoolboy bravura, though never without feeling slightly asinine.

"Man, let's really flap one," I responded briskly. "Who was that guy running off at me out there, Mason? He burnt me up—"

"Some assistant director. Rappaport, I think his name is. Don't let him worry you. He gives everybody a pain. I think Alonzo should give you a job, Petesy boy. You were terrific out there."

"Well, I'm sorry," I began, "if I messed up their scene. I've had a terrible day. I was coming down the highway outside Pompei and I ran smack into—"

"Petesy, you look great!" he broke in. "I'm certainly glad you could come. How long has it been? Three years? Four? I don't think you've changed a bit. A little fatter in the cheeks, maybe, less haunted in aspect—and I should say more self-gratified around the glands. How's all this Italian twat you've been getting, Petesy? I've heard that a man hasn't even begun to *savor* life, until he's had one of these native girls moaning *mamma mia* to him in the sack. Petesy, you look absolutely in top condition!"

"Thanks, Mason," I said, without enthusiasm.

I must have queered the movie-making for the day, for around the cameras there was a tired air of dismantling, and the townspeople, flocking past the ropes, had once again taken possession of their lovely square.

"Don't let it *bother* you," Mason reassured me, as we walked toward a café across the piazza. "They're running this outfit like a carnival. For Christ sake, that scene you just got yourself into wasn't even written until three hours ago. It's the damndest production you ever saw. Writers dropping like flies."

"How long are they going to be here?" I asked, with a twinge of expectation. Through his family Mason had always been in contact with the movie world, but although I had known him off and on since boyhood my acquaintance with the celebrities of that world had been more distant than I might have wished. I had an awe of those people almost teen-age in its dazzlement, and the hope now of some actual fellowship—no matter how fugitive— colored my imagination with a sudden iridescent allure. "Are they going to be here very long?"

"There's that little jerk Rappaport," he said, as if he hadn't heard me. "Don't worry about him. You know what his first name is? Guess."

"I couldn't guess, Mason."

"Van Rensselaer. They call him Rense. Jesus sake." He twitched his shoulder up jerkily, as if he were trying to throw it out of joint. In the center of the square we made our way through a jabbering crowd of movie extras, from which two handsome Italian girls in skimpy black sunsuits detached themselves, slithering across our path with a great deal of pelvic animation. Mason took my arm. "Now just look at that," he said. "Petesy, there's more twat up on this mountaintop than a wise man could possibly handle. Just *look* at that stuff. I'd get a double-indemnity clause in my insurance policy before I'd play humpty-dump with something like that all night. Godalmighty," he sighed, moving in lean long strides beside me, "it sure is good to see you again, Petesy. How *is* this Italian stuff? You must be a veteran."

"Well—" I began, but "So long, Seymour!" he was shouting, flapping his arm at a young man who, perched in the cockpit of a Jaguar at the piazza's sheer edge, seemed prepared for flight into space. "See you in the moom pitchers!" Then, "There goes the last writer," he said to me. "Nice guy. Used to write novels.

"Oh, God only knows how long they're going to be here," he went on, "a couple of days, a week—you never can tell, the way they're making this picture. They only got here just a few days ago, right after I wrote you, as a matter of fact. I don't know what the exact pitch is, financially, except there's something about blocked-up lire, around a million dollars' worth, that the company had to play with, and so they dug up this horrible old costume novel about Beatrice Cenci and then assembled this half-American, half-Italian cast, and then found that the wardrobe and properties strained the budget all out of whack and so they decided to do it as a farce, in modern dress. I don't know. Anyway, they've been all over Italy messing around with the story and hiring writers and firing them, or they quit, because the whole story has gotten so grotesque, and the whole thing finally became such a colossal mess that Kirschorn, the producer—he's sitting on his fat ass up in Rome, at the Hassler—told Alonzo to get the outfit out of his sight and just *finish* the goddam thing. So Alonzo—say, you might have seen him at Merryoaks when we were kids; he was a great pal of the old man's—anyway, Alonzo had been to Sambuco before and decided it would be a fine place to booze it up and look at the view while they were getting the abortion over with. Alonzo and I ran into each other the morning they got here. Say, there's Rosemarie now! Hey, baby!" he cried, grabbing my arm and pointing at me. "Look, Peter's here!"

From an archway near the café we were heading for, the loftiest girl I had ever laid eyes on came ambling along in saffron-colored slacks and halted, tall as a watchtower, shielding her eyes from the sunlight. Then with a sudden pucker of boredom on her lips she minced onward in a giraffe-like promenade of blond and towering beauty, a vast handbag spinning from her elbow. I drew up short, transfixed both by her splendor and her height.

"Is that *yours?*" I said.

"That's her," he said, almost majestically. "Why?"

"She's gorgeous. But—but she must be ten feet high!"

"Calm yourself, Petesy," he said with an indulgent laugh, "she's only a little over six-feet-one. She's shorter than I am." Proceeding toward her, we were silent for a brief moment, then he added: "The first time I got her in the sack I thought I was climbing Kangchenjunga—" which made me writhe a little, but I murmured something appreciative in reply.

"Her last name's de Laframboise," he explained with a chuckle. "And don't laugh. It's her real name. She comes from a very good, loaded-with-dough Long Island family, and she's only twenty-two. French Huguenot. She's had all the best advantages—Miss Hewitt's Classes, Finch, everything." I was unable to tell now, from his matter-of-fact voice, whether he was kidding or not. "She was modeling when I first met her, making enough dough to thumb her nose at her family and hit the road with your old daddy here. Anyway," he added, with what sounded like a gratuitous hint of apology, "she's really a good gal. Absolutely no inhibitions at all, and a heart of gold. She's no dum-dum, either."

Now in the shadows of an umbrella-darkened table Rosemarie bloomed like an immense daffodil, her golden head bent down upon a copy of *The New Yorker*. As we drew near she looked up and regarded me with an equanimity so blank that it might have been plastered on, along with the cosmetic gloss that overlaid the big, elegant contours of her face.

"Hello, Peter Leverett," she said in a throaty voice, "I've *hehd* so much about you from Muffin."

"Muffin?"

A single bright sound of laughter escaped her lips. "Oh, I'm sorry. It's my nickname for Mason. Mason, darling, did that embarrass you? It's the *fehst* time I ever betrayed you." Then, turning to me: "But you are such an old friend, aren't you, Peter Leverett? I just feel I've known you for years." Her face was still no more than a beautiful mask, but her voice—in spite of that clamp-jawed North Shore accent, which not alone by geography has always seemed to me at such close remove from Brooklyn—was warm and amiable, and I sank down in a chair beside her, feeling considerably shortened as I ordered a beer.

"Alonzo said they had to shoot one more scene up the hill, darling," she said, turning to Mason. "Burnsey and Alice said they'd see us tonight."

"What about Gloria?"

"She's got the trots, but she said she'd be up tonight, too. You know what she told me? She said, 'Dahlings, these Italian foods geeve me intestinal wrongings.' Isn't that superb?"

Mason heaved a great roar of laughter. "That's marvelous! It's almost poetry. Shakespeare, isn't it? Cleopatra? That girl's a dream. Wait'll you meet Mangiamele, Peter. Her English has to be heard to be believed. Look, waiter, the beer's for the gentleman over there. I ordered a double bourbon and soda."

"Come, signore?" The waiter, a woebegone, slope-shouldered little man, stood above us stranded in bafflement.

"A double *bourbon* and soda."

"Non capisco."

"Oh Jesus sake, Peter, tell him—"

"C'è del bourbon whiskey?" I asked.

"Whiskey?" the waiter said. *"Si, ma solo Il Vaht Sessantanove. Skosh. È molto caro."*

"Oh Jesus sake," Mason was saying, "some of them are so *opaque*. Why did he take my order in the first place if he didn't have the faintest, wispiest comprehension—"

"Will Vat 69 do, Mason? He says it's very expensive. *Va bene,"* I said to the waiter, *"un doppio whiskey."*

"They're so dim, some of them," Mason said, after the man had padded off. "Now don't look at me like that, please, with that glazed look of disapproval. I know I sound like a horrible American interloper passing out all sorts of passé nineteenth-century sentiments, but honest to God, some of the people up here are really beyond belief, and I don't mean—"

From Rosemarie, face invisible behind her *New Yorker,* came a sudden crash of mirth, amplified deafeningly by the spacious sounding-board of her bosom. "Honestly," she cried, "sometimes I think Wolcott Gibbs is the drollest—"

"Oh stop, Rosemarie," he commanded, cutting her short, "can't you put that down for half a second? Peter's been here precisely three minutes and you're slobbering over that magazine like a basset hound—"

I saw an abashed "Sorry" form soundlessly on her lips, and the magazine slid to the earth with a flutter; then as Mason continued, she was all big blue eyes, all attention, her chin propped up on her hands amid a bouquet of scarlet fingernails.

"—and I'm not simply talking about what they call the language barrier," he was saying. "I'm really not so simple-minded or naïve or arrogant, or whatever you want to call it, to expect them all to speak the language. And I'm not talking about that waiter, who looks like a nice guy with nothing wrong with him that a couple of gallons of penicillin wouldn't cure. I'm only speaking of the stupidity, really, the *economic* stupidity of a café owner in a resort town where at least half the clientele must be English-speaking, who can't or won't employ a waiter who speaks the language. After all, we have to face it, don't we, that English is the pre-eminent language of the world? Well, don't we?"

"Yes indeed, Mason," I said. "By all means." Three gulps of beer, which had rocked me like dynamite, brought new lunatic dimensions to my exhaustion: gazing straight at him through gritty, aching eyes I tried to tell whether it was he, or merely the struggles of the day, that had brought me now to such a numb, anticlimactic despondency. On the outside he had changed hardly at all. Much of his gangling look had gone; the weight he had taken on since I had last seen him was attractive, it hadn't sleekly plumped up his jowls but gave solid lines of maturity to that slim smart pretty-boyishness I knew he had always secretly abhorred. Clothes-horse, too, he remained: the silk brocade sport shirt he wore was bright with glints of threaded gold, made for a princely waist; it must have cost as much as an entire suit of clothes, and no one I knew, except Mason, could wear it with such ease or let it flap out, beach-fashion, as he did, without looking like a clown. Mason was an immensely attractive young man, and the years since I had last seen him had added a suave luster to his beauty.

And with all of this I felt burdened under the blackest sort of gloom. Mason's voice buzzed back into focus.

"I notice you speak the language pretty well, Petesy boy." His voice was abruptly so arch that it was hard to tell whether he spoke with admiration or remonstrance.

"I think Italy's gotten you all upset, Mason," I said wearily. "I had to learn it. I've been here for three years, after all."

"Well, Peter Leverett—" Rosemarie began.

"Call him Peter or Petesy, Rosemarie, or Goo-Goo or Lover Man, for Jesus sake. But not Peter Leverett. Where did this double-name business come from? Is that all the rage now?"

"I'm sorry, darling. Well, Peter—do you mind?—I think I know what Mason's trying to convey. Do you mind, darling?" She turned to him briefly, but whether she ignored the glance of reproach he shot her, or merely didn't detect it, I couldn't tell. "What I think Mason's trying to convey is the sort of— well, trauma that affects one when one comes to a foreign country. Even when you've been abroad before. I don't know, getting off the boat in Naples, the terrible heat and the strange dark little people and all the horrible noise and confusion. Then last May, when we first got here, Mason came down with this dreadful psychosomatic cold—"

"Now, sweetie," Mason protested wryly, "please come off that psychosomatic dodge. It was a cold. Period."

"Well, darling, I'm not blaming you, even if it was psychosomatic. It just fits in with what I'm saying, that coming to a place like Italy can so upset the mind-body relationship that something like a cold is easy to get. That's all. I remember on the way up here from Naples when you took those antihistamine tablets—remember that first day?—you said, 'I'm dizzy and it must be because I can't understand one word these wops are saying—' "

"Sweetie," he said in an exasperated tone, "I suppose by now I've exposed myself *irremediably* to you and to Peter as the most grotesque sort of Rotarian, simply because of my vicious, xenophobic remark about the guy who runs this coffee house, but I want to assure you, baby, that I have never yet used the word wop, and that you are lying through your teeth—"

"I'm sorry, darling," she put in. Her hand flew to the back of his, in a hurried show of appeasement. "I'm sorry, really. I didn't mean to imply—"

"You just said it," he said sourly.

"Well, darling, I didn't mean to imply what you said. All I'm trying to tell Peter is that what I think you were trying to convey was that one can get off on the wrong foot in a strange land simply because the customs and the language—"

"Anyway, they weren't antihistamine pills. They were aspirin. I may be a chucklehead straight out of the Lions Club but I'm not a hypochondriac, for Jesus sake."

"All right, aspirin then. Anyway, the thing I think you were trying to tell Peter—"

Except for that day I can remember no time in my life when, sitting bolt upright, I was able to slip without sensation into unconsciousness, but once again I must have drowsed, for as Rosemarie spoke her voice lost both sound and meaning; past the rim of the sleeping square the vast panorama of sky and sea as if filmed over by sheets of yellow-hued dust lost all dimension, and nodding there and dreaming—what was it?—I felt myself in another land, a boy again upon some lowland estuary or riverside where marshlands echoed the incessant fever of a million humming insects and sails like brilliant kites made upon the oceanic sky patterns as swift and ecstatic as the flight of gulls. But the moment shattered in bits like glass and I must have jumped awake as hurriedly as I slept, for I sensed something moist and warming tumbling from my hand, my eyes snapped open, and the beer bottle exploded in a shower of foam around my feet.

"Peter!" Rosemarie cried. "Poor boy! You look perfectly *extinguished!* Why don't you go lie down for a little while?"

"Well, I would like to go on up to your place and sleep some of this off," I said groggily. "I'm just absolutely beat. If you'll just tell me how to get there . . ."

At this moment Rosemarie's expression reminded me of nothing so much as that chic, touching vacuity seen on the mortuary images of ancient Egyptian queens. What she said now, though, seemed to rise to soothe me through some instinctive, sweet, almost clairvoyant understanding. It was only later that night, looking into a mirror at my wrecked and blasted reflection, at my red-rimmed eyes and grease-smeared cheeks and bum's growth of whiskers, that I realized that, possibly in atonement for her earlier rudeness, she was simply trying to be nice. "Oh, I think you must be absolutely exhausted," she said. "Did you have any trouble getting here?"

"Oh God, it was awful," I said, taking a deep breath. "Near Pompei, this guy came barreling out of a side road on a Lambretta—"

"Petesy, old pal, I've got something to tell you," said Mason.

"I smashed right into him."

"Oh Lord!" said Rosemarie.

"Petesy baby, excuse me for interrupting—"

"Wham!" I said hoarsely to Rosemarie. "Just like that!"

"Oh my!"

"They've got him in the hospital in Naples. I've got to call up about him."

"Oh, Peter—"

"Peter," Mason was nagging patiently.

"It wasn't my fault," I was telling Rosemarie. "The guy already had—"

"Peter, I've got news for you."

"—one eye out. *What*, Mason?"

"Look, Petesy, I hate to say this, but I want to tell you there have been some slight changes. You know I told you in the letter you could stay with us at the villa? Well, what I've done is gotten you this terrific room at the Bella Vista—"

"For Christ sake, Mason!" I blurted. I was nearly sick now with frustration, and I heard my voice rising whiny, petulant, and objectionable in my throat. "What's the big idea?"

"Now don't get sore, Petesy," he said affably. "Lemme explain, dollbaby."

"Dollbaby my ass, Mason," I said, a tone of prep-school bickering creeping into my words. "I come down here to see you and on the way I practically get killed! I can't even get a word in edgewise about it, with all this chatter of yours about antihistamine pills. Then you want me to go squat in some flea-bag after you've invited—"

65

"Petesy, Petesy, Petesy," he murmured, gently shaking his head, "if you'd just let me *explain*."

"All right, then," I said bitterly, "go ahead and explain."

"It's not a flea-bag in the first place. It's a de-luxe hotel. The guy that runs it is our landlord, a great guy. I reserved you the best room they've got, and it's on *me*. I'm paying for it. You know damned good and well I'd consider it not only a duty but a pleasure to pay for it. And the only reason I did this is this—now Petesy, dammit, don't look so glum—the only reason I did it this way is because when the picture unit got here Alonzo got everybody rooms in the various hotels and pensions but—and this is just like Alonzo, the old bear—he completely overlooked finding a place for himself. So I put him in your room in the palazzo—"

"Why didn't he take that so-called terrific room at the hotel you reserved for me? For Christ sake, Mason, you invited *me*—"

"Petesy, dollbaby," he said in his placid, patient tone, "Petesy, listen! Someone, some tourist just *vacated* that room yesterday, after Alonzo was already here."

"I suppose if it hadn't been vacated I'd be sleeping in my car. What's left of it."

"Peter, don't be ludicrous. You know I'd have gotten you a place. You *know* that, don't you, about your old daddy?"

Now so conciliatory, so smooth and lulling, his voice struck old familiar chords of real affection, and my anger melted away, forcing from me as it vanished a drawn-out sigh. "Oh, O.K., Mason, I'm sorry. I suppose so."

"It's a wonderful room, Peter," Rosemarie volunteered. "I made Fausto—he's the proprietor—fix it up this afternoon just for you. It's got a marvelous view. When the Kinsolvings—they're the people who live below us at the palazzo—when the Kinsolvings first came here, they said, they stayed there for a few nights and loved it."

Mason tittered. "All fifty-seven of them."

I rose, no longer outraged, but feeling nonetheless cranky, rude, and somberly disappointed. "I met them down on the road," I said. "The girl—what's her name—Poppy—told me, Rosemarie, to ask you if you'd lend her whozis—the serving girl—to help out tonight. Seems that one of the little ones caught a cold."

"Where are you going?" Mason asked.

"Mason," I said solemnly, "I think I might have killed me a guinea today, but I've got to phone up to find out. Then," I added, turning on my heel, "I'm going up to that terrific room of mine and go to bed."

"Petesy," I heard his voice protesting as I went inside the café, "Peter, don't *be* that way. You're supposed to come to dinner tonight!"

But profoundly drunk from half a beer, my bones like jelly from fatigue, an ominous ticketing sounding in my ears, and, like some stricken diabetic, bizarrely lurching everywhere—with these afflictions I scarcely heard him; indeed, by then so bedraggled was my state that much of the brief remainder of that afternoon I remember in fantastic scraps and snippets, as if illuminated by flashbulbs set off intermittently in the deepest dark. The phone call I clearly recollect: an abortive parley with madwomen, held in a stifling booth which I shared with a swarm of malodorous flies. *"Macché, signore! Chi desidera all'ospedale?"* The lines were crossed, there was a shrill meticulous voice in French—*"Ici Marseille, Naples!"*—and many wrathful replies in Neapolitan; after ten minutes I gave up, leaving the two operators locked in horrible bilingual colloquy. Then with despairing indifference I began not to care about di Lieto, and conceived of him cold and dead, and emerged unsteadily from the dripping cupboard, heading once more for the terrace and the square. A bus drew to a stop in the center of the piazza; from its doors poured forth a horde of middle-aged albinos, haggardly berating each other in German. They formed ranks as I stood there, in *Lederhosen* and dowdy flowered frocks cackling over their Baedekers and clumping forward through a whirling cloud of pigeons toward the church across the way. As I averted my eyes I spied Mason, who rose from the table and hailed me.

"Pierre, you aren't sore, are you?" he said seriously. "Look, if you are I'll just tell Alonzo to switch with you."

And I wasn't really sore at him, I honestly believe, but only tired. This I told him.

"That's the boy, Petesy. Look, you go up to the hotel and sack in for a while, then you're due at the palazzo for dinner at seven-thirty. O.K., man?"

"O.K., Mason. *Ciao. Ciao,* Rosemarie."

A blank spot. I remembered my bags, which were in the car, but how I got there I am unable to recollect. Someone, at any rate, was lounging at the wheel—a big, flat-faced sallow fellow about my own age, who, when I came into sight, gave me a huge smile filled with snaggled teeth and blackened gums, like a blighted sunrise.

"Tell me," I said, "what are you doing inside?"

"*Sto attento alla machina,*" he said, still beaming. "I am taking care of your car."

"Well, descend," I commanded. "You have no business inside there like that."

"*Sissignore! Subito!*" he exclaimed, clambering out. "Had I not come along those boys would have hurt it more than they did. As it is, you see, they have smashed up your windshield and left a large hole in the front end—"

"What in God's name are you talking about?" I said.

"Those boys from Scala. They are very bad. They came along with a big stick and began to beat up your machine." As he said this a poignant and final misery seized me, now after so long almost insupportable; it was as if di Lieto's ghost had stalked me to this mountaintop, for as he spoke the brooding globed skull and vacant eyes, the mouth which, so like that of di Lieto's in the midst of his canceled desolate slumber, twitched slack and forever uncomprehending and benign—all these informed me that this one, too, was mindless as a chicken, and an awesome feeling neither terror nor compassion but part of both swept over me, made electric and vast in my exhaustion along with some ancient, fleeting hunch that what I beheld, though cruelly marred, was indorsed by heaven. "*Io mi occupavo dell'automobile,*" he babbled on. "I chased those boys away. Have you an American cigarette?"

"Pockets full. What is your name?" I said. We sat on the crumpled bumper of the car together while the hazy premature dusk settled in the valley below us, and lit up a couple of Chesterfields. Smelling powerfully of goats, clad in five cents' worth of rags, he sent blue clouds of smoke billowing through the twilight and pondered my question.

"I'm called Saverio," he said finally. "I speak good English. My uncle lived in *la città di Brooklyn* many years ago. He told me. Listen. *Corney Island. Oly Smokes. Skeedo. Wanna pizza tail?*"

"*Bene,*" I said.

"*Skeedo,* that signifies 'hide the red lobster.' "

"What?"

" 'Hide the red lobster,' " he repeated. "Are you with the films? Did you ever hide the red lobster with La Mangiamele? I would dearly love to do that with her. Have you ever? She has such wonderful big breasts."

"No," I said. "Have you?"

"Never," he said, gurgling sadly. "I have only done this once in my life which was with a shepherdess named Angelina in Tramonti many years ago. She died though of the evil vapors. Are you a millionaire?"

I got up, thinking that I heard a faint toy piping sound in the air around us, the sorrowful scamper of naked feet, long ago pursued, long made still. *"Vieni,* Saverio," I said, "earn yourself some riches. Those bags there, those boxes. *Andiamo!* To the hotel!"

Beneath a mountainous load of suitcases, blankets and bedroll and portable radio, books and tennis racket and guitar, slung from him at all angles like a packhorse and like a packhorse foot-sure, burly, and uncomplaining, he preceded me back through town, singing to himself and gabbling the entire way. "Out of the road!" he bellowed at an inquisitive dog. *"Via, via,* son of a whore! Make way for the Americans!" In wild song and in words I could not understand he sent his demented voice, harsh as rattling stones, through the archways and up to the rooftops, and hooted and crowed, and sprayed jubilant globes of spittle through the air. Then I bade him halt and shut up, for at the end of some dark alleyway Rosemarie and Mason were standing in the shadows, and I was conscious of a mechanical racket, basso profundo (one of those mobile generators, it has later occurred to me, which the movie people were forever dragging across the Italian landscape), and the two voices, one husky and male and furious, the other high, placating, touched with chill alarm, both rising up and up in frenzied contest with the roar.

"I did *not,* Muffin!" she pleaded.

"You did, you did!" he yelled. "You *hinted,* you lousy bitch!"

"I didn't mean to, darling. I only meant—"

"You hinted!"

"Muffin, darling, please listen—" she implored him.

"You listen!" he put in. "My sex life is no concern of yours! Like it or lump it, understand?" A dozen of his words went skittering away on the churning din. "—you to know that if I want to get laid—" *Chuckety-clack, chuckety-clack.* "—and *lay* anybody, anywhere—"

"Darling!"

I heard them say no more. With baffling simultaneity the

flowered oblong of his arm went up to hit her just as the generator ceased its roar, then struck, and in that vacuum which rushed in upon the engine's final flutter one flat smack of his hand against her face seemed to echo down the alleyway in wave on hurtful wave, then faded, then lay still.

I drew back for an instant, waiting for some cry or whimper, but I heard no sound at all. So I hustled on (ragtag Saverio, my bedeviled, lustful, gifted Papageno galloping behind me) like a voyeur, ashamed, but undetected.

Later, at the Bella Vista, sprawled on the bed fully clothed and still unwashed, I was kept fretfully awake for a while by the painting which engulfed one whole panel of the wall. It had been pointed out to me by Windgasser, the Swiss-Italian landlord, a soft-handed youngish man with rosy cheeks and burgeoning dewlaps, honey-tongued, flatulent as his name and, at least at that moment, wholly insufferable, who had greeted me at the door with a cry in English like a song, then with a threatening look and a curse, which revealed a lisp in both languages, chased Saverio away, and led me upstairs babbling good evenings, *bon thoirs* and *guten Abends* to his guests and to me obsequious, mystifying amends. "Had I known," he said. "Had I just known. Ah, but this room will be *very* compelling. You thee? This was my father's hotel and his father's before him. But I'm devvistated. Any friend of Mr. Flagg's is Fausto Windgasser's most honored guest. That, thir," he said pointing to the painting and flinging open the blinds, "That painting is by Ugo Angelucci who—I don't know if you know it or not—died twenty years ago in this very hotel. It's his masterpiece."

"Thank you," I said. "Now kindly close the blinds."

When he had gone, allowing me, in a depletion of spirit so profound that it threatened sleep, to lie twitching restlessly on the bed, I found that the empty-faced beautiful woman which was Angelucci's painting was scrutinizing me with half-closed eyes. She was a vapid, heavy-lidded blonde, presumably in bed but hardly tantalizing, for her lower parts were swaddled in what looked like some impermeable rug and a yard of squeamish lace appeared from nowhere to cover both her breasts. Yet as my eyes became accustomed to the darkness I could tell that the painting, whether Windgasser was aware of it or not, was meant to be naughty; the title beneath in rambling Italian script—"Troubled

Sleep"—gave it away, and with a dozing, wondrous sense of discovery I saw that Angelucci, the old rogue, had arranged in artful, subtle lines of chiaroscuro a famished male profile against the woman's shoulder, while tangled around her naked belly, and concealed there just as in one of those drawings for children where you must always find the hidden duck, a cart, or a horn, were the phantom shapes of two groping, ardent hands. With her budlike lips and stiff neck and arctic air of chastity, the woman generated no more vigor or excitement than those old, dim sketches of Madame du Barry—a fraud, a cheat, and a disappointment—and I remember sinking back in the pillows, thinking of Angelucci and listening, as I began nervously to drowse, to hidden bells and boats far down the slope on the placid sea. Who was Angelucci? I wondered, nodding off. What manner of man was he? And for no reason at all, in fantasy still dwelling upon the gloomy damask Edwardian rooms through which Windgasser had conducted me below—the *salone* with its elephantine sofas and yellowing stacked-up copies of the *Illustrated London News* and bookcases dusty with Bulwer-Lytton and Fenimore Cooper and Hapsburg memoirs, and the framed photographs, stained and damp with time, of the hotel's regal visitors (Umberto the First, looking old and sickly, the Duke of Aosta with his pretty family in a box-shaped old Daimler, Queen Margherita in a cloche hat, Ellen Terry, Erich von Stroheim, movie queens and sheiks of the twenties now dead or sunk out of memory)—my mind became a drowsy camphorous collage of antimacassars and dogcarts stuffed with children in pinafores, of *croissants* and governesses and elegant outings to the blue incomparable sea, where men with goatees sunned themselves, and the air was filled with an extravagant babel of tongues. Oh, for that fragrant, bygone, impossible life! And again, across some exquisite margin of desire and longing that separates waking from sleep, the clownish figure of Angelucci cavorted—a Neapolitan lecher, perhaps, with sticky fingers and a Vandyke beard, artist *manqué* in a land of giants, who came each summer to the Bella Vista to simplify his liver, to paint a bit, to bask in the transcendent light of Hapsburg and Aosta and Savoy. *"Vostra Maestà!"* I heard his plea across the decades. "Majesty! If I could just paint—" Or, turned humiliatingly away, sidling now toward the lovely English girl with rose-stung cheeks (how rich she must be!): "Excuse me, signorina, but the color of your hair—" Did he die perhaps in this room? In this very bed? Dimly, remotely, the bells from the gulf jangled in my reverie, my eyes seemed to behold once more those fatuous eyes, those ghostly, licentious hands, and now smitten sorrowfully with the sudden knowledge that this maiden resembled someone . . . someone . . . I began to pass into oblivion. . . .

But I did not go to sleep then—not quite. I only half-dozed, and as I did so a lowland boyhood seascape formed in outline against my brain: a quiet blue waterway, boats, seas, gulls. Then Wendy, propped near me blank and lovely against the cork cushions of a sailboat whispering over foam-flecked Virginia waters, indolently murmuring: "What sunlight. What a divine day." And Mason's voice, merry from the helm: "Stand by to come about!" Then the stilted feminine voice again—"Mason, darling! I *always* get the spray!"—as the boat in ponderous swerve came up to meet the wind, trembled for an instant at standstill amid a flutter of sails, then caught the breeze and turned—gulls, trees, sky and distant riverside all turning too, slowly spinning, moving in languid panorama out of sight. And, *"Mason* darling," the voice cajoled light-heartedly, "I *always* get wet. Let Peter sail, *chéri.*"

"Don't be silly, Wendy-dear," I seemed to hear his reply. "Peter wouldn't know a jib from a jibe."

"But darling, how *uncuhteous* to your guests."

"Shut up. I love you, angel."

"Angel-pie. My sweet adorable seventeen-year-old. Happy birthday, lover. And Peter, dear. Happy birthday, too."

It was not my birthday at all, but a half-dozen martinis had clouded many of her perceptions; when we docked she almost toppled from the boat but, svelte in slacks and nimble, recovered her balance and stood poised at the bow gleaming and joyful, stretching out her arms and whispering, "Youth, youth," to an apricot-colored sunset. It was the day Mason was kicked out of St. Andrew's, imprinted deep in my memory because the havoc wreaked upon Wendy-dear (I rarely heard him call his mother anything else) beginning at the moment that evening when, I think, she sensed the news (he tried to pick the most propitious moment, too, when liquored up, in chirrupy flattery still bestowing upon him garlands of *chéris* and angel-pies, she seemed most able to absorb the shock), sketched upon my mind such a cruel portrait of human turmoil that I often still wonder how, at that age, I survived it.

St. Andrew's was not much as a school, I suppose. Created for the sons of impecunious Virginia Episcopalians, threadbare and creaky, as frigid in December as Dotheboys Hall and chronically short of money, it had more than its share of misfits and nincom-poops who could not find lodging elsewhere, and was a snug har-bor for storm-driven scholars washed up from the academic sea. Our English master one year, I remember, was a young football star from an agricultural college somewhere who kept reading us verses by Grantland Rice; another year, some poor old derelict, a French instructor, was found dead in bed with a bottle of booze beside him. But what there was lacking in scholarship and learn-ing was made up in something called "St. Andrew's spirit"; the football team, clad in cast-off moth-eaten jersies, was regularly trampled by every institution in the state, but rowdily cheered; and the school's situation—its bucolic setting in the lost Virginia tidelands, the surrounding blue and brooding sweep of river's estuary and riverside and bay, nodding cedars around the win-dows close by where we slept, and pines in the woods, and wil-lows at the water's edge which at each morning's tolling bell, I remember, let loose to the sun a flight of exultant birds—made it an agreeable place for a boy to live and grow. What is more, it was a tiny school—there were rarely more than forty of us—so that often I think we felt, though unconsciously, that we were more of a family than a school and that Dr. Thomas Jefferson Marston, the pious old minister who reigned over us, and so Vir-ginian that it was almost heartbreaking just to hear him say "Gen-eral Lee," was more of a father to us than a headmaster. His voice was seraphic—a posthorn, a cello, a psaltery upon which each evening, with artless splendor, he played the liturgy's ravishing song; now when I recall those musty twilights in chapel, and the old man's luscious voice floating over our bowed, dishev-eled heads—*Lighten our darkness, we beseech thee, O Lord*— and then let my mind rove to some other scene, to the river, blue, immaculate blue, where we sailed our leaky boats, and the sur-rounding crickety frog-filled woods lit at night by our stealthy, clandestine lamps and the hill sloping chaste and grassy to the bay, where we went digging for clams and the evening gulls would slant away in full cry eastward toward the sea—when, as I say, in impiety and yearning, in headlong rush toward some departed tranquillity and innocence, I think of those scenes, there soars above them in my memory that reverend voice still crying out in dusk like some celestial trumpet: *O Lord, my strength and my redeemer!*

Into this dutiful Christian atmosphere Mason burst like some debauched cheer in the midst of worship, confounding and fascinating us all. He came out of the North (to all of us a mysterious place; Rye, New York, was where he had lived until the age of twelve), enunciating his "r's" with a brisk, sophisticated lilt, draped in a cashmere blazer, and loaded down with Tootsie Rolls, golf clubs, and contraceptives. Already, he told us with some pride, he had been kicked out of *two* schools. He was seductively glib, winning, quick-witted and beautiful. And at first he bewitched all of us.

Once he told us that he had been only thirteen when he lost his virginity—one summer week end at his father's recently acquired estate on the York River—to a no longer young but still lovely and still celebrated Hollywood actress. The story was outlandish but somehow plausible. We all knew Mason's family moved in movie circles. And considering other tales about this lady (one of them, having something to do with a scandalous act beneath a night-club table, had been powerful enough to unhinge the imagination of a whole generation of schoolboys), I guess we at first believed it. Mason was only sixteen at the time, and he unfolded the story with all the dreamy richness of detail of some rancid old libertine. Yet it was typical of Mason even then to undermine his own credibility, and to ruin a good thing: in later accounts that early seduction was only the first of many skirmishes, and the insatiable movie queen became his mistress for three summers running. There were steamy liaisons in Richmond or Washington, love-bouts in the backs of cars, in swimming pools, on boats; once, he claimed, standing up in a hammock—all these even at our gullible, lascivious age were flights of desire beyond reason and the whole wonderful erotic edifice crumbled finally, broken by Mason's preposterous embellishments. I think our disbelief honestly hurt Mason; later I found out from his mother that the actress had indeed visited the Flaggs—once in Rye when Mason was very young—and had brought him a teddy bear and dandled him on her knee.

His wealth, his glamorous connections, his premature ease with the things of the flesh—they worked on me a profound fascination. Why he in turn should have been attracted to me I have never known for certain. My background, for example, is almost triumphantly middle-class. I have a feeling that Mason's interest in me was largely based on the fact that—at least then—I laughed unfailingly at his jokes, nodded amiably at his lies, and in my sycophant's role mirrored some desperately needed approval for all his greedy desires. Actually I always felt that he somehow admired me—for whatever sentimental altruism I possess that allowed me to tolerate his own excesses. It has taken me years to learn how to reproach people to their faces.

At any rate, Mason at sixteen was more worldly—or gave the impression of being so—than many young men who look wan and deflated at thirty. He dressed in sleek trim suits tailored in New York, smoked English cigarettes, and though he had never left America his voice was the exhausted querulous vibrato of a man who had savored a score of exotic coasts. Already he had outstripped his own adolescence and was lean and handsome, with a supremely becoming suggestion of whiskers and a horrible turn of mind that could cause him to whisper, as he did to me one morning in chapel: "I try to pray but all I can think about is getting laid." It shocked me, for my belief in God, though fading, was still alive and suffered few fleshly intrusions. But my bulwarks were breaking up. I continued to be beguiled by Mason while the other boys were losing interest in him. They were less susceptible to his wealth, became tired of his endless stories, and were finally outraged when Mason, who had the makings of a good athlete, counterfeited something sprained and sat out the whole football season. Of all the boys I think I alone regarded that act as something other than cowardice. In the end I was the only friend he had left—which as I look at it now may well have been a measure of my corruptibility.

The Flaggs were the only people I ever knew who were millionaires. Mason's father was a New Yorker, an investor who had made some sort of a fabulous killing in the distributing end of the movie industry ("About the only one in the business," Mason used to say rather proudly, "who isn't a Jew or a Greek.") and had come down to the fashionable part of Gloucester County to set himself up as a Virginia gentleman. He was a success at it, buying an enormous estate called Merryoaks, which was a Colonial plantation manor authentic in every respect—at least until the addition of a swimming pool, tennis courts, and a stainless-steel boathouse. That year I went there with Mason many times—it was only an hour or so's drive from the school. In the early fall there were often parties for the grownups, New York celebrities going and coming in Cadillacs, and a grove of pastel paper lanterns sprouting each dusk upon the lawn. Once a ball-bearing mogul from Sweden named Aarvold landed his airplane on the grassy meadow which was the Flaggs' back yard. In those antebellum days this was an exploit of spectacular dash, and it took me a long while to get over it. That was the same week end, I recall, that Mr. Flagg hired a whole choir of Richmond Negroes to sing spirituals for the guests, and I remember Mason remarking that the entire proceedings were "impossibly vulgar." "Old Cuhnel Flagg," he said scornfully, with that pained awareness he always had that he was not really a southerner, and that his family were Johnny-come-lately Virginians. That week end, too, I remember everyone was waiting for Greta Garbo to show up but for some reason she never came. Lionel Barrymore was there, though, and Carole Lombard, and a very young starlet of about seventeen—she never amounted to much in the movies—with whom I was feverishly smitten, and who teased me so unmercifully about my tidewater drawl that I eradicated it on the spot. To this day, because of her, my accent has remained as amorphous and orderly as a radio announcer's. My very breath turned to dust around her, and I suspected that she loathed me for the soft patina of acne that hovered rosily about my nose. But I felt blessed just to walk where her shadow fell and would willingly have died after the ecstasy of that night, when doggedly, sweatily, and stricken mute as stone I danced with her until dawn, and until the last of the hired musicians began packing their horns and violins, and the renovated castle in the morning mists loomed with drowsy parvenu splendor amid its garland of extinguished lanterns.

I never got to talk to the elder Flagg at all. He always seemed oddly removed from Mason. I was constantly aware of some unspoken resentment between them which Mason, on his part, would relieve by stealing the old man's liquor. He was a bald, mustachioed, freckled little man with an adjutant's strut and a bearing which I couldn't help but associate with spurs and jodhpurs, rather than with the soft effeminate flannels and sandals in which he was usually decked out. Young as I was and diminutive as he was, I could sniff when I was near him a tremendous power and affluence. It was easy to tell he liked the presence of celebrities, who in turn flocked like famished, irrepressible moths around his opulent flame. He dropped dead later during the war, in South America, where he was financing a huge new chain of theaters. I only realized his eminence—specialized as it might have been—when I saw his obituaries everywhere, making him out as something of a mystery man who had always shunned personal publicity. Resentment, ill-will, whatever, he nonetheless left Mason a trust fund which amounted to nearly two million dollars.

Wendy-dear, however, I knew much better, for she worshiped Mason, and with the blind constancy of some devout communicant, seemed always to be hovering near the image of her adoration. Mason had already been expelled from two New England prep schools and it is doubtful that he would have been admitted to a school less hard up for money than St. Andrew's; even so, it was not hard to tell that she sent him there mainly in order to be close to him, and that those dark moods of apprehension which flickered from time to time across her lovely face expressed a fear, constantly jangling and discordant, that he would get booted out again. She was a marvel to me. Rich flaxen hair brushed with electric perfume and a high flush of rouge at her cheeks, inch-long vermilion fingernails and a jangle and bangle of brass at wrists and ears—these were attributes I had never connected with mothers, who in Port Warwick tended to be portly and subdued, and she seemed to me a fantastic apparition, irresistibly, almost alarmingly beautiful. However, she smoked a lot, and drank; in fact, she was the first lady lush I had ever seen. Three bourbon old-fashioneds after dinner (this was always when Flagg, Senior, was away, which had become more and more frequent toward the spring of that year) made her diction almost as impenetrable as something croaked out by a deaf-mute; she began to weep and fawn over Mason, telling him that for her sake, for his future's sake, for Princeton, he must be a good boy at school, suggesting now with a hoarse sob, now with a martyred shrug or a final haggard grimace, that since his father was seeking another woman's bed, he, Mason, was the only thing she had left on earth. I had lofty southern notions about ladies at the time, and scenes like these left me flabbergasted and depressed.

But when sober, such talk from a mother! Such enchanting, indiscreet, worldly-wise chatter I had never heard.

"But *chéri,* you have so much to learn. You're really so young yet, darling. Sex—I mean the physical union between man and woman—is a beautiful experience, not something foul-mouthed and vile. You'll learn. No wonder Dr. Morrison lectured you. You say he overheard you telling that perfectly horrible joke?"

Still unwitting, still unaware that Mason had been sacked only the night before, she drove us in her convertible down to Merryoaks on that fatal birthday week end, her gorgeous hair flying out behind her in streams of undulating gold. Like his silent pimply equerry I reclined on the back seat behind Mason (it had been no simple joke the headmaster had reckoned with, but some carnal embrace in which the old doctor, fumbling around and with palsied fingers lighting matches in the chapel basement, had ambushed Mason stark naked with the weak-minded daughter of a local oysterman, both of them clutching bottles of sacramental wine; and no lecture—"He whaled the hell out of me," Mason later said—but a public proclamation cast in the form of such black anathema that I still recall how the last part of it read: ". . . a stench and a rottenness in the Nostrils of Almighty God, and I am grieved to say that it is no lingering fragment of Christian forbearance, but only the law of the Commonwealth of Virginia, which prevents my exacting a retribution more severe than silent and expeditious banishment."); Mason, unperturbed and elegant in a camel's-hair jacket beside his mother, would turn his luxurious profile toward her from time to time and lightly peck her cheek, the two of them lost in tender banter, gazing long at one another while the car, swaying from side to side and under no control at all, hurtled down dusty country roads like a runaway rocket.

"Yes, Wendy-dear, the joke about the duchess and the poodle."

"Well, no wonder, it's perfectly *vile*."

"How else then, dear heart, is an unmarried man going to get his kicks? In France—"

"Oh, I'm sorry I ever talked to you about France. You're not a *man*. I hate to tell you this, dear, but when you get to Princeton they'll consider you the merest boy."

"Wendy, sometimes you're such a trial. Besides, remember your promise."

"What promise, angel?"

"That when I'm eighteen you'll take me to—what do you call it?—one of those bordellos."

"Darling! Peter, don't listen to him! Darling, you're absolutely vile!"

I was unhappy for Mason's sake that day, fidgety with apprehension over the scene I knew must come, but Mason and his mother were all high spirits and merriment. Before noon the three of us went sailing in the Flaggs' trim little sloop, landing across the river at Yorktown, where we spread a picnic lunch upon one of the grassy breastworks so lucklessly defended by Lord Cornwallis. To me Wendy had never looked so devastating as she did that day, all sheen and gold and radiance; with a saucy wink for me, prankishly tousling Mason's hair, breathing soft phrases of flattery and devotion to both of us, she seemed hardly a mother at all but some grown-up Dulcinea possessing both sexual allure and incalculable wisdom. It was a hot spring day and we had drinks— for Mason and me beer, for Wendy martinis, which with fetching nonchalance she poured from a Thermos bottle. "Certainly not, my pet," she said to Mason, with a bright little grin, "young lips that touch martinis shall never touch mine. Drink your beer like a nice boy. In a year you can drink anything you like." Later on, recrossing the river, we met a flat calm which set the sails flappily sagging. "Who cares?" cried Wendy, throwing her arms around the two of us. "It's birthday time! Oh *Gawd,* to be seventeen again! Let's drift away, away to the sea!" Even I in my anxiety found her spirit contagious; we all began to sing songs, sprawled out on the deck in sodden contentment while the boat, unhelmed and sideslipping gently downriver, edged out into wide waters toward the sea.

> "In the evening by the moonlight,
>   You could hear those darkies singing—"

we sang, floating past the mouths of tideland streams on the distant shore, sunny meadows on the slopes above, fish stakes in the water, and once an old Negro out tonging oysters, whose eyes rolled white and wonder-struck as we passed. An hour, two hours went by. "Look at him, Peter," she murmured sleepily, "isn't he the adorablest thing? Why, he has practically no hips at all." To which Mason, inured to this kind of talk but flustered because of my presence, said, "Wendy-dear, sometimes you're such a trial," as the wind rose abruptly and whisked us homeward—sunburned, half-stupefied—trailing seaweed in our wake.

I had never been really drunk before that afternoon and I was just sixteen: everything, even my premonitory sense of doom, I remember as in a shimmery haze through which the visions of my mind glowed with beauty and with bright ineffable glamour. Far up its hill above the river Merryoaks stood solitary and colonnaded in imperial grandeur, its windless, porticoed façade serene in shadows above an emerald sweep of lawn where reflections from the swimming pool sent dancing oblong shapes of light against the grass. A Negro, white-jacketed, appeared briefly on the heights, then disappeared. Twilight was drawing in behind the pines, which cast stiltlike silhouettes across the rolling landscaped terraces and flagstone walks. As we approached the dock, closehauled and decks awash in one last windy sweep across the shore,

I raised my bedazzled eyes in almost tearful gratitude to this place, and Wendy took my hand, squeezing it gently, as if to indicate, "Because you are Mason's friend, this too is yours." But again my exalted mood began to fade a little as we docked, when it occurred to me that still he hadn't told her. We were met there by Richard, the thin-lipped, poker-faced Alsatian who was the Flaggs' butler, chauffeur, and factotum, brought down from Rye; a burly fellow, he reminded me of a movie villain, and whenever he smiled, which was practically never, it was with a crude perfunctory smirk that was like a surgical incision. He always left me feeling cowed and intimidated—although this may have been because he was the first white manservant I had ever seen. The two Great Danes leashed to his wrist were as big as panthers and they strained for Wendy as she lurched ashore, whimpering their love as she embraced them and crooned baby talk into their ears, and vaulting finally with great savage groans into the back seat of the Cadillac, where they settled among the three of us licking their chops and shuddering with power.

On the drive up through the pinewoods to the house, Wendy fell softly and suddenly asleep on Mason's shoulder. As for Mason, for the first time since I had known him he seemed despondent, and crestfallen. Drops of sweat stood out on his brow, and as he tenderly held Wendy against him he drew his mouth tautly down and sent me an abject look of dread. Possibly only then, the giddy voyage downriver finished, had he realized the consequences of the brainless thing he had done. Whatever, this pale glance and then his whispered words—"How am I going to tell her, for Jesus sake?"—made me feel a renewed misery, for Mason, but more now for Wendy—who I felt was the most glamorous mother on earth—and for all of her blasted hopes.

She was not drunk yet, not really drunk as I once had seen her; she was only, as she put it when we climbed out of the car, "fagged out from the sun, my dears," and needed a nap. So we watched her weave across the portico, golden hair still in place, slacks still neat and trim around her thighs, but faltering as she walked, so that Richard with a murmured "Moddom" rushed to help her on her way, along with Richard's wife, a parched, aproned little woman who crooked her arm under Wendy's like a nurse with an invalid and led her into the shadows of the house and up the circular stairs in slow, stately, almost funeral procession, the two dogs prancing and bounding behind them. "If she gets good and drunk . . . if she gets really stoned," Mason said solemnly, "maybe she can take it when I tell her." But there was no trace of humor in his voice, and I thought I saw him shiver: he looked cold with panic and fear. In the fading twilight we tried to play a set of tennis, but Mason's game, usually so expert and aggressive, was listless, and although fogged with beer I beat him for the first time, which made him more downcast than ever. Then over us—almost, it seemed, with a crash—night fell, sending a hot breeze through that grove of oaks whose sprightly, trembling leaves had named the whole plantation, scattering westward a flock of crows which squawked dismally in leaden flight toward the last pink glimmering streaks of dusk. In the darkness his racket clattered off the ground. "Ruined! Destroyed!" I heard him cry in about the only tone of self-reproach I had ever heard him use. "I guess I've screwed myself for life on account of a lousy two-bit pig!"

It was the optimism of my youth, I suppose, that led me to hope for a while that Wendy might be unaffected by the news which Mason had to tell her. So blithe and carefree, so understanding—such a *sport*—surely her sympathies would encompass Mason's awful blunder, and she'd shrug it off, and laugh merrily, and indulge him as she always had. Mason, however, knew better. As the evening wore on he grew more and more dejected and at cocktail hour when Wendy, enfolded in organdy and smoke-colored tulle, joined us in the library, he pressed upon her a whole jugful of martinis with the hopeful, hangdog, solemn expression of someone propitiating a goddess. But something had happened to her: though still weaving slightly she seemed chastened, somber even, as if in her nap or somewhere in the upper reaches of the house she had received a sign or signal, a hint that something terrible was being concealed from her, and she flopped down on the couch, saying: "Oh God, this place is such a bore."

"Wendy-dear," Mason began, "I got something—"

"Hush, junior-pie, let Wendy talk. Sit down here. Who's that on the radio? That awful Kay Kyser. Get something sweet, angel." A gray sullen look had possessed her features; her skin sagged in places and those two muscles at the neck which turn the head were firmly outlined. To me, suddenly, much of her beauty had faded—though perhaps it was only the shadows—and I realized she must be old, very old, perhaps as old as thirty-five. "I hate to sound like such a *drip* at your birthday party, *chéri,* but this place just bores me to tears. If you just realized how lonesome this place is, with no one around, and no one but Denise and that horrible Richard to talk to. As for the servants—those darkies—I haven't ever been able to understand a word they say. What do they speak in—Brazilian? Oh Gawd," she yawned. "Oh, who's that? Sammy Kaye? Leave that on, angel."

The library itself was a visitation from the eighteenth century, with its glittering chandeliers and opulent walnut paneling and glossy parquet floors, a vessel of antique elegance set down, as if by magic, into an age of chrome, and demanding almost palpably some saving grace of glowing tapers or of cocked hats and a harpsichord's splashing keys, instead of ourselves, so anachronistic, with beer cans and the sound of squalling horns and trombones. Yet I felt positively embowered in luxury, inflamed by a sad, nostalgic fever. I watched in fascination as Wendy got drunker and drunker. "Your father," she said once to Mason, stroking his hair and gazing dreamily out through the open French doors, "your father has taken flight from Wendy. Your father is now romancing with— No! No names. Where? Tell me, angel-pie. Where's Father? Out on the coast? You won't fly away from Wendy, will you, *chéri?*"

"What coast?" I asked innocently.

"What coast! Jesus Christ, listen," said Mason, laughing for the first time in hours.

"Let's ask Peter, darling," she went on, draining her glass. "No, angel, Wendy doesn't want another drinkle. All right, just a little bit. There. Let's ask Peter, because he loves us and we love him. Peter, sweet, what do you think about fathers who go running around with other girls?"

"It's for the birds," I said, trying to affect Mason's detachment, but I grew hot with confusion.

"See there? Peter knows. Peter can tell what's right." She paused, and I thought I heard a sob, far back in her throat. Then, caught up in some reverie, she began a fretful soliloquy, her fingers never ceasing their meandering course through Mason's hair, and spoke about things largely incomprehensible to me in a voice that grew more and more thick and garbled. "You see, my dears, you never knew Cold Spring Harbor. Well, you did once, Mason angel, but you were such a little boy then. I mean, you'll never know how wonderful it was there, before I met your father. Daddy Bob—oh, that was Mason's grandfather, Peter—Daddy Bob and I lived all alone there after Mummy died. We had horses, a whole stable full. Now why didn't your father have horses?" she said, looking sorrowfully down at Mason. "Why wouldn't he get horses? If we had horses I could stand it here. And ride like we did when Daddy Bob was living. It was so wonderful and green then—green and free and oh, just wonderful, not like it is now with all the horrible old highways and cars. I mean, all the old estates were still there, and it was just like one big bridle path, and we'd ride to Huntington and sometimes all the way to Syosset. But no, your father wouldn't get horses. I mean," she said, her voice growing level and emphatic and harsh, "he just *refused to get me a horse.* 'No!" he said. 'I hate the gawd-damn things! No!' he said. He honestly said this, believe me: 'Gwendolyn, I'd see you riding a rhinoceros before I'd see you *astride* one of those gawd-damn stupid animals.' He said: 'I don't have enough money to buy a stable, Gwendolyn. Who do you think I am, the Aga Khan?' As if I *asked* for a stable. *One horse* is all I asked for. One miserable, single horse. Just to ride around here like I used to do with Daddy Bob. I mean, to break the monotony, that's all." She paused, downing her martini. "Really, that's all. He's got his gawd-damn boathouse, doesn't he? I mean, it's perfectly hideous to stay here day after day after day with nothing to do but stare at that loathsome Richard, and feel life just flow away around you. Oh, it was all right for the longest while. I mean, it wasn't so bad when we were having company and all the people came. But all that stopped. Last winter. I'm *alone!* I don't have *anything to do.* Take Noel, for instance. Or take Norma. Do you think they care for your father? For him? I mean, do you think that they fly all the way to Baltimore or Washington, then hire a car, then drive all the way down here through this miserable country, fifty, sixty, seventy miles, just to bask in the tremendous aura of Justin Flagg? Angel-pie, do you realize I knew *both* Noel and Norma long before I knew your father, when he was a nobody Princeton boy running errands on Wall Street? Did I ever tell you that, angel? They came to see *me,* darling— Wendy, I mean, the dearest sweetest people—of friends, I mean —and he's alienated all of them! Oh, angel-pie, sometimes I get so wretched!" Choked-up now, her eyes filmed with tears, she made a lunge for Mason, throwing one arm around his neck and drawing him against her. "Listen, listen," she murmured in a small stricken voice. "Always be good, my adorable one, always be bright. Manly. Proud and poised. You're all Wendy has. Remember? You see, you're the bright star in my crown. No, darling, no more. I just can't possibly. *No,* angel!"—in a queer convulsive tone now pitched between giggles and grief. "No, Wendy'll *die!* All right. B'just half a glass."

And so the forlorn business continued; the self-absorption of her misery, so omnivorous, seemed to have swallowed up all thought of Mason's birthday and it was way past ten when—still talking and clutching at the two of us for support—she accompanied us to dinner. "I mean, really," she was saying bitterly, as Mason shoved a chair under her. *"Reeshard,* that wine! Really, after all, young as you are, can't you boys see that it's just a matter of simple *ordinary human decency?* Really, it's not as if I were some Hollywood tart he had picked up somewhere. I mean, after all, Daddy Bob and Mummy and I were in the Social Register back then, you know, and the Van Camps were on Long Island two hundred years before the Flaggs even landed. McKeesport, P.A.! Phoo-ee!" She gave a scornful laugh, made an ambiguous gesture with her hand—I thought, just for an instant, that she was about to thumb her nose at Richard, who at the moment moved noiselessly in from the wings—and in so doing sent flying a water tumbler which fell in splintery ruin at Mason's feet.

"Did you call, moddom?" Richard murmured.

"Of course I called," she said. "Don't bother about that glass. Bring that wine. The *rosé.* Did I call?" she added loudly in a simpering voice to his back. "Did I call!"

In the space between drink and drink she had become, it seemed to me, almost dangerously agitated; her fingers drummed nervously on the table and her voice, customarily so silken and tender, had taken on a gravelly, slurred, barmaid's tone. I was by then faint with discomfort. I looked to Mason for solace, found none: holding Wendy's hand in his he peered intently into her eyes as she rambled off again, solicitously kept her supplied with wine, then with gentle admonishments carved her chicken when, stumped by the perplexities of knife and fork, she made motions to gobble it wholesale, and throughout the rest of the whole sad, stricken monologue remained grimly alert and as grave as an archbishop. "One miserable, single *horse.* That's all. You'd think I'd asked him for a stable. And that's it! Listen, angel, you aren't listening to Wendy!"

"Wendy-dear, my heart at thy sweet voice—or something or other." Tensely watching her, he jerked his shoulder convulsively. "Roll on, lover."

"Sweetness. Angel. Where was I? Oh, that's just it! I mean, after all, who was it that gave him a start in the first place? Who was it? Answer me that. I'll answer it! None other than Robert Sargent Van Camp the Second! Do you think Daddy Bob balked *one instant* when your father came to him back then and asked him for enough means to get started out in life? Do you think Daddy Bob balked? No, he didn't. Not Daddy Bob. Daddy Bob—that's Mason's grandfather, Peter, I mean my father—Daddy Bob had a heart as big as all outdoors." She began to sniffle again, her brow propped on her palm in sudden meditation, a forkful of food in mid-air, gravy trickling slowly down her chin. I was on the verge of panic.

"Everybody came to see us then. I mean just everybody. Before Mummy died. Parties. Dancing. Moonlight sails. I mean it was a—a way of life that was—oh, free and wonderful. And just after I got out of Foxcroft, Daddy Bob had the most marvelous coming-out party for me. With just zillions and zillions of people and two bands and everything. And there was this boy that was just mad for me. This boy named Amory Phelps. Poor thing, he got drowned at Bar Harbor. I mean, he was such a wonderful boy, all full of spirit and everything, with this wonderful soft voice. Oh, why am I *talking this way?*" she blurted suddenly. "I'm such a *drip*, angel, I know. Please forgive me. And Peter—forgive me, please forgive me. It's just that—oh, I don't know—it's just that I'm so proud of my handsome grown-up boy but knowing you'll be going far away from me now—I mean, on your wonderful way up, up toward the stars, really all those wonderful proud things you're going to do. It's just so hard thinking you'll be so far away, and yet—and yet—oh, it's just all so *tragic!* I've asked for so little. So little." Her head sank to the table upon her folded arms; in spasms she began to sob, her shoulders heaving. At this moment the swinging doors flapped open, propelling toward us on a hot gust of kitchen air the nightmarish Richard, his face flaming red from the glow of seventeen candles on a cake. I had no idea what to do, knowing that tradition demanded a song. I began to sing "Happy Birthday" in a peepish voice, only to feel the words congeal soundless in my throat. In silence I stared at Wendy. I could barely make out those words she was mumbling so inconsolably and with such raw, tormented grief into the crook of her arm. "—will take me, *chéri,*" she seemed to say. "Take me with you . . . our background . . . *chéri.*" Then "famous" and "man" and "good."

"Wendy-dear," Mason said. "I've got news for you."

"Don' speak."

"It happened again."

"Don' *speak,* angel."

"I ain't going to college, lover."

"Angel, my heart is *breaking.*"

"Wendy, listen, I said *I'm not going to college.*"

"So lonesome."

He seized her roughly by the shoulders, shaking her. "Wendy, I got kicked out of school! Listen, I got booted out. Can't you understand?"

"Angel-pie, always poking fun at Wendy."

I think I would have fled at that instant had I not felt rooted helplessly to my chair. In the minute's dead silence coming after, gongs and chimes went off all over the vast house, crying *midnight, midnight* in a clashing, outlandish counterpoint of tortured clockwork and jangling bells. "Excuse me—" I tried to say, but only my mind departed from the scene, winging outward over moonlit water, pines, and sleeping fields, toward safety, toward home—in swift flight seeking refuge for one blessed instant from all this incomprehensible sorrow and wretchedness, before that awful moment when Wendy, like a swimmer struggling up through asphyxiating depths, drew her face slowly upward from the table and now in grasp of it all, let out a deafening yell.

"Oh no! Oh no!" she cried, staring at him. "Oh no! Oh no! No! No! No! No! No!"

"Wendy, don't take on like that—" Mason began in a faint-hearted tone.

"No! No! No!"

He grasped her trembling hand. "Look, Wendy-dear, it's not the end of the *universe.* After all, it's not as if I hadn't emerged unscathed."

She shoved her face into her hands and began rocking to and fro, like some pitiable mourner. "You promised," she moaned. "You said you'd be good. You said you wouldn't disillusion me again. Oh no, no! I can't believe it! I can't stand it any more! What did you do, darling? What did you *do?*"

For a moment I thought Mason too was going to weep, seeing his mother in such extremity. But he recovered, saying smoothly, almost jauntily: "Nothing you'd be ashamed of, lover. At least this time it wasn't my grades. I got caught playing leapfrog with some dame."

"Sex!" she cried. "Intercourse? Oh, angel! Why couldn't you have waited? No! No! No!"

"Wendy, lover," he said plaintively, "goddammit, I'm sorry as hell. I really am—"

"But what'll you *do?* What'll you do? Oh, angel, how could you disappoint me so? What's going to happen to you now? You can't ever go to Princeton now. Without graduating. They won't take you anywhere! How *could* you disillusion me like this?" Tears in rivulets streamed down her desolate face; she was shaking as if with a violent chill, for an instant I thought she was going to founder. "How could you, when you're all I have? When all my hopes have been pinned on you? When I said, oh so many times, remember, 'Always be good, my adorable one. Always be bright. Manly. Proud and poised. Oh, you are the *bright* star in Wendy's crown!' " She paused, shaking and racked by hoarse, relentless sobs. A knife clattered to the floor. In the darkness of the room the birthday candles flickered and glowed, playing a blowzy light over her quivering lips, her tear-streaked face, her grief-disordered hair. Then I saw a remarkable thing happen. Mason, with suavity born of a communion with his mother so intricate that each impulse, each vagrant gesture, was freighted with a meaning like that of poetry, stuck two cigarettes in his mouth, lit them, and casually but tenderly placed one of them between her lips. Instantly her grief seemed to dissolve; she became placid, soothed. Whether this gift alone turned the trick or whether, so full of gin and wine, she had lost all touch with what was going on, I couldn't tell; whatever, it was like sticking a lollipop in the mouth of a child: her tears stopped, she gently burped, and she turned to Mason with a dreamlike look of concern. "But angel," she said, "what about all your clothes?"

"The old bastard wouldn't let me go back to the dormitory. He made me sleep on a cot in the gym. He said I'd contaminate the rest of the guys. Oh, Wendy, really, the whole goddam thing is so *puerile* that I don't even want to think about it. Really, honey—I mean I got my ashes hauled, that's all. Jesus sake, it wasn't any mortal sin. I was just too stupid not to be more *discreet.* I mean—Jesus sake—that's all."

"But angel, still, what about all your *clothes?* That Burberry—"

"Oh, he told me he'd get one of the niggers to pack them up and send—"

"Who did? Who said that?" she asked sharply.

"Dr. Marston."

"You mean you weren't even allowed to take away your own personal *possessions?*"

"Oh, Wendy," he said wearily, "don't capsize yourself. It's all so tedious. It was a rotten little dump anyway. They couldn't teach you to spell cat."

"I will be heard! Oh, I will!" she cried angrily. "Do you mean to tell me that that old man! I mean that dirty old sanctimonious parson! That Morrison—"

"Marston," he corrected.

"That he can just dismiss a boy like *that!* Without one word of why or wherefore or anything to *me!* A parent!"

"Oh, sit down, Wendy-dear."

"I will not sit down. Does he think that he can just dismiss you without any kind of a trial at all? I mean reason? Or wherefore? To the parent, I mean. Or *justice!* And then talk about contaminating and all? And then not let you have the simple obligation of your *clothes!* That sanctimonious old man? Oh no!" She staggered from the table, a bedraggled scarecrow of a woman now, muttering vengeance and yelling for her car. *"Reeshard!* Where is that dummy?"

"Wendy," Mason cried. "For Christ sake, sit down!"

She floundered across the room. "Oh no! Not on this night! Where's the Pontiac? If that old man doesn't think he's going to answer—"

"Wendy," he shouted, rising now. "You can't drive up there!"

But she might have done so—at least she might have tried—had it not been for the commotion that arose at that moment from the hallway, and the five minutes' chaotic events that followed. For as I watched her retreating back, watched Mason now too in hot pursuit behind her, I heard a tremendous hubbub outside, a banging sound, a man's voice yelling, and the noise of barking dogs—all muffled at first and in fuzzy confusion, until Wendy, on her way out, threw open the door and let in the whole baleful, troubled racket. I heard the Great Danes at the door, roaring. Then the male howls again, not one voice now, but two or three, and the noise of scuffling feet and the lumpish sound of flesh bouncing off timber—all of these projected upon the balmy evening like the sound track alone in some tumultuous scene in a movie. I followed Mason out of the dining room and into the lofty foyer. Here at the entrance to the house I saw Richard, in full livery embattled at the door jamb, bawling in French and in English, and tugging passionately at the Great Danes, who, leashed and foaming, their toenails skidding and chattering against the tiles, made great ferocious lunges toward whoever it was standing on the portico below.

"Go away! You hear!" cried Richard. *"Allez donc!* Quick!"

"Richard!" Wendy shrieked.

"Je vais appeler la police, madame!"

"What do they *want?"* she cried.

"I reckon you know what we want!" said the voice from below. It was a countrified voice, guttural, faintly Negroid—almost Elizabethan—the lazy archaic voice of the southern Chesapeake, one now accented heavily with menace; I felt my scalp prickle as, drawing near the door with suspicion, then certainty, I saw whose voice it was: a rawboned oysterman in overalls, his face like a blade, eyes implanted deep beneath his brows like shiny buckshot and reflecting intolerable outrage and injury. Next to him stood a younger, shorter oysterman, with a square, very red, disconsolate face and a huge club in his hand. "I reckon you know all right," the first man said. "We just want that boy of your'n, to learn him a lesson or two." He shot a warning glance at the smaller man. "Don't aidge up on them dogs, Buddy."

"What are they talking about?" she wailed. "Richard, get Fritzi and Bingo inside! I can't hear!"

"I'll tell you what we're talking about," he said. "Let me lay hands on that boy of your'n and you'll *know* what I'm talking about! Seems like they don't teach nothin' to 'em at that school, nor nothin' homewise neither! Holt still, Buddy, them dogs'll chaw yo' laigs off. Missus, we druv all the way from Tappahannock tonight and don't aim to go back without bruisin' that boy's dirty hide."

Mouth agape, hair astray and tangled around her face, Wendy stood clinging to the door gazing at them in groggy alarm. Mason, along with Richard and the dogs, still bucking and snarling, moved back hastily into the shadows of the hallway. "Wendy," I heard him say in a panicky voice, "shut the goddam door!"

"But I don't *understand—*"

"Missus, I'm right sorry for you," he said. "If I had a boy like that I reckon I'd go drown myself. Anyways, if you want to know what he done, here's what he done: he tuk my girl Doris—she ain't but thirteen, by God, and not real bright in the head, nohow —he tuk her and—missus, I sure hate to say this to you—he tuk her and he got her drunk there, and then by God he *had* her.

Right up in that church at St. Andrew's school! He tuk that poor little girl of mine, that little thirteen-years-old tyke, and he *knowed* her. By the *flesh* I mean he knowed her!"

Wendy began to sob and moan again, but whether over this recital I couldn't tell.

Piety and retribution glittered from the oysterman's eyes. "Missus, I ain't never been no man to take the law in my own hands. I never had no cause to, anyways. Ask anybody around the river from Essex County all the way to Deltaville and they'll tell you that Groover Floyd is a law-abidin' man. But missus, I'll tell you one thing." Here for a second he paused, grimly clenching his knotted fists, and sent a russet jet of tobacco juice into the boxwood. "I'll tell you one thing, missus. Ain't no law nor statute in this state goin' to stop me from undoin' what that boy of your'n done. Warn't no iniquity of Sodom any worse than he done, and right there in the plain sight of God, too, in His holy temple, to a pore little tyke but half out of her didy-drawers. Missus," he said, stepping forward with Buddy now at his heels, the club cocked in mid-air, menacingly, "I don't aim to cause you no hurt. Just step aside, now, because we means to *git that boy!*"

It seemed then, as I too retreated in alarm, that a dozen things occurred to me at once: I saw Wendy first, thrown back against the door as if upon the full blast of his advancing wrath, her arms outstretched against the portal so that, spread-eagled now, her eyes tightly closed and mumbling unintelligible terror to the heavens, she looked like some swooning martyr awaiting upon the fagots her last agony and combustion; the two overalled men, hot-eyed and unrelenting, pressing forward up the steps toward us with stony resolution and slab-handed brawn, the older man now unlimbering from some rear pocket a length of cast-iron pipe which he brandished before him as he moved past Wendy and gained the doorstep; Mason, cowering pale behind Richard and the howling dogs, in abrupt crablike retreat scuttling across the hallway, slipping down, getting up, pleading for help in a shrill child's voice as he raced for the stairs: Richard, himself too frightened to move or to release the dogs, paralyzed, brainlessly yelling, "Moddom, moddom!"—I heard and saw these things all in the briefest fraction of an instant. They passed across my mind in mesmeric slow parade as I stood there groping for a cigarette and until I realized with warm sinking panic in my entrails that the two men, their eyes now level upon me, thought that I was Mason. I tried to cry out, to move, but I was rooted there. And for all I know they might have grabbed me had there not at that moment issued from somewhere in the house behind me an outraged "Hold!"

The voice sounded again: "Hold!" It was Mr. Flagg. Barefooted and in pajamas he emerged from a corridor—it seemed miles away across the hall—and padded noiselessly toward us. Was it that baritone parade-ground voice which alone was so commanding? Or indeed some pure presence, some compelling quality of power and authority which transmitted itself almost instantly to everyone in the place and caused each to stop, transfixed petrified in separate attitudes of anguish and wrath and flight? Whatever the case, as he spoke and came across those infinite distances toward us it was as if by sudden legerdemain we had all been frozen like statues in our tracks: Wendy crucified against the door, her eyes bulging in disbelief—"Justin, I thought—" I heard her murmur; the two oystermen stock-still where they halted at the doorstep, weapons upheld in motionless, powerless frieze against the night; even the dogs became still, struck dumb in a silence that seemed almost more deafening than all their roars; and finally I saw Mason on the staircase looking wildly down, one leg still poised in panicky ascent. And as we watched, Flagg came on. "Hold!" he cried. Bald and short, bespectacled, wearing a foppish sprig of a mustache, he came gliding toward us like a wound-up toy soldier on a drumhead, his fly open, looking neither left nor right, negotiating corners and pillars with precise right-angle turns. I felt I could almost hear a *click* at the corners, and the whir of toy machinery, but as he brushed past me with his face set grimly forward toward the door, I smelled the odor of bath-lotion, still lingering about me as he boomed at the men: *"Get out of my house!"*

It was a display of sheer annihilating authority, of will; it was almost regal; the two men seemed to shrivel and bend before his fury like willows in a gale. Flustered, sheepish, now alarmed, the older man began to croak out again his affliction. "Well look, mister," he started, " 'twas only that boy of your'n there tuk my little girl—"

"Drop that pipe!" Flagg snapped. "I heard everything already. I'll pay you well for whatever you've suffered. Now get out of my house. Get out of my house before I shoot both of you!" He had no gun with him, but I would not have been astonished had he materialized one from the air.

The pipe clattered to the floor. "She warn't but thirteen years old," the man began to blubber. "I swear 'fore God she come to me, mister, and she had a *babydoll* in her arms. A *babydoll* she had, the pore little tyke—"

"I'm sorry for what you've suffered," Flagg cut in. "But it's no cause to enter someone's home with weapons as you have done in the middle of the night. Now you get out of here, do you understand? Leave your name with my man and I'll contact you tomorrow. Now both of you get out of here!"

Standing barefooted at the door, he watched them turn and shuffle silently down the steps.

"Justin—" I heard Wendy say. She took a step toward him. "Justin, I didn't know you were here! Where have you—"

"Shut up!" he said, whirling upon her. "Richard, call Denise in here, and have her put madame to bed."

"Justin," she cried, "oh, Justin darling, where have you *been?*"

"Shut up," he repeated. "That's no longer any concern of yours, Gwendolyn. Where I go and what I do is my concern and it will be that way, do you understand? It will be that way. *It will be that way!* And it will stay that way forever, while I have a common drunk for a wife—a common drunk, a common drunk and a *moron*—you are a *moron,* do you know that?—and a contemptible *swine* for a son!"

Then, padding swiftly again across the gleaming floor—a short little man, stiffly erect—he was gone, leaving behind him, amid the shambles of the room and upon the hectic evening, the strange girlish scent of gardenias.

Much later, still shaken, unable to sleep, I sat in the library with the radio turned down low and leafed half-blindly through a copy of *Town & Country.* Through the windows blew the faint smell of bloom and fern and flowers, the sound of frogs in the meadow and katydids, and in the woods a whippoorwill, broadcasting sweet, piercing word of impending summer. Mason came in after a while wearing an ornately figured bathrobe and a broad, derisive grin.

"Well, it was quite a show, wasn't it, Pierre?" he said.

I would like to have answered but the words, whatever they were to be, refused to leave my lips. I kept looking at the magazine. It was the first of its kind I had ever seen, and it seemed to be full of pale, scrawny people propped on shooting sticks or studying horses. I was close to tears.

"Mason," I said finally, with a strained effort at levity, "why doesn't Wendy get something somebody can read?"

But then I saw that he was face-down on a couch sobbing desperately into the pillows, and so, not knowing what else to say, I let him go on weeping.

After a while I dozed off. There was a sound in my ears, it seemed, of ten thousand alpine horns—slumberous, dim, muted from afar—while in a distant airy room of the mansion populated by whispers, by the footsteps of people I could not name, there came an incessant shuffling and rustling, as of someone packing for immediate flight. "Always love your mother," I thought I heard Wendy murmur, but then, "Peter Leverett! Oh, Peter! Peter Leverett!" a voice called far above me. "Wake up! It's *way* past time!" And I forced my eyelids apart, dreaming for a while that it was Wendy's face hovering over me, until, pushing off the shroud of slumber, I blinked, still half-dozing, and felt the hands of Rosemarie de Laframboise urging me awake, in the dead of night, in Sambuco.

"Don't feel too bad about it, Peter," Rosemarie was saying, "perhaps the poor man will get all right. You know, I've read about people who lie in a coma for just years and years . . ." She faltered, as if with the sudden knowledge that this was no consolation to me at all. ". . . and still live." We were standing at the front entrance of the Bella Vista, where she had waited for me while I hurriedly bathed and shaved and put on my best suit. She had waited patiently, too, while I telephoned the hospital at Naples and learned from whom I took to be some nursing sister, a frosty tight-lipped woman, that di Lieto, still sunk in his dark unflagging slumber, his broken skull packed in ice, was in that condition whose outcome only the Heavenly Father Himself could fathom or influence. As a parting shot—something steely in her voice told me she knew I was an Episcopalian—she enjoined me to prayer, and it was the look on my face, I suppose, prayerful and disconsolate, that caused Rosemarie with all the good will in the world to implant in my mind the vision of di Lieto lying supine, his hair slowly graying, oblivious of all, fed through some miserable tube until doomsday. "I mean," she added hastily then, "what I mean is that this doesn't mean he's necessarily going to *die,* you know."

"I know," I said forlornly.

"Just try to forget about it, Peter," she went on. "I know it must have been a horrible shock to you, but if you—if you can just for a moment conceive of it not as something so personal, but as only a—oh, I don't know, a tiny little thing in the great working-out of the universe. Did you ever read *The Prophet,* by Kahlil Gibran?" Her voice was very sad.

"Oh Jesus, no," I said. We paused to light cigarettes at the bottom of the steps that led into the front courtyard of the Bella Vista. Roses were in bloom here; the night was fragrant and warm and starless. Mild clouds drifted over the moon, leaving a hint in the air of reluctant and improbable rain. It would be sunny and hot again tomorrow. I felt wobbly, depleted still, as if in my recent half-hearted, muddled sleep I had not slept at all, but had walked endless distances, hefted huge burdens, battled giants. Yet as Rosemarie's face, vast and beautiful, moved downward toward the flame in my cupped palm, obscuring the scent of roses with some strong sweet perfume of her own, it seemed that my mind was oddly keen and alert—that old beaten and buffaloed sensitivity again—and with a stab of recognition I knew I had seen her face before: it was of course Wendy's, about which I was in no hurry to draw any Freudian parallels, but even more so it was an exact replica in composite of all of the faces of those at last fetched-up virgins gazing out at me impassive and gentle from a thousand Sunday society pages, their features all but indistinguishable one from another by the soft standardized look in their eyes, so completely American, of conventional morals and moneyed security. *The Prophet.* It was indeed a Finch College notion of poetry, and I could have laughed aloud, except for the fact that now, as she drew back her head, it occurred to me why Rosemarie seemed so sad. She was Mason's "mistress" (I felt she would be the first to put quotation marks around the word), and something abstracted, insecure, and fumbling about her, despite all her smooth big beauty, made me sense that she had come to feel ashamed of the role, or perhaps afraid of it, and yearned for that lost, irretrievable image of herself, gazing out chastely from the engagement pages of the *New York Times.* Was I indulging in unfair prejudgment? I don't think so. Besides, as she turned to take my arm and as we stepped out into the cobbled village road, light from a street lamp fell full upon her and I could see for the first time the shiny blue bruise beneath her eye, where Mason had socked her.

"I'm sorry I didn't come and wake you sooner," she said as we walked along, "but you looked like you needed sleep so badly, poor boy. Mason agreed with me. I hope you didn't mind."

"Not at all," I said. "Thanks for coming for me."

"I'll bet you could stand a drink."

"I could do more with some food," I said. I was famished. I had had nothing to eat all day, except for the bun in Formia, and that seemed years ago. "I wonder if you all have anything, or if I should try to get something at—"

"Oh, Peter, how absurd!" she broke in. "Of course we have just oodles of things to eat. You must be famished! And Mason drove over to the PX in Naples today, and just brought back literally tons of provisions. Oh, steaks and chopped meat and packages and packages of frozen foods. And *milk,* Peter, real honest-to-God milk in bottles! Mason says it's flown down from Germany. I drank a whole quart this evening in place of cocktails. Really."

"The PX?" I began. "But how—"

"Oh, you know he was a pilot during the war. He established PX privileges in Naples as soon as we got here."

"A pilot? But what—" Once again I halted, perplexed for an instant but quickly perplexed no longer as a horde of recollections about Mason came tumbling back. I think I must have suppressed a groan. "I mean I didn't know being an ex—an ex-pilot gave you PX privileges. Unless you were still in. He must have some kind of deal, doesn't he?"

"Oh, I wouldn't know, Peter," she said in a faraway tone. "Those things are so complicated to me. Anyway," she said, her voice brightening, "we have just everything to eat. Just God's own quantity. How would a nice sirloin steak appeal to you?"

I was about to reply with enthusiasm when out from a dimly lit alleyway hopped a crouched and ragged figure that approached us with a husky snuffling noise—a series of rich, porcine grunts that caused Rosemarie to stop and grow rigid in her tracks, clutching my wrist in a sudden powerful grip as she uttered a gasp of alarm. But the subhuman noise, I could tell, came only from my dragoman of the afternoon, Saverio, as he grappled with speech: his flat red face bobbed toward us, fat tongue wagging in the lacuna between his snaggled teeth, and he managed to roar out a phrase in incomprehensible dialect, his features all smiles and glowing, like some inebriate Halloween pumpkin.

"Oh, it's that *idiot!*" Rosemarie gasped. "Tell him to go away."

"He's harmless," I said. "Besides, I can't understand him. Speak *slowly,* Saverio."

"Buonasera, signora!" he howled at Rosemarie. *"Buonasera, padrone!* Look there, signora, I have polished your Cadillac machine!"

Rosemarie shuddered as we moved on. "Ugh! He reminds me of a Charles Addams cartoon. What on earth is he saying?"

Beside us, parked against a wall bordering the shadowy and narrow street, was a convertible Cadillac so red and vulgar and immense that for a moment, although I must have once or twice seen its prototype in Rome, I could hardly believe my eyes. Around it, as around us now, hung the damp and ancient smell of the village, yet the car clearly exuded its own smell—of new paint and plastic and rubber, of volatile newness, of all of the witchery of Michigan—and Saverio had labored until it sparkled in the night like some mountainous ruby.

"He said he has polished your car," I told Rosemarie. "Is it really yours?"

"Well, it's Mason's," she replied, with what sounded like a note of apology. "The color really is—frightening, isn't it? And it *is* too large," she added thoughtfully. As we passed on by the car she gave a gentle caress to one of the fenders; the machine was so enormous that it seemed capable, through some weird mechanical parturition, of having given birth to the midget Italian car parked at its side. "Mason's right about it, you know. He said that when we drive through some of the country villages the peasants couldn't be more startled if we had rolled down the main street on the *Queen Elizabeth."* She made a self-conscious giggle.

At my prompting, then, Rosemarie handed Saverio a few lire ("I didn't ask him to polish it," she said at first, but seemed genuinely regretful when, after telling her that it was the custom for Americans to take such minor extortions with good grace, I added a solemn commentary on the poverty of this southern land); the creature flapped away into the shadows, and a few steps later we arrived at the doorway to Mason's palace just as a church bell deep within the town sounded the last half-hour before midnight. As I pushed against the massive door, a large enclosed courtyard presented itself to view: its vaulted ceiling, supported by graceful fluted columns, disappeared into the shadows high above us where a trapped swallow swooped and fluttered and a skylight in the shape of a fleur-de-lis allowed a vestige of sudden moonlight to pass through. "The tiles," I said, looking toward the floor, "they're beautiful." And they were: the entire surface of the floor was emblazoned with a remarkable pattern of interlocking circles of red and blue that gave an effect of receding perspective at once colorful, slightly dizzying, and resplendent; yet as I accustomed my eyes to the place I could tell that something was wrong here and then saw that it was only the tangle of cameras and arc lamps and booms which emerged from the shadows. "They were shooting here today," Rosemarie explained as we walked across the courtyard. "I can tell," I replied. Wide streaks crisscrossed the tiles where the wheels of the spidery machines had rolled back and forth, gouging out ugly channels in the clay. "You know Fausto owns this palace, too, and he was furious when he saw what they had done to the tiles," said Rosemarie, as if she had sensed my dismay, "but when Herb Wingate—he's the unit manager—told him they would pay for it, he was just like a happy little dog."

Now as we approached the balustrade which led, I gathered, to Mason's living quarters high above, the courtyard became a resonant sounding board; a hell of a racket broke loose. From the regions upstairs, muffled yet distinct behind the alabaster walls, came the noise of a tinkling piano, feet thumping, a high falsetto voice singing above it all, then wave upon wave of hysterical laughter. Close by us, from a doorway at the level at which we were standing and so loud that each crashing bass note had the effect of the tread of elephants, a phonograph erupted the opening bars from the overture to *Don Giovanni*. Together, none of the sounds made any sense; I felt deafened, and I had the childish urge to stick my fingers in my ears. But Rosemarie clutched me by the hand then and as we climbed the stairs up and away from the acoustical trap, the music all around became discreet and reasonable, as if someone had jumped up to turn the volume down.

"That's where the Kinsolvings live," she said, pointing down past the forest of movie equipment to the doorway we had just passed. "They were there when we arrived last spring. It was Cass—didn't you say you met him?—who was the first American we met when we got here. He's—" She hesitated. "Well, he's— he's really quite odd."

"You mean that guy—that drunk I met this afternoon on the road? The guy with the Tarheel accent that runs off at the mouth?"

"Oh, Peter, he's a mess. He's—" She paused, made a strained little laugh. "Forget it," she said.

I would have forgotten it, too, except for the honest concern, the worry in her voice, which made me say: "What's the trouble? Outside of the booze, that is."

"Oh nothing," she said. Then she nervously grasped my wrist. "He *is* such a terrible drunkard. And—well, he's sort of southern and odd and, oh, I don't know, *lower class,* if you know what I mean. A real—well, a real psychopathic, I think. Then there's—there's this girl, an Italian girl that he and Mason—" Abruptly she flushed, turning a bright crimson, and chewed her lip. "Oh nothing," she said hoarsely, shaking her head. "Nothing. Nothing, Peter. Just forget it."

"You can tell me if—" I began.

"No," she said quickly. "Please. Just forget it."

For a moment she seemed so agitated that I shared a bit of her concern. But she obviously was determined to drop the matter—and she tried to.

Yet she was unable to stop brooding. "It's the funniest thing, when we first met him he tried to make himself out as a famous painter. Imagine!" She mentioned a notorious young expatriate artist of whom I had heard. "Imagine! When he's nothing but—" Her voice trailed off and she gave a shudder.

"Watch that wire," I said.

Then we reached the balcony. Over the grimy marble portico a frieze of dryads cried out voicelessly to be cleaned. She turned and paused for an instant. "I—I wouldn't talk about Cass to Mason if I were you. It's nothing important. It's just that tonight —oh, I don't know."

"I hardly even know the guy," I said.

Her face lightened up as at this moment the sound of the jazzy piano once more fell on our ears. "Oh, I'll bet you didn't know," she said. "Guess who came down from Rome and is playing that really fabulous piano? *Billy Raymond!*" Almost as if upon this incantation, then, the doors swung open and we entered Mason's home.

I was charmed, staggered. In spite of my recollection of Mason's fondness for display, I could see that here he had outdone himself. The room was one in which a grand duke would have felt perfectly at ease—a salon of such spacious dimensions that I felt it would not be unnatural to be ushered in by page boys and a fanfare of bugles. On the lofty groined ceiling some nineteenth-century artist with a flamboyant gift had applied his brush, filling the air with a fresco of clouds and lush vegetation and hues ranging from the clear green of the sea to voluptuous purple; the scenes were mythological and obscure, but I did make out what seemed to be Demeter, and Persephone clad in the fashion of a mid-Victorian maiden, her clothes billowing around her as she floated on high and chewed dreamily at a pomegranate. Spaced around the walls of the room, holding up the cornices, were handsome ornamental pilasters, straight out of the Renaissance, which had been polished until they glittered like the purest gold; for all I know they may have been gold, and in any case I was speculating upon this notion when Rosemarie, having paused to exchange a few words in sign language with an impressive, formally attired old man whom I took to be the butler, grasped my arm and led me across the room. "I heard Alonzo tell Mason that it was the most pretentious place he had ever seen," she said, as if reading my thoughts. "And he's seen them all. But Peter, you have no idea; it's so *cheap*. It used to belong to a baron or something, before Fausto took it over."

I walked alongside my towering chatelaine toward the score or so people arranged in sofas and on chairs and around a black grand piano in the distance. Behind them, French windows each half as high as a house gave onto the somber and moonless sea; a faint breeze disturbed the crimson draperies, causing them to move limply in the shadows. There was a babble of voices—vehement, loud, and alcoholic. A confusing amber light played over the scene; perhaps too, tired as I was, my eyes lacked the power to focus. At any rate, what for an instant seemed to my eyes to be a round, jug-eared black vase perched on the piano top proved, as we neared the group, to be the head of a young Negro, whose eyes and mouth sprang whitely open in a kind of paroxysm as he burst once again into song.

"That's Billy Raymond," Rosemarie whispered. "He's perfectly fabulous." Silently we moved in toward the group around the piano. It was a naughty tune he sang; it had to do with bananas and other elongated objects, and as he lewdly anatomized the names of people famous in the world of stage and screen, using the banana motif as a key, his voice crooned lubriciously and he winked at the gathering, and grimaced, or made his eyes disappear altogether, clenching his lids tight as he hunched down and elicited wicked little arpeggios from the keys. But his references, obvious in intent as they were, were for the most part too parochial for me; ill-at-ease, I found myself eying Mason's guests, who, sweating in sport clothes, had bent all their attention upon the raucous Negro and—except for a striking tall man with gray hair who stood propped aloof and sullen in one corner—had collapsed into various stages of laughter. Most of them were persons who by virtue of their position in my own hierarchical scheme of movie values made little impression upon me—what, after all, is an assistant producer, a unit manager, a publicity man?

Of the rest, aside from the stars, three stood out in my mind, and it was these three, cramped side by side on a small gilt settee, who caught my attention as my spirit wandered restlessly away from Billy Raymond. The first was a young woman named Dawn O'Donnell, a slim carrot-haired girl who sat sipping a crème de menthe, and whose complexion for a moment I hardly believed, so chalky white it was, until I realized that it had been painted on —out of some obscure need to shock her beholders—with artful care. She was not pretty; neither was she badly made; she could have been quite attractive, actually, but with her orange hair contrasting so starkly with her ghostly white skin she had succeeded in her desire—and desire it must have been, lacking only a false rubber nose to complete the make-up—to look exactly like a clown. I remembered having heard about her and had seen her from a distance in Rome. Dawn O'Donnell was not her real name —so I had read somewhere—but then little about her at all was real. There had been a period when she had been a minor actress, she had had a one-man show of paintings, had published a small volume of verse. In none of her endeavors, including several marriages, had she shown a molecule of talent, but being the heiress to a vast American mercantile fortune had allowed her to persist in her trifling labors, all the while presuming, I suppose, as Thomas Mann once put it, that one may pluck a single leaf from the laurel tree of art without paying for it with his life. At the moment I gathered she was interested in the art of the film and tagged along all over Europe after the movie-makers, who because of her enormous wealth on the one hand, and her eccentric, childish mannerisms on the other, treated her with a strange combination of deference and indulgence, and called her "Little Carrot-Top" and replied in passionate affirmatives to her never-ending "Do you think I'm beautiful?" I heard all this that night. Rosemarie told me she was sleeping off and on with Carleton Burns.

Now sitting next to Dawn O'Donnell on the settee was a sleepy-eyed, smiling man named Morton Baer, a well-known recorder of gossip for the newspapers whose every word, syndicated in the American-language paper in Rome, I had read with the same intense interest and delight I had once reserved for Keats. I knew him from his photographs. Baer was the only person present outside myself not dressed as if for an outing to the shore;

he wore a fine flannel suit over his small, truncated, slightly hunched form, and a checkered yellow waistcoat, too, and he looked gentle and sheepish, sad even, as he tried dutifully to smile at Billy Raymond's song, which he must have heard a dozen times before, and I couldn't help but feel sympathy for his boredom, over and above the sneaking and mortifying admiration I had for the man—a celebrity in his own right—who hobnobbed almost on terms of blood kinship with movie stars on five continents, and knew J. Edgar Hoover and Herbert Bayard Swope, and had even dined several times at the White House.

The third member of the trio, finally, was a face so familiar from his photographs that I had the impulse to go up and slap him on the back as I would a long-lost friend. But when at last it registered upon me who he was, flabbergasted, unable to tell whether I was struck more by the incongruity of his being a part of this worldly throng, or by a subtly unpleasant reasonableness, I could only gaze and gaze at him as if he were something at a zoo. For this was the Reverend Dr. Irvin Franklin Bell, the exemplary, prolific, and optimistic Protestant clergyman known and loved doubtless by more Americans than any man of the cloth since Henry Ward Beecher. I was, to be sure, prepared for anything that night but not for this ecclesiastical glamour, so offbeat, so rare, and I pieced together from Rosemarie later how it must have come about: Bell, confidant of potentates in industry and business, while on a vacationing, non-evangelical tour of Europe had encountered at the Hotel Hassler in Rome his old friend Sol Kirschorn, the producer. Kirschorn was an admirer of Bell, as were many highly placed American men of substance who found the doctor's simple moral equation of wealth and virtue, virtue and wealth, as easy to abide by as to understand. Learning, then, that Sambuco was on Bell's itinerary, Kirschorn accommodatingly got in touch with his wife, Alice Adair, and told her on behalf of the unit of which he was the producer and she the star, to offer the famous preacher (he was staying at the Bella Vista, too) every hospitality. What I saw at this moment was the result: portly, amiable, mightily sweating, his eyelids visibly wincing behind his bifocals at each one of Billy Raymond's lascivious groans, he tried nonetheless to hold on to his renowned sleek and jovial composure and, like a banker caught with his hand in the till, kept his cheeks plumped up in a sickly, illicit smile. I felt sorry for him in a way. Looking, in his floppy matching slacks and shirt of jade-green silk, like a print I had once seen of the dowager em-press of China, his wet under-lip poised as if to receive a gum-drop, or to emit yet another platitude, he was in an ecstasy of discomfort, and I felt that it was unfortunate that a solitary dirty song should intrude so upon his enjoyment of this sumptuous rich world, by which he yearned to be ravished. Billy Raymond came to the end of his song.

I looked around for Mason but he was nowhere to be seen. As one last rippling chord brought the song to its conclusion, the trio on the couch made, each one, a fugitive gesture with his hands—Baer to stifle a yawn, Bell to straighten his spectacles, Dawn O'Donnell with nervous fingers uplifted to adjust her dangling earrings—so that for the most fleeting fraction of an instant they looked like those three little Oriental apes, mute, dumb, and blind to all evil; turning, I thought I saw Mason mopping his face, passing through the distant doorway to another room, and I raised my hand to beckon to him but he was gone. A roar of applause and hand-clapping went up from the gathering. As I wheeled about to face the piano again, Rosemarie handed me a bowlful of peanuts.

"I've asked Giorgio to bring you something more substantial," she whispered. "He should be along in a minute," she added. "Isn't Billy fabulous? I'll swear he's better than Noel Coward. He's—But shh-h . . ." Silence fell over the house as Billy Raymond commenced singing again, this time the sad limpid words of "As Time Goes By." I'm a fairly good judge in such matters, and it did seem to me that his rendition of the song was inferior to many I had heard, including those of some amateurs. Nonetheless, the people went into some sort of a modified trance as they stood there listening—some propped chin in hands, their elbows resting on the piano; the bare-necked and pretty girls with their eyes closed, arms crossed, caressing their own shoulders—and gradually only myself alert and so famished now I could hardly bear it, I picked out those among the group whom, after all, I had come here to see: the bewitching Alice Adair, slender and blond and with such an opalescent transparency of skin that around her gently dimpled temple, as in that frog's tongue which as a boy I had peered at through a microscope, every capillary and vein was presented to the eye live and mortal and throbbing; Carleton Burns again of the sex-glutted and ugly and dissipated face, the mean demonic dream-incubus of how many millions of women even his employers had no way of reckoning; and finally Gloria Mangiamele, black-eyed and tranquil and exquisite, of a voluptuousness of which all her pictures had provided only the merest suggestion, whose marvelous breasts seemed to call out for seizing and fondling, but who, as she moved back now swaying slightly to the music, revealed a figure somewhat short-waisted and short-legged, like many Italian girls, and an important feature which, from the point of view of my own taste, at least, I can only describe as duck-butted. But I was very hungry. I looked around once more for Rosemarie and just then—perhaps because, worn-out as I was, I was the natural prey of a cold—I sneezed. I sneezed again and again, a wet and exhausting barrage over which I had no control.

"*Can* that, will you, for Christ sake?" I heard a man's voice say as the music limped and rattled to a stop. Billy Raymond's lips hung open pink and tuneless, his tongue dancing in his mouth like the clapper of a bell. I heard the same anonymous voice again; it seemed addressed not precisely to me but to a world full of blockheads and fools, of which I was the major example. "For Christ sake!"

"I'm sorry," I murmured.

"For Christ's own sweet sake!" Someone tittered in the room, someone coughed; a tinkling chord of the piano broke the silence and the husky plaintive song once more filled the room.

And I, rebuffed, sidled gradually away from the group to a cool shadowy place near one of the windows; here I sat with a cigarette between my twitching fingers, sulky, resentful, dreaming of steak.

Yet now as I try to recall the events of that evening in their proper order, it occurs to me that it was along about here that something happened which was the first of a series of mysterious goings-on that got more and more baffling, more and more embarrassing and ugly, as evening wore into night, and night into morning. It did seem odd at the time, but not especially important, and so I have had trouble recalling all the details. Here is what happened, though, as well as I can remember it. As I sat there I saw the dignified old butler—Rosemarie had called him Giorgio—tiptoeing with a tray in his hands through the song-enthralled gathering and up to Rosemarie, who inclined her ear far down to hear what he whispered into it. A worried frown appeared on her face; she peered indecisively about the room until, catching sight of me, she walked over to the place where I was sitting. Giorgio trailed in her wake. Behind her the piano music died in a sort of wan, resigned flutter; the guests, unloosed from their cataleptic dream, broke into wild applause and shouts, apparently in vain, of "More, Billy, more!"—and then slowly dispersed themselves, buzzing, around the enormous room.

"Here, Peter," said Rosemarie, "I hope this will do. It's just what all of us had for dinner, and—" She made a vague motion with her hand at Giorgio, who set the tray down on a table beside me. "And it's real American food and—I mean, it's *real*." Her voice sounded troubled and upset. "Peter, I can't understand what else Giorgio was trying to tell me. I think—" she said hesitantly, "I think he's trying to tell me that Mason was—*cut,* or something."

For a second her words didn't sink in. Giorgio had presented his tray. In the center of it was the steak Rosemarie had promised— a thick rare cut of sirloin. Off to the side was a pitcher, white and foaming, of the first real milk I had seen in years. Like someone half-crazed I made a lunge for fork and napkin, only to be brought up short by the urgent plea in Rosemarie's voice. "Peter, please try to figure out what he's saying."

"Che è successo?" I asked the butler. He was a stooped and aristocratic-looking old man with white hair and a look of bleak concern. I wondered where Mason had dug him up, for he was obviously not a native of the coast. "What's happened to Signor Flagg?"

"He is all scratched around the face, signore. It is nothing serious, but he sent me to ask the signora where is what you call the mercurochromo and the Bond-Aids. It is nothing serious, but—"

"But what *happened* to him?" I said between bites.

"I do not exactly know, signore," he said gravely and apologetically. "There is a certain difficulty of—of communication between myself and Signor Flagg. But I understood Signor Flagg, as well as I was able, to say that he fell into a rosebush."

"A rosebush?"

"Si, signore."

I translated all of this for Rosemarie, telling her about the rosebush and about Mason's need for medication; but just as I did— just as with round alarmed eyes and a startled "Oh!" Rosemarie began to hurry off—I was forced by Giorgio's mumbled insistence as quickly to stop her. For Signor Flagg, according to Giorgio, had told him (and of this he was sure) that under no circumstances was the signora to come personally to his aid. It was nothing serious (and here he turned his sad eyes on Rosemarie, saying with a gentle smile, *"Non è grave, signora."*), nothing serious at all. The expression on his long bony face was now a single ache of embarrassment and apology, and his smile was one of such despairing insincerity that I could not help but feel that he was concealing something.

"He says it's nothing at all bad," I told Rosemarie. "I just think maybe Mason doesn't want to cause any furor, you know. Where are the Band-Aids?"

"In the cabinet," she said in a blank voice. "In the cabinet in the bathroom in the upstairs wing. Tell him that."

"Where did you find this Giorgio?" I asked, after the old man had hobbled off and I had again fallen to upon the steak. "How do you and Mason communicate with the old fellow?"

For a long space there was no answer. I looked up at her. Distracted, with a deep despondent look in her eyes, she was gazing vacantly at the walls; at some time since we had entered the palace she had managed to cover her shiner with a flesh-hued cosmetic, but the bruise must have still hurt her because she was absently stroking it with her hand. "What?" she said finally. "Oh, Giorgio? Fausto got him for us in Naples. He used to work for the mayor or something. We have a maid who speaks English and she sort of acts as a go-between." She paused, then added mournfully: "I do hope Muffin's O.K. Oh, I do hope he's O.K. How could he fall into a rosebush, Peter?"

"Maybe he had one too many," I said, trying to cheer her up. "Why the hell doesn't he join the party?" But it was as if she hadn't heard me; without a word, the same blank look staring out from her troubled face, she moved away from me with slow shuffling reluctance toward the other guests.

I was wondrously revived by the food; with the red meat and the American-style milk inside me I felt a peace of mind—the first of the entire day—so calm and relaxed that it was like a state of beatitude. Giorgio, returning from his mission with the Band-Aids, ever attentive, poured me a snifter full of syrup-smooth cognac. Encouraged by the cognac, not quite so overawed now by the movie stars (indeed, I had begun to feel a kind of brazen and totally unwarranted palship with them), I rose from my chair and with a shifty motion edged over toward one of the windows where Rosemarie, looming over all, was talking to Alice Adair. Next to them stood a stocky, red-faced, crew-cut young man with very good-looking features, and the calcimined Dawn O'Donnell.

"Oh, have you met Peter Leverett?" Rosemarie said. Her spirits seemed to have been somewhat restored. She introduced me to Alice Adair, whose fingers I took between my own, holding my breath, and to Dawn, and to the crew-cut young mesomorph, whose name I didn't catch, whose function was a mystery to me, and who, extending for some reason his left hand instead of right, like a Hungarian, gave my palm a squeeze and without looking at me said: "Hiya." His was the voice, I could suddenly tell, which had told me to shut up.

"But darling," Rosemarie was saying to Alice Adair, "I don't care what Jacques said. I think the lavender thing is adorable."

"Sol does, too," said Alice Adair. Her voice was incredibly sweet, beautifully modulated, and mellow, too, like a note in the middle register on a cello, and for an instant I could almost understand why people might stand in line for hours, in driving rain, to hear it. "I called Sol tonight, and he thinks the lavender thing is great, too. What Jacques is afraid of is that it will look fuzzy in Cinemascope. Or bleed, or something."

"It looks adorable on you though," said Rosemarie.

"It looks terrific on you, Alice," said the young man. "Terrific."

"I think it does, too," she replied, "but Sol said to stick by Jacques' decision. Sol said he really knows color backwards and forwards."

"Too bad," the young man said, "it's a great gown, Alice. A great little gown."

"Sol has wonderful confidence in Jacques," Alice Adair said.

"Are you a Boston Leverett?" Dawn O'Donnell said, startling me.

"Well no," I said, "actually I was born in Port Warwick, Vir—"

"My family was from Boston, and I went to school there," she burst out. "I just love Boston, don't you? We lived on Chestnut Street, in a house with violet windows. My family was very rich. Do you like cats?"

"Well, yes and no," I began to improvise. "It depends—"

"I love cats. I have a Persian cat in Rome with hair the color of my eyes. Blue-gray like the sea. Do you think I'm beautiful?"

"Can that, will you, baby, for God sake?" The young man broke in, playfully grabbing her arm. "Of course you're beautiful." He turned back to Alice Adair, saying: "The pink thing looks terrific on you, too, Alice. Absolutely great."

"Sol thinks so, too," said Alice Adair. "I guess I'll have to wear it after all."

"I'm going to cry," Dawn O'Donnell said. "I'm going to cry any minute now. Where's Burnsey?"

"I wore a pink thing like that in *Going Steady*," Alice Adair said. "Sol thought it was beautiful."

"It was terrific," the young man said. "Really terrific, Alice."

"I thought you looked adorable in that," Rosemarie murmured.

"Do you mind if I cry?" said Dawn O'Donnell, to no one in particular.

Like a swimmer treading water, I strove to keep my nose above the surface, but soon succumbed to the depths of a dreamy, brandy-hazed wool-gathering. Then in a moment Alice Adair wandered off, wrapped in a kind of golden nimbus of loveliness, and Rosemarie—as if she sensed my sudden distress at being trapped alone with the crew-cut young man and Dawn O'Donnell—led me away and across the room. "I'm so glad you feel better," she said. "You really looked quite *ashen* this afternoon."

"Where on earth is Mason?" I asked. But before she could reply we blundered into Dr. Bell, who had adjusted a wicker beach cap on his head and, grinning from ear to ear as if to invisible parishioners, was making his exit with an air of rakish sanctity.

"Oh, Dr. Bell, are you going so soon?" Rosemarie exclaimed.

"I told you to call me Irvin, my dear," he said with a smile, seizing her hand and patting it. "Yes, I've got to be up and away to Paestum early in the morning. Please tell young Mason how much I enjoyed his hospitality. I've got Sol Kirschorn to thank for many things but nothing, pleasure-wise, so much as being put in touch with"—and here I thought I saw him wink up at her through his bifocals—"with such beauty. Good-by, my dear, and I hope the good Lord allows our paths to cross again."

" 'By," said Rosemarie.

"Good night all, and God love you." And then he was gone, trailing behind him an odor of bay rum and sweat.

"He gave me his book, autographed," Rosemarie said. "He writes such—such drivel. But he is—well, he is *famous*," she added after a thoughtful pause. And then she told me how he came to be here. "It was really sort of creepy at dinner," she said. "Everybody was on good behavior for Sol's sake. I thought Burnsey'd have apoplexy, holding back. You know he is the foulest-mouthed person on earth. And he gets so drunk."

Now as we proceeded across the room, I noticed that the man I had observed before standing aloof in one corner had detached himself with a shrug both from the wall and from an importuning Rappaport (the same assistant director who had bawled me out that afternoon) and, throwing the phrase, "Figure it out yourself, Rense," languidly over his shoulder, was making his way in our general direction. There was an indescribable grace and attractiveness about this man, and there is hardly any way I can outline these qualities without feeling that I am being stale and pedestrian. Forty-five or so, with hair turned almost white, he had a face which fell just short of being too handsome; what I guess saved him from a matinée idol's flawlessness of line were his eyes, which were frosty blue and looked intensely outward instead of dreamily inward—like the eyes of most beautiful men—and surveyed the world with caution, with curiosity, and with pessimism. He was a tallish man, rather gangling. As he walked toward us he ambled in the fashion of an amateur champion tennis player—a slovenly gait redeemed by a natural athletic gracefulness. His shoes squeaked; a cigarette holder drooped, cigaretteless, from his skeptical lips. There was something powerfully sensual about him (I felt Rosemarie come electrically alive at his approach, somewhat, I should say, like a mare) but this quality too was cautious and in restraint, as if having seen all, done all, tasted almost all there is to taste, he had gone into semi-retirement from the fray, as a wise man of forty-five should. He did not look jaded, merely passionately and bitterly experienced. I was surprised by his voice; it was softer, higher-pitched than his build would lead one to imagine, and it did not say, "Hiya," but murmured a restrained, perfectly affable "I'm very glad to meet you," as with the merest whisper of a smile he shook my hand.

"Oh, Alonzo!" Rosemarie exclaimed. "You're not going to bed so soon."

"I'm going to try, darling," he said.

"But there's no need, you know, Alonzo dear. You said you won't be shooting until tomorrow afternoon."

"I won't be doing even that if the weather stays like this." He took a deep breath, as if to sniff the overcast.

"Everybody's going swimming down at the pool. Please stay, Alonzo. You know, you're just my favorite person alive. Come on over with Peter and me and let's have a drink."

"My dear," he said in his soft pleasant voice, "for twenty years I've been fighting a war with insomnia. I tried alcohol, until it threatened to land me on Skid Row. I tried sleeping pills until they became such a burden that the cure was worse than the sickness. Now all I can do is go to bed and lie there staring at the ceiling until dawn, but there's an outside chance, as always, that I'll sink into slumber. You wouldn't want to deny me that chance, would you, by luring me again into these nocturnal, meretricious ways?"

"Well—" she began. "Well of course not, Alonzo." But the look on her face was one of such disappointment that, relenting, he sighed: "O.K., I'm weak, darling." He took her by the arm. "Fetch me a plain glass of soda with ice. With a twist of lemon. But mind you, Rosemarie," he added, with a smile at me, "if this night-owl business starts me off on what they call a depressive cycle, I'm going to lay the blame right on your doorstep."

Drifting toward the bar, where a white-jacketed waiter from the Bella Vista held forth, Cripps inquired if I was the friend of Mason who had had the accident on the road. When I said that I was, he shook his head sympathetically. "Rosemarie told me about it. It's a hellish thing to have happen. I've been lucky in Europe so far, but during the war, in Algeria, I was in a jeep that hit a child. It didn't kill the boy but it broke him all up. I know how you must feel. It makes you sick to your soul. Are you insured, by the way?"

"Yes, I am," I said.

"Then you're fortunate. You can't blame them for suing, of course, but the sad fact of the matter is—as you probably know —that an American is considered tender game in Italian courts, even if he's in the right. I hope your boy gets well, poor bastard." He sighed again as he took the drink Rosemarie held out to him. "I love Italy and Italians—most of them. My favorite wife was Italian, as a matter of fact. But the truth is, you know, contrary to popular belief, that they're the sickest people on earth. Except maybe for Americans. Every one of them harbors a suicidal mania. A death-wish. That's why they make such rip-roaring racing drivers and high-wire artists and trapeze stars. And end up like your boy. Well, cheers."

"Cheers," I responded, tipping my glass, thinking gloomily again of di Lieto. "Why do they make such rotten soldiers, then?"

"That's a different matter," he said, running a hand through his hair. "It involves a certain amount of pride. I mean— Put it this way. No Italian wants to kill himself unless it's on his own terms."

A few paces off to the side now I noticed that there was being enacted a strange, tense, and quiet scene. Here half a dozen people had gathered and were standing in a rough semicircle around a small low chess table and two opposing chairs. On one of the chairs was sitting a sweating, black-haired young Italian; on the other chair sat Carleton Burns: between them on the table they had propped their elbows and—perspiring, panting heavily, their faces crimson from the strain—were locked in a game of hand-wrestling, Indian-style. As Cripps and I both turned to watch them, I was able for the first time to observe the face of Carleton Burns straight-on, undistracted, and at close range. And what a face it was! Red from exertion (desperately and grimly he strove to press the Italian's arm to the table), from booze, his face had the complexion now of a ripe tomato, and he snorted with the strain, and allowed a trickle of spit to ooze from a corner of his droopy mouth, so that as I watched his writhing, mobile expression and his inflamed, startlingly homely features—from his eyebrows that sprang up wildly like a satyr's down to his chin which, as in the mug shots of certain criminal psychopaths I had seen, seemed to melt into his neck—I obtained a rapid series of impressions of the man that began with the sense of something diabolical then ranged to corrupt then to just perversely mean. And as I watched the struggle, as I looked at Burns, who despite all his marks of dissipation seemed to possess a wiry strength, and saw him gradually and with a trembling shudder of his muscles force his opponent's arm toward the table, I wondered that such an ugly man should have been always cast as a hero and a lover, until I recalled the recent shift in cinematic fashion which had apotheosized the blackguard, the stupid, and the sidewise look of villainy. Suddenly with a thump, triumphant, Burns forced down the Italian's hand, gasping, "That got you, spaghetti-head."

There was a murmur of amusement and approval from the group around them; as the defeated sweating Italian forked over a fistful of lire, Burns gazed around the crowd with a jaunty smirk and with greenish, bloodshot eyes. "Anybody for a little hand-wrestling?" he said, and belched. "Anybody else want to take on Daddy-O?"

"You're too good, Burnsey," said the Italian as he replaced his wallet with a drained and sheepish look. "You should go into business for yourself. No kidding, Burnsey."

"How 'bout getting me another drink, Freddie?" Burns mumbled to someone lingering at his shoulder, a skinny youth with long sideburns and a glassy, sycophantic expression. Turning back to the Italian, he said: "No, Lombardi, you goofed. You got to keep your wrist straight, like I told you. It's all in the wrist. You can't get by with any of that shoulder jazz. How about it, anyone? Anyone want to take on Daddy-O at fifty mille lire?"

A thin, pretty, bespectacled girl dressed in very skimpy shorts looked up from a sheaf of papers she had been studying. "Tell us the secret of your fabulous success, Burnsey, actually," she said in a wry voice. She looked at him intently and rather sadly.

"It's one-third muscle tone and one-third brains and one-third anchestry," he replied thickly. His benumbed lips scarcely moved. "I've got Chippewa blood in me. That's no jazz. Ask anybody that knows. Good old Chippewa blood, full of crazy red corpuscles. That's what you skinny chicks need, Maggie. Good old hot . . . Chippewa . . . blood." His chin sank down upon his chest. "Somebody might plug in on your socket every now and then."

"Oh shut up," said the girl, turning pink. She half-rose from the low stool upon which she was sitting, thought better of it, and sat down again with her back turned. "You filthy—"

"What you need, Maggie"—he belched again—"is a mercy hump."

"Just shut up," she said, with a catch in her voice. Her distress was as transparent as a glass: she was in love with the odious man.

Burns straightened himself enough to down in one swift gulp the drink that Freddie brought him; then, stretching back in his chair, he looked up at Cripps and grinned. His eyes were filmed and his face was more flushed than ever, and it was a mystery to me how in his soaked condition, Chippewa or not, he had managed to win at his strenuous game. "Hullo, Alonzo. How's your hammer hanging? I thought you'd gone to bed."

"I stayed up so I could watch you," Cripps said in a level voice, without humor. "I always like to see you when you're at your most suave."

"Want to hand-wrestle for fifty mille lire?"

"No thanks."

"What's the matter with all you squares? Where the hell is Mason? I want to go swimming in that pool of his."

"Why don't you go to bed?" said Cripps. "You've been at it all day. I don't want a repetition of what happened in Venice. I think it would be a whole lot better all around if you just went to bed. You'll be dead tomorrow."

"Will you for Christ sake please stay off my back, mother? Where the hell is Mason, baby?" he said, looking at Rosemarie. "Daddy-O wants a cool plunge." Imperceptibly his voice had thickened and he had sunk by degrees down into his chair so that now, his hairy legs asprawl, neck and shoulders almost on the cushion, he was in a position not far from the horizontal. "Where the hell has Mason disappeared to, baby?"

We looked at Rosemarie. She flushed and stiffened. Her eyes grew wide with some undiscoverable but discomfiting emotion and, as her mouth parted round and hovered voicelessly and wretchedly agape, I realized for the first time that she not only *did* know where Mason was but had dark private reasons for being silent about it. "Oh, I—well I don't know," she stammered. "I mean, I think he went up to the Bella Vista."

"Well, tell him to chop-chop down here and take a cool plunge with Daddy-O. He's about the only one who wears pants around here that's not a fag. Mason and me. *Only* ones around here not raving fags. And Freddie. Isn't that right, Freddie?" he said, craning his neck upward.

"Well, gee-whiz, I don't know, Burnsey," said Freddie, looking warily and apologetically at Cripps.

"Now as for good old 'Lonzo," said Burns, gazing up at him with a loose slack-lipped smile. "I'm beginning to think he's the biggest fruitcake of all. That's what I think about old 'Lonzo. Recite us some your poetry, 'Lonzo," he simpered in a high lilting voice. "Play me a tune on the old skin flute. Say, Freddie, go up the hotel and get me my bongo drums. Me and 'Lonzo gonna jive with the old skin flute."

I watched Cripps' expression as Burns continued to bait him; his face wore a look now of faintly amused, faintly weary patience, as if he had been through this many times before, and he squinted at Burns through a blue haze of cigarette smoke with cool slit-eyed nonchalance. It was all in all an impressive portrait of equanimity.

"C'mon 'Lonzo," Burns said. "Own up. Come clean. Ain't you a big frooty-matoot? Gobble my—"

Without a word Cripps strode over to the place where Burns was sitting, or sprawling, and with one swift jerk of his hand at the folds of Burns' sport shirt drew him to his feet. He plucked him, I should say, so casual was the motion and so seemingly effortless. Not for an instant did it appear to me that he lost his serene almost gelid composure, and as he spoke to Burns, with his eyes two inches away from those of the actor and blue and level upon him, I could have sworn that he was smiling—a thin smile, to be sure, but a smile. "Look here, Burnsey," he said softly. "Do you want to know

112

something? I care for you. You're my pal. Am I penetrating? Am I reaching you? Do you read me?"

Dazed and confounded by the turn of events Burns tried groggily to reply, but he only managed to run his tongue nervously over his lips.

"Do you read me, Burnsey?" Cripps repeated.

"Roger, 'Lonzo," Burns said finally, with one limp hand raised haphazardly, essaying a salute. "Wilco over and out." Then swaying there he attempted to say something else, which ended up an incoherent gurgle. I thought for a moment he was going to fall flat on his face. "Read you loud and clear," he croaked.

"Well then, fine. Listen to what I'm saying, Daddy-O. I like you. With you I feel a very close bond. I would lay down my life for you, which is more, I suppose, than I could expect in return. I really care for you, you see? But with all of this kinship I feel, there are times when you are disgusting. There are times in fact when you are so surpassingly repellent that it takes all my will power to keep from kicking you in the teeth. This is one of those times. Now you go to bed, hear?"

"I go to bed, hear," Burns echoed mesmerically, in a faint voice.

"That's right. You go to bed." He gave Burns a feather-light tap on his chest so that the befogged actor, tottering backwards, half-stumbled, half-fell into the outstretched arms of Freddie. "Put him to bed, Freddie," he said crisply. "Take his shoes off and put him to bed."

Converted in the space of a wink, it seemed, from a tough swaggering hoodlum with a virulent sneer to a faltering and harmless drunk, Burns straightened himself partially, readjusting the drape of his sport shirt with fumbling hands, and once more morosely licked his lips. What looked like tears had welled up in his eyes, although this may have been only his habitual rheum. "Ol' buddy 'Lonzo," he said. "Sonofabitch. Ol' mother. Love ya. Love ya, Daddy-O."

"Go to bed," said Cripps more gently. "Go to bed, pal."

"Sorry, Daddy-O," he mumbled. "Didn't mean—" But then he stopped, utterly at sea. Freddie turned him slowly about. Contrite, vanquished, mumbling unintelligibly and swaying top-heavy on Freddie's supporting arm, he lurched off across the room. Somewhere in the spacious distance I saw Dawn O'Donnell break loose from the wall and intercept them. "Burnsey darling!" I heard her exclaim as she took his arm. Then the three figures, weaving like skaters across the glassy floor, were lost to sight.

For me the whole tense little tableau had been rather hollow and disappointing. I don't know just what else I expected but it did seem to me remarkable that Burns—so resourceful, so quick-witted in his professional roles—had been reduced to such shambling debris before my very eyes. In any case, I had little time to reflect on this matter, for a murmurous message had run through the gathering: everybody was going swimming. Turning round toward the window I saw the swimming pool, set like a huge and sparkling amethyst in the garden below, looking for all the world as if it graced some lawn in California and shining splendidly from a host of floodlights. Casually then, in twos and threes, still clutching their drinks, the guests drifted out from the room—fair Alice Adair escorted by the crew-cut young man, Baer and Rosemarie and all the rest, and Gloria Mangiamele, giggling, superbly undulant, her arm entwined about the waist of Burns' demolished Italian. I had more than half a craving to see Gloria in a bathing suit but I was still a little tired, determinedly a non-swimmer; besides, I felt hardly close enough to these people to manage an awkward word or two, much less to splash about with them in the intimacy of a pool; and so I contented myself with another drink, which I poured into my glass at the empty bar, feeling lonesome and abandoned as I listened to the bright noise of hilarity floating up from the bathhouse down the slope. After a moment's indecision I wandered out through a French door to the open balcony, where I thought I would watch the scene, and it was here beneath a dim orange lamp that I re-encountered Alonzo Cripps. He was standing alone at the railing.

"That's a remarkable sight, isn't it?" he said, gesturing toward the sea as I came toward him. Far down upon the gulf a fleet of fishing boats lay spread out upon the black surface of the night; invisible itself, each boat bore a dazzling light to summon the fish, so that now lying suspended between the dark water and the moonless and darker sky the whole collection of lights, twinkling there so serenely, had the appearance of a constellation of fat and vivacious stars. There was an immense silence and peace about these lovely hovering lights, and a hypnotic charm. Without taking his eyes from them, Cripps offered me a cigarette. "I never cease to be fascinated by those lights," he said, "whenever you're lucky enough to get a black night like this, so that the boats really *do* look like stars. Wonderful! I remember seeing them when I first came here during the war. The Army had a rest camp up here for a while, you know. I remember that I told myself that I would come back here, if only to see these lights again. They have an amazing floating unearthly quality, don't they?"

"They're marvelous," I agreed.

"Pretty dreary scene back there," he said without altering the tone of his voice, which was wistful and rather fatigued and stopped just short, it seemed to me, of actual melancholy. "I hope it wasn't too dreary. I'm sorry, what did you say your name was again?"

When I told him, he said: "You were the oddest sort of apparition, you know. Pale as a ghost, dressed like a mortician in the midst of this raunchy crowd. I thought for a while you must have been an acolyte of that old humbug, Bell, until it occurred to me that you were this friend of Mason's. And then I was really astonished. Have you known Mason long?"

"All my life, practically," I said. "Well, not really all my life," I added. "I was at prep school with him near my home in Virginia. Then for a while after the war I saw him in New York. But there's something about Mason that makes you feel you've known him forever, even when you don't see much of him."

"I know just what you mean," he said. *"God,* I know just what you mean. Where in the world——" But he broke off suddenly, wagging his head. There had been more than a trace of sarcasm in his voice. I was puzzled a little, and I could not figure out why he had fallen into this silence, leaving me stranded upon the edge of a small mystery, unless it had been because he had suddenly realized the discourtesy involved in running down Mason, who, after all, was his host. Even so, he was unable to resist hinting at *something* about Mason—whatever it was—that was bothering him. "I mean," he resumed slowly, "I mean—well, he's a weird boy. He's altogether different from the kid I remember down in Virginia."

"How do you mean?" I said.

He seemed not to have heard the question or, if he had, chose to ignore it. "Did you ever go to the Flagg place on the river there?" he said. "What a beautiful place it was. I used to go down every now and then before the war, before old Justin died. What a hard cookie he was. But a good man, really, and I guess I should be forever grateful to him. Actually, in spite of that grim little soldier-boy act he had quite decent instincts. Did you know him?"

"Well, I used to sort of see him," I said.

"He suffered, you know. I mean, really suffered, not the imitation sort of anguish you usually get in this business. He was ruthless in his way but there was an odd side of him that was really quite highly principled. Almost puritanical when you come right down to it. I guess that's the reason he never got a divorce. He really suffered over that. Mason ever tell you what became of his mother? Wendy?"

"I haven't seen him enough to talk to him since I've been here," I said. "The last I heard she was still lushing it up down on the farm."

"Pathetic woman," he sighed. "Christ, what misery liquor can cause! I should know. Even though it's really the symptom, you know, not the disease. I suppose it's simply that our disease is more—pandemic now, which is why you see such a fantastic going to pot. Especially among Americans, I mean. The disease being . . . what? You tell me. A general wasting away of quality, a kind of sleazy common prostration of the human spirit. Like Burnsey there—a really sensitive decent guy beneath it all, and very close to a great actor. Yet what does he do? In his mid-thirties, just when an artist should be hitting his stride, achieving maturity, he sinks into this idiotic infantilism. He becomes a hipster. A juvenile delinquent. A dirty-mouth little boy." He paused, then said: "Ah God, *I* don't know how we're going to finish this—I was about to say film." Then he fell silent.

Below us now the guests were converging on the pool. Some were clad in Bikinis; some were more conventionally decked out, including that fastidious snoop, Morton Baer, who wore no bathing suit at all but shuffled about in his flannel suit at the edge of the pool and puffed on a cigar. There was laughter, a constant chatter rose in English and Italian, and no one went into the pool; beneath a spangled cluster of beach umbrellas they had all disposed themselves at tables, attended by the solitary harried waiter. Crazed by the strange blue light, half a dozen moths the size of small bats swooped and flickered, casting their freakish shadows over all. I kept my eyes on Mangiamele, who was practically naked and had commenced to lacquer her toenails.

At this moment a huge explosion rent the air behind us in the *salone*. It was not an explosion, but it sounded like one: as Cripps and I jumped, then wheeled quickly about—both I think expecting to see fallen plaster and a cloud of smoke—we saw only that the huge front doors had been slammed violently open against the walls. Both doors were still vibrating. In front of them stood Cass Kinsolving. He was drunk. Drunk is hardly the word. He was about as drunk as one could get and still stand up—beside him

Burns would have appeared a teetotaler—and as he came toward us, his hand clawing at the chairs for support, he wore an expression of such desuetude and abandonment of thought that it was like no expression, and I could have sworn that he had only the dimmest notion of where he was, and what he was doing, and where he was headed. A ripped and dirty T-shirt—it was Marine Corps issue, a faded green—exposed his powerful shoulders, but there was something sluggishly decrepit about his progress across the room that made him appear sick, depleted, as if he had left the last ounce of his strength in the courtyard below. At one point I thought he was going to pitch forward across a sofa. And I was surprised when, finally lurching over to the balcony where we were standing, he said thickly but with more clarity than ever I thought such a drunken man could muster: "Hello, Leverett. How's the guy you hit today making out?"

"Hiya," I said. I will have to be honest about my feelings toward Cass at this point: I thought he was a disagreeable lush and an all-around pain in the neck.

He turned to Cripps before I had a chance to reply. "Good evening, Signor Regista, *come va?* How's everything in the flicker business? Making pots and pots and pots?"

"*Va bene,* Cass," said Cripps. "*Come state? Un po' troppo vino stassera?*" He regarded Cass with a smile, but the smile seemed sad, and a trifle worried.

Cass fell against the balcony railing, making it sing and tremble. He gazed at us with drowned hot eyes and a wet lippy grin, panting and heaving while a tic worked nervously at his brow. "Tell me this, Signor Regista," he said, still grinning. "What said the chorus when old Oedipus was at Colonus"—he seemed fearfully close to pitching backward over the rail—"and old Theseus dragged his poor old bones off—"

"Watch it there, Cass," said Cripps, reaching out.

" 'For the long days lay up full many things nearer unto grief than joy,' " he cried, and picked up my glass and downed it in a gulp. "Stand back there, old Buster Brown, old dollbaby!" With one hand he sliced the air in front of him, as if with an invisible cutlass, threateningly, causing Cripps to halt. "Stand back there, old great gray cinematic magician, whilst I keen my song! 'For the long days lay up full many things nearer unto greet'—'scuse me—'grief than joy, but as for thy delights, their place shall know them no more, when a man's life has lapsed beyond a fitting term' . . . *whoo!*" His arm slid off the railing, recovered itself; drawing himself erect he thrust his wrist into the neck of his T-shirt and stood, weaving slightly, in the hot-eyed declamatory pose of an old-time ham tragedian. "Stand back there, I say! 'The Deliverer—the Deliverer,' to continue, 'comes at last to all alike, when the doom of Hades is suddenly revealed without marriage-song or lyre or dance, even Death at last!' " He paused, took a breath. "Now for the bleeding beautiful antistrophe. 'Not to be born is, past all prizing, best, but when a man hath seen the light this is the next best by far, that with all speed he should go thither, whence he hath come. For when he hath seen—' "

"Hold it there, Cass," said Cripps, going up to him. "Hold it there, boy. You're going to land in the garden."

" '—youth go by . . .' " He halted. Neck bent back now at right angles he was trying to drain the glass of its last drop; it was a wide-mouthed glass and the ice cubes perched bizarrely on his eyeglasses and water trickled down around his ears. *"Io mi sazio presto di vino,"* he said with a gasp finally. "This here Scotch of Mason's just dandy. Make tears come to your eyes." He took a step back toward the *salone,* clutching the glass with two hands before him, like a chalice. "I think I'll just get me—"

"Hold on, Cass," Cripps said. "Don't you think you've had about enough?" As he said this a dry laugh, almost as if in spite of himself, escaped his lips and I heard him whisper the words *nursemaid to drunks.* "Why don't you—"

"How 'bout that?" Cass said, suddenly whirling around. "How 'bout that, old sweet gray wizard of the cinematic art? Did you catch the faultless phrasing, the accent, the intonation, I mean the simple pure ordinary bleeding *poignancy* of it all? Each syllable like a shiny round little nugget blooped out from the divine lips of Garrick hisself! Put me on! Put me on, by God! With my talent and this here profile and your noodle we won't have no trouble at all. The girls'll cram the flicker palaces from sea to shining sea. There won't be a dry pair of pants in the house. How 'bout that, old Regista?" He placed a thick arm on Cripps' shoulder. "Take my advice, get rid of these here second-raters, these hand-me-downs from vaudeville, these jugglers and chuckleheads and such trash. Hire you a *man,* a man like me that could bring forth sobs from a cast-iron jockey—"

"Cass," Cripps said, "let me take you—"

"Hold on! Let me tell you what we'll do. Together you and me we'll pull a Prometheus on 'em. We'll bring back tragedy to the land of the Pepsi-Cola and the peanut brittle and the Modess Because. That's what we'll do, by God! And we'll make the ignorant little buggers like it. No more popcorn, no more dreamboats, no more Donald Ducks, no more wet dreams in the mezzanine. *Tradegy,* by God, that's what we'll give 'em! Something to stiffen their spines and firm up their joints and clean out their tiny little souls. What'll you have? *Ajax? Alcestis? Electra? Iphigenia?* Hooboy!" Once more his hand plunged into the neck of his T-shirt. " 'I would not be the murderer of my mother, and of thee too. Sufficient is her blood. No, I will share thy fortune, live with thee, or with thee die: to Argos I will lead thee . . .' "

"Cass," said Cripps, "what you need I think is a nice long snooze. Now if I were you—"

"Hold on!" said Cass again. But then he abruptly fell silent. He scratched his brow. "Plumb forgot what it was I came for." For a moment he wore a puzzled look; then suddenly breaking out into a smile, he clapped his thigh and said: "Now, by God, we'll work a bit of subtle thievery! *Ssst!*" he whispered, bending forward toward Cripps' ear. "You won't tell a soul, will you? You won't breathe a loving word?"

"I don't read you," said Cripps, with his melancholy grin.

"Is the illustrious proprietor away? Old Mason, has he gone away?" He giggled a little, ceased, his face becoming mysterious and grave. "When the rat is away, Regista," he said in a hoarse stage whisper, "old tomcat will play. Now to go fetch the bleeding cure!" At this he pulled loose from Cripps, turned about, and staggered off away from the balcony. Cripps and I both made quick involuntary motions to stop him, but seconds too late: like a blind and incapacitated bull he blundered straight into the piano bench, pitched forward with the crumpled knees and supplicating arms of a man shot in the back, and came down flush upon the keyboard in a thunderous uproar of flats and sharps; for a split instant he lay outspread there like some disheveled virtuoso gone raving mad and then slid to the floor with a groan, one arm trailing a flashy glissando along the keys.

"Sweet heaven!" Cripps gasped as we went to his aid. But even before we reached his side he was on his feet, listlessly probing for broken bones. "No harm done, Regista," he said. He gazed dazedly at the piano. "I think I might have sprung that—"

"Come on, Cass," Cripps said. "Downstairs with you now." Together, with Cripps on one side and me on the other, we maneuvered him back toward the open door. His breath came in short gasps, and he reeked of wine and sweat.

"Take my advice," Cripps said. "Hit the sack."

Cass, still prodding himself, halted at the edge of the steps. "Yeah," he said in a distant voice. "Yeah. O.K." Then with great care, hugging the marble banister, he descended to the courtyard, and Cripps and I were alone.

"That boy is slowly killing himself," Cripps said, shaking his head. "I've never seen anyone put away so much sauce in all my life, and that includes my old pal Burnsey."

"What's wrong with him?"

We moved back toward the balcony. "I'd never laid eyes on him before we came up here the other day. I don't know who the hell he is but he's quite a character. Mason's got him on some sort of hook." His face turned bitter and grim. "I saw something so *low* and *contemptible*," he blurted, "so *disgusting*, really, that you wouldn't believe me if—" His voice trailed off.

"How do you mean?" I said. There seemed to be a lot of mysterious goings-on around this weird palace, and I wanted to be let in on them.

"Oh nothing," he said. He cast a glance at his watch. Then for no reason at all, or as if the watch had allowed him a sudden private insight, he said: "It's the age of the slob. If we don't watch out they're going to drag us under, you know." Delivered of this, he fell gloomily silent. Back in the village the clock struck the hour. As Cripps turned again, brooding silently on the far hovering lights, I felt I had never seen a man in whom resided such bitterness, such gloom. The chime's single vibrating note died and became still: it was one, it was morning. Out of some window now on the level directly below us *Don Giovanni* came again, impassioned, alluring, boisterous, also very loud, as if someone had turned it loose full-blast in outrage. *Rinfrescatevi!* I heard Leporello boom above the flutes and strings. *Bei giovinotti!* And out across the starless night it went, rebounding from the moon-patched slopes across the valley, so far and still so close, and down across the coast above the boats and the twinkling lights—*Ehi caffé! Cioccolatte!* —and on and on, for all I knew, to Calabria and to Sicily. And at this upsurge of sound the golden people near the pool started, turned with puzzled questing faces like a herd of beasts around a water hole, frozen in stiff alarm.

"Look at them," Cripps said slowly. "You know, that boy isn't too far off, after all. Look at them, will you? The greatest art form ever devised by man, and what do you get? A void . . . *cosa da nulla* . . . nothing . . . We are not even barbarians. We

120

are mountebanks." He yawned. "Well, I guess I'll try to go to bed. Did you ever have insomnia?"

"Not often," I said.

"Let me give you some advice. Form regular habits, don't try too hard for anything, forget about—well, honesty, or effort, or it'll all get you like it's got me. You know, I lie there and doze off into something that's not quite sleep and I have a dream. In this dream I am always a victim. A golf pro and a crooner and a drum majorette are all contesting for my soul. Night after night. Sometimes it's the crooner who wins out, sometimes the golf pro. But more often it's the drum majorette. She just stands there and wiggles her behind, and then she stomps me to death." He paused. *"Listen—"*

Don Giovanni had ceased. Now wild and woeful and with scandalous spine-chilling beauty, a hillbilly song had erupted on the night, athrob with shrill messianic voices, male and female, and the strumming of steel guitars. Perhaps it was pure volume alone, or some left-over nostalgia for this music from my native shires, but I thought I had never heard anything at once so lovely and so horrible, and my mind began to swarm with southern weather, southern voices, southern scenes:

This question we daily hear, no one seems to know . . .
Wha-a-at's the matter with this world . . .

Country beer joints, pinewoods, dusty back roads and red earth and swamp water and sweet-fragrant summer dusks: my mind was smothered, overwhelmed by memory. "My Lord," I said to Cripps, "what's that—"

"Shh-h," he said. "Listen—"

Now this rumor we hear: another war we fear,
Revelations is being fulfilled . . .

"Wonderful," Cripps whispered.

Your soul's on sinking sand, the end is drawing near:
That's what's the matter with this world . . .

Pale faces turned toward the source of this anathema, the people below attended to the horrendous noise: a sport-shirted Italian mouthed a voiceless imprecation, another joined him, red-faced; La Mangiamele clapped her hands over her ears.

The precious ol' Bahble says: Sin will have to go—
Wha-a-at's the matter with this world . . .

Across all Italy the music seemed to stream, filled with dolor
and distress, jangling guitars and wild apocalyptic voices joined in
one long throbbing lament—bathos brought full circle and back
into a kind of crippled majesty. I listened until shameful tears
swam in my eyes. And then abruptly, and with the jagged uproar
of a phonograph needle scraping like a raw blade across the evening, the music was strangled off, perished, and we heard drunken
muffled shouts in the room below.

"Scum!" It was Cass' voice. "Swine! Scum of the earth!"

Then after a pause, more quietly now, *Don Giovanni* filled the
night, and the people around the pool relaxed, resumed their
murmurous chatter amid the shadowy swoopings of the giant
moths.

"That boy is killing himself," said Cripps. "What can you do?
He could stop Mason in his tracks, and all his breed. But look at
him. He's killing himself." Then he said good night to me, and then
he was gone.

It was not long after Cripps left that a really rather distressing
thing occurred. What happened was this: after watching Cripps
walk away, I lingered on the balcony for a while, brooding over
the people around the pool. I listened—I should say I was bela-
bored by the music: once again it became raucous and loud, and
the voices of Elvira and Masetto and Ottavio, screeching like alley-
cats while the detestable grandee went about his seduction,
boomed up and around me, and washed away the sounds from the
pool below. I watched the lights floating out upon the sea, ravished
by their beauty, but at the same time sunk in the profoundest
gloom—primarily because of Cripps, who in an odd and oblique
way had so mutilated my happy expectation of America that, if
memory serves me right, I concocted all sorts of alternatives: another job in Rome, marriage to a princess somewhere, headlong
flight to Greece. I was mired in despondency, my throat was itchy
and sore. But after a short time my sadness diminished: to hell
with Cripps, I thought, and I turned to make my lonesome way
back down among the movie stars. It was several moments later,
after I had passed through the long room, that a door burst open a
few feet away from me, exposing a glimpse of an ascending stair-

way, and a girl of eighteen or twenty, who came skidding out into the room as if upon glass, slipped to the floor in a heap, and then leaped up and rubbed her elbow, sobbing as if her heart would break. She was almost faultlessly lovely; even the brief glimpse I had of her, as she stood there indecisively with her brown eyes round with hurt and terror, wrung my heart with yearning. I put out my hand to steady her, for she seemed to be on the verge of toppling once more, but she drew back instantly and threw a hunted, despairing look toward the staircase. Her dress was black and of poor quality, such as that which servants wear; through a rip in the bodice practically all of one of her full, heavy, and handsome breasts was laid bare, and for the entire ten seconds that she stood there, paralyzed, it seemed, by panic and indecision, I too felt rooted there and speechless, torn both by a futile, gallant desire to help and by the beast inside which drew my eyes down to that delectable, troubled bosom. Then, suddenly coverning herself, still furiously sobbing, she struck herself in the face. *"Dio mio!"* she cried in a frenzy. *"Questa è la fine! Non c'è rimedio!"*

"Can I help—" I began.

"Ah my God, please," she exclaimed in English. "No, please, don't—"

And then, recovering control, breathless, she pushed past me with a little groan of anguish, her brown hair in a scattered, lovely tangle about her face as she took to her heels again, bare feet pattering in diminishing terrified flight down the hallway. She had spun me around like a top, and I came to rest on a marble bench, still vibrating. Before I could rise, I heard a thunderous noise once more on the stairs, as of trunks and boxes tumbling down. It was a hell of a racket; the whole palace seemed to be in eruption. Then Mason burst forth, skidding too on the glassy floor, throwing out his arms wildly and righting himself as he slid to a stop before me. Three Band-Aids plastered his face. His hair flew out in all directions. He was clad in a silk dressing gown both too short for him and put on in obvious haste, for his chest was bare, exposing a thicket of reddish sweating hair, and I could see, below, his knobby knees. Rather incongruously, his feet were shod in wooden shower clogs, which is what accounted for all the noise.

"Where is she!" he snarled at me, his face red and ugly.

"Who?" I said. I had drawn back nervously on the bench. I had never seen him quite like this before: he wore a brutish, wild expression, and with his red-rimmed eyes and arm cocked threateningly I thought he was going to paste me one where I sat.

"Where did she go!" he yelled. "Tell me, you bastard! I'll kill her!"

"I'll swear to God, Mason," I said, "I just do not *know*."

"You're lying!" And then with a strange, painful, bowlegged gait, infinitely stiff and slow, he moved toward the hallway down which the girl had disappeared. "You wait right there, Petesy boy, because when I come back I expect to stomp out of you a fat amount of your yellow and treacherous shit." There was a kind of a smile on my host's face but pure malice and venom were in his voice, and hatred. . . .

Maybe you recollect that dream of betrayal which I described early in this story—of the murderous friend who came tapping at my window. Somehow when again I recall that dream and then remember Mason at this moment, I am made conscious of another vision—half-dream, half-fantasy—which has haunted me ever since I left Sambuco.

It goes like this: I have taken a picture of a friend with one of those Polaroid cameras. While waiting for the required minute to elapse I have wandered into another room, and there I pull out the print all fresh and glossy. "Ha!" or "Well!" or "Look!" I call out expectantly to the other room. Yet as I bend down to examine the picture, I find there, not my friend at all but the face of some baleful and unearthly monster. And there is only silence from the other room.

III

"Holy *God*," said Cass one day, as I recalled that evening for him, "was I as bad as all that?"

"I wouldn't say bad," I replied. "Not *bad*. As I recall it you were even quite eloquent, in a soggy way. But—well yes, you were blind, all right."

He reflected silently for a long time on what I had told him. "That piano," he said finally. "Falling all over that piano. I don't remember a thing about it. I swear."

"If you'd done that sober, you'd have been in the hospital for a week."

"And that string music. Jesus, I've still got it somewhere, down underneath the Buxtehude. 'What's the Matter with This World?' Wilma Lee and Stoney Cooper. I got that record up in Petersburg,

Virginia, right after the war when I was visiting my cousin up there. Carted it all around Europe with me, too. But I'll swear I can't remember ever playing it over there. And that night—"

"You played it all right. Boy, you played it."

"Holy God." He fell silent for a while, then he said: "What time do you suppose that was? What time of the evening?"

"Morning, I'd say. Somewhere around one o'clock."

He wrinkled his brow and then looked at me intently. "All right then, that was the last time you saw Mason before—before he was dead. When you saw him chasing off after Francesca. Is that right?"

"That was Francesca, then?" I countered. "The girl he killed?"

His face for a moment seemed unutterably weary and somber. It was his first reaction of this kind since I had come to Charleston; partly through me, I suppose, he had begun to live it all again, and at this moment I could only vaguely sense how much he had cared for the girl. "It was her," he said rather despondently, "it couldn't have been anyone else. Did you see her again?"

"I don't think it was too long afterwards. With you."

"Where, for God sake?"

"Down in that courtyard. You—" I paused. It was an awkward thing to say, and I didn't know if he wanted to hear it. "You kissed her. Or she kissed you. Believe me, I wasn't spying," I added, "I happened to be—"

"No, of course not. But—" With puzzlement all over his face, he ran his fingers through his hair. Then after a moment he said: *"Wow,* you know it is all coming back now. In bits and pieces and little flickers, you see." He fell silent again, then his eyes slowly lit up, and he arose from his chair and began to pace around the cluttered fishing shack. It was raining, and the roof leaked, and water dripped down the back of my neck. "Like what you just said, for instance. I'd forgotten that, too. A total and complete blank. Of course! I did see her. I *did* see her. And—" His voice trailed off.

"And what?"

He scratched his chin. "And she— Look," he said, "this is important. Try to be as accurate as you can. How long do you think you were at that party? That is, before you saw Mason and he hollered at you."

I brooded, straining to be exact. "It must have been eleven-thirty or so when I came in with Rosemarie." I paused. "And about—oh, sometime after one when Mason came downstairs after Francesca. A little less than two hours, I'd say. But why—"

"Wait a minute, wait a minute," he said, gesturing for silence. Then after a bit he turned to me with a wan sad grin, and said: "Now tell me this, will you. When *was* the last time you saw Mason?"

I started to tell him, again with some embarrassment. "Well, at least that's an easy one. It was when he made you go into your trained-seal act. When he made you—" I faltered, horribly.

"Oh Jesus, yes," he blurted, "Poppy once told me a little about that. It got so awful I didn't ever let her finish." He paused, somewhat agitated now, stroking his bare arms. "That was when— when you rescued me, I guess. I don't remember that, but I do remember it afterwards, when you were sobering me up. And after this exhibition I put on you never saw Mason again?"

"Only when he was stiff and cold."

Somber, absorbed, he gazed for a long while through the streaming windows. "Somewhere," he said slowly, "at one point along in there somewhere she told me something." He struck his head shortly with his hand, as if to dislodge the memory. "She told me something . . ."

I was utterly baffled about all this, and my silence must have betrayed my bafflement, for in a moment he turned and said in an even voice: "You've got to excuse this, you know. I'm not pulling your leg, really." He ran some water in a pan and, sitting down beside me, began to eviscerate a large croaker. "I'm going to level with you about something," he went on. "It's not something I've ever wanted to think about, much less talk about. Maybe it's better this way—get it out of the system. But—well, it's like this, you see. That trained-seal act, as you call it. Mason had me coming and going down there that summer. It started out O.K., we were even sort of buddies at first. But then—something went wrong. What with the booze and the weird condition I was in he began to stomp me —I mean really stomped me, and I let him—and it got so bad I was paying him for the time of day. A regular peon I was, if you want to know the truth." He paused. "I've never known anyone in my life I ever hated so much." He became silent, sweating over the fish.

"So—" I said.

"I'll tell you about that sometime. But now— Anyway, the point is this: a while back you said something about how it shocked you, Mason doing what he did and all. How though you could credit him with an ordinary red-white-and-blue American-style rape you couldn't see him doing it in the all-out monstrous way he did it. Well, when you said that, it rang a bell. Because there in Sambuco, when it was all over, that was the way I felt too. I hated his guts, he was the biggest son of a bitch I had ever run across; but later I couldn't see him doing that. What he did took something Mason didn't have. His cruelty and his meanness was a different kind. Only—" He fell silent again, the cords of his arms standing out as he strained away with the knife. "Bleeding croaker," he said at last, as if wishing to banish the subject for good. "Hardly worth the trouble. Skin on a croaker's like—"

I may have been mistaken, but I thought for a moment he was going to weep.

"Only *what?*" I persisted. "Look, Cass, like you say, you can level with me. I'm not trying to worm something out of you that you don't want—"

"Only this," he said, turning calmly to face me. "Only I think now that, by God, I was wrong about all that. Maybe he had it in him, after all. Everything you say—all of this stuff I was blind to —makes it plain that rape was on his mind from the word go. She wouldn't give in to him, so he would take it. That afternoon, for instance; what he said there to Rosemarie that time, just before he belted her. And then this thing you told me about—chasing after her down the stairs. He said, 'I'll kill her.' Isn't that what you said? And then—"

"Then what?"

"Nothing much," he said in a bemused voice. He turned to me again. "Put it this way," he said. "Maybe I'm just being a scoundrel. Maybe I'm just being un-Christian. Maybe I just want to make sure that he really was a monster."

"Monster?" I said. Cass appeared to have lost his reticence about Mason, and I was eager to press this slight advantage. "Tell me," I said, "he really gave you a rough time down there, didn't he?"

He seemed to ponder the question for a long moment, turning over all the angles, absorbed. "Yes, I reckon he did. But how much of all that was due to my own corruption, this old corruption of mine—how much of the whole ruination was my blame I'd like to know. Maybe I'll tell you about that too sometime, when I'm able to be sensible about it and recollect it." He halted to wipe the wet scales off his knife, and dried his hands. "It's really curious, you know," he went on, now in a somber monotone, "this business about evil—what it is, where it is, whether it's a reality, or just a figment of the mind. Whether it's a sickness like cancer, something that can be cut out and destroyed, with maybe some head doctor acting as the surgeon, or whether it's something you can't cure at all, but have to stomp on like you would a flea carrying bubonic plague, getting rid of the disease and the carrier all at once. Not too long ago, as time goes—you're a lawyer, you know all this—they'd hang a ten-year-old for stealing a nickel's worth of candy. Right there in Merrie England, France too. This was the plague theory, I guess. Stomp on the evil, crush it out. Now a kid goes out on the streets—he's not even ten, most likely he's twenty and he goddam well knows better—and he commits some senseless and vicious crime, murder maybe, and they call him sick and send for the head doctor, on the theory that the evil is—well, nothing much more than a temporary resident in the brain. And both of these theories are as evil as the evil they are intended to destroy and cure. At least that's what I've come to believe. Yet for the life of me I don't know of any nice golden mean between the two."

"How does all of this apply to Mason?"

"Well first— Let me explain a little something. I don't mean to be blowing my own horn, or singing the blues, either, but—well, I've come up where I am—I'll admit it isn't very far—pretty much the hard way, as I guess you know. I didn't get past the second year up there in this miserable little high school in North Carolina, even now I have the toughest time writing and punctuating and so on. But I did learn to read and I've read a lot on my own hook, and I guess I've read ten times what the average American has, although God knows that could mean only one book. Anyway, I guess one of the big turning points in my life was right after the war, when I got discharged from the psycho ward of that naval hospital I was telling you about, in California. There was this chief noodle specialist there—one hell of a guy. He was a Navy captain, name of Slotkin. I'd told him about my schoolboy interest in painting, and he got me in one of these therapy painting classes, and I reckon I was a painter from then on out. That's how I ended up after the war in New York instead of back in Carolina, I guess. Anyway, we couldn't come to any agreement whatsoever about my melancholia or whatever it was, with its manic-depressive overtones, but I had a lot of long talks with him, and there was some patient gentle quality the guy had that almost swung me out of my blues, and just before I left the place—uncured—he gave me a two-volume edition of Greek drama. It was quite irregular and all, I guess, this gift from a full Navy captain to a buck private in the Marines, but I guess he saw something in me, even if I wasn't about to buy any of his Freud. I remember he told me this: 'Read this when you're down and out.' Something like: 'The fact of the matter is this, you know, we haven't advanced any farther than the Greeks, after all.' Which you've got to admit is pretty cool talk, coming from a reverend brain doctor. He was quite a sweet guy, old Slotkin.

"Anyway, when you mentioned how I started quoting at length from Sophocles that night, it all came back to me. The sweat and the horror and this bleeding awful view into the abyss. Long before I ended up in Sambuco I'd memorized great hunks and sections. out of those two volumes. And when you saw me that night I was really in a bad way—as blind-drunk off of *Oedipus* as I was off of booze." He paused and fingered ruminatively at the edge of the knife. "Yet here's the thing, you see. Let me explain if I can." He paused again and closed his eyes, almost prayerfully, as if coaxing reluctant memories from the confusion of the past. "I was so completely blind. Stoned. Something you said . . . which has to do with this evil I was talking about." His eyelids parted, and he turned. "Yes, I think I'm getting some of it. More of it's coming back now. I do remember just in the dimmest way going upstairs. The piano, no. But *Oedipus,* and Cripps, and you—yes, a little." He shook his head. "No, there's some connection I can't make yet. Jesus Christ, you'd think we were having a bleeding séance. I was trying to search for something that night . . . But now it's all gone again. Do you think it could be that I had come up there to chew Mason's ass out with a little *Oedipus?* No, I doubt it." He shook his head again, violently. "All I know now is that I had some sort of drunken truth that I'd dredged up out of that play, and that it sure as hell had to do with evil, and that Mason . . ."

He stopped and, very calmly, lit a cigar. "But I might be mistaken," he added. "What did you really think of Mason?" he said then, turning.

"Oh I just don't know," I said. "I don't know how to explain him, I never have known. He was a jerk. A big spoiled baby with too much money and a lot of pretensions. He was the world's worst liar. He hated women. He was a lousy mess. And yet—"

"Yet what?"

"Yet he was great fun to be with sometimes. He was entertaining as hell. But he was more than an entertainer. Remove all the other stuff and he might have been quite a guy."

"How long did you know him, really?"

"That's an odd thing," I said. "I knew him a couple of years at school. And then for a week or so in New York, right after the war. I can't recall how long exactly. Ten days. Maybe a couple of weeks. We'll call it a week. And then that day in Sambuco. And that was all. But—" I paused. "But still and all there was something about him. I mean you could see him for twenty-four hours and he would reveal more about himself than most people do in a lifetime. He was a—" I halted. I really didn't know what he was.

"Tell me about him," Cass said.

"Well, it's not really a whole lot," I said. "I don't think I could exactly—"

"*Tell* me anyway," he said.

So I tried to tell him. I tried to tell him everything I could remember. I told him how at first I had lost track of Mason after that dismal week end down in Virginia and how, though we wrote each other for a while (he was in Palm Beach, Havana, Beverly Hills, New York, usually with Wendy; his letters were lewd and comical), our correspondence petered out and he dropped from sight altogether. I told him, too, how ten years—to the month—passed before I ran into him after the war, quite by accident, in a New York bar. . . .

No doubt it is too easy to say that had I not met Mason again things would have turned out differently, that, having lost touch with one another, we would not have restored our old communion of spirit—a dignified phrase for "palship" or some other term equally American and specious, but which, once re-established, allowed him to invite me down to Sambuco. Most of our existence, though, is made up of such imponderables; the important thing is that we met again. It was in the late spring, a week or so before I got the Agency job and sailed for Europe. I had very little money at that time but a job with a veteran's counseling service allowed me to eat after a fashion and to rent a tiny cardboard apartment on West Thirteenth Street. It was a humid season, with muggy twilights crowned high with thunderheads and a grumble of storms that never came, wilted faces along the avenues, and windows thrown open on the heat-blown air erupting blurred music and voices ballyhooing war, cold war, threats of war. Evenings I tried to read uplifting books in my apartment, but my soul was ill-equipped for the stress of loneliness. My room was a place of subterranean murk with a view of an airshaft and an adjoining hotel where old men constantly shambled by, scratching themselves, flushing remote toilets. But it was only in part because of my surroundings that this time of my life was not a very satisfactory one.

There are certain periods in youth which are not touched by even a trace of nostalgia, one's conduct at that time seems so regrettable. Never very fastidious anyway, I became wholly unkempt, and was sour and spiteful to the girls I tried to pick up in Village hangouts. And to top it all, Mason came into my life—in a jammed bar on Sheridan Square during an evening's prowl that had left me more than usually lonesome and disheveled, and with my carcass burdened with mean-spirited lusts.

Except that he had taken on a little bit more weight, he had not changed at all. He was dressed in an elegant turtle-neck jersey and blue jeans, looking very much the artist from top to toe—though an artist with money—and he seemed to be enjoying himself. I saw his grinning face through the smoke of the room, one hand held high, flourishing a schooner of beer. Even now I remember how our eyes met in the flicker of a glance, my sudden shock of delight darkened by a half-hope that he had not recognized me— both of these feelings almost simultaneous and in such confusion that I had no time to make up my mind whether to rise and shout hello or to steal silently out, before he was on top of me, thumping me on the back— "Hey, Petesy, let's flap off on a wild one!" he cried—and falling around my shoulders with loud hoots of recognition.

"What an absolutely fabulous coincidence," he said, when he had quieted down. "At a dinner I was at last night I was talking to this guy—a very fine painter—and we got to talking about the people we had known at school. I said I couldn't speak for Princeton, having been eased out my first year. Do you know, I got booted out for the most undistinguished reason. Petesy, dollbaby, let's face it, I'm a brilliant man but as far as education goes I'm simply a horsefly on the ass of progress."

I would have had to be a more stolid individual than I am not to have been warmed by his energy, his big grin, and by the note in his voice, as he clapped me on the shoulder, of honest affection. I must have smiled, saying: "But, Mason, how did you get *in?*"

"You mean after I got kicked out of St. A.'s? Oh, Wendy pulled some wires through one of her relatives and got me into a chic reform school up in Rhode Island. They drilled you with rifles and all that crap but I bore down hard—you know, for the glory of Wendy-dear—and I got good grades. That, though, Petesy, is what they call a non sequitur. Because I *didn't* get booted out of college for boffing or drinking or anything sordid. But for my grades! Grades! Can you imagine anything so absurd? And I tested out with an I.Q. of 156! This *gluttonous* widow I was week-ending with on Sutton Place just kept me away from the books. Poor Wendy. The old man had kicked in with I don't know how many bushels of dough to the library, and when she came up to Princeton I thought she was going to take the place apart . . ."

"Look out, Mason, you're spilling beer on your pants. How is Wendy, by the way?"

"Oh, she's fine. She tried to go on the wagon after the old man died. I guess you heard about him. She goes on and off, poor thing, but I haven't had to give her the cure for months and months. Chloral hydrate and Cream of Wheat. You know, it's a funny thing. You know how she used to absolutely loathe Merryoaks? Well, after the old man went to his reward, as they say, you couldn't get her away from there, absolutely fell in love with the place. Sits down there and slurps Old Crow all by herself, and rides around on this big horse. My wife and I—you'll meet the wife—anyway, we were down there last week end. It's the biggest goddam horse you ever saw. And off she goes, loping down the riverbank, with this new boy friend she's got. He's a seventy-year-old Belgian and he's gotten her all interested in something called Zen. I think they shoot arrows at each other. Jesus sake, Petesy," he chuckled, wiping foam from his lips, "I don't know who's sleeping with who down there. I think the horse is getting the best part of it." He began to shake and tremble with quiet interior laughter. "Ah Jesus," he sighed, "Petesy, it's great to see you again. I knew if I ran into you at all it'd be in a purgatory of the spirit like this. You know, Wendy still asks about you all the time. She had a real sneaker for you, you know? I think it must have been because you kept your mouth shut. She was so sick and tired of the old man. He kept yowling into her ear all the time, trying to smoke out her psyche, no wonder she took to the sauce. Poor Wendy," he said, with a sudden wistful look, "I'll have to get her up here so she can see you. What with that spooky Belgian and that horse and all that sauce she'll end up for certain in some laughing academy.

"Anyway," he went on, "that's beside the point." He was not drunk (although he liked drinking, I recalled that even as a boy he was not particularly addicted to it, which always struck me as a noteworthy deliverance) but a bright hilarity burbled up in his voice, and his eyes were twinkly and agitated. "What I was telling that guy last night is that of all the dozens of little schoolmates I ever had there was only one I'd walk around the corner to see again. And then I mentioned your name—old Petesy—and I wondered what you were doing. It's fantastic! It's pure clairvoyance. So what are you doing? Tell me." But before I could pop my mouth open to reply he was tugging at my sleeve. "The love of my life," he was saying. "Come over here and meet her."

I remember my surprise at the idea of Mason's being married, and I studied the girl—a slow-stirring blonde named Carole who gave me a warmed-over smile and kept displaying her handsome bosom in a sort of habitual shrug of weariness. In the booth beside her sat a red-haired, blanched, unwell-looking young couple in blue jeans—I think they were called the Pennypackers—who like a pair of caged foxes stared up at me out of the gloom, fixing me with their feral, glittering eyes. They made no word of greeting, but doted on Mason in a conversation thick with small yaps and noises of innuendo—about a week end at Provincetown and someone named Gus and someone named Wally—and finally, when they got up to go, Mason lent them ten dollars from an enormous bankroll (I thought it must have been a lapse, for even as a boy he had never been so graceless as to be ostentatious about his cash), upon which they battened their little aqueous, lashless eyes in one brief hot glance of conspiratorial greed before slipping out into the night. I recall wondering how these two, who seemed so down-at-the-heel and uninspired, had come to be Mason's friends, but even before I could begin tentatively to pump him, he had answered my question, saying: "He's in Theater"—he capitalized the noun— "he hasn't got a cent and he's a terrible ass but he reads scripts for the Playwrights' Company. He's got the first act of this play I'm writing. If they don't do it I'm almost certain Whitehead will put it on next year, once I get it finished. It's that second act that's such a ball-breaker. Did you catch those two? Funny thing is—did you notice?—they look exactly alike. I really think she's his sister. And she's the weirdest one in the act. Jesus, I'd love to see them in action. I bet it's like trying to stuff a marshmallow into a piggy bank."

None of Mason's drolleries were lost on Carole, who punctuated his talk with throaty little commas of mirth and giggles which she employed without stint whenever he opened his mouth. She was a hefty, good-looking girl with milky skin and a rich, contralto, barrelhouse voice and elliptical green eyes that mirrored almost nothing save an imperturbably confident passion. She looked open-minded and procreative, a soft acquiescent woman, dimly in love. Her raucous voice betrayed her—it was pure Greenpoint—depressing me about Mason's taste in mates, though I couldn't help feeling a bachelor's itch and envy over what he had acquired otherwise.

"Darling, you fracture me," she giggled. " 'Di've another Scotch onna rocks?"

"Actually, these Village dives aren't exactly my dish of tea," said Mason, ignoring her, "but it's good for spasmodic kicks, you know, to see the pseudo-intellectual riffraff in operation."

He squeezed my arm. "We're goofing off, you know. There's a big brawl going on at my place. It's been swinging ever since last night. Come on, let's go." Outside he steadied Carole at the curb. It was a sultry Manhattan night, its stars drowned in a fragile penumbra of neon, its presence odorous with asphalt and drains and a bouquet of gardenias, borne in the hands of a frayed old peddler, floating up to us from the dark. "Baby, do you want something from Max Schling here? The kid's bobo for flowers," he murmured to me as, fumblingly, she pinned them to her breast, "and, frankly, it's her only aesthetic indulgence. Anyway, as I was saying, it's good for kicks, Peter. These people are such *flâneurs*. Jesus Christ, I may not be any Cocteau or Brecht yet, but at least I'm serious." He whistled up a cab. "Come on, let's get back to the studio."

Mason's apartment—"studio," rather—perched five floors above the street in one of the frowzier nooks of the Village, was the only New York dwelling I have ever seen which successfully combined a garrety, blue jean-and-sneaker attitude toward art with real luxury. It was a lofty, cavernous place which had been the property of a once well-known but now forgotten portrait painter. Much of it—the peeling skylight and hideous mahogany paneling —Mason had left as he had found it, but the rest—wall-to-wall carpeting nearly bottomless to the tread, hidden lighting and elegant Chinese bric-a-brac, a Calder mobile and *three* Modiglianis and yard after yard of fine editions—he had furbished himself with great style so that the effect, after panting upward for so many shabby, cabbage-smelling flights, was not of the drab ordinariness of the atelier one had expected, but of a sudden, rich, and luminescent paradise. One anticipated such a place, say, on Beekman Hill, but not here; it was as if a maharajah had taken over a flat somewhere in Queens. With his surpassing flair for the impossible gesture, Mason had fused Beverly Hills and Bohemia: in that dulcet, insinuating light one felt that one could share the lives of the immeasurably fortunate, yet never lose the echo of the rowdy street below, out of which rose, night after night, the muffled tunes of a caterwauling juke box and all the tough, sad accents of Sodom.

That evening the place was jammed with people but soon after we arrived, Mason—disengaging himself from Carole, who by now was quite hopelessly drunk—pushed me toward a rear bedroom, closed and locked the door and, turning round to face me, said with a warm grin: "Now we can catch up on old times, Petesy boy." Perhaps it was the firm bolting of the door but I recall how, even then, the flicker of a dark suspicion passed through my mind, and vanished as quickly as it had come. Being a fairly inward-looking person, and one carefully attuned to the psychiatric over-tones in this age, I have often wondered whether there was not something homosexual in our connection, in my attraction to Ma-son. I think this has bothered me mainly because I am an Ameri-can, and Americans are troubled by the notion that the slightly fevered excitement, the warmth they might feel in the presence of a friend of the same sex portend all sorts of unspeakable desires. That is why, when Frenchmen kiss or embrace without shame and Italians, long-parted, rush baying into each other's arms, an American is reduced to a greeting not far removed from a sneer and a sadistic wallop between the shoulder blades. However, in regard to the allure Mason held for me, I have re-examined it from all angles and have found it tainted enough, but not flawed by *that* complication. I think I simply felt when I was near him that he was more imaginative, more intelligent than I, and at the same time more corrupt (more corrupt, that is, than I could allow myself to be, as much as I tried), so that while he kept me hugely en-tertained he yet permitted me, in the ease of my humdrum and shallow rectitude, to feel luckier than Mason—duller but luckier, and sometimes superior.

That night he was at the top of his form. We compared notes on the years since we had last seen each other, but it took only a few moments to cover my own drab career. Mason, however, had lived —and I suspected with a dash granted to only a very few young men during the war; his story, to one who had seen only Illinois prairies, like myself, was fascinating, for he had been a member of the O.S.S. "Oh really, Petesy, I would rather have done time in Leavenworth than been drafted. And gobble K-rations next to some cretin from Opelika, Alabama? Really, Peter—don't frown—we *do* have to preserve some aristocracy of the spirit." It had been a difficult stunt to promote because of his college debacle, but one which Wendy, who had known a producer who had known a General Something-or-Other at the Pentagon, had expedited shortly after his return from Princeton. "Wendy-dear," he said pensively. "She didn't want me to go at all, of course, but she was positively *adamant* about one thing: she was determined that I get into some outfit where everybody brushed their teeth, even though she had heard that a lot of them were fags."

And then he told a spine-chilling tale about his experiences: about the government school, first, that he attended near Baltimore (I had heard about it somewhere) and its incredible curriculum in which neophytes like himself, in order to test their stealth and cunning, were among other things made to break into heavily guarded military installations in the dead of night, or to purloin top-secret blueprints from the shipyard of the Bethlehem Steel Corporation, or, at high noon, with false mustache and eyeglasses and bogus identity badge, to waltz past the guards at the Glenn L. Martin aircraft plant and, once inside, with the furtive skill implanted in their minds at school, to set token bombs and sabotaging booby traps in the intestines of some highly classified and vital machine, before reporting back to their superiors with a key nut or bolt or a crucial cotter-pin, or even—as once in Mason's case— with the nameplate of some factory vice-president, as evidence of the success of their mission. "Well frankly," he said with a laugh, "it was a hell of a lot of fun playing spy. Call it cloak-and-dagger stuff, whatever you want, it really had its—I mean, colossal moments of excitement. Of course there—at the Division Institute—that was the official name but to the public then it had no name at all, in fact it didn't even exist—we didn't run any real risk. We had what they call a 'check agent' in every installation we planned to knock over; that is, there was always somebody, usually an F.B.I. man, planted there in some sort of security capacity who knew what was going on. At least he knew that the D.I. was running a speed-job that day—we called these raids speed-jobs—so that if you bungled the mission and got nabbed he could at least step in and spirit you out of there." He paused, a ruminative expression on his flushed face, and then began to shake with a kind of tickled, anticipatory laughter. "Oh Jesus, though, some guys really had a rough time of it. There was this little fellow named Heinz Mayer, a funny little German refugee who had been living in Buffalo. He had practically no English at all anyway but he was a raving patriot and would have done anything, I think, to get to spit on the Fatherland. Anyway, they sent him on this solo speed-job into an antiaircraft installation— No it wasn't; I remember now, it was the Naval Ordnance Depot down at Dahlgren on the Potomac. Anyway, what happened was that this check agent, this poor benighted F.B.I. man had been stricken with something—I don't know what, appendicitis, a coronary, something—at any rate he was not there, not on hand when this poor little Heinz got caught snooping around in some building where they were assembling some kind of secret new timing device for eight-inch shells. Oh Jesus," he chuckled, "I can hear him now, telling us about it: 'But dere I vass,' he said, 'dese Marines, dey tought I vass Chermann! Dey vould not believe me ven I said dot I vass American, Heinz Mayer from Buffalo, New York. Und I vaited und I vaited for mein *shack agent* to come und save me but he vould not come!' Oh God," said Mason, "it cracked us up listening to him. I think those Marines were about to give him bastinado with rifle-butts but he got out of there somehow. . . ."

It was a lively imitation of the harried little German—complete with baffled, cringing gestures. I found myself laughing uproariously. "Well, what then, Mason?" I said finally.

He seemed reluctant to add anything more; his face became sober and grave, and he guided the conversation around to the play he was working on, to Broadway, and to playwrighting. Yet I was subtly insistent: the intrigue and derring-do of espionage have always been fascinating to me, and I wanted to hear more. "Well, Peter, it's not all you might have thought," he said. "Like the Army or anything else it was mainly a matter of beastly—I mean, really incessant—boredom. Jesus, I'd like to have a nickel for each of the dead, dead hours I spent sitting on my ass doing nothing but waiting. In Cairo it got so bad, I swear to God, that I got to know every crack in the wall and every bump and every knothole in the bar at Shepheard's Hotel. Waiting on your ass, waiting on your ass until Franklin and Winston cooked up a big deal—and you know it's all based not on strategy, but on some lousy political nuance—a big deal to save some poor, half-strangulated partisan somewhere." And so, since so much of the work of the Strategic Services had been paralyzed by inertia, he had managed to go on only one mission, parachuting along with a Serb-American Army corporal behind German lines in Yugoslavia in an effort to discover first-hand the extent of the partisan leader Mikhailovitch's collaboration with the Axis forces. "It's amazing," he put in suddenly, "talking to people—I mean even, say, British G-2 officers who've done a lot of tough hush-hush stuff and should know better—how everyone thinks of the O.S.S. as filled with brawny supermen who speak seven languages and are adept at judo and are forever prowling some really terror-ridden landscape with a knife between their teeth. Honest to God, Peter, nothing could be further from the truth. I don't mean to say that there wasn't some risk. I mean simply parachuting out into black space at night is no joy. It was the only jump I ever made and by God you can *have* it. But otherwise, really, as far as the blood-and-thunder goes, practically all of it's in the movies."

And he described how, after floating to earth near the town of Dubrovnik on the Dalmatian Coast, he holed up in the seaside villa of a Serb named Plaja in the confidential pay of the Allies—"a terrific old barrel-chested guy," Mason described him, "who'd been educated at Cambridge and had made an incredible fortune exporting slivovitz"—and there for a couple of months lived the life of a total idler, since inauspiciously at that moment Mikhailovitch had shifted his roving guerrilla headquarters to a point far up in the mountains to the east, where, because of the German troops interposed between, he was beyond reach. "We tried to make contact with the pro-Tito operatives we knew were working undercover with Mikhailovitch," Mason went on, "but it just wasn't any go. Stancik—that was Jack Stancik, my Serb corporal from Toledo, a wonderful little guy, hard as nails, who used to be a circus acrobat—Stancik and I tried to poke through the lines a couple of times but the Krauts were really out for blood and the place was hemmed-in like chicken-wire." So, instead of establishing any sort of liaison with the Tito agents, Mason lolled in prodigal comfort at Plaja's villa, drenched in the sunshine of the Dalmatian spring, swimming by night out to the cypress-groved islets which dotted the shore, and guzzling slivovitz, the plum-flavored brandy of which Plaja, its chief entrepreneur, served only the most succulent vintages. "Jesus Christ, Peter," he suddenly burst out, "*that* was the part that was out of the movies. It was unbelievable. Nazis wandering around everywhere. Here I was literally yards from death, but having the time of my life. And then to cap everything, about five or six days after I'd been installed there, Plaja's daughter came on the scene, this magnificent little black-haired dish—she was just fourteen—with these black saucy eyes and ripe red saucy lips set into a fabulous clear olive complexion that the Yugoslavians in that part of the country have. And these terrific hard little breasts like young melons, and a wonderful soft bouncy little tail to go along with it all. I almost blew my top just looking at her, after having subsisted—and I mean *subsist*—off these old fungusy Cairo whores for so long. She couldn't speak a word of English but we got along in a sort of pig-French—anyway, to make that part of a long story short: we made goo-goo eyes for a while—old Plaja didn't care; I think he approved of me handsomely, and besides he was always out falconing, which seems to be the favorite *divertissement* of flush Yugoslavians—and then one night after a lot of preliminary billing and cooing and belly-rubbing we swam out to this little island offshore. Honest to God, the smell of cypresses out there, and plum blossoms—it was heady and sexual enough to make you want to positively retch with excitement. Neither of us had bathing suits, so that when we came out dripping onto this moonlit beach we were as naked as a couple of goldfish. It was her first time, Petesy, but you'd never know it. She just gave a little whimper and melted. It was like taking ice cream from a baby." And this idyll, he said, lasted for weeks. I was ravished by the picture he drew. So much so that I think I was hardly irritated by his childish descriptions of all the "specialties" he had taught her—they can be found in any marriage primer—or even disturbed, while he went doggedly on about "these little jaw-breaking yelps of passion," in my vision drawn straight from his eloquence, of looming threat, of plum blossoms and soaring falcons, and cypress-scented seas.

"God, Mason," I breathed, "it's unbelievable."

"You don't believe it?"

"Of course I do." (And didn't I really? It must be remembered that, four years before Sambuco, I still possessed a larger streak of gullibility.) "It's just that—it's just that it's so—so incredibly romantic. I mean, young Mason Flagg of Gloucester Landing, Virginia."

"I know," he said, musing. "It was really like something out of a book. Sometimes there I thought I was living in a dream."

It was a dream shattered soon, however, for Mason found himself borne away from this beatific seclusion on the winds of violence. A servant in the villa betrayed their presence one night to the Germans. Only by a matter of minutes had he and Stancik managed to make their getaway: a brief fumbling embrace with the girl, a kiss, a farewell—and Mason was gone, together with Stancik, racing and floundering across fields, through olive groves, in a nightmare of confusion and indirection stumbling toward the rescuing British launch that awaited them on the shore, while like avenging and inescapable fury the Germans came on hotly after, inflaming the sky with the pitiless white light of their flares. "The flares were bad enough," Mason said, "I think they must have been firing them out of knee-mortars, or maybe they were using rifle-grenades. Anyway, we'd hear this loud crack! and this was the sign to get down—I mean *belly*-down—and stay down, without breathing. Then in about five or ten seconds we'd hear this little muffled report—*poot!*—way up in the sky, and suddenly, even though we were lying out in this filthy wet field, eyes closed tight, we could feel a tremendous hard brilliance floating down from the sky like brightest daylight, covering us. It was strange. Though I couldn't really see it because my eyes were closed, I could actually *feel* this light stealing into my bones and I just waited there—praying, I guess—waiting for them to blast us. But as I say, that wasn't the worst part, somehow. It was these goddam dogs they had. They had these goddam big Dalmatian dogs that they'd taken from the Serbs and trained as sort of bloodhounds. I'd seen them before, patrolling with the Krauts on the road in front of the villa—these great hungry beasts with red-rimmed eyes and liver-spots on their haunches. Anyway, that night they turned them loose after us. We could hear them snarling and groaning and howling in the hedge-rows, trying to get our scent. And once when a flare lit up the field I peeked out under my arm and saw one of the bastards, way off but still close enough, standing at the edge of some woods beside some big Kraut with an automatic rifle. I swear I felt my blood turn to piss just looking at him: this great monstrous beast with his fangs glinting there in the light and these big round eyes shining like a couple of silver dollars. He was trained to kill, and he'd chop through your spinal cord like it was so much cottage cheese."

Yet by the grace of heaven or by luck they managed to get away; at least Mason did, for his companion Stancik (they were on the beach by now, hiding behind boulders, sliding and slipping down sheer rock faces in one last foot-weary, bone-tired burst of desperation scrambling toward the Diesel launch whose signal, already seeming to flicker and dim as if with the hopelessness of their plight, beckoned to them from the shore's edge), Stancik fell, slipping into a sort of crevasse in the rock and uttering a wild cry of pain which gave away their position. Mason said he could hear the snap of his leg bone as it broke and, turning to help the corporal, was confronted—with a feeling of despair such as he had never known—by the blinding glare of a Nazi searchlight shining full upon them. Pinioned there, helpless and in terrible pain, Stancik tried to stir, but his predicament was fatal. As Mason moved toward him in the excruciating light, a blast of machine-gun fire stitched across the rocks, scattering upon the wind a gritty debris of shale and limestone, sending a bullet through the corporal's belly: Mason said he saw the fount of blood spurt forth like tar from some mortal arterial hemorrhage, heard the corporal sigh, or whisper, in one long last diminishing utterance of his identity and being, and then Mason tumbled himself, pierced through the calf of his leg with pain like a blade of fire. "Well, I dragged myself out of there to the boat," he said. "I still don't know how I did it. But Stancik, the poor sweet little bastard, he didn't have a chance. All he whispered was, 'Go on, Lieutenant. Don't tell anybody that this acrobat fell.' And then he died." Mason drew back one cuff of his jeans, revealing above his ankle an ugly round scar, bluish in hue and a little larger than a nickel. "So that," he added, "is my memento of the war. To be frank, Pierre, I think I'm pretty lucky. And this is a nice little token to have around, because whenever it itches, which it does on damp, horrible New York days, I think of Plaja's daughter and the sunshine and the blue water."

"Wow, Mason," I said, sincerely impressed, "that's one *hell* of a story."

"Yeah," he said, in an offhand manner, "yeah, I suppose it does have all the dramatic elements about it." He paused and looked at his watch. "Well, I guess you'd better get back to the party, dollbaby. Look," he said, "I'm going to hang around back here for a while. I'm getting tired of all those freeloaders. If you want me, come on back."

Since this was Mason during what I suppose you might call his Bohemian period, there were, to my intense disappointment, few movie people in evidence; he had gathered instead a curious and mingled crew. Solitary as ever, I took up my accustomed position, mooring myself in a windless alcove where with practiced hermitical eye I could watch the ebb and flow of the party. There were floaters of various sexes from the Village bars, including the Pennypackers, who cruised in later, giggling, fragrant with marijuana; several middling-to-prominent abstract expressionist painters; an editor of the *Hudson Review;* a famous playwright; a Broadway director whose wife, Mason had earlier breathed into my ear, was an incurable nymphomaniac; three rather hairy young literary critics from N.Y.U., who stood by the buffet and soberly stoked themselves with turkey; an art critic; a critic of jazz; a drama critic; half a dozen sleepy-looking jazz musicians; and a shoal of young and pretty models who zigzagged swishing about the room, or postured in corners, highball glasses clamped before their noses like smelling salts. A bright, frenetic sound of jazz boomed from some concealed source, buoying it all up: whenever the music paused, with a scratchy flutter, the young models seemed to pout ever so perceptibly, and they sagged in their chic spring dresses like wilting bouquets. "That Mason," a hoarse voice spoke at my side, "now there's a boy for you." This proved to be a Mr. Garfinkel, a bald, corpulent small man who like myself was either ill-at-ease or neglected, and had dropped anchor in my alcove. He said he was "with Republic," which I assumed was a steel company until he explained to me with strangled guffaws that he was connected with the movies. "No, my boy. I only been to Pittsburgh once in my life." Then he repeated: "That Mason. Now there's a boy for you. A genius. Figure everything he's got. The eyes. The nose. The *expression*. Everything. It's uncanny, I tell you. Just like his dad." He paused. "Taller, maybe."

"Did you know Mr. Flagg?" I asked.

"Did I know Justin Flagg? My boy, I *suckled* him. I was a mother to him. Hah!" He drew back his lips in a grin, revealing a row of mottled incisors. "It's the Jew in me," he said with a nudge. "In each Jew resides a frustrated mother."

I began to fidget and looked around, and at this moment there passed by us one of the loveliest girls I had ever seen. She was a stunning girl with soft coppery hair: finely spun whorls of it made a fringe of halos around her head. And she had an inward warmth and gentleness that seemed to radiate from her as she moved. "Hello, Marty, having a good time?" she said to Garfinkel, briefly clutching his hand; it was definitely not a show-business voice, being devoid of flimflam and coming from some place other than her sinuses, her throat, to be exact, and with a warm and womanly intonation. Best of all, she didn't call him "darling."

"Hi, Celia," said Garfinkel, as she moved off among the crowd, "where have you been, darling?"

"Who is that—" I started to say to Garfinkel, but again he was talking about Mason. "I see," I said. "So you've known Mason for a long time?"

"Years. The boy's a genius. Just like his dad. Only he's going to be a genius in the field of playwrighting." He was a nice little man, Garfinkel, with a look of stoical lonesomeness. For some reason, I saw him doing the mambo on countless Grace Line cruises to Brazil, with women forever taller than himself.

"You've read his play?" I asked.

"No," said Garfinkel, "but he's told me about it. It can't miss, I tell you. It's a natural. The boy's a genius."

"I see."

"I mean, think of the *advantages* he's had, being born the son of Justin Flagg." His eyes grew dreamy and remote. "Flagg. That's a name with which to conjure—" And he looked up at me significantly. "In certain circles, that is."

There are these women, whose special beauty is such that it is able to break down the reserve of the most unadventurous of men. Celia was one. She fascinated me, and now, as she stood in the center of the noisy room, I was determined to meet her. I coughed and began to drift away from Garfinkel, who was saying: "Levitt. Are you a member of the Long Island and Levittown, P.A., housing firm Levitts?" There must be something basically unsound about the structure of my name; I said I was, and let it go at that, and moved out toward Celia. But as I worked my way across the room in her direction I found myself in a cross-current of bodies and was soon marooned near the buffet table, where I fell into shallow talk with the *Hudson Review* fellow, who did not exactly wince when I mentioned the college I had gone to but made an owlish adjustment with his eyes as if suddenly he were able to see right through my head. I think it must have been then that I decided to go. Celia was inaccessible to me by now, shunted into one corner of the room where, as around some bright blossom, several young men had gathered murmuring like bees. She was lovely, but she would never be mine and now, besides, the *Hudson* man, who had been talking about middle-brow culture, was as tired of me as I was of him. Yawning almost in unison, we bade each other a relieved good night, and I went to tell Mason I was leaving.

Now, was it some exhibitionistic streak in Mason (part of that whole hysteric craze for sex, that incessant hee-haw and jabber about the carnal side of love which was like a hot breath blowing down the neck when you listened to him, which is fine at fifteen or sixteen, but which in a man you expect to become muted—not less hysteric, just muted) that kept him from locking the bedroom door? He knew that I was aware where he was; indeed, he had said that he would be expecting me. If he had bolted that door when he had his chat with me, you would think he might double-bolt it when settling down to doing what I was luckless enough to surprise him at. But this was Mason, alas, not you or me, and I cannot pretend to know what he was always up to. I do know I got the shock of my life when my knock went unanswered and, opening the door, I saw the two of them in the blazing light, Mason and Carole, naked as pullets and frenziedly abed, locked in that entangled embrace all pink flesh and pounding posteriors and arms which I wish I could say fulfilled the fantasist, the Peeping Tom in me, but which instead, in terms of sex or aesthetics or anything you can name, had the effect of a huge shot of novocaine. It seemed somehow so obviously staged that I stood there and watched for a moment with the fascination of one who is witnessing his first autopsy and then, recovering my wits, uttered an inane "Good night, Mason," slammed the door like a startled hotel maid and tramped back down the hallway, cheeks blazing, marveling at the terrible potency of conjugal love which could cause a man to take his wife to bed, drunk as she was, in the midst of his own party.

The point being, of course, that Carole was not his wife at all. (Could I be blamed if, short years removed from Virginia, I assumed that when a man said "love of my life" he meant his wife? Probably.) Because as I started to leave the place, Garfinkel was near the door, and with him was my impossible vision of the evening, the fair and glowing Celia.

"Levitt," said Garfinkel. "You aren't leaving, are you? I'd like you to meet Mason's wife. Celia, this is Peter Levitt."

"Oh, you must be Peter *Leverett!*" she said with a smile, all warmth and animation. "Mason's told me so much about you and those wonderful years you had together in Virginia. That crazy school you went to! Why, I had no idea you were here!"

"Leverett, then. Sorry, my boy," said Garfinkel. "Anyway, I want you to know that right here, right in this little doll here, resides a great deal of credit for Mason's genius."

Mason's *wife?* Too many emotions crowded in at once (Carole, "the love of my life," life: wife, what an idiot!); I looked at Celia and found I could not speak. She was a flute-sound, a bell, a reed; Carole was a moo. And at that very moment Mason and Carole . . . I have rarely felt such squirmy distress, such disenchantment with anything, or everything.

"Art is dead, Peter," Mason said to me at one point or another during that week in New York. "Well, if not dead yet, then put it this way—the dear old Muse is slowly dying, and in a couple more decades we'll watch her as she gasps her last. Science is the new

Muse—it's as plain as the nose on your face. Couple science with a general leveling of taste everywhere, and the demise is inevitable. But there's no need to weep, you know. You can't weep over the determinism of history. Facts are facts. By the end of the century art—painting, music, poetry, drama—all of them, they'll be as dead as the labyrinthodont."

"What's that?"

"A prehistoric amphibian, late Permian period."

"Well then, tell me, Mason, why do you keep on with this play you're doing?"

"Oh I don't know," he said, " a sort of *diehardism,* I suppose. A sailor with any sort of guts doesn't abandon ship even when the rails are awash. Besides, there's always the faint possibility—I mean a really faint one, but a possibility—that history will give a lurch, as history sometimes does, and we'll have a renaissance instead of a burial. There are a couple of things already that make me think that might happen."

"Like what?"

"Well, in painting, abstract expressionism. And in music, jazz. There's a tremendous freedom and vitality in both of them, a fantastic throwing-off of restraint and the dreadful constipating formalism and all the traditional crap that's been such a hindrance to art. So—well, I'll admit it's a dim hope, but if these two ever get really going, we might have that renaissance and of course, as history has shown, all the rest of the arts will start booming, too. Do you see what I mean?"

"Well, I know nothing about painting, Mason," I said. "But as for music, I think some of that early Dixieland is quite marvelous, and Bessie Smith, but after all—"

"After all, what?"

Since I like to express myself exactly, I grope, lose time and ground, and eventually lose out in most discussions.

"After all," he put in, "there is always J. S. Bach. Isn't that what you were going to say?"

"More or less, Mason," I replied. "Though somewhat more elaborately."

"*De gustibus,* Peter," he said amiably. "I'll let you keep your corpse if you let me keep my sexy dollbaby, all alive and singing."

"*De gustibus,* Mason," I said.

"Once a square always a square. But everybody has to have a complement. I think it's because you're so square that I love you." And things like this he would say with such a sweet smile, with such true and honest affection, that there would dissipate as if into the air about him all that, seconds before, I had considered offensive, pretentious, and banal.

We had several weighty discussions that week, about art and related matters. Though college may have rejected him—or he it— he seemed on his own to have read everything, to have absorbed most of it, and he wore his really rather amazing erudition flashily and blatantly, like a man outfitted for a costume ball. If it would please you to know the antique origins of Rosicrucianism; the existence of the Kuria Muria Islands, guano atolls off the coast of Aden; the difference between absolute and apparent magnitudes in the measurement of stars; the origin of female circumcision among the tribes of the Kalahari; of the influence of Ranulf de Glanvill upon law ("You mean you studied law, Peter, and never heard of Glanvill?"); of the high tolerance of sexual perversion, and the modes employed, among the Huron Indians; the difference between fibromyoma and chondroma in the classification of benign tumors; the reasons for German scholarship assigning undue influence of Thomas Kyd upon Shakespeare; the Roman use of the mechanical dildo—Mason could fill you in about all these matters, richly and eloquently, these and a thousand more. Most curiously, too—perhaps though only because, a child of my time, I am a sucker for facts—Mason almost never bored me with his knowledge; he made fanciful play with these useless items, setting them loose in the midst of some joke or story in the way that a magician brings forth from his sleeve rabbits, roses, startling doves. Once more would arise his Yugoslavian experience, which he never tired of telling and which I never minded hearing, if only because new insights, new characters kept intruding—the jovial mayor of the town, an Italian deserter (the victim of epilepsy, and given to murderous rampages through the night), the S.S. commandant who had paid a frightening visit to the villa one day— and from this substructure now arose the most dazzling edifice of fact, history, lore, and legend. "Of course old Plaja was really a full-blooded Dalmatian," he would tell me. "Which is to say that he had a warrior's heart. You see, his ancestors had all fought against the Venetians in the Middle Ages when a real scoundrel of a king they had, Ladislas of Naples, sold out to Venice for a hundred thousand ducats, I think it was. A fantastic gory period! Let me tell you . . ." And off he would go. And somehow, during the telling, I would learn that the chief enemy of the common orchard plum is the curculio, a repulsive small beetle; that the codpiece was proscribed by Pope Sixtus V as a universal threat to chastity; and that the word "falcon" derives from the Latin *falx,* meaning sickle and describing the bird's curved talons. A striking fact about Mason is that, despising the past as he did, he yet knew so much about it.

Now, in my smudged and tear-stained book of memories there are still mounted two photographs. In the first of these (I am trying to remember at what party it was taken) my own white hand is visible, fishbelly-pale in the glare of the flashbulb. Carole is there, too, looking quite dazed and voluptuous, her lips moistly reflecting the light as she bends down her face to give Mason what I'm now sure must have become, half a second later, a kiss on the back of his well-barbered head. What is it that disturbs me so about this picture—and in a way that has nothing to do with what Mason or Carole were doing at all? It is Mason himself who dominates the picture. In profile, he is talking to an invisible someone; he is unaware of the lips, the wet bud of a tongue hovering at the nape of his neck, and at that moment, poised in that split instant of time before the mouth descends, his face wears an expression of total dejection. It is an odd look, one Mason rarely wore—of heaviness, of weariness, and disgust with life (who could he be talking to? it does not matter)—and I have pondered that picture many times, always touched a bit by this fleeting sorrow of his, which I so seldom saw in life. Was he as unhappy during that time as this picture tells me he was? Right now I cannot say. Certainly there is not a speck of sadness in this other picture of Mason. Here we are on his Village rooftop—there I am again, and there is Mason, and not Carole this time, but Celia. It is noontime of a spring day; this you can tell from the light, and from the blooming flowerboxes and trees on the penthouse roofs of the buildings behind, and by the cool spring dress Celia is wearing. As from all fading snapshots, longing and nostalgia emanate from this one: they are in the amateurish tilt of the picture and its yellowing hue and in the sense of springs gone forever, old shoe styles and hair-dos, rooftops that no longer exist (Mason's house was torn down not long ago), in that knowledge which is perhaps the camera's single most poignant gift, of time past and irretrievable. Celia, appearing in retrospect now even more lovely than I remember her in the flesh, has her face and eyes upturned toward Mason, very close to his own, seeming ready to give him a roguish nibble on the cheek with her perfect white teeth. Mason inclines his head down toward her; he is ready to bite her back, but most playfully and joyfully, and his face is suffused with exuberance, with merriment and happiness. As for myself, I am standing somewhat aside, contemplating whoever it was that snapped the picture, and my expression can best be described as glum. And behind us all a flock of pigeons, slate-colored blurs, rove heavenward above the water towers, lending to the whole moment of bygone time a feeling of feathery movement, of space and life. . . .

I must say that Mason really took over my hours, night and day, during that brief period. I had quit my job preparatory to going to Europe and, having nothing to do, I found it was fun to tag along with Mason; he never ran out of steam, there was always something new to do, somewhere new to go, and he always picked up the check. I protested this (I really did) but he had a smooth way to make me rise above my own secret humiliation. "Look, doll-baby," he would say, "those French girls you're going to have soon don't come cheap. Save your money." And then he would pause. "May I be frank about something?" he would continue. "I'm a rich boy and I know it, and I like to spend dough on people I love. Good God, let's don't let Justin's ill-gotten loot go to waste. Now give me back that tab!" Then, pulling out his wallet, he would say: "In a crummy democracy you have to go through the damndest *contortions* if you're rich, pretending you haven't got a nickel to your name."

I relented, with a sort of hoarse catch in my voice. It was a cozy situation to find oneself in—for a short term, anyway. More than once I wondered whether—if I had not already planned to go abroad—it might not be possible to remain under Mason's aegis for the rest of my days, and the thought gave me a shiver. Because if I suspected that there was lust for a kind of ownership in these big gestures of Mason's, I also realized with some shame that my willingness to be owned was stronger than I ever wanted to admit. But who could blame me? Each night (and there were at least five of them) brought me a different girl. And they were all brainless, beautiful, and willing. What a treat to be in the hands of such a casual, big-hearted procurer! I mean it. I have never had so much consecutive sex, and of such variety, in all my life. And I was indebted to Mason for it. I had become the crown prince among his freeloaders. And I knew I was *in* when he showed me his collection of erotica.

When I first saw the collection, I could manage only a long, deep-felt whistle. "Where'd you get all this stuff, Mason?" I asked.

"Friend of mine died of a brain tumor a couple of years ago. It was his bequest to me. Let me give you some more ice there. He gave me the core of the collection, that is," he went on, "most of those books over to the right there. I got interested and added the rest a little bit at a time. What it adds up to, really, is an investment. You know there's a big market for good stuff like this. It's almost as solid as the art market and a hell of a lot more stable than gold or stamps."

The "core," I discovered, was made up of such grizzled entries as *The Thousand Nights and a Night* (London, privately printed, 1921); *The Memoirs of Fanny Hill* (ditto, 1890); the complete works both in French and English of that "really incomparable genius, in his own way," as Mason described him, the "divine" Marquis de Sade, including his masterpiece, *Justine,* and *Juliette,* and *Philosophie dans le boudoir* and *Les Crimes de l'amour* (Paris, end plates, illustrated, 1902); Apollinaire's *Les Onze mille verges;* and half a dozen volumes, in English, of the Paris-printed bonbons for undernourished Anglo-Saxons. But after I finished thumbing through these elementary items there came a tidal wave of delights such as I had never dreamed existed: beautifully embellished works in Italian and French, some dating from the seventeenth century; Priapean celebrations of Roman fashions in love, circa A.D. 79, as revealed by the friezes of Pompeii; delicate and ingenious drawings from Arabia, from India, from Java and Japan, on rice paper and scrolls; love among the Cubans and the Turkestani and the Persians; love even among the Scandinavians, where in a series of photographs a handsome and vigorous blond quartet from Stockholm, slippery-looking as herrings, fornicated amid an aura of gingerbread bedsteads, *smörgåsbord* and *snaps.* One Chinese entry—a kind of apotheosis of depravity, if Mason was to be believed—formed an exquisite round-robin of contortionist perversions, graven on a scroll which he swore up and down was made of human skin. Into this lascivious concourse I plunged giddily, and since hot erotica, like catnip, is meant to arouse, it did just that to me. At least, for a while. Throbbing, I examined the act of love as performed conventionally in New Orleans brothels, in echelon among the Monégasques, even octagonally— in an album of snapshots more chaotic than titillating—among a bedroom full of disheveled Greeks. A pair of Algerian priests made love to a skinny, spiritless nun, and the nun to the Mother Superior; a small volume of oddly fatalistic lithograph cartoons, done in England long before Waterloo, showed Bonaparte himself, massively virile, astride a series of squirming mistresses

labeled *Italia, Germania,* and *Alas, Britannia!* The zoölogical
section, featuring humans with brutes, or vice versa, I found less
to my taste, as I did the huge and synoptic German *Lexikon* of
sex which, explicit though it was in its illustrations, leaned grimly
toward police-file photographs of torn and dismembered children
and other victims of sexual infraction. In fact, of the arts of mankind, this entire mode of expression has, to all except perhaps the
pubescent and the unbalanced, the least staying power of all, so
that it was not long before I was betrayed by a certain repetitive-
ness in what I had seen, and, numb—really numb—I turned to
look at Mason, feeling terribly blue about the whole enterprise.
"You mean this junk is really worth a lot of money?" I said.

"You're damn right it is. That Chinese scroll alone I paid five
hundred dollars for. Early Ch'ing dynasty. Here's an interesting
item."

It was a large photograph, some decades old, of a strapping,
grinning, coal-black African in mettlesome coition with an ostrich. I gazed at it for a long time, bemused.

"Sex is the last frontier," he was saying somewhere behind me.
"In art as in life, Peter, sex is the only area left where men can
find full expression of their individuality, full freedom. Where
men can cast off the constrictions and conventions of society and
regain their identity as humans. And I don't mean any dreary,
dry little middle-class grope and spasm, either. I mean the total
exploration of sex, as Sade envisioned it, and which makes a library like this so important to the psyche, and so rewarding. It's
what you might call *le nouveau libertinage.* Because, you see, it
was Sade's revolutionary concept, his genius, to see man not as
what he is *supposed* to be—an inhumanly noble creature whose
nobility is a pseudo-nobility simply because he is hemmed in and
made warped and sick in an impossible attempt to free himself of
his animal nature—but as he *is,* and forever will be: a thinking
biological complex which, whether rightly or wrongly, exists in a
world of frustrating sexual fantasy, the bottling-up of which is the
direct cause of at least half of the world's anguish and misery. It's
a strange paradox, Peter, that Sade should become synonymous
with all that is cruel and causes pain, when in reality he was the
original psychoanalyst of the modern age, seeing more evil in the
fruitless repression of sex, and more pain, too, than in what to
him was the simple answer to that repression, and the panacea—
release from the fantasy world, and the working out of sex on a
functioning, active level. And again that doesn't mean some

151

tepid little convulsion in the dark. It means group interplay, for one thing—and there's no one alive who hasn't yearned at one time or another for community sex—and the free airing of bisexual impulses, among other things, and the final orgiastic purgation which has been a cleansing aspect of the human experience, at least among those humans who have been bold enough to break convention, since the dawn of recorded history. And it's going to be the future major crisis in art. Because only when the sexual act is able to be portrayed in art—in prose and in painting, and on the stage (though I'll admit that's a problem)—then and only then will we have any kind of freedom. Because for one thing—"

Brooding over the outlandish picture, I had become wildly tickled in a helpless in-dwelling fashion, and I felt chuckles of laughter rising up in me and I turned around and let out a loud yuck, finally, which caused Mason to halt in mid-sentence, eyes level upon me.

"What's so funny?" he said in an irritated voice. And as he spoke, the words he had been saying, so solemnly and with such passion, registered upon my mind belatedly, abruptly, as if a door had been thrown briskly open to let it all shamble in.

"Oh I don't know, Mason," I said, still grinning. "You aren't serious about all this, are you? I've always thought sex was a lot of fun—wonderful, great, fabulous. The best thing on earth. But you seem to want to turn it into a cult, and a gloomy one at that."

"You reveal yourself, dollbaby," he said. His voice was airy, but a touch of irritation remained. "At its greatest, sex has always been a cult. Nurtured and refined like any other high art." With a thin smile he removed the ostrich picture from my hand. "Squarest of the squares," he added affably.

"A matter of taste, Mason," I said.

But these two photographs—the one with Carole, and the one with Celia—still haunt me; they are as mnemonic as a fragrance, a scrap of music, a familiar voice which has not been heard for many years. I turn back to the first one, trying to extract its mood, comprehend it, place it in time—then all of a sudden (perhaps it's only the memory in turn of the ostrich that does it, or the bedroom full of Swedes) I know what it is and I know what it means. Like one of those trick effects in the movies where for a long instant the scene becomes motionless—a skier suspended in mid-air, a diver rigid in a somersault or a comic prat fall with legs and arms stilled in frozen chaos above the floor—then once again rolls on, this picture suddenly achieves movement; indeed now, with very little effort of the imagination I am able to persuade myself that I am no longer viewing the scene, but am within it as I was so long ago, that my hand moves back just a bit, fidgeting, as, still half-blinded by the flashbulb, I watch Carole's protuberant bulb of a tongue reach Mason's neck and linger there, wet and fluttering, while at the same moment her well-fleshed paw steals forth to unzip his fly. Shades of the divine Marquis! How, after Mason's dilations upon "group interplay" several nights before, it never occurred to me, until it was almost too late, that he had brought me to an orgy, mystified me then as it mystifies me now; I can only say in all honesty that I must have known, or suspected, that it was going to be one, and that deep down I desired orgiastic purgation, too.

Our host that evening, in a large, flossy apartment near Washington Square, was a famous young playwright called Harvey Glansner. Immediately after the war he achieved an astonishing success on Broadway with a play that with great courage, insight, and pity had laid bare, in terms of a lower-class New York family, the neurotic agony of our time. Then he had had several failures in a row, which in America, especially on Broadway, is the equivalent of the grave. Thereafter, to the distress of many who still saw in him the hope of American drama, his talent had gone to pieces; he took to writing a knotty kind of prose—articles mainly for the small quarterlies—in which he hymned and extolled the then burgeoning signs of juvenile delinquency, psychopaths, rapists, pimps, dope addicts and other maladjusted wretches until, finally descending into a sort of semicoherent pornography, he became unreadable (though not, as I expect he wished to be, unpublishable), except by a rather specialized intellectual in-group which applauded any sort of wicked stir, no matter how puerile. He wrote much about the solemnity of the orgasm, its lack and its pain, and its relationship to God. With all of this, he was a gifted writer, even after his fall from Broadway grace, and he might have found more general favor except for the fact that all of his essays gave to sex a reference of horror, discomfort and disgust: you may sentimentalize sex by confusing it with love, and still be read, but if you equate sex with unpleasurableness, you may expect your audience to be obscure, whether your bias is puritan or pornographic. "Like Dante, Harvey's a real hater," Mason said, adding that he was writing a biography called *Karl Marx: Giant in Orgasm*. I think it was from this Glansner that Mason drew his erotic inspiration. A pimply-faced, cadaverous young man, with a pot belly, beaked nose, and horn-rims, Glansner greeted us at the door with a meaningful (though to me, then, meaningless) smirk, and passed out the marijuana. I should describe the cast, which for an orgy I suppose was a meager one, though maybe not. There were eight of us—the forever-present Pennypackers, foxy as ever; Glansner and his wife, a sinuous golden-haired beauty with harlequin glasses, whose name I forget; and, as a kind of anchor man, myself, accompanied by a girl named Lila—whom Mason had dug up for me—a ripe and amiable stripper who from the beginning seemed far more knowing and dubious about the setup than I, drawing me aside early (it was not hard to do, for the sound of jazz was deafening and blue lightbulbs everywhere cast on each distant face a bruised, mortuary gloom) and saying, to my puzzlement: "Don't let on now, baby, but I think I smell a fish."

Now then, like many hectic recollections this one comes back to me in bits and flickers—blue lights, howling saxophones and the bittersweet odor of marijuana predominating. Glansner meandered back and forth for a while, snapping pictures with a huge Graflex. I think it was then that Carole went through the routine with Mason's fly, only to be chided by him for her crudeness. Eschewing the weed, which seemed to have almost no effect on me, I stuck to a little red wine, and for most of the time sat hip to hip with Lila on a large white leather ottoman. Jazz, the music not of fusion but of fission, was a constant explosion in my face, and when it ceased, to allow the record-changer to softly whir and plip-plop, the silence was eerie and burdensome, and I recall wondering at the *tone* of this gathering, which from the outset had the mingled features of despair, hostility, and the deplorable inertia of a meeting of southern Baptist young people. I have since learned that marijuana stills the desire for speech; it certainly laid a heavy hand on conversation that night. Only Lila and I, islanded on our ottoman, tried to talk; as for the others, they had paired off on sofas and were puffing from cupped palms, wreathed in bluish fumes. After a time, however, came a slight stir of activity; there was now considerable faint, high, hollow giggling and our host arose to put some dance music on the phonograph: it had a soft bourgeois sound after all the jazz, but it must have been part of the ritual, because for one thing it allowed Mason to get up and with a tight tense look on his face to take Glansner's beautiful wife in his arms and conduct her around the dim room in the semblance of a dance, rather falteringly, and with a great deal of unabashed and mutual hanky-panky in the lower regions.

I wish I could go into more generous detail about this orgy, but at just about this point the whole affair—for me, anyway, and for Lila—began to terminate. Outside of Mason's pelvic work the only overt sexual act I stayed long enough to witness was between the Pennypackers, who climbed atop each other on a couch and, fully clothed, went through some frantic copulatory motions which, since they were married, brought from the others lazy, tolerant sniggers of laughter, as one might laugh at children who know the rudiments but nothing of the spirit of the game, and are also a bit touchingly anxious. A little later, while Mason danced, Glansner was nuzzling Carole in the shadows, muttering to her in a strange you-all, cotton-picking dialect (a few years later this became known as hip talk, but I did not know it at the time); the words he crooned drowsily were the gamiest in the language, and there was a compulsive, metronomic desolation in the way he said them that chilled me to the marrow, but if he calculated them to excite, and if my Lila was any barometer, he had made a serious miscalculation. Lila was a big healthy girl with a fine elastic bosom; she had been around, and there was no nonsense about her. When I turned to her—more than smelling that fish now—she said in a low voice: "I stopped smoking pot when I was sixteen years old. Somebody ought to tell that poor square to grow up and stop diddling himself. Does he think he's giving her *kicks?* Look out, honey, here comes trouble." The Pennypackers, down off their couch, were slithering toward us; we rose in unison, Lila and I, self-protectively, and danced off through the gloom, hugging the walls. "When I was performing in London," she said, "they called a deal like this a n*ah*sty. Which is just about exactly the word for it. Mason should have better sense. I'm a good party girl, but this is strictly not my cup of tea. What does he think I am, anyway, some sort of *tart?*" And then she pressed close. "Let's get out of here, baby, and have something good and private."

We danced for quite some time, close together, monogamously welded. There was a lot of stirring and groaning behind us and when at last we decided to go I turned to see Mason, standing fully illuminated in the doorway to the bedroom, his arm around a glassy-eyed and now unbodiced Mrs. Glansner, the two figures obscuring all except the face of Glansner himself, propped against the headboard of an enormous bed, and wearing (to my surprise, for I had expected something more mellow) the impotent, sepulchral look of a man separated by five minutes from the gallows.

As for Mason's own expression: I think I must have anticipated the smoldering lust that one reads about in romantic novels, but all that was there—or so it seemed to me—was a kind of miserable and forsaken innocence.

"What's the matter, Petesy?" he said. "You aren't leaving, are you?" If there was not what one might call anguish in his voice, there was a sudden broken sense of loneliness, of abandonment, and as he said these words again, his voice rising—"You aren't *leaving,* are you?"—I realized that he was honestly hurt by my defection. "Come on now, dollbaby," he said cajolingly, though the hurt was still there, "you're not going to chicken out, *really.*"

"Lila's not feeling well, Mason," I lied.

I do not want to say which of us, Mason or I, was right or wrong; the question, if there is a question, is not a matter of either. But at the moment, aflame though I was with desire for Lila, I felt that it was exceedingly thick of Mason to fail to understand why I might not wish to take down my trousers and in harsh light, sweating cheek by jowl with the whole crowd—their eyes on me and mine on them—despairingly perform the joyous rites of love.

"O.K., Peter," Mason said. "Back to Squaresville."

Next morning, breakfasting with Lila after a full night, I think we discerned the most fitting irony of all when it occurred to us that though Mason might have had Mrs. Glansner, and Glansner Carole, the Pennypackers—like an abbreviated Paolo and Francesca—had most probably had only each other. But then Lila grew sad. "Gee," she said. "What do you suppose is eating Mason? With that wife of his—you know her?—a real doll. I think he must be flipping his lid, if you want to know the honest to God's truth."

There are gestures that linger in the mind. One bright day as Mason and Celia and I were driving to Long Island for lunch, Celia's hand went up to the back of his head. "Look at his hair," she said. "Look how it shines in the sunlight. Isn't it just beautiful, Peter?" I cannot help but remark upon this characteristic that Celia shared with Wendy: the most outrageous flattery of their darling boy. But here the resemblance ends. Celia was something apart and by herself.

If Carole remains in my memory a large nocturnal blur, Celia was leaf, cloud, light, a daytime creature who had no part at all in Mason's night-crawling. Indeed, so separate were Mason's evenings and days, his life with Carole and his life with Celia, that except for one or two instances I cannot remember Celia except in daylight, as in that photograph, her face upturned toward Mason's, as toward the sun. How she adored him! And with what inner restlessness I watched the casual fashion in which he accepted her adoration, her tenderness, her flattery. Not just because I had fallen for her myself, in a distant hopeless way, but because like Lila I could not understand how he could reject this *haute cuisine* in favor of Carole's slumgullion.

Yet to give Mason credit, he was courteous and even gentle with Celia—at least when I was around; in conspiracy with the sunlight she seemed to be able to alter his character, subdue him, tenderize him. She was as soft as silk; she had a kitteny way about her that was not in the least coy or undesirable, and in her splendid voice there were all sorts of warm, delectable modulations, all of them sexy, and all of them fine. She had dignity, too, and that kind of radiant poise, so rare in beautiful women, which comes from the consciousness that one's beauty is meant to please men, and not oneself. I suspect that the single thing she lacked was the small streak of bitchiness that even the most angelic of women can muster, given the provocation: there are some men who despise a good woman even more than a virago, and I would be inclined to guess that it was Celia's decency, generosity, and goodness that drove Mason into Carole's swollen embrace, were it not for the fact that Mason would always find his Carole, no matter what.

Anyway, we had a fine time, the three of us, during the last four or five days before I sailed to Europe. I had to some extent moved in on Mason, using my apartment only to sleep in; I breakfasted with Mason and Celia, had lunch with them, and with the two of them I spent long and lazy afternoons. A rather sedate and platonic *ménage à trois* it was, come to think of it; we felt very close, warm, familial. Mason curbed his tongue when around Celia, I noticed; the nagging, compulsive smuttiness in his talk was gone, as was all the leering cabala about *le nouveau libertinage,* and every now and then, when he would tell an amusing story, and as I stole a glance at Celia and watched her gay charming face crinkle up in delicious merriment, with the innocent and wonder-struck delight of a child who has seen some strange new animal, some clown, some fresh marvel, I had a difficult time envisioning her as a helpmate sharing Mason's interest in pyramidal arrangements of naked Turks, or having anything to do with Glansner's stews. Though naturally I need not have concerned myself on this account because, as I have said, Mason kept his nights and days distinctly apart: toward the end of the afternoon I would leave them and when, later, I joined Mason, it would be in some smoky Village pad thronged with people who, it seemed to me, were always in a state of desperate lethargy and hunched-up near-collapse (though, "Peter, these cats are crazy," Mason told me once. "Kicks and excitement are all they want, they're the last rebels left.") and where there was always Carole, slow and sleepy-lidded, asking for another Scotch.

"What are they rebelling against?" I asked.

"Against the H-bomb. A world they never made."

"But, Mason, look here. If they just seemed to be having any fun, I'd—"

"Fun?" he said. "They're too *desperate* for fun. They understand the legacy that's been left us."

I let it go at that.

Indeed, the more I saw of Mason in this dual role of daytime squire and nighttime nihilist, the more I saw working in him the antinomy of Carole-Celia, the more it became apparent to me that here was a truly distinctive young American—able in a time of hideous surfeit, and Togetherness' lurid mist, to revolt from conventional values, to plunge into a chic vortex of sensation, dope, and fabricated sin, though all the while retaining a strong grip on his two million dollars. At the time it seemed to me not entirely unadmirable: at least it took more flair, more imagination than most rich boys have, or use.

The day before I left for Europe has a recollected purity that some rare summer skies have—hazeless, cloudless, with a flagrant immensity of blue that, at least for a moment, allays all the painful mistakes of the past and promises rewarding things to come. Never before or since has New York had such a magnanimous day, and as we drove out to Long Island even the dismal boulevards of Queens seemed odorous with spring. But it was not only the weather that made it so fine. It was Celia, fragile and mild, with a scarf around her hair, in broad daylight glowing like a candle. It was in the sports car, a Ferrari which Mason—always in the vanguard—had bought only the day before; such machines still attracted curiosity then, and as we drew up at stoplights (Mason and Celia in front, myself crouched behind, in a kind of nest of jacks and wrenches, much as I had been years before when I sat curled up in the luggage behind Mason and Wendy) we were the cynosure of Forest Hills. But more than anything, almost, it was in Mason; he was in command of the day: as we zoomed toward the far green reaches of the island he talked his head off, and with a sorcerer's charm. Jokes tumbled from his lips, and witty wicked allusions, and airy ballooning puns; his spoofery was a marvel, so wild and preposterous that Celia, rosy with laughter, had to implore him to stop, put her head down in his lap and cried, "Stop! *Stop it!*" while I collapsed in merriment among the wrenches. The night-creature, the psychologist, the solemn apostle of the groin—he was no longer any of these. He seemed three times as alive as any other mortal could hope to be, brimful with warmth and wit, playing to the hilt that role which God alone knows why he did not work at harder, so much pleasure did it give to the people around him. Suddenly, as if aware of this gift to the two of us, and perhaps aware also of the source behind it, he wrapped his arm around Celia and held her close against him, purring gratefully—which gave me a spasm of envious pain.

Later, after a fine lunch with wine at a North Shore restaurant we sat far into the afternoon on a terrace splashed with dappled, leafy sunlight. Riders on horseback cantered past us; somehow again I thought of Wendy. Thoughtful, contented, stripped of the nighttime's high frenzy, and holding Celia's hand in his own, Mason told me what to expect in Europe—he'd been there, after all, and I hadn't. "You won't find it all pleasant, Peter, it's still recovering from the war. And there's a dead, dead feeling everywhere. Art really has come to a finish over there, and that's why—though I love to travel—I could never live anywhere for very long, except in America. I don't mean to sound platitudinous, but we *are* the nation of the future and anybody who *cares*, really, and who casts his lot with Europe—permanently, that is—is simply missing out, in my opinion. The so-called treasures of the past are all very well—a necessary experience, in fact, for anyone who pretends to culture—but significant form, as Clive Bell calls it, is dependent upon constant change, constant renewal from the resources of the present, a perpetual shaking-up and reordering, and this it is beyond the powers of Europe ever to do again. Which is why without any embarrassment at all I'm proud to call myself unswervingly modern." Yet, relieved of this—about his only heavy statement of the day—he went on to describe the fine things I would find in Europe ("If you look at it as a kind of still-enchanted playground, you won't go wrong.")—Paris and the sunny delights of the Midi and the Côte d'Azur, the fantastic beauty of the Alps, the Costa Brava, the Balearics. And I sat studiously, rapt, listening to this travelogue; he made magic of the scenes he described, the people he knew ("Here, I'll write a little note to Papa Albert. The greatest *coquilles St. Jacques* in Lyon, which is to say in all the world. A one-legged little fellow . . ."), the sanctums and hideaways, the cafés and beaches, the sheltered inlets unbeknownst to any American save himself. . . .

He made magic of these, and infused it all again with his own brand of bright hilarity; Celia would gaze at him with longing, tickled half to death, her teeth biting down charmingly over her lower lip, repressing laughter. Then out it would come, and all of us would laugh, and as we sat there in the lengthening shade of this gay spring day, with its smell of salt air and its white sails aslant against the distant blue and the nearby graveled spatter and crunching of riders along the paths, I thought how fortunate I was, after all, to know this vivid and inexhaustible young man, and count him as a friend. Rich, gloriously handsome, erudite, witty, gifted, a hero of the war, with a wife over whom the goddesses must grind their teeth in rage—what else could a man wish to be? Could the earth hold more youthful promise? Beside him that day, suddenly, I felt pitifully small, and I gloomed over all that was so paltry and commonplace in myself—that forbade me to see all that I disapproved of in him as a superb Renaissance spilling-over, manly as a stud horse, instead of corruption.

Of course—to mention only one thing that allowed me to view him somewhat less poetically—he was not a hero of the war at all. To be more exact, he was a draft dodger (the scar on his leg he picked up as the result of a bicycle collision at Princeton during his luckless semester), and as for Yugoslavia, he had come no closer to it than an enthusiastic reading of Rebecca West's *Black Lamb, Grey Falcon*—from which he had acquired enough color and historical minutiae to gull far less credulous souls than myself. How did I know all this? Celia told me.

She told me that same night, during what I suppose you might call a visit to me. It was morning, rather—it must have been past three, while I was still packing for my trip, when it happened: a frantic rapping at the door, the door itself flung open without a pause, and there was Celia. It had been raining outside. Her hair was plastered down around her forehead and her cheeks. She stood there for a moment and gazed at me with a most stricken look of pain and anguish; her lips parted as if to speak, then her hand went up to the back of her head, came down again, covered with blood. She said nothing at all. After a moment she stared at her red and trembling fingers, once more opened her mouth as if to say a word, and then collapsed in a heap upon the floor. Sweet Celia. I was shocked.

I brought her around easily enough, with cold water on the brow and instant coffee, hastily made. As for the wound at the back of her head, there was a lump the size of an egg but the cut itself was small and shallow; soon the bleeding stopped of its own accord, and she lay back with a soft moan against the pillow, breathing heavily, and with one arm flung across her eyes.

"What happened?" I said.

"Oh, my head hurts!"

"What in God's name *happened?*"

"He hit me with a plate," she said.

"A plate? What kind of plate?"

"A Lowestoft plate. A kind of platter. Oh, my head hurts!"

I gave her a couple of aspirin tablets and now (for she had begun to tremble violently) covered her with a blanket, insisting that we call a doctor. But she would have none of this: she would be all right—he had, after all, hit her before, and harder than this, much harder.

"The bastard," I said. "The swine. Why did he do it? Has he hit you often?"

"Oh, I don't know why he hit me, Peter." She made a move beneath the blanket, as if to rise; I gently pushed her down. Now she opened her eyes and I saw how red they were from weeping. "I shouldn't have come here, Peter," she said. "I'm really terribly sorry. But I get so terrified of him sometimes. And you were so— well, you were close and I just didn't know . . ." Her voice trailed off. "No, he doesn't hit me often." (A wifely remark, loyal even *in extremis,* if I ever heard one; you either hit your wife often, or not at all.) "I'm really very sorry, Peter," she said again.

"Don't be sorry, Celia," I said. "Don't be. I just wish I'd known about it sooner." Inside I had begun to feel a great helpless stormy torment of outrage: that someone should do violence to this warm, gentle little lark of a girl seemed, at least then, in the midst of my distant infatuation, the foulest of all foul sins. "Where is he now?" I said bitterly. "Where is the bastard? I'll lay him out." I would have, too, or tried.

She had come around a bit and now, after easing herself up on her elbows, sat propped with her legs curled beneath her and with her head pillowed against the wall. In this pose—smeared hair, dirty bloodstained fingers, red-rimmed eyes and all—she looked both lovely and cruelly hurt, a flower upon which has been impressed the print of a dirty boot. For an instant I came very close to throwing my arms around her and telling her how madly and completely I adored her, but I was brought up short by her words, which mingled incredulity and desolation within me in equal parts.

"Don't call him those names," she said gently. "I love him, Peter. I love him, you see. So you mustn't call him things like that. Please don't. I love him."

"You *what?*"

"Yes, I do," she said placidly.

"After *that?*"

"Yes."

"Why, for God sake?"

It was simple, she said. She loved him because he was funny (it certainly wasn't money, her Long Island family was *terribly* well fixed), because he made her laugh, because he had taught her so much. And not the least—would you believe it?—because he was so good-looking! And she would go on loving him, no matter what. "I'm just *mad* for him," she said. There was a preposterous, avid, debutante tone in her voice which for an instant made me want to show her the door. But of course I did nothing like that. I sat listening instead; for two hours or more I sat listening while she told me of her life with Mason—of what it was, and what it had been, and what even now (a shadow passed across her face, and her fingers went up lightly, though still trembling, to the place where he had struck her) she hoped that life could be. No, she was not going to whitewash him; she knew his faults as well as anyone. He was a liar, yes, that she knew; the Yugoslavia business was an example of that, and he had used—well, some kind of *influence*—to escape Army service. That scar on his leg? Oh, it was just some kind of traffic accident. But really, didn't I see? Didn't I see how all of his wild lying was only a part of that breadth and vastness of his whole personality, part of his *vision* of life, which was so broad and encompassing that it just had to include exaggeration and stretchings of the truth? Didn't I see that? Didn't I see how necessary it was for him to tell these things— they were harmless, after all, they could hurt no one but himself —if only because they represented left-over energy, expansion of his whole terrific imagination? Didn't I understand that?

"I'm trying to, Celia," I said.

And yes—well, Carole too. His sex life. No, she wouldn't pretend that it made her happy. It had caused her worry, pain—all right, then, real *anguish*. Sometimes at night she had gotten into such a lonely and frenzied state that she could barely stand it. And Carole wasn't the first. There had been Anya and Nancy and Kathy and—oh, she couldn't count them all. But wouldn't it be some kind of poor excuse for a wife who, married to a man of such incredible animal magnetism, such vitality and genius, couldn't put up with a thing like *that?* Yes, those parties—she knew about them, all right. They were disgusting. Childish even, to get right down to it. And those pictures. He'd made her look at them (O.K., it was blind of him to think that that would excite her, when, as anyone should know, dirty pictures don't excite women—very much anyway) and they'd done nothing but make her squirm. But after all, he was a *man,* and a different kind of man, too; he had needed those kinds of things, as the expression of *ambivalence*—the good and the bad—that is bound to be mixed up in such—well, in such a really enormous personality. He was an adventurer in the arts, a discoverer, and he just needed to have this kind of release, that's all. . . .

I asked her how she knew he needed it. I had begun to pace the floor. Despite my passion for her, she was losing ground with me, steadily, each time she opened her mouth.

She said he just needed it, that's all. He had told her he needed it, explained it all very philosophically from the artist's point of view. And she had understood. And she had complied. It wasn't too much of a sacrifice to make, was it?

Because otherwise he was so good to her. Oh, if I only knew how much he had taught her. And the places he'd taken her, and the books he'd made her read. Well, to be sure, it wasn't all a bed of roses. What marriage ever was, really? Most of his friends bored her, especially the Village crowd, who were just a bunch of grown-up babies, actually. And as for the rest—well, he had no *real* friends, she knew that. They were all dreadful spongers, mostly. Mason knew that, he'd told her sadly that a rich person has no real friend but himself. . . .

And—well, yes, their tastes weren't exactly the same. And he *was* difficult about it sometimes. Music. Ever since she was a child she had loved music. Brahms. Chopin. Wagner. Especially Brahms. How she loved that wondrous sad finale of the C-Minor Symphony, and the *Academic Festival*. They reminded her of far-off, dark, sweet, autumnal things—twilight and woods with falling leaves and mountain lakes covered with evening mists. Brahms. He must have been a man who knew how to grow old, who welcomed growing, and maturity, and even age. And Mason —well, no, sometimes she found it hard to take. He never let her play those kinds of records—oh, every now and then, yes. But never it seemed when she was in the mood. And she remembered one time when she longed to hear Brahms so that she took a taxi all the way to Thirty-fourth Street and sat smothered up in a record-store booth for a whole summer afternoon, listening and listening. . . .

No, sometimes things like that were hard to take. She would admit that. But didn't I see how a wife had to *defer* to her husband in such matters? After all, it was the husband who was the—well, if you want to call it that, the guide. It was *his* career, not hers, that really mattered. And if he was so dedicated and devoted to his work (and it was going to be such a *wonderful* play, full of swagger and wit; no, she hadn't read it but he'd told her about it— the Yugoslavian scene, the young American officer, the lovely Dalmatian girl), if he was so dedicated, then nothing mattered really, even if one wanted babies . . . She stopped talking.

Outside, the weather had cleared again. Dawn was draining silver down the air shaft, and across the way the old men were setting up a noisy commotion in the plumbing. Along the avenues, far off, buses began to growl, and when I turned from the window I saw that Celia's head was bent down, exposing the raw and sorry wound, and that she was weeping now, silently and hopelessly. I sat down beside her and took her in my arms and for a long time we remained there, amid the debris of departure, saying nothing.

When finally she raised her head, she said in a low voice, so faint that I could barely hear it: "Once when we were first married we had a house upstate, in the country. It was really a nice place, simple but comfortable, you see. I don't know, Mason was somehow—*different* then. I mean, he believed in, well, simpler things. We were going to live there and we were going to have children, and he was going to write his plays. I'll never forget when we moved in and that first night, when we stayed up until dawn. It was fall and it was cold—but that dawn, I remember how clear and beautiful it was outside. I remember how Mason went out to burn some trash and how I sood there beside him all bundled up, watching him, watching the quiet countryside getting light, and the cold with a sort of wonderful *promise* in it, and Mason standing there by the fire with the wind whipping his hair and the fire blazing up in the dawn. And then he put his arms around me, I remember, and we shivered and laughed and I remember thinking how happy I would be there in the country with him, having children and helping him while he wrote his plays. What more could a girl ask for? I thought. There were ducks flying across the sky. He hadn't ever hit me then."

Once more she was silent, but now I felt a tremor run through her body. "He scares me when he hits me like that." Her lips were trembling and I held her very close against my side, as I would a little girl. "But that's all right," she blurted out suddenly. "I'm mad for him, just positively *mad* for him!" Now she had begun to shake and twitch violently, all over, and she pulled away from me and gazed straight into my eyes. "He can do anything to me," she said, her voice rising, "anything at all! I'm just *mad* for him!" And I too pulled away, for it seemed to me she was telling me something that lay deeper than her words.

Can one detect in the eye—like a mote of dust or a beam of light—the peculiar glint of madness? I do not know. Perhaps it was only the echo of that word she used over and over, like an incantation. But now as she slid with incredible speed into hysteria, I did know that whatever Mason was doing to her, hitting her with plates was not necessarily his worst oppression.

"He hasn't made love to me in two years!" she cried. "But it's all right! Because *babies!* His career, you see! I mean it's *all right* if we don't have children! Don't you see! I mean as he says, bringing innocents into this hellish world! It's all right! And for the best! Anything he does! I'm still just *mad* for him!"

I finally had to take her around the corner to St. Vincent's Hospital, where they were very sympathetic: they gave her a sedative and put her to bed. She would pull out of it in a while, they said, and they would send her home. But as I left there in the full light of day—with a kiss on her cheek, the saddest of my life—she was still babbling.

Ask me why, after all this, I came to see Mason in Sambuco, and my answer would be a vague one. But maybe what happened on shipboard that same morning would partly explain it.

I was quite without sensation when, four hours later, I entered my economy-sized cabin on the *Queen Mary*. And for a moment I thought I had gotten the wrong accommodations. Crammed into that tiny space was the most óutlandish assortment of delicacies that I had ever seen: not a single bottle but a whole case of champagne, two enormous wicker baskets of fruit, a flat box of candy the size of a paving block, a high stack of books on the floor, a clutch of whiskey bottles neatly done up in a huge red ribbon, and several baskets of nodding flowers which, shoved together for want of space, had already begun to shed their soft fresh petals upon the floor. Other luxuries were heaped up: half a dozen cartons of cigarettes, a pile of magazines, and an iced tin of caviar. As my eyes took in this scene I was aware of the smoke which in rich blue swirls wreathed the room, and of its smell, which had a pungent herby fragrance that only for the briefest moment I couldn't define. Then as I took one step forward, trying to penetrate the gloom, my eyes made out two huddled forms squatting on a bunk: a sallow young man, throttled by a turtle-neck sweater, with evasive, foxy eyes, and a Negro boy of twenty or so who wore velvet ballet pants and a purple jersey and who, shifting now sluggishly in the darkness, leaned out toward me into the light of the porthole, which cast a bright oval of sunshine onto his thinly mustachioed, inky-blue, and cataleptic face. It was a den full of vipers, I knew, and I backed out in haste calling for the steward, who came on the run and in emphatic Cockney tones insisted that I had the right cabin. So I eased back in, introducing myself with as much hardiness as I could muster to the two youths on the bunk, and when I got no response except what sounded like a soft *tee-hee*—far-off, indistinct, almost ethereal, as if it came from outer space—I turned to examine the candy occupying my bunk, and saw by the card it was for me: "For Petesy from his old daddy." Intently then, with anger and shame, with gathering resentment yet with some left-over feeling, too, of warm, degrading gratefulness, I went among the other gifts: they were all for me, to each one was attached a card—"For Petesy"—and in my chagrin I burst out into a fit of sneezing, to which the colored boy, in a voice softly modulated and faraway, said: *"Gesundheit,* man. You're just gonna have to excuse this here fog."

"Thanks," I said.

There was a long pause before he spoke again. "Great big tall cat brought all that stuff in here. Said he'd be back tout de suite."

Another faint titter came from his companion. "Let's cut out, Johnson. Let's do the poop deck."

"Jesus Christ," I said aloud in disgust.

"Naw," the colored boy giggled. "Not *J.C.* A big tall cat with a real groovy yellow-headed chick. Said he—"

Just then Mason, with a be-orchided Carole in his wake, burst into my cabin and fell about my shoulders with loud brutal cries of greeting.

"*Allons-y,* Petesy!" he yelled into my ear. "*Pour chercher la twat française.* I got half a mind to ship on board with you for this cruise and flush out some of that quail on the Rue Bonaparte. What's the matter, Pierre? You look rather down in the mouth for a man who's going to clash head-on with the choicest flesh in Christendom." He drew back, his fingertips on my shoulders, and surveyed me with a mild, reproachful look. I must have groaned, or something; at any rate, I know he sensed my resentment—that whole-hearted disapproval of him which had made me stiff as a board at his touch and had kept my eyes averted and downcast. Oddly, though, still burning with anger as I was over what he had done to Celia, I could not bring myself to say a word to him.

"Let me tell you, Peter," he went on, "I've cased this tub from stem to stern and although about half of them are a bunch of randy-looking Limeys who look like they take it in the elbow, or somewhere, I saw a couple of broads, American girls, who look ready for anything. 'Course, I had a couple of pals in England during the war said these British dames are positive *cormorants,* jazz you till your ears drop off. But I don't know. *Chacun à son goût.*"

Another giggle floated up from the shadows. "Man, dig that crazy Frenchman."

Mason wheeled about, looking down at the colored boy, upon whose blue eroded features now dreamed a sleepy smile. "Well, look here now, Petesy," he said very loudly, grinning. "I thought when I smelled that tea burning I'd discover a couple of lotus eaters." He began to laugh at the top of his voice. "Leverett in Bopland!"

Turning to my shipmates he said: "Boys, you've got a square on board, but he's a good man. Don't put him down. Where you off to? What are you going to do—set the Left Bank on fire? Where the hell's your beret?"

"Right here, man," said the colored boy, pulling drowsily from his pocket a floppy Basque headpiece the size of a pie plate, which he set in rakish slant on his brow, all but obscuring his eyes. "Groovy, *n'est-ce pas?*"

"Look at it," his companion giggled. "Like, man, it's the absolute most."

Mason burst out in a roar of rollicking amusement. "Bless your bulletproof head," he cried. "Give my regards to Sidney Bechet.

Come on, Peter, it smells like swampfire in here. Let's go up topside and get some air. In the meantime, boys, keep your fingers
out of that caviar. My friend here is Prince Peter of Yugoslavia
and he eats hipsters for breakfast." Clutching my arm with one
hand, and a champagne bottle in the other, he propelled me toward the door, where Carole—forgotten by me for these past
moments—now stood with a forlorn, distraught look on her
creamy face, and with a pinkish hue around her eyes, as if she
had just stopped weeping and was about to begin again. She gave
me a wan, apologetic smile and her lips parted on the breath of a
greeting. But before I could reply Mason said, "Excuse me a second, Peter," and moved her briskly aside to the end of the companionway, where I watched him for a moment deep in agitated
colloquy with her, his words muffled but clearly annoyed, his head
pressed down close to hers, his arms buttressed against the wall
and hemming her in like those of a top sergeant as he chewed out
a fractious recruit. Escape was high in my mind; I felt rotten
enough as it was, and with a kind of insane clarity I knew that if
I had to participate, this morning, even as a bystander, in one of
Mason's delirious scenes I would surely end up babbling and sobbing myself. Yet something held me there, and I watched in
fascination as his face grew red as an apple, the veins like tiny
throbbing pipes rampant at his brow, and as finally, with an outraged toss of his hair, he bellowed: "Then *go,* you lousy bitch!
Back the hell to Coney Island . . . or whatever dump—" I thought
for an instant that now with his hand drawn back he was going to
strike her, but he didn't, allowing his palm as if carried forward
by the momentum of an arrested then rejected idea to fall with a
sharp crack against the wall. "Go!" I heard him say again. "Go!"
And then Carole simply collapsed. She gazed up at Mason in dismay, with piteous amazement.

"Ah please," I moaned aloud and turned away.

"I'm fed up!" I heard him say behind me, and again I awaited
the sound of his clobbering hand. But when I turned back now,
Carole was beating a sinuous, big-hipped retreat down the corridor, keening like a Hindu, sending through the bowels of the ship
ponderous, contralto moos of despair which brought heads popping out from a dozen doors. When these sounds diminished,
finally dying out, I turned back to Mason. His brow was propped
against the wall, and the single word he uttered—over the celebrant noise of tourists and the distant throbbing of engines—

seemed laden with a burden of ten thousand years. "Women!" he said.

"Now what's the matter, Mason?" I asked impatiently, as he came near me.

"I don't know," he said with a grunt. "I don't know!" he repeated, looking seriously into my eyes. "I seem to have a run on woman trouble recently. Carole! The bitch. Oh, she'll be back. She'll be back. I'm not worried about that. Peter, I'll tell you, women are another *race!* They're like cannibals. Turn your back and they're ready to eat you alive."

"What happened, Mason?" Again, it was none of my business but I couldn't think of anything else to say. He seemed to me ineffably tiresome.

"Come on," he said, steering me down the companionway, "let's go topside. Oh nothing. *Nothing,* really. We'll be mooning at each other by noontime. She's got the curse or something and she decided to take it out on me. Yak, yak. Wants me to make her a movie star. Wants me to buy her a Jaguar or something. Thinks I'm Darryl Zanuck. I don't know, every time she gets the rag on she gets positively *moon-struck.* It's the worst thing about women —that really screwed-up plumbing of theirs. A big jumbo sewer flowing through the Garden of Eden."

To this sort of poetry I am the type of person who usually mutters a complaisant "Yeah." That's what I said. "Yeah." And still, for the life of me, I could not bring myself to mention Celia.

But, "Really, Peter," he blurted suddenly. "I'm sorry as hell." His voice as we bustled along became worried and solicitous, almost beseeching. "Really I am. About last night, I mean. You must think I'd gone absolutely bobo after last night with Celia and all. She came home just a while ago. We made it up all right. Mean trick of hers, making you patch her up like that. On the other hand, I sure as hell should have kept my paws off her. I was all nerves, that's all, with the play. And she was yammering about kids. I'll *give* her kids some day, but can't she understand that the play comes first? First time I ever laid hands on her! I don't know what made me do a thing like that!" There was a lack of conviction in his voice, as if he realized I knew better. "Anyway, I sure didn't expect to impose on you something like just now. Oh, Peter, women! Sometimes I think I'll switch to beavers. Or moose. Or Rotarians. I don't know. Or maybe go back to Merryoaks and have Wendy rub me down with Baume Ben-Gay."

But when, gaining the outside deck, we pushed up toward the bow through a tourist group of Portland Oregonians, he had recovered from his depression and chattered away at me with jolly gusto. It was a balmy day with a hazeless and sapphire sky across which two planes had sketched straight white trails of vapor, like scratches from phantom fingernails. Erect against the blue, the towers of Manhattan rose up in monolithic glitter, and before this backdrop Mason posed me, talking the whole time as he fiddled with his Leica. "What *seized* you, to go tourist class?" he said. "I mean for kicks a couple of guys like that are fine, but a week in the same room—murder. Oh, Peter! I can tell you already just who you're going to share a table with. I saw the list. A chiropodist from Jackson Heights and a hideous old Lesbian with a hearing-aid. Why didn't you fly?"

"I'm trying to save dough, Mason," I said. "What do you mean you saw the list?"

He snickered and clicked the camera. "I was just kidding, doll-baby. Don't worry. The trip's going to be a dream."

For a minute, without speaking, we drank champagne from paper cups at the rail. In the silence I was embarrassed, but I felt a slow, intolerable hardening of my heart toward Mason, not in spite of his generosity but almost because of it, and because now, singled out so uniquely for his grotesque affections, I felt no rare warmth or gratitude but only resentment, a soiled and debased feeling, as if I were the receiver of bribes. Anyway, something— my pride, or only an outraged sensibility—refused to let me speak, and it was Mason finally, in solemn, even sorrowful tones which surprised me, who broke the silence. "Well, Peter, I'm going to miss your homely face. Drop me a line every now and then, will you? I'm going to miss you, boy. I don't know why. You're really outrageously dull and prissy as an old biddy of seventy-two. But you know, I guess, how fond I've always been of you. Celia put her finger on it, I think. She said, 'He understands people,' whatever the hell that means. You probably conned her into that thought by nodding gravely and stroking your whiskers and nonchalantly scratching your ass at the right time. Anyway, Pierre— anyway, I'm going to miss you."

"What are you going to be doing now, Mason?" I said idly.

He was silent for a moment. It was a peculiar and meaningful silence, one that I had learned to arm myself against. It involved an amount of deep rumination, a sparkle in the eye: and by now I felt I knew him so well that I could almost hear the crafty currents of his brain at work, regimenting those shamelessly naked false-hoods which when made vocal—made glib and honey-smooth by his expressive tongue—would wear the illustrious garb of truth. Inelegantly, he spat over the side. "Oh, I don't know, Petesy. Finish the play, I guess. That's first on the agenda. Whitehead's about to go out of his mind, he wants me to finish it so badly. But, you know, a play isn't something you can do right off the top of your head, like a Ford commercial. You've got to think and think and suffer and suffer and think. Then there's that eternal problem of accuracy—verisimilitude, I should say. For instance, this play of mine—well, I might as well tell you. It's about those ex-periences I had during the war in Yugoslavia. Did I tell you that? The fact just in itself slows me down from the very beginning. Be-cause in order to get this—this verisimilitude I need so badly—well, for instance, details about the Serbian language, and certain street names in Dubrovnik, and various partisan passwords that I've forgotten, things like that—well, in order to get these things really down pat the way I should, I've been having to carry on this endlessly long correspondence with old Plaja. Remember the old guy I was telling you about—"

"You mean that old *hoax?*" I said. "That old *fraud?*" To have to contain myself any longer, to continue to allow myself to be stuffed with his forgeries and fictions, with his crooked inventions, with all the other indigestible by-products of his peerless quackery, was a prospect which at this moment I couldn't bear. I felt that at least he should have spared me the degradation of a final lie; but he hadn't, and I was bursting to tell him so. "You mean that fig-ment!" I said.

He hadn't caught on. "You remember old Plaja," he said, "the old guy's still hale and hearty. Plans to come over for a visit soon. He's been sort of my technical advis—"

"Look, Mason," I said, "why do you feel you have to lie to me? Do you think I'm a—a *fool* or something? An idiot? *Do you?*"

His face went pale. One shoulder pitched upward and he raised his hands, fingers outstretched placatingly toward me. "Now I don't understand, Petesy. Don't get me wrong. I haven't said—"

"What do you mean you haven't!" I said. "You tell me these creepy cock-and-bull stories, standing there with a solemn look on your face like a Baptist deacon, and expect me to believe them! What's the matter with you, anyway? You think I'm a moron? You think I wouldn't eventually somehow learn what's true? You call me your confidant, your pal, your dollbaby, and pull all this buddy-buddy stuff and every time I turn around you're telling me a dreary *lie!* You were never in Yugoslavia! You were a draft dodger! That play of yours is a *soap bubble!*" I was choking with fury, the dreadful callow American prep-school words ("creepy," "pal," "buddy-buddy") I uttered with the hysteric rage of a fifth-former, and, aware of all this even as I shouted at him—aware of how stupidly and impossibly and absurdly young we remain in this land—I thanked God I was leaving Mason and going to Europe, and I felt tears compounded of rheum, of indignation, and of an old weary worn-out pity and love for him brimming up in my eyes. I turned away from him. *"What,* Mason?" I cried, my voice growing loose and incoherent. "Do you think I'm that much of a fool? You'd better get your goddam head looked at!"

Above us at the funnel's mouth a plume of steam exploded forth, followed by the whistle's horrendous blast. As it went off, booming thunder around us, I felt his hand on my shoulder and turned, deafened, to see his gray, stricken face and his lips mouthing the contours of words. Around us, people with fingers in their ears moved slowly forward toward the gangways. "—hurts me!" he cried, in a sudden silence that was profound and astounding. "That hurts me, to hear you say stuff like that." His lips trembled; he looked on the verge of tears. "Stuff like that," he said bitterly, "stuff like that is—it's *irremediable.* I mean, to think that you—you of all people—can't make the subtle distinction between a lie—between an out-and-out third-rate lie meant maliciously—between that, and a jazzy kind of bullshit extravaganza like the one I was telling you, meant with no malice at all, but only with the intent to edify and entertain." His shoulder was twitching badly now, a wide arching seesawing movement; I could almost hear the ligaments snapping with the strain. "Jesus sake, Peter!" he burst out in a voice that was indeed hurt—hurt and aggrieved. "Don't you have enough *prescience* to see that I was telling it all to you under the guise of truth only to see your reactions? To see if it would stand up as a play? To see if it was convincing to, say, someone like you whose sympathies I trust and whose aesthetic orientation—"

"And that dear, fantastic wife of yours!" I broke in. "What's the matter with you? Lay off her! Lay off her, God damn you!" And then I stopped, my mouth agape, rattled by the sudden knowledge that this was the first time I had ever really talked back to Mason—my first outburst, my only reprimand. For a moment I had no words. Then after a breath, I went on more amiably, "Really, Mason, maybe we're all a bit neurotic and all that, but for heaven's sake—"

He was not to be deflected. In shaken tones he added: "If I can't have any faith in your reactions, Peter, then the Lord knows —" But then he made a futile gesture with his hand, turning back toward the rail, and wrenched from his throat a few awkward words that hurt me to the core. "Lord knows I've *tried* hard to be decent and sociable enough. But every time I open my mouth it seems I turn into a great pile of . . ." He paused, lips trembling. It was awful. "I just always end up with everybody using me. Or hating my guts."

"I don't hate—" I began, turning, but another blast from the whistle nearly lifted us from the deck. Far off in the lower depths sounded a carillon of jangling bells. "Well, Mason," I said instead, "it looks like it's time to break up our party." I stuck out my hand, feeling like hell. "Many thanks for all the nice presents. Thanks really, Mason."

He moved toward me with a somber little smile, reaching for my hand. "Bon voyage, old dollbaby," he said, "don't get clutched up. Down one for me, will you, every now and then?"

It was the last I heard him say. His shoulder still heaving as if with palsy, he took my hand, turning that simple gesture of farewell into the sorriest act of loneliness, of naked longing, I think I have ever known.

For like that forsaken boy—his face unremembered now, even his name—who lingers dimly in my memory of childhood, the rich little neighbor boy who—so it was long after told to me— warped or crippled or ugly, perhaps all three, when asked one day by his elders why and how and whither all his nickels and his quarters and his dimes had so swiftly vanished, burst out the confession that they had gone, each one, not for candy or toys or Eskimo pies, but to pay for the companionship of other children —five cents for an hour, twenty for an afternoon, a small fistful of nickels for a whole summer day: like this lost child's, Mason's gesture was one of recompense and hire, and laden with the anguish of friendlessness. Before I could say another word, or recover my wits long enough to really understand what he had given me, he was gone, swallowed up in the shorebound throng, leaving my hand clutched around a wad of French money he had got from somewhere, all notes of ten thousand francs—enough to buy a solid-gold Swiss watch if I had wanted one, or a suit of Harris tweeds, or bottles of brandy without number. Mortified, I tried to call out after him, but already he was lost from sight—except for one last brief glimpse I had of him at the top of a distant stairway: with his head bent down there seeking the steps he looked curiously clumsy and inept; not the old breezy magician but vulnerable, bumbling and for an instant wildly confused—future's darling, a man with one foot poised in the thinnest of air.

Then within minutes I felt a throbbing beneath my feet and the boat began to move. Propped against the rail with the money still in my hand—feeling even at this terminal moment that my virtue had been pre-empted, that somehow, irretrievably, I had been bought and procured—I slipped seaward toward Europe with all Manhattan aglitter in my eyes, its cenotaphs and spires exorbitant and heaven-yearning.

With my cabinmates I got along very well: they were really gentle, accommodating fellows—somewhat hard to get next to, maybe, but far less depraved than Mason, it seemed to me, and a lot better adjusted. In Paris I got a letter from Mason, telling me that Celia had gone to Reno. I remember one characteristic phrase, which seemed—as with so much of Mason—to emerge from some insubstantial shadowland unacquainted either with sorrow or joy: "Weep, weep for Mason and Celia, Peter, we've gone to Splitsville." And it was not long after this that Mason faded from my mind. Yet I wish now I could recall the details of that shipboard dream I had, far out in mid-ocean, when I shot erect in my bunk and listened in a sweat to my fellow voyagers snoring in the dark, and smelled the sweet scent of those blossoms, slowly dying, that he had given me, and was touched all over with the somehow-knowledge of Mason's certain doom.

IV

When Mason, clattering down the hallway in his shower clogs, left me vibrating on that marble bench in Sambuco, I found it hard to get a decent grip on all my emotions. I was furious, God knows. Yet my anger, mixed as it was with a bewildering and indefinable fear of Mason, had the quality of anxiety; flight—from the palace, from Sambuco—seemed essential, and I sat there nursing the insult I felt, and pondered the ways in which I could make a decorous, unseen escape from the whole neighborhood. Two or three minutes must have passed. I was about to get up then, when I heard Mason's wooden clogs click-clocking slowly back down the hallway. He entered, still walking with his strange bent-over hobbled gait, but he stood a bit more erect now and he was looking at me with such grinning, callous good humor that my fear of him instantly vanished. No longer my Polaroid monster, he was himself, desperately plausible from top to toe. "Bet I gave you quite a start," he said. "How about a drink, Petesy? I haven't had time to—"

"Go to hell!" I retorted. "Who do you think you are, talking to me like that! We aren't back at St. Andrew's, and by God if you think— I'm not just another one of your crummy freeloaders!"

"Petesy, Petesy, Petesy," he murmured in his old plaintive cajoling voice. He sat down beside me and gave me a slap of palship on the shoulder. "Old Petesy with the tissue-paper skin. Look, I want to tell you—"

"You look!" I exclaimed, getting briskly to my feet. "I don't know what the hell's going on around here, but I can tell you I've *had* it! Do you think I'm some lousy *contadino*—some peasant you can push around? You invited me down here as your guest and I've felt about as welcome as a case of typhoid! If it hadn't been for Rosemarie, understand, I wouldn't even have gotten fed! I think I'll take a raincheck. *Mille grazie!* Wise guy! Jerk!" I shouted miserably as I began to shuffle off. "Invite me back sometime when I won't be such a strain on your resources!"

He leaped to his feet and caught my wrist. He was still panting from his recent pursuit, still sweating, and he wore an expression about as close to being shamefaced as he could ever approach. "I'm sorry," he said. "I really am. I didn't know what I was saying. I was—well, I was *hacked,* upset. Please forgive me, Peter. Please do."

"Well, I'm going, Mason," I said faint-heartedly. "See you around the campus."

"You'll do nothing of the kind," he replied. "You're going to forgive me for being a bastard. And you're going to stay here with your old pal."

"What did you mean, saying you were going to *stomp* me?" I said. "What's gotten into you, Mason? What have I done. I'm not a criminal, a bum you can talk to like—"

He ran one hand nervously over his brow. "I—I don't know, Peter. I'm sorry. That girl. She's been robbing me blind. Just lifted a pair of Rosemarie's earrings. I was upset, that's all. I dunno, I got so exasperated I thought everybody was trying to side with her. Crazy of me! Look," he pleaded, "say you forgive me! I really didn't mean it, I swear. Soon as I said it I felt like a worm."

Incorrigible to the end, I allowed nostalgia and sentimentality to win out. I averted my eyes and gripped his hand, saying: "Well,

O.K., Mason, O.K." All my life I've been addicted, in such situations, to weird self-implication. I added: "I'm sorry, too. It was half my fault, I guess."

This seemed vaguely to cheer him up. "Right," he said vacantly, "let's call it bygones and to hell with it. We all make mistakes. Look, wait here a minute while I go up and put some clothes on, and I'll show you around the plant." And as I stood waiting there while he vanished up the stairway I was left feeling—like one bamboozled in an old familiar con game—that it was he who had pocketed *my* apology.

He was gone for five or ten minutes. During that time I wandered aimlessly around the deserted room, puffing at a cigarette; I still felt nervous and rattled, especially troubled over the girl he had chased down the hallway, and whom he had obviously molested in one way or another. I think that for a while it must have drizzled outside, for as I lingered, peering again up at the melee on the ceiling (the Huntress this time, harpooned squarely through the navel by a latter-day electrical conduit) I heard voices buzzing below as the poolside crowd began to disband and made their way back up through the garden and into the palace.

When Mason returned he had on a white jacket and freshly creased Bermuda shorts, and he wore a preoccupied look. "Come on, Petesy, let's look over the plant." His voice and manner were terse; nonetheless, he was trying hard to please and impress me. In the next half-hour or so he showed me his den, a leathery relaxed place done up like a whiskey ad, with elephant guns, books, bullfight posters, an ottoman made from the foreleg of a rhinoceros, and the head of an African buffalo he claimed to have slain —a rather pathetic beast that gazed down from the wall with the sweet, dumb, glassy expression of a Brown Swiss cow. This was a new phase of Mason's, I reflected—the sporting life—and here in the den we lingered for a while, drinking brandy, while he told me of his friendship with various flashy matadors, showed me his great bullhide-bound volumes on tauromachy, which is the word he used, and, lastly, with an effrontery and shamelessness advanced even for him, described in detail the safari he had made through Kenya with a sensitive Canadian blonde. She had taken her Ph.D. at the University of Toronto, on Baudelaire's imagery . . . but I won't go into it: such a rich amalgam of jackals howling in the night, and nerve-racking trails of blood spoors down draws and gullies, and bwanas and memsahibs, and petrifying waits for a wounded beast to come plunging from the brush, or bush—all of this laced with *Fleurs du mal* and strong draughts of fornication on the veldt—a romance the likes of which you never heard. I think I must have feigned interest but my mind was far away; all I wanted to do was to make an escape from this palace and go to sleep somewhere. Next he took me through the rest of the "plant," showed the basement with its General Electric oil furnace—trucked over from Naples, he said, at great expense and effort—the frozen food locker, and then the stainless-steel kitchen complete with Frigidaire, an expanse of cabinets, ovens, and ranges whose buttons, controls, and indicators glittered in multi-colored ranks. I looked around. At a gleaming sink two local scullery maids toiled in a cloud of steam, scraping plates for the nearby dishwasher, which grumbled and hummed like an idling Diesel engine; beyond them in one corner old Giorgio, stripped to his galluses, was moodily amusing himself with an electric knife sharpener that sent a spine-chilling wail through the air.

"I got everything wholesale at the PX," Mason said. "Well, what do you think of it?"

"Mason," I said, "I think it's just grand. But tell me something —how did you get PX privileges?"

"There are ways," he said inscrutably. And then he led me into a nearby alcove and showed me a newly developed American fire extinguisher, the extinguishing element of which—a type of gluey foam—he claimed you could actually eat.

"Fantastic, Mason," I said. Culturally he had shifted his poles, that was plain to see; he seemed no more self-conscious over this sudden display of pelf than he had been before over his forays into the demimonde. "Tell me," I went on, "how come you've got a Cadillac now? Isn't that rather square?"

"Oh, sports cars," he said. "They've become such a cliché." I should have known.

Then we returned to the kitchen and were confronted by Giorgio, looking this time sour and mournful as he gave Mason what appeared to be some kind of note. *"Da Francesca,"* said Giorgio.

"Francesca?" Mason exclaimed, his eyes growing wide. "Where is she?"

"Dov'è, signore? Non lo so. Ma credo che sia giù, nella strada."

"Speak up!" he said excitedly, then to me: "What's he saying, for Christ sake?"

"He said he believes she was downstairs, on the street."

"What does he mean, 'believes'?" he said, tearing open the note. "Doesn't the old fool *know?*"

"*Se n'è andata,*" Giorgio said with a shrug, spreading his hands wide. "Finish."

"She's gone, Mason," I said.

"Well, tell him to go find her."

I told him. More knowledgeable, apparently, than Mason knew, he shuffled away, mumbling resentfully that he was nobody's fool. I began to fidget. Mason in the meantime, digesting the message in a glance, had turned scarlet; puckering his lips up as if to spit, or to blurt out some blasphemy, his face became redder and redder, and he let the note fall to the floor, his eyes bugging out and looking wild as, finally, he found words to speak. "The little slut," he said in a low, mean voice, "the unspeakable, filthy dago slut."

"Mason," I said hastily. "I think I'll go on up to the Bella Vista. I'm really quite beat and—"

"They've got the minds of criminals, I'll swear to God," he said. "Every goddam one of them are filthy, sneaking thieves. It's born in them, I'll swear, Peter, with the same predestination that makes the Germans born with blood-lust. They've got robbery and embezzlement in their *bones*. No wonder they're so goddam poor. They must rob each other blind!" As of yore, he had begun to gyrate his miserable shoulder.

"Look, Mason," I said, "all this is very well and good, but it's not true and I don't want to talk about it. I'm dead tired and I want to go to bed—"

"Jesus Christ!" he said, paying me no attention. "To think that filching little bitch would promenade right under my nose for two —no, three whole months, robbing me baldheaded—at the wages I pay her, too!—robbing me with no more compunction than if she thought I was a gibbering idiot. Wiggling her criminal little twat around the house as if she owned the place—" And as he stood before me there in the steaming, grandiloquent kitchen, he sailed away upon a harangue so absurd and so mad that I actually thought for a brief moment he was joking: had I not heard, for Jesus sake, of Willie Morelli and Tough Tony Anastasia and such thugs as The Dasher Abbandando and Bow-legs Sarto—not to speak, for Jesus sake, of Luciano and Costello and Capone? Was that not proof enough, if proof was needed, that the principal contribution of the Italian people to America if not to all humanity (and *please,* Peter, he knew all about the Renaissance) was a thievish and corrupt criminality so murderous, so immoral, that it was unrivaled in history? "Jesus sake, Peter!" he said angrily, as if he sensed my silent rebuke. "Use your head!" Didn't I know that Murder, Incorporated—that vicious mob of professional assassins —was made up almost wholly of Italians and that moreover gangsterism in America was totally controlled by a wicked pack of dope-sellers and connivers in Italy? (Dear old Italy.) I had heard that, but I didn't see that—"*Jesus!*" he cried. "Use your head!" And then he indulged himself in one final, flamboyant, pathetic lie (the last of his I was ever to hear): about a young friend of his, a Harvard-bred assistant district attorney so brilliant that his name had been bruited about New York as candidate for mayor, who, having declared a personal war on the mobsters, went out bravely incognito among them, only to be found slain one night in a vacant lot in Rego Park, Queens, mutilated so horribly that even he, Mason, was loath to tell about it (but he would: a hot poker rammed up his bowel; his genitalia . . . etc.). I made my mind a blank. "And the Mafia had branded their mark on his chest!" he concluded, shaking with fury. "A bunch of miserable Italian thugs with the mentality of beasts. Look, you know I'm not a—a *xenophobe,* of the lunatic fringe. But isn't that proof enough that the Italians have become degraded to the point of *bestiality?* Do you see why I might be peeved," he asked, with a heavy load of sarcasm, "when this dirty little twat of a housemaid has the temerity—the gall—to walk out beneath my nose with practically everything I own? Can't you see how I might be *vexed,* to say the least? Well, can't you?"

I said nothing. I couldn't even bring myself to look at him, as he stood there panting and heaving. Then all of a sudden he smacked one fist into the palm of his hand, startling me, forcing me to look up at his face. And as I stared at him, he muttered beneath his breath something which made no sense to me at all: "So it's a lot of lowbrow diddling, that's what it is. A cheap smelly roll in the hay." Then he paused again, the sweat pouring off his face, smacking his palm. "Well, we'll see about *that!*" he exclaimed. He turned on his heels then and charged back through the door past the fire extinguisher, his shorts flapping around his knees as he hotfooted it down the hallway.

I picked up the note he had let fall to the floor. It was in English, but in a messy, lacerated scrawl so splintered that it was barely legible. *Youre in deep trouble,* it read, *Im going turn you in to bait for buzzards. C.* I thought it some sort of joke.

I pocketed the note, then I trailed after Mason, despondent but curious. I followed his gaunt and hustling vision, multi-reflected, down the mirrored corridor; breezing into the foyer, past the marble bench upon which I had so lately tumbled, he made no sign or word of recognition to the scattering of guests returned from the pool, who had gathered there, but threw open the door to the stairway of the courtyard and raced out onto the balcony. I followed in his wake, passing through the foyer too, where I had a brief glimpse in the distance of several people dancing and the black indefatigable face of Billy Raymond as he pounded the piano. And when I reached the balcony I saw that Mason was leaning over the stone parapet, bawling down into the courtyard.

"Cass!" he shouted. "Hey, Cass! Come on up!"

But from the green door down in the shadows below there was no stir, no answer.

"Cass!" he yelled again. "Hey, Cass! Come on up here!" His voice, oddly, had none of the anger nor the agitation his recent movements would have led me to expect; it was instead only rather blunt, peremptory, as if it expected to be heard, and obeyed, and it echoed in hollow waves around the dark and lofty courtyard. "Cass!" he cried again, but there was still no answer from the door; he turned to me with an exasperated look, saying, *"Now* where the hell has he gone to?"

"I wouldn't know, Mason," I said, utterly baffled.

Some emotion shivered and shook him as he stood there—God knows what emotion it was. He trembled, ran his hand again across his sweaty brow. I thought he was going to burst into tears. "The jerk!" he said in a choked voice. "The miserable jerk!" And then, brushing past me, saying in a voice that was almost like a gasp for air, "I'll bet Giorgio knows!" he flung himself back through the doors and into the palace.

My mystification was complete.

Now was the time to go. And I would have done so, no doubt— my foot even then poised in liberating descent upon the stairs— had not the green door opened at that very moment down below, sending a shaft of light across the courtyard and causing me to draw back like some hooligan (such was the infection of Mason's personality) into the shadows of the balcony. Two figures emerged from the door—Cass Kinsolving and a girl. I heard a soft sobbing noise from the girl, exhausted, infinitely touched with grief, and saw Cass half-stumble against the wall; then, as they moved on slowly out into the rectangle of light, I saw that the girl was none other than the black-clad servant girl who had fallen to her knees before me in the *salone.* I heard them talking in low unhappy tones—indistinctly, spiritlessly— their voices rising and falling alternately and then in unison in a curious, small threnody of distress, and rent at intervals by the girl's soft, remorseless, heartbroken sobs. Irresistibly, I leaned out over the parapet. I saw Cass stagger and slump against the wall, almost toppling down, and heard the girl's voice again, as she appeared to clutch out for him, in a renewed surge of half-hysteric grief. For a long moment, leaning there against the wall, they melted together in a tormented embrace. At last I heard the single word *Basta!* Then one of them said *Ssss-ss,* and their voices died to whispers, and for a long minute I heard no more until with a soft pitipat of bare feet the girl scampered across the courtyard, still weeping, and was gone.

Alone, Cass stood at the doorway, swaying back and forth. At last with a sudden clumsy motion he turned about and pressed his cheek against the wall, clutching at the gray stone with his hands, as if trying to embrace it. I thought I heard him groan; then the sound died and all I could hear was his heavy breathing as he stood there, the noise sibilant and greedy and agonized like that of a distance runner at the end of a race. And at this moment the door burst open once again behind me, and Mason flew to the parapet, leaning over.

"Cass!" he cried. "Come on up here! Come on up and have a drink!"

There was no movement from the figure below: only the steady, laborious breathing. Mason called again, still not harshly but with rising impatience and with a blunt imperative tone, like that of a military person to a slow-thinking or half-deaf subordinate. *"Sonofabitch,"* I heard him mutter fretfully. Then he turned abruptly and clattered down the stairway, taking the steps two at a time and landing flat-footedly in the courtyard, where he paused for an instant, arms flailing about as he regained his balance and then sprinted past all the movie machines across the tiles to Cass' side. I heard them mumbling to one another, first Mason's voice, affable and insincere, saying, "Come on up, pal, and join the fun," then Cass' mumbled unintelligible reply, and Mason's voice again, growing more and more impatient but still under control as he gave Cass a big swat between the shoulder blades—"Don't be a miserable spoilsport!" I heard him say, louder—and turned him around, half-supporting him about the waist, and led him slowly back across the courtyard to the stairway. Cass was drunker than he had been an hour before, if that was possible. He looked now like a man pitched on the edge of total ruin, his eyes making comic-strip X's behind his glasses, his arms limp and powerless at his sides. At one point, as he climbed the stairs, I thought he was going to topple over the balustrade. Mason steadied him, grimly. Then when he finally lurched up to the balcony where I was standing, Cass' eyes floated to a point several inches from my face, and I thought for an instant that he winked at me but because of the condition of his eyes I could not be sure.

Mason, panting and excited, released his hold around Cass' waist. "Come on have a drink," he said to him sharply. Then to me: "Cass is going to put on a little show. Cass is a real actor, when he's had one or two under his belt. I might even get Alonzo to get him to turn professional. Is that O.K. with you, Cass?" He tried to smile.

Cass stood before us swaying, hair still in his face, grinning now—slackly and rather stupidly. "Sho', boy, anything you say, anything you say." A crazy, witless chuckle emanated from the back of his throat. " 'M a real actor. Melpomene and Thalia. The sweet goddesses for which—for whom, I should say—old Unc Kinsolving would die. Willingly." He paused and hiccupped. "Willingly. No bullshit, boy. Born to the buskin. Thespis me middle name. Unc'll do anything for a drink." Sweating wildly, he looked up at Mason through his befogged glasses. "Anything for a drink, man. None of this old cookin' whiskey, either. None of this ol' rotgut that'd burn the craw out of a turkey buzzard. *Sippin'* whiskey! That's what Mason serves. *Gentry* whiskey! Good ol' sour mash what never saw the light of day for eight whole years. Tell me, old Mason buddy," he said, laying a big hand on Mason's shoulder, hiccupping again, "tell me, boy, you got any that Jack Daniel's we picked up at the PX today? Any left for old Unc Kinsolving?" From the eloquent, warm-natured, animated person I had encountered that afternoon he had changed into a played-out lush, wheedling and foolish. I felt undermined, disappointed. He was just another one of Mason's sycophants.

"Sure, Cass," said Mason. "You can have all you want. Soon as we put on our little show." And he laughed as he once more grabbed Cass by the arm and propelled him toward the door, but there was a mean glint in his eye. The back of his neck was the color of a boiled lobster; he was seething, and I knew that I could expect the worst. "Come on, lover man," he said sarcastically, pushing Cass along with soft pokes at his shoulder. "Come on, boy. Let's show the folks some *real* entertainment."

Just then—just as we were about to enter the foyer—I heard a small shrill cry from below and another patter of feet crossing the courtyard. I drew back several steps and looked down. It was Poppy. Dressed in a flowered kimono and socks, her yellow hair now most unbeautifully cemented to her head by curlers and bobby pins, she mounted the steps pell-mell, gasping, puffing as she reached the top, where, with small fists clenched and her face red with pouty outrage like a child's, she fell on Mason and began to tug furiously at his arm. "Mason Flagg!" she yelled. "I heard you! I heard what you're up to, you mean person! You let Cass *alone!* Do you hear me? You let him alone!" In her faded kimono, she looked worn and poor, but she was lovely.

Mason turned on her. "Go on away!" he snapped. Then he added more temperately, with his forced smile: "Take it easy, Poppy. We're just going to have us a little fun. Isn't that right, Cass?"

"Don't say anything to him, Cass!" Poppy shrilled, in a frenzied, broken voice. "He's going to mistreat you! He's just going to shame and humiliate you like he did before!" She glared up at Mason—bristling with fury, her eyes brimful with tears and hugely round —still tugging at his arm. "Why *are* you such a mean, evil person!" she cried. "Why do you want to do this to him! Can't you see the condition he's in? Don't you know he loses all *command* of himself when he's like this? Oh please," she wailed, with a despairing, imploring gaze, "please leave him alone and let me put him to bed! Don't shame him any more!" She glared at me, pleading. "Please, Mr. Leverett, please make him stop. He's so sick, Cass is! And now Mason wants to put him on *display!*" She wheeled again on Mason and stamped her foot. "You brute! It's not *funny* any more, Mason! It's horrible. Oh, I hate you! I hate you! I hate you!" And she put her face in her hands and began to cry.

"Maybe you'd better let him alone like she says," I suggested. "Maybe you'd better, Mason."

"You keep out of this, Buster Brown," he retorted, throwing me a look of contempt. I think it was at this moment (and it came with staggering belatedness, considering what had passed between us since I landed in Sambuco) that I realized for the first time that Mason, in the midst of all his gross and preposterous dissimulation, actually disliked me as much as I did him. Each of us had changed, at last, beyond recapture. His eyes lingered on me. "You keep out of this, hear?" he repeated, and he turned briefly to Poppy, casting her a look of amusement and disdain. Then, "Come on, Lochinvar," he said brusquely to Cass, "in we go."

Cass stumbled heavily against the door. "Thass all right, my girl, my little girl," he said in a thick garbled voice to Poppy, regaining his balance. "Don't you cry for me. Me an' ol' Mason gonna have us a ball, isn't we, pal? Fun and games, like always. How's about a little tiny nip of that Jack Daniel's, Mason, just to start everything off right?"

Mason said nothing and pushed Cass forward. Poppy trailed in their wake, tears streaming down her face.

"Quiet, everybody! Quiet, please!" Mason clapped his hands, and his voice boomed through the huge room, bringing the music to a stop and causing the dancers to halt in their tracks. "Quiet, please!" Mason shouted again. He was grinning broadly but his jacket was drenched in sweat: he seemed eaten up by some furious inner agitation. "Quiet!" he cried. "Will the ladies and gentlemen present please gather around for the evening's special attraction! Kindly step forward in this direction if you will!" Slowly the guests edged forward to the place where Mason and Cass were standing in the foyer. The party had thinned out considerably. It must have been close to two, and many of the people had retired, I supposed, to the Bella Vista or to their rooms in the palace. Alice Adair was gone, as were Morton Baer and Dawn O'Donnell, but I saw Gloria Mangiamele undulating toward us and, among the others, Rosemarie and the crew-cut young man, who had become cross-eyed drunk, and my other *bête-noire,* the assistant director Van Rensselaer Rappaport. In all, I imagine a dozen people were left, and while Mason shouted and clapped his hands they gathered in a cluster around him.

"Wot happen your pretty face, darlings?" said Gloria Mangiamele with a giggle, sidling up to Mason and putting an arm around him.

"I fell into a thicket," he replied abstractedly. "Will all you people—"

"Ticket?" said Mangiamele, puzzled. "How can one fall into a ticket?" I glanced at Rosemarie: she was a pale portrait of misery.

"Will all you people please come closer? Thank you. Tonight we have for you a special surprise attraction," he said, gesturing toward Cass. His voice had become rich and magniloquent, like that of a circus ringmaster, and his face still wore the stiff, absurd, almost painted smile. "I want to present to you ladies and gentlemen Cass Kinsolving, the greatest personality, the greatest one-man show since the days of the great departed Jolson. Isn't that right, Cass? Speak up, Cass. Let's have your pedigree."

For an instant in the background I saw Poppy, biting her lip and fighting back tears, reach out to clutch at Cass, but he was lurching forward now, grinning his foolish grin, and with lumbering steps he moved up and came to a standstill next to Mason, where he remained weaving and grinning like some shambling burly bear in the center, so to speak, of the stage. His T-shirt hung sloppily out around his hips, his pants were stained, his glasses askew upon his flushed and perspiring face; standing there yawing precariously he looked husky and vaguely professorial and afflicted by some profound, voiceless melancholy, despite his grin, like a lost and drunken scholar on a Bowery corner, contemplating his inward ruin. Among these suavely varnished people, he did indeed look as out of place as a Skid Row bum. I heard Mangiamele giggle, then someone else laughed. There was a stir of anticipation in the crowd, a rustle of dresses. "He's simply priceless," I heard a French accent murmur, and turned to see the neck of an elderly fairy craning over my shoulder. Rosemarie had pointed him out to me earlier: a celebrated couturier—Jacques Something-or-other—of whom I should have heard, but hadn't. His neck was a pinkish neck, and wattled, like a vulture's. "Where on earth did Mason find *him?*"

"Come on," Mason repeated impatiently, "come on, Cass. Let's have the old pedigree."

Cass hesitated for a second, scratching his head. "In answer to your application, my parentage and age, et cetera," he said finally, in a thick voice, "my mother was a bus horse . . . my father a cab driver . . . my sister a rough rider over the arctic regions . . . and my brothers were all gallant sailors on a steamroller." It took no time at all to say. He said it mechanically, dreamily, as if by rote, and when he had finished he grinned again at Mason, in search of approval. It was a look that seemed so automatic, so predetermined, that I almost expected Mason to throw him a fish, or a hunk of meat. For a moment there was a complete silence—a silence you could touch, fraught with an overwhelming, general bafflement and uneasiness. I felt myself tensing up and sweating. No one uttered a sound. And then as Mason, still smiling, fixed upon Cass his intense, magisterial gaze, someone on the other side of me laughed. It was a hoarse, masculine laugh—raw and side-splitting—and it had the instant quality of contagion: someone next to me began to guffaw, then another, then another, until the whole crowd was let loose upon a flood of whooping, hysterical laughter which rebounded from the ceiling and the walls and washed around us in wave on senseless wave. They laughed and laughed; and they laughed, I suppose, because they were at that stage in drunkenness, or inertia, or boredom, where they were ready to laugh at anything. In the midst of it all Cass stood with the sweat glistening from the bristles of a stubbly beard, dreamy and remote, oblivious of the racket, grinning and swaying as if upon his far-off and desolate street corner. There was a quality about him so totally spent, so defeated, that it was almost repellent. All of his vigor and manhood seemed drained away, and his big muscular hands fell limp and flaccid at his sides; he grinned, giggled a bit, gave a sudden lurch sideways, righted himself. Then finally the laughter diminished, died. Mangiamele, who I was sure had not understood half of Cass' brief speech, still wheezed and trembled with convulsive laughter, breasts heaving, hands upthrust in helpless mirth to her lovely empurpled face. Between spasms she paused to stare at Cass with a look of simple idiocy, and I suddenly realized that she had no more of a brain than a gnat. Mason disengaged her arm from his waist, stepping forward.

"Well done, Cass boy," he said. "Now how about the Honest Abe bit?"

"Sho', man," Cass replied sluggishly. "Sho'. Anything you say."

"Billy," Mason said to the colored piano player, "how about a few bars of 'Old Black Joe'?" He turned and addressed the gathering. "This, good people, is a song about Honest Abe Lincoln. For the benefit of the non-Americans present, Lincoln was a president of the U.S.A., the Great Emancipator, also something of a liar and a slob, though you'd never know it." There was an appropriate titter as Mason once again retired, pushing Cass forward, and the piano, maestoso, set loose the first chords of "Old Black Joe." Cass sang, in a thick glutinous voice.

"I'm Honest Abe,
With whiskers on my chin . . .
I freed the slabe,
My face is . . . on . . . the . . . fin . . ."

The tempo was excruciatingly slow. I thought he would never get the words out. Worse, he had no voice at all, so that as he stood there with his eyes squinted shut and strove to track the gentle melody down its labyrinthine way, he hit no note at all on key but hoarsely blurted out each word almost at random, and was several beats behind everywhere. His voice was almost drowned out in the hoots and wails of merriment.

"I nev-er tole
No-thin but . . . the . . . truth . . .
Howcome you pulled the trigger on me,
John . . . Wilkes . . . Booth?"

The laughter showered around him, wave on wave. He stood with his eyes closed, as if dreaming, grinning his sleepy grin, deaf to all. "Now the Rebel yell!" Mason shouted above the uproar. "Don't forget the Rebel yell!" And at this Cass, much as if he had been shocked out of some profound and amnesic sleep, came suddenly alive. He threw back his head and cupped his hands around his mouth and let out an ear-splitting, screeching noise which sent shivers running up and down my back.

"YAlHeeeeeeee!" he howled. "YAHOO-eeeeeeee!" Over and over he roared the pointless, bloodcurdling phrase, screeching like a banshee or like one demented, while the crowd around me, convulsed, visibly wilting beneath the onslaught, clutched one another, grinning as they averted their faces and clapped their hands against their ears. Cass howled on, like some ferocious horn or whistle running wild, unstoppered by Mason's perverse and unfathomable will. *"YAlHeeeeeeee!"* Senselessly he kept bellowing his outlandish cry, until I thought it would bring the plaster crumbling from the walls. The two scullery maids, trailed by Giorgio, popped out into the hallway wringing their hands, eyes rolling white with terror, and a Persian cat sprang from nowhere, its fuzz raised in stiff alarm, and sailed like a rocket out through the door. And then other people appeared. Like a churchyard transfigured by the trump of Judgment Day, the palace began to disgorge its slumberers, who with dressing gowns and bathrobes wound around them came forth squinting, barefooted, and with the aspects of those who foresee unspeakable horror. Pasty-white, Dawn O'Donnell was first, followed by Alice Adair, and then a couple of wild-haired Italian men in their underdrawers, and finally Alonzo Cripps, looking tense and insomniac and with a cigarette twitching upon his lips. It was he—when Cass' screams finally subsided—who approached Mason with an air of incredulity, and became the first to speak up. "What the hell's going on, Mason?" he said.

"Just having a little fun, Alonzo. Cass here's entertaining the folks. He's what in show business we call a laugh riot. Isn't that right, Cass?"

"Sho', boy," Cass replied in an empty voice, between wheezes. "Sho', boy, anything you say. How's about a little nip of that Jack Dan—"

"We thought someone was being murdered," said Dawn O'Donnell.

"Well, how about keeping it down a bit," Cripps said. "Some of us have to work tomorrow." He was in a spot: he was obviously raging but he kept himself in check, I'm sure, because Mason was his host. He turned then, and his eyes fell on Cass, registering pain. "Why don't you lay off him, Mason?" he said quietly. "I don't think this sort of thing is particularly funny any more. What's the point, anyway? I'd think you'd had enough by now. Look at him."

Cass turned groggily, and made a slow military salute, British-style, palm turned out over his eyebrow. "Good evening, Director. Glad to have you aboard."

"Leave him alone, why don't you?" Cripps said almost amiably, holding himself back. "Don't you ever get enough, Mason?" It was a moment which should have been tenser than it was: what Cripps had said, after all, had been in the nature of a challenge, and a public one at that. But the guests—harmoniously convivial, well soused, and desperately bored—echoed none of Cripps' feeling. They buzzed and chortled: "Go on back to bed, Alonzo," I heard someone say; their cheeks were red and their armpits were wet and they were out for entertainment—or blood. Even the roused sleepers joined in the happy mood—Alice and Dawn, moving in closer for a better view, and the two Italians who in their jockey shorts looked as poised and unruffled as a couple of ambassadors and scratched their hairy bellies, sniggering, and relaxed.

"Don't be a hard-nose, Alonzo," said Mason airily. "Jesus sake, get yourself some sleep. The party's just begun."

And then Mason made Cass recite a long series of limericks. Everyone came very close to collapse. If they had been amused before, they were now nearly helpless, and in their merriment they got careless with their elbows and stepped on each other's feet, and my own, and sloshed whiskey all down their wrists.

"The director of the American Academy," Cass recited in his solemn lethargic tone.

"Has a most peculiar anatomy . . ."

His eyes were glazed, and he was no longer smiling; all the blood had drained from his face and the sweat seemed to have evaporated from his brow, leaving him looking parched and dry and accentuating that expression he had had at first, on the stairs, of pale sickness or of poison. He finished the verse in a husky, broken voice, tinged and tired with melancholy. The laughter crashed around him.

"Hoo! . . . hoo! . . . *hoo!*" The voice of the French dressmaker was shrill in my ear, and I suddenly realized that it had been steady and constant all along—an unwavering high-pitched squeal.

"Now the one, Cass," said Mason, chuckling, patting him on the back. "Now the one about the maiden from Nassau. And then the one about the lewd Prioress—Chatham, or you know what."

And then, as Cass began to croak out another limerick and as I gazed at him, keeping Mason in the corner of my eye, all of those feelings and suspicions and apprehensions which had been stirring about at the back of my consciousness suddenly jerked into place in the forefront of my mind, made vividly clear.

Mason *had* Cass, had him securely in hand, just as in an entirely different but no less impregnable way—up until this night, at least—he had had me. And as I looked at Cass, and as then I looked at Mason—at that slick, arrogant, sensual, impenitently youthful, American and vainglorious face to which I had paid for so long my guilt-laden fealty—I shuddered at the narrowness of my escape, and at my ignorance. And I felt sorry indeed for Cass. The Prioress of Chatham wound up upon a thunderous hullabaloo, surpassing all yet for hysteria, and now it occurred to me that stranger, even more abominable things were taking place. "This'll shatter you," I heard Mason say, in what seemed a remote and unreal voice—only half-heard because my attention was now fixed upon two babies in nightgowns who had crept wide-eyed through the door. They were Cass'—the oldest boy and the oldest girl—and they gazed with searching, lovely, bewildered eyes around the room until they spied Poppy and hand in hand marched swiftly to her side. Deep silent sobs racked her gentle frame, and she bit in anguish at the sleeve of her kimono, and with one hand gathered her children to her as she watched the scene. Rosemarie, I noticed, had vanished from the room.

"O.K. O.K., Cass," I heard Mason say, his back turned now. "You'll get something to drink. After the *exhibition* bit."

"Oh, stop him someone, please!" Poppy's thin wail soared above the hubbub. "Stop—"

"This is an authentic re-creation of a Paris *exhibition,* as practiced only in the highest-class establishments of Montmartre. Proceed, Cass, old dollbaby."

And in cold horror I saw Cass get down onto his knees. *"Messieurs, dames, c'est comme-ci que l'on fait l'amour en Norvège."* He leered up drunkenly at the bemused guests, amber disks of light glinting from his glasses. As big and as hulking as he was, hunched over like a great desolate animal in this ignoble posture, his voice with its flawless accent was a simper, a prissy obscene lilt at once high-pitched and vacuous and dripping over with apathy —a perfect imitation of a Paris whore. "In Norway, the way they do it . . ." And then, stupidly licking his lips, adjusting his feet, his long maniac's hair dangling down over his face, he poised himself to duplicate in parody that act which even the Paphian gods above—had they had the eyes—would have mourned to see brought to such degradation. *"En Norvège . . ."* But he never made it, and the crowd had no more time to laugh. For an instant I saw myself in that same position—clownish, prostrate, and dishonored. I sprang to his side—beaten there by Alonzo Cripps, who, pulling Cass to his feet, supporting him, looked at Mason with black loathing.

"That'll be enough of this, do you hear?" Cripps said.

"But Jesus, Alonzo—" Mason began in a whine.

"That'll be *enough,* I said."

Poppy pushed through the crowd toward Cass and fell on his shoulder, sobbing. His head was lolling on his chest. "Sorry, my little girl," I heard him say in a muffled, stricken voice. "Oh Christ, I'm sorry."

I suppose Cripps sensed in me an ally. "Why don't you help get him downstairs?" he murmured. I was holding Cass up with all my might. "I never saw such a disgusting business in all my life." This was an aside from Cripps, but I know that Mason heard it.

"Jesus sake, Alonzo," Mason began, "it was only fun and games—" But Cripps had already vanished down the hallway. An admirable man, above sordid involvements.

The guests dispersed quietly, melting into the night. I have no clear idea what their reactions were, being too busy with Cass to tell or care, but they were silent, and the silence seemed to be an unregenerate one, full of sulkiness and disappointment rather than shame. Together with Poppy, and with the children tagging after, I tugged and labored Cass toward the door.

"Why are you *up,* children?" Poppy said, sniffling. Then she turned back and looked at Mason, standing alone with a baffled, unhappy expression in the foyer. "Mason Flagg!" she cried. "You're a dirty, wicked man!" He made no reply.

"You and your goddam phony buffalo!" I added, as we staggered out the door. Since they were the last words I said to him ever, they have caused me more than one twinge of remorse, in spite of all he did.

"I've got to get sober, I've *got* to get sober," he muttered beneath his breath, over and over. "Got things to do. Thanks, Leverett. Poppy, make me a whole lot of hot coffee. I've got to get sober." We pushed and pulled Cass through the cable-tangled courtyard.

"Well, for heaven's sake, Cass," said Poppy in her small childish voice, panting as she tugged him along. "Heaven's sakes alive! I told you to get sober this morning. You just won't listen to me! You're just a—a reprobate, that's all."

"Reprobate," he mumbled. "I've got to get sober."

"You're so *obstinate,* Cass," she mourned, still sniffling. "Think of the children! They saw you doing that disgusting thing!"

"We saw you!" the children chimed in from behind. Slim in their nightgowns, their eyes dark and grave, they looked as bright and beautiful and fresh as a couple of daisies. "We saw you, Daddy!"

"Oh, *Mama!*" Cass groaned, stumbling over a cable. "Did I really do what I think I did?"

"Think of your ulcer!" Poppy said.

"Jesus God, I'm a lunatic. Sober me up!"

We entered through the green door and into the Kinsolvings' part of the palace. This—or at least as much of it as I could discover at first glance—was a cavernous, dimly lit room with large French doors at the far end which, like Mason's, gave out upon the somber, twinkling sea. Otherwise there was no resemblance to Mason's dwelling, and perhaps it was just the comedown, or letdown, from the magnetic grandeur above which fortified my sense here of anarchic housekeeping and grubby disorder. Or perhaps it was the diaper on the floor at the entranceway, which made a wet sloshing noise beneath my feet. Whatever, as Cass lurched forward and fell face downward on a ratty couch and as Poppy hurried off with the children into another room, I was certain, as I stood there blinking, that I had never seen such squalor. Dishes and coffee cups were everywhere. In the air hovered a troublesome, gamy, enigmatic odor not precisely, but not far removed from, decay, as of a place where garbage cans languish days on end in unfulfillment. The piled-up stumps of cigars protruded from half a dozen ashtrays, or had been squashed down into empty wine and Coca-Cola bottles, one of which still fulminated with greenish, greasy smoke. Comic books in Italian littered the floor, where Mickey Mouse had suffered a change to Topolino, along with Stefano Canyon and Il Piccolo Abner and Superuomo. Across one half of the room a bediapered clothesline sagged damp-looking and redolent, while from the only hopeful-looking object in the room—a large wooden easel—a tattered rag doll grotesquely dangled with stricken button eyes, as from a gallows. Upon his couch Cass called out loudly and hoarsely to Poppy for coffee. Then as I accustomed my eyes to the haze in this benighted room, I saw what at first I was certain was the wraith of Pancho Villa come out from the distant shadows—a young, round-faced, mustachioed *carabiniere,* bandoliered to the neck and flashing his white front teeth in a yawn, who clanked and rattled obscurely as he approached through a swarm of flies and greeted me with a melancholy *"Buonase'!."*

I fairly expected, in the morbid state I was in, to be arrested, but the cop—languidly picking his teeth as he strolled past me—paid me no attention as he sauntered over to the couch and laid his hand on Cass' shoulder. *"Povero Cass,"* he sighed. *"Sempre ubriaco. Sempre sbronzo. Come va, amico mio? O.K.?"* His voice was subdued, sad, almost tender.

For a moment Cass said nothing. Then I heard his muffled voice from the pillow, in lazy, fluid Italian: "Not so *O.K.,* Luigi. Uncle's had a bad night. Sober me up, Luigi. I've got things to do."

Bending over him, the cop spoke in his gentle tones. "You got to go to bed, Cass. Sleep. That's the best thing for you. Sleep. What you've got to do can wait till morning."

Cass rolled over with a groan, laying his forearm over his eyes, breathing hoarsely. "Jesus," he said, "it's all going round and round. I'm a lunatic, Luigi. What time is it? What in God's name are you doing here at this hour?"

"Parrinello put me on night duty. The swine. Again I'll swear it's because I'm an intellectual, and he's an unreasoning blockhead who despises thought." (An intellectual policeman! I could hardly believe my ears.) "I more than half-expected it. You remember my telling you—"

Cass interrupted him with another groan from the couch. "Come off it, Luigi. My heart bleeds for you as ever. But I've got *real* troubles. I've got to get sober. Poppy!" he yelled. "Hurry up with that coffee!" He rolled over on his side, blinking up at the policeman. "What time did you say it was? I've got bugs in my head."

"After two o'clock, Cass," said Luigi. "I was up by the hotel. There's some cinema equipment outdoors that I'm supposed to keep an eye on. You know these peasants from the valley; they'd dismantle a steamboat and haul it away, give them the time and the opportunity. Anyway, I heard the glorious strains of Mozart, very loud, coming from the palace, and I knew you were up. So I came for a chat, and what did I find?" He spread his arms wide. "Nothing. You gone. Poppy gone. The *bambini* gone. Only the record machine going *ss-put, ss-put, ss-put!* I shut it off, and sat down to watch after the other two children. It wasn't like you to leave the machine on like that. You'll ruin *Don Giovanni* that way."

Cass eased himself up and sat on the edge of the couch, looking woozily around him. "Thanks, Luigi," he said. "You're a prince. Jesus, I really saw a big vacuum there for a while. A big fantastic vacuum. You could hear me all the way to the hotel? It's a wonder Sergeant Parrinello himself wasn't down on me." He shook his head violently, as if to clear it of the obstructing shadows. I sensed a battle and a struggle: he seemed, very gradually, to be emerging from the shrouds of his drunkenness, like a beleaguered swimmer hauling himself up inch by inch onto the dry safeguarding shore. He shook his head again, then banged it with the flat of his hand, as if dislodging water from his ears. "Let me think," he said, then more loudly: "Let me think! What have I got to do?" His eyes caught mine and he gave a start: I think he had forgotten about my presence entirely. "Well," he said in English with a smile, "old man Leverett. By God, I think I owe you something, although what," he added, taking off his glasses and massaging his weary, red-rimmed eyes, "what, and for what, and how much I have no way of telling." He got up, his arm outstretched to shake my hand, but stumbled on one of the unnumbered nameless objects littering the floor and, collapsing back onto the bed again, began to cough hoarsely and in racking spasms. *"Questi sigari italiani!"* he howled at Luigi between fits of coughing. "What are they made of, these cigars! Dung of goats! Excrement of priests! Luigi, I tell you—hack! hack!—I've got to be x-rayed. I'm turning to mush inside—hack!—the way I torment my poor old bag of guts! Sober me up, for the love of God! I've got things to do!"

"Povero Cass," Luigi breathed sympathetically, "why do you persist still in drowning yourself, abusing yourself, annihilating yourself? Why don't you take a pill and go to sleep?"

I scrutinized Luigi in the dim light. He was a well-built, neatly barbered young man, not unhandsome despite a tendency to beetle brows and an expression, common to cops everywhere, of dogged, almost prayerful humorlessness. Frowning down at Cass, he looked tired and discontented: cops the world over are underpaid, but where the blue eyes of a New York policeman are often terrifying, and those of a Parisian spiteful and hysteric, the eyes of an Italian *carabiniere* reflect only a ceaseless, calm, melancholy yearning for money, which is possibly the reason why, more than a policeman almost anywhere else, he is constantly being bribed. "Why do you persist on this dangerous course, Cass?" he said. "Haven't I been trying to impress on you for months the terrible hazards of this way of life of yours? Don't you know that the consequences may very well prove fatal? Don't you know that the trouble in your stomach is no longer a laughing matter? And without, I hope, sounding too pompous, may I ask you whether in your heart of hearts you have really pictured to yourself the whole horrible vista of eternity?"

"Gesù Cristo!" I heard Cass moan. "An Italian Calvinist!"

Luigi looked at me mournfully, briefly, the expression that of a doctor who has just divined the worst. "No, Cass," he went on to the supine figure, still racked with coughs, "no, my dear friend, I am not a religious man, as you all too well know—"

"You're a Fascist, which is no better," Cass replied in a tempered, casual voice. "How *could* you be a Fascist, Luigi?"

"I'm not a religious man," Luigi went on, ignoring him, "and this you well know. However, I studied among the humanist philosophers—the Frenchman Montaigne, Croce, the Greek Plato, not to speak, of course, of Gabriele D'Annunzio—and if there's one thing of the highest value I've discovered, it is simply this: that the primary moral sin is self-destruction—the wish for death which you so painfully and obviously manifest. I exclude madness, of course. The single good is respect for the force of life. Have you not pictured to yourself the whole horrible vista of

195

eternity? I've told you all this before, Cass. The absolute blankness, *il niente, la nullità,* stretching out for ever and ever, the pit of darkness which you are hurling yourself into, the nothingness, the void, the oblivion? Yet are you unable to see that although this in itself is awful, it is nothing to the moral sin you commit by willing yourself *out* of that life-force so celebrated by D'Annunzio, and by willing thus, to doom your wife and children to the hell of fatherlessness, to the unspeakable—"

"Luigi, you're a crackpot," Cass said in an offhand tone, getting to his feet. "I love you like a brother—" He turned to me with a grin, planting, at the same time, his big hand on Luigi's shoulder. He was still as high as a kite, and he swayed a bit, but he had lost that distant look of oblivion which had been all over his face during the fiasco upstairs. "He's really a great fellow, Leverett," he said, still in Italian. "Why don't you two shake hands, you two intellectuals?" Gravely, and with a polite dignified bow, Luigi took my outstretched hand. "Imagine a lovely fellow who's a Fascist! And a humanist! Did you ever hear of anything so absurd in your life? Look at him—a Fascist! And he wouldn't hurt a little bird!"

"I'm no one's weakling," Luigi said stiffly.

"Of course you're not," Cass said, gouging him amiably in the ribs. "Of course you're not, my friend. But you're a crackpot. You shouldn't be an Italian cop, making next to nothing in a little miserable town in Campania, getting corns all over your feet. You should take off that uniform and go to Southern California. You'd make millions! Luigi Migliore, Consultant in Humanist Philosophy! With your looks you'd make a treasure, besides getting all the loving you could possibly handle. Why all those crazy, desiccated, brainless women would be over you like grease. You'd have an office, and a couch, and you could get one of those beautiful dumb California blondes on the couch and gabble to her about that noble humanist philospher, Gabriele D'Annunzio, and the whole horrible vista of eternity, and in about two seconds you'd be up to your groin—pardon me—in love, you'd—"

"It's tasteless to joke about such matters," Luigi said bleakly. "Besides, as you know, I have no desire to go to America. I'm earnestly worried about you, Cass."

"Sciocchezze!" Cass said, throwing up his hands. "I never heard such nonsense in my life. All Italians want to go to America. *All* of them! Why don't you break down and admit it, Luigi? You *love* America. You *adore* it! Don't try to fool Uncle Cass."

"I should prefer not to talk about it," Luigi replied, frowning. "And I see no point in remaining here if it's your scheme in mind to make me out a fool. You try my patience, Cass. You protest your friendship but you joke too much. I attempt constantly to be your friend, because I've felt that you and I are fellow spirits." He paused and shrugged. "I've simply been trying to help, and you make jokes."

"I know it, Luigi, I know it," said Cass. "I'm a hopeless drunk on the skids, and I need a helping hand. I love you like a brother. You've been my shield and defender, besides drinking up all my vermouth. But please don't babble on about the horrible vista of eternity. How in God's name do you know what eternity is like? You're just trying to scare me, Luigi."

"Eternity is horrible to contemplate," he said without humor. "*Nullità, oscurità,* like never-ending snow. That is my conception of it. A dark whiteness—"

"What absurdity, Luigi! Suppose I told you why dying was good? Suppose I told you that eternity was a soft quiet place, with grass and rocks and running water, and blue sky above, and sheep in the fields, and the sound of pipes and tinkling bells? Suppose I told you, my dear friend, that eternity was not too unlike the lovely little village of Tramonti back in the valley, which you so ignore and despise? Suppose I told you that eternity was like slaking one's thirst in a spring of waters that comes down from the snows of the Apennines, where one may lie under the cedars and see all the sweet girls dancing and capering far off on a sunny lawn, and lie there, in endless serenity and repose? Suppose I told you that? What would you think, Luigi? Would I be right or would you? Would you believe me?"

"I would think," said Luigi, solemn as an owl, "I would think that you would be indulging in middle-class romanticism. You would be telling me a mawkish fable. As D'Annunzio says, 'All life is here and now—' "

"*Vero,* Luigi! I do believe you're right. But let's cease this feverish chatter. I have things to do yet. You distract me from becoming sober. Hey, Poppy!" he yelled again over his shoulder. "*Porta il caffè, subito! E due aspirine!*" He turned to me with a slow grin, continuing casually, almost unconsciously, in that limpid, flowing Italian at which he seemed to be as enviably adept as at his native tongue. "I can only offer you a glass of Sambuco *rosso,*" he said, adding, "my wine steward absconded with the keys and left us clean out of Jack Daniel's."

197

"No thanks," I said in American, "but I could do with some coffee and a couple of those aspirins."

"*Quattro aspirine!*" he roared at Poppy. Then, sitting down on the couch once more, his shoulders lurching unsteadily, he proceeded to go about uncorking a bottle of red wine. Luigi regarded him sadly and soberly. "I have to be going back to my *giro*, Cass. I find myself greatly upset at leaving you in this condition. Are you proposing now to drink another whole bottle of wine? I think you're mad." He put his cap on his head and made a slow move toward the door. "Now I think you're mad. I find it impossible to deal with madmen. They will surely take you to Salerno and put you in the lunatic asylum. And everyone will be grievously sorry —except no doubt yourself. But there's nothing more that I can do. *Buonanotte.*" And with a lingering, dismal, hangdog expression he drifted out through the doorway, popping his head back in for one last minatory utterance: "I have seen the madhouse in Salerno with my own eyes. I have seen it, Cass. It surpasses anything you can imagine. It is *medieval.*" Then he was gone.

"Wonderful guy," Cass said, struggling with the cork. "Should be a lawyer in Naples or something, instead of a hick cop, but I guess he's too much of a nut. You never saw such a weird mind. Imagine! A Fascist humanist! I'll tell you about him sometime. Also a mystic. Jesus!" He uncorked the bottle with a pop. "Have a shot of Sambuco *rosso*."

"No thanks," I said, "I'll stick with that coffee." I paused. "Why don't you lay off it for a while, Cass?" I said as offhandedly as possible. "After all, you said yourself you wanted to dry out, you had things to do . . ."

He gazed long at the bottle and at the floor, then looked up at me with an ingratiating smile. He hesitated; several flies began to make a drowsy, buzzing sortie around our heads. "Well by God," he said finally, "you know, you couldn't be righter. A bleeding sweet guardian angel, that's what you are. Come down from the heavens to deliver poor old Cass from the gorge of the predacious nobby anthropoid. To deliver from his wan lips this cup of—" He looked at the bottle sourly and bitterly. "Of poison." Suddenly he heaved the bottle away across the room; falling unbroken, miraculously, among the litter on the floor, it left a long splash of crimson against the wall. "I never did that in my life before." He chuckled. Then he flopped back on the couch and with his khaki-clad legs in the air began to howl in English and in Italian. "*Brutto maiale!* The filthy dog! God give me strength, give me fortitude! Mother-

defiling jackal! God make my hand strong!" He commenced to
shudder and hack at the same time, horribly, and raised one big
muscular fist toward the ceiling. *"Vigliacco!* Masturbator of small
children! Putrescent shark! Oh Jesus, give me strength! *Jesus!* Is
there no justice? Must I be deprived of wealth and wit and sanity
and pride, and then be deprived of *guts!* Jesus love me!" he roared
as if in entreaty to the heavens. "Is there no way to down the
slummocky obscene swine? Is there no way, Lord! Ah my my,
give me the guts to face him down and I'll drag him by his moldy
balls through the new Jerusalem!" Abruptly he ceased and lay
back with a tremendous shudder and a sigh. Then after a spell of
silence he said with a groan, and in a leaden stricken voice which
had no longer any exuberance in it, or humor, but only the pure
accents of despair: "Somebody's dying, Leverett. Somebody's
dying and I've got to help. I've got to be sober enough to be a
clever thief." He paused for a moment, and while I tried to figure
out what he was getting at I heard his breath going in and out in a
husky agitated whistle. "I hate to put you out. You've been a
prince. But somebody's dying. And I don't mean me. No bullshit,
boy. This is a heavy matter. If you could—if you would sort of
deal with me and smack me around or something, and give me a
shot of something, and help fix me so I could—so I could burglarize
this item, I'd be eternally grateful. I've got to steady up, boy.
You've done a noble—" At this moment Poppy in her sleazy
kimono, still coifed in unsightly curlers, rustled through the door
with a potful of coffee.

"Well, Cass Kinsolving," she said with a scowl, "will you please
finally just quit hollering like an elephant or something and go to
bed?" She set down two cups before us and poured the coffee; on
the surface of mine I saw rising one of her blond hairs. "You're
the limit, Cass," she said as she swished about. "The very limit!
Getting drunk over and over again and letting Mason shame and
humiliate you like that. And now you're keeping the children
awake! Why don't you try to be *nice* for a while?" As she fetched a
sugar bowl and a shriveled-up lemon from the cluttered sideboard,
I studied her charming little face. Even in curlers and with cold
cream in shiny gloss upon her cheeks she was like a sprite,
touchingly, unelaborately lovely and slightly wild; there was something about her both unearthly and demure: she looked as if she
might have flitted out of a wood. "And you use your awful words,"
she went on. "When you get this way. I've been trying to teach
the children proper English and proper Italian and you use those

terrible words. Not to even speak," she added, her nostrils flaring angrily, "of the name of Our Father. Jiminy, Cass! Don't you see what it can do to their psychology!" She threw two orange-colored pellets onto the table.

"What are these?" Cass inquired unhappily.

"Baby aspirin," she said. "That's all there is. It's from that bottle Mason got us— Oh, that terrible person!"

"Lord God," he said with a groan, thrusting his face into his hands. "Lord God, Poppy, why don't you *minister* to me! I've got a headache!" He looked up at her briefly and dizzily; then he looked at me, as if calling upon me to witness his affliction. He shook his head and slurped noisily at the coffee. "It's a trick on the menfolk," he said sadly. "He filled us full of hormones and He made us commit the act of darkness and in the glory of our youth He struck us down with a blight of screeching tadpoles. An evil trick. Look around you, Leverett! Did you ever see such a misbegotten abomination of a draggle-assed quagmire? This is supposed to be my studio—pardon the pretension. I used to paint and things like that. Look at it, for Christ sake! Mickey Mouse. Diapers. Dolls. Old venerable anchovies underneath the couch; that's that stench you smell, they've been there for months. Are you a single man, Leverett? Absorb if you will then this portrait of dosmes—excuse me, domesticity, and take heed. Marry a Catholic, and it's like being retired to stud. Did you ever see anything like it? I'll swear before Christ nothing exists like it west of the slums of Bangkok. Did you ever see its likes before? Lord, my head aches!"

"The place looks fine to me," I said, lying extravagantly as I gazed up at Poppy.

"Well goodness, Cass," she exclaimed, "it's not as neat as it could be, but if you're so smart why don't *you* take care of four children and everything, and cook, and wash clothes and everything, with only a part-time girl to help, and then—"

"Go to bed, Poppy," he cut her off abruptly, without emotion. "Just go to bed. I've got to go out."

"Cass Kinsolving! You'll do nothing of the—"

"Go to bed now!" he said. His voice was that of a father with a headstrong child, not unkindly but very firm. "Go the hell to bed."

Her face blazed up and she tossed her head, but she gathered her kimono about her and swept in insult toward the door. "You just go to the dickens!" she said, with a catch in her voice, as she sashayed out, lyric and lovely and impossible. "Sometimes I think you're absolutely *pazzo* in the head!"

"That's two tonight who've pegged me for a loony—two besides myself," he said morosely when she had gone.

I watched him as he sat there in gloomy silence, staring down into the dregs of his coffee. I didn't see how he would be able to go on. Yet again I sensed the urgent interior struggle: out of sheer power of will, right before my eyes, he seemed to be casting off the layers of drunkenness and obfuscation that encompassed him, much in the manner of a dog, rising from the mud, who by successive violent shakes becomes purified and cleansed. It was as if he were actually thrashing about. Something held him in torment and in great and desperate need: I never saw anyone I wanted so to get sober.

All at once he rose to his feet. "Now you've got to be my will power, boy," he muttered. "Come on." I followed him down the steps into the dank darkness of the lower level of the house, puzzled by what he had just said, until he explained that he had to take a cold shower—in order to complete the process of purgation—but that he lacked the strength of character, at this point, to keep from turning the hot water on. He snapped on a light in the noxious bathroom, where more diapers lay in soggy disarray upon the floor. "Me, I've gotten used to it," he said with a note of apology as he undressed. "I come in here and shave, and I pretend I'm on a hillside somewhere, smelling the pungent fern and the trailing arbutus. Now—" he exclaimed, climbing over the rim of the tub and standing rigidly with closed eyes beneath the shower. He thrust out his arm toward me. "Here, hold me glasses. Let her rip." I turned on the cold water, frigid from mountain streams, full blast. He let out a yell. "That's it!" he cried as the water splashed and cascaded over him. He shivered and trembled and held his breath, groaning, his lips working as if in prayer. "That's it! Keep it up! Mother of Christ! . . . I'm a bleeding Spartan! . . . Keep it up, Leverett! . . . *Sacramento!* . . . I'm turning into a . . . bleeding stalagmite!" He howled and screamed there for five minutes beneath the driving spray but after a final whoop, like some crazed mystic announcing divine revelation, gasped that he was Methodist-sober, boy, and with his hair plastered down around his face clambered dripping from the tub.

"Well," he said, stamping around with his eyes closed. "Now I can get down to business." He groped for a towel, but there was none to be had, so he slapped off the water and slithered wetly into his pants. As he dressed he kept up a steady monologue. "No, that's a lie," he said while hopping around on one foot, trying without sitting down to put on a shoe, "I'm not that sober. But I'm sober enough to commit this—this most necessary larceny. Larceny! You know, I haven't stolen anything since the war. I was on this island and I swiped a gallon and a half of grain alcohol from sick bay and I never got over being guilty about it. What a party we threw, though. What a marvelous party! Whenever I think of that party it plain long eradicates all my sense of sin. Sitting down there on the palmy beach with sand between your toes, looking at the moon, downing all that booze. Triple bleeding God! Did you ever drink grain alcohol? You know, you can hardly taste it. And my God, what a thirst I had! Now hand me that comb, will you?" He began to comb his hair at the mirror; his eyes were brighter, his hands steady now. He seemed to be finally in some command of himself, capable of most anything. "A proper thief's got to be well groomed. Whoever heard of a second-story man who wasn't the nattiest thing around? Besides, this is going to be the cleanest wholesome-like little piece of burglary you ever heard about. No grubby old automobile tires or greasy money from a cash register or common degrading articles of merchandise—cigarettes or cameras or fountain pens or anything like that. My God, no! This is going to be *special*. But look!" he exclaimed, staring down at his feet. "I can't wear these clodhoppers. They'd wake up the dead. A proper thief, you know—above all—has to be quietly accoutered around his foots. Else he'll bump up against a prie-dieu or a taboret or a trundle bed or something, or set the joists and beams snapping with his clumsiness, and the whole household in their nightshirts will be down on him like a bunch of hawks. No, my friend. He's got to be shod like a bleeding elf." And, taking off his shoes, he padded across the darkened hallway, where, in a cluttered wardrobe or trunk, I heard him rummaging about, breathing heavily. After a moment he came padding softly back, wearing a pair of sneakers. His expression was tense and solemn. "It suddenly occurred to me," he said, "in my great self-preoccupation, that I might be boring you out of your head. I'm sorry, Leverett. I haven't meant to. Please just say kiss my ass, and get out of here, if you want to. God knows, that's what I'd do if I were you. I—I don't know. It was very decent of you to—to intercede for me up there."

"Mason's a *swine!*" I blurted. "Tell me, Cass, did you—"

He cut me off with a bitter, ugly look. "Don't talk about it," he said. "Just don't talk about it, please. I'm going to do a little burglarizing, that's all, and I don't want to forget myself and foul up.

Look—" he said after a pause, "look, as plastered and fried and piggish as I've been today, there are a few cracks of light I remember. One was you, down on the road this afternoon. I don't know why, but I have the feeling I insulted you. I'm sorry if I did, and I'd like to apologize. I guess I thought you were another one of Mason's tiresome shitheads—"

"You don't have to apologize," I put in. "I was beat, and you were, well—"

"Boiled. Anyway, that's beside the point. What I'm getting at is this: that somehow through all the evil red haze I remember beating your ears off about Tramonti—this little town back in the valley. I didn't mean to be trying to give you a message or anything. I only meant—" He turned away and moved slowly down the hall. "You've been a fine guy, Leverett, and I hope I see some more of you. Soon as I relieve Mason of one of his treasures I'm going to light out down into the valley. It's quite a place to see, even at night, this place I'm going. If you want to hang around, I'll be back in fifteen minutes." He disappeared without another word into the shadows, where I heard his feet sneak away, soft and stealthy as they climbed the stairs.

I wandered back upstairs into the littered, rancid living room. Night-dwelling flies bumbled and buzzed in the stillness. It was a sad place I beheld, this room: chaotic, unkempt, stinking, it reminded me of nothing more than some of the living rooms I had seen at home during the weary thirties, when poverty was more than a lack of money and seemed to display itself, as in this room, by a simple bedragglement of spirit. A cheap plaster Madonna ogled me from the wall with dreamy, credulous eyes; nearby a calendar marking the days of all the saints advertised the blood-red word *Marzo,* the month already half a year gone. A sardine can lay open on the table, filled with chartreuse-yellow grease. On an artist's sketch pad flung out beside it were these words, with a pen frantically gouged, as if in splinters, and in a crazy, drunken scrawl: *I hold to my Dear ones and now should I die I were not wholly wretched since ye have come to me Press close to me on either side Children cleave to your sire and repose from this late roaming so Forlorn so grievous!!!* The pen had been laid aside after the first words of another phrase, unintelligible, below it—thrust aside with its nib punched in one violent jab through the paper, as if in sudden fury. Beneath all of this there was an impossible jerry-built child's house with a chimney, in red crayon, a flight of prehistoric-looking birds, a spindly horse with ears like mammoth swollen carrots, also in red crayon, and the notation below in enormous red letters: AMƎRiCA GO*HOMƎ!! MARGARƎT KiNSOLViNG AGƎ 8 POO. I thought I heard a mouse or rat stir in a far corner of the room, and I looked up with a start; then with a shiver, feeling as if the decrepitude and inanition of the room had stolen into my very bones, I moved out onto the balcony. The starry lights on the water had not moved or altered, resting upon the sea like some untroubled constellation in the serene dark reaches of the firmament. There was not a sound anywhere. Closer, the swimming pool lay blue and trembling, abandoned of all save the incessant crowd of moths which like wind-blown petals fluttered and danced around the garish floodlamps. *I hold to my Dear ones and now should I die* . . . I could not get rid of the chill I felt in my heart and bones. I was touched all over by a clammy, insubstantial dread; if I had been a woman, I think I might have had trouble suppressing a scream.

The door slammed open behind me, turning my flesh, momentarily, to jelly. I wheeled around, beholding Cass, who in a great flurry and agitation went to a mountainous pile of junk in the corner of the room and began to rummage about, pitching socks and shoes and belts into the air behind him. "Where's that miserable sack?" he said. "It was as easy as pie, Leverett! I could have walked in there in chain mail, rattling like a bagful of clamshells. The Hollywood riffraff were still whooping it up and so I snuck in there as pretty as you please and copped it. It was like hooking candy."

"Copped *what?*" I said.

He didn't seem to notice. "Funny thing," he went on. "Some big oaf of a Roman movie type met me just as I was coming out the bathroom with the goods in my hand. I never saw him before and he knew I was up to no good. He just stood there with his big lower lip drooping and said, '*Che vuole lei?*' And, says I, thinking rapidly, 'Up yours, gorgeous, I work here,' in my best English, and breezed on past him beaming like a friar. It takes a lot of brass and cunning to be a proper thief."

"*What* goods?" I demanded.

"Oh," he said, looking up casually. "I quite forgot. Thoughtless of me. This." As I approached he held out a bottle, and when I bent down to peer at it I saw that it contained pharmaceutical capsules. The label read: PARA-AMINO SALICYLIC ACID LEDERLE U.S.A. The bottle glowed opulently in the dull light. "Pure magic," he said, softly now and rather wryly. "A hundred capsules.

Enough to cure half a dozen romantic poets. What they do, they use it along with this streptomycin to cure T.B. Now if we'd had this back in the thirties my dear old cousin Eunice Kinsolving would still be alive and kicking up in Colfax, Virginia."

"Where did Mason get it?" I asked.

"Ah now," he said evasively, "he brought it forth from the clear and shining air."

"But—" I persisted, "but just what would he want with a hundred capsules of that stuff?"

"Ha!" he said, without much humor. "Well, that's quite a long story. That there is a story, my boy, that would make your toes curl up."

"But he couldn't have gotten it without a prescription, could he?"

He stared at me. "Why, man, I thought you *knew* Mason. Didn't you know that when it comes to worldly goods that boy can get *anything*? Anything!" He paused, regarding the bottle soberly. "The point is that you don't hardly see any of this stuff in this benighted country. Oh, it's here, all right. They've gotten around to making it, just like in the good old U.S. and A. But try to get your hands on any of it. Why, for the price of this bottle you could ransom a whole clutch of Christian-Democrat senators."

"What are you going to do with it?"

For a long moment he was silent. "I don't know," he said, in a voice that was like a small cry. "Jesus Christ, I don't know! The doctor—Caltroni—this misery of a Sambuco doctor . . . To hell with that! Anyway, it's supposed to work all sorts of wonders. I think it's going to be too late in this case, but there's an outside chance. But why in God's name are we standing here talking like this! Come on, let's go." Into a dirty knapsack he dropped the bottle, along with several cans of sardines, half a loaf of bread, and three or four bruised apples long past their prime. Then together we plunged out into the night.

The main street of Sambuco up which we hastened was hardly a street at all, but a series of cobblestone steps too narrow and too steep for vehicles of any kind, damp with the steady seepage of water, slippery from this damp and from the smoothing wear of the centuries. As we toiled upward, panting, barely speaking, silent slumbering houses lined our route, illuminated by dim street lights for perhaps a mile or so, and then by nothing as the town itself dropped behind and we found ourselves walled around by darkness. It suddenly smelled like country. Cass turned a flashlight on. "The path begins around here somewhere," he said, playing the light over a weedy patch of ground. "That's it," he murmured suddenly. "Come on. It's a good half-hour's hike, but it's along the rim of the valley, and pretty level all the way, so we won't get too pooped." His light caught a lizard in its beam—a ghost-eyed, anxious-looking little creature which fled our approach and scuttled away over a wall. "A million years old, the poor bastard," Cass said. "Come on." We set out down the trail. A smell of lemon trees blossomed in my nostrils. I don't know what it was—perhaps only escaping at last that palace-hemmed chicanery—but the night seemed suddenly touched with rapture. An odor of clean earth, of lemon blossoms, of pine-scented air from the mountains came over us. Out from the edge of a roving cloud the pale full moon appeared, outlining the woods and slopes below, and a stream way down in the bottom of the valley, bright as quicksilver, madly babbling and gurgling. I heard sheep baa-ing far off. The valley seemed enchanted. As we walked along Cass turned out his light; we could see by the moon: its light engulfed the entire valley, showering silver upon the pine groves and rocks and the peasants' huts scattered here and there upon the slopes, looking lonely and marooned and asleep. Far up on the heights a waterfall noisily splashed: around it a rainbow quivered, then vanished. Again I heard the distant bleating of sheep, a somnolent, gentle noise. Finally Cass spoke up: "It's like some crazy Arcadia, isn't it? You should see it in the daytime, or at dawn." There was a pause. "What's your dodge, Leverett?"

"What do you mean, what's my *dodge?*"

"Don't get me wrong. I mean, what do you do? To make the world go round, and the gardens grow and all that."

When I told him—or when I told him what I *had* been doing, in Rome—there was another long pause. "I remember now," he said. "Mason told me." He paused. "Seems like you boys could have spread some of that aid or assistance or whatever you call it down here." He stumbled against a stone, clutched at my arm for support, righted himself. " 'Scuse me," he said, "still a little wobbly around the ankle bones."

"I wasn't the boss up there," I began mildly to protest, trudging along beside him. "I was just an expediter, a what you call—"

"*Aha!*" he broke out in a hoarse, unhappy laugh. He pulled a beret out of his hip pocket, yanking it down rakishly over his brow; it was an odd, brisk gesture, full of scorn and anger. "Ha! Yes, Jesus Christ, I know you weren't the boss, God bless you. I see the boss' picture every time I pick up the newspaper. A great shark-faced elder of the Presbyterian church. What does *he* know about the world, I ask you! What do any of them know, the sleek stuffed bastards! Why don't they come back *here* and take a look?" He paused, breathing hard. The valley around us swam in tender, silvery loveliness beneath the moon. "Look at it!" he said, stretching forth his arm. "It breaks your heart, doesn't it? And I'll swear before God, Leverett, it's the saddest place I know on earth."

Without altering his stride, Cass lit a cigar. Smoke billowed back around us in reeking gusts. Then, after another brief spell of hacking and coughing, he spoke to me over his shoulder. "Tell you a funny story about this valley. Very, very funny story. Around Sambuco it breaks everybody up when they hear it. Especially the fat Christian-Democrats who run the town. It *really* breaks *them* up. Now you know, no one makes any money back here. They try to farm but the land's been so poor for so many years that they're lucky to turn up a few dry peas in the spring. You should see the chickens! They got a whole little fable about that. About how the valley of Tramonti's the only place in Italy without foxes, the foxes got so disgusted years ago about the chickens that they just packed up and left. Anyway, that's not the funny story. The story is about milk. You should see the cows, Leverett. They don't get any fodder, of course; they graze on the hillsides and they're about the size of goats. Well, about five years ago, so the story goes, the government sent a bunch of agriculture inspectors around the province, testing samples of milk. Big deal, you know. They had a fancy sort of portable laboratory and all that, in a big truck and so on, and anyway, they came to Sambuco. Well, all the farmers from all the valleys around came to the square with buckets of milk to be tested, for tuberculosis and fat content and mineral content and all that sort of thing. They tested this milk all day there in the square, and finally the farmers from this here valley—hell, there couldn't be more than a dozen or so of them—these Tramonti farmers came up with their samples to be tested. Well, they took this Tramonti milk into their big portable laboratory and tested it and sampled it, and finally after a long time the head technician stepped out with the results. I can just visualize the whole scene: this big fat slob of a government man from Salerno with his test tubes and his charts and so on, and these poor sad hopeful yokels gawking up at him from the piazza. Well, the man drew a big breath finally and said, *'Questo qui non è latte. È un'altra cosa.'* Can't you see it, the whole ridiculous scene: these poor draggledy-assed bastards gazing up at this pompous fat chemist fellow, while

he very gravely told them that what they had given him, whatever it was, was certainly not milk. 'This is not milk,' he said
again, I guess in that pompous voice government officials have,
'it is something else.' And then, very pompously, while all the
Sambuco citizens gawked and snickered, he proceeded to give a
chemical analysis of the Tramonti whatever-it-was: water, rat
turds, hair, and a certain blue coloration which could only be made
out as something really negative and horrible—a total absence of
fat or minerals or any bleeding food value whatsoever. And then
he said: 'Take it home, this stuff. It is not milk.' " After a pause,
Cass said: "Very funny story. Every time I hear it, it breaks me
up." His voice was spiritless. "Very funny," he repeated. Sending
out clouds of smoke from a corner of his grim, clamped lips, he
fell into an impenetrable silence.

We had walked for nearly half an hour when, trudging up over
a rise, we beheld in a hollow below the moon-silvered shape of a
peasant's hut. We took a side path toward it, passing through a
meadow busy with the scratching of insects, across a brook, beneath a shadow-haunted cypress grove, over a rickety stile. Descending onto a patch of soggy, spongy ground, we found ourselves
in a farmyard. There was a smell of manure in the air, and the
rustle and stir, somewhere in the shadows, of chickens in clumsy
slumber. A broken-down dog approached snarling and snapping,
quieted down at Cass' murmured tones, gave a whimper of delight and scrambled about us, his ribs stark and scurvy in the
moonlight. We approached the hut across a stretch of parched
earth. Inside the hut, what seemed to be a single dim lamp was
glowing. And as we moved closer to the place, I was aware for the
first time of a sound which broke in upon the serene moonlit quiet
of the valley like fingernails against a pane of glass or the scream
of braking wheels—not a loud sound, nor a low sound either, but
one long, long protracted steady wail of anguish and despair which,
emanating from the darkness of the hut, was like a laceration upon
my eardrum.

"My God," I said. "What's that?"

Cass said nothing. The wail in the hut ceased abruptly, as if
strangled, and after a few seconds there came in its stead a low
series of groans, almost inaudible now, but touched with the same
insupportable and desolating anguish. Nearer, we could hear a
scuffling of feet within; a child cried, a pot or pan fell, then all was
silent as before.

"*Chi è là?*" came a voice from the shadows. It was a woman's voice, oddly heavy and masculine, and slow and torpid, suffused throughout with the deepest weariness.

"*Sono io, Ghita,*" said Cass softly. "It's just me, Ghita—Cass. With a friend."

The woman stood in the doorway, her arm upthrust against the frame, supporting herself, her face harshly illuminated in the flooding moonlight. It was an awesome face—fearsome, I should say, in the attitude graven upon it of suffering. Her lips were contorted downward, her eyes had become as dull and as sightless as two black stones; like wild grass her hair flew out around her head in unkempt strands. And she stood there motionless except for her breathing, which heaved up the sagging breasts beneath her tattered bag of a dress, and seemed to shake her all over. She looked like one whose grief had borne her miles beyond the realm of simple tears. "*Buonase',*" she said in a dull voice. "We were waiting for you."

"How is Michele? How is he tonight?"

"He fails," she said. "He asks for you. It's his pain now. It's as if his pain were my pain, so that when he cries out I can feel it in my own bones. I think he will die soon. I can't get it out of my bones."

"The morphine? Shut up about dying."

"It's of no use now. He no longer feels it. Besides, the glass instrument one uses fell and broke. *La siringa.* Alessandro took it in his hands—"

"I *told* you to keep—" Cass began with a note of anger. Then he said quietly: "Ah well, we'll arrange to get another."

Her voice was parched and dry. "I feel it in my bones," she said, "in my flesh. Here. Everywhere. Maddalena came tonight. She says that the disease possesses me now. The children. That it will devour us all. She gave me a philter—"

"Keep that witch out of here," Cass interrupted. The groans commenced again from the recesses of the hut. The woman stiffened and her eyes grew wide. "Keep that witch away from here, Ghita. How many times have I told you to have done with these idiotic charms? She'll do nothing but make things worse. Keep her out of here. Poison! Hasn't Francesca told you, too? Where is Francesca?"

The woman made no response, turning toward the sounds like an automaton and melting into the shadows of the hut. The groans faded, and suddenly died. "What it is," Cass said to me as he removed the knapsack from his shoulder, "is a case of miliary tuberculosis. Galloping consumption. This man's riddled with the stuff from head to toe, bones and kidneys, liver, lungs, and lights. Broke his leg a while back, which don't help any. It hurts him, and it's like a bleeding sponge. There's not a hope in the world. I wouldn't go inside if I were you." He weaved a bit, as if still half-drunk, but steadied himself. He took the bottle of capsules from the sack, peering at it closely in the moonlight. "As for me, if I'm going to get it, I've got it already. Mother of God! A bleeding amateur sawbones! Now what the hell did the book say? What's the dose? Oh yes, three grams four times a day. Well, we'll see. It sure won't hurt this poor bugger. Nothing in this world." He turned and made a move toward the door. "There's no point in your taking a chance. I won't be very long."

"I guess I'll go on in with you," I said.

"Suit yourself," he replied.

The stench of the place met me at the door, clamping itself down over my face like a foul green hand. It was an odor of many things —of manure again, of sourness, of dirt and offal—but mainly it was the odor of disease, a sweet tainted odor as of meat gone bad which blossomed in the air as vividly as a color. It was the odor of the morgue. Fumbling my way in the smirchy light, I blinked and gazed around me. Flies generated a steady buzzing in the stillness: they were everywhere—in the air, on the earthen floor, and upon each inch of the windowless walls. In sticky nocturnal fidget they crawled across the wan faces of three feverish, sick-looking children who, oblivious to the stir around them, and to the racking wails, slept soundly in one corner on a tick of straw. Nothing adorned the walls, not even a Madonna, while for furniture there was a table and three chairs and that was all. A huge shadow stirred clumsily in a nether corner of the room, startling me, until I saw that it was a cow, separated from the room by a low wooden partition, who gazed up at me from her repose with a sweet fune-real expression, all the while sedately masticating. Then another groan roused me, and I saw the sick man on his straw pallet, only his face exposed beneath a thin and tattered U. S. Army blanket, the face itself taut, immobile, as pale as wax, and such a wondrous portrait of emaciation, of sunken and ravaged flesh, that I thought for an instant that he must be dead. Cass and the woman had knelt down beside him. I heard Cass' voice, soft and gentle: *"Come va, mio caro? Soffri molto?* It's me, Cass, Michele."

Michele opened his eyes, and slowly looked around him. It was as if he had been in some rapt communion with his agony, a meditation upon his pain as profound and consuming as the deepest sleep, so that now, encroached upon by the outer world, he was indeed like a man who wakes to marvel at his surroundings. Slowly his eyes roved about, searching the ceiling and the walls. Then, as his gaze finally lit upon Cass' face, he gave a stir beneath the blanket and his sunken mouth with its lack of teeth suddenly parted wide in an unexpected, beaming smile. He spoke: his voice was almost unintelligible, stricken like the rest of him with the mutilating canker flowering within, cracked, hoarse, and sepulchral. "Cass," he said, "I've been waiting for you to come! I have a bottle of wine. Francesca brought it today. Real Chianti."

"What you need is sleep, Michele," Cass said. "Then also I've brought you this special clever medicine which will put you on your feet in no time at all. How is the pain in the leg?"

"It is bad, Cass," he replied, still smiling. "Very bad, Cass. But when you come, I—I do not know. There is a difference. We talk, you know. Make jokes. There is a difference in the pain. It is not so bad."

"How about the fever?" said Cass. "Have you been taking the aspirin I gave you for the fever?"

The woman Ghita spoke up. "He has been pissing blood. That is a bad sign. Maddalena says—"

"Hush about Maddalena," Cass said. "What does she know? Keep her out of here." He turned toward the woman with a look of patient remonstrance. "And the flies, Ghita! Look at them, *millions* of them. Do you want the babies to get poisoned, too? What about the bomb Francesca brought you?"

The woman shrugged. "It is all used up," she said. "Anyway, the flies always come back. You cannot have a cow without having flies."

"Give me some water, Ghita," said Cass.

"Right there, Cass, beside you. In the glass."

Cass uncapped the bottle and plucked out two of the yellow capsules. "Here, Michele, swallow these now. Then take one with a lot of water every six hours until I tell you to stop." He eased his arm under the man's frail shoulders, drawing him up half-erect on the pallet. It was an arduous procedure; straining, with droplets of sweat standing out on his brow, Michele forced himself up on his elbows, yowling in a sudden new onslaught of the pain. *"Ahi!"* he gasped. "Ah God!" He rested for a moment with his eyes closed. Then as before his eyelids parted, and he smiled his gentle collapsed smile. "What are these, Cass?" he said, his lips hesitating at the rim of the glass. "Is it true that in America there is really a cure for *il cancro?* Then this is it, Cass?"

I saw Cass' hands tremble as he placed the pills upon Michele's lips. He seemed to have trouble speaking for a moment. Then he said firmly: "You *know* you don't have cancer, Michele. We've been all through that. This is for your kidneys and the bone of your leg. It will make you well. Now swallow them down."

As Michele gulped at the water, the woman began to moan—a low-throated, placid, soft threnody of despair; so gentle it was, so untroubled by hysteria, that it was almost as if she were humming a tune. After a moment she stopped. "I have seen the black angel," she murmured in her dull voice. "I have seen him this night. He is all around us in the night." Turning, I watched her eyelids droop and close, like someone drifting off to sleep, as once more she began her gentle, grief-filled acquiescent lullaby, hands clutched together like great raw red wings to her withered breast.

"Hush, Ghita," Cass said. "Hush now. Don't be foolish. Quit torturing yourself."

"I have seen—" she began, her eyelids parting.

"Quiet," Cass said, more firmly. "Where's Francesca?"

"She never came," the woman replied listlessly.

A wrinkled, worried look appeared on Cass' face. "What do you mean, she never came?" he said crossly, and before Ghita had time to let her eyelids slide closed again he clutched her by the arm. "You mean she's not in the little room!" he exclaimed. He made a gesture with his head toward the single doorless doorway, hung with a curtain of burlap, which gave off from the interior of the hut. "But she said she was coming right here! She said she would sleep here!"

"She never came," Ghita repeated.

Cass rose abruptly from his place by the pallet. He stalked toward the doorway and looked in, returned, squatted again by the pallet and looked up into Ghita's flat impassive face. "Well, where could she be then?" he said. "It doesn't make sense for her— And something happened tonight which—" He paused. "Suffering God," he whispered in English. "That miserable snake! If he—" He rose again abruptly, as if to leave the place, when Michele croaked from the pallet.

"Cass." He had risen up and thrown off part of the blanket, revealing, through the shirt of his dingy pajamas, striped like those of a prisoner, an intolerably thin chest. "Cass," he said, "don't worry about Francesca. Often you know she stays with Lucia, you know, the daughter of the gardener at the Albergo Eden. All the time. Don't worry, *amico*. She's there tonight. Don't worry. Come here and sit beside me. The medicine has made me feel better already."

Cass hesitated. "Well—" he said, pausing. "Well, don't you think she'd have *told* me, Michele? I've got to go."

Michele forced a dreadful gurgle of a laugh. "Why tell you, my friend, when she has never in her life told her own papa? Come, sit down. Francesca is all right. You know Francesca! Sit down here, Cass. I feel I can almost walk."

"I don't know," Cass said glumly. But the anxiety and concern had begun to fade from his face. Saying, "I had forgotten about Lucia," he gave a sigh and bent his attention once more upon Michele. "You must lie down on your back, Michele," he said in a determined voice. "Like this. And you must not talk so much. Those are the rules."

"Ah *Dio!* Slowly!" Michele cried out. And his wife rocked back and forth again, moaning.

I sat there across the room, hearing in my brain the fanciful ticking of a clock, that imaginary tick-tock which, even in the absence of a clock, seems to accompany all wakes and nighttime sufferings and watches of the dead. And, as the woman rocked back and forth, softly moaning, and the children jerked and stirred, whimpering, in restless sleep, and the cow gazed at me in sweet brown incomprehension through the fly-swollen air, I finally understood that this Italian was actually dying. Dying—aware of it, too, in spite of all—he seemed only wishful now of wresting from Cass a last testimonial to that impossible vision which he had harbored in his mind, how long the Lord only knew, but I suppose all the years of his miserable life. So that now, between sounds of anguish, which Cass would soothe with a word and with a touch of his hand, I could hear his voice struggle up buoyantly in hope and wonder, as he asked about America: Was it true that even the poorest laborer had a car, Cass, and a stove, and a house with windows? Would it be possible, Cass, when he got well, and they all went to America together, to get Alessandro and Carla, and even the littlest one, a fine pair of shoes? He had asked Cass these things before, but persisted in being told the glory of their truth anew, like a small boy with visions of elephants and tigers, and of far exotic shores.

"Yes, *amico*," I heard Cass' patient tired voice. "Yes, it's all true like I have told you."

"I should like to live in Provvidenza, where my brother lived long ago. It is a fine city, is it not, Cass?"

"Yes, Michele." But to me, in English, turning: *"Providence, can you imagine?"*

Michele was tired. He stretched himself; a soft whistle escaped his lips and he closed his eyes, clenching them tight for a moment, then shuddering all over as if with a chill, as without a sound now he mounted rapt guard over the dominion of his pain. Save for the woman moaning and rocking, and the flies in their incessant pestilential drowse and drone, no one stirred or made a sound. Cass, hulking over the man in an attitude of frozen genuflection, wore upon his face a desolation so complete that it drained his skin of all color, and his eyes of all vestiges of light. Then after a while Michele roused himself a bit and opened his eyes. "It should not be so," he said in his choked faltering voice and now, for the first time, with a look of desperation. "It should not be so, Cass."

"What is that?"

"That a man should hurt so. That a man should work hard all of his life and make ninety thousand lire a year. And then end up like this, hurting so."

Cass said nothing for a moment; his lips trembled, as if searching for words. Then he said: "I truly agree, my friend. But you must not fret about that. *Animo.* Courage."

Rising on his elbow, Michele gave another groan, fixing Cass with his despairing hot eyes. "No, it should not be so, Cass!" he croaked. "He is evil, is He not, to put us down in this place where we work and slave for fifty years, making ninety thousand lire a year, which is not even enough to buy *pasta.* Ninety thousand lire! Then all the time He sends the tax collector from Rome. Then after draining us dry—of everything—at last He throws us away, as if we had cost Him nothing, and for a joke He punishes us with this pain. He loves only the rich men in Rome. He is evil, I tell you! I shit on Him! I shit on Him because I do not believe!"

Like a shot, as if waiting hawklike for just these words, the woman sprang erect from her trance. "Blasphemer!" she cried. "Listen to him, Cass! Like this he's been all day, ranting and raving. In his state! He will go straight to perdition!" She turned and looked down at the prostrate man. "And what he did, Cass, I perish to say. But in his wrath he got up from there this morning, right where he is lying now, and on his one good leg went to the wall, swearing like a Turk, where he tore the crucifix down and hurled it out of doors! Blasphemer, Michele! In your state! It is no

wonder that you have begun to piss blood. It's a sign from heaven!
You will drag us all down to perdition with your blasphemy!" One
of the children began to bawl.

"No worse—!" Michele commenced howling from the floor, his
voice throttled and choked and awful. "No worse than the charms
and amulets and potions you get from that sorceress! How can you
talk about blasphemy! When Cass has warned you against this
magic! *Ahi*—!"

"*Silenzio!*" Between the two impassioned, embattled theologies
Cass' voice rose like a wall, silencing the pair. But as he shouted at
them I fled the accursed place, unable to take any more. And
somewhere outside, in the newborn and ancient dawn looming
like a great limitless pearl over the sea, amidst the twittering and
chattering of birds and the soughing of pine trees that was like a
noise of rain, I found myself thinking, unaccountably, of other
dewy, radiant dawns I had known in years past, in Rome, and
the morning's plunging view from the balcony of the smooth young
benefactor, with his Ginevra and his Anna Maria and his girl from
Smith College, and then I found myself foolishly—albeit discreetly and out of a deep sense of failure and loss—blubbering
against a tree.

But there was none of this about Cass. He emerged shortly from
the hut, raging at the top of his voice, wobbling, and for an instant
I thought he had again in some mysterious fashion managed to get
drunk. But he was not drunk, only wild and inflamed; he was
ranting about the Communists and the Christian-Democrats and
Mrs. Clare Boothe Luce, and he said something which to me
seemed at that moment curiously apt.

"You can take politics, see," he said, "and you can stuff them up
your ass."

I slept that night—or that day, I should say—in a spare bedroom
in Cass' part of the palace. In the light of dawn, as we tramped
back up through the valley to Sambuco, he seemed subdued and
spent, and he said hardly anything to me at all. I, too, felt drained
of everything, and for the most part I kept my mouth shut. When
at last we paused to say good night at the gate of the Bella Vista,
when I ventured some final word about Mason (saying that he
would doubtless no longer feel obliged to pay my expensive bill),
Cass looked at me and smiled his tired smile, and said: "Come

stay with us." It was as simple as that; he was merely being generous. It sleepily occurred to me that it would be a kind of retaliation—a mild one, perhaps, but retaliation nonetheless—to flaunt myself for a few days under Mason's nose as the guest of Cass, and so, after the standard grateful show of refusal, I accepted the invitation. I checked out of the hotel, paying my bill to a dormant and pottering night clerk. Then Cass helped carry my bags down the still-sleeping street to the palace. His amiability and kindness were almost too much; he began to seem a bit unreal as he jockeyed my luggage down the stairs and into a bedroom—a fairly clean and well-kept place, in contrast to the "studio" upstairs—and joined with me in making the bed, and fetched me a couple of worn but freshly laundered towels. But for the most part he was tight-lipped, and his face wore a distant look of worry and concern: I thought nothing of it at the time—although it had all the bearing in the world on the events which followed soon—when he downed a great tumbler of red wine and, bidding me to sleep well, left me to myself, saying in a remote and abstracted voice that he had "to go check up about this friend I know."

I heard his feet tramping back and forth on the floor above me as I tried to sleep. Unconsciousness seemed a long time coming; I was stiff and sore and nagged by fugitive sorrows and regrets. First I wondered about Cass: who was this tormented, sad, extraordinary character? I worried about Cass for a long time. Soon I began to wonder if di Lieto was still among the living; then try as I might I could not force from my mind the vision of that hut, doomed in its lovely glade. With the muddled irrationality that goes with complete exhaustion, I remembered the pornographic pictures that Mason had asked me to bring him, and I kept trying to decide whether I should somehow see that he got them, or, as a last gesture of my defection, throw them away. I began to scratch and fidget and I yearned for a cigarette, for I had smoked my last. Then I began to think of a girl I once had made love to in Rome, which made me sweaty and earnest with desire, and I got up and drank a glass of cold water. The feet above me finally ceased their pacing. Cass Kinsolving! Who was he? At last, with the sunlight streaming down upon me through the rustling blinds, I slipped off fretfully into sleep, listening to the shrill cheery chorale of birds among the vines, and the clip-clop of a horsecart, and a girl's velvety sweet voice, somewhere far off, singing *"Caro nome."*

I woke up sopping with perspiration how many hours later I could not tell; in the room it was almost completely dark, and my watch read a few minutes past noon, but it had stopped. I thought it must be night again. For a while I lay there still, thankful that I was alive and breathing, for the dream-landscape I had visited seemed now more grim and malignant than any I had ever known: a nightmare at the beginning so fearful that I could not recall it, which was in itself an abomination—a curtain, dropping straight down like a shutter in my mind, which seemed to be made of the interlocking black wings of ravens crawling and loathsome with parasites, and which shivered and rustled as it sealed off the nightmare from recollection. Then all the rest, for all the hours I had slept, was nothing but a huge and barren place where I stood and witnessed a country in cataclysm and upheaval—a land of insurrection and barbarous acts and slaughter, where across the naked countryside wild hairy men ran with torches, and women gathered shrieking children to their breasts, and strange-looking dwellings flickered and burned, sending fetid clouds of smoke into a boiling, overcast sky. And throughout it all, through the unnumbered hours I stirred and tossed and groaned, I seemed to hear remote screams and yells, and wails of terror, and the anguish of the flayed and the crucified, until finally, without respite or calm, I woke up drenched, and with an outcry of supplication half-spoken on my lips. And as I lay there on the bed collecting my senses, watching the last pale glimmerings of light fade from the room, I was assured that it was not all a dream. Sambuco seemed windlessly, intolerably still. Not a sound came from outside, where there should have been that chuckle and buzz and tintinnabulation of Italian towns: it was as silent as a churchyard. Yet as I lay there listening to the slow leakage of water somewhere in the depths of the palace, I heard something in the distance which echoed from and explained my nightmare: a woman's single cry—a high-pitched, caterwauling sound of grief which wavered on the still hot air, soared higher and higher, then ceased, abruptly, as if shut off by a bullet through the head. Then all became as it had been—deathly still. After a time, puzzled and depressed, I got up, feeling a sharp pain in my neck where I had twisted it. I wiped the sweat off me with the bedclothes. And all the while, as I got dressed in the shadows in a troubled, dopey fashion, I heard other separate and isolated cries of lamentation, some close by, some indistinct, which like the cries in my dream sounded like those of souls in immortal torment. I expected to walk outdoors and find the town in siege or ablaze; no, I didn't know what to expect—least of all, as I left the room, to find that it was not night but late afternoon. There was daylight now, and a clock ticking in the hallway told me it was five o'clock, which meant I must have slept nearly twelve hours.

There was not a sound in the house; the upstairs living room lay as depraved and messy as it had the night before, and abandoned. It occurred to me then that the disturbance outside might be only a contribution on the part of Alonzo Cripps and his crew of movie-makers, but when I stepped out into the courtyard I saw that all the movie equipment had been dismantled and taken away. In its place there was a huge stack of suitcases, golf clubs, and other luggage, prepared as if for evacuation. Standing guard over the pile was a tacky-looking old townsman who tipped his cap and mumbled something mournful and unintelligible as I passed. There was no other sign of life here save for the trapped swallow I had seen the night before, which swooped down among the fluted columns, then upward, and still beat its wings against the skylight in flight toward the inaccessible sun. At the top of the stairs I had climbed—it seemed so many days before—Mason's door stood ajar beneath its frieze of dingy nymphs. No one came or left: the silence was appalling.

Outdoors I stood blinking at the deserted street. It was still a bright clear day, hot but tempered by a breeze from the sea. The shops across the way were barred up and shuttered; not a soul was in sight. For long moments I stood there. Then I heard a woman's cry, doleful, high-pitched, and piteous. Turning, I saw her rushing toward me down the street, a white-haired old woman in billowing black, keening grief at the top of her voice: all in a slant she came past me, tears running in rivulets down her ancient face—"*Disonorata! A sangue freddo!*" I heard her gabble—her black tempestuous skirts held up around her ankles, still keening and in miraculous slant as like a witch on a broomstick she sailed around the corner and vanished, leaving behind her an eddying whirlpool of dust. Suddenly I realized that I had been holding my stiff neck at an angle, causing woman, street, and sky to slant, and I painfully untilted it. I gazed after the woman, stupidly expecting some kind of explanation, but the street remained deserted and silent as before, calcimine-white in the Tyrrhenian sun and looking as shuttered and withdrawn as if once again the town were being beleaguered by the Saracens. Violated, as the woman had said, in cold blood.

In bewilderment I strolled up the street toward the hotel: there was a sort of terrace restaurant there, where I knew I could get an orange and a sandwich and a pot of coffee. But in the gardens at the entrance to the hotel no one was about—only a big bobtailed tomcat, a mouse trapped between his jaws, who eyed me discreetly and edged out of sight beneath a camellia bush. The terrace, too, was devoid of life; feeling footless and now creepily abandoned, I wandered through a sea of tenantless chairs and white tablecloths to a place near the edge of the terrace where I could watch the well-advertised panorama. It was a spectacular day: the sea, cellophane-clear, seemed to allow the eye to plumb the very limits of its blue cool depths; the green humpbacked mountains all around had the sunny, three-dimensional quality of stereopticon slides. With only a small straining of the vision, I felt I could see all the way to Africa. Yet why, I kept asking myself, was everything so totally, absurdly quiet? Far down the slope on the coast I watched a truck, no bigger than a pea, begin its winding ascent up the mountains: although I should have been able to hear the coughing of its engine, I heard no noise at all. Sound seemed drained from the whole visible world around me, as from a vessel. For what must have been ten minutes I sat there waiting for service, but no one came. At last belatedly, thick-headedly aware that something somewhere was seriously wrong, I made a motion to get up and leave, when I saw approaching me from the gardens an agitated figure, pitched between a fast walk and a trot. *"Non c'è thervizio oggi!"* he cried, and then I saw that it was my erstwhile *padrone* Fausto Windgasser. "There's no thervice today!" he lisped in English, recognizing me; he came on at a gallop, halted, beckoning me with frantic gestures out of his preserve. And I arose and sauntered toward him, touched already by the contagion of his hysteria and feeling an abysmal premonition. "What's wrong?" I said as I neared him.

The dapper little man was all but frothing at the mouth: his eyes seemed glazed, and the silky strands of hair on his balding pate had sprung erect, like those of a terrified and cornered animal, and fluttered in the breeze. "Yes, it's you, Mr. Leverett! Fortunate you checked out. Fortunate you are leaving!" All suavity abandoned, he clutched me by the arm. *"Quelle horreur,"* he gasped, in a lapse of tongue, *"quelle tragédie,* oh my God, have you ever heard of such a thing!" As if aware of what must have been a strange prickling at his scalp, he took out a silver comb and, releasing my arm, began to run it through his hair. His eyes were swimming with tears, his lower lip drooped and quivered; I thought at any moment he might collapse in my arms.

"What in God's name has happened!" I demanded. I began to jabber too: his aspect of horror was so consuming that I felt my own strength fail, and the blood draining away; for a second I had the insane notion that another world war had begun. "I've been asleep all day!" I cried. "Tell me what's happened! I don't know!"

"You dunno?" he said incredulously. "You dunno, Mr. Leverett? About this devvistation in our town? We are *ruined!* The town is veritably in ashes! After this eventuality there will be no more *turismo* in Thambuco for ten—no, my God, for twenty years. Overpowering twagedy, my God. It's like the *Gweeks,* I tell you, but far worse!"

"Well, *tell* me!"

"A young girl, a peasant girl," he said in low wretched tones. "A peasant girl from the valley. She was found ravished and dying on the valley road this morning. She is not expected to live out the day." A great racking sob wrenched itself from his chest. "I tell you, it's the first *mortal* act of violence in this town since the last thentury. Before my own father—"

"Go on!" I commanded.

"I *demur,* my God, because—" He was weeping now, blubbering, a soft fluid mess of a little man, turned to water. "Because—Because, it is so *twagic,* I tell you! Mr. Flagg—"

"What the hell has *he* got to do with it?"

"Oh, Mr. Leverett," he sobbed, not entirely heedless of some innate dramatic flair. In his voice were all the echoed intonations of that strange dead hotel library of flamboyant gestures and fevered diction—Mrs. Humphry Ward and Bulwer-Lytton and *Lorna Doone* and other swooning, improbable chronicles left behind by drowsy English gentlewomen—which, I suppose, were the only books he had ever known. "Oh, Mr. Leverett, Mr. Flagg is dead. He lies even now beneath the precipice at the Villa Cardassi, where they say he threw himself, in remorse over the—the deed he committed."

For a long moment I had no notion at all of what Windgasser was trying to convey to me: who was this soft, foolish, soggy little man, combing his wind-blown hair? Make him repeat it, my mind said, you misunderstood. I grabbed him by the arm.

"Yes, I mean it," he said, sobbing. "Mr. Flagg lies below the Villa Cardassi. Dead, dead, dead." He blew into his handkerchief. "He was such a kind, decent, generous man, too. It is difficult to believe. So big-hearted, so courteous, so *affluent*—"

I waited to hear no more, tearing myself from him and out of the garden and into the street again. I had no idea which way to go but I headed down the slope toward the square. Presently I increased my pace and soon I was running, my feet stumbling and sliding on the cobblestones. On the run I passed clots of people who stood in open doorways, some silent, some wildly gesticulating, all looking wide-eyed and stunned. I galloped on in the warm windy sunlight, half-overturning a boy on a bicycle, dodging a stray goat, in dreamlike flight through empty space vaulting down over half a dozen precipitously pitched stone steps; at last, gasping, I debouched in flapping seersucker from the cobbled street and found myself in the buzzing, people-crowded square. Everyone had gathered here, it seemed: townsfolk, tourists, peasants, policemen, movie stars. In groups of four and five and six they were solemnly talking—the townspeople in the center of the square, the tourists in seamy, be-Kodaked clusters near their buses beside the fountain, the movie folk at café tables, gloomily drinking. A squad of *carabinieri* entered in a riot truck, stage right, with groaning, descending siren, scattering a flock of geese in obese waddle. Save for one or two anachronistic details, the cluttered piazza might have been a set out of *Il Trovatore*. Above this jam-packed mob a hum and murmur of conversation floated like a black cloud—speculative, lugubrious, flecked with nervous laughter that bordered on hysteria. And as I stood there trying to gather my wits about me, I heard a church bell begin a jangling, discordant requiem, high in the air where pigeons wheeled about in the gusty sunlight—no more melodic than falling dishpans yet heavy and plaintive with woe. CLANGBONG! DING! BANG!

"Che rovina!" spoke a voice at my elbow. It was old Giorgio, the butler: huddled up in an American Navy pea jacket, though the day was sultry, he gazed with blue watery eyes into space, tugging at the folds of his neck and looking miserable.

"Is it true, Giorgio?" I said. "Is Signor Flagg really—"

"Si, signore," he said listlessly, still gazing into space. "He is truly dead. By his own hand."

LACRIME! the bells clang-clattered.

"What happened, what did he do, where can I see him?" I said all at once.

The old man was like one drugged. Blindly he plucked at his neck, snuffling, quietly mourning. "He who lives by violence shall die by violence," he mumbled sententiously. Then he paused, all aflounder in his unhappiness. "That one so fair and kind should meet such a bitter end," he said finally, "is the greatest tragedy in the world." And it took me a moment to realize then that it was not Mason, around whom all my thoughts had been revolving, he had been talking about, but the ravished and dying girl. Beneath the canopy of clashing bells I tore myself away from Giorgio's side, plunging and sidestepping my way through the crowd toward the edge of the square. Here between two buildings was the entrance to a shadowy alleyway and down upon it were galloping the recently arrived *carabinieri*, who were armed to the teeth and blackly scowling and began to muscle their way through a crowd of gawking peasants, sending up bright flares of profanity and working their elbows like pistons. I stood there for a moment feeling shaky and rattled; then, undaunted, I pushed through the crowd of peasants, cursing too, and hustled after the cops up the alleyway. Very shortly the alley became a cobbled little street, the street a labyrinth winding narrowly between rows of dank, deserted houses, and the labyrinth finally a walled path which straggled away from the center of the town and mounted gradually the side of a dizzying precipice so vertical and so smooth that it was as bare of vegetation—even of moss or lichen—as a crag in the remotest north. Along this path I made my way, following the track of the cops whom I could hear clumping and toiling up ahead. People were coming down—spectators, I presumed, of the aftermath of tragedy: natives of the town, ragged peasants from the valley, several crestfallen dogs, and even two German tourists, a dough-faced fat couple sporting alpenstocks and green Bavarian hats, who edged past me with a strange glow of satisfaction and left the air echoing with soft chortles of eerie succulent laughter. I trudged along. The waning day was gold and green and summery, viewed as if through the clearest pane of glass. Lizards preceded me up the protecting wall, unloosing in their iridescent scramble bits and pieces of crumbling stone. Unnerving heights rose up and fell away on either side of me: I was at the level of a cloud which was plump and fleecy, its underside a dissolving pink, floating over the valley like cotton candy. Back in the town the bell ceaselessly tolled its jangling lament. Of the rest of that half-hour's climb I remember nothing save that somewhere along the way I encountered Dawn O'Donnell coming down the path. She was making a weak-kneed descent, and her carrot-colored head was bent tragically low upon a wad of shredded Kleenex, and she was escorted by the crew-cut young man of the night before, who as he passed, I swear, was saying, *"Can that, baby, will you?"* He looked at me but whether he saw me I couldn't tell.

Halfway up the steep hill which led to the base of the cliff the path widened out, joining here a spacious, grassy ledge perhaps a hundred yards across which several scores of people had collected—townspeople, more tourists, more dogs, and at least two dozen policemen. Above the ledge the precipice rose heroic and dizzying to the Villa Cardassi: by craning my neck I could see the Moorish roof floating on high in the slanting sunset, and the stunted, wind-bent cedars which clung to the villa's fortressed walls. It was a sickening drop. A few yards away near the base of the precipice a rope had been strung, one end secured with a metal hook in a crevice of a rock, the other end tied to a pole in the ground fifty feet away. It was against this rope that most of the onlookers were pressing, filling the air with soft morbid whispers of rumor, of conjecture and speculation; behind the rope stood half a dozen *carabinieri,* most of them looking solemn and self-important, and sweeping the crowd with beady-eyed glances of contempt. One of them was Cass' friend, Luigi. I pushed toward him through the humid mob, signaling to him with my fingers. His sleepy eyes parted wide in a look of recognition; as he did this, a gap of space appeared between two craning, brilliantined heads and I saw Mason at last—my heart giving a huge lurch of misery as I saw his long familiar outline beneath a blanket, covered up all but for the lower part of his white pathetic legs which stuck out shoeless and fly-covered and slew-footed. And at the sight, incongruously, I thought that the legs were still no doubt wearing a pair of Bermuda shorts, bottle-green and sharply pressed.

"*Buongiorno,*" I said to Luigi.

"*Buongiorno.*"

"*Come sta?*"

"*Bene, grazie, e lei?*"

In my confusion, our greeting had such a quality of ludicrousness that I found myself forcing back in my throat a bubble of bereft and crazy laughter. I calmed myself. "I don't know," I said. "I think I'm going mad."

"I can understand. *Via!*" he snarled at two urchins who tried to edge past him. "I can well understand. You were well acquainted with this man, Mason. Is that not so?"

"I was," I said. "Tell me, Luigi, what in God's name happened?"

There is something about death, violence, and calamitous happenings that brings out in Italians the wiseacre, the frustrated savant; of the many details I recall from that hellish day not the least is how, in my search for particulars, I ended up with a collection of aphorisms. "Who knows," he said, gazing at me gently through heavy-lidded eyes, "who knows what terrible things lurk in the mind of a man who kills? Who—"

"Can I see him, Luigi?" I broke in. Why at that moment I wanted to see Mason (I think I have an aversion to the dead more than ordinarily squeamish) will forever remain a mystery to me, unless it was only to prove to myself, in my stupefied disbelief, that it was really Mason's mortal shell beneath that blanket, instead of some living, breathing Mason who, pink and supine, would gaze up at me with a wink and a lunatic cackle, full of claptrap to the very end.

"*È vietato,*" said Luigi. "No one is allowed on the scene until the investigation is completed and the body removed."

"But I knew him, Luigi," I pleaded. "He was. . . he was"— and out came the calumnious phrase—"he was my best friend."

Luigi pondered for a moment. I could not help but feel that the fact that I was an American—despite, or perhaps even because of, his comments of the night before—gave me a certain status in his eyes. "Very well," he said finally. He moved away across the grassy ledge to the place where Mason's body lay. Two men stood there brooding over a ledger—a mountainous fat sergeant of the *carabinieri*, with spectacles, with a fuming cigarette pasted upon his lips, and with a triple chin folded away toward his neck like the buttocks of a baby; the other a thin, bony, intense-looking man in a trench coat and a fedora which came down over and all but hid his eyes: he was assiduously chewing gum, and a pistol divulged itself lucidly through a bulge in his coat, like a plain-clothes cop in a funny movie. Only, he was not funny. This man, I was told by a wide-eyed boy standing beside me, was *l'investigatore*, from Salerno, and while Luigi murmured in his ear and gestured toward me, I humbly awaited his decision, ungrieving, unmourning, but with a pain of desolation in my heart such as I had never felt before.

"O.K." said Luigi, as he came back. "You can talk to the investigator." He enunciated the title in oval meticulous syllables, investing it with glamour and ponderosity. "Be brief, though," he added. "The investigator has much to do. Have you seen Cass, by the way?"

"Not since last night," I replied.

"Strange," he said, with a puzzled look. "I can't find him anywhere. Or Poppy or the children, either."

I ducked under the rope and walked toward the investigator; he scrutinized me narrowly as I approached, looking up from his notebook, suspicious, guarded, glacial, a regular monk of a policeman, with pious and austere eyes and a lean, monastic, lowering stance, his jaw working strenuously against its burden of gum. The sergeant, a behemoth beside him, intercepted the rays of the sun, casting an oblong of darkness over Mason's prostrate form, like the shadow from a gigantic tent. Welling up inside with my ancient atavistic dread of cops, I walked toward them with a great deal of hesitation. *"Buongiorno,"* I said.

"Do you know this man?" said the investigator in a peremptory voice.

"Yes," I said. "Yes, I do. I should like to see him, if I may."

"He has already been identified," he replied, somewhat illogically. There was no discourtesy, no harshness in his voice, yet there was no trace of gentleness either. He seemed rather to have trapped within him, like steam in a simmering kettle, a seething anger, and was taking pains to control himself. "He has already been identified," he repeated, fixing me with his competent, gelid eyes. "What is this man to you?"

"Why I—I don't know," I replied. "That is—what do you mean?"

The voice of the mammoth sergeant behind him was like a wheezy little reed: emanating from that ton of mountainous flesh it had a fluty, canary-like quality, the voice of a boot-licker—querulous, eunuchoid, and sarcastic. *"Ascoltami!* You heard *l'investigatore!* What is this man to you? How do you know this Flog?"

"Quiet, Parrinello," the investigator snapped. His voice grew more equable as he turned back to me. "I mean, signore, how do you stand in relation to this man. What is he to you—the deceased. Relative? Friend?"

"He was a friend of mine," I replied.

The investigator leveled upon me his frosty gaze; again there seemed to be no hostility in his look—toward me, at least: if anything, there was now even a touch of cordiality in his manner. But he was still all business: I was no doubt a source of information to him, so perhaps he did not want to fluster me by giving vent to the anger raging within him. He shifted his gum and cleared his throat, saying: "So he was a friend? Let me ask you this, signore. Was he a psychopath?"

Nourished all my schooldays as I have been on the thin porridge of psychology, I am as given as anyone to tagging people with labels; with Mason then, however, in his ultimate, pitiful state of defenselessness, I didn't know what to say. "Well, I'm sorry—" I began. "If he was, it was because— No!"

"How long have you known him?" he put in. "Understand, signore, you're under no obligation to answer these questions. However, you would be doing us a kindness by whatever information you can offer about this—" And he looked down at Mason, his lips parted as if upon some distasteful word. "This man here. You have known him how long?"

My glance stole down to the blanketed form. I might say that there was a smell of death about this scene, except that there wasn't; all I could smell was my own sweaty, unstrung self, while death resided only in the eye—in the blanket-shrouded body, shockingly immobile, in those shanks and feet with their hue and texture of milk glass, and in that plague of demonic scavengers, whose mindless winged presence, at least at that moment, seemed once and for all to dispose of any idea of a caring and beneficent deity: the thousand sucking flies, rankly festering in a metaphysics of their own, which swarmed on the blanket and upon Mason's ankles, and sought out private mysteries between his toes. And for an instant I pondered just how long I had known Mason, realizing that by any definition whereby one might feel me competent to judge him I had not known him long—two swift boyhood years, plus a week, plus these last feverish hours—but that with all of this I had the notion I had known him all my life. That is what I said, finally: "I've known him all my life."

"And he never exhibited any tendencies which one might call psychopathic?" said the investigator.

"Not to my knowledge," I said. I don't know whether I lied to him, and still don't know to this day. One thing I did know: that Mason, upon whom short hours ago I would have turned my back in his direst need, now was so defenseless that it was the least I could do, in my own way, to stick up for him, if only as a last, nostalgic gesture. I said: "He was not psychopathic, signore, not to my knowledge." And one sudden remembrance—that I had not bade him even a decent good-by—touched me with withering sorrow.

The investigator still held himself in check, but it was an effort, and on his thin dry lips there was an expression of restrained exasperation. He handed the ledger to the sergeant and drew his trench coat around him with an angry, silent flourish. ("Thank you, my Captain, thank you, thank you," the sergeant said insistently.) Far down in the village I heard again an old woman's shriek of lament, distant, echoing, drowned in a renewed clamor of bells which swept up the valley on a gust of wind. A small cloud darkened the day with a moment's somber light; the grass rustled about Mason's body, I heard a chirruping of crickets. The cloudlet passed: flooding sunlight swept over the valley like a yellow noise, like a thunderclap. The investigator wiped sweat from his brow with two slender bony fingers. "I cannot let you see him," he said. "For your own benefit. He is terribly mutilated. Look up there." He jerked his neck toward the villa and the promontory high above. "One cannot fall that distance without suffering a change of—of features. *Inoltre*—" He paused, gazing at me with a look part bitterness, part reproach.

"Furthermore, what—" I said.

"Furthermore, I do not believe you when you say this man was not psychopathic. *Per prima cosa*, it is apparent to me that he was a suicide. That does not in itself necessarily mean that he was a psychopath, but such an act is always at the very least the product of a deranged mind. *Secondo*"—and here I began to detect a tremor in his voice as the anger, the outrage gained dominance within—"*secondo*, signore, I cannot believe that anyone but a psychopath could commit such an insane act of violence. Therefore, it is no doubt a charity to call this man one. Never in my life have I seen a person violated so horribly as that girl. Never! Signore, you were his friend and I will spare you—"

The sergeant's piping, female voice broke in; his face was tomato-red and his lumbering body shook like jelly, scarily, as if his whole bladdery, epicene form were about to tumble down upon me. "Never in your life! Her scalp ripped back from her head as if seized by a bear! Never in your life! Gangster of an American—"

"Shut up, Parrinello!" the investigator commanded. "Shut your mouth!" Then he turned back to me and said in a savage whisper:

"But it is true! The man was a devil." His eyebrows bristled close to me, he breathed an odor of peppermint. "A devil!"

"Untrue," I said. "He was no devil." But I didn't know. They seemed to be talking about a total stranger. Over my drooping consciousness, like a shawl, I felt descending a kind of blessed unbelief, and I heard a strumming in my ears which I thought might be the first onslaught of dementia.

MISERIA! the bells sounded from the town. DOLORE!

It was dusk by the time I got back to the village. No, of course it was not dusk but only that illusion of premature darkness which came as the sun sank down behind the towering hills, allowing the stars to shine in the afternoon and the chickens beside the hillside huts to go off clucking dolefully to sleep amidst the hazy lavender. Everything had become more peaceful, though, as this false night fell. There were lights burning in the houses I passed, and I smelled fish cooking; I even heard a snatch of rowdy laughter. The first shock had worn off, it seemed, and now with a clatter of pans and a cautious whistle people were beginning to go about their ordinary ways. Down a dark alleyway a radio was blaring music; it was an old record of Artie Shaw's "Frenesi," and I felt a pang of nostalgia, made doubly grim because I associated the tune with my days at St. Andrew's and, unavoidably, with Mason. Yet curiously I refrained from thinking of Mason: it was not something I could think about. He was dead, that was all, and for all I was able to feel deep within my heart he might have been dead for twenty years. Having accepted this fact, I could no longer feel even my original sense of loss, of desolation: shattered though I might have been, I felt no grief, and my eyes were as dry as marbles. It was indeed over some other death that I brooded for a while when, approaching the gate of the town, I spied the wreckage of my Austin, unmolested by seekers after spare parts, so far as I could see, but now the lime-splotched roost of a flock of pigeons. I didn't want to have anything to do with the car and passed it by, but the sight of it made me heavy with thoughts of di Lieto: in dreary alternation, I saw him swaddled mute and helpless in hospital, plasma dripping into his veins, then still in his denim overalls, purblind, gimpy, grinning, presenting his shabby credentials at the everlasting doors. But di Lieto, too, I put out of my mind: I wanted nothing so much as to get away from Sambuco, and I was seized by the final demoralizing notion—made more troublesome by some nagging, left-over feeling of obligation to Mason—that I would have to "arrange" for his disposal.

I reached the piazza: here the citizenry was still milling about, but the place was not nearly so crowded as before, nor so stunned, nor so frightened. As my anxiety and tension faded, I felt hungry again and I sat down at a café table and ordered a sandwich. But the waiter, a sleek stuffed young man with a Mussolini jaw, seemed so positively brusque and unfriendly that I settled for a hasty cup of coffee and left. There were murmurings in the square as I passed; for the first time it occurred to me that, in so small a town, I was easily picked out as one of Mason's associates: I felt distinctly uneasy as I slunk across the square in my espadrilles, the target of a score of hostile eyes. Bells of doom and grief hammered in my ears as, passing beneath the church's stern façade, I walked up the street to the palace. Muttering, the townsfolk gave way on either side of me, as if from a leper. *"Orco!"* I heard some-one hiss among the shadows. "Ogre!"

At the top of the hill the oaken doors of the palace were flung open, while on the street before them moved a slow procession of trucks and cars. Here there was a frenzied air of demobilization: a crowd of local navvies were manhandling equipment onto the trucks; there were shouts, threats, curses; baggage poured forth from the palace doors on a human chain; a Chrysler station wagon backfired, enveloping the twilit scene in a blue pall. In the midst of the commotion stood one of the Italians I had seen the night before in his underdrawers: in pin-stripes now, and sun glasses, he bellowed orders from the tailgate of a truck. Then as I approached, my eyes picked out familiar figures in the gloom: Dawn O'Donnell and Alice Adair, despondently clutching hat-boxes; Billy Raymond, engaged in what seemed forlorn conversa-tion with Morton Baer; and Carleton Burns, finally, who emerged from the palace looking green and sick, blinked up uncertainly at the sky, and then, hoisting to one shoulder a bag of golf clubs and cradling in his arms a pair of bongo drums, veered shaky and somnambulant toward a waiting Cadillac. For several minutes I was unable to get into the palace. Then at last I found an opening; I pushed through the mob toward the courtyard, almost colliding as I did with Rosemarie de Laframboise, who was on her way out. She had the look of one who had been weeping ceaselessly for hours; her wide cheeks were ravaged and inflamed, devoid of make-up, thus lending startling contrast to the livid bruise around her eye which she wore still as testimony to the warmth of Mason's affection. She half-stumbled as she walked, a mink stole was wrapped around her pale and beautiful shoulders, and from her mighty bosom came hoarse tormented sobs; beside her, supporting her by the elbow, was the pretty bespectacled girl, named Maggie, who had endured the insults of Carleton Burns. I put my hand on Rosemarie's. Her grief moved me honestly and deeply, and I hardly knew what to say. "I'm—I'm so sorry, Rosemarie," I began.

"She's in a state of shock," Maggie informed me. There was a touch of awe in her voice, which had the vacant intonation of Southern California. "She's full of phenobarbital. Jeepers, the poor girl—"

"Oh, Peter," Rosemarie broke in with trembling lips. "Oh, Peter—" And then she halted, her eyes round, goose pimples sheathing her marble arms, unable to speak.

"God," I said, "God, Rosemarie. I—I just don't know what to say." No state of human emotion renders me so fatuous as bereavement; vainly I sought the proper words to comfort her.

"It's all so—so *impossible*," she managed to say finally; her eyes suddenly opened wide, lighting up her face briefly with a look of such stunned wonder and disbelief that she appeared for a moment half-crazed. "He just couldn't have done that, Peter. Couldn't have. *Couldn't* have. I know him!" Then, standing there, she thrust her face into her hands and once more began to weep.

"Rosemarie—" I murmured. Beneath my touch her skin was like a toad's, pulsing wildly, moist, cold as ice.

"She's in a state of shock," Maggie repeated. "Alonzo wants to get her to Rome as soon as possible."

"Where is Alonzo?" I said.

"He went to Naples to see the American consul or somebody about—well, you know, about *arrangements,* I guess."

"Is he coming back?" I said. Cripps alone was the one who I felt might bring a touch of sanity to this bedlam.

"There, baby," Maggie was saying to Rosemarie, patting her heaving shoulders. "Don't cry, baby. Everything's going to be all right." She glanced up at me. "No. Everybody's leaving. Sol Kirschorn heard right away about what happened and he sent a telegram from Rome. I saw it. It said: 'Get out of town *subito*. Repeat *subito*.' I guess he didn't want to get mixed up in everything. There, baby sweet, everything's going to be all right. Come on now, let's go out and get into the car."

Rosemarie raised her head, her mouth working wordlessly, and gazed at me. For an instant I had an awful vision of her sorrow: her black eye alone was witness to the loyalty she still bore for him, far beyond the memories of his misdeeds, his clouts and bruises, and his unfaithfulness. What part of him she was grieving for I could not tell: how grieves the lady fair of such a man as Mason? But I had a quick sad vision, as I say, and I guessed she must be grieving for the times when he made love to her in the night, or when she whispered "Muffin" to his sleeping tousled face, or those mornings when, in the first fever of love, he appeared to her a staunch knight, not only rich but tender, too, and alive and quivering with promise. Her arm rose in a sudden nervous gesture to her hair; her tresses became dislodged, unloosing a bunch of bobby pins which skittered to the floor. "Peter," she said imploringly, "he didn't do these things. I *know*. He just—"

"Come on, baby sweet," said Maggie.

Rosemarie's hand rested chilly upon mine; again she tried to make her mouth say words, but her lips moved soundlessly, and with a great shudder she turned and walked—hobbled, I should say, so tortured was her progress—across the tiles toward the door. I watched her go: a good girl, she seemed to me, victimized by Mason even to the point of this towering grief, a kindly girl trailing a spoor of bobby pins from her disheveled golden hair and with a copy of *The New Yorker* crumpled clumsily beneath her arm.

"If you ask me," murmured Maggie confidentially as she moved away after her, "the jerk deserved it. He must have been a *monster*. They say that girl didn't have one unbroken bone left in her body."

I lingered long enough outside to watch the movie folk go. Their escape was hasty and frantic; no military unit forced into sudden retreat could have made such a determined exit from the scene. In vans and trucks, in station wagons, on motorscooters, in Fiats, in Alfa Romeos and in Buick convertibles, they rumbled in caravan fashion like refugees from disaster past the palace door. At some point I remember feeling sorry that I would not see Cripps again. A bus full of technicians was the next to the last to pull out, trailed by an open car in which sat Gloria Mangiamele, still giggling over something, and Carleton Burns, whose haggard hound-dog face was upturned, taking a tremendous belt out of a bottle of Scotch. Not one of them had any kinship whatever with tragedy, and it was evident, for in less than a minute they were all past sight, leaving the street with its gleaming fireflies and flickering bats as quiet and serene as it had been under good King Roger of Sicily, a thousand years before.

At the end of this day, then, I came back to the Kinsolvings'. For God knows what obscure motives I closed the big wooden doors behind me: perhaps only to shut out the far-off incessant doom-tolling bell, perhaps to insulate myself, no matter with what temporariness, from the town itself with its hovering commingled burden of gloom, of fright, of menace. The courtyard lay deserted and still, littered with paper and cartons and other debris of leave-taking. My eyes automatically searched the ceiling: high in the air the imprisoned bird still sought freedom through the moonlit fleur-de-lis of glass, yet with a less frantic fluttering of its wings now, almost feebly, and soon it would plummet down to these gouged-out and desecrated tiles, where it would die. Its plight, which had touched me before, moved me not at all now. I felt as drained of emotion as if there had been piped away from my bones and tissues all strength and all will; I was as limp and as pliant as a green reed beneath the streaming water. I heard the sound of feet tramping above: Am I accurate in recalling that I expected Mason to appear on the balcony, flapping at me his lean long arm, with a querulous "Petesy" on his lips insisting that I join him in a drink? As a matter of fact, for a deranged moment I did think it was he—they were of the same height—but it was only a local workman, one of Fausto's minions, who came out through Mason's door, pitching downstairs a boxload of rubbish with an inane, instinctive *"Prego,"* and casting me a lip-curled glance of disdain.

I went through the green door, where in the glow of a single dim light Cass' living room lay untouched and silent in its squalid disarray. It was quiet; no one was at home. Not a thing had altered since the night before: soggy clothesline, easel with its dangling doll, scattered comic books, cigar butts, bottles—each occupied still its own grubby disordered place. The smell of the place was riper, gamier; as I switched on the overhead light three big fat mice catapulted like fuzzy musketballs from the table, making sharp separate reports as they hit the floor then scuttled for shelter behind the wainscoting. Nothing here, though, discouraged my hunger; remembering that somewhere around I had glimpsed a room that looked like a kitchen, I began to prowl around on the top floor, barking my shins, lighting matches as I went. Finally I saw an ancient icebox in the hallway and opened it: the ice had long since melted and the interior was warm and damp and sour-smelling, harboring within its gummy, unclean shelves a single tepid Coca-Cola, a bottle of infants' vitamin solution, and a desiccated piece of cheese. I squeezed out a few drops of the vitamins into the Coca-Cola and took this, together with the cheese, back into the living room. There I unearthed half a loaf of bread; it was bone-stale, but I ate it, too, as I sat there sunk in a condition of pulpy, emotionless inertia. For a long while I sat, wondering what to do next.

At last—it was dead of nightfall by then, close to nine it must have been—I heard the sound of voices down past the garden and beyond the swimming pool. Remote at first, they sounded like the voices of shrill and quarreling women, but as they came nearer the high piping notes defined themselves as the noise of children. I heard feet below tumbling across the flagstone walks of the garden, there was a swishing in the bushes and a patter and a sound of banging doors. Then on the stairway I heard their strident calls, in English and Italian, ascending, until at last with a noisy scuffle on the hallway landing they burst into the living room like children everywhere on a summer night—panting and damp-browed, scratching mosquito bites. Trailing hard behind them was Poppy, holding in her arms the youngest little boy, who was fast asleep, heedless of the racket.

"Peggy!" Poppy commanded sternly. "Timothy! Felicia! Everybody to bed! I'm not going to have any *arguments!*" I arose and coughed. "Oh, Mr. Leverett, it's you!" she exclaimed. A faded bandanna covered her hair; she looked worn and haggard and unhappy. Her pretty little face was of that fragile and transparent sort which like litmus paper responds to every mood: the shadows of weariness beneath her eyes were like smudges of soot. "Have you seen Cass?" she cried, wide-mouthed. In her voice was an anguished plea, a wail, with no nonsense about it and no refinements; she was like a three-year-old who had lost her doll. "Have you seen him? I've looked for him everywhere! I haven't seen him since last *night!*"

One of the children began to howl. "Mommy, I want some *cioccolato!*" Another took up the cry. *"Cioccolato!"* And in the space of a wink, right there before my eyes, a general tantrum ensued, all but the oldest girl—who sat gravely and primly in a chair—shrieking for chocolate at the top of their voices, joined by the baby in Poppy's arms, who, terrified out of sleep, turned an abrupt and pullulating crimson and commenced screaming. I have always been reduced to bald despair by screaming children; I took out a cigarette and lit it, obscuring the sight in a cloud of smoke.

"Stop it!" Poppy shrilled. "Stop it, children! Blazes!" Her chest and shoulders heaved, and she was on the brink of tears. "Just stop it now," she implored, as the children quieted down. "You can't have any chocolate. There isn't any. There just isn't any. I've *told* you. Now you've got to go to bed." She began to whimper herself as she rocked the crying baby in her arms. *"Haven't* you seen Cass?" she said, turning back to me, beseeching me in a way that made me feel she thought I really had seen him.

"No, I haven't," I said. "Can I—"

"Did you hear what happened today?" she said with an awed, frightened look. "Isn't it awful? Isn't it just the awfulest thing you ever heard of in your life?"

"What happened, Mommy?" said Timothy. He was running his hand around in an empty sardine can, licking off gobs of congealed green olive oil from his fingers; he looked so famished I could hardly blame him. "Tell me what happened, Mommy," he persisted in a casual, artless voice.

"I know what happened," said Peggy from her dangle-legged perch on the chair. One eyebrow was raised, her lips turned down in sly superiority: she was a jewel of a little girl, with sparkling eyes and resplendent golden hair. "Old Nasty-face Flagg jumped—"

"Taci!" Poppy commanded. "You just close up your mouth, Peggy Kinsolving! Just for that you're all going to bed right now, you hear! Downstairs, right away!" With a blandly probing finger stuck up inside, she checked the condition of the baby's diaper. "Oh dear, he's got full pants again. I just *changed* you," she crooned to the little boy, "and now you've gone and done it again, Nicky. You little pumpkin pie." She pressed her nose against the child's, smilingly clucking and fussing. Her voice was a brief sweet carol of delight. "Yes 'um did, I just *changed* you," she cooed, wiping her finger on her skirt, her distress drowned in the fount of maternal love. Then all of a sudden she herded the children together and, with the baby on her shoulder blinking drowsily at me over pink jowls, marched the brood downstairs, caroling sweetly all the way as if nothing had ever troubled her.

But when she returned ten minutes later she seemed as rattled and distraught as before. Gusty little spasms shook her as she talked and wandered aimlessly around the room. "I just couldn't believe it at first, when I got up this morning. I just couldn't believe my ears! But it was true. Everything was so funny when I got up. And you, Mr. Leverett, there you were—"

"Call me Peter," I said. "What do you mean?"

"Didn't you hear me? When I came into the room and woke you up? I thought you were Cass. He sleeps there sometimes when he's been up late and doesn't want to wake me. I shook you and you rolled over and groaned. I was greatly taken aback, I will say." She paused, twisting a damp handkerchief in her fists. "Of course, we're delighted to have you," she said politely.

"Where did it all happen?" I put in.

"You mean what— Oh dear—" She flushed and a look of pain came over her face. "Oh dear, it's so awful. I just couldn't find out anything. But I saw Mr. Alonzo Cripps just before he left, and he said that it occurred on the path going to Tramonti, just outside of town. There's an upper path and a lower path, and I think he said it occurred on the upper—no, maybe it was the lower. Anyway, some peasants found her on this path this morning and they lifted her up and took the poor creature to a house just inside the walls." Her voice broke off, a tremor passed through her, and two tears slid slowly down her cheeks. "Oh it's so awful! Jiminy Christmas, it's like out of the Dark Ages or something. I mean, Mason and all. I mean he was an evil cruel man and all, and he persecuted and took advantage of Cass' condition and everything but, golly, Mr.—Peter—it's just so hard to believe *that*. He must have become *crazed*." All at once she broke down and fell to sobbing into the tiny handkerchief, helplessly and weakly.

"How is the girl, Poppy?" I said. "Francesca. How is she? Do you know?"

"She's going to die," she said with a moan, still sobbing. "That's what they all say up the street. Oh, I wish I could find Cass!" She wore blue jeans now, there was a charm bracelet of yellow gold around her wrist; frail, hipless, with baggy socks and a smear of grease on her cheek, she looked like a pretty teen-ager who had fallen off a bicycle and was nursing her humiliation. My heart was wrung with sympathy for her. I glanced around at the proliferating mess of the room, which, I supposed, she tried somehow to cope with: that she should be a mother four times over touched me with awe and bafflement. I put my hand on her shoulder. "Take it easy, Poppy," I said, "he'll be back soon."

She raised her tear-stained face. "But where could he be?" she cried. "I've looked just *everywhere*. In the piazza, up by the Villa Constanza, in the market—everywhere! He's never gone away like this before! Never! Oh—" Her face lit up suddenly, inspired. "Oh yes, I forgot. I know where he might be! He might have gone to Salerno with Luigi. They often—"

"I saw Luigi. He said he hadn't seen Cass," I had to tell her.

"Oh golly Moses," she whispered, her face falling, looking desperate and scared. "Listen, Peter, I just know he's mixed up in it all somehow."

"What do you mean?" I said.

She was ashen-faced, and as she rose slowly from the chair I could have sworn I saw her teeth chattering. "Oh, I wish I could tell you! He's so sick and all, you know. I mean, he's an alcoholic as you doubtless know, and he's got this ulcer and all and he shouldn't drink, and then he's been having these dizzy spells. What I mean is—"

"What *do* you mean, Poppy?" I insisted. "How could he be mixed up in anything—"

"I don't know!" she blurted suddenly and tearfully. "Yes I do!" She had gone to the wall and pulled down a yellow rain slicker (it was not raining), and this, three sizes too large, she wrapped around her. "Women have premonitions, that's all. I mean—" she said with quivering mouth, "I mean, I know Cass! It was probably a profound shock to him, knowing Mason and knowing Francesca, who worked for us and all. So knowing Cass, what he has doubtless done is to get drunk and raving, and has gone and said some ugly, insulting things to the *carabinieri* about their conduct of the case, and they've locked him up in jail! He hates that Sergeant Parrinello! Phooey!" she said, stamping her foot, adjusting her bandanna. "He's so irresponsible, that Cass Kinsolving. Maybe," she added, drying her tears and staring at me with an air of haughty, worn-out patience, "you know, just maybe he should be committed to the Alcoholics Anonymous or something." She went to the door. "If the children should holler or anything, I'll be back in *venti minuti*. I'm going down to see if I can't get Cass out of jail. Just look in the icebox if you get hungry or anything. *Ciao!*" And with all her tender strength she slammed the door behind her. Her rapid queer reasoning, her motivation, left me flabbergasted, powerless to move: it suddenly occurred to me that she might be somewhat backward.

I went downstairs and got my luggage together. I could hear the children brawling in a bedroom: to hell with them, I thought, they could take care of themselves. I felt sticky and begrimed; as I sponged myself off in the bathroom I laid out for myself a plan for withdrawal. Money for me at that point was a minor concern; from a schedule I recalled seeing in the hotel lobby I knew the last bus to Naples had left, but I was certain that for the equivalent of ten dollars or so I could easily hire a car and driver to get me there. My boat to America, to be sure, did not leave until five days later, but I felt that it would not be unpleasant to mooch around Naples for a while, revisit the museum, go to Capri and Ischia and Ponza. And so I started to leave Sambuco. As I prepared to go upstairs I remembered the Austin: junk heap that it was, it had cost me thirteen hundred dollars, second hand, and I was not prepared to sacrifice it to the elements or to marauding Italians. But in the end I really didn't care. Perhaps I would wangle out of Windgasser a hundred thousand lire for the wreck—enough to pay for my Naples sojourn; failing that, I would let it stay parked where it was forever, shat upon by pigeons.

I did not see Cass at first when I reached the top of the stairs and went back through the living room. He must have come in quietly, or maybe his entrance had been drowned out by the scuffling children: I was almost to the door when, startled, I heard a noise behind me and whirled around to confront him. I didn't know what there was about Cass that made him seem at my first glimpse of him another—a different—person. It was Cass—he was dressed the same, in disheveled filthy khaki, and the beret was still cocked in fierce slant above his gleaming glasses—but it didn't quite look like Cass, an indefinable weird displacement of himself, rather, as if he were his own twin brother. Otherwise all was familiar: he was drunk, as I had first seen him. A bottle of wine dangled from one limp big paw, and he could scarcely stand erect, propping his hip for support against the table, just perceptibly and limply swaying. In his other hand he held the butt of a shredded and beslobbered black cigar. Very plainly in the stillness I could hear his deep and heavy breathing. At first I thought there was menace in his eyes, so constant and searching was his gaze upon me, but then I realized that, profoundly discomposed by alcohol, they were striving merely to focus. Finally when he spoke his voice was thick-tongued, hoarse, barely articulate. "Well, by God," he said slowly and deliberately, trying to master his tongue. "You caught me red-handed. Saw Poppy go out just now. Thought I could sneak in here and tend to my own business, unbeknownst to man or monster. Only I forgot all about you. I guess I'll have to put you out of the way, like they do in the flicks. You know too much, buddy. Where you off to so fast? You look like you just robbed a race track."

The suitcases slipped from my hands and clattered to the floor. "I—I don't know," I began "I was just—"

He cut me off with a wave of the wine bottle. "By God, it's good to see you, Pete," he said with a flabby-mouthed grin. "Man I can trust. Man I can talk to. Thought you was one of those wise movie boys for a while. Southern boy, ain't you? Georgia? Loosiana? Ole Virginia? Knew I could tell by that sweet corrupt look you got around the jowls. But then—ah, loving God!"

"What's the matter?" I said, in place of anything else. "Can I help you, old man?"

He recovered himself momentarily, focusing upon me his hot drowned eyes. "Yes, I'll tell you how you can help old Cass," he said somberly. "Now I'll tell you, my bleeding dark angel. Fetch him the machine, fetch him the wherewithal—a dagger, see, a dirk, well honed around the edges—and bring it here, and place it on his breastbone, and then with all your muscle drive it to the core." He paused, swaying slightly from side to side, never removing his gaze from my face. "No bullshit, Pete. I've got a lust to be gone from this place. Make me up a nice potion, see? Make it up out of all these bitter-tasting, deadly things and pour it down my gullet. Ole Cass has had a hard day. He's gone the full stretch and his head aches and his legs are weary, and there's no more weeping in him." He held out his arms. "These limbs are plumb wore out. Look at them, boy. Look how they shake and tremble! What was they made for, I ast you. To wrap lovely ladies about? To make monuments? To enfold within them all the beauty of the world? Nossir! They was made to destroy and now they are plumb wore out, and my head aches, and I yearn for a long long spell of darkness."

I tried to speak but my tongue clung to the roof of my mouth as slowly and ponderously he shuffled toward me, dropping the wine bottle which broke in splinters on the floor. He jammed the cigar butt into his mouth; his glasses made shiny half-dollars of reflected light. And as he came near me he seemed so full of clumsy sodden threat that I poised myself on the balls of my feet, ready for precipitate escape. But with astounding speed, quick as the strike of a rattlesnake, his arm went out and I felt my wrist go numb in the engulfing, savage grip of his hand. Reeking of sweat, pressing

238

close, he held me more now by his grasp than by his wild drink-demented gaze.

"Seddow," he said, releasing me.

"What!"

"Set down!" he commanded.

And I sat, transfixed.

"Well, he went and done it, didn't he?" he said, breathing hard. "At long last he went and done it."

I began to say something but he cut me off, swaying, let loose a tremendous belch, and then spat on the floor. "You'd think the bugger'd known better, wouldn't you?" He began to say something else, then came to a halt, his eyes wide and wild, lips apart. Then very slowly he said: "He couldn't die but once, and that's the bleeding pity of the matter. One time—"

"Take it easy," I mumbled, rubbing my wrist. I got up. "Loosen up, Cass. Just take it easy, will you?" Gingerly I patted him on the shoulder, trying to calm him, but he pulled away from me with a jerk and then slowly sank into a chair. He thrust his head into one hand and for a while was silent and still; squatting rigid and immobile, his muscles tightly contorted beneath his wet stained shirt, he looked almost as if he were sculpted there, a great aching lowering figure like Rodin's "Thinker," caught in an attitude not of meditation but grief. I listened to his breath escape whistling and tortured through his nostrils; far off beyond the walls the tolling bells rose muffled, clangorous, doleful.

"What happened to the flicker creeps?" he said.

"They're gone."

I thought he grinned. "When the old boat founders it's the rats that's first to go."

Then again he fell silent. When at last he spoke, in a dull, hoarse monotone, his words made so little sense to me that I felt that it was not wine which had so bested his mind, but something far more unhinging and profound: *"Exeunt omnes.* Exit the whole lousy bunch. Enter Parrinello, gut throbbing, with a fat theory. *Gentilissimi signori, tutto è chiaro!* With his own remorse he slew himself. Mother of God! A brain stuffed with mohair soaked in piss. Show me a smart policeman and I'll show you a girl named Henry." His shoulders began to heave with laughter, only I could see—as he slowly raised his face—that it was not laughter at all; his convulsions were those of a man who was weeping, if it is possible to weep without shedding tears. Dry-eyed, racked by spasms of grief, he arose and cast me such a look of envenomed wrath that I flexed myself once more for quick flight from the room.

"Longer'n I can remember," he said in a whisper, "I been hungering for my own end. Longer'n I can remember! Now there's a justification. Give me odds, boy. Give me odds! Listen. Tell me. Tell me that ten million times I got to die, to find beyond the grave only darkness, and then be born again to live out ten million wretched lives, then die again and so on, to find ten million darknesses. Listen, boy! Tell me this! But tell me that *once* in ten million deaths I'll find no darkness past the grave, but *him,* standing there in the midst of eternity, grinning if you please like some shit-eating dog and ready for the fury of these hands, then I'll take your bet, boy, straight off, and be done with living in half a minute. Oh, I should not have let him off so easy! Oh!" he repeated. "I should not have let him off so easy!"

"What do you mean?"

"Nossir," he said, in a remote voice now. "Can't get *to* the bugger. Old Mason's dead as a smelt."

He staggered to his feet. He made a curious, importuning gesture with his hand, as if beckoning me toward him, then clapped it against his brow. His voice as he stood swaying there remained distant, ruminative: "You know, it seems to me that today sometime I was laying on the high slopes above Tramonti, up there where the cool winds blow and the earth is full of columbine. And streams of water, boy—streams of cool water coming down from the hills! And I dreamt that my love was in my arms and we was all home at last. Then along came this here doctor, rousing me out of sleep, this doctor with a long bush of a beard and a boutonniere and a red nose. And do you know what he said to me as I lay there, this old doc? Know what he said?

I couldn't speak.

"Said he: Have you heard that your lady, who was so fair, is slain? And he put ice on my brow and he cooled my fever, and I said to him: Estimable Signor Doctor, do not fool with old Cass. Bleeding doctor! Say that his lady still lives, she whose solitary footprint in the dust was more precious than all the treasures of the world! But it seems to me that then he said: No, it is true, your lady is truly dead. And then I knew it was true enough."

He ran a limp hand slowly across his eyes. Suddenly his arm snaked out for a wine bottle on the table, an awkward motion which, unbalancing him, set him teetering against the chair, where for a split second he swam with his legs out in mid-space at an impossible gravity-defying angle before coming down hard upon the floor, legs and arms asprawl and upsetting the ponderous easel with a crash. He lay inert and motionless on the floor in a spreading, shimmering cloud of dust. Rigid with horror, I could not move to help him, stood there wondering if indeed at last he had killed himself. After a time, though, he stirred and with great effort, still prone and akimbo, composed his limbs and slowly pried himself up into a sitting position on the floor. He shook his head dazedly, pressing his hand to his brow, where, through his open splayed-out fingers, I could see trickling a tiny stream of blood. I spoke to him: he said nothing. Behind me I could hear a slow clumsy patter of feet, and I turned: aroused, I suppose, by the crashing easel, two children came into the room with frightened eyes. "It's Daddy. Oh look, he hurt himself!" They stood watching him for a moment. Then silently, ghostlike, as if wafted toward him by the breeze which suddenly blew up the slope and set some shade or blind to chattering in a remote corner of the room, they crept weightlessly into his arms.

Bloody, with dazed and glassy eyes, he drew the children next to him in a smothering embrace. "Press close to me on either side—" he began, then ceased. Abruptly, gently, he pushed them aside and struggled to his feet. He looked at me but he no longer saw me, I'm sure, his eyes fixed instead through me and beyond me upon some vista mysterious and distant and sufficient unto itself. His lips moved, but made no sound.

Then as swiftly as his lurching gait could move him, he shouldered past me to the door. There, ignoring Poppy, who had just returned, ignoring both her shrill squeal of anguish—"Oh, Cass! You've changed!"—and her tumbling collapse as she fell forward toward him, swooning, in a crumpled heap upon the floor, he staggered past her through the courtyard and out of sight. And it was only seconds later, bending over Poppy (watching her eyelids slowly part as she murmured to me, "Oh, Cass, you've changed"), that I realized at last that all this time his face had been a face which, in the space of a day, had aged a dozen years.

PART TWO

This shaking keeps me steady. I should know.
What falls away is always. And is near.
I wake to sleep, and take my waking slow.
I learn by going where I have to go.

THEODORE ROETHKE

V

One day on our riverbank in South Carolina, Cass said to me: "I always figured you knew I had killed him. Not that it worried me too much, for some reason. I remember blabbing to you that night, running off at the mouth, but I never could remember just how much I said. I thought I'd given myself away, though. The funny thing is that it really didn't bother me. Maybe it was because I knew the Italians had closed up the case, it was a suicide, and that was that. You couldn't much blame them. Two people found dead like that—almost at the same time, you know—and there sure wasn't much reason to look around for a culprit, much less to pin it on the Deacon Kinsolving, who was the soul of rectitude." He paused. "Anyway, I didn't ever have any worry about your going and spilling the beans. Put that out of your mind. Maybe the simple fact of the matter is that when it was all over nothing really mattered any more. I'd gone the limit, and what anybody might do or say meant nothing. See this gray old head?" He stroked the side of his brow and there was neither pride nor self-pity in the gesture. "I guess it was kind of small of me to keep up the pretense with you down here for so long. Somehow I knew you knew. But it's a tough thing to come out and say. To admit. It puts you in the position of having to explain the whole bleeding miserable business, and that hurts. Do you understand?"

"Of course I understand," I said. "But one thing. I didn't ever *know*. I suspected it. You had said some rather odd things. So I suspected it. And those few days there, when you didn't *come back,* and I stayed and—well, helped out Poppy and the kids, it really weighed heavy on my mind. You were suffering, and—well, if this doesn't sound too embarrassing, I cared for you. You'd done something to me, opened my eyes about a lot of things, and I just didn't want you to drift out of sight. So when I left Poppy and the kids finally and came back to New York without having seen you again, without ever having known what the real story was—how you stayed alive and all, much less stayed out of jail—I just kept wondering about you, that's all, wondering how the hell you made out. And wondering what the real story was. Yet it's strange how one rationalizes. When I wrote you, when I invited myself down here that first time, it was really I thought just out of the hugest curiosity, about Mason and what he'd done that summer to bring himself to such a—a godawful end, and knowing that you'd probably be able to tell me something about him. Still saying to myself that it was a suicide, after all. Yet I know that part of my reason was—well—" I found it difficult to say the word, or words.

"The suspicion that I'd killed him," he said, somewhat morosely. "Don't be bashful, my friend. Say it. It's not as hard for you to say it as it is for me."

"All right, that you'd killed him. Understand," I began to explain, "I wasn't snooping. I wasn't being any bloodhound. You could have done away with five hundred Masons, for what he did, and as far as my moral position in the matter—"

"God sake, boy, you don't have to tell me. I knew you weren't *after* anything." He paused. "On the other hand, maybe you can understand why I didn't send an answer to that other letter of yours. There's some things you'd just as soon forget."

"I shouldn't have stuck my big—"

"Don't get yourself in a sling about it," he put in. "I shouldn't have said that. These things you've told me. They've made me mighty glad we've thrashed this out after all. You've lightened some dark spots."

"Like what?"

"Oh, about Mason, for one thing—what kind of a man he was, and so on. Outside of Sambuco, that is. And then—as I've said—about that night. What was going on in the midst of my black, blind, grizzly, suffocating darkness. It's made me see things that I really didn't know before. Wild things." He halted for an instant. "Terrible things, really," he added in a bleak unhappy voice. "Things that shift it around somehow. Things I've always suspected, had hints about, but never really knew—due to the aforesaid darkness. Whoo!" He shivered a little and rubbed his eyes. "Not that anything can really be changed," he went on, "being so completely over. But you might say it's fascinating."

"What, for instance?"

"Oh, like when I came up and fell over the piano and you and Cripps salvaged me. You see, it comes back to me now. It came back to me when you told me about it. Remember that drug—that bleeding wonder-drug antibiotic? *That's* what I'd come up there for that time; it sure wasn't to babble any Sophocles. That's what was on my mind."

"So—"

"Well, so if I'd managed my slick little bit of thievery *then,* the whole crazy evening would have been changed. I'd have gotten down to the valley and gotten back and—" But he stopped and threw up a hand. "Bugger it, you just can't trifle with fate, I guess."

"Lord, if I had known—"

"Forget it. How the hell *could* you have known?" He gazed at me gently, with a sort of sad benign tolerance all over his face. "You'd think that you had something to do with it all. I've got enough guilt about it to equip a regiment of sinners and now you want to horn in with your own. What's the matter with you, boy, anyway?"

"Nothing," I said. "Nothing much. Small clues. Little items like the fact that I knew something mean and ugly was going on between you and Mason. That note of yours for one thing. That was one of those things that was in the back of my mind for months. And—oh, I don't know—some of the things you said. I should have gotten Cripps or someone— That is, somewhere along the line there I should have just waked up and taken hold of myself and tried to get you strapped down in some position where you couldn't do anybody any harm." I paused. "I'm working on the assumption, of course, that you wish it hadn't happened, in spite of what Mason did. Right?"

"You're right," he said, and the look of sorrow on his face was abruptly so total and painful that I turned my eyes away. "Boy, you're sure right."

"Tell me something, Cass," after we were both silent for a long time. "What *was* it between you and Mason?" I hesitated for a moment. "I don't mean to sound stupid. All right, there was the girl. Francesca and— You—well, you know what I mean. He ravished her, killed her. And for that you finished him off. All that's evident and plain. But what were these other things? That horrible act he made you go through, and—"

"Ahhh!" he said. "How do you know? How can you ever tell? How can you ever know where the blame lies? What part was Mason's and what part was mine and what part was God's. Sometimes I've had nightmares about it—or I used to, before I got ahold of myself—and in these nightmares someone or something told me that it wasn't Mason who was the culprit—wasn't Mason who was the wicked party—but only your old friend the preacher here, who was the evilest man who ever walked. Sometime I'll let you look at my journal, and read the story as she is writ. It didn't start in Sambuco, either, if you really want to know. It started—a lot of it anyway—in my own heart, on the day I was born. It started—" He paused for a long while, then rose up on his elbow and looked into my eyes. "I'm going to ask you a funny question. Do you believe in —well, what they call the supernatural? I know that's a queer word."

"Are you kidding?"

"Neither do I," said he, "not one bit. But do you want to know something? When I look back on it—or at least take it back as far as I can, to Paris, say, where you know Poppy and the kids and I were before we went to Italy—when I look back there and try to get a perspective on it, I can't help but believe that something *forced* me to go to Sambuco. These nightmares I had. I put them in my journal, too. Strange ones. Half out of the devil, half out of paradise. They forced me, *drug* me there—do you understand what I mean? It was as if I had to go there—and that what happened there, to be fancy, was some sort of logical end-product of what had been prefigured in these dreams. Shithouse mouse! This is hard to get at. Do you follow me?"

"I don't know if I do or not," I said. "Things that are not

strictly of this world tend to give me the creeps. Tell me this. Did you like Mason at first? I mean when you first met him down in Sambuco, did he—"

"It didn't *start* with Mason, I'm telling you," he insisted, emphatic now, earnest. "It started in me, early, way back. I suppose it started on the day I was born, like I say. But it really started in Paris the year before, when I was sick and these here nightmares began to come upon me. It began *then,* and without knowing about that you couldn't know how and why it ended with Mason. Do you understand?"

"I don't really—" I began. I only dimly realized that he was prompting me for a blast.

"Get this clear," he said. He had risen to his feet, I thought somewhat agitated; his voice even more than before was heavy with emphasis, urgency. "This has got to be made clear, because, Peter, I don't really think you quite understand about Mason. Beast, bastard, crook, and viper. But the guilt is not his! I been asking and asking and asking it from you, hoping you would show me he was *evil.* But no. He's still just scum. Don't you see? Nossir! The guilt is not his!"

"No, I don't see," I said positively.

There was a long silence. Then he said, more gently now: "No, there's really no reason why you should. There's just no reason why you should at all." And he stopped, then said: "He *didn't kill* Francesca, that's what I'm trying to tell you."

It came as quick as that.

"No, goddammit," he said, "don't look at me like that. Straighten up, boy. Do you want to get the facts now? Or the truth?"

"The truth," I managed to say, somehow, straightening up.

"Well, visualize the Kinsolvings in Paris, if you please." (In the fishing shack again, another night, after my mind had slowly adjusted itself to a lot of things.) "We'd been there a year, I guess. We were cramped together enough, God knows, in the palace, but what we had in Paris wouldn't have accommodated a proper clutch of dwarfs. Two only halfway-big rooms for the six of us— Nicky had just been born—and a two-by-four john and a huge big window that covered the entire wall. Sometimes I think if it hadn't been for that goddam window I really *would* have gone nuts. What I mean is, a big elephant vine had grown up on the outside and it covered the entire window, so that in the spring and summer and fall when the light streamed through, it passed through these huge green translucent leaves and filled the whole room with a kind of shimmering jade light. That sounds like it might be annoying but it wasn't: it was quite marvelous in a way and sometimes it kept my mind off of—well, off these *fleas* of life that were constantly biting my back. You know what I mean: Poppy, bless her heart—forever blameless Poppy—and Nicky's colic and not painting and lack of money, and so on et cetera. And my miserable ulcer, though it was fairly quiet at the time. Sometimes when I think back I wonder which flea was the biggest—lack of money, I suppose. Well, Poppy had some money coming in from Delaware, from some trust fund her father had set up, but it wasn't a hell of a lot, for my type of ménage. And I had a little coming in from that disability pension—not much, either, but altogether we got along somehow. No, I don't guess that was the big flea after all. I guess the real monster was—well, my *condition* at the time, if you want to put it that way.

"You know, you can't work without faith, and, boy, I was as faithless as an alleycat. Godalmighty, the rationalizations I used, and the lies! I told myself I had no talent, you see; that was the first evasion. Yet, hell, I knew I had talent, knew it in my soul, knew it as well as I know my own name. I *had* it, there was no getting around it, and the knowledge that I had it and wouldn't use it or was afraid to use it or refused to use it just made my misery that much worse. Hell, I knew I could paint rings around anyone —at least of my own age and experience. Anyone! Yet in front of a sketch pad or a canvas I was like a man who had suddenly had both hands chopped off at the wrist. Completely paralyzed, I was. And I'd go snooping around the galleries or a modern show at the Orangerie and sneer and snicker and pooh-pooh all the amateurish stuff I saw—just like some miserable little fag or a dilettante— yet deep down I was hurting: boy, I was hurting! For at least they had produced something, and I was still a mean little cesspool of bitter, pent-up, frustrated, hopeless desires. Well, you know you still have to have reasons. So, when I examined myself and found that the no-talent excuse wouldn't go, I dreamed up all sorts of other answers: the time was out of joint, society was against me, painting had been supplanted by photography anyway, all of that. Boy, Kinsolving pitted against Kinsolving, what a dreary battle! Anyway, I couldn't work. I was perfectly blocked, dammed up like the inside of some miserable, pussy eardrum, and hurting like crazy. But it would have taken all the *flics* in Paris to drag me to a brain-healer, which I guess is what I needed."

"We Christians have to stick together," I said facetiously.

"It's not a matter of being Christian," he said, "it's a matter of common sense. Unless a man's gone completely berserk, he's got to work out these problems for himself, that's all. It's a matter of pride. Besides, I knew a nut doctor once—not Slotkin, but a real phony—on the psycho ward of that naval hospital I told you about I was in, right after the war. This guy, I'll swear before God, could barely count to ten. He had a tiny little brow about a quarter of an inch high and a red nose and hair sticking out of his ears, and the only other thing I remember about him is that he had never even *heard* of Daumier. Pronounced it Dow-Myer, like some bleeding psychological test. Jesus, how could a guy like that ever get together with somebody who had my problems—at least the ones I had in Paris? Anyway, to go back to where it all started: all this pressure was in me, as I've said. There I was in the most beautiful —no, second most, Florence has the edge—city on earth, all in a sweat and fever to capture something, to get it down, to crystallize it, to preserve it, leave a record or something, and I had no more ability to do it than some blind old dropsical eunuch of ninety-five. What a setup, what a perfect way to become a whiskey-head! Well, I plunged in head-on. And that started me off on this jag—well, you know how it ended. I don't know how it came on—gradually, I guess, but the first thing I knew it had me squarely by the balls. You should have seen me, boy—no, I remember you did. But if I was bad in Sambuco, in Paris I was even worse, maybe because it hadn't beaten me down yet and I could just take on a bigger load. I was like some bleeding camel who'd just staggered in off the Gobi with a big hump waiting to be filled to the brim. God, the stuff I put away! If there's such a thing in lushdom as being a nymphomaniac about booze, I was it—a regular hard-on I had for the stuff, half-insane, I guess, like some fat repulsive little kid turned loose in a soda fountain. *Ah,* I don't even want to think about it."

We sat in silence for a minute, but obviously he wanted to go on.

"Dragged me, that's the way it felt. I felt like I was *dragged* to Sambuco. And I still don't know whether or not I might just be imagining the whole thing: it could have been a series of coincidences, after all, which in the end just seems to add up to one thing. Anyway, visualize once again the Kinsolvings in Paris. Are you conjuring it up, boy? Well, visualize this: a top-floor studio on a sad dusty little side street not far from the Gare Montparnasse, a big room where elephant vines cast these trembling jade shapes of light. It is a Sunday afternoon in the late spring of the year. There is the fragrance of bread in the air, and of sadness too, because Paris always smells sad even when she is most sunny and beautiful. That's the God's truth. There is a dog barking down on the street. Upstairs there is a sound of chaos and havoc. *Entrons.* Behold the occupants of this noisy den. First there is Poppy—née Pauline Shannon—Kinsolving, the châtelaine of the house, scioness of a large Delaware family—not the du Ponts, regrettably—unique in all this world in her strange blend of childish wisdom and elfin (Christ, I hate that word!) charm, the pride and joy and despair of her husband's life—sweet-souled, generous, loving, and the world's most catastrophic housewife. She is dressed only in a pink slip. Her hair is festooned with aluminum curlers. With one hand she offers a bottle to an infant in a bassinet (Nicky, just born by Caesarean section), and with her voice she is shrieking at three children who romp in pandemonium through the steaming room around her. Let's see: they are eight, five . . . No, Peggy must have been six then. Anyway, to hell with it. They are beautiful noisy children and they so resemble their mother that she is often mistaken for their sister. Poppy is screeching at the top of her voice. 'Children!' she yells. 'Children! Children! Be *qui*-yut! Yull scare the *baby!*' Her words avail her not; she has no more control over her offspring than she would have over a pack of timber wolves. In despair she rolls her eyes, turns, drops the ice-cream cone she has been licking and screams in desperation to her husband. 'Cass!' she cries. 'Make them shuddup!' "

He paused for a moment. Then, "That Poppy," he said, with a soft wry chuckle. "Boy, she took a lot of crap from me, and all without a murmur hardly. She's Catholic, as you know, and I—well, I don't know what I am, or was, but I surer'n hell wasn't a Catholic, and I guess I used this religion of hers as a sort of scapegoat for all my meanness. Actually I had quite a religious background myself, and I'd forsaken it about as completely as you can get (still have, for that matter) but at the time I must have built up a whole lot of guilt about it, a real head of steam. My father was a minister, you know. Well, after he and my mother were run down by this train in Rich Square, North Carolina—I was ten at the time —this old uncle of mine took me over and brought me up. He and my aunt were Methodists, real pious and all, and he always wanted me to become a minister because his dear wife's brother had been one, and because of tradition and all. But I wanted to be a painter. I didn't want to become some dewlapped young fraud hobnobbing with the seraphim, and swapping the sweat of my palm each Sunday with a flock of usurers and bankers, and softening my brain telling a bunch of used-car dealers how righteous they were. So I didn't. So after the war, when I was going to art school in New York, I met Poppy. Love at first sight. Her family had a little dough, which didn't hurt any, either. Anyway, she tickled the hell out of me. She was on her way to flunking out of her first year at Vassar, not because she's dumb, you know, but because—well, I think she was a little what you might call *ethereal* for that kind of setup, and anyway I fell for her like a carload of bricks, Catholicism and all. I didn't realize at the time how I'd start to use this really mean backlog of ignorant Protestant prejudice against her, bludgeoning her with it to shore up my own inadequacy. It must have been horrible for her sometimes. I should have been taken out and shot.

"Anyway, to get back to Paris . . . Let us examine the old man, this terrible blob, the master of the house—this vegetable, this wreck, this painter without portfolio. Half-supine, he lolls against the pillows of a shabby day bed, a cigarette dangling, *à l'Apache,* from his lips, a bottle of very low-class cognac suspended in his hand. He is reading a copy of . . . oh, I guess *Confidential.* Or *Front Page Detective,* or *Wink,* or *Whisper,* or any of a couple dozen darling American magazines I used to pick up in this store on the rue du Bac. That was how low I'd sunk. Anyway, regard him again, this newt, this ox. Poppy shrieks again. 'Cass! The baby's got *stummick* trouble and you just lie there! Cass, *do* something!' He obviously hears her, for he stirs and groans, and a flicker of annoyance, if not of actual displeasure, passes across his spongy features. Without saying a word, he continues to pluck through his catalogue of white thighs and white tits and ripe round behinds. Poppy shrieks again, the dog howls on the street, the children dance and scream. Over all, the repulsive odor of boiling turnips. At last, just as this . . . this frail young maiden's voice reaches its terrible shrill crescendo, a pot falls from the stove in a roar and a splash and an explosion of steam. The ox heaves to his feet. And stands there, bellowing. 'Get out of this goddam house, you pack of slimy maggots!' he roars. 'At once! All of you!' he shouts, gazing glassy-eyed at the beautiful children, fruit of his loins. 'All of you goddam people, *out* of here! Jump in the river! Die! Get run over! Out of here! Stay out! Stay out! Get out of here and stay out, do you hear, before I turn on the gas!' He sends them packing, all right. Babbling hysterically, the whole brood sobbing and bawling with fright and panic, they flee down the stairs and into the street. Poppy is so frightened that she puts her skirt on backwards and is shaking so that she can scarcely get through the door with the poor colicky baby in her arms. . . ." He paused.

"And then—?"

"Ah well," he said, in a leveler tone. "It was gruesome. You know, the great trouble with self-disgust is not the ruination it works on oneself—though that's bad enough—but the way it so easily can begin to upset other people's lives. Oh, I'd had difficult times with Poppy off and on—who the hell who's married hasn't? —but this was the first time I'd ever done something like that. It was sickening, really; and what I'd really done, it's plain enough to see, was to simply turn the loathing I felt for myself outward upon Poppy and the children. Ah God, it was sickening! Once in Sambuco, during one of my better—or sober—periods, I remember I awoke from a dream. I can't recall this particular dream, except that it had a written message for me. It was one of the strangest dreams I ever had, because it was as if some fruity old moralist of the subconscious had risen up and written in chalk this maxim right straight across my brain. For a moment I thought I was the reincarnation of some great philosopher, it all seemed so perfectly true. It went like this: 'To triumph over self is to triumph over Death. It is to triumph over that beast which one's self interposes between one's soul and one's God.' It's true as hell, you know. Anyway, I had no such notions or insights there in Paris. Self! Self! God, I was a regular *puddle* of self. I mean I felt I could hear— almost see—every contraction of my ulcerous stomach, and watch my kidneys straining away and sieving out all the crud, and see the loops of my intestines slick and gray and sweaty in their battle against all the poison I was guzzling down, and my bronchial tubes all filthy with French cigarettes, and my *brain!* My poor old aching, suffering brain! God, I was a mess. Of self. Conscious of nothing in the world so much as my own miserable ambulating corpuscles.

"Well, that day I suppose I got as low as I could get. Later that day, anyway. I remember that after they had left I went to the window and watched them scampering down the street. Whenever I think of it now it near about breaks my heart, but at the time, as I say, I was in a perfect alcoholic fog, absolutely unmoved by the picture: Poppy, not much bigger than a mouse, with the baby in

her arms, hustling down the street with its dusty springtime light—
a real Utrillo street—and the kids tagging and galloping after, all
of them heading for God knows where. Then they were gone
around a corner. They were gone, and I was alone in the house,
sort of sagging there with my nauseating self. I had an old beat-up
record player at the time—you saw it in Sambuco. A man can't
live properly, of course, without music. Even though music itself,
when abused, is a form of corruption. I remember reading somewhere in *The Republic* a passage where Plato says that in the ideal
State music will have to be curtailed and regulated by law, its appeal is so powerful—it's so likely to dope the spirit. There's truth in
that, I know, because at the time along with all the booze I was using music as a sort of—oh, an auxiliary drug, which gave me even
bigger kicks and let me tear loose my emotions. Just like everything else that's good you've got to use music wisely. Anyway, as
I say, I had this record player that I'd picked up at the Flea Market for a few thousand francs, and I'd oiled it and fixed it up. It
played loud as hell. It was a scratchy hoarse monster but I had a
few records: *The Magic Flute* and *Don Giovanni* and some early
Haydn and Christian Bach and the *St. Matthew Passion* and a Pa-
lestrina mass and—oh yes, I had an ancient Leadbelly album with
about every record held together by Scotch tape. Old Leadbelly.
Every time I heard 'The Midnight Special' I got right back to
Carolina. Anyway— So that day, I remember, after they had gone
—gone forever at that moment, for all I cared or knew—I opened
another bottle of this crummy brandy and got my *Magic Flute* out
and put it on and staggered around the joint for a while, hating myself, hating Poppy and my own glands and the life-force or whatever it was that caused me to produce such a useless, snotty-nosed,
colicky tribe, and I began to trip over things—one of Poppy's ga-
loshes or some goddam toy—and I fetched it a lick with my foot,
and missed, and kicked the wall, which almost broke my toe, and
that set me to stamping around again and cursing and hating myself even more, as if I was caught up in some endless circle of self-
loathing and venom and meanness. Well, I began to simmer down
—gradually, I guess—most likely the music was stealing into my
bones, and I took another terrific slug out of the bottle, and then—
I remember the moment so clear and plain—I walked over to the
window. Now, ever since—well, ever since I've straightened out,
or whatever you want to call it—I've tried to figure out what was
happening to me at the time, inside of my body, that is. I've
thought about it and I've read about it, and the only conclusion

that I've been able to come to is that these—well, these *visions* I had were not psychic, that is, they weren't mystical or supernatural or anything except the simple fact that I was a soggy lush-head in whose scrambled brain all sorts of hallucinations could happen— must happen, in fact. I don't mean the D.T.'s, either. It's a simple fact that when you set out, as I had been doing, to destroy yourself and don't eat, preferring instead to slop down each day about two quarts of swill lacking vitamins, minerals, calories, corpuscles, hu- mors, gray matter, or any other substance necessary to both health and sanity—when you do this, I say, and flog your lungs with *Gauloises Bleues* (and cheap cigars) and stumble about the streets of Paris breathing the fumes of incinerated gasoline and get so low as I did, I swear, so depleted and exhausted, that even the old pecker refuses to twitch at the most wildly pornographic fan- tasy—when you're in this state, all I'm trying to say is that some kind of hallucination, some kind of weird displacement of the mind, is not only likely, but bound to happen.

"As I say, I remember going to the window. It was a spring af- ternoon, warm, full of pollen; you could almost touch the air and have it turn to yellow dust in your fingers. Then there were these elephant vines, huge and green and tropical. These shiny harmless little ladybugs—the French have a wonderful name for them, *bêtes à Bon Dieu*—they were swarming all over the leaves, so that when I bent closely down to watch them, watching these spotted black backs and russet-colored glossy wings, with the great green leaves behind, they looked like some strange surrealistic armadil- los crawling through a jungle. A big golden spider had built a web in the crotch of one of the vines, and I wondered why she hadn't trapped any of the ladybugs, until I remembered that ladybugs are supposed to secrete a smell or something that's repulsive to spiders. Well, I stood there for a long while looking at the leaves and the ladybugs, smelling bread baking down below, listening to the mu- sic. And then finally, in a sort of doze, and with all my hatred and poison lost for the moment, or forgotten, I looked up. And I'll swear at the moment as I looked up it was as if I were gazing into the kingdom of heaven. I don't know quite how to describe it— this *bone-breaking* moment of loveliness. I was almost sick with desire and yearning for what I saw. It was only this same street in Paris, of course, this sad and nondescript Paris street with its lean- ing gables and tarnished doorknobs and weatherworn, filigreed lamp posts, and a shabby plane tree or two, and now an old woman had come out of a door massaging her hands, and there was a dog vanishing into an alleyway. Way down the street was the wall of the Montparnasse Cemetery and above it the sky rose up blue, blue, and now there were pigeons up there, a great flight of sun-flecked wings, all wheeling around in space. And over all this the sense of afternoon, of Sunday, of spring, of tranquillity and repose. And behind me in the room Mozart splashing away, mad and sane and tender and—what?—*good!* Brought straight down from the Maker of us all! Ah my God, how can I describe it! It wasn't just the *scene,* you see—it was the sense, the bleeding *essence* of the thing. It was as if I had been given for an instant the capacity to understand not just beauty itself by its outward signs, but the other—the *else*ness in beauty, this continuity of beauty in the scheme of all life which triumphs even to the point of taking in sordidness and shabbiness and ugliness, which goes on and on and on, and of which this was only a moment, I guess, divinely crystallized. God, the magic of that moment! What was it, really? I just don't know—the weakness, the light-headedness, the booze, the vertigo. Yet it was there, and for the first time—the first moment of reality I think I had ever known. And the strange thing was that it was in the midst of this, in the midst of a time when I was most wrapped up in self and squalor and meanness, I had a presentiment of selflessness: I mean, it was as if the crummy little street had been for an instant transformed into some grand, gay boulevard of my own spirit, where I no longer walked alone, but where so many countless generations of lovers and old women and dogs and children had walked, and where there would walk generations of lovers and old women and dogs and children yet unborn. It was no longer a street that I was watching; the street was inside my very flesh and bones, you see, and for a moment I was released from my own self, embracing all that was within the street and partaking of all that happened there in time gone by, and now, and time to come. And it filled me with the craziest sort of joy. . . ."

He paused for a long time, concentrating, as if to summon all that he could of that afternoon.

"I've done it badly," he said finally. "I feel that I've only gotten a little bit of it over. I've done it badly. But that's the trouble when —when you try to describe a—a state like this. You end up like some shaggy tenth-century anchorite, hooting and hollering that he's been raped by a platoon of angels. It's like the criticism of a painting: it just can't be done, you've got to look at it yourself. Well, anyway, maybe you can see how, if I got such a boot out of these spells, I didn't want to give up the very thing that caused them, even if the very thing that caused them was a self-destructive thing of booze and slow starvation and nervous exhaustion. Suicide, really. No, I wouldn't say I didn't want to give it up. Like anybody who's hooked, who's wrassling with the beast, I'd have given anything to be free, to be clean. Besides, a—a *seizure* like the one I was telling you about didn't come too often, even when I was pouring it on the most. But I must say the prospect of having one again sort of took some of the curse off—off the horror. Even if the worst—"

"The worst what?" I asked, when he failed to finish the sentence.

"Well, let me go back to where I was. I can't say how long this moment of *rapture*—I guess, that's what it was—I don't know how long it lasted, maybe not more than half a minute, I suspect even less than that. Then a strange thing happened. Again it was something I had never experienced before. I fainted, blacked out. One moment I was standing there with my heart pumping away, watching the street and the plane trees and the dog trotting up the alleyway and the pigeons high above, and then the scene just dribbled away before my eyes, in rivulets, as if it had all been no more substantial than a rag doll left out in the rain, and I saw all the colors and outlines draining slowly out of sight, and all went black then as if I had been accepted gently but positively into the very bosom of death—I even thought that as I melted away—and I felt nothing except a kind of endless black repose and peace. And yet, do you know something? With all of this—with all of this sense of eternity crowding around me, and passing into some space of infinite time—I didn't move an inch from the place where I was standing. My head—only my forehead—had drooped down and banged itself gently against the windowpane, and I snapped my neck up and saw not the night or passage of time that I had expected but the woman, by God, still standing there massaging her hands, the plane trees trembling, casting the same shadow, and the pigeons high up still whirling around over the cemetery. Only the dog had finally vanished, and even his shadow I could still see against the far wall of the alleyway with a leg uplifted as he watered a tree. The woman singing Mozart was still soaring off on the same aria, the same measure, in fact. I hadn't even dropped the bleeding cognac. And I was standing there in the green light from the elephant vines, rubbing the bump on my forehead and breathing like a maniac, and troubled, and close to weeping, feeling that

I had tied into the space of a minute more emotion than a man should have in a couple of years."

The recollection seemed to shake him and sadden him, and so gradually I somehow managed to change the subject. Yet later I happened to touch on that afternoon, inadvertently, and before I was scarcely aware of it he was reliving the whole thing again. But first there was a diversion.

"That reminds me," he said. "Once, you know, when I was a kid, sixteen or seventeen or so, and living up near Wilmington on this river I was telling you about—once, I remember, one Saturday afternoon I went into town all by myself. Listen! This has a whole lot to do with it all. . . . I got slicked up and put on my patent-leather shoes and my pin-stripe suit from Montgomery Ward and I went to Wilmington. I was quite a sight, I guess, a young hayseed with big gawky hands and store-bought glasses and a hand-painted tie and a wide simple country-boy's leer on my face. I don't know, I might even have had a touch of a mustache then; I remember I grew one at some time: we lived in a mighty depressed area in those days. It was right around the beginning of the war, I remember: the streets were packed with soldiers and Marines, and it was hot, and I remember I had only one thing on my mind and that was to get me a piece of nooky. I hadn't ever had a girl, you see— hell, never even touched one!—and I figured they were going to put *me* into the Army, too, and soon, and ship me off to a place where there weren't anything but colored girls or something, and so I guess I made up my mind that it was now or never. Well, I remember walking around the streets of Wilmington all afternoon, feeling my oats and snooping around and poking my nose into little beer joints, and getting chased out on account of my age, and feeling hornier and hornier, like some young billygoat, really, and making the terrible discovery as I went along that there just weren't any girls to be had: what few of them there were, the soldiers had. I got pretty downcast after a while. You know, there's nothing more pitiful on earth than a boy of seventeen and his clumsy, suffering desire. So it got to be evening, finally, and it got later and later and I still hadn't found me a girl. I remember a soldier told me that I could get a good piece for five bucks at a certain hotel, but five bucks for me in those days was close to being a millionaire.

"Well, I dragged on back toward the bus station finally, figuring that it was a bad job all around. Then just as I turned a corner, standing full in the gorgeous light from the windows of this Rexall drug store, she appeared to me: the black-eyed, heart-stopping, resplendent girl of my dreams. My God, I can even remember her name! It was Vernelle Satterfield. And do you know what she was doing? She was standing there—this little ripe peach of a girl, this delectable nymph in bobbysox, this marvel of nubile and ravishing womanhood—she was standing there in the dazzling Rexall light and she was hawking *Watchtowers* at five cents a copy for the Jehovah's Witnesses. For a moment she struck me almost blind, she seemed so beautiful. And she was: all brown hair and round young breasts and soft contours and rose-gold Botticelli flesh. Well, I don't guess I was any paragon of—of suavity in those days, but somehow I managed it; maybe it was just the force of my unbridled passions. Anyway, I hove to alongside her and gave her a nickel for a *Watchtower* and then another nickel for a lot of other junk she had, all the time hemming and hawing and trying to act benign and elderly, and finally I laid out fifty cents for the collected sermons of the Judge whatever-his-name-was who ran the outfit, and that clinched it: I told her my name and she told me hers, and she said she was plumb exhausted from having to fend off soldiers all afternoon, and that I was the only gentleman she'd encountered in some time, and though she would have to decline my invitation to have a beer, as her religion forbade it, she would join me in an ice-cream sundae. So I took her into the Rexall's. Mother of God . . .

"Vernelle Satterfield!" he exclaimed, with a look of long reminiscence. "Christ, I'll remember that girl till the day I die! Never on earth was a ripe, toothsome, palpitatingly carnal reality touched with such a glow of virginity and innocence. She was sixteen and a half, she said. Imagine, saying sixteen *and a half*. She was dressed in what I suppose you would call décolleté—though I expect she wasn't aware of it—and every time she would lean over, ever so innocently, she'd expose this pink full brassière and then she'd heave backwards a bit and stroke her lovely hair and say in her gentle sweet voice that she was glad there was one gentleman left in Wilmington, North Carolina. Funny thing, too, was that there didn't seem to be anything snippy or priggish about this: she was just pure, you see, pure as hell and full of religion, and she thought a whole lot about the verities, as she put it. I remember she said, just as gravely and honestly and sweetly as you please: 'After all, Jesus Hisself was a gentleman.' Well, after about half an hour of this, what with all the leaning over and all this pristine, silky crossing and recrossing of her legs, I was just one solid sweaty torment, and I asked her if I could take her home. She raised these little plucked eyebrows a bit, and considered, and then she said yes, she supposed I could—again because I was so well-mannered and moral-looking—and so I picked up all the tracts and prayer books and hymnals and we got a bus and went back to her house. She wasn't really *heavy* about it, as I remember—she could talk about other things, if pressed—but she seemed to focus pretty consistently on religion, and on the way out on this bus she kept asking me what my affiliation was, and whether I felt I was really *prepared* and so on, while I kept my hot eyes (do you remember those short skirts girls used to wear then?) on her round plump sweet knees. You know, if you could turn into tiny bits of—of *feathers,* every word said by all men, in just *one year,* to all women when the men were thinking of something else; when they were trying to be smooth and polite but when their minds were fixed on that single all-compelling goal, you'd have enough hypocrisy to plug up the entire known universe with feathers. Well, sterling gentleman that I was, I tried to carry the ball, and I tried to focus on the truth. I told her that I was an Episcopalian by baptism and all that, and how my father had been an Episcopalian minister—which was true, of course—but that I'd been left an orphan at ten, and had been brought up by an uncle and aunt who were Methodists. Which was also true. But, as I say, lust brings out the hypocrisy in man or boy—those plump knees and that heaving little bosom, I could hardly think straight by then—and so I told her that, in spite of all this, I'd been powerfully drawn toward the Jehovah's Witnesses, who always seemed to me to represent the *highest-type* religion, and I must say this clinched things even further: she said she was an orphan, too, which gave us a kind of kinship, didn't it, and she thought it was real nice that I might become a Witness, and by the time we got out to her house we were mooning at each other a little and I had hold of one of her sweaty little hands. I was about to burst. I remember saying, 'Lord, ain't it sad to be an orphan,' which was true enough, but not at that moment, because all I was thinking about was whether I'd have the courage, and whether God (and then I did believe in a nice loose-type God) would permit me to have my way with this luscious handmaiden of His. And then I heard her say: 'Lord, ain't it true? Jesus called Momma and Poppa away when I was only five.' I was literally about to burst.

"Maybe I seem to be getting away from the point. But you see, it was this girl and this moment in time which were so important to me that day in Paris, and I'll tell you about it. But I've often thought that it was not the girl so much—maybe because, whatever it was, it wasn't love—who was important to me, but the moment, the mood, the sad nostalgic glamour—call it what you will: the crystallization of a moment in time past which encompasses and explains and justifies time itself. Because, say what you will, the loutish seduction of an adolescent might be funny or ludicrous or pathetic or even sad, but it isn't hardly anything in itself to waste a whole lot of time in making it significant or tragic or profound. No, with sweet Vernelle it was something else—the moment surrounding her, the clouds of time through which she bore like a pair of chalices her witless carnality and her innocent love of Jesus. I mean, think how few of us—of our age, at least—ever escaped the moment, whether for better or for worse. I wasn't a soldier then but in less than a year I was, and that fact hardly matters. The mood is the same—the mood, the glamour, the emotion that justifies time. It was a part of the fact of going to war, with all of us, and with me it was heightened by being a southerner anyway, I guess. Hell, you know what I mean about that. Someone said the Second World War was fought just like the War Between the States—between the Potomac and the Gulf of Mexico—and my God it's true. Think of all us millions of men and boys prowling the streets of a thousand dusty southern towns, and the boredom, and the beer joints, and the bus stations, and the bootleg whiskey and the endless, endless search for girls. And the rain and those dead, black skies of winter and the M.P.'s. How few of us escaped it! It's a mood that lingers in the heart of a whole generation. And behind it all, shadowing all of it, is the memory of the time when all the lovely girls had vanished from the land. The time when only the whores were abroad. The whores, and Vernelle Satterfield. Every one of us at one time or another briefly found Vernelle, you know.

"As I say, she loved Jesus, all right. She lived in a ratty sort of one-story clapboard house with her aunt, who was a high priestess or something in the Witnesses. The aunt was out, Vernelle said, and my heart swelled at the news. Well, you know what kind of house it was, because you were there with *your* Vernelle: a beaded overhead lamp and two overstuffed plum-colored chairs and linoleum on the floor and a kerosene stove. And there in the corner is a maple chest of drawers, called the chiffonier, and an old upright piano, and a Westclox clock ticking on the table." Pausing, he grinned a little, and said: "Actually, it wasn't too different from the house I was brought up in. It near about breaks my heart. Anyway, there's a sort of rump-sprung davenport and there's a pillow made of iridescent pink-and-green silk, and it has a picture on it of The Alamo or St. Petersburg and a poem, or an apostrophe to Mother. There's a rack on the floor with about twenty-five movie magazines in it. And on the piano are two tinted photographs of boys in uniform, signed Buddy or Leroy or Jack Junior or Monroe. They are grinning. One is Vernelle's cousin, and the other is her boy friend. That's the God's truth. It's one of the prime facts of this mood in time that Vernelle always had a boy friend. My heart sank like a rock. But, do you know, she could not have loved either me or Buddy so well, loved she not Jesus more. Sometimes I think it was at that moment I decided to become a painter. Because in her little bedroom—she led me in with great piety and dignity, but that bed really *loomed,* I'll tell you—she had the goddamdest gallery of Jesuses you ever saw: Jesus crucified, Jesus staggering underneath the cross, Jesus weeping and before Pilate, and in Gethsemane and upon Calvary and risen from the tomb. Miracle-working Jesuses and ascending Jesuses and suffering Jesuses—every bleeding one of them made in Atlanta. It was like a regular Jesus cult. It would have put some of those Italians back in the Abruzzi to shame.

"I almost queered myself then. Even back then I loved painting; I didn't know a damn thing about it, but the earth seemed to move whenever I saw, say, a Leonardo drawing in a book, and this terrible crap of Vernelle's almost turned my stomach, so when she asked me what I thought of her pictures I allowed as how they seemed to me long enough on religion but powerfully short on art. Her pretty little face got all flushed and angry and she said I didn't know anything about painting. I was a gentleman, maybe, but a gentleman without any eye, and my poor heart plummeted again, and I thought surely that that was that. But she recovered after a bit, and said she was hungry—up in my old neck of the woods they say *hongry*—and so I went out to a little stand and got a bagful of hot dogs and a couple of Pepsi-Colas and brought them back and we sat there on this rump-sprung couch munching away, and Vernelle got on religion again—*got* on it! she was always on it—and asked me who my favorite apostle was. Then I said something—I wasn't thinking—and came out with a prophet instead, Ezekiel or someone like that, and she gave a tinkly little laugh at my ignorance, and I could feel a chill rise up between us like a sheet of glass. I thought it was a chill, anyway. Ah God, I was suffering!

Every capillary in me from head to toe was absolutely tumescent with desire, raging, and I couldn't do anything but sit there and chomp away at the hot dogs and plot and connive and plan hopeless stratagems, and sweat and suffer. There's no misery more acute on earth than the plain ordinary *horniness* of a boy of seventeen. It got awfully late finally and I was so full of religion I was close to tears. I was scared as hell, really, but determined, and ready to try anything short of rape, and even that, to enter this pure undefiled vessel of the Lord. Miserable transgressor, half-drowned even then in original sin!

"At last, just as I thought I was at the final insupportable bursting point, she got up, and with a sort of mincing pristine swaying motion of her behind she walked over to this old Victrola and put on a record—some hillbilly record, I remember, I can hear it right now as clear as a bell—she put on this Roy Acuff and turned around and said just as calmly and blandly and sweetly as you can imagine: 'Would you at all care to dance?' I can see her now: this mellow, unblemished, plum-ripe little virgin with a smear of mustard on her lips, one hand outstretched graciously—so—just like she'd seen it in the movies. And I was flabbergasted. Would I at all care to dance, my God! At that moment I would have danced with her barefoot on broken glass, or under the sea, or straight into the maw of hell. But I didn't understand, I didn't believe it! Dance with this dove of Jehovah? And I said: 'But ain't it against your religion?' And she said, real calmly, without a flicker: 'That's one thing you'll find out about us Witnesses. We're right liberal as concerns social contacts.'

"And by God, do you know that that did it! Me and my wretched suffering! Why, do you know that she'd been just waiting for me to make a move as soon as we stepped into that house. As quick as I got my arm around her she was all belly and thigh and groin and mustard-smeared mouth wide open, groaning 'Lover boy' and all in this swooning movieland passion, saying over and over, 'Dawling, what took you so long?' And in a fake Stork Club accent, at that. Vernelle Satterfield! A Messalina in the guise of a vestal virgin! Not a treasure of the Lord, but a junior-sized harlot! Why she was no more of a virgin than one of those little trulls of fat King Louis! And she kept saying, 'Dawling, what took you so long?'—in this real clickety-clack godawful phony voice, as if she wished my name were Rodney. And then, well, what man can't remember the first girl he ever touched, the smell of perfume—gardenias, you know—and the elastic, and the pitiless garters, and the simple feel of young *flesh* beneath your fingers, which is so hopelessly sublime, I suppose, because at that age it's beyond your power to conceive of it as anything but immortal.

"Yet I was a failure. A hopeless, flat-assed failure. Who wouldn't have been, in my condition? I was like a great gorged mosquito. But it didn't matter. It just didn't matter one bit at all. The mood remains in time, it lingers, and that's the important thing. My God, Vernelle Satterfield! I can still see her as the lust consumed all the simple piety in her eyes, and as she screwed up her face and still in this elegant huskiness moaned: 'Come on, Lover boy! Hurry! Hurry! Aunt Lucille might be coming!' And with my hair standing on end and every arm and leg atremble, she dragged me like some big limp reluctant half-grown hound dog into the bedroom and onto the sagging springs. And there I had her, in the dim light beneath the eye of three dozen proliferating, suffering Christs, and with Roy Acuff howling like a spook possessed about the great speckled bird, and the Bible, so envied by the swan. No, I *didn't* have her, as I say. I was a failure, because one single caress of her hand brought me down against her blubbering in delirium. And spent. But it doesn't matter. The other things remain—the guitars, the gardenias, and the sweat and the hurry, and Aunt Lucille coming, and far off outside the sound of soldiers singing, and war, and the Lamb of God with great oval merciful eyes peering down at me over the billowing bedclothes. And Lord, her words! I'll never forget her words! I'll never forget her words as she sat up in bed and put my weak trembling hand to her young breast and said: 'Why, you *pore silly*. Look down there! Look what you done! Why the divine spirit just flowed right on out of you.' "

He ceased talking for a bit and took off his glasses, as he sometimes did, in order to press his fingers thoughtfully against his closed eyelids. Then after a spell of silence he made a small noise which was partly a laugh, but even more a sigh, and then he said: "Well, as I say, all this was somehow tied up with that day in Paris. And I've never gotten it quite straight. I've never really gotten it quite fulfilled in my mind. I remember not too long ago you seemed to be trying to get at something important. You were talking about that strange moment sometimes just before you fall asleep, which is so inexplicable and indescribable and mysterious, when you're in a state that is neither sleeping nor waking but something miraculously in between, where the antennae of the subconscious are all alive and aquiver yet drowsy, deliciously drowsy, and all sorts of random memories come flooding back with this really heart-stopping and heart-rending immediacy, as if it were not simple memory you were conjuring up but the beauty and sadness and joy of all things real that had ever happened to you. Well, there in Paris that afternoon I was telling you about, after that spell or seizure at the window, after I blacked out and recovered myself, I remember that the first thing I wanted to do was to go to sleep. Most of it was the booze, I guess, but something else had happened, too. I was baffled by what I had seen from the window, and confused, and a tiny bit scared, too, I reckon. I just didn't know what the hell was going on. But the funny thing was that with all of this I felt wonderfully serene and composed, for the first time in as long as I could remember, and I had this boozy calm drowsiness in all my bones— the troubled and trembly and creepy feeling I'd had at first wore off in about half a minute—and so I turned away from the window and went over to the couch and lay down there. But I couldn't sleep. Or rather, I could only doze partly off and half-listen to *The Magic Flute* and find myself in that miserable poetical borderland where a thousand memories began to crowd in on me and twist my heart without mercy. And I thought, without lust at all but only with this hopeless wild desire, about Vernelle Satterfield and all that lost and lovely pink-hued flesh. And that in turn made me think of home and the dusty roads and the marshes with the long-necked water birds flapping high above at dawn, and a bunch of Dr. Pepper signs hung out on a rickety little crossroads store, and how that store would look at noontime on a hot summer day when I was a boy, with the sun burning down around it on the blazing tobacco fields and buzzards roaming in the sky and a solitary nigger coming down the road with a kerosene can or with a pig under his arm, or with a croker sack dragging in the dust, and the nigger humming. And then I began to think about other things—random, you know, and without order, and drowsy, but each one piercing my heart like a bleeding skewer —about the jungles and the beach at Cape Gloucester and how misty and spooky they looked at dawn, and the smell of the sea when we went in, and the palm trees uprooted on the shore like dead giants. And then home again and the water birds and the nigger shacks at dusk. And then when I went to New York and the way Third Avenue looked on a summer night, beneath the El, and the sound of passing trains and barges on the river, and being young in the city, and alone and full of glory on a summer night.

Then home again and Vernelle Satterfield, and the way it was when my aunt took me to the circus and the merry-go-round wheeling, and my aunt holding my hand and saying, 'Son, don't stand too close.' Then . . . But it doesn't matter. I just lay there for a while and twisted and turned, neither awake nor asleep, and dozed off, then caught myself, and all the while these memories swarmed in my mind like great birds, so real that they were not like memories at all but fragments of life touched again, and heard and seen and breathed. I don't know how much time passed—maybe a half-hour, maybe less. Anyway, I finally got up. I couldn't take it any more. The joy, serenity, the calm—they were all still on me, like a spell, you see, as if that feeling of wonder I'd had at the window were something I couldn't shake out of my bones. As if whatever insight, whatever knowledge or revelation I'd been informed with there still persisted, still dogged and haunted and consumed me with its simple immaculate truth. So that again, as I got up from that couch with these memories still flapping around madly and fabulously in my brain, I was aware, just as I had been aware of the beauty in that shabby little Paris street below, of the—well, of the beauty, the beauty and the *decency* in my own life which was continuing and indestructible in time, the beauty which was the water birds at home and the merry-go-round and the nigger shuffling down this dusty road in summer and, God knows, Vernelle Satterfield, and which, since it existed not just in the past but now and for all time, could surely conquer over my own momentary sordidness and selfishness and meanness, if I only gave it half a chance. . . ." He got up and walked to the window.

"Anyway, as I say, the joy was on me, the joy and the calm. It was a real euphoria. And, God, how stupid I was not to realize that the whole thing was a fraud! That I was in real danger. That I was sick, really, sick from booze and abuse of the flesh and semi-starvation. That all this—this vision and insight was the purest hokum, pleasant maybe, pleasant as hell, really, but phony none-theless, chemically induced, and no more permanent or real than—well, than a dream. But I didn't know that then; I didn't know that the higher you kite upward like that the harder you hit the ground when you fall.

"Well, here's what happened then. I got up off that couch, feeling like I could chew nails. Drunk as a hoot owl still, but bright-eyed and bushy-tailed and ready to take on a whole crowd of giants. You remember I told you how I'd been unable to work for so long. Well, right then in the midst of all this phony euphoria I felt I could even give a lesson to Piero della Francesca. I had truth and beauty right squarely by the nuts, see, and I was raring to go. I staggered around the joint for a while with this big fat smug smile on my mouth, listening to *The Magic Flute* and getting together all my equipment: you know, sketch pad, virginal all these many months, and charcoal, and bottle—I had to have that bottle. I reckon I'd forgotten all about Poppy and the kids. I plunged outside, out into this Paris afternoon. I don't know exactly when I started to fall, when this cloud I was riding on began to dissolve underneath me. As I recollect it, though, I don't think it was too long after I left the house. But first I was still all electricity and bubbles and vitamins and piss-and-vinegar. I can remember walking down the little street which had seemed so beautiful, marveling at its lines and colors, really marveling, and ravished by its perfection. Then I remember walking—rolling, rather, thinking that I had the suave gait of a boulevardier but in reality about as graceful as some swab-jockey on liberty—staggering down the rue Delambre toward the Dôme with this great big grin on my face and my heart like an open door to Paris in the spring. And what is Paris in the spring? You know what it is. All pollinated air and gold and leaf and shadow and cotton dresses and the coquetry of behinds and—what else? Ah—

"The come-down began gradually enough. I remember the first sign, though, the first warning. I was heading in the general direction of the Luxembourg Gardens; there was a certain corner there that I'd seen and I had this fuzzy idea that that would be a good place to sit down and sketch. On the way I stopped by at the Dôme and got a couple of cigars, and on my way out of the place I ran into this whore I knew—on Sunday patrol, I guess, working overtime. There's no point in going into that particular relationship. It wasn't much of one. Her name was Yvonne or Loulou or something. About the only thing I can recall about her was that she was from Lille and that she wasn't particularly good-looking but splendidly built. I'd spent a night with her once—a black, carnivorous, exhausting night after a drunk argument with Poppy which had left me feeling miserable and guilty as all hell. The night, I mean. You know, the old Anglo-Saxon hellfire which we just can't ever get rid of. I felt goddam guilty over the lapse and even guiltier, I reckon, over the fact that that month I'd spent my disability check on booze, so that the ten bucks or so that I'd paid to this floozy was actually Poppy's money. My God, what contortions we go through! Anyway, as I say, I bumped into this broad coming out of the Dôme. Somehow or other I'd managed to avoid her ever since that night of catastrophe. I'd put her out of my mind, so that when I blundered into her it was like a great big black cloud passing across my sunny day. She was a nice friendly girl, actually, not like most whores who in spite of the myth don't have hearts of gold but are mean bitchy hornets, or just plain stupid, or bull dykes at heart. I remember that for a moment she tried to put the touch on me again, but then this strange stark solemn look came over her face as she stood there talking to me, and finally she just stopped talking and twisted her neck to one side and said in this throaty somber voice: *'Cass, tu es malade!'* And she put her hand up to my brow and stroked it and said that it felt like the belly of a trout, all wet and cold. Then she told me I should go home and call the doctor, because I looked sick, very sick, and she was concerned for me. And she wasn't kidding, either.

"I shook her off, a bit brusquely, I reckon. No Montparnasse tart—especially one who had confronted me as if she were my own guilt made incarnate—was going to spoil my balmy day, see? So I suppose I said something rude, and sideslipped off jauntily down the boulevard, tipping my bottle to old bronze Balzac at the intersection and spreading a general benediction all over the place. But the come-down had already begun. I was—well, to put it mildly, I'd begun to feel poorly. God knows, I didn't want to— and whether it was the girl who'd been the catalyst for the thing I just don't know—but I wasn't more than a few blocks down the street when I began to feel real seasick. And the thing was, you see, I *was* sick. I'd been sick for months without knowing it, and sick from what? Why, from the aforesaid booze and from abuse of the carnal envelope—as I once heard a fancy Methodist preacher call it—and in Paris, God help us, the headquarters of all that's magnificent in groceries, from an almost insane campaign of slow, steady malnutrition. But that wasn't all I was sick from, of course. That was the least of my sicknesses, if anything. What I was really sick from was from despair and self-loathing and greed and selfishness and spite. I was sick with a paralysis of the soul, and with self, and with flabbiness. I was sick with whatever sickness men get in prisons, or on desert islands, or any place where the days stretch forward gray and sunless into flat-assed infinitude, and no one ever comes with the key or the answer. I was very nearly sick unto death, and I guess my sickness, if you really want to know, was the sickness of deprivation, and the deprivation was my own doing, because though I didn't know it then I had deprived myself of all belief in the good in myself. The good which is very close to God. That's the bleeding truth.

"And to top it all, I was a *fool,* you see? I thought all that bliss and wonder and insight and peace had come to me because at last I'd been given the key, because I was a genius and if a genius waits long enough he'll be handed revelation on a silver platter. But I was wrong. I was a fool. That hadn't been any real revelation I'd had: it had been a sick drunken daydream, with no more logic or truth in it than the hallucination of some poor old mad starving hermit. No wonder there are so many visions recorded in the register of the saints. Flog yourself long enough, starve yourself, abuse yourself, and any meathead alive will start seeing archangels, or worse. Yet I didn't know all this that day. I didn't know it, and for the life of me I couldn't figure out why it was, as I kept on walking toward the Luxembourg, that I'd begun to feel weak and dizzy and ill. Or why it was that all my elation and delight had begun to fade away. Maybe the whore had something to do with it. No, what was going to happen was going to happen, but I've often thought she helped bring it on quicker: the guilt, you understand, and the dismal, messy image coming back to me—the sour sheets and the whorish counterfeit lust and myself, slobbering and humping away while Poppy lay home weeping. Triple bleeding God! Anyway, by the time I got to the Luxembourg I was feeling *bad.* I was clammy all over and trembling and as I passed a store window I looked at my face in a mirror and I was a pasty white ghost, just like the girl had said. And to top it all, worse than this was the anxiety I'd begun to feel—this dread, this fear that something horrible was about to happen. I remember stopping outside the entrance to the gardens. I took a tremendous wallop out of the brandy bottle, and I stood swaying there for a minute, waiting for it to lift me, to bring me back up to the summit; but I was gone, I was plunging, and I didn't know it: at last I was getting my rightful punishment and I was plunging fast. Not a goddam thing happened: the brandy only made me feel worse. But in the midst of all this I was still determined to draw something. I was still determined to prove to myself that I could, that all this crazy passion and glory I'd felt hadn't been a fraud, a hoax. Well, somehow I managed to maneuver myself into the gardens. It was crowded with sun-worshipers and I stood there for a bit waiting for this little wrinkled custodian of a woman while she scurried around and found me a chair. She seemed to take hours. During a spell like this, you know, time becomes elongated, pulled out like a hunk of taffy. You just sit and suffer and squirm and wait in agony for the next event to happen—because it's that event which will show you that you're still alive and in touch with the universe, rather than suspended in a timeless, crushing terror—but the event takes ages and ages to come. As I say, the woman seemed to take hours to fetch this chair. I just stood there, weak and hollow and terrified, shaking like a bishop with the clap. And when she finally brought it I had a surge of momentary relief and sank down into it as if it had been a throne.

"And that was the beginning of the end. Because as I sat there with the pad limp and useless in my hand, the terror and the dread came back like a great cold paralyzing blast of wind. Just sitting there in this Paris sunlight, I never felt so lost in all my life before. I was like some hulk which has slipped its moorings and drifted out onto the sea, surrounded on all sides by reefs and ruin and yawning deeps. I wanted to cry out but I had no voice at all. I had a panicky need for escape—flight—and I had the desire to run away in all directions at once, but I figured that wherever I ran I would be chased as if by a wolf by this unimaginable, nameless, ravening terror. The Luxembourg Gardens seemed to spread out on all sides of me in light-years of space—I swear to God—and the people were as far off and as unreal as people in a dream. And through all of this, as I sat there shuddering and hammered by fright, I felt that the most precious, the most desirable, the most marvelous thing on earth would be to be shut up tightly—alone—in the darkness of a tiny single room.

"And I know where that room was. It was back home, back on that little street where I'd come from, and I knew that if I didn't get there quick, if I didn't get back into that safe, dark, enclosing space within a matter of minutes, this terror would conquer me, break me down, and I'd turn into a goddam lunatic right there in the midst of that peaceful Sunday in the Luxembourg, and begin hooting and shouting, or start clobbering people or maybe worse, or just gallop out and down the street and climb to the top of St. Sulpice and jump off. So I got up from that chair as steadily as I could, knowing all the while that people were looking at me—well, curiously, and I edged myself on out of the gate to the gardens, and then I began running. Not fast, and not slow, either—just this pounding, steady, determined dogtrot down sidewalks and across streets and through red lights and in between moving cars, all the while saying to myself, half-aloud, in a sort of under-the-breath monotone: If I stop running all will be lost, I'm scared now, more frightened than I've ever been in all my life, but if I just keep running and get back home I might be saved. And I remember somewhere crossing the Boulevard Raspail seeing a *flic*, and hearing him shout as if he thought I was a thief and half-expecting him to pull out a gun and shoot, but trotting on heedless, still babbling to myself, and leaving him far behind. And on a side street near the Avenue de Maine, too, colliding with two little girls playing jump-rope and hooking my foot on the frigging rope, half-falling down, but recovering myself without missing more than half a step and then plunging on, all awash with sweat and horror. Then finally I was on the little street again, and then at the doorway to the house, and I burst in and ran up the stairs two at a time and exploded back into the studio with my mouth wide-open like a gargoyle in a frozen voiceless scream. And how I managed the last part I don't know, but I got the shades down all over the place, shutting out the light and the street below, and I got into bed and pulled the blanket over my head, and lay there trembling and whining like some miserable old woman who thinks she hears someone outside trying to break into the house. . . ." He came back from the window and, sitting down, lit a cigar.

"Well, as I say, I lay there for a while, trembling and screaming inwardly. But I felt a little bit better, I guess: I was home, at least, I was in the dark, I was safely back in the womb. Some of the fear went away finally, and so with the cover still up over my head I drifted off to sleep. It's not a very pretty picture, is it—this newt, this hot caterpillar, wrapped up in woolly slumber?"

"Quit running yourself down so," I said with honest irritation. "It's all over and done with, you know."

"You're right," he said. "Well, anyway, I went off to sleep. Only it wasn't sleep. Instead, I was in a car with my uncle and we were driving along a street in Raleigh, and he was taking me to the state prison. Funny, how I can remember the details just as clearly and vividly as if it had really happened. He was taking me to the state prison in his car. I saw the high stone walls up ahead and the guard towers. And I can remember the feeling of despair I had, because for the life of me I couldn't figure out what my crime was, or anything about it, other than that I had done something unspeakably wicked—surpassing rape or murder or kidnaping or treason, some nameless and enormous crime—and that I had been sentenced not to death or to life imprisonment but to this indefinite term which might be several hours or might be decades. Or centuries. And I remember my uncle saying in his calm bland voice not to worry, son, he knew the governor—I remember him calling him Mel, Mel Broughton—and was contacting him, and that I'd be out in no more than a couple of hours. Yet as my uncle stopped and let me out at the gate and said good-by, and as I walked through the gate and heard it clang behind me, I knew that my uncle had already either betrayed or forgotten me and I would rot there in that state prison forever. And it was funny, too—because, when I dreamed this, I was long emancipated (or at least I thought) from that kind of ignorance—how as the gate clanged shut my next thought filled me with a despair that was almost as great as my uncle forgetting me: and that was that just about half and even more of the prisoners were bound to be niggers, and I'd be spending the rest of my life among niggers. But then after that the dream got all switched around, as dreams do, and the real horror commenced: it wasn't the niggers—though a lot of the prisoners seemed to be black—but my own crime that dogged me and terrified me. Because I was in the prison uniform now, and the prisoners had all gathered around me and were pointing at me, and sneering, and looking at me with hate and loathing and disgust, and calling me filthy names; and I heard one of them say: 'Any man that'd do that should be gassed!' Then I heard the others start to hoot and holler and shout: 'Gas him! Gas the dirty sonofabitch!' And it seemed that only the guards, who were themselves scornful and mean to me, kept the other prisoners from coming at me. And I kept struggling for speech and trying to say: What have I done? why am I here? what is my terrible sin? But my voice got all lost in the shouts and the cursing of the other prisoners. Then again the dream became confused, and time seemed drawn out into infinity, and the days and months and years passed forwards and backwards, and I seemed to be forever climbing endless steel prison ladderways and going through clashing gates and doors, chased down by a guilt I couldn't name and burdened with my own undiscoverable crime. And all around me not even the companionate misery, but only the loathing and the hatred, of my fellow-damned. And throughout this the wretched and ridiculous hope: that somehow and at some time my uncle would get the governor to turn me loose. Then the dream got switched around again and once more I heard the other prisoners saying: 'Gas him! Gas him!' and then as God is my

witness I was suddenly stripped to a pair of black skivvy drawers
—that's the way they gas you in North Carolina—and with the
warden at my side, and two frock-coated preachers fore and aft,
I was being led off to the lethal chamber. Well, I guess only up to
a certain point is a dream like that supportable, even to one like
me who was plunged into his own handmade hell. And so then I
woke up beneath the blanket half-smothered and howling bloody
murder with the vision in my brain of the dream's last Christ-
awful horror: which was my uncle, my kindly good old baldheaded uncle who'd reared me like a daddy, standing with a
crucible of cyanide at the chamber door, grinning with the slack-
lipped grin of Lucifer hisself and black as a crow in his round
tight-fitting executioner's shroud. . . ."

He halted, then shivered as if from the cold. And he didn't say
anything more for a long while.

"Well, I jumped up out of bed sucking for air and clawing at
space, and I stood in the middle of the room, shaking in every
bone. I don't know how long I'd laid there but outside it was
night. Through the cracks in the blinds I could make out a glow of
lights over the Gare Montparnasse and far off a couple of red beacons shining on the Eiffel Tower. And there was a radio blaring
somewhere down on the street, I can still hear it: the applause
and the laughter and the whistles and the voice booming: *'Vous
avez gagné soixante-dix mille francs!'* And there I was in the middle of the room, shaking and clattering as if I had St. Vitus dance.
And trying to get something said—a half-assed prayer or a word
—but unable to move my lips, as if every voluntary impulse inside me were frozen and paralyzed with horror. And thinking over
and over: If I had a drink, if I just had a drink, if I only had a
drink—but knowing I'd left the bottle along with my sketch pad
in the Luxembourg Gardens. And then not knowing what to do
. . . suffocating again with anxiety and dread, and hopelessly
burdened, as if the weight of all this air-filled void around me
were pressing me down with invisible hands. Then I called out
for Poppy, but still no one was home, and I saw them all dead
and drowned, lying beneath the streaming Seine where I had told
them to throw themselves. Then for the first time in my life, I
guess, I honestly, passionately yearned to die—I mean in a way
that was almost like lust—and I think I would have willingly done
myself in in an instant if it hadn't been that the same dream
which pushed me toward the edge also pulled me back in a sudden
gasp of crazy, stark, riven torture: there wouldn't be any oblivion

in death, I knew, but only some eternal penitentiary where I'd tramp endlessly up gray steel ladderways and by my brother-felons be taunted with my own unnameable crime and where at the end there would be waiting the crucible of cyanide and the stink of peach blossoms and the strangled gasp for life and then the delivery, not into merciful darkness, but into a hot room at night, with the blinds drawn down, where I would stand again, as now, in mortal fear and trembling. And so on in endless cycles, like a barbershop mirror reflecting the countless faces of my own guilt, straight into infinity. And so, lacking a way out, lacking anything, I went over to the bed and crawled back under the covers and hid myself from the night.

"And then, some time later, came that abominable old dream that I've had over and over again all my life—waterspouts and storms and volcanoes boiling.

"This time I didn't panic. There was no crying out, no shaking, no sweat, no fear. It was late. It must have been past midnight, and still Poppy and the children hadn't come. Well, I knew they would come, sooner or later, and I'd be waiting for them. Outside it was as quiet as a graveyard, and the glow had disappeared from over the station. After a while I heard footsteps on the street below and someone whistling *"La Vie en rose,"* then a rustle of laughter, and a girl's voice, then the footsteps got softer and softer and disappeared up the street, and all was quiet as before. And I got myself ready. I didn't have any more muscles than a jellyfish, and my ulcer was acting up, but I didn't care, and I was as sober as a Knoxville parson. And it's funny, as I went about my business I kept thinking of the headlines I'd read, things like: *Farmer hacks, slays family, kills self,* and how I'd always visualized the man—some mad, sweaty, hairy ox with foam on his mouth and eyes balled-out like pigeon eggs, laying about him with a hatchet and shouting, Whores of Sodom! Satan's offspring! and cutting down his own flesh and seed like so many saplings and then with one last shriek at Jesus and all the saints to bear witness to his affliction taking a twelve-gauge loaded with buck-shot and blowing off the roof of his head. And I kept thinking that maybe that was the true picture but more likely my own was closer to the truth. That a man bent on annihilating his own and dearest and best might be a lunatic but he might too be someone else and contain within him the cool clean logic of eternity: a man just like me, maybe, who had dreamed wild Manichean dreams, dreams that told him that God was not even a lie, but worse, that He was weaker even than the evil He created and allowed to reside in the soul of man, that God Himself was doomed, and the landscape of heaven was not gold and singing but a space of terror which stretched in darkness from horizon to horizon. Such a man knew the truth and, knowing it, would take the best way out. Which was to remove from this earth all mark and sign and stain of himself, his love and his vain hope and his pathetic creations and his guilt, and be duped by life no longer. And he'd be cool about it, and collected, because it wouldn't pay to bungle.

"So what I did was, I went over and checked the gas range—the oven and the four burners—and turned them on full blast for a moment, then turned them off again. There was plenty there. They would do, I knew, they would suffice. Then I went back to the bed and sat on the edge of it, waiting. I was as calm as I could be and I had it all fixed in my mind: playing possum when they came in, I'd allow them all to go to sleep, then sometime toward morning I'd get up and do the job. And finish myself off after. Then I thought: Suppose it don't work, suppose they wake up in the strangling gas? Christ love us, what mortal fear! They had to go easily and swiftly, just like sleep. So I got up again and rummaged around in the dark in the pantry and found a claw hammer and brought it back with me to bed. Then I just lay there on my back with my eyes wide-open, waiting for them to come, thinking of nothing but sort of rocked by great soft silent waves of emptiness and loneliness, as if I were the last man left in all creation. Then, before I knew it, something strange seemed to come to me: it seemed as if I were reliving that nightmare again, only it was not the part that was so soul-ruining—the waterspouts and the storm and volcanoes and the perishing shore—but the other part, the good part, the heart-breaking and lovely part that had been hidden to me before, and it all seemed to be beckoning me toward it. And I saw some southern land with olive trees and orange blossoms, and girls with merry black eyes, and parasols, and the blue shining water. There were majestic cliffs, too, and gulls floating about, and there seemed to be a carnival or a fair: I heard the strumming music of a carrousel, which wound through it all like a single thread of rapture, and I heard a liquid babble of tongues and I saw white teeth flashing in laughter and, Lord love me, I could even smell it—this smell of perfume and pines and orange blossoms and girls, all mixed up in one sweet blissful fragrance of peace and repose and joy. And over all of it, somehow, vague and indistinct but possessing the whole scene: a girl's sweet voice calling, some southern Lorelei calling me and beckoning me on. And as I lay there, sometimes it was as if I saw the whole thing entire, and a voice in my mind told me this was Andalusia, and another voice the slopes of the Apennines and another Greece. Then I'd see it in small joyful fragments, like magic lantern slides in color, and my eyes would pick out the cliffs, or the gulls, or the clear and shining sea, or the girls with flowers in their hair. Then there'd be a spell of darkness and I wouldn't see anything at all, but suddenly it would return in a great blossoming flood of color—magentas and blues and cherry reds and limpid greens—and I'd hear the voice of the girl again, calling, and after a time I was groaning in my sleep with delight, and I knew I had to go there. And then finally somewhere in the midst of it all I heard this chattering sound. I woke up again. I opened my eyes and outside it was broad daylight. The blinds were drawn up and there were great green blotches of sunshine all over the walls from the elephant vines. I could smell bread baking and down below someone had set a parrot out into the courtyard and he was chattering his head off.

"Well, I didn't have any more strength than a newborn mouse. And hungry! I could have eaten a slab of asphalt. I sort of rolled slowly out of bed, and stood up and blinked and walked softly into the other room where Poppy was sleeping with Timothy and Felicia and the baby. They were sound asleep. I went into the bathroom and there was Peggy, sitting on the can in her nightgown and reading a funny-book. She looked up and grinned at me and said, 'Hi, Daddy,' and I tried to say something, but my tongue got caught between my teeth, and I couldn't say anything. So I turned around and went back into the bedroom. I knelt down beside the bed and very gently drew Poppy next to me. Her little face was moist and soft and warm and—well, fabulous. She woke up slowly and opened her eyes and blinked at me, then closed them, then opened them and blinked again, and yawned, and finally she said: 'Cass Kinsolving, if you don't get a haircut I'm going to buy you a dog license!' I didn't say anything, just knelt there beside her with my head against the pillow and my eyes closed. Then she said, drowsily and gently and without bitterness: 'I hope you feel better today, darling. You certainly were cranky yesterday. I do hope you feel better.' I still didn't say anything, just biting my lip and softly stroking her and feeling her ribs small and frail beneath the sheet. Then I felt her stir as she sat part-way up in bed and said: 'I do hope you weren't worried last night because we were so late. What time is it? I've got to take Peggy to mass.' Then, 'Oh, Cass!' she said. 'Guess where we went? We went to the bird market and guess what we did? We bought a parrot! A wonderful little parrot with green and blue wings and all he can talk in is Flemish! He's just a *daisy* of a parrot, Cass! Can you talk any Flemish?' I couldn't say anything for a moment, then finally I made my mouth work and said: 'Poppy, sweetheart, I think we're going to leave this town. I think we might just move on down south.' But she hadn't heard me, and in her wonderland world of birds and parrots jabbered on in the morning, and I lay my head against her shoulder and I thought of the day before, and the long night, and even Vernelle Satterfield and what she said about the divine spirit, which had indeed flowed right on out of me, and which to save my very life I knew I had to recapture."

VI

The next day Poppy made Cass go to a doctor. The office was in an expensive-looking house far over on the Right Bank, and the doctor himself, an Austrian, was a stolid, wrinkle-browed, officious man who listened to Cass' heartbeat and took his blood pressure and peered into his ears and then, after x-raying his stomach and examining him up and down and hearing a somewhat abridged version of all his recent debauchery, came bluntly to the point. In an amazing French heavily accented with gargled r's and g's, he told Cass that, except possibly for his ulcer, he was as healthy as a plow-horse, but the fact remained that even a horse might kill himself if instead of eating oats he drank nothing but bad cognac for a long enough period of time. No wonder he had spells of anxiety (Cass had only been able to hint at how bad the "anxiety" was);

the mind, after all, was not an entity distinct and separate from the body. Waste away your substance while you're young and you'll live only to regret it. Stop trinking! he said in English. And he prescribed two months of therapeutic vitamins, and a week on a mild barbiturate, for sleep, and a new drug, Pro-Banthine, for the restless ulcer, which didn't seem to be in too bad shape. Then, as Cass was on his way out, the doctor sort of loosened up and dropped his stodgy guard, putting his hand on Cass' arm and saying gently, Don't be a fool, you're young yet. And he charged him five thousand francs, which was more than he would have paid on Park Avenue; it made him feel unconscionably old.

All the rest of the month of May and on into the months of summer, Cass embarked upon a regime which he was later to call his period of "dull reasonableness." It wasn't easy; it took a lot more will power than he thought he possessed, but he managed it—or at least the better part of it—and he began to feel more relaxed and composed than he had in a long time. He obeyed the doctor's instructions almost, but not quite, to the letter. He took exactly four vitamin pills, and then forgot the rest, which finally melted and ran together like gumdrops on the bathroom shelf. He was conscientious, however, about the ulcer balm, which after a while seemed to put an end to the gnawing pain in his belly; then, most importantly of all, he swore off the murderous brandy. He drank wine instead. To be sure, this was not just what the doctor ordered, but it was far easier to handle than cognac, and he was still able to see Paris in a pink romantic glow. He began to eat food again. He began to work—not precisely with gusto perhaps, because whatever blocked him still blocked him, but at least when he picked up a brush or a pencil his fingers no longer trembled with the old enmity and dread. Like something not only intolerable to the mind, but now utterly implausible, he put out of his thoughts that night of Gehenna; he could not countenance it, and didn't, save for the mild reflection, which would sometimes steal over him, that maybe in order to think straight a man just needed to be dragged, every now and then, to the edge of the abyss.

His entire posture and stance in the midst of life seemed infinitely more graceful. He no longer staggered, but walked—with his brow up to catch the sun. His sense of taste improved—a notable reaction of the restored lush—as did his eyesight: his children, who had for so long been dim blond blurs, emerged upon his vision as bright and beautiful as a sudden handful of daffodils.

And he found himself inordinately and embarrassingly nuzzling their sticky faces. Even his hair had taken on a surprising luster. And though his mood fell somewhat short of ecstasy ("I've always been wary of these bastards who are all the time *embracing* the world," he said once, "and that includes me.") he felt composed and restful: sitting in the café in the morning light with a croûton and a carafe of wine (gentle eye-opener), gazing clear-eyed and alert at the sparrows in the sycamores or the old men passing or the skirts (the skirts, always the rounded frisky skirts, retreating!), he would sometimes feel so liberated, so alive, that he might only be aware in the dimmest way that part of a cloud had effaced the edge of the sun, and the air had become faintly chill, and that his eye, catching the suddenly shadowed wall of the cemetery of Montparnasse, had communicated to some inner part of him a vague fidgety restlessness and a breath—just the merest breath—of the old fear. And he would begin to wonder how long all this peace could last.

Then one morning early in August, as he sat reading in a café on the Boulevard St. Germain (and the logic of the whole sequence of impressions, as he later recollected it, seemed beautiful, reading as he had been that great chorus from *Oedipus at Colonus,* which begins: Stranger, in this land of goodly steeds thou hast come to earth's fairest home, where the nightingale, a constant guest, trills her clear note in the covert of green glades, dwelling amid the wine-dark ivy and the gods' inviolate bowers, rich in berries and fruit, etc.) he heard a woman's voice, shrill against his right ear, which, both meaningless and meaningful, had the effect of a cheese grater scraping against all his senses and caused him to look up wild-eyed, letting fall to the floor as he did Volume One of Oates' and O'Neill's *Complete Greek Drama.* "I will not pay!" said the voice, in the purest accents of America's prairie hinterland. "If you 'spect us to pay seven hunnerd francs for *tha*-yut, you're just outa your head!" And as Cass looked around, it suddenly struck him that, save for the browbeaten waiter who stood shrugging automatically at the woman's elbow, there was not a Frenchman in sight. As if, while deep in Sophocles he had not seen the bad fairy enter and cast some malign hocus-pocus over all, the place had been whisked two thousand miles across the sea. And although the phenomenon, he knew, should not have left him so wonder-struck, he could not repress a feeling of awe as his eyes roved around and searched in vain for one Gallic eye to return his glance. Mother of God, he thought, I'm in a

Howard Johnson's. He was hemmed round by a sea of camera lenses and sport shirts; the noise of his compatriots assailed his ears like the fractious harangue of starlings on a fence. "Willard!" the voice persisted. "Tell him off! In French, I mean!" No, he thought, you couldn't even caricature it. Shakily, he retrieved the book, opening it: *And, fed of heavenly dew, the narcissus blooms morn by morn with fair clusters, crown of the Great Goddesses from of yore. . . .* As he recalled it later, it must have been, as they say, a simple concatenation of circumstances, the only question remaining being why, after all, it had not come sooner: like a great wild dolphin exploding from the depths of a murky sea, the memory of the dream he'd had—the blue southern waters, the carrousel, the laughing girls—vaulted into his consciousness, no longer just a promise and a hope, but a command, rather, and an exhortation. It was as simple as that: Why, he wondered, feeling an inner joy, had it taken so long to move him? Paying for his wine, he arose and sauntered over to the benighted couple from Baraboo, or wherever. "Pardon me, madam," he said without rancor, almost courtly in his softest Carolina voice, as he clamped his beret down over one eye, "when we are the guests of somebody we don't shout. We positively *do not holler.*" Her eyes grew wide as saucers; a broomstraw would have toppled her to the floor.

"Well, never in my entire— *Willard*—" But Cass, wheeling about, had gained the open boulevard, and he hurried homeward to tell Poppy that they were bound for the sunny south.

"The town's full of Americans!" he shouted. "Go down to St. Germain and see for yourself. Morticians, beauticians, *matrons!* All sorts of riffraff. Bleeding Saviour! Take a look, Poppy! We've got to get out of here! We're going to Italy!"

Poppy was forlorn. All the time they had been in France she had pined for America, for the sandy coast of Delaware, for home and mother; she had, however, grown accustomed to Paris, even fond of it, as Cass well knew, and his proposal—or rather his insistence—sent her into a flood of tears. "Just when I was getting to like it, Cass!" she wailed. "And speak a little French and all, and now you just want to bust it all up and take the children into a new environment and everything!" She turned crimson; he hadn't seen her so honestly bereft since the day her father died. "Oh why, Cass?" she implored him. "If we've got to go somewhere, why can't we go back to the U.S.A.? Why, Cass? Oh *why* are you so anti-U.S.A.?"

"Because," he raved, a little damaged by the Beaujolais. "Because— You want to know why? Because it's the land where the soul gets poisoned out of pure ugliness. It's because in the U.S.A. everything looks like a side street near the bus station in Poughkeepsie, New York! Lord love me, Poppy, do I have to go through all this again? It's because whenever I think of stateside I can't picture nothing else but a side street in Poughkeepsie, New York, where I got lost one night when I came to see you, and whenever I think of it I get consumed with such despair over its sheer ugliness that I feel great waves of anguish rolling over me, and I want to cry. You don't want me to start crying too, do you?"

"Well, no," she said, drying her eyes, "but jiminy, Cass, you know yourself it's not *all* like that. You've said yourself—"

"Don't misquote me! Whatever I've said in—in *mitigation* of the horror America afflicts me with, strike it out. Strike it out! I was just being sentimental. Why," he said, improvising, "there was a woman I saw from Racine, Wisconsin—*Racine,* imagine, isn't that ironic?—and she had a great jowly husband named Willard who looked exactly like that Daumier caricature called Monsieur Pot-de-Naz, and this woman, Poppy, I'll swear, when I gazed into her eyes she had dollar signs there, as if they'd been glazed on in twin shining symbols of avarice and venality and greed. Why—"

"Good gravy, Cass!" Poppy cried. "You've said yourself that the French were just about the most money-mad people on earth! How can you be so—so prejudiced! I've seen these Americans in Paris myself. They're not so bad. Some of them aren't nearly so mean-looking or money-mad as some French people I've run into. You're just prejudiced, that's all. And I think it's just a sin to be prejudiced against your own flesh and blood!"

"Flesh and *blood?* Flesh and blood my eye! Those horrible— those *marmosets* my flesh and blood? Lady Willard, maybe? That great big rude midwestern blob of a woman with her squashed breadfruit of a face, that auxiliary Elk? Why, by damn, Poppy, sometimes you try me to the limit! How can you say that? Shithouse mouse! What's the matter with you, anyway! That's the trouble with you bleeding Irish Catholics. Talk about prejudice! You're a curse and a plague on the human race! The whole miserable lot of you!" He found himself waving a schoolmasterish finger in front of her face. "You're a bunch of superstitious, nose-picking peasants who swept down like a blight on the U.S. and A. when it still might have become something great, when it had hope and promise and a chance for glory, and with your larcenous aldermen and bigoted priests and bishops and other monstrous witch doctors you helped turn it into the nation it became, and is —an *ashheap* of ignorance and sordid crappy materialism and ugliness! God's own eyesore! The whole lot of you is nothing but a bunch of rummies and fat-assed cops and ward-heelers—brainless scum! St. Patrick's Day in New York! Christalmighty! A whole city at the mercy of a bunch of garbage collectors and bartenders! And that religion of yours! That mealy-mouthed, bigoted, puritanical, unbeauteous religion! Why, by God, I wouldn't trade one of Vincent Van Gogh's *farts* for a fistful of certified whiskers from the beard of St. Patrick hisself! What do you people really know about God! What do you—"

"You just *shuddup* about my religion, Cass Kinsolving!" she squealed. "Thank goodness the children aren't here to hear such talk! My great-granddaddy was starving! The Irish were *destitute* when they went to America! They had to fight against your kind of prejudice! Quit talking about rummies, you rummy! I've never seen such an unhappy man! Maybe," she said tearfully again, preparing to leave, "maybe if you had some of that religion you'd be happier. Maybe you wouldn't drink so much and could work and wouldn't be in such torment all the time! Just maybe," she called over her shoulder as she sailed out of the door, "you'd start in making the people who love you just a little bit happier! And that's the truth!" Slam!

"Maybe"—poking her outraged rosy little face back through the door—"just maybe you'd begin to see that America is a great country and you have no right to criticize it for—"

"I have every goddam right to criticize!" he heard himself bellowing, with a touch of self-pity. "I came close to dying for it! I left half of my brains and my peace and my composure rotting in the jungle for it! If I don't have a right to criticize, who the hell has! As for the Irish being poor, so were the Italians! So were the Jews! But they had enough heart and humanity to—"

"Go peel a grape!" Slam!

Shame. For a while he felt bitter shame. He had no cause at all to talk to Poppy like that. And he became glum and downcast. And remorseful, feeling in an access of imagination the old guilt-ridden fear. (Wringing his hands and thinking: What if something should happen to her? A truck or something. *God,* I love that girl.) But since it was a scene that had been enacted many times before—since, like some subtle antitoxin, a thousand household battles had inured him finally to *too* much guilt—he absorbed the shame easily and let the whole thing pass from his mind. Later that day, when Poppy came back from the playground with the children, there was a gentle adjustment of feelings. Still later at night, when they were in bed together, Poppy said: "Oh, Cass, I do love you so, darling, and I'll just go with you anywhere you want in the world." Stroking his belly. "How is your stummick feeling, darling?"

"What's that I smell?"

"Oh dear." Half-asleep. "Felicia made a poopy in her pants and I left them on—"

"Oh Jesus."

"I'll get up—"

"Forget it. Forget it, Poppy. Forget it, sweetheart."

She was like a pretty child. He did love her deeply, in his fashion, and sometimes he thought that the knowledge of the pain he often caused her was his own single greatest pain. How could he tell her that it was not, after all, a plague of Americans which was causing him to flee southward, but only this indescribably innocent yet all too voluptuous and seductive fantasy? In his mind he tried but couldn't, and so he fell asleep.

The next day he counted up their money, cashed some traveler's checks with the talkative Jew near the Hôtel de Ville, and began to pack up their baggage. Such junk a family piles together in a year! Then, working awkwardly and somewhat haphazardly, he mapped out an itinerary. First he'd treat Poppy to a taste of the Riviera—it was not his dream at all, but it was south —then on to Italy, almost anywhere would do. . . .

Somewhere along the left breast of the Rhone valley, on the railroad route leading south to the Côte d'Azur, there is a lonely, humble grave. A solitary oak sapling, transplanted from its native soil nearby, marks the isolated spot; perhaps now even the sapling has perished, or has been blown away by the winds, so that the searcher for some mortuary relic will find nothing there at all save the tangled anomalous weeds, and the wind and sunshine, and the far, bleak, sun-swept cliffs standing sentinel over the immemorial flood. There was a gnarled apple tree too, though, Cass remembered, and a time-roughened fence, so that, triangulating upon a line of poplars which stood erect like a file of green soldiers upon the horizon, he might still, if he ever wanted to, find the sad and forsaken place. It was south of Lyon and north of Valence and it was the place where, when the train halted for a long inexplicable hour, they all debarked from the stifling and noisome third-class compartment to bury Ursula, the Flemish-speaking parrot. It had been an astonishingly speedy ending. From the moment in the draughty halls of the Gare de Lyon when Ursula had ceased her healthy, piercing harangue and had shuddered, greenly wilting, and had begun to fuss and grumble in a feeble, senile plaint and then withdrew nodding to a far corner of her cage, where her feathers became tacky and plucked-out and lusterless right before their eyes, to the moment when with rheumy eyeballs and a final croupy hack, she expired, toppling from her perch with a feather-duster plop and without—as Peggy, who was of all of them the least sentimental, put it—"even saying good-by," the time elapsed could not have been more than two or three hours. It was an evil omen, Cass knew. The two middle children, Timothy and Felicia, filled the train with wild heartbroken cries of lamentation; even Peggy was affected, even he was. The baby wailed sympathetically from his basket, and Poppy—Poppy was the worst of all, leaking ceaseless tears, trying to control herself for the children's sake, and with trembling lips, as if by words alone she might ward off grief, telling the baffled, perspiring countrywoman who shared their compartment that the *"pauv' petit perroquet"* had had at least "a very happy life."

The confusion, the grief, the noise became almost intolerable. Yearning for a drink—a stiff one, hating his hard-won self-discipline, and oppressed by a life in which certain insupportable moments, such as now, could only be made bearable by an elixir which he himself could not support, he drew a funereal cloth across the parrot's cage (actually it was a species of parakeet), loudly told the mourning assembly to shut up, and with a pillow wrapped around his head went to sleep. But the sense of it all being an evil omen persisted in his dreams. When the train stopped, and when, waking, he learned from the conductor that there would be a long delay, he followed Poppy and the family into the lovely field. It was a sparkling, meridional day, dry and hot and cloudless, blindingly blue, and humming with the jittery noise of insects in the underbrush. Poppy carried the still-warm Ursula in a shroud of green cloth which had served to cover her cage. Each for the occasion had his solemn role: Poppy was the parrot's mother, Timothy her beloved husband, Felicia her little sister; Peggy, somewhat removed from it all as usual (she had never forgiven Ursula for biting her, two months before), chose only to be "a friend, kind of a bird friend," while he himself, through no choosing of his own, became both grave digger and priest. How could he be a priest, for Christ sake, Poppy? he asked. But she said he could, for a bird. It was, he thought, as with a stone he sweatily hacked a hole in the parched ground, a soft and sickening thing, the limits to which Poppy would carry the poetry of her faith—and perhaps even blasphemous—but priest he was chosen, and priest he was, reading the Mass for the Dead from her prayer book in orotund phonetic Latin, while Poppy and the children stood about with bowed heads and the listless passengers on the train, fanning themselves, gaped at the scene in quiet dismay. At last it was over. Into the hole they all cast handfuls of dust. Cass planted the sapling, and as floral tribute Poppy picked a blue-bonnet for Felicia, who in sisterly fashion—at the time she was two—stuck it in her mouth. Good-by, Ursula, adieu, sweet oiseau, good-by, good-by. . . . Cass felt gladly shut of the blabber-mouthed bird. But in spite of all the stickiness, he thought as the cortege filed back toward the train, he had been oddly and ob-scurely moved: his children, good Catholics all, who would be saved, patient with heads bowed and as fresh and as fragile as the wildflowers they stood among. It was then, he recollected long afterwards, that he felt Peggy falter and stagger against him and, looking down, saw how wild-eyed the child was and saw fever glowing on her cheeks like flamboyant rouge. The omen, he knew, was fulfilled. Psittacosis! he thought. Monstrous bird! Parrot fever, fatal to man! Triple bleeding God!

His diagnosis was not correct, but the child was horribly sick, and it gave him as rough a time as any he could remember. The port city of Toulon, where they arrived after several racking hours, is almost identical in size and aspect to Norfolk, Virginia, present-ing to the eye a similar unsightly waterfront of jagged cranes and shipyards and an oily harbor and a general atmosphere of tran-sient and maritime busyness. It is no place to take a vacation or to sightsee around or to bring a sick child, and Peggy, they knew long before they got there, was about as sick as a child could possi-bly get. She had puked all over the train and she throbbed with fever and her pretty blond hair was plastered wetly against her neck and brow and, in less time than it took to traverse the two hundred miles or so across the suffocating landscape of Provence, she had gone quite out of her head with delirium. In foolish head-long panic, and instead of going straight to a hospital, they went to a hotel—a barnlike place with potted palms, reminiscent of quick liaisons and commerical travelers. At an outlandish price (*"La saison, vous savez,"* said the manager, as if Toulon had a season) they took two connecting rooms and put the younger children in one and themselves and Peggy in the other. Then right before their eyes, at dusk, lying moist and disheveled on a pillow, the child's face turned a blazing crimson, except for a circumferential pallor around the mouth, chalky white, which gave her the horrible aspect of a painted clown. *"C'est la scarlatine,"* said the pleasant young doctor, finally summoned, who needed only one glance to tell. Then, explaining that this case of scarlet fever seemed exceptionally severe, he ordered her taken to the hospital. Somehow, in all the confusion, the manager managed to find an old woman, who looked responsible, to take care of the children, and then, haggard and wretched and numb, not speaking, they wrapped Peggy in a blanket and took her to the hospital down palm-lined streets in a careering taxi driven by an eager and conscientious maniac. Sometimes life, Cass thought during the drive, holding the hot child in his arms, sometimes life is even worse than war. In a cavernous hallway of the hospital, smelling of carbolic, lowering and mysterious with cream-colored, flapping, soft-footed nuns, they waited until morning. Neither he nor Poppy said a word. At dawn the doctor's face was drawn and grave. She was not responding well to the penicillin. It might, though, be still too early to tell. Go home and get some rest. Come back at ten o'clock. At their hotel room the old baby sitter met them with trouble and worry on her face like a mask. *"Les autres aussi,"* she whispered. *"Ils ont la fièvre!"* More bleeding scarlet fever!

Then at ten in the morning, leaving Poppy with the babies (after another doctor had come with more penicillin, then departed), he went back to the hospital. There he discovered that Peggy had gone into convulsions; a spinal tap had been made, revealing a terrible complication: something with the sound of infamy in it, and doom—streptococcal meningitis. Not uncommon, the doctor said, in extreme cases. Cass stole into her room and took a look at her: she seemed barely to be breathing and beneath the lobster-red of her face there was a subtle quality of flesh—a consistency—like that of wax. "Oh, baby, *don't*," he whispered. The outlook, the doctor was grieved to tell him (they actually did shrug, the maddening Frogs!), the outlook, *le prognostique,* was definitely not hopeful.

He went reeling out into the violent sunlight with a dry, rusty taste of fear in his mouth, and a clammy touch of mortality on his flesh and in his bones. Sleepless, and with splintery pain in both eyes, he could not tell how at last he found himself where he was —by a clamorous pier on the waterfront where the air was filled with a fine powdery grit from some ship's hold, and the wind was odorous with salt and gasoline, and an unseen riveting hammer stitched bullets of pure noise across his eardrums. Less distraught, less exhausted and unhelmed, he later reasoned, he might not at that moment have been quite so fatalistic, but all things had conspired to make him think one thought: all my children are going to die. All my sons and daughters. The thought was so desolating as to be beyond the realm of sorrow. Try as he might to down the image, he could not get it out of his mind: of Peggy, his first-born, and of all the dear ones the dearest and the best, who, with lovelocks atangle, flower-face uptilted to celebrate her devotion, always kissed him like this: grabbing him by the ears and turning him around to face her, as if her adoring father's head had been a jug. Chasing the intolerable vision from his mind, he lifted his eyes to the sky: two jet planes swooped in low over the harbor, screaming, skimmed ships and rooftops, were gone. Adoring? Of course he had adored them, but in his surpassing self-absorption how little *real* love he'd shown them in return. Had it not been Poppy who had brought them presents, who had cared for them and watched over them, who in her aimless and scatterwitted fashion had nonetheless taught them everything they had ever known, while he, content indulgently to pat their rumps and dandle them on his knee and smile with condescension at their tricks, had only taken them all for granted? God knows, it served him right. It served him right for the presumption. For his foolish, childish presumption. Because it was true, he knew: by some limp and witless Sunday School reflex—throwback, he supposed, to all of Poppy's subtle pious influence—he had thought that his regeneration of the past few months, his temperance and his more or less sober habits might somehow quite erase his recent years of footlessness and laziness and dissipation, could atone for all the time—irrevocably, miserably lost now—when he had been drunk, when he had refused to work, when he had left undone those things he should have done, and the other way around. Why, by God, he thought with real anguish, he had behaved like a bleeding Catholic! Expecting to be *shriven* like that! Expecting to evade retribution through the unworthy simple-minded premise that an act of evil could be erased, like so much chalk-dust from a slate, by the easy expedient of replacing it by an act of good. Why, he'd forgotten his own upbringing—overlooked the fact that God was really not a gentle benign Christian who, as Poppy would have it, let you get by through honest penance, but was a mean old Jew with a dirty beard and flashing eyes and nostrils snorting smoke and hellfire who had graven upon Cass' mind The Law in the same way that those mad-eyed foot-washing prophets with paint cans flapping through the low country of his youth had inscribed the blazing, merciless slogan on every barn and pillar and post: THOU SHALT NOT—! He would get you if you done wrong, and if He got you, you were doomed. That was the simple sum total of the whole situation. It did not matter that you cried out "Father!" or "Forgive!" or beat your head bloody in contrition against the nearest wall— He got you in the end. And finally, with the same magisterial wrath that made a hundred million Hebrews tremble at His very name, He fashioned the punishment to fit the crime. How fitting it was, Cass thought, that he himself, whose life until now had been dedicated to such senseless self-flagellation, should both more than half-believe in and yearn for a God who was such a sadistic monster. How fitting, really, that that God (had He had His gloating eye upon him that fearful night such a short time past?) should take it all in His own vengeful hands now and, as if to indicate His displeasure with one who had so clumsily and gropingly and vainly striven for some specious immortality, should snatch away all of him that was, in truth, immortal. Sons and daughters! It did not matter that they were as fragile and as lovely as flowers or that, in their brevity, they were hardly more than small eyewinks into the glory of His own sun. He would get them, too. "Take them then!" Cass heard himself whispering aloud, in fury and hopeless remorse. "Take them! *Take them!*"

Later, in a waterfront bar, he tried to get drunk on Pernod, but for some reason he couldn't. Long, long afterwards he was willing to admit that something essentially honest in himself saved him from this sort of last failure. But at the time the feeling of being a worthless derelict was almost insupportable: sensing that in some vague, secret, hopeless, irremediable fashion he was the slayer of his own children, and that God, whoever He was—He who like some uneasy phantom kept changing shape and form within him —had abetted the crime, he walked back to the hotel to tell Poppy the news about Peggy, bitterly weeping the whole way. Bawling out loud, in fact.

But one of the exciting things about life is that some of our worst trials have miraculously kindly endings. There is no way out! This is the very end! I am dying, Egypt, dying! Then all of a sudden we are relaxing by the fire, talkative, immodest, faces all aglow as we tell of the horrible ordeal safely maneuvered, its details still bright but already dimming. The point being in this case that the children began to recover completely within thirty-six hours. Peggy, after huge injections of penicillin, rallied, shouting at the top of her voice for *de la glace au chocolat,* while Timothy and Felicia, similarly filled with the almighty drug, having had mild cases anyway, lost their rashes and their fever and by the end of the second day had crept from their beds to disturb the hotel corridors with rowdy cries. As for the littlest one, he was protected by the immunity of his age, and had not got sick at all. There was a week of convalescence for Peggy, during which time it was made fairly certain that she had suffered no permanent ill effects, and there were big bills to pay, but in less than ten days—all of them swatting mosquitoes on the rocky beach at Hyères, where they had rented a cottage—one might have scarcely known (save for the towels on a clothesline which each bore the legend *Clinique de Provence Toulon*) that the household had been ravaged by disease. Poppy, wet, brown, slippery-looking in a polka-dotted Bikini the size of an eye-patch, would call from the foaming shore: "There's Daddy! Cass, come in and take a swim!" But Cass—sneaker-shod and in a baggy sweatshirt, sucking at the licorice candy which tasted like Pernod and took the place of booze, and aggravated by athlete's foot he had picked up God knows where—would retreat into the shadows of the cottage. He alone still remained somber, detached, subdued. . . .

"Everything here like Cézanne's paintings of L'Estaque," he wrote in his notebook one day, marked *Friday le 24 août,* "which is to say blazing sub-tropical light, and greens & blues so riotously mixed that one feels one MUST, at any cost, discover the mystery behind this spectrum. Yet I cannot lift a hand. (Note en passant, how this journal or carnet or whatever moves in cycles, i.e., this being the first entry since long time ago when in Paris the gut blockage & the paralysis was just as hot and heavy as it is now). Yesterday, armed with implements of the trade, feeling oddly unpusilanimous for a change went by ferry alone, to Porquerolles expecting to find crouched among the honeysuckle a handful of ripe bacchae and a passel of niaids (sp?) and a clutch of water-sprites in assorted colors. Found instead several hundred Buick dealers from Geneva, convening, so sat on a rock by the sea & went fast asleep. This place is NOT the dream. Have had no recurrence yet—possibly Im too healthy lacking the shredded nerves and sick liver I had in Paris. Would almost risk the OTHER part to get it all straight in my mind again. Poppy & kids happy as clams but here I feel like I'm at Daytona Beach, hemmed around by motels and barbarousness. Frenchmen on vacation surpass all people on earth for flashy loud mouthed vulgarity including my fellow-citizens on the Cape in summer, or at Myrtle Beach, S.C. which I never would have believed. All possibly a reflection though of whatever it is thats biting me and wont let go. Nonetheless I must approach P. calmly but firmly telling her that mans only salvation lies in Rome (the TOWN), from whence after all she came and perhaps that will do the trick. In the meantime I am astonished and overwhelmed at my will-power vis a vis the murderous grape. First dim sign of regeneration. Very dim. Eyes as bright as prisms, scent like a blood hound, appetite would shame a stock-yard full of pigs, & havent heard a peep out of Leopold in three whole months—though at that I shouldnt be surprised since sawbones in Paris said simple abstinence would cure an ulcer straight off. How fiercely keen the senses can get! The sea shore beyond loops in a long white arc out toward Corsica, & the gulls above are like petals adrift on a pure ocean of aquamarine, and the greens, the shocking shaggy almost self-radiant yet oddly tender greens of the land hemming it all in, are beyond imagining. It is a Cézanne in truth. A KINSOLVING rather, purely visualized. Yet somehow the joy is out of it—the JOY is not there—and I cannot lift a hand. Poppy has something hideous smoking on the stove. I see her splashing with the children in the waves. A fish jumps from the blue water far out flashing like quick-silver. A kind of haze over all too, stealthily and belatedly observed which encompasses all—shore-line & blooming greens & petal gulls and makes somewhat indistinct (like Turner's approach to Venice) and dingy the whole seascape including the Porquerolles ferry which lumbers tub-like to sea, puffing out smudges of black smoke. Formidable! I cannot raise a hand. Remember an essay I read—was it Montaigne?—which said that a man should pursue no goal the pursuing of which does not give him the greatest un-selfish joy. Which pegs me for a looney, alright. At least I have in a manner of speaking accepted it—

though—which is to say that it is removed anyway you look at it from ignorance. For no reason at all (maybe the warm air, maybe the sonofabitchery in me which I guess is unregenerate?) I find myself with a hard-on. In less than 10 minutes I can draw a picture of two luscious 15 year olds screwing that would peel the scalp off the moldiest old pornographer in Montmartre. It might be a good thing to fall back on. But something stops me now. I steel my spine. L'après-midi d'un crapaud. In the empty Acadia of our souls we still have left to us our lust. Who said that.??

"(Later. Dusk.) A 'peintre manqué' like me I suppose can always at least try to write notes, like Delacroix who made a damn good job of it besides being a fabulous painter to boot or in his own way, like Berlioz who as someone said did a greater service to literature than he did to music. Who said painters not articulate?? Anyway its a fair rationalization. Anyway to Hell with it. Funny thing going into town this afternoon on the bus, to get something for my supurating toes how it occurred to me, that in less than a week I'd be turning 30, and how it shocked me—though I suppose the shock of being 30 is the corniest thing in the world. Dans le trentième an de mon age, etc. etc. I kept wondering if it is really true as Ive heard it said, if a man at thirty has not through his own blood & sweat & toil seen the first glimmering light of success & acheivement he never will. Suspect that theres more than a little truth to that—especially in regards to the world outside of affairs & business—art that is—but again literally to Hell with it. At least I understand the quality & the quantity of what I do possess which is a mysterious self-hatred so prideless & engulfing it would turn a Hitler or a Himler purple with envy and which I at least understand enough to keep it (roughly speaking) within the bounds of reason. Perhaps I will plumb it some day. Until then I will try to be not too ashamed of it but will humor and tolerate it much as I might tolerate a cold in the head that I knew was going to last a lifetime. And even though it is as Montaigne said the most bestial emotion that can afflict a man. It is mine. Let me suffer it. (Timmy came in just now screaming bloody murder, saying he'd been bit in the nose by a crab. I kissed the wound and made it well and he departed saying happily he had the crabs. Don't know where he got that.) The dusk here is magnificent. It seems appropriate to the sea which is like a gentle lake & needs muted goodbys and untroubled endings—whereas dawn is for the ocean & the ocean alone which needs tumultuous beginnings and sunrise like a trumpet blast. Perhaps its the air here, the clarity, some relative restlessness or falling off of humidity at twilight—I dont know. The colors are already a kind of model arche-type for impressionism, ready made—no wonder the boys did what they did. All running together the sky already jet and sprinkled with stars yet not really discrete at all but merging, melting, partaking of both the final ribbon of sunlight at the horizons edge and the water, blue, astoundingly blue at this late hour. All of a piece. And nearer— Poppy and the children on the pebbled shore no bigger than mites there, still playing and calling in the dusk. Were I only half a man Id be worthy of it. And I mean it. Not to believe in some salvation, to have disbelief rolled over on top of ones head like an un-removable stone yet at times like this (soberly, calmly too) to see such splendour and glory writ across the heavens & upon the quiet sand and to see all certitude & sweetness in ones own flesh & seed scampering tireless & timeless on the shore, and then still not believe, is something that sickens me to my heart and center. I should have been brought up north in N.Y. suburbs Scarsdale or somewhere on that order, where I might never have learned the quality of desire or thirst or yearning & would have ended up on Madison Ave. designing deodorant jars, with no knowledge or comprehension of the freezing solitude of the bereft and prodigal son. Meantime I just thirst and my thirst is like the thirst of a dying man who sees streams of cool water flowing down from the high Himalayas thousands & thousands & thousands of miles beyond his maddest dreams, I would sell my soul for one single drop of it. Poppy the wicked little nymph has it all taped up with no fuss or bother. Sometimes I think our relationship is what it must be for a fairy to be married to a lady wrestler. All harmonious dis-harmony. Last night I mentioned the Toulon business to her. It was a casual & trivial thing. The children looked brown & healthy & happy & I said how marvelous how wonderful, something like that, and how for a long terrible moment there I had thought they were all goners for sure. Why Cass she said with a sort of nonchalant sniff, what on earth made you think that. Why I just knew all the while they were going to get well. And I said, how did she know. And she said—why I had FAITH, thats all, silly. And then I blew my top— saying something on the order of Faith my ass, it was a *man* named Alexander Fleming who did it you idiot, and penicillin & 75,000 francs worth of medical care product not of faith in some dis-embodied gaseous vertebrate, and an hermaphrodite triply-damned incestuous one at that, but of mans own faith vain per-

haps, but nontheless faith in his hardwon decency & perfecta-
bility & his own compassionate concern with his mortal, agonizing
plight on a half burnt out cinder that he didnt ask to be set down
on in the first place. Not a SPOOK I told her. It didnt phase her a
bit. She just yawned and called me an intellectual bully which is
about the only polysyllabic phrase she knows. Then she said
again quite firmly & finally: I had faith. Then she primed the
pump squeezing some milk out of her little tit and stuck it in the
babys mouth and rolled over & went to sleep there, still nursing.
Theyd all be dead if it werent for that, I shouted but she didnt
stir. What can you do. She gives & loves & I take & thats that.

"(Later—much. After mid-night). Quiet now. Only the mosquitoes, & a beacon flashing out among the islands and what looks
over to the East like distant sheet lightning a thunder storm out
of Italy or somewhere. Its so quiet I can hear my watch ticking.
Should keep this carnet with some degree of consistency. Funny
how sometime this evening for the first time since I was a boy I
remembered what old Uncle said to me once—which was if some-
things eating you, if you cant seem to get straightened out about a
thing, then go out in the woods and chop down a tree. Which is
fine I thought as long as your still a boy in a state of cleanliness &
grace & innocence, before that time when suddenly you are a
man, at 30, with no tree to cut down in the desert & no axe or
hatchet for the cutting even if there was a single bleeding tree.
Which in turn reminded me of when I came to N.Y. after the war
all full of piss & vinegar & ready to tear out my guts or die or anything for art—an un-educated Carolina clod-hopper with the lint
still in his hair & that in spite of four years marine corps etc., &
then after all the sweat & toil it gradually dawning that no one
gave a god dam. That jewish boy too—Dorman? Dorfman?—
standing in the rain on 14th street with his hair prickled out &
paint all over his hands & murder in his eye shouting—I want
nothing, all I want to do is to give of myself & the swine are too
blind to even see much less receive, they will go un-recorded &
they deserve it. They are a race of blind ciphers, he shouted &
three days later they found him in his hole in the wall hanging
from the gas meter. I dont know maybe the paralysis began way
back there even. What has happened I dont know. Maybe they deserve us and we deserve them & the guilt & the blame is split right
down the middle. Sleepy now. I risked a 'marc' grape tasting,
after supper and didnt seem to hurt any or lead me on so maybe
Im getting better & some day will be able to shore up my founda-

tions if not for my own glory then for the sake of those gentler & sweeter & dearer who have already come after. So tomorrow or the next day Ill tell Poppy that we are going on to Italy where the earth is milk & honey & well load down some slow train with fat legged babies & orange peels & melted chocolate & rubber dollies and off well go again hanging from all the windows, saying goodby France, adieu beau pays, goodby beautiful land. . . ."

Florence, with its splendor that hurt and intimidated the eye, was too beautiful to stay in long. By the middle of September, Cass and company were living in Rome in a sun-shy apartment—which might have its replica in Brooklyn—on the Via Andrea Doria not far from the western limits of the city and within easy hiking distance, for Poppy, of the Vatican, which loomed over her consciousness as never Mecca did to the most worshipful Mussulman. Cass, walking the shaky tightrope of respectability, blew hot and cold—alternating hosannas for his new-found health with black moods of dejection whose origins he could not determine.

In Rome, one thing that baffled and enraged Cass more than anything else about the curious steeplechase that went on inside his skull was that no matter how long and hard he tried, no matter in what clever combination he placed his bets, he seemed destined forever to lose. When, for instance, by force of determination, or out of desperation or whatever, he made himself play safe and went on the wagon—or climbed halfway up, at least—and in a dozen other ways became a good family man, striving for the sunny ideal of *mens sana,* etc., removing himself from the seductive world of the night and from erotic daydreams and sour semi-suicidal moods, brushing his teeth twice a day and polishing his shoes and cleansing his breath with Listerine—when he did all this there were indeed manifest benefits and blessings, the most important one being simply that he began to function at least biologically as a human. The world of taste and sight and sound—all the sweet sensations Nature granted to the most uncomplicated mortal—were his once more; the air dripped sunlight, his nostrils quivered to long-forgotten odors, he felt he might live to a ripe old age. Yet this state in itself had its drastic shortcomings. Chief among them was the fact that the closer he approached this condition of palmy beatitude—the whole man operating with all his God-given faculties wide-open—the closer, paradoxically, he saw himself coming to be a nice young fellow with a blurred grin, a kind of emotional eunuch in whom that necessary part of the self which saw the world with passion and recklessness, and which had to be flayed and exacerbated and even maddened to retain its vision, had been cut away. Nor was this theory, upon reflection, merely a romantic one: the simple truth of the matter was that he had become dull. To be sure, he finally broke the listless spell which had seized him on the beach at Hyères, and he began for the first time in a year to work in earnest, but his work, he knew inescapably, was flat, stupid, sterile, with all the hollowness about it of the art school, the academy. His eyes were still "as bright as prisms," his ears attuned to Rome's rowdy music like singing reeds. And Leopold, his ulcer, was as quiet as a dormouse. Yet no doubt there is such a thing as too much well-being; with all of it he felt that, long before he reached any ripe old age, he might perish of health, good intentions, and dullness.

But if all this was true it was equally true that he couldn't afford to repeat the months-long bender which had brought him so low in Paris. The memory of that last day and night still lingered in his mind like the faint echo of a nightmare, its moments of frozen beauty etched distinct and clear upon his memory yet adumbrated and made malign as if from the shadowy wings of spooks and goblins. The very thought of it gave him the shakes. Any way, he was bound to lose.

Sometimes, he thought, sometimes I think I should have stayed in New York. I could have become an abstract expressionist and I'd smoke pot, which is healthier than booze, and I'd be a bleeding Eisenhower success. It wouldn't take anything out of me, and I'd be chic as hell, and I'd make a mint. . . .

But in winter Rome can be fabulous and grand. Although for a while the money problem was a headache, a bonanza came one day in the form of a rebate check on his G.I. insurance and with part of this he bought a second- (or third-) hand motorscooter and began to tool around the city, bescarfed and bemittened, spectacles smoking over, and with his beret flat around his ears to keep them from the Tiberous fog and damp. Americans were few at that time of the year, and he was happy. He saw everything the tourists saw, and more. When his eyes were weary with galleries and churches and ruins, with Domenichino and Guido Reni and Tiepolo and a lesser horde of his sainted forebears, he sat in cafés and bars, peering intently at Roman faces, listening to everything, and, with the rueful moderation of an elderly clergyman, sampling *fiaschi* of white lukewarm Roman wine. The Romans made him feel gregarious. In his brighter moods he would go to the jammed cafés of Trastevere, where he argued with bartenders and talked to learned grandmothers with cats, with a withered old liar—a regular at one bar—who claimed to have stormed Porta San Pancrazio at the side of Garibaldi himself, and with a group of noisy young Communists who, each one, longed to go to America yet loved Cass because he loathed the place, and serenaded him with guitars. In this way he learned a more than passable Italian, which was no great feat, since long before in France he had discovered his effortless knack for tongues: it was, he thought sometimes with sadness, the only real gift he owned. Where had he read that a multilingual talent was prevalent among psychotics? This fact occasionally made him ill-at-ease. In his darker moods, while Poppy took Peggy to school or, in the housewifely way she had of dropping in on her favorite saints, shepherded the toddlers from church to church, Cass would stay home in the Canarsie apartment, smoking Sicilian cigars, groaning, and painting his dull pictures. Sometimes he listened to the phonograph, which had all but lost its voice. Sometimes he read Sophocles, who always bewildered and unnerved him and made moist the palms of his hands; more often than he cared to acknowledge he read *Oggi,* or rather—since he could not *read* the language—looked at the pictures, drooling, in the fashion of all but the most detached male humans, at Gina Lollobrigida and Silvana Mangano and Sophia Loren, and discovering new delight in photographs of Texas tornadoes and Illinois murders (*un triplice assassinio a Chicago*) with the bodies laid out beneath bloodstained sheets. Sometimes he slept all day. Sometimes he did nothing but sit and think—inert, mouth dry, nerveless as a stone—wondering what it was that was eating him. Now and then he wrote in his journal. He was gentle with Poppy and the children. He committed no harm upon himself or upon others. In this way he passed seven months in Rome.

Then, during a cold and blustery time in March (it happened to be Holy Week, Cass remembered) there occurred a series of troublesome events that once more pointed him southward in the direction of Sambuco.

It all came about like this. Poppy, whose religious activity had been intense enough all through the Lenten season (at times Cass had thought that if she brought one more fish into the house he would throttle her), reached a kind of peak of fervor during Holy Week; unremittingly, she had addressed herself to all sorts of complicated rites and offices, in pouring rain dashing out to see the various Stations—whatever that meant—and it was at one of these, Cass knew not where—at the Church of Santa Maria Maggiore, perhaps, or that other one, with the Giotto fresco, San Giovanni in Laterano—that she encountered an American couple, the McCabes. Purely encountering these two, Cass later thought, might have been all right, and who was at fault in promoting the relationship (it could not have been Poppy, who was usually diffident, and Cass later had a vision of the ham-handed, fat-lipped McCabe, with his concavity of a Galway nose and a Rolleiflex lolling on his breast, standing among the jostling throng and twitching inwardly as his eyes lit on Poppy's radiant pious face) he never knew for certain. In any case, someone struck up a conversation. All innocence, Poppy cottoned to these pilgrims, and they to her, and she made the grave mistake of bringing them home. It was late in the afternoon when they arrived; molecules of rain floated on the air in a greasy drizzle, it was gray, and Cass, gray as a shad himself, had been brooding all day upon their now shaky financial state. McCabe, a raffish fellow of thirty-five or so in a mackintosh and a snap-brim cap, was full of grins. He dealt (bitter irony!) in retail wines and liquors in Mineola, New York; he referred to Poppy as "this sweetie here," and he called Cass "pal." His wife, who wore her hair in bangs over—or to conceal—a somewhat foreshortened brow, was a plain, nondescript, asexual young matron, and her name was Grace. Cass scarcely could believe that it was all happening to him.

"What in Christ's name has come over you?" he said to Poppy as softly as he could, in the kitchen, while she was fixing supper. "You invited them to *eat* even!"

"Well, I'm sorry, Cass," she said determinedly. "They were very sweet to me and all. They bought me some *gelato* and everything. And they looked so lonely and kind of lost there, after we got to talking. They're sweet. Besides," she added, with a look of sorrow, turning around to face him, "we don't ever see any Americans— ever!—and I'm just tired of it, that's all!"

Which the Lord knew was true enough, Cass thought ruefully (for Poppy's sake), he himself having retreated so far from contact with his native land that in his years abroad he could count on his fingers and toes the sum of the words he had spoken, beyond his family, in his own tongue to his own compatriots. Yet this fact alone he could not square with the desolating McCabes.

"You didn't have to drag in a couple of *Micks,* for the love of God! From Mineola yet—"

"Hush about being a Mick!" she said, eggbeater quivering in her hand. "I'm a Mick, and the children are *half,* and you're just about the biggest bigot I know. I've—"

"Why didn't you invite a couple of plumbers, and a half a dozen Odd Fellows—"

"I've invited them, now shut up!"

At supper, which was *merluzzo*—a form of oily codfish—and spaghetti, McCabe, blind to the litter of paint and canvas strewn about the room, asked Cass what his "line" was. When told, he grimaced, grinned, but said nothing. In the Eternal City even the Pharisee cannot be unkind to art. The conversation swung, as it logically should, to the spiritual aspects of the season.

"Father Cleary," said Grace, "you know we came over with him, well, he said that the Holy Father would probably be canonized some day. That's what the rumor is, anyway."

"You know how rumors are," said Cass, plucking a fishbone from his mouth. "You know how they get around. Scuttlebutt. Sound and fury, signifying *niente.*"

There was a moment of silence, a suggestion, almost audible, of forks and knives in mid-air, suspended. Then as Cass raised his eyes, Grace said, with only the faintest touch of asperity: "On the way over, your wife told us—well, that you weren't a Catholic."

"You're goddam right I'm not a goddam Catholic." The sentence rose in the back of his throat, pulsating, surly; he could almost see it, inverted commas and all, but the words stopped short of his lips. "That's right," he mumbled instead. "Never got the bug."

Seething, he managed to get through the meal, picking his teeth and rising for restless tours to the bathroom and then, drifting on the tide of his own thoughts, idly sketching on the tablecloth doodles with a spoon as the puerile chatter unspiraled—about Pope Pius, whom the McCabes hoped to see sometime, at an "od-dience," and Cardinal Spellman, who was not nearly so fat— "large" was the word Grace used—as his pictures made out. Poppy, deeply impressed by this news, was nonetheless one up on the McCabes, for she had had, already, an audience with the Pope ("up real close") and she had a moment of modest glory when, at

Grace's breathless urging, she was able to describe the Holy Father—his hands, the cut of his nose, the size of his ring, or rings; "a fine glorious man, to be sure," she said, shiny-eyed, lapsing into her ancestral brogue.

"Pardon me," Cass put in abruptly. Something had jogged his memory; it had tickled him before and it tickled him now. "You know what," he said, already laughing, "you know what the cardinals in the Vatican call Spellman?"

"No, what?" said Grace. *"Cardinal* Spellman."

"Guess."

"I really couldn't guess," she said with a hopeful look.

"Shir—" He had begun to laugh so hard that he could barely get the words out. "Shir—" Convulsed, he pressed his head against his hands, weakly heaving. "Shir— Oh Christ. Shirley Temple!"

"Cass!" Poppy cried.

"No, I mean it!" He giggled, gazing into Grace's scandalized face. "He comes winging in from the U.S. and A., by this Super Constellation, see—"

"Cass!" said Poppy.

"No, I mean it! I was told this by a *priest,* mind you. In he comes to Ciampino, and the news gets around the Vatican that *Shirley Temple è arrivata!"*

"Cass!"

"Haw haw haw!" Gusts of laughter exploded forth from the table, startling Cass, who looked up to see McCabe, mouth wide-open like his own, shaking in helpless mirth. "That's rich, pal!" he said, wiping his eyes. "Shirley Temple, that's the most! You hear that, Grace?" He could hardly wait, he added between wheezes, to tell Bill Hurley that one.

"I don't think it's funny at all," said Grace sharply.

It was at that moment, Cass recalled later, that the evening took a vigorous turn for the better; to be sure, when all was said and done the change was illusory, lulling him, leading him into a trap, and engaging him in a tangle of emotional crises which he was not to shake off for a long time. At that moment, though (who knows what might be the repercussions of a single hairy joke?) he felt full of himself, transformed by McCabe's surprising, appreciative laughter from a sour introvert into a talented clown. As for McCabe himself, who still sat across the table shaking his head and letting out loose wails of merriment, he basked for Cass in a new and more kindly light. That he was simple-minded and an ass was one thing; that in the face of his wife's ambitious and tedious piety he could laugh gave him, in some odd and obscure way, more solid dimensions. Cass felt himself actually warming a little toward the man, "pal" and all.

"No, I'll be confidential with you, see?" McCabe said after dinner, when Poppy and Grace were washing the dishes. "I'm a good Catholic and all that, but I'm not *thick* about it, see? Now Rome is great, I'll tell you, but me and Grace have just come for two different reasons." And, describing the curve of phantom breast or buttock with his hand, he said with a long vaudeville wink: "Know what I mean, pal?"

"I sure do, Mac," said Cass benevolently.

The fatal moment had arrived. The transmogrified Mineola Eve, proffering forbidden fruit. "Say," he said in a hoarse whisper. "You look like it's been a long time since you had the real American article. How about some Old McCabe?"

He was not joking, and Old McCabe was no fiction: it was one hundred proof sour mash bourbon whiskey, bottled in Tennessee and sold in Mineola under McCabe's own picturesque label (shamrocks, harp, Hibernian pipe), and he had a quart full of it in the sagging pocket of his mackintosh. Cass heard a groan, mingled in equal parts of joy and despondency, escape his lips as McCabe held the bottle, flashing amber, up to the light; he groaned and he fidgeted and he sweated and finally he said, in tones of purest affliction: "Well, Mac, I haven't had any of that stuff since I left the States, and I'd like to. But I can't."

"Watsa matter? It's the real article, pal. I never travel without it."

"I can't handle the booze," he said simply. "It takes me. It gives me problems. I stick to a little wine. If you want to know the truth, I'm a whiskey-head. Also, Mac, I got an ulcer."

He might have known better than to temporize this: within an hour, during this the cruelest night of his recent reckoning, he was on his way to becoming the drunkest man in Rome. And why? Why! Why on this night, under these particular circumstances, with this foolish and irksome stranger? Why, after so long a struggle to keep his balance, should he go off now, on a dull drab night in Rome which demanded the stuff neither for celebration nor mourning? Why, he kept asking himself, as in despair and in rapid succession he downed three half-tumblers full, straight, was he such a weak-kneed slob, unless he had simply been set down in a situation over which he had utterly no control? Suddenly (this was when McCabe, moist-mouthed and stripped to his red, white, and blue suspenders, had begun a series of gamy Irish jokes, full of Pats and Mikes and begorras) he began to wonder if this storekeeper were not really a sort of bizarre *advocatus diaboli,* sent not merely to test but to prove, through the irresistible sour mash, his inability to survive in the world of his own will. Mother of God, he thought as with mumbling lips he downed his third glass, I'm slipping again. But Old McCabe was, in truth, the real article: Cass began to glow inwardly and outwardly and all around; he abandoned himself to the jokes, hee-hawing with mouth wide-open and, like the meanest smoking car poltroon, slapping his haunches, rooting at his crotch, and telling McCabe a few of his own. When "the girls" returned from the kitchen, half an hour later, his face was aflame, he had torn off his tie, he was awash in sweat, and he was prancing the room like a billygoat.

"So this Irishman was on the train," he was saying, "next to this little Middle Europe Jew who couldn't read English and kept asking him to translate from the newspaper. So this Irishman said to himself, 'I'll play a joke on this little guy.'—You know this one?"

"Cass Kinsolving!" He heard behind him Poppy's cry of distress. "Oh, Cass, you've started all over *again!*"

"Hush, Poppy! I'm telling a story!"

"But, *Cass*—"

"So every time the Jew would ask 'What's this?' the Irishman would say something like 'Syphilis' or 'Gonorrhea' or—"

"Cass! You listen to me!"

"So finally the Jew said, 'What's this mean? This word right here,' and the Irishman said, 'That means the clap.' So the Jew just shook his head slowly back and forth and said, 'Oy! Is that Pope a *sick* man!"

"Haw haw haw!" McCabe roared, rolling back on the couch. "Haw haw haw haw haw!"

Limp himself with mirth, free now of despair, regrets, recriminations, he wheeled about to face Poppy's unhappiness: "You said you *wouldn't* any more!"

"I was kidding," he said, beaming, throwing an arm around her. "Forgot what fun it was."

She jerked away from him. For a moment her mouth parted, trembling on speech. Then, as if canceling whatever it had been in her mind to say (God love her, he thought in a dreamy haze, she has never once nagged me in her life), she cast McCabe a ruinous

look, turned silently about and left the room, either unwilling or
unable to see him once more embrace his demon. She slammed the
bedroom door.

Then strange things happened. Grace, still prim and aloof for a
while, slowly dropped her guard and, prompted by her husband's
loud and deprecating wisecracks ("Come on, Gracie, don't be a
drag, so it's Lent, you haven't swore off the Old McCabe."), sampled some of the product; finding it as good as ever, she soon
became well lubricated, loose of tongue and hair-do, and by midnight, just before their game of three-handed blackjack began,
she had abandoned all airs and religiosity, hinting with a snicker
that she might also have come to Rome "to pick up a couple of
alligator bags," and letting slip several hells and goddams. Cass
should have known better than to gamble when drunk (especially, it gradually dawned on him, with someone like McCabe,
who, holding his liquor like a grenadier, quickly dropped all pretense at conviviality and settled down to the game with falcon eye
and stony hand), but when McCabe had said, 'How's about a
little cards?' it had been in the nature of a clarion and resistless
cry: of all his memories of the war, poker was the one remaining
which had a shred of decency, of charm. He was—at least he had
been in the past—an expert. Indeed, a virtuoso. It had even
brought him, in his Marine Corps outfit, a kind of middling fame.
Money in those days, accumulated pay, meant nothing. On half a
dozen Pacific islands, in hotel rooms in Hawaii, on stateside
bivouacs, and in the steaming holds of Navy transports he had
won and lost what would have been, for him, a prodigal fortune
at any time; once in a three-day game in New Zealand he had
won sixteen thousand dollars, only to lose all of it within a week in
a luckless and inferior game of craps. Once he had won over four
thousand dollars in a single hand, by the skin of his teeth, to be
sure—on an inside straight touched by the hand of the Almighty.
And once, on the psychiatric ward of the naval hospital in San
Francisco, playing with an accredited schizophrenic, two con-
stitutional psychopathic inferiors, and a D.U. (Diagnosis Un-
determined) like himself, he had won twenty-eight million dollars,
and a sense of triumph that was not diminished by the quixotic
nature of the stakes. He loved the cards, he had not played—
though he always lugged with him cards and chips wherever he
went—since he had been in Europe, and he fell to with passion
(God knew they needed the money) and with the illusion that he

would clean out the dreary McCabes—which was a mistake. If the Old McCabe had been the proscribed apple, it was the game of blackjack through which he found himself expelled from the Garden.

Tense and quiet, the brief camaraderie gone, the three of them played through the early hours of the morning; groggily, hazily, almost hypnotically, he watched the whiskey in the bottle (he alone now drinking) fall to the mid-point level, then lower, shook his head from time to time to keep his swiftly blurring mind in focus, and wondered why he seemed to be losing in such a headlong rush. It was his own reckless fault, he thought, for setting so high the limit of the bets—three hundred lire, or roughly fifty cents; even so, drunk or not, or simply rusty, he had had too good a set of cards—nineteens, twenties all along—to have lost by one o'clock nearly all of his available cash. By one-thirty he was out of pocket eighteen thousand lire and he was forced to go to the kitchen, to rummage around in the dark and pluck ten thousand more from the tea can which served as Poppy's household exchequer. Bleeding God, he thought as he stumbled back through the shadows, I'm acting like a bum in the flicks; we just don't have this kind of cash to throw away. Sitting down heavily, he glanced squint-eyed at the McCabes. Rapt in stony concentration, cigarettes dangling from their mouths, cold-sober, and silent save for the brisk, peremptory way they each muttered "Hit" or "Stick," in the tone of someone who had played cards for profit all his life, they had lost all aspect of the devout pilgrims they had first pretended to be, transformed like twin Cinderellas by the alchemy of midnight into avid, consecrated, hungry sharks. And for the life of him, Cass could not get a blackjack, that fortunate marriage of ace and face-card which would make McCabe relinquish the deal. They gave him the willies, these two dough-faced Micks; he felt ganged-up on, and he saw the ten thousand lire begin to vanish like water poured down a drain. He beat McCabe three times running; he thought his luck was changing. The deal passed from McCabe to Grace; Cass lost again, with a consecutiveness of ill-luck that made him writhe inside and caused the sweat to pop out in droplets on his face. Then he got the deal on his first and only blackjack: the deal lasted two hands, on both of which he lost, and reverted once more to McCabe.

"Mothera God!" he cried out in disgust, as for the fifteenth time his ace and nine—a solid twenty—were beaten by McCabe's twenty-one. "You don't need no Pope, Mac. You got the god-damdest luck I ever saw." He was down once more to a dollar's worth of lire.

"I know what you mean, pal," said McCabe, in his longest speech of the game. "That's the way the breaks run sometime. Gimme a match, will you, Gracie?"

By then it was past two o'clock. Although he was still function-ing after a fashion—functioning in the realm of the game, at least, taking no rash chances, cautious when caution was called for, forc-ing his luck, such as it was, only to the most barely tolerable limit —the whiskey, he knew, had begun to work upon his mind a most un-subtle demolition. He felt hemmed-in, depressed, claustro-phobic. The room had suffered a slight, secret yet nonetheless weird and unnerving displacement of dimension: smaller now, wreathed in clouds of smoke, it seemed almost to have become tilted a bit—somehow with a premonition of menace—like the cabin of a ship at sea moving slantwise in the troubled yet still noiseless waters that presage a violent storm. His head was giddy (it had just been so *long,* he kept thinking) and an uncomfortable nausea had begun to gurgle at the pit of his stomach, and from the high pitch of his early delight he had been brought down—by his tragic losses, by a surfeit of booze, maybe both—to the clammiest sort of anxiety and depression. And it was symptomatic of the deep-dyed lush he was, he thought even while ritualistically he groped for the bottle, that he should assume that a whole lot more of the Old McCabe could ease all of these problems.

"Have another," he heard himself saying thickly to Grace, hold-ing out the bottle, which was (inconceivably!) only a third full. "How 'bout some more the Ole Mac here?"

Whatever slight inebriety had loosened her up before had fled from her, in spirit and in countenance. Her face was as cold-looking as a clamshell. "Me and Mac don't believe in mixing liquor and the cards," she said austerely, shuffling the deck like a presti-digitator.

Intolerance, of the sort Cass bore toward Catholics in general and the Irish in particular, breeds brooding; brooding breeds sus-picion; and suspicion, in this case mingled with financial loss and an out-of-hand drunkenness, breeds an infuriate conviction. The conviction being that night, as he stood in the dark once more groping for lire in Poppy's tea-can treasury, that between the two of them the McCabes of Mineola comprised a crooked house. In the darkness he felt his brain lurch like a seesaw; pinpoints of ruby-red fire dotted his vision, and he swayed top-heavy against the sink, cracking his elbow. He drew out from the can a fistful of lire—greasy, shredded, of all denominations; as he did so, it occurred to him, in a kind of explosive and vindictive flash, in an access of imagination or fantasy so intense that it was truer than truth, that McCabe, the miserable sonofabitch, had been bottom-dealing from the deck throughout the entire game. Thrice-punctured Christ! he thought. He had been trusting, stupid, and as blind as a bat. Pilgrims your ass! They were two miserable low-brow suburban sharpers, and they had tried to take him for the sucker that he deserved, but at this point, by God, refused, to be. Pros they were, an old-time Mississippi twosome, crooks in pietists' clothes who had lushed him up, fattened him for the kill, and plucked him clean as a pullet. A tremendous belch tore itself from his gorge, reverberating around the black kitchen. He felt a damp and queasy sensation in his palm, and drew back his hand from the place where he had propped it, unfeeling, in a plate of cold spaghetti. He began to tremble in total, towering, Protestant wrath. And though his wrath was a moral one, it was also the wholly uncomplicated one at having been taken by these sharp punks, who should have assumed that he, disciplined through a thousand deadly games (for *stakes,* not for peanuts) to sniff out the slightest funny-business or skulduggery, was too dumb to detect a simple bottom-deal, and would be blind to what (and of this he was sure!) had been going on all along, revealed by the flesh of McCabe's somewhat pudgy knuckle—middle finger, left hand—as he performed his slippery fraud. Well, we'll see about that! he thought. And he lumbered grim as Armageddon back into the living room, lurched into his chair, and said: "Deal!"

"What'd you say?" said McCabe.

"Deal! And *bury* and *burn* those goddam cards, this time."

"Don't get touchy, pal. We all have bad nights every—"

"Deal, I said. Up the limit."

"What?" said McCabe incredulously.

"Up the limit! One thousand lire."

"Well, it suits me if it suits you."

Cass watched him narrowly, or as narrowly as he could with his inflamed, wayward, by now nearly antipodean eyes. McCabe was not a frail man by any means: he had chunky, solid shoulders and beefy hands and there was a sort of flinty Celtic meanness in his face that indicated he might be capable of a decent scrap. Yet Cass, unworried, even eager, knew he could be handled. Boiling now, and itching, Cass watched him as he dealt the cards—to him first, then to Grace, then to himself. There was no revelatory flicker of knuckle-skin beneath the deck; Cass made a clucking sound, aloud, beneath his tongue: the bastard was playing it cool, he thought, perhaps he even knew that *someone* had pegged him for the crook he was. Cass had three thousand lire riding on a five and a six, showing, and a seven in the hole—a restful eighteen. "Good," he said. Grace stuck. McCabe turned up his cards, said, "Pay twenty," and took the pot.

"Baby, you're hot as a firecracker," said Grace, in a marveling voice. To be both crooked and lucky was just too much. As McCabe dealt again, Cass took the bottle in both hands, somewhat like a baby, and downed in raw flaming gulps what was left of the whiskey to its palest dregs: perhaps to forestall what happened then and what seemed "forever after," he should have made a libation to the gods of Rome; perhaps not even the gods can hinder a greased slide down toward disaster; either way, as he felt his brain reel and rock with instant concussion and, still gasping like a fish, caught what was—or what seemed to be—a cheating finger flashing white across the moist ruin of his vision, he knew with despair that he was gone again for good. "McCabe!" he roared. "You bottom-dealing swine!" And it took him no more than two brief seconds to fling off his glasses, heave the bottle over his shoulder, and, like a man swimming frantic strokes underwater, to flounder across the collapsing and wildly splintering card table, amid cards and chips and clouds of floating paper money, where he fell with outstretched, encircling hands upon the horrified McCabe.

Little else—try as he might—could he ever remember. He had begun to black out only seconds before he attacked McCabe, so that all that happened afterwards receded by degrees ever more dimly yet certainly into oblivion. He remembered Grace's screams, unbelievable sounds—ear-splitting, cataclysmic: the voice of a woman in quadruple childbirth or in the throes of rape —high-pitched, relentless, and everlasting. He remembered McCabe's front tooth splitting his own knuckle, painlessly, as he landed a lucky blow in a fight where all else seemed to be round-house swings, aimless staggerings, sightless and punch-drunk wrath. He remembered McCabe's hairy fist as it connected with his eye, blinding him. He remembered more of Grace's screams. At some point he remembered Poppy and the children, screaming too, and the tenants above and below all screaming—*Zitti! Silen-*

zio! Basta!—and the taste of blood in his mouth. He remembered getting a strong fingernail-splitting grip on McCabe's pants, finally, and hurling him out into the night. He remembered retrieving his glasses and stuffing his pockets with lire—his own and McCabe's —and staggering away from the place. And that was all.

When finally he came to, he knew neither where he was nor how he had gotten there nor the hour of the day or night. He was in a shuttered, silent room, dark as Hades; his head ached and throbbed like a monstrous boil, as did his hand and his half-closed eye, and he was lying naked on a bed. For long perplexing minutes he grappled with the question of how came he there, and when, and why; there was a terrifying instant when he could not recall his own name. The terror passed. The hell with it. All identity had fled him and he lay there quietly breathing— pulsing, rather, like some low amoebic form of marine life— without fear or anxiety or sensation of any kind, save for pain, which he tried to exorcise through a vain attempt at going back to sleep. After a time, by the slowest of stages, he regained his bearings; memory and reality came slipping back, as did his name, which he spelled out slowly to himself—K-i-n-s—with a sense of charm and discovery, like a young lover. Then a cold crazy panic seized him and he shot out of bed, padding clumsily about on icy tiles until he found a light switch, turned it on, and in a full-length mirror stood revealed as naked as Adam, one-eyed, bruised, hair upended like a Hottentot's, standing half-frozen in a hotel room so foul and sleazy that it would have shamed a Panama brothel. An antiseptic smell floated on the air. Dirt in great sausage-shaped cylinders festooned the moldings of the walls, the rungs of two rickety chairs, the edges of a tattered rug. Of furniture, beyond the bed and chairs, there was none; for plumbing there was a plugged-up bidet, gorged with some unspeakable liquid that gulped softly and stagnantly. As for decoration there was only the omnipresent Virgin, gazing down on the grizzly sagging bed where, amnesically and with the collaboration of God knew whom, he had added his chapter to its dateless chronicle of fornication. Whoever she was (and try as he might with his bursting head to recall her, he could not; he might as well have gone to bed with a wraith) she had been thorough: not only had she taken all his money, down to the most frayed and crumbling five-lire note, but she had managed to make off with all of his clothes. Even his underwear was gone. No—charitable whore!—she had left him his glasses; these he found on the floor near the bed, along with his beret, which, being dilapidated, he supposed she couldn't pawn, like the glasses. He put the glasses on, and the beret, and gazed at himself in the mirror: noble animal. His pelvic bones ached from the sinister, Lethean romp; looking down, catching sight of something that moved, he saw that she had left him, too, what appeared to be all the vermin in Rome —if that in truth was where he was. Murder! he thought. Murder! Triple bloody murder!

So he had no money, no clothes; recalling the night before (if it really was only the night before), he had no doubt that he was being hunted by the police, by the Pope, by the right honorable lady ambassador Mrs. Luce herself. He had a case of crabs. He was certain his finger was broken. He was on the verge of catching pneumonia in an unheated hotel room in a remote part of Italy (at least he was sure it was Italy) whose location he did not know. He had had, indeed, the debauch he had so long pined for —and one must pay—but did he really deserve this disheveled ending? His plight, in its quality of helplessness and exposure, seemed the closest possible approach in reality to that universal nightmare where one passes in nude parade down the crowded main street of some city—vulnerable, all divulged, without a fig leaf, without anything. There was only one thing to do, at least at that moment, and he did it: he crawled back into the lascivious bed and lay there, bereted, bespectacled, fiercely scratching, pondering a way out of his low condition.

Then who was it that called him? And from whence did it come, that rapturous voice? Was it only some place in his mind's imagining—some island or magic coast never seen on earth—or was it in all truth a land, previsioned, real, where he knew that some fine day he'd set down his lover's triumphant feet? He put up a hand to his aching brow, feeling sweat there now, and fever. Water! he thought. Water! Somewhere in the depths of the building a door slammed hugely, an explosion that brought forth from the woodwork a tribe of affrighted bugs; drowsily watching them shuttle about in the blinding light, he fell once more, terrifyingly, into sleep, dropping not into the oblivion he had so gluttonously yearned for but dreaming of that old abominable seascape upon which, floating helpless as a twig, he found himself eternally undone and foundering. Here, so familiar, was the black gulf, the solitary unpeopled coast rimmed round by palm trees, by the weathered slopes of volcanoes which from horizon to horizon sent plumes of smoke into a sickly overcast sky, devoid of sunlight, troubled by premonitions of thunder. Here on this gulf, in a tiny boat so frail that each black foamy wave threatened to swamp it, he was rowing with confused, exhausting strokes toward an island far out to sea where amid whirling carrousels and orange blossoms and the black eyes of girls there existed a slumberous southern repose so sweet, so voluptuous, so soothing to his flayed and bedeviled senses that not to reach it would mean his ruin and his end. And from somewhere in the depths of this green vision one single girl's voice called to him in a strange language filled with soft liquid syllables, remote, importunate, and ripe with the promise of love. Love me! she cried, in those words he could not fathom. Love me, and I shall be all salvation. Yet now as he stroked on the heavy oars he seemed to be carried far and away from the voice, borne even more perilously toward the land; huge currents and riptides washed him toward the barren inhospitable shore: a storm blew up, the gulf became as black as night, and upon the horizon there sprang to life a forest of whirling waterspouts, bearing down upon him as darkly as vengeful tornadoes from the western plains. The waves beat against him, black and cold, and with the waves came an explosion of torrential rain. In cataclysm, the great range of volcanoes erupted fire; the marvelous green coast or island, the enchanted land unseen at his back, perishing with its freight of unborn and untasted love, toppled into the sea with a hissing noise—*"Dio non esiste!"* he heard himself shriek—as at last one black and mountainous wave, washed to this gulf as if from the uttermost boundaries of the earth, bore him up and up through a sky snowy with the falling bodies of gulls, and descending now, onto the wretched and irremediable shore. . . .

"Non c'è Dio!" he found himself sobbing, lying outstretched on the floor. "He is dead! He is dead!" And even as he awoke on the wet tiles the contracting, seashore rhythm of the dream still lingered, and he was again wafted in one long last dwindling shiver of memory, screaming, to his mean and worthless extermination. Light had filtered through the shutters; still he could not tell whether it was dawn or dusk. . . .

Poppy came and got him, bearing a cardboard box full of clothes. He had mustered enough strength to bang on the door and yell, summoning a limping, evil-looking porter, whom he bribed with the promises of fortune to make the telephone call. The man also brought him a bottle full of water, which he downed at a gulp. Distraught and red-eyed as she was, Poppy was relieved to see him and—as always—was forgiving. In wrenching guilt over what he knew he had really done, he told her how—in a bar on the Piazza Mazzini—he had fallen in with bad company: two fuzzy-headed Somaliland Negroes who could scarcely speak Italian and who, dropping some tribal potion into his Strega, had rolled him for his money and his clothes. This Poppy believed implicitly, which aggravated his guilt. Bouncing homeward in a taxi through the morning light, he lay with his head in Poppy's lap, suffering and suffering, and muttering recriminations. From her he discovered that the hotel had been on a miserable slum street far out off the Via Appia Nuova—barely in Rome at all—and that he had spent a full day and a full night in the place. It was Good Friday, with a salmon-streaked and radiant sky, touched with sorrow and hope, and the bells were silent all over Rome.

VII

With raw meat on his eye and a bandage over his cut finger, and with blue ointment smeared upon his nether parts, he convalesced, for three days gazing like a sick cow upon the ragged edges of sleep. The nightmare did not return, although he brooded about it a lot. What did it mean? Passionately he tried to make the dream give up its meaning; each detail was as clear in his mind as something which happened only yesterday, yet when he tried to put them all together he ended up with black ambiguous chaos. Perhaps, he thought, it was a species of madness.

Be that as it was, he was hooked, he knew, hooked by the treacherous grape, and he felt that this time he'd be forced to ride the merry-go-round for a long, long spell. Above all, now, escape —the desire for flight, anywhere, so long as it was swift—loomed in his mind as the foremost necessity, thus bearing out the prophecy of Slotkin, the kindly old Navy brain doctor, who once had told Cass just that: "You will be running all your life." His voice had been fatherly, and there had been in his eye the rueful look of one who had tried, but failed, to help runaways and escapists before; yet the words had stuck, and as Cass struggled to his feet on the day after Easter he remembered them, hating that dim old father symbol whose presence seemed fated to dog him until the day he died.

One thing he knew was that he must head south again, and so he did—alone—and that is how he finally came to Sambuco.

He was later able to recall some of his suicidal journey; in pouring rain, wobbling southward on his motorscooter, it was only a miracle (or perhaps Poppy's tearful blessing, together with the steel Testament carried safely by her dumb brother Alfie all through the Normandy campaign, which she stuck into his breast pocket) that prevented his *grappa*-blurred trip from coming to an end beneath the wheels of some truck or bus. Rain poured down his neck, rivulets of water flowed into his shoes. He sang hymns to keep up his spirits, Methodist hymns, throbbing with passion, meekness, and love for a pansy savior. *And He walks with me,* he roared to the highway, *Andy talks with me, Andy tells me that I am His own.* Smitten with a sudden religious tic, giggling yet close to tears, he gulped *grappa* as he weaved steering with one hand down precipitous concrete slopes. *At the Cross, at the Cross where I first saw the Light!* Huge trucks passed him with their backwash drenching him to the skin; in the rear of one he thought he saw perched his old uncle, who waved a receding, remonstrating finger. *And the burdens of my heart rolled away . . .* A low, black, ancient Maserati veered close, skidding, brakes squealing in a mist of rain, and nearly clipped him off the road. Memory, in the form of an iridescent penumbra of tears, fogged his eyes. *Blessed assurance—Jesus is mine!* All Italy lay shrouded in wet and cold. *Oh, what a foretaste of glory Divine!* Presently he ceased singing, and lapped back moistly into dark inner recesses of his self. He brought the scooter into a semblance of control. What he was searching for, what impossible prize or vision he was seeking, as he bumped along in the monstrous damp, he did not know; yet he felt some premonition not too far removed from delight when, toward noon, he saw the sun flame out over the slopes of Vesuvius and Naples below it, cluttered and blue, sea-girt, smoky, and as prodigious as Jerusalem. Yet he did not stop here, to eat, or even rest. Something impelled him on. Stiff and saddlesore, veering wildly as he sidestepped in and out of a web of trolley tracks, he put-putted down the drizzly Via Monteoliveto, assailed by a grim ecstasy of southern smells—of salt sea and pimientos and sewers —and a jazzy amorous hubbub, and snapping, black and insolent eyes and, quick as a wink, by a raucous pimp no more than ten and hardly higher than his knees, hideous and imperishable in his memory for the fluted blue cavity that replaced an ear, who trotted alongside and badgered him for five blocks about screwing his sister. "Hey, Joe, maybe you like my *brother!*" Maybe I would, Cass thought, with a sad strong inner stirring, thinking of a boy's slim hips, maybe I would, I don't seem to be making it with the ladies any more, but then banished the thought, banished the child with a few lire and a soft boot in the pants, throttling up as he found the road to Sorrento.

Yet again it rained, and still he did not know why he pressed on. Between the snow-capped peak of Vesuvius and the calm dark bay, a jetty, seaweed-slimy in the low tide, lay poised like a cliff in the green of summer. At its edge three bare-legged urchins, shivering, and a solemn fat priest stood fishing in the downpour, and Cass paused thoughtfully, wondering if he had the talent to sketch the sweet and crazy scene—decided he didn't, passed on. The *grappa* bottle was nearly empty. In Sorrento, in midafternoon, he found himself in a grimy bar somewhere at the edge of the sea, drinking Strega, learning songs in tongue-twisting dialect from a sweaty barkeep in B.V.D.'s, playing mechanical football with a cross-eyed boy in American Army clothes, and washing his hands at a scummy sink whose drain emptied onto the water fifty feet below; there, inanely winding his watch, he fumbled it into the sea with a splash, and was immediately dissolved in loony grief. "*Sono pazzo!*" he exclaimed tearfully to the barkeep. "I'm mad! Mad!" And before he knew it he was on his motorscooter again, blundering around the hairpin turns toward Positano and Amalfi. Above Positano he blew a tire, squatted by the roadside and repaired it with numb fingers. Farther on he ran out of gas, which in terms of Sambuco was either a curse or a blessing, depending upon how one views all that came after. For as he stood drenched at the roadside, a truck carrying barrels of wine drew to a halt, and from one window a most peculiar face peered out. Hooked like a scimitar, a majestic nose rode adventurously forth, dominating, indeed almost overshadowing, the face; upon its stately arch small wens were sprinkled like pumpkin seeds and from the two caverns beneath, great thickets of hair sprouted black and luxuriant. Of the chin there was almost nothing: above the point where it should have been, and shadowed almost to obscurity by the huge bowsprit of a nose, a mouth with thin red lips described a V-shaped smile, wet and lubricious. Something about the man's face, the nose especially, gave it a look at once humorous and benign, like a cross between Punch and Torquemada; his hair, like Franz Liszt's, hung seedily to his shoulders. *"Che t'è successo?"* he said. To which Cass replied: "No gas, my friend." The face smiled. "Hang onto the back," he said. "You look cold. Open the *tappo* and have some wine, but be careful not to spill it. Hang onto the back and I'll take you where you're going."

Which was the most curious part of all. For the face in the truck could not have known where Cass was going, any more than Cass did himself. And a long time afterward, thinking that without that offer he doubtless would never have landed where he did, he wondered if that face had really been as queer and sinister as he remembered it. Yet as Cass hung himself with one hand to the rear of the truck and allowed himself to be pulled behind, he felt the road rise beneath him, and now through pouring rain he felt himself being towed higher and higher along the margin of some wild and yawning gorge, where foaming torrents rushed a thousand feet below, and the sea fell away in the distance like gray water in a dishpan, steaming and indistinct. Directly in front of his muzzle the bung of one barrel was riven through by a wooden cock, and with his free hand he gave it a twist, so that the wine spurted red and bubbly into his out-thrust lower jaw. Higher and higher the truck climbed, towing its drinker. When they reached the peak level ground, Cass had gulped a pint without wasting a drop, and now as the truck halted in a strange rainy piazza, before he could thank the weird face in the cab, he had fallen from the motorscooter in a soggy, deplorable heap, a red and white banner floating insanely across his vision:

BENVENUTO A SAMBUCO
BIENVENU A SAMBUCO
WILLKOMMEN IN SAMBUCO
WALCOME TO SAMBUCO

The truck was gone. Merciful God, he thought, heaving slowly to his feet, I'm in a bleeding infantile neurotic cycle. He climbed dreamily back onto the motorscooter, tried to start it, remembered his lack of fuel, and was about to push it toward shelter, when at this moment Saverio came splashing across the square, stuttering, snaggled mouth ajar, nearly toppling him again as he took possession of the knapsack riding aft. *"Bella Vista!"* he roared. *"Tutti i conforti . . . panorama scenico . . . prezzi moderati!"* Through the downpour the creature gazed at him imploringly, with wild dislocated eyes. Cass shivered. I have gone to sleep, he thought, I've gone to sleep and am dreaming of hell. He sneezed, swaying groggily, aware that the day was verging on darkness and oblivion. *"Dica,"* he said to the idiot, "where can I get a drink?"

"At the Bella Vista!"

There was no one in the lobby of the Bella Vista. It was grim, cold, deserted, and silent save for a hideous rococo clock whose pendulum snapped back and forth slowly and dolefully in the stillness. There were potted rubber plants, an umbrella stand, and a massive walnut armchair whose mirrored back reflected the oval specter of himself, pale-faced and dripping. It was like the waiting room of a funeral parlor, and the adjoining *salone* revealed even grimmer secrets: plush chairs bedecked in graying antimacassars, a chandelier once meant to cast a glory of light, in which one bulb glimmered dimly, more rubber plants in pots, and a wide view of the sunless valley with its churning rack of clouds and mist. Then in the gloom his eyes picked out a fireplace and a grate filled with feebly glowing coals. Drawn up close beside it an aging couple in sweaters and lumpy tweeds were playing backgammon with broken, haunted expressions and with chilblained, visibly trembling hands. They seemed to be the hotel's only guests. Somewhere out of sight a canary chirped submissively. The place smelled of wet wool, old books, fish, and Great Britain. Staggering through the hallways, he located the bar. Almost as an afterthought, it was cramped into a tiny, dim, airless anteroom, and there could not have been a gloomier place to drink in all of Europe. By hammering at a bell long enough, he finally summoned an oppressed-looking waiter, who sold him a bottle of caramel-tasting Italian brandy. He took this back into the *salone* and sat down, trying to dry out, but without hope, since the air of the hotel seemed damper even than his clothes. He picked up a copy of the *London Daily Mail,* put it down again—it was six months old. The brandy, foul as it was, warmed him, allaying some of his nervousness and depression. After some minutes he actually felt a kind of deceptive, dull-witted sense of well-being, and told himself that he was not drunk, after all. He looked at the backgammon players, and sneezed again.

He must have sat there for half an hour, brooding, gazing out at the tragic landscape. It conjured up all scenes which in his imagination existed as places to be shunned: Blackpool; Winnipeg; Finland; Shamokin, P.A. The land was darkling and accursed. He tilted the bottle up and drank. In the shadows by the fire the Englishman and his wife massaged their fingers. All of a sudden, try as he might to repress it, a pressure which had been building up all day tore loose, and he broke wind loudly, a prolonged tattoo which he squirmed vainly to muffle, finally relaxed sheepishly and let go—a slow, erratic crepitation, like marbles falling into a hopper. There was a commotion at the backgammon table. He barely noticed it. His disturbance ceased. He brooded some more. Then, after a while, rising unsteadily from the chair, only half-aware that he had begun to fret out loud, and to mumble, he took an infirm step forward, wondering if now was not the time to go back to Rome, and in spite of the rain. "You can take Sambuco and bugger it!" he said aloud. "Bugger it!" He hardly knew he spoke: the Englishwoman, followed more slowly by her husband, snapped erect at the table like a startled doe. He lurched toward the mantelpiece, in the hope of eliciting some warmth for his pants from the meager coals. Suddenly he was trapped, cornered, utterly hemmed in by Sambuco: he felt like one of those gallant cowboys who, pinned to the edge of an abyss by Indians, must turn around to face a storm of arrows or plunge horse and all into the horrendous gully. There was nowhere, he thought with mounting terror, nowhere at all to go. His affliction returned. Windy, turbulent, he edged past the slowly rising, cherry-red, bristling old man and in complete despair fell heavily against the mantel, feeling, as he did, something give way ponderously at his shoulder and fall to earth with an ear-splitting crash.

Slotkin, he thought, old father, old rabbi. Patience, discipline—that's what I need, and he was still thinking this in dim self-congratulation at his insight, when hell broke loose around him. For the huge vase, in falling—it could not have weighed less than fifty pounds—had narrowly missed the old man; even now as Cass looked dully down at it lying splintered in green shards on the floor he saw two wool-lined slippers shuffle forward, heard a voice quaking and elderly and half-hysteric with rage. "Drunken foul-mouth! Blightah!" the old man quavered, brandishing an invisible riding crop, and Cass, looking up in pity and wonder at the inflamed, mustachioed face, was for the first time aware of what he had done.

" 'Scuse me—" he began, but it was too late, for the *salone,* awakened by the sound of the crash, came alive like a mausoleum overrun by vandals. Three waiters appeared, and several maids; what looked like a cook came on the run, chef's hat flopping, and a horde of lesser minions—busboys, gardeners, porters. As they surrounded him, and as the old man, still fuming, shook a chapped fist in his face, he could only think that with all this help around, the place surely must be losing money.

"Look here! Ruddy side of the man!" the Englishman was bawling to the assemblage. "Look at him! Who is he, filthy drunken beggar! Nearly brained us, he did, with that vahs!" Dumbly he watched the old man, watched his wife now plucking at his sleeve, watched the parlor as it filled up with spectators, and said to himself over and over, metronomically: This is not happening, this is not happening to me. Then just as his longing to melt through the floor became so intense that he did, for an instant, seem to feel his feet sink beneath him, a wild-eyed little man came on the scene, gesticulating with a menu he held in one plump hand. This, he made out, was someone named Signor Windgasser, a small human, wholly terrifying. Sputtering apologies to the old Englishman, he turned to face Cass and began to flourish the menu beneath his eyes. "You!" he cried. "That vase was worth two hundred thousand lire!" Cass was too dazed, too confused, too inextricably lost to stir; in a blur of muffled sight and sound like the wildest hallucination he watched Windgasser's lips moving in convulsive outrage, yet could make no sense of what was being said; hand cocked upon his spectral swagger stick, the old man still fumed and fussed; from somewhere in the crowd there was a hoarse croak of uneasy laughter. A frieze of dingy damask curtains swam like water upon his vision; uptilted, the distant valley seemed to slope like a ski chute wrapped in mist toward the unbelievable sea. Nauseated now, weakly heaving, he tried to reply, tried to discover some meaning in this preposterous inquisitorial dream; just then, just as he made his benumbed lips function and, trying out a mouthful of thick strange-sounding words of apology, staggered toward Windgasser with placating hands uplifted, he felt an unyielding rod or bar or fireplace fender clutch his ankle, tripping him, and the parqueted flooring of the Bella Vista rose up to meet him full and shocking in the face, like a slammed door. He lay there, aching, watching ten thousand minute blossoms of fire. Then he felt himself being hoisted by strong hands, by brawny white-sleeved arms that propelled him forward across the room and into the lobby, where someone muttering Italian oaths rammed his knapsack down around his neck and by the seat of his pants hurled him forward again, half-suspended in air, feet paddling like a comic bicyclist's, out of doors and into the rain. *"Cacciatelo via!"* he heard someone shout, and the jeering word *"Ubriacone!"* A door slammed, and the muffled words came back—"And stay out!" And he was alone once more in the rain.

Then—perhaps it was the intolerable rain again, or the swelling beneath his eye, or the insulting *"Ubriacone,"* with its false imputation that he had drunk too much—something popped like a valve inside him; he took a deep breath, shot his soggy cuffs, and charged back into the hotel like a tormented bear. A grave error. The marble steps, slick from the downpour, were like glass beneath his feet. He was only halfway up to the entrance when like a doormat the earth was whisked away from beneath him. Still roaring, he saw the hotel's façade spin madly sideways, and at the door one solitary waiter, pop-eyed in dismay, reaching out vainly to arrest his fall. Then he felt his skull crash down upon the edge of a step, and he was sped into oblivion upon great baroque chords of organ music, obliterating shock and pain. . . .

When he awoke, with an ache in his head but curiously in command of his senses, he smelled an institutional smell of wine and grime, and knew almost at once that he was in a police station. He was lying on a cot, and he heard his own groan as he struggled back to consciousness; though it was a little death to do so, he rose to a sitting position on the cot, gingerly touched his cranium, and felt a lump the size of a small doorknob, fiercely painful to touch. And as he raised his eyes he saw two policemen. One, an immensely obese, bespectacled sergeant, scowled at him from behind a desk. The other, standing, was a young corporal with a mustache, who seemed to regard Cass less with suspicion or hostility than with a kind of bemused speculation, though even this was hard to be sure about, for much of his face was obscured as he spread his jaws wide and with a large hand began industriously to pick his teeth. No one spoke. Cass watched dully as a bewhiskered rat peered out from a hole in the wall behind the sergeant's desk, sniffed the atmosphere and, like some café trifler idly emerging at midafternoon, serenely waddled away out the door and into another room. Rain drummed steadily on the roof overhead. Still drunk, his pain numbed, Cass heard a thin brainless giggle at work in his throat.

"*Molto comico?*" said the fat sergeant, with ponderous irony, "*molto divertente?* Well, we'll see just how funny it is." He spread out a sheaf of papers on the desk before him. "Get to your feet and come over here."

Cass rose and moved unsteadily to the desk, where by stretching his neck he was able to look down and make out the list of charges, all the while attending to the sergeant's high-pitched epicene voice: "You are first charged with willful and malicious destruction of property. *Secondariamente,* with the use of obscene language in a public place. *In terzo luogo,* with disorderly conduct in a public place. *In quarto luogo,* with attempted assault upon a person, by name Signor the Vice-Admiral Sir Edgar A. Hatcher, Southsea, Hampshire, Gran Bretagna. *In quinto luogo,* with drunkenness in a public place. How do you call yourself? Passport, please."

"*Come?*" Cass said.

"Your *passport!*" the sergeant commanded.

"It's with my motorscooter, in the piazza," Cass mumbled, forcing back demented hilarity.

The sergeant made an exasperated motion with his pudgy hands, turned to the corporal: "Go get the motorscooter. Get the motorscooter and the passport."

The corporal, disheartened, rolled his eyes toward the roof and the rain, torrential now, a cloudburst.

"All right, wait until the rain stops," the sergeant said, and then to Cass: "*Nazionalità? Inglese?*"

"*Americana.*"

"How do you call yourself?" the policeman went on, brusque, provincial, pen poised above a ledger.

"Domenico Scarlatti." The name, like a flute-sound, like an incantation, had appeared at the forefront of his mind for no reason at all; now it had simply escaped his lips, spoken with gravity, dignity, self-possession. The sergeant looked up at Cass, scrutinizing him with ignorant small eyes.

"Then you are an Italo-American," he piped, with bitter censure in his voice. He drew back in the chair for an instant, folding his hands over his elephantine paunch. "It is the case with such people as you. It is your stock of people which has gone to America and made a fortune, only to come back to the land of your ancestry and flaunt your money and your uncouth ways. It is a great pity that we do not have Mussolini now. The Duce would enforce laws against the likes of you. Well, let me tell you something, Scarlatti. Here in Sambuco we will not tolerate your type of behavior, do you understand?" Again he leaned over the ledger. "Where were you born, and when?"

Oh, my heart, Cass thought, improvising: "June 6, 1925. But tell me, Sergeant, how is it that I am accused of assault? That vase. I meant no harm—"

"Answer the questions," the sergeant snapped. "Birthplace?"

"Put down Tuxedo Park. Then, comma, New York," he persevered. With fingers delicately outstretched, he steadied himself against the desk.

"Tuxedo Park, New York. Spelling?"

"T-u-s-s-e-d-o. Like the capital of Japan."

"Curious. Father?"

"Alessandro Scarlatti. Deceased now."

"Mother?" The sergeant scribbled laboriously.

"Gypsy Rose Scarlatti. *Defunta,*" he added. "Also deceased." All of a sudden—orphan that he was and had been—he felt close to tears.

The sergeant leaned back again and, with an air of sagacity, of magnitude, began to lecture him again: "You are in very serious trouble, my friend. We do not like to arrest Americans. Not because we have any qualms about it, see? But only because you now are strong and we are weak, and your country brings—how would you say it?—pressure to bear. When the principles of the Duce are restored"—and here the dimmest facsimile of a smile appeared on his porcine face—"all that might change. But at the present we do not relish arresting Americans." He paused and looked down, drumming with his fingers on the desk. "But we cannot tolerate your kind of behavior. And we *will* arrest you! It is emigrants like you, bearing an Italian name, who give Italy a bad smell all over the world. The Duce himself pointed out," he went on with an erudite gleam, "the Duce himself pointed out in a speech at Ancona in July, 1931, that democracies must fall out of the weight of the corruption and license they allow their citizens, citizens I suspect like you—" He doubtless would have gone on, except for the uproar which rose at that moment from the single adjoining room. There was a man's large, rough, argumentative voice, then another voice, then another voice—a girl's—vituperative, high-pitched, and filled with angry scorn. Something seemed to strike heavily against a wall. The girl shrieked, the man began to shout. And the sergeant got up heavily, wheezing, and lumbered back into the other room. *"Zitti!"* Cass heard the sergeant squeal, and the hubbub subsided, save for the sound of distant heavy breathing, and the sergeant's *castrato* voice, now in command of all. Cass turned then and saw that the corporal was still gazing at him, speculative, not unfriendly, attentive.

"What will I get?" Cass said with a groan, apprehensive now.

The corporal removed a fingernail from between his teeth. *"Straordinario,"* he mused, ignoring the question, *"assolutamente straordinario."*

"What?"

"The *vacuum* of the man. Born and brought up in Naples, home of the Scarlatti. And he has heard of neither one of them. What is your real name?"

Cass told him, feeling somewhat more sober now, but the ache in his head burgeoning and blossoming and, along with it, pangs of anxiety creeping up secretly, darkly inside his breast. For an instant he had the crazy impulse to make a break out the door. Then he forced himself to remain calm and asked the corporal for a glass of water.

"What will I get?" he said again, as the corporal ran water into a glass.

"Here, drink it down. It will be good for you," said the corporal. "You speak excellent Italian. I suppose it is the fact that you are an American that makes you so naïve in such matters."

"What do you mean?"

"Sergeant Parrinello, that is what I mean. When a police officer is intent on making an arrest he simply locks the culprit up. And that's the end of it. When on the other hand he is persuaded that he might in some small way profit by the desperation of the accused to be released, he gives long dissertations on this and that. The Duce. Ancona. 1931. Democracies. Corruption and license. Do you not see the method in this procedure? It is merely to allow time. To allow time for the accused to make an appropriate mental calculation—that is to say, whether he should perhaps give up the price of an enormous meal in a de-luxe hotel or whether, under the circumstances of his own malfeasance, an even more handsome sacrifice might not be in order—that new gown for one's wife, perhaps, or—"

"I'm not going to *bribe* that pile of blubber!" Cass protested, too loudly, in the spirit—suddenly resurgent when it came to money—of Calvin, Wesley, and Knox.

"Sssh-h," the corporal warned him. His face was quite solemn. "Take it from me, Luigi, this Parrinello can make it hard. He does have a charge against you; you might squat in jail in Salerno for a whole month, awaiting trial. Our procedure for obtaining bond is different from that in America. And Parrinello is basically a cheap fellow." He moved toward the door, fingering his mustache, and, lowering his voice, said: "In your situation I should think ten thousand lire might be right, so long as you also pay for that broken vase. But don't be obvious, stick it in his ledger there. I have seen nothing."

"But why are you doing this for me?" Cass wondered aloud. "I mean—" But the corporal—enigmatic, exuding conviction, creepily benign—had vanished into the other room. What a monstrous swindle, he thought, ten thousand lire. A week's pay for the fat bastard. It nearly cleaned him out, and this fact in truth sickened him far more than the hubris of the matter, overshadowing even his loathing of the huge wet bladder of a sergeant who had committed the extortion. Head throbbing, gut aching, feeling nearly as low as any low day he had had in Paris, he extracted the bill—his last of that size—from his wallet, and breathed it farewell as he tucked it into the sergeant's ledger so that it coyly divulged itself, like a pink inner patch of thigh.

The sergeant returned with heavy footfall. "Now then," he began sternly as he sat down behind the desk, "now then, I wish to say again that you are in a very serious predicament." He reached for the ledger; as he did so, Cass saw his eyes light upon the banknote. "A serious predicament," he went on without changing expression, and with such an artful modulation of tone that it was almost breath-taking, "which however you might be able to find your way out of." He looked up at Cass, at the same time clapping the ledger shut. "You have made a serious mistake here in Sambuco. We will not tolerate your kind of misbehavior. At the same time," he said in a tempered, expressive larghetto, "at the same time, you do look like a decent sort, Scarlatti. I'd even be willing to say that this is your first encounter with the police. Am I right?"

"Right as rain, Chief," Cass said, lapsing briefly into English, now again wildly outraged.

"Then I tell you what I am going to do. With the exception

that you must pay for the broken vase at the Bella Vista, I am going to liberate you from these charges. I suggest that you watch your step in the future. You are free to go. You owe this office one hundred and fifty lire for the *carta bollata.*"

"For the *carta bollata?*"

"For the revenue stamp on the charge, for the official—"

"I know what it is, for the love of Christ," Cass said, voice rising, "but do you mean to stand there, you despicable lump, and tell me—"

Later Cass recollected that at that instant he might easily have undone everything, but the sergeant had not heard his words or, if he had, chose to ignore them, for right then the noise and the shouting outside recommenced. *"Bugiardo!"* a girl screamed. "Liar!" "Bitch!" a man howled. And almost at the same moment Luigi the corporal, sweating, cap lopsided, propelled before him into the room a sunken-cheeked unshaven man in a tradesman's smock and, directly behind him, a peasant girl. The girl, who was eighteen or so, wore a shabby moth-eaten coat several sizes too large and darkened with rain at the shoulders. She was barefoot, and a faded scarf concealed her hair. Still shrieking her fury she came in, and for a desperate, sinking moment all Cass could think of was how extraordinarily beautiful she was. Like the draught of wind that makes a fire blaze up, her anger seemed only to excite and inflame the loveliness of her face; Cass noticed that it was only Luigi's big hand, grasped firmly at the belt of the girl's coat, that kept her from climbing like a wildcat straight up the tradesman's back. "Liar!" she screeched. "Liar! Liar!" And the tradesman, who had some dusty inflammation of the skin which patched his cheeks like frostbite, came back with that antiphonal low-throated groan, like a sob of hurt and disbelief, which punctuates Italian Donnybrooks: *"Ah-uu!* Tu *sei bugiarda! Puttana!* Liar yourself, you bitch!"

"Silence!" the sergeant commanded. "Maybe you'd better stand over here," he suggested to the man. "And *you,*" he said with a jerk of his head to the girl, "you stand on this side of the desk and keep your mouth shut." Cass could almost hear an audible clink as the scales of justice, balancing sex upon one side, sank in the interest of commerce. The girl's eyes flashed as she moved to where she was told to move, but she was close to tears. She bit the inside of her cheek, and her lips began to tremble, and as Cass stared at the soft-eyed oval of her face, smeared with rain and dirt, he wanted to clean her up, make her happy, and press upon her lips a full and passionate kiss. She was exquisite, and he gazed at her helplessly as he rubbed the knot on his head, aching to make sure that the rest of her body measured up to her legs, which were perfectly formed though like her face smeared with reddish dirt.

"Let's get this clear," said Parrinello to the man. "You are claiming this girl stole something from your store."

"She attempted to," the man said. "I caught her in the act."

"I did not steal!" the girl burst out. "I was outside and I had it in my hand, but I was going to *pay!*"

"Another lie!" the man retorted. "What could you pay *with?*"

"Silence!" the sergeant ordered. He eased down into the seat, quiet for a moment, mysterious, and the swivel chair with a sound of singing springs swung him ponderously and heavily far, far back, so that he lay nearly horizontal, hammocked in the bloat of his paltry and terrible authority. Then after a bit he said to the store-keeper: "Tell me. You have not told me. Just what is it that the girl stole from you?"

"This," the man said, *"this."* He pulled out of his smock one of those gaily colored celluloid windmills, fastened to a fragile wand, which children run with or hang out of car windows. It was possibly worth the equivalent of a nickel or a dime. "I had it displayed outside upon the street," the man began to explain rapidly, "when along came this peasant who snatched it up and ran away with it. Admit it!" he said with a snarl at the girl. "Why don't you admit it!"

Suddenly broken, the girl put her face between her hands and began to sob.

Parrinello took the windmill. With an absurd and stagy air of nonchalance he blew upon it, puffed cheeks distended and with puckered pink lips, like some lewd Wind that blows from the corner of an antique map. "Tell me, slut," he said to the girl at last, in his querulous eunuchal voice, "tell me something. I think I've seen you before, haven't I? I can't see now, but it seems that I remember that you have a nice big behind on you. A sweet behind. Now why does a grown girl like you with a sweet big behind want to steal a child's toy like this? You should be down on the coast peddling that sweet nice behind to rich tourists." It was, pure and unadorned, the voice of impotence, and Cass saw the sergeant's face tinge pink as he crooned and sucked and smacked, getting his labial kicks. Luigi stirred nervously, now gazing with

326

an air of stiff despondency out the window. "Why did you want to steal a thing like this?"

"It was for my little brother," the girl said in a muffled faint voice, helpless now, mortified, tears streaming out from beneath her dirty fingers.

"Listen," Parrinello went on. "You're from Tramonti, are you not? You need money, I'll bet. Let me give you some advice, *carina*. What you should do is save enough money to go to Positano, maybe Naples—maybe even Rome. Rome is a fine place. There you rent a room in a hotel and you pick up a rich man on the big street—hey, what is the name of that street, Corporal, where all the rich princes go?"

"Via Veneto," was the stiff remote answer, spoken so frostily that it could barely be heard. Heartbrokenly, miserably, the girl continued to weep.

"And you go to a room, see, and you take that lovely sweet behind of yours and you spread it out on a set of nice pink sheets—"

The wretched storekeeper had begun to make yucks of appreciative amusement. For an instant, shutting out from his mind the dreadful scene, Cass looked out the window, following Luigi's gaze. His skull had begun to throb like some huge inflamed carbuncle, but now he saw that something strange had happened to the weather—a miracle. It was spring, and he could feel the warmth stealing into his bones. Dissolved like dew before the sun, the scud and rack of clouds had been washed clear of the valley. It was suddenly so bright, so vivid in the Mediterranean light, that he felt he could reach out and touch each detail; he saw a postcard in color of majestic peaks and a sky so shockingly blue that it looked like some madman's overpainting and orange groves dropping in a ladder of terraced greenery toward the sea. Somewhere there was a dripping noise, last remnant of rain and winter. A flock of sheep was bleating, inebriate, on the far slope of the valley. And, Lord love me, he thought, there was even music: someone far off in the town had turned on a radio full blast, as if to celebrate this delinquent sunlight. It was not, to be sure, the carrousel which in his dreams had always foreshadowed this moment; it was Guy Lombardo, all glucose and giggles, but it struck some buried chord in him and as he glanced back at the girl, who had raised her begrimed, sorrowful, lovely face now, he felt like letting out some kind of a scream.

"Perciò," the sergeant was still needling the girl, "you will have a lot of money. It is a matter of using only that nice well-built part of yours. As it is"—and here the lilting soft lubricity faded from his voice—"as it is you cannot afford to steal. Do you know what the fine is for stealing?"

"No," the girl said hopelessly.

"In your case, it will be one thousand lire. Do you have it?"

"No."

"Of course not. Then do you know what we must do?"

"No."

Cass saw the sergeant's face go pink again, winding up. "We take that big sweet behind of yours—"

Rage, possible to give voice to only in his native tongue, burst inside Cass' head like a ball of insanity. "Lay off her, you miserable sonofabitch!" he roared. "Lay off her, hear me? Lay off her or I'll stomp your teeth out! Lay off her!"

Alarmed, pale, the sergeant let his hand go back to his holster, where it rested caressing with nervous sausage fingers the grip of a Mauser automatic. "What does he say, Corporal? *Che cosa significa* layofer?"

Luigi made a helpless expression. "I don't know. I have no English, Sergeant." And as Luigi spoke, Cass calmed himself, though still quivering and with some difficulty. Heedless of the commotion, the *flâneur* rat meandered in from the other room, halted sniffing, plunged back into his hole. Through the window Cass smelled flowers. He was sweating. The warmth in the air was not of spring but of eternal summer; outside through the doorway, around the blooms of immense white camellias, bumblebees droned, mnemonic with the sound of South and home. The sergeant stared at Cass, momentarily daunted, fidgeting.

"I'll pay for the thing," Cass said to the storekeeper. Then to Parrinello, in a crucifixion of restraint and decency: "Forgive me for my outburst, *Vossignoria*. But if it may please your lordship, I have a very personal difficulty. I am subject to fits often—harmless."

The sergeant relaxed.

"I should also like to pay the fine, if I may." The sergeant shrugged his acquiescence. Cass took out his wallet. "Here is two thousand lire for everything. I hope this amount will suffice."

Then he turned and made his way from the room, into the spring air outside.

It was late in the afternoon. Bells were chiming through the bright translucent air. A flight of pigeons thundered up as if from nowhere, bedecking the air above the fountain with tumultuous slate-colored wings. As he walked up the cobbled street to the hotel he turned, and he thought he saw the girl, head hunched down in her baggy coat, hurrying from the police station, and he started to call out to her but already she had vanished down an alleyway. He turned again and was walking on when he heard a voice.

"How does the head feel?" It was the corporal, Luigi. Reserved, cool, remote, very unlike an Italian, he seemed at the same time longing, even desperate, to communicate, and he fell in beside Cass as he climbed the hill. "I was sent by Parrinello to make sure that you pay for the vase."

"The head is better," Cass said. "You Italians run a strange police force."

The corporal was silent for a moment. "I suspect that it is no better or no worse than anywhere else."

"It is a wonder that someone has not eliminated that chief of yours. He is the grandfather of all reptiles."

"Yes," Luigi said, "he is—troublesome. Tell me, you are an educated man, are you not?"

"No," said Cass, "I have no education. I have read books but I have no education. Why do you ask?"

The corporal had stopped walking, and now Cass paused too, looking into the grave, earnest, somewhat humorless face. "I do not know why I ask," he said. "I do not know. Perhaps you will pardon me. But I so rarely see an American like you. That is, your little joke with Parrinello, your command of this language. Then—what you did for that girl, who was simply a poor peasant, of no account whatever. That appealed to me. That was a humanist gesture, I thought. What an educated man would do. That appealed to me."

"I liked her looks," Cass replied, faintly annoyed. "She was of some account. She was a very good-looking female. Why? Aren't you an educated man?"

"No, I am not," he went on in his formal, meticulous way. "Like you I have read many books but I had no opportunity to continue my education. I wished to become a lawyer, but circumstances forced me to—" He paused. "I became what I am. Most people do not get much education in this country. They must work too hard, so they do not read anything."

"Also in America they do not get much education," Cass said.

"They do not work hard, and they do not read anything either."
Cass resumed walking.

"It is sad that they do not read, missing so much. One of the great revelations of my life was reading *The World as Will and Idea* by the great German philosopher Schopenhauer. More than anyone I have read he points the way toward what I have come to regard as a creative pessimism. Have you read Schopenhauer?"

"Never," Cass said shortly, with rather more rudeness than he meant or intended. His head had begun to throb mercilessly. "No, I haven't."

"I'm sorry," said the corporal sensitively. "If I have intruded, forgive me. I find it so rare a thing these days to be able to talk to a kindred spirit. Your little joke with Parrinello. That was delightful! How I wish—" But his voice trailed off, and now, coming to a rise in the street, Cass caught a glimpse again of the sea, far below, and the orange and lemon groves and vineyards terraced against the gigantic plunging hills. From distant gutters and drains there was a steady trickling and gushing; earth and sky seemed burnished, brushed, cleansed, and there was a sound of water everywhere as the debris of winter was swept gurgling seaward. The sun was going down, cresents of fading light glowed on distant barren hills. *"Madonna! Che bello!"* some woman's voice shouted, celebrant, as at the light of the Second Coming. For no reason at all, Cass felt himself shivering.

"That girl," he said, turning to the corporal, "that girl in the station. What is her name?"

"I do not know," Luigi said with a shrug. "A peasant from the valley. I cannot say that I have seen her before."

"She was beautiful. Do they all come that way?"

"It is rare that peasants are born with beauty. When they are, it is almost never that they keep it past childhood. I did not notice this peasant's beauty."

"Corporal, you must be blind."

"I did not look at her carefully. Peasants do not interest me. They are a scummy lot for the most part, hopelessly inbred like animals. Most of them are mentally defective." He shook his head solemnly. "It comes from eating nothing but bread. Sometimes I think that they should all be exterminated."

"Why, Corporal," Cass said with good humor, "you talk like some sort of Fascist."

"I *am* a Fascist," Luigi said in a bleak matter-of-fact voice, though adding as if in extenuation: "Please do not misunderstand me. Insofar as extermination is concerned, I do not mean that cruelly. Fascism is not Naziism. I only mean it—" And he paused for an instant, and clenched his fists together as if struggling for articulation, for reason. Then in a voice which would have sounded foolishly pompous had it not at the same time been resonant with conviction, he said: "We are *all* damned, you see! All of us! But somehow we get along. They"—jerking his hand sideways, toward some invisible peasant host—"*they* are damned forever. They do *not* get along. They are less than animals. They should be exterminated. They should be put out of their suffering."

"Creative pessimism," said Cass, blinking.

The corporal for the first time made the suggestion of a smile and then he looked at his watch. "It has been a pleasure talking to you," he said. "I hope I have not offended you. Life is strange, is it not?"

"How do you mean?" said Cass, in honest wonder.

"Existence, I mean. Do you not sometimes wake up from a long sleep and for those few moments before you are completely awake feel the terror and the mystery of existence? It lasts but for a few seconds but it is the only time when one moves close to eternity. And do you know something? I do not believe in God. Yet for me the awful part is that in a twinkling I am fully awake, and I do not know whether it was that in that movement toward eternity I have come closer to God—or nothingness."

Cass blinked again, and for a moment he wondered whether the corporal was not slightly loony. Fascist-humanist, intellectual, scourge of the peasantry, creative pessimist, metaphysician, with long sideburns poking down from beneath his visored cap, mustached and honey-eyed like some *borghese* matron's movie dreamboat, he had nonetheless communed lonesomely with his soul; suddenly the words—and were they as true as they seemed, and as terrible?—came through to Cass like vibrations from a titanic gong. He looked straight into Luigi's eyes, realizing that the corporal, whatever else odd he might be, was as sane as they come.

"I often feel very lonely too," Cass said. "Very lonely. Very terrified."

"Then you understand what I mean?"

"Yes."

"I'm sorry that I have talked to you in this way," Luigi said after a pause, and then put out his hand. "I hope you will come back here sometime. You *are* going to pay for that vase?"

"I'll pay for it, Luigi," Cass said, "many thanks. Many thanks." And then the corporal was gone.

It was easier than he thought it would be to get into Windgasser's good graces. Cleaning himself up in the bathroom of a café, quite sober now, he put on his courtliest manner and presented himself at the hotel, apologizing elaborately for breaking the vase. At first cool and forbidding, Windgasser broke down and became surprisingly sympathetic, even warm, and listened with anxiety on his face, and understanding, as Cass described the diabetic condition he had been forced to live with since adolescence, and the insulin shock he was sometimes precipitated into, accidentally, and without warning, causing him to acquire the thick speech and the inhibited powers of locomotion and, yes— most abominably!—even the loose-lipped coarseness of a drunkard. "My stars, I had no idea!" said Windgasser, offering his own apologies while perhaps sensing a client, and he mentioned his own affliction, a fistula *in ano,* inoperable these many years despite consultations with doctors in Geneva, Zürich, and Basel. Getting back to the issue at hand, Cass said that as for money he was somewhat reduced, and he was on the point of offering to pay in installments when Windgasser, a brick of a man, allayed all Cass' distress: the vase, he said, like all his furniture, was insured by a solid Swiss firm which (unlike the Italians) always paid off, and there was a satisfied tone in his voice which indicated that the vase was possibly even better off in splinters. Cass went to the window. It was almost dark. On the gulf, against the softest aquamarine of an evening sky, fishing boats with lights aglow moved seaward; the lights glittered and twinkled, a tiny galaxy of drifting vivacious stars. The air was warm and a scent of orange blossoms was heavy all around him. "It is beautiful here," he said aloud. "I don't think I've ever seen anything like it." Windgasser behind him, eagerly breathing, allowed that it was beautiful, indeed just the place for an American to live, especially a painter, especially an American, so unlike the Italian tenants of years past, so raucous, so uncouth, whose children wrote obscenities all over the walls. The palace annex, the famous Palazzo d'Affitto, owned by the Windgasser family for three generations . . . There was an apartment, *commodious, most engaging* . . . Perhaps Mr. Kinsolving would like to take a look?

A wild cry came up from the valley, a cry passionate and young and wild, and darkness came quickly and heavily, odorous with spring and the scent of oranges. Cass stood for a long time at the window, like Richard Wagner before him (*"Parthifal* was written here," Windgasser lisped), filled with lust and longing and tawdry romantic urges.

I think I could work here, he told himself that night, I think I could really get cracking. He lay in a bed upstairs in the Bella Vista, unable to sleep. His head ached. *Thirty years old and I haven't even stuck my toe in the bleeding door.* He thought of the peasant girl in the police station (Assunta? Paola? Desideria? Laura?) and he dozed off with a sense of trouble, hungry with tenderness and desire.

The next morning, he recalls, he had completely forgotten the girl. But the spring weather was like an ecstasy. Inspecting the palace apartment with Windgasser he found it much to his liking. He decided to go up to Rome and bring the family down right away. He paid two months' advance rent with a check on his and Poppy's joint bank account, and left for Rome—without the realization, however, that he had just paid out almost the last cent either of them had.

Another move! Poppy was less than pleased.

"Just when I've learned to speak a little Italian and all, now you want to move again! Jiminy, Cass! I *like* Rome!"

"They speak Italian in Sambuco, Poppy, for pity's sake! This city gives me claustrophobia! We're moving out on Friday. You'll love it, Poppy. Sea and mountains and sunlight! My God, it's a bleeding paradise!" He paused. "I've got to get some new paints, new brushes. I've got to stock up because I'm going to do a lot of work down there. I'll need some dough." He paused again. "Speaking of which, how about telling me where our little kitty has gone to?"

She was sitting by the window in a bright splash of sunlight, working on her stamp collection. Some years before she had acquired a big album and a dollar's worth of stamps from a mail-order house ("1000 assorted, all countries"). Everybody should have a hobby, he remembered her saying, and since then she had built up a sizable collection, largely through the habit of hoarding duplicates of any and all stamps, no matter how common the issue, and depressing even the infinitesimal value of these by scorning detachable cellophane hinges and pasting them into the book with glue.

As he walked toward her he saw her placidly stick a small brush into a paste pot. Then she looked up and said: "What kitty?"

"What kitty do you think?" he said. "Where you keep the dough. The tea can. I stuck my hand in there just now and all you had in it was tea."

"Oh, Cass!" she said. "How did you know I hide it there? Peggy must have told you!" Her lips quivered a little, quivering at his knowledge of her secret, which had been no secret to him since a month after their wedding. "How did you know, darling?" she said despondently.

"A bird told me," he replied. "Look, baby, I've got to have five thousand lire to buy some paint and some brushes. Hasn't your check come this month?"

"What check?"

"You know, Poppy, the *check*."

And then it happened. She said she hadn't received any check. When he asked her why, she hedged a bit, bent over and stuck a stamp in the album and screwed up her mouth, saying she really didn't know but maybe "those letters" would explain it. What letters? Why, those letters that came with the checks from the bank. And where did she keep those letters? Why, there in the kitchen drawer, of course. And there he found the appalling answer, in half a dozen syrup-sticky envelopes from the trust department of the bank in New Castle, Delaware, which he dredged up out of a hell of rusted knives and unwashed eggbeaters and hair ribbons and coffee grounds. One of them contained the key to the whole thing:

We wrote you time and time again [this is the way it began, without preliminaries; Cass could see some thin-lipped old small-town banker snapping his Dictaphone on and off as he tried to master his chagrin and outrage] but received no answer to our repeated requests that you allow us to dispose of your properties. Under the terms of your father's will, as you know, you have been receiving approximately $400.00 a month from these two properties, known most recently as the OK Motel and Winnie Winkle Burger Bar & Drive-In, both located in the Second Tax Dist. of New Castle Co., Del. At the time when the construction of the Delaware Memorial Bridge and Highway Approach was still theoretical we felt certain that we could sell these properties for a sum which when invested would still yield you a substantial monthly return. *Since we failed to receive your permis-*

sion, however [italics Cass'], as stipulated in the terms of the trust, we had no alternative but to hold on to these properties. With the final construction of the Delaware Memorial Bridge and Highway Approach these properties, having been by-passed and the road they are on cut off to thru traffic, have become virtually worthless and since the present lessees have failed to renew their leases we have to inform you that the check deposited to your account in the Bankers Trust Company, New York, on or about March 1 next, will be your last. . . .

The rest of the letter, compounding insult with injury, had to do with the matter of taxes that Poppy would be liable for.

"You didn't give them permission," he whispered, with wonder in his voice, and grief.

"Well, yes—" she began.

"Well, no!" he said, his voice rising. "And why not?"

"Well, because— Because I didn't read them!"

"And why the hell didn't you read them!" he began to shout.

"Because— I don't know. Because I couldn't *understand* them, Cass! I tried—"

"Didn't you think *I* could understand those letters? Didn't you think that *I* might be able to divine their secrets? Why by damn, Poppy, you haven't got the brains God gave to a mushmelon! How could you? How could you throw away four hundred dollars a month, just like that! Just when we got to the place where we might decently live off it—Sambuco, I mean. Do you realize what this means? Do you realize, Poppy! Who the hell are we going to borrow from? St. Peter? Who? *Who!* Answer me that!"

"I don't know," she began to moan. "I don't know, Cass. Oh jeepers, I'm so sorry—"

"It's too late to be sorry!" he roared. "You know that compensation check of mine? The one I get for being a nut? It won't even keep us in catchup! How do you like that! What are we going to do now, go to the poorhouse? Beg? Borrow? Steal? What! Do you realize where you are now, Miss Deadhead? Four thousand miles from old New Castle, without a pot to pee in! How do you like that? Oh, Poppy, how could you be so careless?"

"Well, you said it yourself," she began to reason. "I heard you say it yourself! How you thought the capitalist system was corrupt and dishonest, and investments and all were a terrible delusion."

"Christ!" he said. "Shut your yap! You're a living, breathing, walking prefrontal lobotomy! This is a perfect lesson in capitalism! One dumb move and you're broke! You know what's going to happen to you, you idiot—you're going to be swabbing floors for fifty lire a day, that's what! And the kids! They'll be living off *grasshoppers!*" (Jesus, he thought, maybe *I'll* have to go to work.)

"Oh, Cass!" she cried, wilting beneath his assault.

"What have we got?" he demanded. "What! I can sell the motorscooter, but how much spaghetti will that buy us? We've got to go to Sambuco now anyway, see? The place is already paid for, two solid months. But what in God's name are we going to live on? Answer me that!" Desperation ran through him like ice water. "My God, Poppy, what you've done!" And his eyes rested for an instant on her hand. "Your engagement ring!" he said, snaking out his arm. "That diamond should fetch a hundred thousand lire, it cost me three hundred and fifty bucks when I bought it. Here, lemme have it."

"Go take a shit in your bleeding hat, you filthy misbegotten prick!"

"POPPY!" He stood nearly paralyzed, rigid with shock and horror. Then in a small voice he said: "Poppy, where did you learn those words?"

She had begun to bawl, mouth wide-open, and the baby propped in a chair beside her began to howl, too, at the top of its voice.

"Where did you learn them?"

"Where do you think I learned them, you dumb bunny," she sobbed. "Where do you think I learned them?"

For a moment he was utterly crushed. He tried to touch her shoulder, trying to get close to the mystery of her decency and her sweetness and her innocence, but she shrugged him away. He left the room.

The next day he sold the motorscooter, and what he got from this, together with his compensation check, would be enough to last for a month or so. And they were going south again. Everything was fine, everything was adventurous. Poppy said: "Oh, Cass, it's going to be dreamy!" But as they rode southward on a bus through the greening spring fields of Campania, he felt a foreboding, and he could not erase the vision from his mind: of elegant passengers in Cadillacs on that blackguard of a bridge across the Delaware, all of them gazing aloofly down, and the OK Motel and the Winnie Winkle Burger Bar & Drive-In, stucco ruin below, mossy and crumbling in a rubble of shattered neon and toppling television antennae and corrupt encroaching weeds.

But in Sambuco, of course, new worlds did not open for him. He thought he would be able to paint. Windgasser loaned him (rented him, rather, for two thousand of his diminishing lire) an easel, left years ago in the hotel basement by a ninth-rate Edwardian painter named Angelucci whose barbarous encrustations, like the work of some crazed Burne-Jones given the muscles but not the mind of Michelangelo, still covered every wall and ceiling of the palace. On this easel Cass placed some canvas, and the canvas remained bare. Restless, he began once again to drink too much. He went without eating. He felt presentiments of the same anxiety which had afflicted him in Paris. Hung-over, each morning he sought out Luigi, who idled away his off-duty hours, cool and philosophical, over a single Campari and soda at the café in the square. Luigi was fond of what he called, somewhat heavily, *dialettica;* their conversation was usually an argument, conducted however on amiable terms.

"A Fascist you say," Cass would prod him. "Now how could this be? Here you are a man of culture and wit and reading and yet you're a Fascist. How can this be, Luigi? How can you be a Fascist and call yourself a humanist at the same time?"

"It is easy," said Luigi, picking his teeth. "What your trouble is, friend Cass, is that like most northern people you are too willing to pin labels on people. Or put it this way: you believe that a label fully identifies a man, either black or white, with no room for chiaroscuro. Thus your so-called liberals will grant the possibility of an Italian embracing Communism, which is a monstrous ideology, but will call an Italian Fascist worse than a dog. While with your anti-liberals the sentiments will be precisely the other way around. All it shows is that none of you Americans knows anything about Italians. We are not Germans, after all, or Soviets either. I think it is this dogmatic tendency that has made you people so lacking in the field of the arts, not to speak of diplomacy." He sat back and made his humorless grin.

"Go ahead," said Cass, somewhat grimly, "you haven't answered my question."

"All right, I'll tell you how I can be what I am. For one thing, I am not a spiritual Fascist. No Italian is a spiritual anything in politics. He lives too much for the moment to be idealistic about what is going to govern him. With one or two gaps it has always been a tyranny in one form or another and he has gotten so that he doesn't care. As for myself, I am an opportunist. A well-meaning opportunist. That is why for the moment I am a Fascist. Let me explain: Presume first that I am a humanist—this is so. All decent people are humanists, basically, even decent policemen. Presume then that I must get a job, to feed myself and to help support my mother and father and my sisters who live in Salerno. Presume further that the only job open to me—because of my superior intelligence—is that of a policeman. *Please*, Cass, don't smile, this is true. I must become a policeman or work on the roads or have no job at all; so I choose to become a policeman. It is not much but it is something, and I am lucky to get the job. Now for a minute, reflect. Could I be a policeman in Italy and be a Communist at the same time? What a preposterous thought. Even if it were possible, my revered superior, Parrinello"—and here he made a look of disgust—"is a Fascist sub rosa, and if I were a Communist what kind of life would I lead—"

"What a cowardly way—"

"Please, Cass, no insults. Let me explain. It is not just that. In my extreme youth, as I've told you, I was a Communist. But that was a mistake. I was stupid then and had not learned much. Gradually I came to discover, after much pondering, that it was a betrayal of the soul for any man to embrace Communism, which is anti-human, barbaric, and a monstrous despotism—in short, a repudiation of all that is fine and noble in over two thousand years of Western culture—"

"So when you joined the cops you junked all•that and became a Fascist. You forgot all about that camp in Poland where they melted down millions of little Jewish babies for butter and saddle soap, or that cave up near Rome where they took several hundred of your innocent countrymen and mowed them down with machine guns in one fearful senseless slaughter. You forgot how twenty years of Fascism turned Italy into a desert, a wasteland. And don't tell me anything about Mussolini's fine roads. You forget— Ah, Luigi, what a short memory you have!"

"Please, Cass," he remonstrated with a sour look. "Don't get hysterical. We are not Germans. You're really trying me to the limit now. Are you going to listen—"

"Go ahead." Go ahead, you ignorant bastard.

"So even in order to eat, to hold myself together—not to speak of my family in Salerno—I could not remain a Communist, practically or morally. Then what ways were open to me?" he asked rhetorically.

"I should think you might have tried the way of the Christian-Democrats, or of the Socialists. Or of anything, Luigi, for the love of God, besides this gruesome—"

"Patience, my friend." And he laughed, dryly and briefly. "Could an honest man be a Christian-Democrat, I ask you? As the great German philosopher Nietzsche" (great names, with Luigi, were always explicated: the famous Frenchman Descartes, the illustrious painter Bellini) "pointed out, it is such corrupt and self-satisfied dregs of society that threaten a nation with its greatest harm. Could an honest man embrace the party of the clerics and the fat bourgeoisie and all those who would kowtow to that *orribile* foreign minister of yours"—he pronounced it, somewhat Gallically, Dew-lays—"who wishes only to turn Italy into an image of the American Protestant church? Being so poor, we are willing to accept a decent charity; but no charity can come from this man, only pious words, and graft for the rich men who make typewriters in Torino. Could an honest person respect whoever respects him? I ask you, Cass. As for the Socialists, they are soft and soggy and offer only daydreams."

"You could have remained nothing, Luigi, you know. What I think is known as an independent—"

Again Luigi flashed his annoying grin. "An Italian has to be something, Cass."

"He has to have a label," Cass said, thinking he had scored a point.

"So he has to have a label—yes, but the important thing is he does not have to be what the label says he is. That is where we differ from everyone else. As for my forgetting, as you put it just now, let me ask you how many Jews were put to death by the Italian Fascisti. Your expression tells me that you are aware of the fact that the sins of Germany are not the sins of Italy." He paused and gave Cass an amicable pat on the wrist. "Let me tell you something. Italians are the most expedient people on earth. What could be a sin has turned out to be a very great virtue."

"We do not call it expediency. We call it hypocrisy, and it's not a virtue."

"Call it what you may. We Italians are too poor and we've been through too much to make a virtue of perfect honesty. Instead we believe that just a measure of honesty spread out thin enough is generally more valuable than the terrible weight of your Anglo-Saxon self-righteousness. As for myself, I can be a Fascist with no sense of compromise. It's the safest measure. I've got to look out for my own skin. And I bide my time, hoping for nothing but keeping my eyes open. Who knows but whether some day I might not be able to do somebody a little bit of good?"

To this sort of argument Cass had no reply. He would sit sullenly, drinking, and by and by the talk would turn to other things, Luigi carrying the ball: What is matter? What is reason? What is reality? Had Cass ever read the esteemed Spanish-Dutch philosopher Spinoza? Cass would say yes or no, depending upon his mood, but at this point the wine would usually have laid waste to his powers of concentration, his head would sag down upon the table, he would be too drunk to care. . . .

"You drink too much, Cass," he would hear Luigi's voice, along with a *tsk-tsk-tsk,* "it will bring you to disaster, mark my words."

"You talk too much, Luigi," his own voice would say as, in the bright morning light, he fell sound asleep.

But there were times during that spring when he was at least partly sober. Forsaking his usual headpiece, the jaunty beret which had grown gamy with the advent of hot weather, he put on a straw hat, sandals, and baggy blue pants and thus accoutered like Paul Gauguin went for long walks back into the hills. In this way he found Tramonti, which was a vale, or glade, or dale—at any rate, something poetic—so far removed from this century that if ever, from where he sat in the cool shadows of a willow tree, a faun had reared his head to give a goatish laugh or a shepherdess with a crook appeared to cajole him in the language of Virgil, he would have only been half-surprised. There was a brook here, spongy-smelling and cool with water iris and fern. Peasant huts were scattered through the valley, and a few stray sheep. Stretched out on the mossy bank, reading a book, or just lying there gazing aslant at the motionless blue sky, he would hear sounds—sheep softly bleating or the tinkle of a cowbell or the far-off cheering of birds. A breeze would come up from the sea, bearing with it an odor of cedar and pine, and like fat snowflakes a flurry of dandelion seeds would swoop and dance, pirouetting, and drift to earth. The scent of cedar and pine would linger, and he would nod off to sleep, all terrors dissolved in the alloy of memory and desire and his heart wrung, even at the borderland of darkness, with foreshadowings of repose. Yet even then all was not well: presently phantoms would distort his dreams, small violent outrages of the most grotesque and fanciful recollection, and he would awake with a start in his bucolic glade, sweating, thinking of nymphs and shepherds, but aware above all that he had heard—indistinct and remote but real enough—muffled sounds of toil and tribulation that were worse than grief. Once, awakened in this fashion, he scrambled to the top of a knoll just above him, and saw what it was that had rattled his dreams. Three women in rags, ageless, their skin stained the color of walnut, labored up the side of the mountain toward Sambuco, carrying on their backs loads of brush and fagots which would have burdened down a strong man or a small mule. Indeed, there was something mulelike about the women. What it was he could not exactly define, except that here, at a point where the path took a steep and brutal lurch upward, the going was so rough that none of them could suppress sounds of the most purified and bone-bare anguish, anguish rent not from the soul—for these crooked shapeless things could possess no souls—but from tormented gristle and flesh, as if from animals. And he watched wide-eyed and in confused misery himself as the three creatures, ragged brown bags, gained the crest, stood there for an instant with the fagots balanced mountainously and perilously above them, then clumped away as under a cloud, one brownly diminishing, dustily merging image of stooped and downcast bondage.

The sight distressed and saddened him—so much so that, guiltily, he found another spot in the valley to read and dream, far away from the women and their groans of torment and their crushing loads. He could not forget them, though. Try as he might to put them out of his mind—even on the bank of his new brook, amid new pastures—he could not escape the feeling that each day the valley had fresh shadows, as if sullen shapes prowled around in Arcady.

Then sometime after this, early in May, the real anxiety returned, heavily, inescapably. One night, with an obscure urge to get supremely drunk upon him, he bought five bottles of red Sambuco wine and, enthroning himself by the phonograph in the living room, alone, with Poppy and the children safe in bed below, he proceeded to get merrily potted. Only, after long hours fortified by Leadbelly and by seedy visions of grandeur, it was not so merry. At three o'clock, perceiving all earthly beauty in the way the lamplight fell in a coppery pool across his own hands, he was Van Dyck (living in luxury, too, and keeping several mistresses); at four, with such majestic concepts of color and form afloat in his mind that he hardly knew where to start, he was revolutionary, legendary, without a peer; at four-thirty he was swapping theories with Rembrandt in heaven; at five, when dawn came up ablaze across the sea and he seized a brush and took an abortive swipe at the canvas, his ballooning rapture split, burst, and collapsed in a heap, and he began to stalk the room like one dungeon-bound. His nerve-ends were frayed, a dull and unnameable panic had come over him, and Leadbelly had sung "Poor Howard" close to a hundred times. Sleep was beyond all possibility. Grabbing his last bottle of wine, he left the house and walked through the cool and sleeping dawn toward Tramonti. There in his glade he sat down with the bottle propped between his knees, and there he sipped and nipped until the insects began to fidget and stir and the birds began to sing and until dim chiming notes from the town told him that it was ten o'clock. The only thing he remembered thinking, as he sat there crouched embryonically by the clear stream, was that God surely had clever ways of tormenting a man, putting in his way a substance whereby He might briefly be reached, but which in the end, forever and always, sent Him packing over the horizon trailing clouds of terror. At last he staggered to his feet, hurling the empty bottle into the weeds. He was making his way back toward town, stiff-legged and with glazed eyes, somewhat like a zombie, when like apparitions straight out of the realm of everlasting fire three women fantastically burdened—were they the same ones, always the same ones? he did not know—trooped up over a crest in the path before him, stood there motionless for an instant, dumb. Then, descending, gaining momentum, spines at right angles to their spindly legs, they shuffled toward him and past him, uttering no sound at all—"Good morning, ladies," he heard himself murmur idiotically—and were gone. He stood there for a moment, gazing at the place where they had vanished, beyond a hillock and into the lovely valley. And he wandered back toward town, with an oppressive sorrow in his flesh and bones.

Then as he approached the gate of the town he saw a sight which in his shredded and jangled condition demoralized him even further and which, together with the women, had the power to lay a troublesome spell over him from that moment forward. A quiet crowd had gathered outside the gate. A blue Pullman bus with its motor still chugging had halted too, and nearby the crowd was milling in a rough circle, all heads bent down upon an object lying in the road. It was a dog, Cass saw as he approached, and something—the bus?—had run over him with such weight and impact that his entire lower parts from belly to tail had been mashed flat against the asphalt pavement. Yet, wondrously and horribly, the dog still lived. He still lived, and his jaws were wide-open in a snarl of pain, but he made no sound. His upper parts—head, chest, and legs—possessed power and life, and Cass saw now that the crowd was intent upon seeing whether the beast, piteously straining and scratching with his forelegs against the pavement, would be able to lift himself up from the earth. It was impossible, of course, for the dog already was dying, but the crowd watched his struggles sadly and with teeth bared in fascination, and Cass watched in fascination too as the wild-eyed creature scrabbled against the pavement and through a blood-flecked mouth tried voicelessly to utter its agony. *"Ah Dio!"* someone said. "Put him out of his misery!"

But still no one stirred. It was as if they were watching a struggle that held them revolted and horrified but which, because of some obscure meaning there in which they themselves were profoundly implicated, they were powerless to alter or resolve. *"Buon Dio!"* the same voice said again. "Somebody finish the poor animal!" But again no one made a move toward the dog. In foaming, sparkle-eyed anguish he still jerked and twisted and floundered with his forelegs against the road, and with fangs bared barked into the air soundless torture. Then at last somebody stepped forward—a portly man in a business suit with a thick gold watch chain strung across his paunch. He was holding a stick in one hand, and Cass, hearing someone mention the word *"medico,"* recognized him as a man he had once seen briefly in the piazza—Caltroni, the local physician. He wore a pince-nez and his bald head shone like glass. The doctor took a step toward the dog and with a hand glittering with rings raised the stick high in the air; when it descended, badly aimed, it struck the animal not across the skull but along the snout and muzzle, knocking the beast's head to the road and bringing forth from his nostrils a gush of scarlet blood. The crowd gasped. The dog once more raised his bloody head and commenced to struggle. Again, sweating now, Caltroni lifted the stick on high—"Some doctor, eh?" Cass heard a voice snigger, inevitably—and brought it down hard upon the dog's head, where it made a single explosive, excruciating crack and broke into two ragged pieces. The crowd gasped again, this time on a wild, unified note of pain. *"Datemi un bastone!"* the doctor cried out in despair, calling for a proper club, but Cass with his mind and guts in turmoil waited to see no more. He fled in sudden cowardly haste, for no reason at all—it was only a dog—

furious and cursing. The last glimpse he had of the scene as he stumbled off toward home was the dog's head, mutilated, bleeding, still mouthing its silent, stunned agony to the heavens. And the doctor, bent on euthanasia, shouting for a stick.

That afternoon and night while he lay in feverish sleep it seemed to him, as he crouched deep in the womb of his slumber, that he kept waiting for the nightmare—volcanoes, gulf, perishing shore—to wash over him. But he dreamed instead of women with burdens, and dogs being beaten, and these somehow all seemed inextricably and mysteriously connected, and monstrously, intolerably so, so that when he awoke—full in the morning light of the following day—it was with an outcry of terror on his lips. He lay there for a while in the shadows, shuddering, hung-over, still impaled upon some cruel, swiftly dimming image of a thing being hurt and flayed. After a time he became aware of the world about him: he heard Windgasser's gardeners jabbering outside the window, then, sniffing nearby an odor, foul and fishy-smelling, he turned and pushed off the pillow next to him a newspaper-wrapped package of sea food which Poppy or someone had mysteriously laid there.

He got up, shuddering. Dementia seemed to hover over the day like a mist. There was a displacement, a sense of reality unseated and uprooted all too reminiscent of that terrible day in Paris. He took a shower, which only chilled him. He got clumsily into his clothes and hurried toward the piazza as swiftly as his rubbery legs would take him, hoping against hope that enough wine might kill the fear to which he was shackled like a fellow prisoner.

"Ma la volgarità," Luigi was saying as Cass ordered his *rosso,* "the vulgarity of our age is not confined to America, you see. It is a world phenomenon. Did you ever read the famous Spanish philosopher Ortega y Gasset?" He paused to stir with a hairy-knuckled finger the slivers of ice in his Campari. "No? It might cure you of your romantic naïveté about art and its corruption. Italy. It is the most vulgar country in the world. You must stop complaining, Cass. Nine hundred and ninety-nine people out of a thousand don't care a dried fig for art, and they never will. Art is a silly accident, really. Why do you think millions of Italians migrated to America? To be free to enjoy art? No. Why then?"

"Moolah."

"Come?"

"Una parola americana. It means money." The wine came and Cass poured it with shaking hands.

"Precisely. Money. Perhaps you are beginning to see." He paused. "You look ill, Cass. Do you think it would be wise if you did not indulge yourself in so much alcohol."

Cass gulped wine: though red it was icy cold, Sambuco-style, and when it hit his stomach it was as if there had been turned on suddenly a jet of flame. "*A-ii!*" he gasped. His eyes blurred; the golden piazza, blue peaks beyond in the brilliant sunlight, all were engulfed in shimmering water. Then, "Sonofabitch," he blurted in Anglo-Saxon, his stomach heaving. "I think Leopold has finally waked up. I won't even be able to drink any more, Luigi."

"Leopoldo?" said Luigi, with a puzzled look. "Ah, *Leopoldo!* The stomach you were telling me about." His dark face wore a sudden sad-eyed, canine expression, full of honest concern. "Has it really come back, Cass?"

"I don't know," he replied in a flat voice. In apprehension he waited for another twinge in his gut, but the pain diminished, subsided. "I don't know. It would have good reason to."

"You'd better be careful," said Luigi. "If you don't take care of that ulcer" (he said *ulcera al duodeno,* bringing forth a crumb of medical knowledge which sounded, with all those liquid syllables, doubly ominous) "you'll hemorrhage some day and who will be able to get you to Salerno in time? Why don't you stop drinking, Cass? Why do you Americans torture yourselves with so much drinking?"

"Simply, Luigi, for the same reason I gave you the other night." Brightening now with the wine, after the sunken and imperiled first few waking hours, he felt a glow stealing over him; it was the old familiar reckless glow, banishing the hard core of trouble, and it was made somehow all the more pleasant by Luigi's reproach. He glanced sideways to the square. Two skinny nuns, astoundingly black and beautiful, flapped past like ravens across the immense and cobbled sunlight, diminishing, by their vivacious fluttering patterns of jet on gold, some of his morning gloom. "Simply, Luigi," he repeated, "because Americans are so wealthy. That's why they drink. They have to drink because drinking drowns their guilt over having more money than anybody in the world. My God, Luigi, let them have *some* pleasure."

Although he felt that he had said this without bitterness, he was aware that Luigi, morbid snooper, had caught the irony. Or perhaps it was because at this point, almost without thinking, he turned his pocket inside out. More grave than ever, the *carabiniere* bent toward him, saying, "What's the matter, Cass? I thought you said there was money coming in the mails. I thought you said you weren't going to have to worry."

"We're broke, Luigi. Dead broke. There's no more money coming in the mails."

"But Cass, that's terrible! Didn't you say—"

"No more money, Luigi. I think we are down to our last five thousand. We are slowly dissolving, the benighted Kinsolving." This last he spoke in English. He gulped wine again.

"Does Poppy know?" the corporal asked, squinting now at him against the sun. "Is she aware of this financial—this *difficoltà?*"

"She knows, of course," he said, "but she, as you well know, is even less able than I to grapple with the hard realities. Poppy! Luigi, I should have been born an Italian. Then I should feel no compunction whatever at seeing my wife in the role of a slave. A drab, a scullery wench. An inept one at that. As it is, I suffer. As it is, just an hour or so ago I woke up with my head throbbing as usual, completely unhinged and undone I am, still wrestling with my nightmares, and what do you think I find on the pillow beside me?"

"What?" said Luigi. His face wore a sober look of expectation (a nymph? a snake?).

"Two kilos of shrimp. Imagine the indelicacy. And the stench! Poppy left them there—why *there* I don't know. She—I don't know the phrase in Italian—she gathers wool. She dreams. In her abstraction she dropped everything, and the shrimp, done up in a page from *Oggi* with the big broad rear end laid out there of some movie blonde, you see, were propped up next to my chin. Oh Christ, Luigi, the place stank like a charnel house! Luigi, she can't *do* anything without help. God knows, the places we lived in were horrible enough when there were just the two of us— candy wrappers, I remember, and cookie boxes all over everywhere—but with four kids! Anyway, I dragged myself out of bed and stepped into a diaper full of shit. I just howled there at the top of my voice for a while. Then after I took a cold shower I went upstairs. The confusion! The chaos! Timothy writing on the walls with my crayons. Felicia pouring milk on the cat. Nicky screaming in the corner with wet pants. And in the middle of it all, at a table with sunshine streaming down on her fair head—Poppy, sobbing as if her heart would break."

Luigi made a clucking sound. *"Povera Poppy,"* he said. *"La vita è molto dura per la bella Poppy."*

"Life is hard for pretty Poppy," Cass echoed. "An Italian

would *do* something—" he began, but then he fell silent. He could put down his own kin no further.

Pursing his lips together, Luigi made ready for a pronouncement. "Somewhere in one of the plays of Gabriele D'Annunzio," he said, "there is a certain line, relating to the innate conflict between man and woman. A magnificent line. I believe it's from *Il sogno d'un mattino di primavera*. Although now that I think of it, it might come from *La città morta*. It goes"—his eyes revolved about as he considered—"it goes, '*La donna e l'uomo* . . .' Something, something, something. Confound it, I can't seem to recall the words. Something about the necessity for a man to escape from women, or something on that order. '*La donna e l'uomo* . . .' I'm almost sure it's from *La città*. . . ." His voice trailed off. "Are you listening?"

By God, he thought, it was Leopold, after all. The burning sensation—part pain, part hunger—had begun to creep upward into his gorge, causing him to yearn for a belch that would not come; he felt weak and giddy but this feeling, he knew, would pass away as soon as the wine's blessed anesthesia took hold. He gazed up into Luigi's dejected face, thinking: *Down, Leopold, down.* "I'm listening, Luigi. Speak."

But Luigi, already, had lost touch with D'Annunzio. Suddenly his eyes brightened and he snapped his fingers. "Cass! I just remembered, I have the very thing for you!"

"Have they invented a plastic stomach?"

"No, no. No joke. Someone to help you." He nodded his head toward the shadowy interior of the café. "The *padrona* here. Signora Carotenuto. Early this morning she told me about an aunt of hers. She is an elderly woman of some means who used to live in Sambuco but who now lives in Naples and comes back here from time to time to engage in charitable work with the nuns. Now just by chance there came to the convent last evening while Signora Carotenuto's aunt was there, an ugly peasant hag from Tramonti in the most pathetic state imaginable. Please pay attenion, Cass."

"I'm spellbound, Luigi."

"Now this woman, along with her entire family, is the victim of the most terrible circumstances. Which is to say," he drawled, savoring a dramatic pause, "which is to say that she and her family have been assaulted by fiendish calamities the likes of which it would take the mind of a Dante to devise. According to Signora Carotenuto, whose aunt was present at the time, the woman was in a terrible way. Claiming to be forty, though in every way she looked twice the age, she came to the door of the convent last night hysterical with grief and desperation. Her eyes were glassy, her lips were streaked with spittle, and upon her cheeks there were crimson flecks of blood. Thinking her possessed of the fits, the sisters took her in and laid her down on a pallet, where, finally coming to her senses, she babbled out the most harrowing tale of woe. The blood, it turned out, came from biting her lips and tongue. You see, she had *run* the whole five kilometers to town up from the valley of Tramonti."

"Why, for the love of God?" Cass said.

"Patience, my friend. I'm coming to that. What evidently had happened was this, according to the story told by Signora Carotenuto's aunt. The woman's husband, a tuberculous farmer who owns one sick cow whose milk he sells here in Sambuco—this woman's husband had the misfortune to fall off the roof of the cowshed which he was repairing and break his leg. Frantic with anxiety, the woman left the children in the care of the eldest daughter and ran, as I have told you, all the way to Sambuco to summon the doctor. Now here comes the distressing part. The doctor—do you know him, Caltroni, a plumpish man with a pince-nez?"

"Plumpish? Fat, don't you mean, Luigi? Yes, I know of him. I saw him yesterday, flailing away at a dog." The image came back, and it lingered troublesome and haunting in his mind as Luigi spoke. "Incompetent, I'd say."

"There's no need to run down Caltroni, Cass. In spite of his background, Dr. Caltroni is no quack. He is a competent physician, poorly recompensed and overburdened by work and by patients who either cannot or will not pay for his services. Which is in line with the story I'm telling you. For this peasant woman came to him and demanded that he come right away and attend to her husband's leg. He turned her away—"

"That was a miserable thing to do—"

"No, not at all. Rightly so, as a matter of fact, because although it was an unfortunate thing to have to do and although I'm sure that Caltroni, who is a true humanist at heart, was saddened by her plight, it nonetheless transpires that for ten years he has been attending to the ills of this wretched family without receiving one lira for his services. There is, after all, a point where one must draw the line."

"I don't follow you, Luigi. Suppose the poor clod was bleeding to death. Where would you draw the line on that?"

But Luigi was not interested in this ethical caution. "Let me go on. I'm getting to something that might fascinate you. The woman, as I have said, came in desperation to the convent. Now although the sisters there are not members of a nursing order, it happily turned out that one of the nuns, a big burly woman, had training in the care of the sick. Together with the peasant woman, she and Signora Carotenuto's aunt hurried back to Tramonti, where they found the peasant as described, writhing in pain on the earth outside his hut and calling upon heaven—according to Signora Carotenuto's aunt—to end his suffering. And indeed such suffering, she said, had to be witnessed to be adequately expressed. I myself can certainly imagine it, for although I have not been back to that *paese* since before the war I can remember seeing it as a youth and having indelibly engraved upon my mind its sordidness and corruption. Signora Carotenuto's aunt apparently was quite undone as she described it. It turns out that not only the father was tubercular but at least two of the children —all of them hacking and wheezing there in one room no larger than your bedroom at the Palazzo d'Affitto. Well, into the windowless place they brought the peasant and laid him down. The nurse-sister set his leg in a splint and there he now lies helpless and no doubt doomed."

Interrupting his recital, Luigi sat back, looking sorrowful, though, like a fat cat, contented. Over the square now the sun rose flaming-white and scorching in a clear blue sky. A bustle and stir had commenced in the vicinity. A blue tourist bus halted near the fountain, and down upon its blinking passengers bore Umberto, publicity man for the Bella Vista, weasel-faced, wearing the headpiece of a major general, able to harass and annoy in five languages. On flat heels two skinny American college girls slatted past, breastless and without buttocks and bandy-legged in the sagging costumes of their *Wanderjahre;* one, Cass heard, was called Bubba, or Barba, or something: each bearing trophy-like a quality of innocence through the sunny, swarming air, they passed out of sight. Saddened and depressed by Luigi's tale, but also pricked with irritation, Cass turned back to the corporal, saying: "So what do you want me to do, vote Fascista, so this terrible situation will be corrected?"

"No, Cass, I'm not talking politics now." He paused. "That was meant as a sly joke, wasn't it? Well, I'm a tolerant person and I'll ignore it," he went on, with some sort of approximation of a humorous wink, "but you might just incidentally reflect that Tramonti, after having been under the control of the Communists, who didn't do anything, is now in the hands of the Christian-Democrats—the *American* party, you know—and it is still as miserable as it ever was. Now I'm not saying that the Fascist—"

"Go on with your story." God *damn* Luigi.

"Well, it's simply this, Cass. The eldest girl of the family—I think she is about eighteen—just got down on her knees and implored the ladies to find her work. The interesting thing is—and I suppose it's why Signora Carotenuto's aunt took special note of it—is that the girl up until about a month ago used to work right here at this café. She can cook well, it seems, and do housework, and she is willing to work for next to nothing. Indeed, so cruel is the condition of the family that I would not be surprised if she would work for only the food that she would be allowed to take away. For you it's a perfect—"

"Look, Luigi," Cass said, "all this is very well and good. Let's say that some miracle happened and I could afford her. Let's say I just gave her food. For Poppy's sake—which is to say for the children's sake and my own sanity—I'd do anything to get somebody who would keep the place habitable for humans. But do you want to add T.B. to the endless list of ulcers and hangovers and colic and head colds that *la famiglia* Kinsolving—"

"Ah, I should have *explained*," he broke in, "this one—this wench—is free of the disease. I think she had it once, according to Signora Carotenuto, but she worked as a domestic in Amalfi for two years, where the cool air and salubrious climate was for her a complete remission." He spoke of Amalfi as if it were as remote as Denmark. "It is said that she speaks some English, too, which for Poppy— It would be a real charity, I think, if you'd— But here, I'll go get Signora Carotenuto and let you talk to her yourself." And before Cass could say anything, Luigi had risen from the table, stalking off into the café to search for Signora Carotenuto.

He looked down at the table, amazed to see that in less than half an hour he had consumed a full liter of wine—on an empty stomach at that. He turned toward the waiter with the command, half-spoken, for another *mezzo litro*. At this instant there passed close by across his vision a depressing, mean tableau which darkened the day like a cloud. For not ten yards away, in clamorous full view of the bright morning, there took place a brutal catastrophe. Here one of that ragged procession of women from the valley had wheezed to a halt; she was of any age at all, pop-eyed with toil, sweating, bent over like a broken limb beneath the everlasting load of fagots. Behind her stood a little girl in tatters, sucking on her thumb. As Cass turned, the woman made a final desperate humping motion with her back but the enormous hummock of wood, badly balanced and off-kilter, came tumbling off her shoulders and fell to the cobblestones with a clatter. Then as he watched, the woman threw up her arms—it was a noiseless gesture, touched not with anger or despair but only inevitability, acceptance of a world in which heavy loads fall and must be forever rehoisted—and with the little girl pushing too, she huffed and puffed the bundle along the ground to a nearby wall. At once there took place something that caused the sweat to roll down beneath his armpits and to stand out in cold droplets on his brow. For now the woman had backed up with her shapeless rear end against the wall; stooped over donkey-like she began to bray hoarse commands to the child, who with skinny arms aquiver, flower-stalk legs trembling with effort, commenced to tug and heave the load onto the woman's back. The child strained and tugged, the woman arched her back, and for an instant the bundle rolled up and onto her shoulders, awesomely, as if hoisted there by some block and tackle invisible in the heavens. But it went up not quite far enough, it teetered and tottered, the phantom ropes were severed, and the bundle came back down to earth with a mighty crash. The child began to weep. The woman began to stomp about the bundle, muttering and flailing her arms. As if forced, sympathetically, into some rebellion by the sight, Cass' stomach knotted up in a swift paroxysm of pain. He started to rise from his chair, thought better of it, sat down again. What in Christ's name could he do or say? Madam, permit me if you will to carry your burden, to whatever remote and heartbreaking destination. He heard a groan pass his lips and turned away: Filippone, the slant-shouldered waiter, came drooping out from beneath the awning. Fixing his eyes on a distant wall, Cass made his mind a blank, conscious only of a greasy thumbprint on one lens of his glasses, through which he read, unthinking, three blurred white faded words: VO-TATE DEMOCRAZIA CRISTIANA. *"Un altro mezzo litro,"* he half-whispered, not looking up. When, finally forced by the urge to make himself even more distressed, he turned back again, the woman had shouldered her prodigious load. Stooped, misshapen,.

of another century, she padded bare-soled beneath her tower of wood across the square, trailed by the child with legs like the stems of flowers.

Far off in the valley toward Scala, grindingly off-key, church bells banged and clattered in remote confusion like celestial pots and pans. Filippone came and went. Cass took a deep gulp of wine, downing in fact half the bottle before removing his nose from its rim, conscious now that in some stale and left-over fashion, he was once again drunk, but exhaustedly, unpleasantly so, and that the day already had begun to gray over with the old apprehensions. His bright brief moment of elation had drained utterly away. Heavy weights seemed to burden him. He sought urgently for something to buoy him up, some merry swirl of color or motion in the near-deserted square, found nothing—fat chinless Saverio, scrounging mindlessly at his uplifted pecker, boldly outlined through his pants. With a whistle Umberto summoned him toward the luggage piled around the bus, and like a baggy animated scarecrow he took off, still tumescent, uttering magical paeans. Now the square lay level and deserted, like a lake becalmed. On a green promontory half a mile across the valley someone laughed, a woman called, *"Non fa niente!"* in a silvery voice, as clearly as if it had been spoken into his ear. In the hush that followed, he raised his eyes from the piazza toward the sea: there a streak of blazing light reflected from the zenith-ascending sun caught him flush in the eyes, making him for one stupefying instant as blind as a mole. And at this very moment from the belfry high above him a flock of pigeons erupted forth like feathered rockets and filled the unseen air around him with a tumult of wings. Hallucination! His heart was seized by a despairing clumsy terror. Blinded, he heard drumming all around him a multitude of wings; a yellowish taste like that of sulphur rushed up beneath his tongue and in the darkness he thought he heard thunderous footsteps from afar, approaching on the surface of the sea. Once again the woman seemed to be crouched nearby —*"Shpinga!"* she was croaking to the child, in that all but impenetrable dialect, and the air about his head was sweet with the odor of blossoms he had never smelled before. Instantaneously, with the speed and majesty of light, a cold wind blew through his mind: footsteps, blossoms, birds, terror —all were gone, while in their stead came a familiar clear white space, clear as water, of illimitable repose.

He caught his head before it had fallen to the table top, and snapped erect with a shudder. He blinked. Somehow in his seizure his spectacles had fallen away from his eyes and dangled down suspended from one ear. Retrieving them with trembling fingers, he adjusted them upon his nose and focused his eyes on the square. Miracle of miracles—as in Paris—hardly five seconds had passed: Saverio, still galloping, had not yet reached the bus; the pigeons in bottle-green and fluttery glide had only at this instant gained the parapet around the fountain. A hand crashed down violently between his shoulder blades. *"A-hii!"* he cried, in an ecstasy of terror. Bleeding Christ!

"It is all taken care of, my friend!" said Luigi in a jaunty voice. Cass forced himself to listen, wide-eyed, composed, afraid to reveal his inner condition. Far off on the sea, like some last remnant of his hallucination, he thought he saw waterspouts—a black forest rushing toward the horizon, the sea itself boiling faintly in convulsion. Then all was still. His heart thudded against his breastbone like an overworked pump. "It is all taken care of. Signora Carotenuto has seen the girl today, and she is at this very moment somewhere in town. She is going to send Saverio to hunt for her and bring her to you."

"But you—" He found it difficult to speak. "Saverio?"

"Yes. I myself would wish for a more respectable messenger." He halted. "Saverio is what you might say—" His voice, rather solemn, trailed off.

"What?"

"It is just that Saverio— Nothing. I'll tell you something about him some day. It is all right."

Near the bus now Cass saw the café owner—a fat woman with a bun at the back of her neck—talking to the half-wit, gesticulating. After a moment Saverio turned from the woman and hustled up a cobbled street. As he did so, a maroon Cadillac nosed its way into the piazza, a sport-shirted young man at the wheel, a blond girl beside him, the eyes of both shuttered behind dark sun glasses. The car eased past the fountain, the sound of its horn piercing, chromatic, very loud. Like a shoal of minnows, a gang of boys began to wriggle and twist round the car, shouting. The young American, smartly handsome, once more sounded his harmonic, turgid horn. *Wonk!* The car halted, throbbing with power barely audible, in the middle of the square.

"One of my countrymen," Cass murmured, somewhat recovered. "I think I will go to Russia."

"Here, Cass, I brought you some mozzarella," Luigi said, sitting down. "Eat it. You've got to eat, my friend. You're going to kill yourself with this wine."

"I think I will go to Russia."

"How alike you are, you Americans and the Russians!"

"Come?"

"I mean it is true, Cass. Your similarities are much more striking than your differences. And neither of you seem to be aware of it. There are dozens of them, besides the obvious one of the wish for world power. Your reliance on science and the scientific method. Your puritanism. That is quite true, Cass. Have you never thought that in spite of the emphasis on sex in the United States it merely comes out as the same unhealthy puritanism that exists in Russia?"

"I don't know if I have thought of it or not."

"And your concentration upon material things. You were talking about art in America. I should hate to be an artist in either country. As for your own, you are free I gather to create as you wish but you have no real public. The people really do not care. In Russia, on the other hand, there is a vast public which cares, but one which the artist is not free to create for. You see, it is all the same thing." He paused. "But I sympathize with you. I would choose the dictatorship of the Kremlin—if I had to choose—to the dictatorship of the mob. Because there is always the matter of your respective leaders."

"How do you mean?"

"Why, it is quite apparent. Your president and the dictator in the Kremlin. They are both peasants. But yours is a cretin, and the other is shrewd. I would always cast my lot with a shrewd man, no matter how ruthless."

"You would?"

"It is just this, Cass. Some day the Russians will have the refrigerators and the bathrooms that you Americans have. But though it is repressed at the moment, the Russians have a fund of spirituality which you Americans have never developed. They will be educated people with refrigerators and bathrooms. You will be ignorant people with refrigerators and bathrooms, and the educated people will triumph. *Capito?"*

"Um." Barely listening now, Cass took a generous bite out of the cheese: creamy and ripe, impossibly delectable, it plummeted into his stomach, pacifying there almost instantly the ulcerous raging pain of which he had hardly been aware. But he was severely, dangerously drunk. He felt his head sinking downward, with racking weariness toward the table. A vagrant cloud, shaped like the face of Africa, rode serenely across the sun, bringing nostalgic shadows to the corner of the piazza and now a sudden, frivolous gust of wind: Luigi clapped his hand to his head, too late: his green cap went kiting off in a cloud of dust. As he rose to retrieve it the wind died, suffusing all with radiance and peace. "Muffin dear," the tall blonde called, sidling out of the car, "tell him to bring the green hatbox *fehst.*"

"But it is free there," Cass heard himself say, half-giggling and in a muffled voice against the wet table. " 'S a democracy. Everyone eats. It is free." For what seemed many minutes he sat there like this with his head half-buried in his arms. What made it seem so long, he later recollected, was the dream which appeared out of nowhere, passing across his blackened gaze with all the detailed immediacy of the previous night and loading his spirit with the same intense despairing fear he had felt just before his spasm ten minutes ago. "Cass," he heard Luigi dimly above him, "Cass, why don't you go home, get something to eat, go to sleep?" But ignoring him, only half-aware of his voice at all, he allowed the dream to march in stately black parade across his mind— terrified by it, utterly captured, and stricken with wonder at the final treachery of his drunkenness which brought no ease to his anxiety and fear, as by all rights it should, but sharpened to the point of torture his most unholy apprehensions. Then all of a sudden he knew why it had been the woman with the fagots who had set off this seizure. He raised his head from the table, fixing Luigi with his blurred, unsteady gaze. "The woman," he said. "The woman carrying that wood. Who is she?"

"What woman, Cass?" Puzzlement was all over his face. "What woman do you mean?"

"You know what woman," he said sharply, scarcely able to manage his impatience. "The beat-up scrawny woman carrying those fagots. The one with the little girl. Who is she?"

"*Iddio!*" Luigi exclaimed. "How should anyone know, what peasants! All of them," he said in tones reminiscent of those sleepy-faced storekeepers of Cass' youth who went on so about Negroes, "all of them look alike. Cass, indeed I do not know what you are talking about."

But he had it now, plain! Of course, the woman had merely resembled the woman in his dream, and to be sure, as Luigi had pointed out, they did all look alike. One way or the other, though,

no trivial detail such as this could diminish the whole encompassing truth of his dream—a truth which seemed to him now so un-
impeachable, so invincibly clear, so grounded in the bedrock of
existence that he felt an exultant laugh rise up in his throat as he
poured the whole thing out to Luigi, who had begun to fidget.
"Don't move about so like that, Luigi," he heard himself say with
a chuckle. "Keep still a minute while I tell you about this—this
visitation I had last night."

As he spoke his fright receded; he felt almost exhilarated,
touched by a roguish gaiety he could only compare to those times
long lost in the past when he was able to create, to work; it was
so odd a sensation as to be, in a way, unbelievable, and something told him that it was not right to feel this way at all, but a
spillway had been opened and he felt himself being borne buoyantly along upon the flood. "It was like taking ether, you see, this
dream I had. Like waking from an ether dream, when all the
indescribable mysteries have been made clear. I was in one of
those Pullman buses, you see, and we were driving up the road
from Maiori that goes over the mountain toward Naples. The bus
was crowded and noisy. It seemed very hot. I remember I kept
fanning myself. There were some loud *vitelloni* from Salerno singing and playing a guitar, and making passes at the girls. We were
going up the side of a deep ravine, that big gorge up near the top,
just before the summit—you know where I mean? Then suddenly we picked up speed. We went through a little village, driving very fast. I remember calling out to the driver to go slow, that
he was going to kill us all. But we kept picking up speed, roaring
down the street of this little village. Then suddenly we struck
something. I could hear the soft thumping noise beneath the
wheels. It's hard to describe. It was as if he had run over a bag of
flour or meal. I remember calling out again to the driver, this time
to stop. We stopped and I got out. Strange, now that I think of it:
I was the only passenger in the bus who got down—do you follow
me?"

Mournfully, without speaking, Luigi nodded his head. He began to mop his brow—a restive, unhappy motion. Then, "Cass—"
he began.

"Wait a minute, can't you? I got out and walked back to see
what it was we had struck. I kept thinking it must be a bag of flour
or meal—I don't know why. It seemed to look like one as I went
up to it. But as I approached I saw that it was not a sack of anything at all. It was—it was a dog. It had been brutally crushed. All

of its hinder parts right on up to its chest had been smashed flat—
flat as those cutlets that that butcher down the street makes out of
those thick slices of beef after pounding on them for half an hour.
You know? The back part of the dog was crushed just as flat as
that—"

"Listen, Cass—"

"Yet the poor beast was still living! Lying there so horribly
mangled he was nonetheless still alive, and as he lay there he gave
a heartbreaking whimper and tried with his forepaws to raise
himself from the earth. This part was so vivid, I remember: watching the animal as he moaned and whimpered and with his eyes
rolling white and anguished tried to get up from the road. Then
the driver came down from the bus—it's strange, because although he looked familiar to me he seemed to have no face at all
—the driver came and stood beside me watching the poor dog's
struggles and kept saying, 'I wonder whose dog is that?' Then all
of a sudden there appeared beside us this peasant woman, this
bent-over scrawny woman I thought I had seen just now. She just
stood there with us for a bit, watching the dog too, and then she
said, 'The dog was mine.' Then the bus driver went to the side of
the road and picked up a big stick. He came back—still without a
face, you see, that was one of the strangest parts—and he began
to beat the dog in the head furiously with the stick, saying over
and over again, 'I must put him out of his misery, I must put the
poor beast out of his misery!' Furiously he kept pounding at the
dog's skull and muttering over and over to himself these stricken
words. But the dog refused to die! Oh, it was frightful to watch!
To watch this animal in its desperate suffering, whining and moaning there in the road, his eyes rolling in agony, still trying to rise,
while all the time the fellow kept thrashing away at his skull, hoping to free the beast from his torture but with each blow only adding to his pain! Then—"

"Then what?" said Luigi. The corporal's face seemed now to
loom up through murky, unfathomed depths of water. For an
instant Cass thought he was going to faint but caught himself; no
longer elated by his discovery but, indeed, horrified by it, he was
pressed toward its ending by some force far beyond comprehension or control, and was sick to his soul with a profound,
clammy dread.

"Then—" he said. "Then I looked down through the billowing
dust, and this is what I saw. It was not now the dog's head he was
beating, but the head of the woman, this scrawny peasant woman

with the fagots. Somehow she had turned into the dog. Lying there crushed and mangled, with her poor tormented body pressed against the dust, she let out piteous cries, shrieking, 'God! God!' over and over again. 'Release me from this misery!' And each time she called out, *down* would come the flailing stick which would knock her bleeding head against the earth, only for the head to rise again to cry out for deliverance from all this agony, and each time again the stick would strike her, futilely, releasing her not into death but only into an endless mystery of pain. Do you understand? Don't you see!" Cass began to shout, hoarsely and drunkenly. *"Liberatemi!"* she kept screaming. 'Release me! Release me!' And then far aloft I heard the man's voice saying again and again as he laid on with the stick: 'I'm trying! I'm trying!' And I heard his terrible sobs of remorse as he kept beating her, and as he kept saying then, 'I cannot!' And as in the depths of my dream I realized that this was only He who in His capricious error had created suffering mortal flesh which refused to die, even in its own extremity. Which suffered all the more because even He in His mighty belated compassion could not deliver His creatures from their living pain. Which—" But now he halted. He felt his lips trembling. *"Che—"* he resumed. "He is *beating* us, yet *mercifully*—" he tried again. But it was no use. His wits, such as they had been, had abandoned him. Luigi gazed back at him with the half-dead expression of a man trapped by a lecture in some unknown language. Luigi had not understood him and beyond this, he knew, suspected him of being crazy. His suspicion he could take but his incomprehension seemed to him now a form of betrayal, and Cass heaved himself up from his seat unsteadily, knocking over the chair. "Don't you understand what I mean, Luigi? Why is it then," he demanded in a distraught voice, "when we erase one disease another comes to strike us down! Is it not His own feeble way of trying to get rid of us? Answer me that! Is it not? Is it not?" There was no reply.

He felt strangled in the grip of an almighty fear. *"Stupido! Idiota!"* he said with a belch. "Disease of the minds!" Then he turned and fled the corporal, lurching away across the square from his entreating outstretched hands, appalled at the fool he had made of himself and at the furious braying sounds he heard heaving up from his chest. . . .

Not too far west of the village, near an old ruin called the Villa Cardassi (its original owner, a Victorian Englishman, was a classicist: the motto DUM SPIRO, SPERO can still be seen engraved above the marble portico) there is a promontory among the rocks where people go to watch the sea. Here the trees are stunted and bent from incessant winds. A stone wall surrounding the point protects the maladroit, or the drunken, or the unwary: the drop, straight down upon the rocks in the valley, is almost a quarter of a mile. On clear days from this point the whole vast Mediterranean seems to open up from horizon to horizon: the sheer cliffs of Capri far off in the west, and the lazy umber coast marching southward to Calabria, and all around, infinite and glistening, the emerald sea. Here Cass found himself a short while after— though how he got there, he later recollected, he scarcely knew, except that he must have been a sight as he zigzagged up through the town with his hair in his face, belching and hiccupping, with a maniacal glint of terror in his eye. At the wall he stopped short, breathing heavily, and peered down over the familiar brink. Someone hardly larger than a gnat toiled far below in a toy-sized lemon grove; a swollen torrent in the valley, white with spume, looked no more forbidding than a rivulet of milk. Dizzied, bereft of all save the merest whisper of self-preservation, he leaned far out over the frightful gorge, tormented by a horror of these gallant heights so ardent and so powerful that it was almost like love. *"Prendimi,"* he whispered. "Take me now." As he leaned, a powdery crumble of mortar gave way beneath his hand, pitching him forward, and he had one instant's foretaste of oblivion as groves and vineyards and distant flood all spun lopsided and immense before his vision, all beckoning. With a cry strangled in his throat he tried to regain balance with his other arm and began to strain and tug himself back over the parapet. But all was lost. Lost! More mortar gave way; he slipped again. For a moment he dove forward into thin air, arms thrown out, supplicant, and all space seemed his destiny. Spread-eagled in nothingness, he held himself by his aching thighs, and by his heels, miraculously trapped beneath some rock or stone. At last with floundering arms and straining legs he pulled himself back up over the ledge, inch by inch and in a softly raining shower of dust. Then he was safe; he felt as if he were drawn fast, secured by unseen hands. He sank down shuddering on a stone bench beside the wall. With his eyes closed he sat there for long blind minutes, feeling the sun and the warm wind which soon dried the sweat that had drenched his hair and lulled and pacified his fright and his infirmity and allowed a dim light of sobriety to reach his brain. The yodel of a bus in the valley startled him; he opened his eyes.

A rustling behind him in the underbrush caused him to look around. The bushes parted, revealing the spade-shaped head of Saverio, who like some depraved and hellish apparition out of Hieronymus Bosch came vaulting on all fours from the foliage, then stood erect before him, grinning and gesticulating. From his tatters an aroma of filth and poverty rose like steam, and his right eye, demoralized by one of God knew how many thousand blown fuses littering the inside of his skull, rolled bloodshot and unruly in its socket and fixed itself with a demonic sidewise leer upon nothing. His lips flew frantically, conveying with groans the tortured outlines of a message and filling the air around him with globules of spit. Then as if someone had given his head a dismayed and impatient kick, his words became sensible, the spray around him diminished, and his apostate eye, like the little white bulletin in those spirit jars wherein one discovers one's fortune, rolled greasily into place. "I've been hunting for you, *Signor Keen*," he said. "The girl who wishes to work for you! Here she is!"

The girl who came walking up the path was the girl of the police station. Sweet-faced, slim, full-breasted, she approached him gravely, though with the faintest breath of some forlorn and disconsolate smile. She had put on a pair of shoes, perhaps for this occasion; they must have been borrowed, for they were sizes too large and they flapped about her brown ankles as she came near him.

"She wishes to work for you!" Saverio yelled in his ear.

"I have no money," he said in a whisper, still shaken, gazing at her, wondering at her beauty.

"She wishes to work for you!" Saverio repeated senselessly.

"Shut up," he said. And he opened his mouth to speak to the girl, but suddenly he felt so weak and depleted that his sight blurred and the earth made a lurching motion beneath him. He thrust his face into his hands. "I have no money to pay you," he said again. But he realized that if he could not hire her, neither could he allow her twice to walk out of his life. So he said, "Come see me tomorrow," in a tone of dismissal. And for some reason he could not trust himself to look at her again as he heard her turn and leave, followed by the shambling half-wit, flip-flapping in her enormous shoes back down the path.

Self, he thought. Merciful Christ. *Self.* If I don't find a way out of it soon I'll be over the bleeding edge for sure.

Journal entry *Sabato 4 Maggio:*

"What saves me in the last analysis I have no way of telling. Sometimes the sensation I have that I am 2 persons & by that I mean the man of my dreams & the man who walks in daylight is so strong and frightening that at times I am actually scared to look into a mirror for fear of seeing some face there that I have never seen before. Like today for instance & its not just the wine either but some kind of God or daemon that's got hold of me with his fangs and brittly crackling claws & will not let go til my flesh is parted from my soul. I mean, for instance after going berserk as I did, shouting, raging at Luigi & getting up as I did & rushing head-long to the brink of the cliff it was as if the dream had posessed me & I was dwelling in that self-same dream & a voice was telling me—NOW. Now is the time. Wait no longer. Come to me & all will be peace & quietness & repose. What saved me I don't know. Some reason within me so far has always prevailed & prevail it will I pray, prevail prevail. Lest old Cass go bug house & bring down his abode & dwelling place in confusion & in dust.

"Resolution made this date & sworn to by the name of all thats left that still makes sense: to let no drop of C2H50H pass these lips til June 15, which is Poppy's birthday & perhaps then she will vouchsafe me the celebration. It is the booze which is the grave digger & the spade & the earth & the grave diggers wife & family too. Each man picks his own brand of poison.

"2 A.M. At least I am not so far gone that I am not able to see & feel those fabulous lights on the surface of the deep. I am not blind yet. Luigi told me with his bland & exasparating sarcasm that the fishing boats are not nearly so pretty—*graziose,* his word—since the U.S. army left & the fishermen took to using those old surplus gasoline pressure-lamps. When they used plain old kerosene lanterns, they were much more graziose said he, curling his mustachiod lip around a cigar. Ecco Luigi. He is worried & confused. He is not yet really sure how to approach the U.S. with me, maybe because he feels in some instinctive way that deep down my emotions are as ambiguous as his own. Anyway the lights are marvelous, gasoline or not. Not so much like stars either, as first I thought but blurred & swollen if you get to looking at them long enough until at last with all boundaries effaced & all frame-work & all perspective lost in hypnotic limitless dark they look only like pure white blossoms, fat chrysanthemums lost and swarming in the black bosom of some oriental notion of eternity. They have some kind of message I think, but I can only look. I can not divine. Nor plumb. Nor lift a hand if my very life were staked upon it. There are times when I am vulnerable & look at it most honestly when I think Captain Slotkin was right, when he looked at me with those sad dark jewish eyes and said something on the order of, O.K. son if you want to put it on the ethical level & remove it from the psycho-analytical then put it this way— self destruction is the last refuge of the cowardly man. And I remember saying somewhat self pityingly—not at all, self destruction is the triumph of a man whos back is to the wall, it is at least one cut above imperishible self loathing. He had no come-back to that though I could tell from his look that he knew I was hedging & knew I knew that what he said was truth. Why he seemed to care for me in some kind of non professional and non-navy way I don't know unless as Ive often thought theres more kinship deep down between a southern methodist & a jew from Brookline Mass. (even a psycho-analytical one) then there is between two Pennsylvanians, & no doubt two people who have known Isaiah or Job 38 are more like to feel some strange & persuasive bond than a couple of mackeral-snappers who have never known anything but N.Y. Journal American in their life. In the end maybe it was just that I conned him somehow & being a jew I think he was impressed that a buck assed marine private from Columbus County N.C. only one cut above a share cropper actually, & with only 2 H.S. years could have cared & I mean really care for Sophocles and old Michel Eyquem not to speak of all the rest which came as easy to me as water & at 21 or so had a workable theory of painting worked out all my own. I wonder what happened to Slotkin, probably practising in Boston or somewhere & making a mint. But whenever I think of him & maybe thats only because he was about the only person I ever felt I could talk to about what was eating me, I get an extraordinary feeling in my bones, & can recall as clear as the shining air that day when I quoted that line from Oedipus that hit me so between the eyes, from the book he gave me, now should I die I were not wholly wretched etc., & he said something on the order of—yes we fail often but it is our birthright no less than the Greeks to try to free people into the condition of love. Which was a moment he seemed to make so much natural & gentle & decent sense that I almost gave into the bastard.

"And I suppose its true, some twisted connection or crossed up circuit between love & hate in me is the secret of it all, & to go in on my own from day to day like some scared electrician & try to fix the circuit will be in the end, I mean if there is an end, my only way out. I could not give up my thoughts or my dreams even to a Slotkin. It is awful & desperate enough to give them up to myself. A man must be chary with his daemons & who knows whether it is not better to suffer a dream & see Hell fire & the gulf & sink in the perishing deep & have volcanos exploding around ones head for a lifetime, than to know its final meaning. Who can say that its meaning once made naked & clear, wont make a man anything but triply damned & free him not into love but into a hatred so immense that all before would seem tender & benign. Who could safely say anything about that, I would like to know that man. Maybe it is just that in the end some secrets should be hid forever. Meantime I am my own soul diviner & I do not hope to dredge up out of the depths any thing but that which would momentarily solace me. And the blame is my own to bear. So that when ever I dream as I have done of old Uncle standing there as my own executioner I do not place the horror in his hands. If he was sweet & gentle though a miserable & dirt poor farmer & burdened & if the most he ever did was whallop me once when he caught me pulling my pork in the outhouse, or that time time at Lake Waccamaw when he caught me at 14 all beered up and drug me home by the ear—then he was not very progressive in many ways I guess, but I dont blame him for my present letchery nor for the fact that Im a whiskey head either. Slotkin kept wanting to dig at this, at my being an orphan & at old Uncle, but I guess he was barking up the wrong tree. Its not old Uncles fault any more than it was Cape Gloucester, which scared the living shit out of me just like it did everyone else. Nor when I look into my heart of hearts is it the U.S. I can blame at all though many times I would like to & do, a bleeding expatriate that would put a Bowery bum to shame. Because though say even somebody like Poppy dont know it there are times when just the thought of one single pine tree at home, in the sand, & a negro church in a grove I knew as a boy & the sunlight coming down hot on a Sunday long ago & the sound of the negros singing In Bright Mansions Above (?)—then I feel or know rather that all I would need is that one trembling word to be whispered or spoken into my ear.

AMERICA. And I could hold myself back no longer and blubber like a baby.

"Though for the rest of the time I figure you can have the whole smart-Alex, soft-headed, baby-faced, predigested, cellophane wrapped, doomed, beauty-hating, land. And thats a fact. No in the end maybe its good to get to know some of the horrors of the night, & to get old Uncle off the hook I suspect that whosoever it is that rises in a dream with a look on his face of eternal damnation is just ones own self, wearing a mask, and thats the fact of the matter."

VIII

Curious to relate, there was at this time living and working on the Adriatic coast a young American painter and sculptor named Waldo Kasz. A native of Buffalo, with a great mop of reddish hair and an expression which, at least in his rare photographs, mirrored a very special and personal detestation of the human race, Waldo Kasz had for a whole year enjoyed a vogue unparalleled by any young artist of his generation. He was of Polish descent; presumably his surname was a simplification of more unpronounceable consonants. His haunting, twisted, abstract forms in oil and gouache, his compressed and tormented statuettes in terra cotta, his larger figures in bronze—skeletal, attenuated, crypto-humans whose knobby outlines and strange, sudden concavities seemed to express the very essence of exacerbated and outraged flesh—all of these had won him, while still in his early thirties, the kind of acclaim for which most artists wait in vain a lifetime. An expatriate, a self-confessed hater of all things American, he lived in sulky exile in a little village on the seacoast not far from Rimini with only (according to a New York fashion magazine) his mother and three Siamese cats for company, and one solitary diversion—this being to prowl the lonely Adriatic shore in search of wild driftwood shapes from which he often took inspiration for his macabre, vaguely anthropomorphic masterpieces. Rumor had it that he was aloof to the vanishing point, a locker of doors and a slammer down of windows, and had even threatened violence upon those persistent souls—chiefly reporters and photographers from popular American journals—who had managed to penetrate his lair. The rare interviews with Waldo Kasz are records mainly of monosyllables and grunts. An article in the *Herald Tribune* called him "the grim young prophet of the 'beat' generation." One of the few photographs taken of him—a huge mug shot in a widely circulated magazine which also ran a three-page spread in color of his works—shows the tousled reddish hair, the glittering eyes two blue pinpoints of near-blind fury, the rather simian brow knitted in furious ripples and, in the foreground, a splashy blur of crimson—wine, so the caption explains, flung without ceremony at the prying photographer. The picture is titled "Angry Young Genius." It was because of the awful though not very precise coincidence of their names—Cass and Kasz—that Cass had his first encounter with Mason Flagg.

Unless you have been to Sambuco in May, you have never known the spring. This is what many Italians say, and it is no doubt hyperbole, but there is truth in the matter. Spring in Sambuco is something to know. It is odor and sweet warmth, bud and blossom, and, in the sky, ecstatic aerial tracings—sunbeam and bumblebee and hummingbird, and silvery, innocent showers of rain. Then the rain is gone, and it comes no more. Perhaps it is the height, the looking downward, that makes spring here the marvel that it is. Flowers clamber up along the hillsides, donkeys bray in the valleys and over all is that sense of the strut and glamour of newborn life. And you are so high, miles above the common earth. Girls, slender in cotton dresses, walk the street arm in arm in gay parade, while old women in doorways seek the sunlight with upturned faces and drowsing eyes. People shout to each other from open windows. There is an odor of pepper and pimiento and cheese in the air. From the depths of the dank café and into pure sunlight moves the eternal card game, kibitzed by two pink-cheeked priests and by Umberto, the Bella Vista's major-domo, decked out in gold-sprayed summer whites like a Spanish admiral. Radios everywhere give voice, unrestrained, to *Pagliacci* and sad songs of Naples, bittersweet *stornelli* that tell of rapture and betrayal, to loud pitches for spaghetti and toothpaste and suppositories, and to Perry Como. Athwart the piazza, portly and grave, moves the begabardined form of Piero Caltroni, M.D., fanning himself with his mail. Rumors buzz like bees in this gentle weather: a cow across the valley in Minuto has given birth to a three-headed calf; *turismo* will be booming this summer— the West German mark is as solid as the dollar; Sergeant Parrinello, the town despot, is due for a transfer—bravo!; the caretaker at the Villa Caruso has heard ghastly moans in the small hours, and has seen flickering green lights. Specters! Ghosts! Rumors! At two in the afternoon all falls silent. There can be heard only cowbells clanging in the valley or the sound of a bus horn, or, far off, the whistle of some coastwise ship plowing southward toward Reggio Calabria or Sicily.

It has been said that most suicides occur when the air is balmy, the sky blue, the sunlight unclouded, jovial and golden; the writhing amputee, skewered upon life like a wingless June bug, finds the climate of spring a heartless last insult, and so gives up the ghost. No doubt it was just this weather that caused Cass, on the morning of the day he met Mason, to dream this fearful nightmare, so poisoned and festering with the casts of self-destruction.

He was in an airplane. High above the Andes he flew, in drifts of cloud and mist, above Aconcagua and Cotopaxi and Chimborazo, their peaks threatening, billowing with the dark fleece and rack of a thousand soundless storms. The plane was crowded with faceless people; there was a constant dim murmuration—a faintly heard, barely discerned babble of humming and chuckles and remote sibilant whispers—and this murmuration chilled him to the bone, touched as it was with the sound of doom. Music, too, attended this flight of his through space, a discordant, atonal sound as of some bizarre ensemble playing off-key yet in unison, a saxophone, a harpsichord, a tuba, a kazoo; and the music like the constant ebb and flow and hum of voices seemed tinged with premonitions of death. Presently then he got up and went to the bathroom. There was a shower stall here—a strange accommodation, he thought, for an airline, for it was vast and made of concrete and in the corners there were damp, enormous webs where spiders as big as saucers feasted upon struggling insects. Panic enveloped him, and terror; the plane pitched and rocked, and as it did so he found himself taking off all his clothes. Then—wonder of wonders —he had withdrawn from himself. Standing aside, clammy and wet with horror, he saw his other self, naked now, step into the shower and, with the numb transfixed look of one already dead, turn on all the faucets full blast. The spiders trembled in their webs, shriveling; a sense of strangulation, of asphyxia. Christ! he heard his watching self dream, for it was not water which emerged from the nozzles but the billowing jets of suffocating gas. The murmuration grew in volume and tempo, joined by the tuba, ponderously belching, and the panic kazoo. Now naked and blue beneath the rush of gas, his other self grew rigid, skin shiny as a turquoise bead, and toppled soundless to the floor, all life extinct. And he, watching, tried to reach out to his corpse, but here several sporty Negroes entered, shouldering him aside, and leaned over the blue body, shaking their heads and grieving. "Man, why did you kill him?" one said, looking up. "Man, why did you let him die?" But before he could answer the Negro, the plane pitched again, vibrating as if rent by mammoth claps of thunder. And now a ripe mulatto girl, entering too, seeing the cadaver, shrieked, shrieked again and again and, as if to obliterate the sight not just from her own but from all eyes, pulled down a shade upon which was written, in blood, this message . . .

He awoke half-strangled beneath the bedclothes, blotting out the message from his mind even as he awoke, and with chill after chill of terror, of insight and knowledge and recognition, coursing through him like the recurring rhythmic ague that accompanies fever.

"Nossir," Cass told me, "I didn't know what that message was, but I knew something else. I mean this crazy chill and thrill of understanding that kept running through me as I lay there in the shadows. I knew *something*."

"How do you mean?"

"Well, dreams, you know. I never put much stock in them. That is, those naval wig pickers in San Francisco used to try to worm a few of them out of me, figuring that they'd be able to plug in on my most intimate circuits, I reckon. I knew they probably had something there and all—I wasn't *that* ignorant—but it did seem to me that it was pretty much my own private business, so whenever they asked me what I dreamt about, I just told them I dreamt about pussy and let it go at that. . . ."

"So?"

"Except, as I say, I knew they were probably on the right track. It really doesn't take any supreme genius to know that these various horrors and sweats you have when you're asleep add up to something, even if these horrors are masked and these sweats are symbols. What you've got to do is get behind the mask and the symbol. . . .

"Well, God *knows*. Jigaboos everywhere! Ever since I'd been in Europe about half of whatever nightmares I'd had—the ones I remembered, anyway—had been tied up with Negroes. Negroes in prison, Negroes being gassed, me being gassed, Negroes watching me *while* I was being gassed. Like that terrible dream I had in Paris. There was always a nigger in the woodpile somewhere, and you'd have thought that as a nice southern boy who was maybe just a little brighter than some of my cornfield brethren I'd have had it all doped out a little bit sooner. But the fact of the matter, you know—and it's probably a blessing—is that dreams, even horrible nightmares, have a way of slipping out of sight once you're awake, with the cobwebs out of your eyes. I say it's a blessing, because I'll bet you there's not one white southerner over the age of fifteen—ten! five!—who hasn't had nightmares just like the one I told you about, or at least variations upon it, replete with Negroes, and blood, and horror. Suppose these nightmares lingered? You'd turn the Southland into a nuthouse. . . ."

He paused. "Well, I don't want to sermonize. I guess like your old man—or what you've told me about him—I'm a way-out liberal, for a southerner anyway. Comes from living with the Yankees for so long and marrying one. On the other hand, I despise these goddam northerners who've never been south of Staten Island and are out to tell everybody down here they've got to hew to the line, right now by God, with no wait and no pause and because we know it's good for you, and it's humane, and it's decent and American, and who pretend that Harlem and the Chicago ghettoes don't exist. The bastards just don't *know* what's going on down here.

"But no sermonizing. The point is that there in Europe I was being wakened up in many different ways. God knows it was tough, and sometimes you'd never know it from some of the things I did, but I was being awakened, and now I can see that some of these dreams and nightmares which I remember so vividly were a part of the awakening.

"Take that dream I told you about. Well, first—try to remember. When you were a kid did you ever holler 'nigger' at anybody?"

I reflected for a moment. "Yes," I said. "What kid hasn't? I mean in the South."

"Did you ever do anything else—*mean,* that is—to someone who was colored? Really mean, that is?"

Pondering my early youth, I could dredge up nothing more sinister than that sorry old epithet, hoarsely shouted. "We'd yell at them from the school bus I used to ride on," I said. "Maybe some of the other boys would heave a rotten orange. Nothing more than that. They're rather genteel about such matters in Virginia, you know."

"That's what you think," he said sourly, but with a sort of smile.

"What do you mean?"

"Well, that morning—the same morning I ran into Mason— when I woke up with that dream still hovering in my mind, these chills were still going up and down my back, these chills of recognition, you see, and all of a sudden I knew what it all meant. No, it wasn't as clear and as pat as all that, but right there simultaneously with my waking up I remembered something wretched and horrible that I had done when I was about fifteen years old— something really dreadful and wicked that I must have kept way back in my mind all these years. And floating over me like the palest big fat blob of a balloon you ever saw was the image of this guy I hadn't thought of in so long that for a while I couldn't remember his name. Then it came back to me. Lonnie."

"Lonnie," he repeated.

"Lonnie?"

"Well, let me tell you about it." And now, on the lovely river Ashley, lolling against a pine stump, he told me of something which, seventeen years before, had brought him for the first time into the slovenly presence of shame. He told of the summer of his fifteenth year—or was he sixteen? One year either way, no matter how you looked at it, could not mitigate the crime—when his uncle bought him a bus ticket and farmed him out (as had been his habit from time to time during those depression years when the bottom dropped out of the bright-leaf tobacco market) to a first cousin once removed, Hoke Kinsolving by name, who lived up in southside Virginia in a dinky sun-blistered town called Colfax, pop. 1,600, altitude sea level, in a part of the commonwealth no tourist intent on Williamsburg palaces and elegant river mansions had ever seen or heard of, and boasting in the business way only a peanut warehouse, a lumber mill, a sagging cotton gin and a Western Auto store. Cass remembered that summer for many things (fifteen! He *must* have been, for he came to manhood then, neither early nor late, but enormously and unforgettably, as all men do, in this case after watching Veronica Lake in the sweltering one-horse movie house, and later half-fainting in the throbbing dark, among the summery-smelling mimosas behind his cousin's house)—for the mimosas themselves and their pale pink watery blossoms, and the dust rising from the scorched back alleys of the town, and old ladies fanning themselves on front porches drenched in green shadow, and mockingbirds caroling thunderously at sunup—for a hundred gentle memories, purely summer, purely southern, which swarmed instantly through his mind, though one huge memory encompassed all. Vaguely, this involved his cousin Hoke, who, being a corn and peanut farmer nearly as poor as his old uncle, got him a part-time job at the Western Auto store, working in the back among the stacked-up tires and cartons of radio tubes and hubcaps and tools odorous of rubber and oil; more distinctly, more clearly, more threateningly, it came to mean someone called Lonnie (if he had a last name Cass never knew it), who was a man of twenty-one or so with bad teeth and a caved-in sallow face and a broad plastered-down wig of unparted, Lucky Tiger fragrant, custard-colored hair. Lonnie was the assistant manager. Now, had I ever been to Sussex County and seen a real Virginia gentleman in operation? No? *Ecco* Lonnie then, who to be sure was somewhat unlettered, a Baptist and only half a cut removed from trash and all, yet a soul neither deluded nor demented and the fairest flower of southern manhood. Let us remember, too, that this was Virginia, Peter, my own Virginia, the Virginia of stately châteaux and green carpeted lawns and bony aristocrats on horseback, the Virginia of the outlawed lynching and the soft word and the enlightened (mildly) Jeffersonian notion of justice—not Mississippi, not Alabama, not Georgia, but the Old Dominion, home of conservatism leavened by gentility and breeding and by a gentlemanly apprehension of democracy. To be sure, Colfax was not that Virginia so dear to chamber-of-commerce pamphleteers—the sunny commonwealth containing so many varied riches: eighteenth-century ladies richly draped in velvet and crinoline, by candlelight shepherding the credulous fritter-stuffed visitor through opulent hallways at Westover and Shirley and Brandon; or darkies starched to the neck and in cocked hats and satin pantaloons looking just like they did when Marse William Byrd owned the whole James River from Richmond to the sea; or that quaint ivy-shuttered church where Patrick Henry voiced his immortal cry for freedom —no, this was a Virginia that no one ever knew, the flat hot Virginia of swamps and scrub pine and sludgy lowland rivers and pigs snorting among the peanut vines, and flop-eared mules, but all the same Virginia. And Lonnie.

Well, Lonnie had a queer way with Negroes, Cass went on, the shy, faltering field niggers who in that county were well over half of the population. A really queer way, around the store. Not that there was any hostility in him, any meanness or severity; indeed, it was all quite to the opposite. Badinage was his trick, and cajolery, and such a light-hearted tomfoolishness marked his way with the customers that you might have thought that he was the darkies' original friend—not a nigger lover, understand, for his manner was loaded with too much condescension for that. Nonetheless, with all of his raillery and banter, his knowing digs, the teasing patter he'd keep up through some fifty-cent transaction, you might never have suspected that behind those mashed-in features and beneath that blond pomaded hair raked so slickly back was boiling trouble, ready to explode. Certainly Cass, if he could remember having given Lonnie and his breezy ways any thought at all, was full of approval; he was old enough to appreciate that southern remark, "He gets along good with the niggers," which in mercantile circles is meant as a compliment, and implies good business. Take that afternoon in August, for instance—the one Cass recalled so well—and take the way that Lonnie dealt with a certain grizzled old-timer, black as doom itself, who shambled in to buy a radiator-cap ornament for his 1931 Model-A Ford. Blazing heat, and the smell of oil and a vulcanized odor, and sticky flies zigzagging over all. "You mean this ain't fancy enough, Jupe?" says Lonnie, yellow teeth bared in a cackle of wicked laughter. "You say you want that nekkid woman anyway? Why by damn, Jupe, an old buzzard like you oughta be ashamed of yourself! Haw! Haw! Haw!" The old man stands sagging in his overalls, a shy smile creases his face. "Taint for me, boss. Like I says, it's my youngest boy's—" "Don't give me any of that, Jupe," says Lonnie, grinning, bare elbows on the counter. "I know why you want that nekkid woman. It's because an old buzzard like you hasn't got any more lead in your pencil. You just want that nekkid lady sittin' there out front *all the time,* so you can get just one more hard-on before you die. Now ain't that right, Jupe? Haw! Haw! Haw!" The old man remains perplexed, embarrassed, grinning, runs a finger through his sparse grizzled hair. "Nossuh, Mistah Lonnie. To tell the truth, my youngest boy—" The words avail him nothing; for five minutes Lonnie teases, nags, cajoles. Large issues are joined: blasted virility, the ravages of age, waning powers, rejuvenation; Lonnie mentions monkey glands, goat serum, a doctor in Petersburg who has done wonders for old buzzards like Jupe. Jupe sweats; Lonnie babbles on: it is hot, business is off, he is bored. At last Lonnie calls to Cass. "Get me that nekkid lady, Cass." Then, "O.K., Jupe," he says largely, "that'll cost you a dollar more'n the other kind."

Later, Cass recalled—sometime later that very afternoon— Lonnie stuck his head into the stockroom, with a quick jerk of his neck said: "All right, boy, come on. We got to go out toward Stony Creek and dispossess a radio. Hump it, boy." Cass humped it. He climbed into the cab of the pickup truck next to Lonnie and they headed out of town. Had Lonnie been afraid, afraid to go through this simple operation alone, so that he required the company and support of a fifteen-year-old boy to redeem a defaulted radio from a Negro farmer who he knew would or could make no protest even if he had been at home; or did he concoct the whole plan beforehand, assuming that the man and his whole family would be in the fields most likely chopping cotton, and needing Cass to bolster him morally not to say physically in an act which already had taken outline in some far fuzzy corner of his brain? Or did what happened occur as a simple impulse of the moment? Cass never knew, nor until that morning he had been awakened in Sambuco by his nightmare had he ever really wondered—but did it matter, after all, since he himself had partaken so inescapably in the blame? He remembered the ride out through the flat hot fields of peanuts and soybean and cotton, and pinewoods blinding-green and tinder-dry, seeming almost to crackle with a parched quality of dryness both dusty and verging on combustion, the stench of gasoline seeping up through the rump-sprung seat as they jounced along, and above all Lonnie, crouched forward bare-elbowed against the wheel, mouthing over the clatter of the unmuffled engine gusts of

countrified, come-to-manhood wisdom. "There's all types of cul-
lud, I'll tell you. Good, bad, and in between. Some like that old
Jupe there you could trust with every nickel you got. Almost
like a white man." Blue sky and fields, and a stretch of riverside
stagnant, foam-flecked, greenly decaying; and a rickety brindle
barn crazily aslant with signs on it: COPENHAGEN, NEHI, BULL
DURHAM. "What this nigger Crawfoot is is a crook, criminal
type." Dusty fields, riverside again, a blue Greyhound bus, tires
clattering and awhine, roaring southward. "And uppity, boy.
He's got a son lives up in Philadelphia, Pennsylvania. Never
saw such monkeyshines. . . . Most niggers'll pay, see, give 'em
enough time. Get a crooked nigger like this Crawfoot and he just
plain don't *intend* to pay, in no way, shape or form." A moldering
columned mansion, set back from the road among ponderous
oak trees; a white metal sign of the commonwealth, glimpsed in
a blur: PLUMTREES. HERE IN APRIL, 1864, UNION DESERTERS
FROM THE ARMY OF GENERAL BURNSIDES . . . "Criminal type
like this Crawfoot is a disgrace on the whole nigger race." On a
rutted side road they turned off, bumping, toward a grove where
a frame church stood with that breezeless, shadowed, weekday
air of benison and tranquillity of Negro temples on a summer afternoon: SHILOH A.M.E. ZION CHURCH, REV. ANDREW SALTER, PAS-
TOR, *Matthew V, 6: "Blessed are they which do hunger and
thirst after righteousness, for they shall be filled."* VISITORS WEL-
COME. Nearby, with a castoff rubber tire taller than themselves,
two Negro children only a shadow beyond babyhood played in the
dust of the road, turned in white-eyed apprehension at Lonnie's
command. "C'mere." Stock-still, they made no move or sign. The
truck pulled ahead twenty feet, stopped. "You kids deaf? Where's
a nigger named Crawfoot live?" No answer, only the wide-eyed
look part incomprehension, part fear, or more exactly that emotion which is perhaps far less fear than the ordinary mistrust
engendered by how many overheard hours of their elders' bitter
and wrathful and despairing complaints of injustices done and
afflictions borne only young Negro children know, and which,
reflected imperfectly in small black faces, white men mistake
for reverence, or at least respect. Neither of them uttered a sound.
"Cat got your tongue? *Crawfoot!*" he repeated. "Where's he live
at?" One thin young black arm finally went up, pointed down
the road toward a cabin, dimly discerned among the pines and a
shimmering gauze of pollen-white dust. "Young'uns near 'bout

worse than the grownups," said Lonnie, grinding gears. "Nits breed lice. That's what Daddy always says."

And then the cabin itself, effaced these years from his memory, or if not effaced then only a dim blur amid the congeries of blurs that made up all his boyhood recollections, but now looming like some habitation whose every sagging board and termite-riddled sill and rusted nail he had committed with the solemnity of an oath to his mind and heart.

"Fantastic!" Cass said beneath his breath, hardly aware at all of whom he was talking to now, as he brought forth a vision of this solitary and forlorn and benighted hut, surrounded by hollyhocks and a bumble of bees and tattered washing on a line, with three creaking rickety steps that rose to an unlocked door which Lonnie, shirt sweatily plastered at his back, threw open with a clatter. "Fantastic!" Cass repeated. "What we did!"

They asked no permission, permission being not only unneeded but beyond remotest contemplation. "Jesus Christ, smell it!" said Lonnie, as the stench—of dirt and sweat and rancid fat cooked up a multitude of times and of too many human bodies in one place, of bathless crotch and armpit, of poverty naked and horrid and unremitting—struck them in the face; Cass drew back gasping. "Nigger house stinks worse than a whorehouse!" Lonnie bawled. "Whoop! Let's get that radio and get out of here!" The radio was not directly found; every country nigger had spies in town, Lonnie explained as they tramped through the deserted cabin; they knew when you're coming to get something, and they hid it. Crawfoot had hid it well. Remorselessly Lonnie searched, with Cass trailing indifferently after, behind the woodstove, beneath the bed and beneath the single stained and reeking mattress, down behind the soot-smeared sills underneath the roof, in the privy outside and in the tiny lime-smelling chicken coop and, backtracking, in the house again, where Lonnie, stubbing his toe against a sprung floorboard, finally reached down behind the planking and, triumphant, fished up the pathetic radio —white, plastic, already cracked, not much larger than a box of salt or rice, which had brought witchery in the night and tinny bright sounds of singing and laughter. "Hid it!" said Lonnie. "The *wise* sonofabitch." A great slanting beam of yellow sunlight, trembling with dust, gushed through the door and filled the house with hazard, with immensity, with flame; Cass remembered this, and the buzzing flies, and joining indissolubly with the whistle of a train in the pine barrens far off, high and rending in that captured moment of South and summer, the single photograph on a table which caught his eye—the family, the man and his wife and his many children and two quizzical white-haired old matriarchs of some other generation, all solemn and standing stiff and straight in cheap Sunday-go-to-meeting, the two-for-a-dollar snapshot already fading and taking on the bluish hue of age but imprisoning still behind its cracked pane of glass one sweetly gentle, calm-visaged mood of solidarity and pride and love. He remembered, too, how this dissolved—or splintered, rather, right before his eyes—as Lonnie (spying the crack on the radio's plastic side he let out a wounded yell which broke in on Cass' reverie like the sound of broken glass) in a frantic swing of rage and frustration and unstoppered resentment thrust his hand violently forward, sweeping with his arm every jar and bottle and can of beans off the shelf above the stove, the momentum carrying him on so that in a sort of final flick or encore of wrath he lighted upon the photograph and sent it spinning across the room, where it tore apart—frame, glass, and all—into two raggedly separated pieces. "Shit!" Cass heard him cry, in a voice pitched near hysteria. "Not only he don't pay for it, he went and broke it, too!" Nor was this the end, it was only the beginning. For as Cass, struck now with horror (though with a queasy visceral feeling of excitement, too), looked at Lonnie, saw the mashed-in face break up into a commotion of pink patches like rouge, he made an involuntary step to retrieve the picture but was fetched up short by Lonnie's voice again: "Well, we'll see about who breaks what!" And then pivoted on his toes, and with the other leg outthrust like a fullback punting a football shot a cowboy-boot-shod foot out against the flimsy kitchen table, hard, and brought the whole clutter of china cups and plates and saucers, sugar in cans, flour and meal and bacon fat, down to the floor in one monstrous and godawful detonation. And from then on he was quiet, giving forth only the faint asthmatic wheezes of a man possessed and in extremity as he went through the cabin upturning chairs, yanking from their moorings the dingy curtains, raking to the floor all such gimcrack mementos as had brought to this place color and loveliness—china dolls, a plaster bulldog brightly enameled, picture postcards (one of which Cass snatched up: *Hell-o All Haveing fine time up hear Love Bertrim*) and a pennant, he strangely, wrenchingly recalled, which read University of Virginia. These came to the floor, as did a maple Grand Rapids chiffonier, a patent heirloom, which Lonnie pried away from the wall and toppled earthward with a squeal of sliding drawers and the snapping uproar of sprung joints and pegs and corners. "That'll teach him!" Lonnie howled. "Where you goin'?" Cass, panicky, had raced already to the open door, froze in mid-stride at the sound of Lonnie's voice. "Come on!" he commanded. "This'll teach every black son of a bitch in this county!" But, *"Ain't you done enough! Ain't you done enough!"* These words, Cass recalled, hung unspoken at the back of his throat—troubled, horrified, but unspoken—and therein, he knew, lay his ponderous share of the blame. For although he was sickened to his entrails in a way he had never been, his newborn manhood—brought to its first test—had failed him. Not only did something within him refuse to allow him to give voice to the monstrousness he felt at his heart and core, but this—

"So he told me to come on," he said, gazing out over the river, as if to summon up all of that bereaved moment entire—ravaged hut wrapped in its stench of poverty and decay, and summery afternoon, and flies buzzing, and bumblebees. "He told me to come on. What was I standing there for? We had to teach every crooked nigger in the county. So we went over to the stove. It was one of those big black cast-iron jobs, I remember, and it was heavy. And what I mean is this. It was wrong, I knew. No, not just wrong—awful, monstrous, abominable. I knew this to my very soul. That goddam picture, and that postcard I'd picked up where he'd thrown it, with this scrawl on it—and that broken plaster bulldog—my heart was near about torn from its roots. But what, for God sake? What made me do it? What?

"That bleeding stove. It was a heavy bugger, see? And on top of it I remember there was a big dishpan filled with dirty water. Well, what happened was, Lonnie grabbed hold underneath, and so did I, and we began to heave and heave until it started to tilt and the dishpan began to slide off. And then you know I remember this, see, how as we stood there bent over heaving and sweating a tremendous warm excitement came over me, a feeling that—well, it was almost a feeling of anger, too, as if I'd picked up some of this young lout of a maniac's fury and was set on teaching the niggers, too. By God, this feeling, you know, I remember it—it was in my loins, hot, flowing, sexual. I knew it was wrong, I knew it, I knew it—bestial, horrible, abominable. I knew all this, understand, but it was as if once I'd lost my courage anyway, once I'd given in—like some virgin, you see, who's finally stopped struggling and said to hell with it—then I could actually do what I was doing almost even with a sense of righteousness. All the clichés and shibboleths I'd been brought up with came rolling back—a nigger wasn't much more than an animal anyway, specially field niggers, crooked niggers like this Crawfoot—so I heaved and pushed there with Lonnie, and the legs of the stove became unstuck and it tilted more and more and finally the whole bleeding mess went toppling over with one hell of a roar and a crash, water and all, stove and stovepipe and dishpan, until it turned that poor little house into what looked like something hit by a tornado. . . ."

He fell silent and although I waited for him to speak again, he said nothing.

"Well, what happened then?" I said finally.

"That was all," he said. "All. We left then. At least it was all I ever heard about it. Oh, maybe Crawfoot complained, I don't know, but if he did nobody ever said anything to me or Lonnie. Of course Crawfoot *should* have complained—he'd probably have gotten a fair shake from the sheriff—but there was that radio, after all. I don't know. I went back anyway, soon after that, back to Carolina. But you know it's true," he added after a pause.

"What?" I said.

"Until all those well-meaning people up North understand characters like Lonnie, and characters like this young Epworth Leaguer Cass Kinsolving, this downy Christian who was age fifteen and pure of heart and mind and didn't mean no harm, really, to nobody, but was cruel and dangerous as almighty hell —until they understand about such matters and realize that they've got as many Lonnies and as many young Casses in dear old Dixie as they've got boll weevils, they'd better tread with care. It's *those* two guys that's going to make the blood flow in the streets." He paused. "But what I'm getting at is something else, you see. It was bad enough to do what I did. Certain things are so monstrous there is no atonement for them, no amends. I reckon I should be able to tell you a nice redemption story, about how I maybe robbed the auto store at night and went back to that cabin and laid a hundred dollars on the doorstep, to pay for all the wreckage. Or ran down Lonnie with a truck. Something clean and honorable like that, very American and all. But of course I didn't. I went on back home and put the whole thing out of my mind." He fell silent for a moment again, then said: "Except I didn't put the whole thing out of my mind at all." He rose from his seat against the pine stump, and stood erect, gazing out over the river.

"No, there are no amends or atonement for a thing like that. But there is another thing, and though it won't bring back any busted stove or plaster bulldog or picture either, it's something, and it's strong. What I mean is, you live with it. You live with it even when you've put it out of your mind—or think you have—and maybe there's some penance or justice in that.

"I think maybe sometimes you'll be able to see how this figured in with what happened to me there in Sambuco. I remember that morning so well. The nightmare, and the chills running up and down my back—these chills of pure recognition and understanding—and then, after that, just lying there, for the first time in as long as I could remember thinking of Lonnie and his ugly flat mug, and the cabin and the smell, and the picture and those sweet sad proud black faces, like ghosts still haunting me after so many years. And the guilt and the shame half-smothering me there in bed, adding such a burden to the guilt and shame I already felt that I knew that, shown one more dirty face, one more foul and unclean image of myself, I would not be able to support it.

"And then that morning! Staggering out into that lemony spring morning afloat with pollen and bees, and a strumming of music and rich-throated huckstering shouts and cries and a great shrilling choir of birds as if the Lord Himself had turned into a field full of fat larks gone all berserk with beauty and joy. And me adrift in the midst of all this ecstasy—hung-over, hacking up my guts, and feeling about the size of a gnat. That nightmare kept working on me, coming back in sort of fitful flickers. I felt like slitting my throat.

"And then on top of that there was Mason and this damn Kasz business."

"What was that?"

"Well, this painter fellow Kasz that Mason got me confused with. One thing, I'd never even heard of him, famous as he was. That's how far I was removed from America and the art world and so on. It was really quite comical—the first part—in a grisly way. What apparently happened, you see, was this. Mason had just landed in Naples with Rosemarie and this cerise Cadillac of his and he came up to Sambuco and became so smitten by the place that he figured this would be just the spot to settle down in and write his play. Well, what I gathered later is that he fell into conversation with Windgasser, who not only sold Mason on taking up quarters in the palace, but also let drop the fact that there was an American painter living downstairs. Now you know that marble-mouthed way of speaking Windgasser had. He says 'Cass' in an offhand way probably, and Mason jumps to the conclusion that it's the famous mad painter of Rimini. I don't guess it was very sharp of Mason, but it was an honest enough mistake, given Windgasser's diction, and given Mason's personality, and you know this kind of letch he had for—well, capital-A art and artists, this Bohemian streak he had. And even someone as coony as Mason could forget that Kasz was a bachelor and lived in Rimini with his mother and so on. Anyway, what he obviously thought was that I was this crazy Polack, this wonder-boy of American art, and he moved right on in upstairs. God only knows what he was really thinking, but it might have been something like: This is it. Man oh man I'm in clover. Me and old Kasz, living it up art wise on the Amalfi coast. Shuck all that phony movie and Broadway world I've been in so long and finally get cracking on the *vie artistique*. I think he figured it'd be just him and Kasz, living it up together from then on out. Sort of like all the great historic friendships—you know, Van Gogh and Gauguin—only he'd be the writing end and Kasz'd be the painting and sculpting end and they'd go down through the ages together, hand in hand, as cozy as two burrs on a hound-dog's ear. Only to really get this good thing going he had to be quite cool and calm and collected about it, if you see what I mean. That is, he couldn't present himself and go in there with a couple of big paws stuck out and drooling all over like some auxiliary Elk. Especially I guess when he must have heard that this guy was something of an oddball and might take a poke at him if he looked like he was some tourist on the make. No, he had to be real cool and reserved, you see, and all the ass-kissing had to come in very subtly, and that's just what he done.

"Well anyway, that morning I was standing there on the balcony, trying to get that nightmare out of my system, when I heard this big commotion out in the courtyard. What it was, of course, was a bunch of Fausto's slaves tramping about and carrying Mason's junk up to the top part of the palace. Such elegant paraphernalia you never saw—aluminum luggage and leather luggage and golf clubs and a dozen hatboxes and God knows what all. I just stood there blinking for a while in my skivvies, trying to figure out what was going on and who had come to stay, and then just as I started to go back inside, the outer door to the courtyard flung itself open, and there he stood—this loose long lanky Mason, handsome as a Vitalis ad and looking about as American as it's possible to get, with his huge beautiful Rosemarie clutching at his arm. I can remember it as clearly as I can remember anything in my life—Mason standing there with this sort of expensive white flannel costume on, and sun glasses, and a pleasant inquisitive half-grin on his face, as amiable-looking as you'd ever want to ask, along with this really ingratiating quality of being somewhat lost and confused and being ever so grateful if you'd just point him in the right direction, and with that great blond undulating hunk of sex, that wonderful Rolls-Royce of a humping machine draped over his elbow. And then as I stood there with my mouth hanging open, Mason stepped forward with Rosemarie slinking beside him and came up to me and said, cool but oh so infinitely polite: 'Cass?' He was just chock-full of politesse and humanity and good breeding, and he stuck out his hand and without knowing it I stuck out mine and took it, and then he gave a thin well-bred friendly little smile, saying, 'I've been wanting to meet you very, very much,' and it was all done with such grace and aplomb that it would have melted the heart out of a brass monkey. Well, what do you do in a situation like that? I guess at first it flashed through my mind that this was the beginning of some kind of a con game, yet he really didn't look like a man who was out to sell me anything— he was too beautifully decked out for that—and I suppose I just figured that if he wanted to call me by my first name it was a little forward and familiar coming from a total stranger, but he was an American, after all, and Americans were glad-handers in general, and that if he wanted to meet me very much it was only because Windgasser had told him I was an old hand, more or less, and he wanted to get checked out on life in Sambuco. Anyway, I was a real pushover, I'll tell you.

"So I allowed as how I was me and just as I tried to apologize for being in my underdrawers he introduced me to Rosemarie, and she gave a sort of whinny—I think she must have been as awe-struck at what she thought was the golden boy of art as Mason was, or even more so—and bubbled that she was so pleased to meet me and all, and stuck those beautiful knockers in my face, and said, 'We'd heard you were ever so unapproachable. Why, there's nothing stand-offish about you at all!' I remember that word, stand-offish. Frankly I didn't know what the hell she was talking about, but if that's what she had heard about me and I wasn't that way at all, and if she was willing to come here and parade that beautiful lush body around and give me the impression that she was ready to smother me with it on the spot, then I didn't care what she was driving at. All that flesh! That tremendous heaving wonderland of a groaning carnal paradise! To think that that great walking Beautyrest of a woman was all wasted on Mason. It's enough to break your heart, even now.

"Anyway, there wasn't too much else to do but invite them in. I put on a pair of pants and of course the place looked like an accident ward, but as a matter of fact I imagine that's just what they were set up to expect from a mad genius. On the way in I remember Mason patting me on the back and saying, 'Somehow I expected a more frail and wiry person.' Well, I guess it crossed my mind that Fausto had given him a complete if inaccurate run-down on me, and I vaguely wondered why, but I was still in the dark, see—deaf, dumb, and blind—so I shrugged it off and muttered something pleasant and got the conversation switched around to him. Because up until then he hadn't explained himself at all. So while I was fixing up the coffee on the hot plate and Rosemarie stood at the window ooh-ing and ah-ing at the view, old Mason just plunked himself down in the armchair and rared back and really gave me the works. What a snow job! Said he was doing Europe and all, said he was fed up with the New York rat race, and said he finally realized that here in Sambuco was the place he'd always longed for. And it's funny, you know, the impression he created while he talked—it was all as charming as hell. These little wry jokes about himself, and funny little puns and sour remarks and so on. And the way he conveyed to me that he was a playwright and a man of talent—it was subtle as hell. Things like saying in a flat, offhand, mildly disgusted voice, 'Critical success in the theater, you know, is synonymous with popular success,' and you must hand it to him, that's about as cagey and collected as you can get in the fine art of prevarication, because it was in regard to a play of his he said had been produced the year before, and had flopped. I mean, a real clumsy cross-eyed blunderer of a liar would have fallen all over himself trying to snow a person with his success. But not Mason. No, you see, too *fragrant* a lie would get found out. So he works on the premise that Waldo probably don't keep up with the theater, being so far away and doubtless having little interest in it anyway, so that a nice soft medium-sized lie will do, and he very artfully mentions his play, and says that it flopped, and tags on this kind of embittered but manfully stoical remark about critical and popular success, so that in the end the effect is simply that of a dedicated artist who has been hooted down by the rabble and the dim-witted critics yet has the courage to keep his chin up and struggle on. What an actor Mason was! He could have sold rotgut whiskey to the W.C.T.U. He sure impressed me, all right, so that by the time we'd finished the coffee and he'd dropped a few names—but tastefully, you see, and just the ones anybody might recognize in the theater—we were almost what you might say buddy-buddy—no, not that exactly, but I'd taken a shine to him, in a casual way.

"Well, along about then began the really touching part. We sat there in the sunlight on the balcony for a while, chatting and admiring the view. About this time Rosemarie looked over and gave a kind of mental nudge to Mason. Then a little flicker passed across his face and he turned and beamed at me and said in the nicest way: 'I wonder if you'd do us a really extraordinary favor. I know—' And he paused, then went on: 'Well, I know how reticent you are about showing your work to strangers. And the Lord knows I don't want to appear *presumptuous*. But I wonder if you'd do us the great favor of letting us look at some of your work. We'd just—" And then he paused again with this sort of half-flustered and abashed look on his face, as if he felt he was being presumptuous after all. Then Rosemarie clutched her hands together and turned them outwards and tucked them into her crotch like women do, and she leaned forward and chimed in with a 'Please do! Oh please do!' Well, you could have dropped me on the spot with a broomstraw. Would I show them my work? Would I show them my *work*? Why, it was like asking some beat-up lifer of a convict if he'd care to have the keys to the front gate. Bleeding God, what a question to ask! In going on close to ten years I could count on my fingers the number of people who had wanted to see my work, or had seen it—outside of maybe Poppy and the kids, and the strays you pick up looking over your shoulder in the park or somewhere, and a couple of goofy dogs or so. Now here comes this nice, clean-cut, charming young American, and he's not only so engaging and witty but he's also dying to see my work—can you see how I might have been taken by the guy? Well, I guess I beamed

383

a bit, and blushed, and went through the old gee-whiz routine, and then after a while I relented and said something like: 'Well, if you really want to.' And they began to look happy about that, and expectant, you know, and then all of a sudden it occurred to me that maybe all of us, both them and me, had bitten off a little bit more than we could chew. Because the fact of the matter was that—well, I just didn't have a hell of a lot to show off. In the first place, I simply hadn't done much in a long, long time. In the second place, practically everything I'd done that I considered halfway decent I'd done in America and had stored at Poppy's house in New Castle, and all the rest I had with me—this really grim, interior, tight-assed stuff I'd done in Paris and Rome—was work I really couldn't be proud of at all. But Mason and Rosemarie were still insisting and prodding me, you see, and as I say I was in quite a glow over all this attention—it still hadn't occurred to me to wonder just who in hell had told them I was reticent—and so finally I got to my feet and gave a sort of boyish grin and said: 'Well, if you really want to see them, it's not much but—O.K.' And I remember them giving these sly, knowing, tickled little looks to each other, pretty much for my benefit, all as if to say, 'Heavens, how charming this guy is with all his modesty.'

"So I went downstairs to the *guardaroba* where I had everything stored and I drug up all of this miserable, pallid, ineffectual, self-centered stuff I'd done for the past several years: five or six dreary figures and landscapes in oil, and some water colors, and seven or eight ink and crayon sketches—that was about all. And I brought the whole pathetic mess back upstairs and got some books out to prop up the unrolled canvases against the wall, and rummaged around and found some tacks to peg the upper corners to the molding, and set out the water colors and the sketches around the room so that they'd be displayed with the proper delicacy and dignity. And even as I was doing all this—proud and hopeful in a way, see, and just itching and itching for some kind of praise—I began to sweat and tighten up inside, knowing every second that it was all an outrageous disaster from beginning to end. But as you know, Mason was never one to be daunted by the mere realities of a situation, and neither was Rosemarie, for that matter. If this character was the young—the young tycoon of American art, the big wheel, the golden young Leonardo of the mid-twentieth century, well by God you can bet your hat and ass that Mason and Rosemarie were going to make no gaffes in the maestro's presence. Nossir. They were going to be properly rever-

ent and humble—not abased, see, not inferior or servile or anything like that, because that would be pretty unsophisticated—
but just properly reverent about this magic art, and humble, just
like anyone should be, after all, who doesn't know or feel a
goddam thing about painting, but is *up* on it, having gotten all the
latest poop in *Life* magazine. So in they slunk from the balcony,
wreathed in rosy expectation. Godalmighty, you should have seen
them. For the life of *me,* I couldn't figure them out. You couldn't
have asked for more wonderment, for more fatuous credulity,
from a pair of beauticians on a pilgrimage to Albert Schweitzer.
Or some other Great Soul. Yet still they were playing it cool, you
see. They wanted to think about it a bit, to ponder and muse and
absorb—to soak it up, if you see what I mean. So they began to
pass very slowly around the room, lingering for a long time before
each painting or sketch and murmuring to each other in these
voices that were almost inaudible, and they were holding hands,
and every now and then—with their backs to me, you see—I'd
see Rosemarie's hand clutch his in a kind of convulsion and she'd
give a little gasp of wonderment or delight that I could barely
hear, and they'd be cocking their heads to one side and another
like a couple of parakeets. 'Aha!' Mason would say. 'I see you're
flirting with the representational. Interesting phase.' And I really
mean it—I was snowed for a long while there. Because although
I felt deep down that this stuff I had done was pretty feeble, who
after all was I to tell? These two certainly didn't seem to be fakers;
if anything they seemed to be more honest and earnest—more
genuine, you might say—than almost any young Americans I
had seen in Europe. They seemed to really *care,* if you know what
I mean, and perhaps I was all wrong about what I'd done. I remember that it passed across my mind with a sense of delight that
was almost like rapture that maybe this, after all, was the turning
point. I mean, maybe what I had done all this time was really
terrific, was basically first-rate stuff, only my own miserable self-
loathing had not allowed me to accept the fact or to grant the
worth, so that all that had been needed all along was somebody
like this guy Mason to hop out of nowhere like a genie from a
bottle and put me on the road to acceptance and affirmation—
salvation, even. What crap.

"It wasn't really too long before I began to sense vaguely that
something really was quite screwy somewhere. They were just a
little bit too wrapped up in this personal awe of theirs, you see.
What with all the hand-squeezing and the sighing and so on, and

Rosemarie's little gasps and the husky sort of half-whistles Mason put out every now and then, I began to feel—well, somewhat ill-at-ease, I guess. And besides, I guess they figured it was time to open up a little, it was time for Act Two, and they began to make more comments. And they were the goddamdest comments you ever heard. I remember one in particular. In Rome I remember I'd gone up on the Palatine and made two or three sketches one day, each one worse than the next. I can't describe them. They were tight-assed, if you know what I mean. That is, the basic idea was good, but nothing in them gave or flowered, spread out, encompassed, whatever the word is. They remained fidgety, selfish little corners of some private view, a bunch of aborted, stunted notions wriggling in a vacuum. I kept them anyway, I don't know why—maybe because the idea at least had been good—and anyway I showed them to Mason and Rosemarie with all the rest. A school kid could have seen how aimless and pointless they were, but not Mason. And not Rosemarie, either. Because, as I say, the second act had begun and they had decided to show just how bleeding sharp and sensitive they were. Mason turned around and looked me square in the eye and said, 'God, man, the sense of *space*. It's absolutely uncanny.' And Rosemarie wasn't missing a trick, either, I'll tell you. Without turning, and before Mason could open his mouth again, she stood there, with her head bent down on this poor little strangulated fetus of a drawing and I heard a long inspiration of breath and then she said, so help me God, 'Not only space, Muffin. The incredible humanity.'

"Well, I began to get a sneaky feeling right then and there. There wasn't no more space or humanity in those drawings than you could stuff up the back end of a flea, really, but in spite of this I was about to put them down as a couple of misguided people who were nonetheless trying desperately to be kind, when Mason opened his mouth again, staring at me with these sort of soft, compassionate, wonder-filled eyes, and said: '*They* were right. You have a true vision. True and pure.' Then wheeled about again quickly, as if he couldn't trust his own emotions, and commenced looking and cocking his head and whistling once more. Well, now who in the hell were *they?* This time I guess you can imagine my suspicions really began to rise. They had me really buffaloed, these two, but mind you I still didn't catch on to what was up. I guess it was too big an experience—I mean, having somebody interested in my work—for me to see clearly much farther than my own flattered ego. I just stood around behind them as they wandered around the room, clenching my hands together like Charlie Chan and licking my lips and coughing self-consciously every time they sighed or made a remark. Finally, after about ten minutes of this, they drew up to a halt before this canvas I'd done in Paris the year before—it wasn't too bad, either, a sort of impressionistic thing with a lot of color of Montparnasse rooftops—and Mason went into his familiar spasm and turned and clenched his teeth and said something—oh, I forget exactly what, but it put me several hundred miles past Matisse—and then after a long pause he said: 'Haven't I seen this before?' Then before I could say anything, or even think, Rosemarie picked up the cue and said: 'Muffin, I was thinking the very same thing!' But then, she said slowly, and rolled her eyes: 'I know it couldn't have been in that show in New York. Because wasn't it true, dearest, that they didn't have any of his oils?' And then she shot me an artful glance, and let it slide off, and said: 'I think it's maybe because it has that—well, that *je ne sais quoi*—that universal quality that reminds me of *all* paintings.' So help me God. Well, of course, that did it. I finally knew that something was really hideously wrong—I didn't know what exactly, but these two people sure had blundered into the wrong shop—and I was about to open up and very delicately try to get the whole situation straightened out, when in Poppy bounced with about twenty-five balloons and the kids, and half a dozen village children shrieking and trailing after."

"Tell me," I said, "how in the world did you get the terrible business over with? What did you say to them? What did you do?"

"Well, it was tough, you know. I've always been twisted completely out of shape by such situations, even ones less serious than that. I don't know what it is, because I don't think I'm a real coward when you get right down to it. I guess I'd just rather see people have their illusions, rather than break them up and in the process make them seem even slightly stupid or silly. It's a failing, I guess, but I've never really been able to conquer it. When I first went to art school in New York, I remember, the instructor thought my name was Mr. Applebaum, don't ask me why, and for the longest kind of time I let him believe it—afraid to make him look like an ass—until it went on so long that it really became too late to tell him—then we both would have looked like idiots, you see—so I guess to this day if he ever remembers me he thinks of that nice Mr. Applebaum, from North Carolina.

"Anyway—Jesus Christ, lead us not into temptation. . . .

Well, just like McCabe up in Rome, you see, Mason had him a bottle of whiskey. Twelve-year-old Scotch it was, too. He poured me out a stiff belt and had a weak one for himself, and pretty soon the glow was on. I remember along about here he went over to the balcony again and stood there looking out. And he was silent for a while, sort of musing; with his nose sticking out over the rim of his glass, and then he came out with this whispered line in German. *Kennst du das Land wo die Zitronen blüh'n?* Then he turned and looked at me with this little wistful half-smile on his face and said: 'At last I know. Honest to God, it's crazy beyond belief. At last I know, Waldo, what Goethe meant when he had his vision of Eden.' And I reckon I was getting a little dreamy, on four ounces of Chivas Regal too, but I was damned if I was going to let this guy outdo me in the poetry line, so not to be topped, I said that yes, I understood what he meant, it was an earthly paradise, all right, and that it oft reminded me of those lines in praise of Attica to my old friend Oedipus at Colonus—to wit, and I quoted: 'Nor fail the sleepless founts whence the waters of Cephisus wander, but each day with stainless tide he moveth over the plains of the land's swelling bosom, et cetera.' What a real collusion of frauds! Except, as I say, I was still worried deep down how I was going to straighten out this confusion of identities. You have no idea how embarrassing it is to be called Waldo in all earnestness when your name is something else.

"As usual, the booze took care of everything and worked the situation out in its own sweet way. Which of course is to say that it wasn't more'n about fifteen minutes before I was plastered to the eyeballs. And now that I look back on it, I don't suppose that Mason could ever forgive me for what I said and what I had done. He was being so phony and he was trying so hard, you see, only he had the wrong man. He was barking up the wrong tree, and when I finally got going there—spilling out all my bile and poison—I must have really hit him where he lived. Anyway, along about then Poppy took Rosemarie and the kids out for a stroll down into the piazza and Mason and I were alone. We started chatting again and I remember I had gotten up to pour me out another shot when at this point the damndest thing happened. . . ."

Cass fell silent, and closed his eyes briefly, as if trying to recapture the moment in its reality. "As soon as I caught sight of her I was struck that I could have seen her these two times and each time forgotten her, and then see her again and be touched all over by the same sort of million-fingered joy and delight at her beauty. What she had done, you see, was to give a timid little knock at the door while Mason and I were talking. We hadn't heard the knock and she was just standing there, God knows how long, in this sort of frowzy, shabby croker-sack of a dress and her naked feet were planted firmly on the floor and as I came toward her she reached up and slapped at a fly and then she folded her hands together in front of her. It would be easy to romanticize that moment, you know, and tell you how her hair had the fragrance of camellias and her skin the hue and sheen of fairest marble, but you saw her—you know how she looked—and the fact of the matter is that she smelled like a cowshed and she had streaks of reddish dirt running up her bare legs. But no matter. She had brushed her brown hair till it shone with a silver luster and she didn't crack a smile when I came over and looked into her grave and lovely face.

"Funny thing, I had noticed Mason had gotten up and was giving her the once-over. It was really a hungry look he was giving her. It annoyed me somehow, boozy as I was. I motioned her out into the courtyard where we could talk. I said, 'Are you the girl that Luigi and Signora Carotenuto sent?' And she said yes, then I said, 'What's your name?' and she said 'Francesca, Francesca Ricci.' My heart was pounding like a bleeding schoolboy's, and I must have had an oafish look on my face, because I was suddenly aware that she was looking up at me with a puzzled expression and then I heard her say anxiously. 'I knocked, signore, but you didn't hear me, you didn't hear.' As if I suspected her of robbing the joint. Then, as much as I hated to, I came to the point instead of beating around the bush and prolonging the contact, so to speak. I said: 'I'm sorry. *Mi dispiace.* But you will have to go away. There was a mistake made. I just can't afford to hire anyone.' And then this terrible look of sorrow came over her face, and she looked out into the street with her eyes full of the purest grief, and I thought she was going to blubber at any minute. I've often wondered whether a quality of pity wasn't rooted in the heart of love just as much as beauty is, or desire; whether a part of love wasn't just the perfectly human, uncondescending, magnanimous yearning to shelter in your arms someone else who is hurt or lost or needs comfort. Anyway, there she stood looking so raggedy and shabby and wretched—so *poor,* there doesn't have to be any other word—that I could have bit off my tongue for causing her such misery and disappointment. But I couldn't very well back down; what I'd said was true, and that was the simple fact of the situation. I said: 'I am very sorry, but I've had a recent *disgrazia*. You'll just have to go away. It is something beyond my control. I know you need the money very much and I'm terribly sorry but you'll just have to go away.' Pretty soon she looked up at me again with her lips quivering and said: 'I can cook and sew, signore. I can scrub clothes and clean the house.' And then she said in a sort of quick anxious gasp in this horrible English she had picked up: 'I can wash over the kildren!' Then I said: *'Che?'* And then I understood what she meant and I found myself laughing. But not much, because as I laughed her eyes got more and more lost and mournful and despairing, and finally she broke down and stuck her head into her hands and began to sob. And at this point I began to tramp up and down the courtyard muttering to myself and coughing behind my hand, all in an absolute sweat, you see—wanting her to stay if only for a few more minutes just so I could feast my eyes on her, but at the same time trying to figure out a way to get her out of there before I busted out bawling myself. Finally I went up to her and took her by the shoulders as gently as I could and said firmly: 'You *cannot stay.* I have no money to pay you. Don't you understand?' She kept on sobbing, and it was all I could do to keep from taking her in my arms and soothing her and telling her that everything in the end would be all right, but I knew that everything in the end would not be all right so I just stood there and patted her on the shoulders and snuffled and groaned to myself. Then finally she looked up at me and here is what she said. It's hard to describe her manner, because in the midst of her grief she was proposing something that a girl might find hard to do even in the midst of composure or good spirits or joy, but she looked up at me with these woeful red-rimmed eyes and said with the merest pathetic suggestion of some wan dispirited coquetry: 'I know you are an artist, signore. I could pose for you well, and do *anything*—' But I shushed her up and said, 'Yes,' because if she had to go as far as this *anything* then her distress was deeper even than the distress she had been weeping over, and I figured we'd be able to work out an answer somehow. So I said: 'Yes.' And then I said: 'You won't have to pose for me or anything. You just come and cook for us and wash over the kildren. I'll find a way to pay you.' And in a moment she had vanished, and I felt an undertone of trouble myself, but with you might say a kind of warm gentle joy along with it, like a man who knows a tremendous secret. . . ."

Again he fell silent, and when he resumed talking, after a long pause, it was with a laugh that had very little humor in it at all. "Now that I recall it, I don't think Mason had been eavesdropping. Bald as he could be and all, he was careful about most of the more obvious amenities. But when I turned around he was standing there in the doorway, gazing at the outer door of the courtyard where Francesca had gone. But even if I thought he had been listening in—in which case he couldn't have understood a word, since the Italian language remained as dark to him as Icelandic right up to the very end—it wasn't this that griped me and tore at me so as what he said then. 'Now that looks like real tail, Waldo,' he said, rubbing his finger up against the side of his ear. 'There's nothing like a round little behind to make me bloom like a rose.' Then he said: 'Where did you dig her up?'

"Maybe this was meant as a really *virile* observation, to offset all the art appreciation and the poetry. But the look on his face was pink and greasy and what he said was like a slap in the face in this hot and disrupted condition I was in. Now that I look back on it I can understand that maybe he didn't mean anything insulting by it, and actually he was even trying to impress me. Hell, it was a remark I might have made myself, about somebody I didn't care anything for. For one thing, she was obviously just a poor little peasant and he couldn't have suspected how she had set me rocking and churning. But the other thing, of course, is that Mason was just like that. The universal man he thought of himself as, the bleeding equilateral triangle of the perfect human male, an aesthete who could quote you half a line from Rilke and Rimbaud and you name it, and dream of himself potting tigers in Burma and getting gored in Seville, and balance himself off as the most glorious stud that ever crept between two sheets. And since he was none of these things to no degree he had to talk a lot, to make you believe he was all of them." He hesitated for a moment. "Christ, I'm trying to be fair to this guy!" he said with sudden passion and bitterness. "He was bright, too, bright as hell—a marvel even, in his amateur way. What made him such a swine? Such a—" He stopped, lips trembling.

"I don't know," I said. "I just don't know." For the briefest space of time I had the notion that Mason, sprung forth in spirit from the grave, was sitting in judgment on our judgment upon him. We turned away from each other—I with a counterfeit yawn, Cass fidgeting.

After a moment Cass went on. "Well, I reckon I simmered down pretty quickly. That Scotch he was putting out was on the de-luxe side, and it was too much to forgo just because of a single crude remark. Yet I remember, as we went back into the room there, I remember thinking about him, brooding, trying to size him up. In those days, especially when I was drunk, my judgments on America and Americans tended to get a bit somber and harsh, to say the least. And Mason now—well, I can't say that I actually out and out disliked him, even with that remark of his—seeing Francesca again had left me feeling very warm—but you might say that there was a whole lot about him that I didn't exactly cotton to. And all this quite aside from the Waldo business, which had begun to set my teeth on edge. No, there were these other things—all his slickness, and his suavity, and that bland arch pretty-boy face of his, and yes, even those goddam sun glasses he was wearing indoors, too, where there wasn't no sun. In this haze I was getting into, all these things added up to something, and that something didn't seem to be much more than the man I had come to Europe to escape, the man in all those car advertisements— you know, the young guy waving there—he looks so beautiful and educated and everything, and he's got it *made,* Penn State and a blonde there, and a smile as big as a billboard. And he's *going* places. I mean electronics. Politics. What they call communications. Advertising. Saleshood. Outer space. God only knows. And he's as ignorant as an Albanian peasant."

He paused. "Maybe it was partly envy in those days. Mason had a lot more than this, I guess. After all he wasn't a type, he was his own self. But then, as I told you, I always had it in for these young American dreamboats, who've had it handed to them on a silver platter—education, especially, books, the opportunity to learn something—and then never used it, but took a couple of courses in water-skiing, and then dragged-ass out of school barely able to write their name and believing that the supremest good on earth was to be able to con a fellow citizen into buying a television set that would reduce his mind to the level of a toadfish or lower even. Millions of them! Because I never had that chance—though if wasn't nobody's fault directly, except maybe the depression and my uncle's having to pull me out of school to go to work—and I resented it, and having to learn the little I know on my own hook, so to speak. Anyway, put part of this feeling down to envy. Nonetheless, with Mason here, you see, he had begun to look and smell a little like that certain man, in spite of *Kennst du das Land* crap and the playwrighting, and my enthusiasm for him had pretty much wore off, you might say. As a matter of fact, he had begun to look phony as a boarhog with tits. What the hell are you laughing at?"

"At Mason," I said. "I want to cry, but I'm laughing at Mason. Go on."

"Well, we got to chatting there by the balcony, and we got on various subjects, abstract expressionism—he had all the proper things to say about that—and I remember somewhere along the line there he started in on jazz. I think he must have seen my phonograph, or maybe my Leadbelly album, and figured that naturally I was pretty well gone on jazz. Though of course what they call modern jazz and Leadbelly are two different things. Well now—jazz. You know, some of it's pretty good, and I'd probably like it a lot more than I do if it weren't for some goddamed avant-garde creep always jamming it down my throat. And Mason was basically about as much avant-garde as J. P. Morgan. Anyway, I guess you've got to be something of a heretic—a bleeding *infidel*—to say that you don't like jazz. In New York, say you don't like jazz and it's like saying you're an F.B.I. man. It's a shame, you know. Because good jazz should be taken for what it is. Music. It isn't great art but it's music, and a lot of it's fine, only about half the people who listen to it think that it's some sort of propaganda. They're worse than the bleeding Russians. Like that time in New York, I was in a bar near the Art Students' League and I told this young girl that I thought Negro spirituals were very beautiful, and she said: 'Oh, they went out in the thirties. You southerners just want to see Negroes remain in a state of primitive religiosity.' She was one of these jazz nuts, of course. But it's true, really. Most of the people who say they like jazz couldn't whistle "Yankee Doodle." They're tone deaf. They like it because they think it *stands* for something. Or because it's chic. Well, believe me, it's not that I have anything *against* jazz, but until my ears improve there will be very little in it that will ever turn me to fire and ice inside—like the day in Paris when I was listening to the radio, and heard that aria from Gluck for the first time in my life, where Orfeo calls out to Euridice in his grief, and I sat there shivering and burning, with my hair straight on end, and near about keeled over like a log.

"Anyway, Mason moved in on me pretty quickly there, and he began talking about Mezz and Bird and Bix and Bunk and Bunny and God knows who else, and I just pretty much gave him the helm, sitting there brooding and listening and sipping away at his ten-dollar luxury bottle. I guess almost a half-hour must have passed, and I was getting woozier and dreamier and—I don't know—sad, I guess, half-listening to him yack away about this horn player named Bird, who had a terrible death-wish and finally croaked, and gazing down into the sea and the valley, which were all blazing gold at that time of the day, and so beautiful, and forever out of my reach. And I kept thinking about Francesca, too— things that excited me but scared me, too, if you want to know the truth—and his voice came back into focus all of a sudden, and I realized he was talking about parachuting and Yugoslavia, and this jump he'd made into the black, black night. Well, I listened more intently now, and I believed it—there wasn't any reason not to, especially since his manner of telling it was really so modest, and even funny in a way. As you know, it was quite a tale.

"Well, I reckon what started me off was this. This— After he finished his story he asked me where I'd been, and I told him the Solomons and New Britain, and then he asked me—all in the smoothest way, you understand, without seeming to pry at all—if I'd gotten hurt any, and I said no, I'd been lucky—physically, that is—but that I'd gotten pretty beat up mentally for a while, enough to put me in a hospital for a spell, at any rate. Then he wanted to know if this experience hadn't deepened me, hadn't added to my work; then tacked on something heavy about how this Yugoslavian business, and fear, and suffering there, was the key to his own talent. And it's a funny thing, he wouldn't let it go at that, you see; in the nicest way he kept wanting to know what happened to me. So I poured myself out another Regal and I told him: about landing at Gloucester in the mists, in that tremendous hovering jungle, and how it wasn't anything that exactly happened to me that eventually cracked me up, but how the Japs were way back in the bosky dells, waiting, and when we advanced—lucky old Cass being *point,* lead man in the lead squad of the leading platoon in the leading company, et cetera—it was like being pioneer in an experience so nightmarish and scary that all reality just drained away from your consciousness on the spot, and that being waist-deep in this incalculable muck anyway, the fact of sudden death from some invisible machine gun or sniper stuck up in a tree somewhere seemed at once so inviting and so foregone and so inevitable that from then on, once you miraculously pulled through it all, fear was never the same again. It was a land and an empire whose citizen you would be for the rest of your life. And no doubt for the rest of your life you would be paying it homage. That was my *experience,* I said, and as I droned away there—getting a little mawkish, I guess, what with the memory and the booze and all—my eyes misted up and I told him this. I told him we done a good job in that war. I told him that it was a war we had to fight, that if there's such a thing as a just war it was no doubt juster than most. But as for *experience,* I said, you could keep your goddam experience and give me back those days when I could have been swimming on the green coast of Carolina, washed over by clean green waves and left upright and ready for living, instead of half buckled-over remembering some misbegotten quagmire of a jungle, and with the dirty taste of fear in my mouth. Experience, I said, was for the birds, when it *diminished* a man. Bugger that kind of experience. Bugger it. Bugger it forever.

"Then came the snapper, you see. Mason's eyes were all glittery by now. Looking back on it, it must have been just the sorehead renegade talk he was led to expect from this Polish what's-his-name. Anyway, as I ended up my little outburst, feeling all mean and bitter and drunk and sorry for myself, as I finished up there Mason's beautiful lips parted and this, so help me God, is what he said. He leaned back in his chair and folded his hands gracefully behind his head and said: 'Well, I don't consider myself a member of the beat generation, Waldo, though I certainly sympathize. But I think I can understand why you're considered one of the leading spokesmen.' Which is a pretty sweet piece of ass-kissing, you must admit. He had everything all sewed up. With a couple million bucks he couldn't exactly be *beat,* and he knew it, but to be beat was fashionable, and he sure could sympathize. Old Mason. He would of sympathized with cancer if he thought it was à la mode. Well, anyway, that did it. What it was I don't know—an accumulation of things, I suppose. Him pretending to care for my art, which was so poor. Francesca, and the booze, and this sudden memory of the war again, and my general misery and inadequacy, and on top of that this glib young fellow with his fast chitterchatter about abstract impressionism and jazz and this guy Bird with his death-wish and now, drug in by its heels, the beat generation, knowing that was pretty chic, too. I mean, whether justly or not, for a moment there he seemed to be the bleeding shallow and insincere epitome of a bleeding neo-yahoo snakepit of a fifth-rate juvenile culture that only a moron could live in, or a lunatic. He burnt my ass.

"So I let him have it, number-two shot in both barrels. I got up and I looked down at him and I said, very gently: 'You want to know something, my friend? I think you're as full of shit as a

Christmas goose.' Then I said, very softly, very even-tempered, see: 'Let me tell you something. I don't know what you're driving at, but those bums don't know what *beat* is. They're just a bunch of little boys playing with theirselves. Get me some *men,* friend, and I might set myself up in the spokesman business. In the meantime, don't call me Waldo.' Well, you'd have thought Mason had been cold-cocked with a wrench. He gave a little jump and his eyes got as gray and washed-out as a couple of oysters. And then that shoulder of his started to jerking and twitching and heaving and he looked like he was trying to say something, but what could he say? Either I wasn't Waldo at all, or I was sort of a super-Waldo who had transcended even himself, and was so way-out that here I was repudiating the generation I was supposed to be the mouthpiece for. He looked absolutely clobbered. And before he had a chance to collect himself I was charging on, half out of my head, I guess, with drunken spite and bitterness and general all-around anti-everything. And I said: 'Who the hell are you, anyway, some bleeding smart-aleck Joe College with half a semester of art appreciation and several fancy chapters from Bernard Berenson who's come over here to yawn over whatever Renaissance genius is passé this year?' (He wasn't that, of course, but I didn't know it. Mason might have heard of B.B., but anybody who painted before 1900 was on his shit list anyway.) 'People like you give me a king-sized pain in the butt. The whole suave smooth Ivy League lot of you should be made to run high hurdles from here to the Strait of Messina, barefooted like one of these *contadini* and nothing to eat but some week-old bread full of weevils, then by God maybe you'll know a painting when you see one!' His shoulder was heaving like mad and—I don't know—he looked so *displaced,* all of a sudden, that I sat down and altered my tone a bit. 'The trouble is, you see, it's not that you're not *nice,* you young Americans, it's just that you don't know anything. Take the Greeks, *par exemple.* Do you know anything about the Greeks?' He just sat there for a moment, looking walleyed, then he said somewhat stiffly: 'Of course I know something about the Greeks.' Then I said: 'Quote me something! Quote me from *Iphigenia,* quote me from *Orestes.*' And he said: 'You don't have to be able to quote to show your knowledge, for Jesus sake.' Which the Lord knows is true enough, but I said: 'Ha! See! A man who can't quote one line from Euripides hasn't got no education whatsoever. And you a play writer? What *is* your line, my friend? Communications? Some sort of drummer? I thought so. Well, let me tell you something, friend. You'd better prepare for doom. Because when the great trump blows and the roll is called up yonder and the nations are arranged for judgment you and all your breed are going to be shit out of luck. They don't allow communicators into heaven, or traveling men either.'

"Well, I was getting quite a kick out of needling this guy, and I sloped off on a general tirade against America, its degradation of its teachers and its men of mind and character, and its childish glorification of scoundrels and nitwits and movie trash, and its devotion to political cretins—military scum and Presbyterians and such like whose combined wisdom would shame some country sheriff's harelip daughter—and its eternal belief that it's God's own will that illiterates and fools shall lay down the law to the wise. *Ad infinitum*. Right on down the line. And Mason was taking it all in, nodding and looking sad and hurt, and with his shoulder going up and down. Except that, talking about America as I had been doing, a swarm of memories had begun to rollick in the back of my mind, and then they calmed down and began to flow through me in one clear continuous stream, clear as water, so that even as I halted, then tried to speak again, there came upon me this spell which I had had in Europe so many times—where touched a bit by this wine, you know, I would glimpse such simple homely things as the fold of a curtain or the knob of a door or a frosted windowpane, and these I would somehow connect with the same things at home, and then I'd remember a house or an old tobacco barn and the way it looked on a wintry evening in the full light of sunset, or the gulls white and motionless in a mad wild gale over Hatteras, or a girl's voice would come back to me, clear as a bell on some street in New York many years ago, and her eyes and her hair, or the scent of perfume as she passed, or then the sound of a freight train lumbering up through the pinewoods near home, and its long whistle in my ears both a monotone and an ecstasy. So as I say, this reverie came upon me as I sat there, and as I thought of all these things and the memories flowed through me I began to feel like a total stranger, and the anguish and mystery of *myself,* you see—of who and what I was and had been and was to be—all of these were somehow tied up with these visions and sounds and smells of America, which were slowly breaking my heart as I sat there, and I knew I had to get up and get out of there and be alone. It was as simple as that. I remember I cleared my throat and looked at Mason, who was sort of suspended there in a yellowish winy fog, and then I got up. 'The only true experience, by God,' I said, 'is the one where a man learns to love himself. And his country!' And as I said these words, and turned around, why so help me God that nightmare I'd had came crashing back like a wave, and then those Negroes and that ruined cabin so long ago and all of that, which seemed to be the symbol of the no-count bastard I'd been all my life, and I became absolutely twisted and wrenched with a feeling I'd never felt before—guilt and homesickness and remorse and pity all combined—and I felt the tears streaming idiotically down my cheeks.

" 'How will I ever forgive myself, for all the things I've done?' I said to him, hardly knowing what I was saying.

"And then Mason said: 'What *have* you done, Waldo? What's the matter? Why, man, you've got it *made!*'

"But I said: 'The name is Kinsolving'—spelling it out—'journeyman cartoonist from Lake Waccamaw, North Carolina.'

"And then I got out of there. I went hunting for Francesca, thinking that I might be able to find her and buy her an ice cream or something. But then I realized I didn't have a nickel to my name. So I staggered down the mountainside and sat and looked at the sea."

"Tell me, how did you ever get so involved—so chummy with him?" I asked Cass later.

"Well, I'll tell you a short little incident that I remember very clearly. One morning, you see, not long after that day I got up and started to go down to the café for my daily workout with Luigi and the wine bottle. I had just stepped out into the street there when down the cobblestones cruised Mason in that monstrous pneumatic barge of his, loaded down to the gun'ls with the damndest pile of boxes you ever saw. I mean cartons of Maxwell House and Campbell's soups and catchup and Kleenex, this and that, anything you can name. He'd just come back from the PX in Naples, you see. He was really setting up housekeeping in a big way. He had enough there to outfit Admiral Byrd.

"He drew to a halt and pitched me a big grin and got out and started unloading all his loot. I remember in the back he had a huge big boxful of cans—Crisco, I believe it was, or maybe Fluffo—anyway, it was some kind of fancy American lard, and he had enough of it to fry potatoes in till kingdom come—but the box was heavy and he was having a little bit of a time with it, so I shuffled over to help him out. Funny, this must have been about a week after he arrived. I hadn't seen much of him up to then, but we'd waved to each other and smiled as we passed in the courtyard— both of us pretty sheepish, I guess, over the jackasses we'd made of ourselves that first day. As a matter of fact, once we'd even stopped there and mumbled a few apologies at each other—he for mistaking me for old ding-dong what's-his-name from Rimini, and me of course for getting so drunk and outrageous and insulting. Mason must have been in a sort of pickle at the time, you know. I mean he was pretty well stuck there in Sambuco, for one thing. He was committed. Then at the same time, this blow job he'd given me about his work—I wasn't the Polish boy, to be sure, but after all he *had* told me that my work was right up there with Matisse and Cézanne, and he couldn't very well go back on his judgment without looking like a perfect cluck. Well, I didn't think of all this at the time. Inside he must have been boiling—at himself and at me—but there was no way out, really. If he'd showed his resentment and, say, cut me dead, why he'd look all the more foolish and asinine, that's all. But maybe, you know, he wasn't boiling at all. Because maybe I had something else to offer him.

"Anyway, as I say, at that point we were on decent enough terms, even though possibly somewhat distant, and I figured what the hell, I'd help him out with his Crisco. So we huffed and puffed the box into the courtyard, making sort of stiff little formal wisecracks and so on, and while we were doing this I said to myself, for God sake, I'd been pretty stinking and rude to this guy, he really seemed like a decent enough type; if he was going to be around Sambuco—sharing the same house, too—we might as well be friendly, so I just went on and helped him with the rest of his groceries. All that lard! It *did* seem maybe a little too much at the time, I guess, but who was I to begrudge him all his dough, and besides, he had boxes and boxes of books, too, which sort of excited me, and I remember thinking that maybe he'd loan me one or two. He said he'd picked them up at the dock in Naples, shipped over from New York. And there were a lot of other things that came along behind just then, in a truck he'd hired: that damn buffalo head, and these paintings—a Hans Hofmann, and a couple of de Koonings, and a huge black-assed Kline—and a Toastmaster. And a bunch of fancy elephant guns all crated up and packed in cosmoline. . . ."

Cass paused for a moment, scraping at the gray stubble on his chin. "I honestly don't know what must have been bumping around in my subconscious. I knew I was stone-broke, and I knew that Poppy's last ten thousand lire had dwindled down to almost nothing. I was really quite desperate, if you want to know the truth—way behind on the rent, and a wine-and-Strega bill down at the café half a mile long. I didn't know what I was going to do. And here was this solid-gold young Santa Claus, this patron of the arts, moving in right on top of me. I don't think it would be honest if I told you that I didn't say to myself something like: Man, this is some gravy train. He sure doesn't want all those goodies just for his*self*. No. No, maybe nothing quite so crass and *outright* as that—after all, I still did have one or two scruples left. But when things like food, and milk for the kiddies—the lack of them, that is —is not just a vague possibility but an actual threat, and then along comes this guy who not only looks like he's going to open up an A. and P. right on your doorstep but has brought along two or three cases of booze to boot, and he looks so generous and all, why your scruples really aren't the same thing any longer. What was once hard pure diamonds turns into something soft on you. Anyway, this initial polite gesture of mine—helping him with that box of Crisco, that is—had suffered a rather tremendous change, and it wasn't long before I was sweating there like a coolie. There wasn't any need for this either, see; he'd gotten a couple of Windgasser's boys to help him by then, but there I was anyway, hauling boxes around and toting these cases of Jack Daniel's and Mumm's champagne up the stairs, and by the time a half-hour had went by and we'd gotten everything securely tucked away upstairs, why Mason and I were jabbering away at each other like a couple of old college chums who were about to bunk together in the Phi Delt house. 'Well, by Jesus, Cass, this is all damn white of you,' he'd say. Or then, 'You'll have dinner with us tonight, won't you, you and Poppy?' Or then, 'Those paintings. That de Kooning. I'd like you to take a look at it and tell me where to hang it. You know a lot more about such matters than I do.' " Cass paused again. "And what—" he said, then halted. "And what," he resumed, "what was he after then? What was he trying to do, to get? Here I was, shaggy, down-at-the-heel, not his type at all. I had insulted him, furthermore; and it was because of me that he must have suffered a really miserable humiliation. I was not any chic figure in the firmament he wanted to dwell in; I was a bum and a drunken rascal and he must have known it. Yet here was Mason—generous, putting out for me, all sweet friendliness and hospitality. What was he after, do you suppose? Was it because he had no friends in this crazy hot exotic scary land, and needed a protection against his loneliness, and preferring to that a broken-down artist to no artist at all? Maybe.

"Well, soon after that I made my mistake. Soon after that I did the thing that, once I did it, I was in up to my neck with Mason and there was no turning back. We were standing around there among the crates and boxes, chatting and talking and so on, and I heard Poppy call for me downstairs, and I figured it was time to go, because she'd be ready with lunch. So I said I'd be delighted to help him hang the painting, and then—well, even here there was probably more than a little *guile* behind my thoughts, thinking of that wad of lire Mason must pack around with him—then I asked if he and Rosemarie would like to join me in a game of poker. 'Poppy will play,' I said, 'and this woman I know that runs the café, I've taught her how to play a decent hand. Plain old stud or draw, none of these ladies' games—baseball or spit-in-the-ocean or anything like that.' But Mason said that all he knew about was gin and bridge, and so I figured that the cards was one way I'd never get a penny off him. Well, I was about to leave then, when it happened. He leaned down into one of those liquor cases and he pulled out a bottle of whiskey. Then he said, 'Here,' holding the bottle out to me. 'Here, why don't you take this along?' And he just stood there, holding it out, with this little sort of sideways grin on his face, and these elegant knuckles of his all white and bony with *noblesse oblige*. Very cool of him. Not a case of Rice Krispies, but just what he knew I'd not be able to resist. And then he said: 'Oh come on, Cass, take it along.'

"It was not exactly a tip for my services, yet it was a tip, too. I'll swear, I never saw anybody give something with less feeling, less charm. It was neither a gift nor a gratuity, and maybe if it had been either I wouldn't have taken it. I don't know what it was, but whatever it was—or maybe it was just his manner, holding it out there and that terribly well-meant and sincere yet lofty and slightly tired 'Oh take it along,' and Rosemarie had slunk in, in a pair of those toreador pants, so I felt that here was the lady of the manor watching the baron himself as he dealt with one of the serfs —whatever it was, it was bad. It was bad and I knew it, I knew it right down to the bottom of my guts, but I couldn't resist that sauce. So I took it and I mumbled my humble thanks, and then I got out of there, flaming like an oven. If I had offered to pay for it, why even that might have taken a little of the curse off it. But I didn't offer to pay for it—not because I didn't have any money anyway, but because decency had left me, and good sense, and pride. I just took it, that's all.

"Then again I heard his voice, calling down at me, just before I got down to the courtyard. 'Say, Cass,' he hollered, 'you wouldn't like to make the PX run with me next time, would you? Maybe pick up a few things for Poppy in the grocery line. Something for the kids?' And I just hollered back: 'Sure, Mason, sure. That'd be just swell. Sure, I'd love to.' Which was not a lie, but only the wretched truth. . . .

"Funny thing," he said after a long pause, "that last awful day —the day I met you on the road for the first time, remember?— that day I'd just finished what he always called a PX run. I lost count of the times I went over to Naples with him; it became a habit, like booze or dope, then at last I was tied to him, bound to him for reasons of pure survival, and not just my own, either, but of all those around me that I in turn had committed myself to save.

"Mason," he said slowly. "Uncle Sugar. I got so that with Mason I was as helpless as Romulus, sucking on the fat tit of a wolf. But this day here, this day he gave me that bottle, I had no idea how far *in* I would get with Mason, how deep and involved. Any more than I had the notion that in another way I'd rouse myself—God knows how I did it—and grasp a truth about the shabby and contorted life I'd been leading and make at least a stab at salvaging something out of the wreckage. . . .

"I just *took* that bottle, that's all." Then, *"Mason,"* he said after a long moment of silence. "I guess I've died a thousand deaths since I killed him. But never as long as I live will I forget standing down there in the courtyard, with that bottle like a big warm cow turd in my hand, and him hanging over the balustrade, so lean and so American, with the hungry look of a man who knew he could own you, if you'd only let him."

IX

"Art is dead," Mason was saying. "This is not a creative age. If you look at it that way—and really, Cass, I'm not trying to pull your leg about this—if you look at it that way, you won't have any worries at all. As capable as you are—and I *mean* that—do you think the world has any use for your stuff, even if it were not representational, as it is? Put the whole thing out of your mind. A kind of Alexandrian, patristic criticism will fill the vacuum, and after that—nothing. The Muse is on her last legs—look around you, can't you tell?—she is tottering toward the grave and by the year 2000 she'll be as dead as the ostracoderm." Above the slip-stream noise of wind sliding past the Cadillac, Mason sneezed; removing handkerchief from gabardine slacks, he wiped his nose. "What's that?" Cass heard himself say gummily, his tongue (though it was not yet noon) already bethickened. "What's an oshtracoderm?" In the V of his crotch he nursed a pint bottle, gripped tightly in both hands against the car's pneumatic rise and sway, and he hoisted it to his lips and drank. Gurgle and glug, a sweet taste, burning. "A fishlike animal," Mason said. "It vanished in the late Devonian. Just a fossil now. I mean really, Cassius," he went on persistently, "that being the case, how can you take all this so seriously?" He saw Mason's foot go up against the brake pedal, felt momentum urge his own spine forward as the car paused: a red and white stop sign, the sea blue, glittering beyond, gay with boats. Atrani—slimy fish nets, bedecked with seaweed, drying in the sun. "Now which way do I go, on this new route of yours?" *"Take a left."* The words thought, spoken simultaneously, and uttered upon the fag-end of a half-hour-long program of hiccups which now, after much breath-holding, much squinting, more concentration, mercifully ceased: *That's what you get for drinking without any breakfast, enough to make Leopold give up the ghost.* "Take a left, Mason. What's patristic?" There was no reply to this; the voice continued, lilting, high-pitched, avid, tireless: "So look at it in this light. Hypothesis: art is dead. Corollary: after art's death, *talent* must be put to expedient purposes. Final deduction: you yourself, Cass Kinsolving, have done nothing wrong. I desired the expediency of your talent—namely, a certain picture, commissioned in the way pictures have been for centuries. You needing goods I had to offer (Cellini and Clement the Seventh, all right, I'll agree, the parallel's absurd like you say, but there's a similarity in *outline*), you needing goods painted me a certain picture. I in turn made the appropriate recompense. So it isn't art. Who cares? The deal is done. Could anything be simpler than that?"

Blinding blue with July's clear weather, the sky arched above the topless car; cool sea-wind fanned Cass' face. The Cadillac clock, aslant on the glittering panel, registered eleven on the nose. In his mind, a dilatory quality seemed to inform all of Mason's words: they made their imprint on his brain seconds after they were uttered, like an echo. On the pebbled beach below, brown-legged children played; past the beach there were white-hulled boats; past these, flashing sea birds; past all, a blazing eternity of blue: slowly, replacing the bottle in the cradle between his legs, Cass brought his eyes back to the clock, then the road ahead, hearing the echo—*Could anything be simpler than that?* "I still—" Cass said. Just that for an instant: "I still—" Even he himself could not hear those muttered words. He cleared his throat. *"I still* want that picture back, Mason," he said. The hiccups commenced again, pain lurched in his guts: *Bleeding Christ, stoppit!* "Still," he repeated. "I still—*huke!*—still want that picture back, under- stand? I reckon I'm ashamed of it, that's all." Mason was silent, though was that the engine making that chiding clucking sound, or something that Mason was doing with his tongue? Like a dog who averts his eyes from his master's face, Cass could not, this mo- ment, bear to look at him; he gazed at the sea again and though he tried to repress it the painting rose up in his mind, horribly super- imposed against the seascape's blue: a nude and lovely young girl with parted mouth and the fairest of hair, supine, eyelids closed tight in passion's grip, the gold and rose-petal flesh of her thighs entwined round the naked waist of a boy, somewhat Grecian of cast, black-haired, nostrils aflare, who made his sturdy entrance into her at the very vortex of the painting, assisted by a young, fair, yet most urgently contorted hand. Pure realism, it had been done in encaustic (with waxes Mason had bought for him in Naples); though sickeningly plastered during the three sessions it had taken him to complete the job, he had used no model save his imagination, and Mason had pronounced it a work of genius. The contrast! The light flesh and the dark! The perineal area—ah, said Mason, he had never seen a perineum so "moistly stimulated," and as for the lovely youth—why, each delicate bluish vein seemed to throb with a gathering, pitiless increment of desire. (And that hand, that girl's sweet young hand: it was absolutely frantic.) And for all this: seventy thousand lire—just enough to pay back rent— three bottles of French brandy, three vials containing ten cc. each of streptomycin sulfate (Squibb), and, now, the burden of an all but unbearable shame. "No really, Mason," he heard himself mutter, "I want that painting back. I'll pay you for it, see?" But Mason, unhearing—unlistening?—had switched on the radio. *E adesso le sorelle Andrews nella canzone 'Dawn fanzmi in.'* . . . Christ! He flinched, grabbing the bottle as Mason swerved past a donkey cart loaded with bags of meal, gained the straightaway, gunned forward, leaving behind meal-motes floating in air, a stooped old man with skin like wrinkled mahogany, eyes rolling in blank belated terror. Give me land lotsa land under starry skies. . . . The bleeding Andrew sisters, a Red Cross canteen in Well- ington, New Zealand, ten thousand years ago, and that song, a girl. . . . Gorblimey, Yank, you do cut a fawncy caper. . . . But the memory faded as Mason said now: *"Really,* why do you want it back so bad, dollbaby? If you'd just give me one honestly logical reason I'd—" But it was his turn to remain silent, thinking: Because of the bleeding abyss. Because I feel how close I am now. Because even in futility's supremest futility I cannot let my last and only creation be a perineum, a moist membrane and a bunch of pulsing veins, in short, a *screw*. . . . He held his breath, the hiccups stopped. I got to watch out, he thought.

Smooth and serpentine, the road wound far above the sea. The sun blazed down. On the heights above them wild roses bloomed, and water from springs poured forth out of the cliffsides, purling and splashing in whispery gush over the noise of the motor, the whistling wind. Far off, smoky Salerno sprawled against the shore, baking. He took another glug from the bottle, thinking the thought he had thought for many days: What I should do is *really* rob the son of a bitch. Let me be by my-saelf where the West commences! *le sorelle* sang, in wild throbbing treble. A power wire sagged above the road, cutting through the sisters with a blast of static. A seaside vacation village, smelling of caramel.

"Where is this new road of yours?" Mason said, as the car eased to a halt. Hard by the seashore, where spangled umbrellas flowered on the rocky beach, there was a stone fountain, trickling rusty water. From this piazza, somnolent and sticky with morning, three asphalt roads branched off into the steep hills. "What'd you say, Mason? Wish I had a paper cup. 'Bout half of this here whiskey's slopping down my neck." "What I said was—" He sensed the sharpness in Mason's voice, was aware that Mason had turned to stare at him, leaning slightly forward, his left arm curled around the steering wheel. "What I said, Buster Brown, if you care to listen," he said heavily, sarcastically, "is where is this new route to Naples you were telling me about. This short route, which presumably—if it's shorter—we should have been using for the last dozen trips. If you can just remove that bottle from your lips long enough—" Two priests, one fat, the other rail-skinny, bounced past them on a sputtering Vespa, slanted black and billowing around the fountain, were gone. Neither Cass nor Mason spoke. For a moment motionless, they sweltered in the car, amid the smell of leather. Barely hearing Mason, Cass turned his eyes toward the sea; above Salerno, aloft, unbelievably high in space, there seemed to hover a mist, a churning rack of cloud, terrible and only faintly discerned, as of the smoke from remote cities sacked and aflame: he gave a stir, touched on the shoulder by an unseen, unknowable hand. He closed his eyes in sudden inward fright, trembling again on the marge of hallucination. *Jesus Christ, not again today, not today when I got these things*— Mason's voice broke in: "Well, Buster Brown, do you navigate or do I?" Opening his eyes, Cass spoke. The mist, the stratospheric rack had vanished. "Ah, see that sign; says Gragnano? Take that one, Mason, dead ahead." The car eased forward with an oily meshing of gears, barely perceptible; the sea slid out of sight behind them as they began the northward climb. On the outskirts of the village the road followed a stream bed where, shaded from morning heat by towering bay trees and willows, women with hiked-up skirts and brown bare legs scrubbed away at clothes. And now the way ascended, smoothly, through vineyards and lemon groves. Screaming, red-necked and with panicky flapping wings, a starved rooster rose up in front of them, escaping death by a feather. "So put it out of your mind, Cassius," Mason said tersely. "The picture's bought and paid for."

Gentili ascoltatori! the radio blared. *Canzoni e melodie, un po' di allegria di Lawrence Welk!* Murder! Mason's hand went out, fiddled with the dial, the voice complaining now about Italy, the dearth of jazz, the lack of this, of that—what? A short stretch through a tunnel in the rock, black as midnight, filled with the sound of rushing torrents, obliterated the voice. In an explosion of light they emerged from the cavern, Mason's voice flat, insistent, haranguing: "—but you may not think so, Cassius old boy. I don't mind missing a little chow once in a while—a can of beans here, a loaf of bread there, et cetera—you're going to get that from servants anywhere. I think you'd agree, however, that there's a slight difference between a little totin' from the kitchen and lifting jewelry right out from under your nose. Those earrings were one of Rosemarie's heirlooms. I've done my damndest, I tell you. I've eliminated Giorgio; I've eliminated those two wenches in the kitchen. Then who else is left? Much as I hate it, all the evidence points to—" Wrenching pain gripped Cass' heart. The name Francesca on Mason's lips, as always, spoken in that flat fatuous northeastern *cum* Hollywood voice larded over with some acquired lounge-lizard accent, faintly British, faintly phony—the name was like filth on his lips. *Say one thing against her, do one thing out of line, friend, and I'll pop you in the bleeding mouth.* But Mason: close to the line as he often came, he had not stepped over it, *yet;* there was a wariness here, a caution, one area of Cass' existence that Mason had hesitated—or feared—to violate, possibly dating from that day weeks and weeks before when

Mason, in the very act of appropriating Francesca for a servant—
after all, he could pay; Cass couldn't—had said something crass
and lewd, making plain in his broad wisecracking way not only
his desires but his designs, and then had turned around blanched,
wide-eyed, even apprehensive at the sound of Cass' sober words,
just those: *Say one thing against her, do one thing out of line,
friend, and I'll pop you in the bleeding mouth.* It had been a tense
moment, but he had failed to drive the wedge in tight. For if there
had been a single point during the past two months when Cass
might have gained the advantage, at least come up to Mason's eye-
level, made this plain: *There is some shit I will not eat*—that
surely was the time. But instead the hard moment had become
soft, blurred, blunted: Mason had said something querulous, vacantly apologetic— *Arright, Cass, sorry, don't be a hardnose about
it, sorry*—and he himself—in deathly outrageous panic lest his
harsh words cause Mr. Big to withdraw the *bambini's* fresh milk,
plus Life Savers, bubble gum, frankfurters, bacon, liverwurst,
booze (not the least)—had been soft, conciliatory, deplorable.
*What I mean, Mason, is don't get any ideas, that's all. She's just a
kid, can't you tell?* And now Mason went on warily, cautiously:
"She's good around the place, works her little tail off. I remember
when she was working for you and Poppy, how you told me what a
terrific worker she was. And she is. That's what's so rough about
it. I know how hard up she is. You've told me all about her trouble. My great heart bleeds, Cass. But I can't think that it's anyone
but her. The evidence is in. The place, the time. Am I supposed to
stand around and let her steal everything in the joint?"

Drowsily, he heard himself say: "You're barking up the wrong
tree, Mason. Get you another goat, hear?" "What?" Mason said.
"Goat," he repeated. "I said get yourself another goat. You're
barking up the *wrong tree."* Mason was silent. They were climbing now, steeply, along the rim of a gorge, a savage place where
only scrub oak grew upon granite outcroppings strewn with gigantic boulders. But as they climbed, the air grew cooler, touched
with a high mountain scent of laurel, fern, evergreen. Down
through a space between the buttresses of the ridge they were ascending, the sea flashed by like blue enamel in bright sunlight,
lakelike, a thousand feet below. Then the rocks and scrub oak returned—dusty abandoned country, conjuring hints of wolves,
banditry, bleached and scattered bones. "This looks like the San
Bernardino mountains," said Mason. "Where's that?" Cass said.
"Out on the coast," Mason replied, "sixty, seventy miles east of

L.A. Parts of them wild as hell. Up around Lake Arrowhead, you know?" He fell silent for a moment. Then, "Well, all I can say, Cass," he went on, "is that there's going to come a reckoning with Francesca, *wrong tree* or not. I can take anything but sneak thievery. It's the worst sort of thing, this sneaky Italian malady of theirs. I'd almost prefer the out-and-out gangsterism they brought to the U.S.A. Violence. You can deal with violence. Anything but this mean, behind-the-back petty larceny. As for Francesca, I know you have all sorts of *sympathetic insights* about her that I don't"—for a moment, again, the voice was touched with sarcasm, then became solemn as before—"but she didn't work very long for you. I don't believe you ever saw the sly little bandicoot in action. I could pay for a trip back to New York just on the sugar she's stolen." He felt Mason's eyes turn toward him. "Look, dear dollbaby, don't take my word for it. Ask Rosemarie. You just don't know—" The voice became a nag, a slurred complaint, a monotone barely distinct from the sizzling and strumming of tires upon the macadam, the obbligato of fruity saxophones, muffled, half-drowned in a steady nickering of static. "You just don't know, you see, how—" A sound, half-giggle, half-moan, rose up softly in Cass' throat. You just don't know. I just don't know what? he thought. Old buddy, I know more than you'll ever find out. For if Francesca had finally been reckless enough this day to steal something of value—and he had no doubt that she *had* fleeced Mason (or Rosemarie) of earrings—what Mason still did not know was this: that for the rest—the sugar, the butter, the flour, the cans of soup which several times with a desolate whine Mason announced had disappeared from the pantry shelf—Cass had engineered their removal, encouraged Francesca in her depredation with all the smooth calculated craft of a Fagin, tipped her off as to Mason's comings and goings, schooled her as to the amount of goods she might safely get away with, and in the end performed the feat, through Francesca, of depleting Mason's supplies almost every evening in respectable proportion as he helped him augment them —through these insane, ceaseless trips with Mason to the commissary—almost every morning. He had cut a large hole into Mason's cornucopia.

"It is not chauvinism at all," Mason was saying, by way of extension upon Francesca, thievery, Italians in general. The road had been torn up here; they were forced to drive slow, and billows of dust, raw umber, swept through the car. "It is not chauvinism in any way when I say that, Cass. But it's a sickening thing when you consider the money the U.S.A. has squandered here, and find only that you're regarded as some witless nincompoop of a fat rich uncle who's meant not only *not* to be treated with ordinary decency, but robbed and swindled at every turn. Now you know my orientation is essentially liberal. But sometimes I think the greatest disaster that ever happened to America was that fountainhead, or fathead, of good will, General George Catlett Marshall. An old pal of mine in Rome just quit his job with E.C.A. or whatever it's called, you'll meet him; hell of a nice guy. Should be here today, in fact. If you want to get the low-down on the monstrous way our dough has been mishandled, just ask—" Cass belched, stuck a finger in the bottle's mouth, protectively, against the dust. "Tell me something, Mason," he said. "That movie star. That Alice what's-her-name. Does she put out?" He found himself giggling to himself disgustingly and without reason; rocking slightly, reeling, the sky above seemed to cloud over—though the sun still blazed down—touched with presentiments of dementia. *Merciful God, let me hold out, let me endure this day.* He chuckled, helplessly. "Down in Carolina we call stuff like that table pussy. Tell me, Mason, do you think old Alice would—" "They're all narcissists," Mason said shortly. "Make it only with themselves. No, I mean it, Cass, our whole foreign policy needs a complete overhauling. Everything political can be reduced to human terms, a microcosm, and if it's not utterly plain that this petty thievery is not the *reductio ad absurdum* of what's going on, literally, on a higher general level, then we're all blinder than I'd thought. What we—" What we're going to do is get that picture back, Mr. Big, he thought, then we're going to cut out. He nipped at the bottle, delicately. *Una conferenza sugli scienziati moderni!* the radio squawked. *Stamattina: il miracolo della fisica nucleare!* Madness! He felt his soft helpless interior chuckles diminish and die out. The car with a rubbery bumping regained the pavement and the air cleared, greasily shimmering with heat waves high above the sea. His mouth felt sour and dry, he began to sweat. Above, the sun, pitched close to its summit, rode like a heat-crazed Van Gogh flower, infernal, wild, on the verge of explosion. *Che pazzia!* he thought. *Madness! Madness!* All that he had done, that summer, all his thoughts, motions, dreams, desires had evaded madness by a hair, and this, at least, *was* madness, the maddest of all. Madness! The drug (Was it the heat? the whiskey? In a ghastly moment of fugue he forgot the name of the anointed medicine, gave a gasp which made Mason turn. Then he recalled it again, murmured the name aloud.), the *pa-ra am-i-no-sal-i-cyl-ic acid,* would be waiting at the PX pharmacy, of this he was sure. But to think that after all this—hovering next to the D.T.'s as he was, an amateur sawbones with nothing to support him save an intern's manual, desperation, and the marvelous but uncertain drug—he could bring new life to that forsaken bag of bones in Tramonti: this, all this was madness. . . . *Christ, Mason, slow down!* His head bobbed forward, eyes fixed upon the gorge which fell seaward short feet from the road (often during the first trips with Mason he had wondered at this frenzied desire for speed, considered it a species of reckless courage even, until that now dim and distant moment on the Autostrada when, casting a glance at Mason, watching that flushed yet tight-lipped face facing the road at ninety miles an hour, he realized it was not courage but if anything its vacant opposite—an empty ritualistic coupling with a machine, self-obsessed, craven, autoerotic, devoid of pleasure much less joy) and he said softly, aloud: "Mason, for pity's sake, kindly slow the hell down, will you?"

The car slowed, though it was not due to Cass' plea, for here as they rounded a wide bend in the road there was a flock of sheep, fat-rumped and filthy, sturdily trotting, tended by a solitary boy. Mason hissed between his teeth, stopped, eased forward slowly. Sad bleats filled the air; the car moved ahead, parting the flock like shears. The boy called out, words high and indistinct. *"In bocca al lupo!"* Cass shouted back, waving the bottle; there was another bend, the sheep and boy were gone. "Strictly from Creepsville, sweet Alice Adair," Mason was saying, *"Née* Ruby Oppersdorf in Tulsa, Oklahoma. Couldn't act her way out of a wet paper sack. She was a dumb little New York model when Sol Kirschorn got hold of her. I don't know, she may have known a special bedtime trick or two—though frankly I doubt it—but anyway she got him by the balls and he married her. So now he's cast her in everything he's done. Such *hébétude* you could not possibly imagine. And yet she's been cast as Joan of Arc and Madame Curie and Florence Nightingale and *Mary Magdalene,* for Jesus sake . . . she's barely bright enough to come in out of the rain. . . . I told Alonzo that in this Beatrice Cenci role the only possible thing to do would be to concentrate on . . ." The voice became splintered, dim, remote. In a sort of shadowy grove the smell of hemlock bloomed around them; then, emerging from the wood into blinding sunlight, they mounted a long and level ridge: on one side was the sea again, on the other a field full of wildflowers, shimmering in the heat, smitten with light and summer. A shepherd's hut lay in ruin, crazily blasted and aslant amid dockweed, yellow mustard, dandelion. A brisk wind blew toward the sea, cooling Cass' brow. For a moment he closed his eyes, the flowers' crushed scent and summer light and ruined hut commingling in one long fluid hot surge of remembrance and desire. *Siete stato molto gentile con me,* he thought. *What a thing for her to say. You have been very kind to me. As if when I kissed her, and the kiss was over, and we were standing there in the field all body and groin and belly made one and wet mouths parted this was the only thing left to say. Which meant of course I'm a virgin and maybe we shouldn't but you have been very nice to me. So— So maybe I should have took her then, with gentleness and anguish and love, right there in that field last evening when I felt her full young breasts heavy in my hands and the wild way she pressed against me and her breath hot against my cheek. . . . Siete stato molto gentile con me . . . Cass . . . Cahssio . . .*

"Crackerjack," Mason was saying. The sunny meadow with its sweet conjuring mood of another field, another moment, had slipped behind them, yielding to a sloping ascent through the last stretch of woods before the summit, precipitous and awash with water from the roadside springs; beneath them, the tires whispered and splashed. With a shudder Cass raised the bottle to his lips and drank. "An absolutely crackerjack director, completely first-rate. Do you remember *Mask of Love,* back in the late thirties? And *Harborside,* with John Garfield? It was one of the first films ever done completely on location. That was Alonzo's. But the trouble with Alonzo is that he's neurotic. He's got a persecution complex. And so when that Hollywood Communist investigation came up, even though he wasn't remotely connected with anything to do with the Party—he was too bright for that—he got disgusted and came to Italy and hasn't been back to the States since, making a lot of wretched two-bit pictures in Rome. I think it's only because Kirschorn has a guilt complex—a sort of fair-weather liberal, you might say—that he signed Alonzo up for this monstrosity. Poor bastard, Alonzo hasn't—" Cass tapped Mason's shoulder. "Bear right here, Buster Brown, the right fork." The car swerved to starboard, with a soft lurch and a squealing of tires. "Christ, Cass, stay on the *ball,* will you?" He barely heard the words, maddening, insistent as they were. *I cannot say it is not sex yet if it were sex pure and simple I would have took her long ago. No there is this other thing. Maybe you could call it love, I do not know* . . .

Abruptly, the summit gained, all Italy rolled eastward, in haze, in blue, in a miracle of flux and change. Steaming with noon far below, the Vesuvian plain swept away toward the Apennines, a ghostly promenade of clouds dappling all with scudding immensities of shadow. A rain squall miles away was a black smudge against the horizon, the enormous plain itself a checkerboard of dark and light. Westward Vesuvius loomed, terrible, prodigious, drowsing, capped with haze. Beyond these heights—invisible—the gulf. Blinking, with odd and sudden panic, Cass turned his eyes away. *Frattanto in America,* said the meticulous radio voice, *a Chicago, il celebre fisico italiano Enrico Fermi ha scoperto qualcosa.* . . . Cass blinked again, shut his eyes, drank. The gulf, he thought, the gulf, the perishing deep. The volcano. Merciful bleeding God, why is it always that I— "So they can say what they will about Alonzo. You should see what Louella wrote about him, by the way. He might have been foolish, he might have had a bit too much of what is commonly known as integrity, and all that nonsense, but give him some film and a great actor like Burnsey to work with and he'll turn out something first-rate. It might not be Eisenstein, or the early Ford, or Capra, or even Huston, yet there's something individual—" Yatatayatata. His eyes still closed against mad Vesuvius, Cass thought: That voice. That bleeding outrageous voice. Cripps. Yatatayatata. Cripps. Why was that name now so sharply meaningful? Then suddenly, even as he addressed himself the question, with dark revulsion and even darker shame, he knew: recollecting dimly some sodden recent night, an assemblage of faces—the movie yahoos—leering and howling, Mason standing above him flushed and grinning and with his ringmaster's look, and then himself, finally, impossibly murky with drink, rubbery-limbed, mesmerized, performing some nameless art even now unrecollectable save that it was clownish, horrible, and obscene. The limericks, the dreadful exhibition bit, the filthy lines—and what else? Merciful Christ, he thought, I think I must have took out my cock. But yes, Cripps. Had it not been Cripps, alone among that mob sympathetic, who with face at once enraged and compassionate had approached him sometime after, steadied him, guided him downstairs, splashed his brow with water, then gone off on a tirade about Mason the words of which meant only this: Courage, boy, I don't know what he's doing to you, or why, but I'm on your side? Let him try that again and he'll answer to me. . . . Good old Cripps, he thought, nice of the guy, I'll have to thank him sometime. He opened his eyes. But for Christ's sweet sake it's not Mason who done it after all, it was me!

He looked down, saw that his legs were trembling out of control. "I'm gonna cut out, Mason," he said, turning to stare at the lovely profile, cool, swank, sweatless, scrupulous, a silk scarf beneath, chaste polka dots. "I finally decided I've just about had Sambuco. So soon's I clean up this little job back in Tramonti I'm gonna cut out." The booze had made him bold; it was out before he had time to think: "Now if you could just see your way clear to advancing me say about hundred and fifty thousand lire I could get me and the family back to Paris. See, in France I could get some kind of a job, and pay you back, and besides—" "How much do you owe me already?" (The voice peremptory but, withal, not unkind.) "Oh I don't know, Mason. I got it all down some place. Somewhere around two hundred thousand. Except that I—" Mason spoke again, affable still, yet in tones inhibitory if not adamant: "Don't be silly, Cassius. A hundred and fifty thousand couldn't get you as far as Amalfi. Quit worrying about the money, will you? Stick around, we'll have us a circus." He turned, with a sort of wink, faintly apologetic, adding: "I mean a ball, dollbaby, not what you think I mean. A *ball*. Picnics in Positano. Capri. Just a good time, that's all." (In spite of nausea, weariness, fidgeting legs, Cass began to giggle again, without a sound: *Merciful Christ, a circus.* Thinking of that delicious *crise,* somewhere in the depths of June, when Mason, propositioning Cass at a fuzzy vulnerable moment with the idea of a circus, coyly divulged the information that this would engage the four of them—Mason, titanic broad-assed Rosemarie, himself and, implausibly, insanely, *Poppy*—in some co-operative bedroom rumpus; more tickled and bemused than horrified by the vision of his saintly little Irish consort sporting with Rosemarie, all naked as herring, he had laughed so uproariously that Mason gave up the venture straightaway, though sulking.) His giggling ceased, died out as suddenly as it had come. So the guy really is going to hold out on me. Which is all the more reason I guess for shaking him down on the sly. He glanced at Mason again, sideways, wordlessly addressing him: If you'd just come on out and admit you was basically a plain old sodomist and wanted to get into my fly you'd be a lot more attractive person, Buster Brown.

"So cut the crap, Cassius. Quit this silly talk about leaving. Look, I know it's a rather banal observation, but the grass always looks greener on—" At horrifying speed now they moved north-west along the spine of the ridge, tires humming, above the enormous plain. Focusing his eyes upon Mason's knee, Cass again opened his mouth to speak, thought better of it, belched. And for a long moment, almost as if in delicate, easily shatterable opposition to the volcano which he could not bear to allow himself to see, he thought of the crazy mess of incidents and misadventures which had brought him to this day, this ride, this horror and this hope: the vision of Michele on that doomed, suffocating afternoon when first he'd seen him (the day itself had been touched with premonitions of ruin, somehow, for far off down the coast a highway crew was blasting and gusty tremulant explosions all too reminiscent of warfare and death accompanied them, Cass and Francesca, as they walked back into the valley and as she told him of her father's consumption—*tisi, la morte bianca*—which was, *Dio sa,* bad enough in itself to have, yet surely He must have had special vengeance in mind to compound this disease with such a wicked accident: the time between the moment she heard his helpless frantic cry and the instant he struck the ground could scarcely have been ten seconds, less than that, yet seemed a long eternity—for the cowshed roof, wet and slanting, offered no grip at all to his clutching hands, so that when he stumbled and fell he lay there for a moment spread-eagled against the peak and for that instant she thought he was safe until very slowly he began to slide feet first and belly down along the glassy incline, uttering not a sound and making futile grasping motions with his hands, slipping still, skidding faster and faster to the eaves, where, a limp figure catapulted into empty space, he soared outward, and down, his leg snapping like a piece of kindling beneath him as he struck the earth), that stifling afternoon when, with Francesca at his side, gazing down for the first time at Michele, at the great blade of his nose and his sunken cheeks so pale and cruelly lined, the mouth like a gash parting in a whisper of a smile, revealing jagged teeth and a mottled diseased patch of bright red gums—at that smile, was it not then that he had come to his own awakening? Or was it later, sometime after those sick fevered eyes, gazing up from the hammock in the shade, had rested upon Cass gently and questioningly and not without wonder, and the voice in a croak had said: "An American. You must be very rich"? There had been no reproach in this wan and worn-out remark, no indignation, no envy; it had been merely the utterance of one to whom an American and wealth were quite naturally and synonymously one, as green is to grass, or light is to sun, and Cass, who had heard these words spoken before though never by one so unimaginably far gone in misery and desolation, had felt clamminess and sickness creep over him like moist hands. The man, he saw, was not too much older than himself. Perhaps his awakening had begun then. For, *"Babbo!"* said Francesca then, sensing his embarrassment. "What a thing to say!" And runnels of sweat had coursed down Michele's cheeks, while Francesca moved to his side, mopping his face with a rag, crooning and clucking soft words of reproof. "For *shame,"* she had said, "what a thing to say, *Babbo!"* Then carefully she had ministered to her father, stroking his brow and rearranging the folds of his threadbare denim shirt, smoothing back the locks of his black sweat-drenched hair. So that with pain and distress in his heart and a hungry indwelling tenderness he had never known quite so achingly, he had watched her as she attended to the stricken man, and all her beauty seemed enhanced and brightened by this desperate, gentle devotion. An angel, by God, he had thought, an angel— And then, embarrassed, he had turned away, and stepped into the doorway of the hut. Here in the hushed light his eyes had barely made out the dirt floor and a single poor table and, beyond, empty, the cow stall with its meager bed of straw, and his nostrils were suddenly filled with a warmly sour and corrupt odor that bore him swiftly into some mysterious, nameless, and for the moment irretrievable portion of his own past, thinking: Lord God, I know it as well as my own name. And then he had inhaled deeply, almost relishing the sour and repellent smell, then almost choking on it as he filled his lungs with the thick putrescent air, in a hungry effort to dislodge from memory that moment in years forgotten when he had smelled this evil smell before, when suddenly he knew, and thought: It is niggers. The same thing, by God. It is the smell of a black sharecropper's cabin in Sussex County, Virginia. It is the bleeding stink of wretchedness. And then, exhaling, he had stepped back puzzled and distressed into the sunlight, and Francesca raggedy and lovely bending down over Michele, then standing up. A great collapsed grin had spread over Michele's face, and with an aimless gesture in the air of one limp and bony hand he scattered a cluster of green hovering flies. For a moment they were all silent. A thunderous detonation sounded once more from the sea, borne on a hot blast of air which shuddered in the pine trees around them, welling up thudding through the valley distances and died finally with a rumble like that of colliding kegs and barrels diminishing in murmurous echo against the hills. "It is a *festa?*" Michele said. The sunken grin creased his face again, and for no reason at all an awful chuckle gurgled up in his mouth, terminating not in the sound of laughter but in one long agonized spasm of coughing which set his arms, shoulders, and spindly neck to jerking like those of a puppet on wires, so loud and prolonged, this fit, that it seemed not simply the effort of one frail body to free itself of stifling congestion but a kind of explosive, rowdy anthem to disease itself—a racking celebration of infirmity—and it was at that instant that Cass, belatedly and desperately, at last awakened, understood that the man was dying. And had thought, turning, his eyes closed tight against the sun: I've got to do something. I've got to do something and do it quick. And remembered the women carrying fagots. And thought again: And I have been poor, too. But never anything like this. Never.

"Why is he not in a hospital?" he had asked furiously. "Why is he lying here like this?" Ghita, the mother and wife, had come then—wild-haired, consumptive herself, feverish, wobbling ever near hysteria—trailed by an evil old crone from the hills, carrying amulets, potions, charms. "Ask Caltroni!" Ghita had screeched. "Ask the doctor! He says there is no use! What hospital! Why put a man in a hospital when it is no use! And when there is no money to pay!" (All this in front of the squalling children, in front of Michele, sunk in his hammock dreaming his gentle smile, while cackling Maddalena, the rustic thaumaturge, hovered over, gattoothed and with swelling blue varicose veins, waving the amulet like a censer.) "He is going to die anyway!" she had yelled. "Ask the doctor! You'll see!" And, some days later, he had indeed gone to see the doctor, climbing the dark fish-smelling stairs to an office aerie where, munching on a piece of stringy goat cheese, pompous and vain, evasive, a wop Sydney Greenstreet paradoxically radiating a quality of ignorance and ineptitude so overpowering that it was like a kind of brownish aureole around him, Caltroni held forth, amid a magpie's nest of rusty probes and forceps and speculums superannuated at the time of Lord Lister. "*Perchè?*" he had said, and spread pudgy nicotine-brown fingers. "*Non c'è speranza. È assolutamente inutile.*" And had paused, savoring the pronouncement. "It is what is known as generalized consumption. There is not a hope in the world." And Cass, feeling the blood knocking outrageously at his temples (by then his need to do something had become like a panic, a fierce drive up-

ward and outward from his self that had begun to cut like flame
through the boozy dreamland, the nit-picking, the inertia, the
navel-gazing), said loudly and impatiently: "What do you mean
there is not a hope in the world? I'm no doctor but I know better
than that! I read the papers! There are *drugs* for this now!"
Whereupon Caltroni, stupidity like ooze around his pink lips, had
closed his eyes behind his pince-nez, pressed his fingers together,
a rich wise gesture, absurdly vain, sacerdotal: *"Vero.* I do believe there is a drug. It is somewhat like penicillin. The name
escapes me." And opened his eyes. "It is an American product,
I believe. But it is in exceedingly short supply in Italy. I myself
have never had the opportunity to use it, although in Rome—"
He paused. "In any case it could do no good with the *peasant"*—
speaking the patronizing word, *campagnuolo,* delicately, as if it
were a germ—"he is far gone, and besides he could never be in
any position to pay—" But Cass had risen, stalked to the door,
shouting over his shoulder: *"Che schifo! Merda!* I wouldn't let
you perform an abortion on my cat!" And felt instant shame,
aware even as he slammed the flimsy door shut that the ignorant
doctor's sin was only the venial one of being born in the south of
Italy, where, soggy and defeated, even his vanity a sham, he
would be reconciled in despair until the end of his days to pricking
boils and salving the teats of mangy cows and prescribing quack
pills and ointments to people who repaid him—because that is
all they had—in goat cheese.

But still Michele continued to get worse: he had no strength
to lift himself from the hammock, he had a constant headache, he
began to complain of pain in his leg, his attacks of coughing
were monstrous to see and hear. Through Cass' tutelage in plun-
dering Mason's storeroom (once he took off for a week in Capri
with Rosemarie, which made for a field day among the groceries),
Francesca saw to it that Michele was fed, and Ghita and the children too, but the sick man's appetite was poor. Every day Cass
visited him; they talked endlessly of America, land of lost content, of gold. For Michele's sake, he embroidered long lies,
baroquely colored. Once, describing in much detail, of all places,
Providence, Rhode Island, which Michele, for reasons known
only to himself, longed to see, Cass felt sudden pain and longing
himself, and annoyance at the demeaning nostalgia, and, breaking off in mid-sentence, wondering at the feeling, realized simply
that whatever else he might say against his native land, there
would not be this particular gross wrong and insult to mortal flesh.

And he looked down at Michele, consumed by a tenderness that he could not understand; seeing the man's eyes closed in sleep, he thought for an agonizing moment that he was dead. Then shortly after this, sometime around the middle of June, an odd thing occurred which Cass considered a good omen: one day there had come to the Bella Vista a young doctor from Omaha, Nebraska, and his wife, obviously honeymooners—the doctor a short, intense type with a reddish butch crew-cut and square red mustache like matched hairbrushes, his bride gangling and plain, possessing an earnest athletic look and the flatly contoured powerful legs of a miler. The couple was obviously distraught to begin with; they stayed long enough to play one or two desultory sets of tennis on the Bella Vista's single dusty court, and then (doubtless it was fear of heights, Windgasser observed unhappily, that morbid phobia which had caused even more extroverted-looking tourists than the doctor and his wife to flee the towering crag of Sambuco) had skedaddled sweatily away—possibly all the way back to flat Omaha—frantically chartering a private car to take them to Naples and in their haste leaving behind them, among other things, their tennis rackets, a set of barbells, a douche bag, and several books. It was one of these books—*The Merck Manual of Diagnosis and Therapy,* subtitled: *A Source of Ready Reference for the Physician*—that Cass, having come to beg from Windgasser another extension on the rent, saw on the hotel desk that very evening, and then tucked into his pocket with a secret glow of discovery. And it was through the manual that he finally set up shop as an M.D.

GENERALIZED HEMATOGENOUS TUBERCULOSIS. *Subacute Form: The onset of this form of the disease is . . . insidious. Fatigue, loss of weight, malaise, and fever develop over several weeks. The infection is less overwhelming than in the acute form and fewer lesions are established in the various organs. A greater variety of manifestations develop, however, because the patient lives longer, allowing for the development of local lesions. Lymphadenopathy is more prominent, splenomegaly more frequently seen, and progressive ulcerative pulmonary tuberculosis often develops subsequent to miliary "seeding." Symptoms and signs of genitourinary tuberculosis, bone and joint tuberculosis, or skin tuberculosis frequently develop during the illness. A majority of the patients die within three to six months but some live for many years with partially healed lesions in the organ systems involved.* He committed such passages to memory, finding in this one, or at least in its final line, almost as much to hope for as to cause him despair. For if it was true that *some* did live for many years, was there not an outside chance that Michele might join the saved? In the Bella Vista library, between *Middlemarch* and *East Lynne*, he discovered an enormous rat-chewed dictionary and looked up "splenomegaly"; rushing down to Tramonti that very evening he prodded gently at Michele's spleen, found that it was swollen, outsized, like a rubber tire, and figured that at least Caltroni's diagnosis had been correct. *Streptomycin or dihydrostreptomycin is of considerable value in the treatment of the acute and subacute forms of the disease. In addition to specific antibiotic therapy, active supportive treatment is indicated for the patient with severe acute miliary tuberculosis. He may be so ill as to require I.V. hydration and alimentation and vitamin supplements. Blood transfusions may be helpful.* And he thought: Shit a brick, how am I going to give him any blood? But that problem he would grapple with when he came to it. The drugs were the immediate, the pressing thing and by dawn of the next day—his mind aswarm with monstrous words like sarcoidosis, histoplasmosis, coccidioidomycosis, but with a rage to cure flaming in his breast—he knew at least where he could get his hands on some streptomycin. That morning he had presented himself early at Mason's door, for once neatly attired, as befits an up-and-coming doctor of medicine.

And Mason had held out on him. No, he had not really held out on him at last; he *had* given in, languidly accoutered himself in his spotless flannels, and with Cass had tooled over to the PX pharmacy, where, making use of his elaborate connections, he had obtained the thirty cc. of streptomycin—plus two hypodermic syringes, and ten ampoules of morphine, too, to ease the pain in Michele's leg: that was part of the bargain. For bargain it was, a deal—there was no largesse involved—and for this alone, almost, Cass would be unable to forgive him. He had made his plea, straight and simple ("Mason, see, it's Francesca's father, he's in *awful* shape and what he needs, you understand, is this new wonder drug that I'd figured you might be able to get for me . . ." And so on), and had elicited only an Olympian shrug and *this* rejoinder: "Crap, Cass, now *please* don't consider me the Flintheart of all time but you know as well as I do that if each individual American went around nursing every sick distressed Italian that came along he'd go broke in about a week even if he had twenty million dollars." And swiveled in the bright morning sunlight, immaculate, swank, streamlined, and scrutable in his flannels, and poured two cups of coffee from the spout of a gleaming electric Koffee King. "I'm a bastard, I know," he said, self-mocking, "but face it, can't you? If one must accept the notion of a welfare state with all of its committed millions, and European Recovery or whatever it's called, then one must realize that one has already done his bit. Really, Cassius, I mean this. If I told you how much Federal income tax I paid last year you'd call me a liar. I mean, dollbaby, I've already kicked in with a couple of gallons of antibiotics." Yet a bargain was finally struck after several hours' conversation during which, for the first time, Mason broached his opinions upon the value of erotica, and in fact showed Cass a stack of his juiciest lithographs. "It might just be the thing, dollbaby," Mason had said, "to get you around that psychic block of yours." In his morning haze, the prospect was deceptively titillating. And later he regretted it. But the bargain was struck. For one filthy picture, to be skillfully executed: rent money, brandy, streptomycin. They took off for Naples at noon. And late that same evening, just before he started to fulfill his part of the bargain and began painting the atrocious picture in encaustic, meticulously applied, he had at least the satisfaction of seeing a full gram of the hard-won stuff flow from his own syringe into Michele's veins. All he lacked was a diploma.

Yet it became a month of disconnected days, verging, it seemed, ever closer to some shadowland frontier separating reason from madness. He drank, he went without sleep; at Michele's side at least six times daily and often more, he lost count of the hot treks he made into the valley and back—compelled to do so because hysteric Ghita could not be trusted to make the proper injections, even if in a valley which had never known a cake of ice, much less a refrigerator, there *had* been a place to store the drug (once he struggled into the valley with a huge block of ice, which quickly melted, and he saw that this scheme would be more arduous than a careful program of hikes)—and established a kind of hallucinated rhythmical schedule in which a certain familiar cypress that he passed, or the shallow place where he leapfrogged across a brook, or a boulder that he mounted to short-cut up a slope were only way stations, arrived at without the variation of a minute, upon the route toward that final destination where, pooped and logy with wine or Mason's booze, he would rest for a while in the fly-swarming heat and talk to Michele (America! America! What lies he told! What paeans, what eulogies he bestowed upon the nation!) and then with great care insert the boiled needle in the rubber stopper of the vial, extract a gram of the *rosé*-colored fluid and slowly pump it into a vein of Michele's wasted, unflinching arm. Yet Michele, perhaps more slowly than before, but still quite visibly and plainly, grew worse, wasting away like the thin attenuated white stalk of some plant deprived of water and the sun. He saw Michele wither away, and blind outrage seized him as he hiked back up through the valley, storming and raving at his own inadequacy, at Italy, at Mason (thinking: Bleeding God, he could get Michele fixed up just out of his petty cash . . .), at that black, baleful and depraved Deity who seemed coolly minded to annihilate His creatures not in spite of but almost because of the fact that they had learned to heal their bodies, if not their souls. . . .

"Questi sono i soli esemplari che si conoscano," said the finicky scientific radio voice, *"a rigor di termini—"* Mason had fallen silent, and now, as the Cadillac moved swiftly along the spine of the great ridge, a single fleecy cloud eclipsed the sun, bringing a sudden, momentary chill. Feeling the sweat evaporate on his brow, a cool prickle up his back, Cass raised the bottle to his lips and drank. Below in the valley the shadow of the cloud passed westward at tremendous speed, the ragged gray silhouette of some prehistoric bird engulfing fields, farmhouses, trees; behind its trailing edge the sunlight moved voraciously, pursuing the ghost. Slowly the cloud itself passed from the face of the sun, bringing heat to the car once more, and dazzling light. "Say, Mason," Cass heard himself say with effort, "say, old buddy, tell me something. Are you sure they've got that stuff?" "What stuff, Cassius?" he said amiably. "You know, the P.A.S. Last time, I mean Tuesday, are you sure they said you could get it today?" (*Merck* again, the viscous terminology committed to his memory as unshakably as a nursery rhyme: *Para-aminosalicylic acid is indicated chiefly as an adjuvant to streptomycin or dihydrostreptomycin therapy, since it delays the emergence of organismal resistance to these drugs. It may be used alone, however, when streptomycin and dihydrostreptomycin are contraindicated or have proved ineffective, since it possesses antituberculous activity itself.* The last bleeding hope and chance. And how, after watching Michele wither and fail for the last two weeks, it had taken him so long to root this precious information from the manual he would never know; no matter, stumbling upon the passage by sheerest chance as he half-drowsed by Michele's

hammock only three days before, he knew he must get his hands on this stuff whether it prove the ultimate miracle or only one last desperate and futile gesture.) "You sure they said you could get it today?" he repeated. "Sure I'm sure," Mason said. "Put it out of your mind, dollbaby." "I can't—" Cass began, sweating. "I mean, Mason, like all the rest I won't be able to pay you back right away. I mean, if you can just put it on the tab with all the rest of —" But remarkably, impossibly now—could it really be true?— Mason was saying: "Come on now, Cass, don't be absurd. I'll take care of it, call it a gift if you want to. For one thing I priced the stuff Tuesday. It's cheap. It's synthesized out of coal tar like aspirin, the pharmacist told me, and they have P.A.S. up the ass. But even"—Cass was gazing at him intently; was that a gentle smile on his face, a smile of benevolence even, or only something else, more complicated and devious, he was doing with his lips?—"even if it were really precious, Cassius, I'd want you to have it—for nothing." And for an instant he paused, rubbing one lens of his sun glasses with a Kleenex, magnanimously smiling. "I mean, God knows, it's the very least I can do. She's a *virulent* little sneak thief—I'll argue that with you right down the line— but if the old man is as bad off as you say it's the least I can do to chip in a little bit myself and try to put him back on his feet. After all, it's not his fault that she's—well, you know what. So forget about it, Cass, this one's on me. O.K.?" He didn't answer. Drowsing now, peering at the valley through half-closed eyes, he felt his jaw drop, the muscles of his limbs growing limp with exhaustion as he thought: I don't want any of your bleeding charity. Not for Michele's sake, anyway. I'll pay you back, Buster Brown. I'll pay you back for everything.

Vesuvius, looming nearer beneath a blue arch of sky, seemed horribly to swerve and lumber, lurching in ponderous independent motion as the Cadillac squealed, breasted a curve, and began the descent toward Naples and the plain. At this point, what all day he had been so fearfully dreading, happened. Merciful sweet Christ, he thought in terror. Again. Again I'm going to hallucinate; and indeed for a moment—as his hand clutched the door handle not for support, but out of his own quick involuntary arrested impulse to hurl himself to the road—he saw superimposed against the volcano's blue flank the outlines of a hairy tarantula, disturbingly red and with clumsy groping arms, the whole writhing obscenity as vast as the Colosseum: in seconds, fading into the landscape, it was gone. He shut his eyes tightly, heart thumping, thinking: Think of nothing, think of light. Slowly his hand relaxed its grip on the door, fell back into his lap. So I must really have the D.T.'s, he whispered to himself. And now in the darkness the radio voice had fallen silent, but Mason's rattled on, garrulous, persevering, unfatigued: "No, getting back, Cass —in an age of cultural collapse, of artistic decline, people still must find some valid outlet for the emotional and psychic dynamism that's locked up in the human corpus. I remember that time we drove to Paestum I was trying to convince you of this, but I think you'll buy the theory finally. Remember what I was telling you about Nietzsche's concept of the Apollonian and the Dionysian—a marvel of romantic yet totally acceptable logic, really. . . . So now with art in decadent stasis society must join the Dionysian upswing toward some spiritual plateau that will allow a totally free operation of all the senses. . . . What you don't seem to realize, Cassius, is how basically moral and even religious the orgiastic principle is . . . not only because in a secondary way, flouting bourgeois convention, that is, it is a form of living dangerously—again Nietzsche . . . but it is the yea-saying of the flesh . . . the Priapean rites, you know . . . time-honored . . . your friends the venerable Greeks . . . neo-Laurentian . . . age-old ritual . . . phallic thrust . . . like jazz . . . *pro vita* not *contra,* dollbaby . . . it's what the hipster and the Negro know instinctively . . . bitch-goddess . . . a kind of divine sphincter . . . and the penultimate orgasm . . ."

Horseshit, he thought drowsily, triple bleeding horseshit. Impotent, now soft and faint, the voice lulled him for a spell and then was lost to hearing, for as he dozed a wild and agonizing fantasia possessed his brain: Poppy spoke to him, surrounded as ever by her children. "Cass," she said sadly, "I know," and moved away, and now he was once again with Francesca. In some sun-drenched field strewn with the cup-shapes of anemones, white, purple, and rose, they strolled together and the clear bright day was filled with the sound of her soft chatter. *"Mia madre andava in chiesa ogni mattina, ma adesso mio padre. . . ."* And she fell quiet, sadly, and now together they were crossing a stream, and she raised the hem of her skirt to expose her soft sweet thighs. Was this indeed something beyond a dream? For on the bank beside her, on a grassy mound where willows cast a constant cool shade, he was naked as, at last, was she, and he held her warm body tightly in his arm. *"Carissima,"* he was whispering and he was pressing long kisses on her mouth—and he felt her hands, too, loving and soft on his chest—and in her hair. Gently he touched the nipples of her heavy young breasts, even more gently that tender warm wet inner place which brought the word *"Amore!"* to her lips like the cry from a madrigal . . . yet now there was a sound in his ears, a rumbling, as of the confluence of traffic from a hundred drumming streets, and the meadow, the anemones, the willows—his blessed Francesca—all were gone. A smell of putrefaction swarmed through his brain, a sweet-sour outrageous stench of dissolution, of death. On some wet black shore, foul with the blackness of death's gulf, he was searching for an answer and a key. In words whose meaning he did not know he called out through the gloom, and the echoed sound came back to him as if spoken in an outlandish tongue. Somewhere, he knew, there was light but like a shifting phantom it eluded him; voiceless, he strove to give voice to the cry which now, too late, awakening, he knew. "Rise up, Michele, rise up and walk!" he roared. And for the briefest space of time, between dark and light, he thought he saw the man, healed now, cured, staunch and upright, striding toward him. *O rise up Michele, my brother, rise!*

"Sharon's a Johnny Ray fan, she can't stand Frankie Laine," an American voice chirruped somewhere above him. He awoke slowly, with a dull headache, everywhere drenched in sweat. He was racked with lingering sorrow, lingering desire. Pulling himself to a sitting position from the place where he had lain sprawled across the seat, he found himself alone in the car, now motionless, absorbing the full blast of the sun in the familiar parking lot. Two chattering bobbysoxers rosy with acne, in babushkas and blue jeans, both of them licking on popsicles, strolled past discussing culture: "Sharon can't stand anybody but Johnny." He was stupefied with drink and the remnants of the all too brief nap; he looked for Mason, saw no one now save a blond soldier with an incredibly square head who strode whistling toward the PX. Sudden panic seized him. Maybe he's not going to get the P.A.S. he thought. Maybe for some reason he's going to get all his booze and his groceries and he's not going to get that P.A.S. after all. The bugger just might be going to hold out on me. Half-stumbling down on the asphalt as he hooked his foot beneath the seat, he lurched from the car and weaved toward the squat, barrack-like PX, muttering to himself, sweating like a Percheron, and belatedly aware (the flushed, tight-lipped look, the suddenly averted eyes of some Army wife told him this) that he was displaying through his trousers a large erection. He paused and composed himself and then proceeded toward the glass door, where, pushing through along with a crowd of sport-shirted countrymen, he was met by a frigid blast of conditioned air and a gum-chewing master sergeant with mean blue eyes and a large scuttle-shaped chin. "Where's your pass, buddy?" he said, gazing up from his deck. "I'm looking for a friend," Cass said. "You gotta have a pass." "I don't have a pass," Cass began to explain, "my friend has a pass and I usually—" "Look, soljer," said the sergeant, laying aside a copy of *Action Comics* and gazing at him without sympathy, "I don't make the rules. Uncle Sambo makes the rules. To get into this Post Exchange you've *gotta have a pass.* Signed by the C.O. and endorsed by the adjutant. How long you been here? What outfit you in? Guard Company? H. & S.?" Cass felt sounds like sobs welling up in his chest, a red mist of fury began to glaze his eyes. "And another thing, buddy, let me give you a tip," the sergeant went on, "if I was you when I got into civilian clothes I'd be a little bit more careful about my appearance. Especially when you're taking a load on. You look like something the cat dragged in, soljer. I'd just go somewhere and sleep it off if I was you." For a long moment, incredulous and confused, stirring with insult, outrage, Cass stood looking at the sergeant, mouth agape; through the icebox air, muted, sweet, floated a syrupy confection of recorded dance music, saxophones, clarinets, and whining strings; from some other source, competing with the goo, a crooner softly blubbered, adding a mawkish dissonance. He smelled a drug-store smell, as of ice cream, milk, and spilled Coca-Cola. One more word out of him, he was thinking slowly, dimly, deliberately, and I'll flatten his bleeding nose. And he was not precisely sure, but in his daze and stupor he did seem to be making a clenched fist and a lurching gesture in the sergeant's direction when he felt a touch on his arm and then saw Mason, intervening. "That's all right, Sergeant," he was saying, "let him in on my pass, if you will. He's—uh—my *man,* and I'll need him to help carry some things out." He turned to Cass, his voice ill-tempered: "You're a big help, Buster Brown. I tried to wake you up for fifteen minutes. Let him through, will you, Sergeant?" "Yes, sir. Right you are, sir." And so, trailing Mason, he pushed into the place—his *man,* now. It was close to the last bleeding straw. . . .

He felt himself slowly going. The booze he might have tolerated. Or he might have sustained himself even in the depths of pure exhaustion. But booze in company with his exhaustion (how many hours of sleep had he averaged daily in the past weeks —four? three?—he did not know, aware only of a weariness so profound that it threatened thought, sanity, threatened sleep itself, which in turn was so racked and haunted by his nightmarish six-times-daily ritual hike that even in his dreams his feet kept steadily plodding over rocks and boulders, his mind counting landmark cypresses, his fingers pumping life and sustenance into Michele's ever-outstretched arm)—whiskey and exhaustion were too much, and together they conspired to unseat his senses. "Mah BAH-lews will be yo' BAH-lews," the voice was crooning, in a vindictive whimper, "some day, baby"—and as Cass trailed after Mason toward the food market he felt overpowered, in spite of himself, by a kind of numb, despairing hilarity. In front of him a red-faced rawboned Army matron in slacks loomed up. "Harry!" she crowed. "They don't *have* any Reddi-wip!" And Cass, squeezing past her, mumbled, "Merciful God, think of that." The remark unnoticed, he passed on in Mason's train, staggering slightly athwart pyramidal towers of canned soup, dog food, and toilet paper, and blundered for a moment into a queue—between two hulking figures, one of them, he dimly discerned, a major in crisp khaki, who scowled and said: "Just a minute there, you. Go to the end of the line." He giggled, hearing his own lethargic dreamlike voice: "Don't you believe what they say, Major, peacetime Army ain't all a bunch of bums, why take you, now, you look like a fine upstanding clean-cut . . ." but at this moment felt Mason's clutch on his arm, heard Mason's smooth apologies—*Just a joker, Major, don't pay any attention*—and now Mason's voice in his ear, the peremptory command: *Straighten up, you idiot. I'll let you make a clown of yourself tonight, any time you want. But not here. Do you want me to get that drug or not?* "Sho', Mason," he was saying. "Sho'. Sho', buddy. Anything you say, anything at all." Shortly after this, briefly separated from Mason in the jostling throng, he found himself half-sprawled across the camera counter amid stacked-up orange boxes of Kodachrome film, amid lenses and light meters and leather camera cases, solemnly sighting through a Brownie. "But what I mean is," he was cajoling the corporal-clerk, "what I really mean is, is it made for all eternity?" He had begun to wobble dangerously. "I mean can I take and snap a little shot of Myrtle and all the kids, and maybe Mom and Dad too, and Buddy, he's my brother, and Smitty, he's my best pal and—" But now he went no further, for almost simultaneously with the clerk's shouted

"Bates, c'mere and help me get this drunk out of here!" he felt Mason's presence again, heard the apologies, all followed by a moment of blankness so perfect that it was as if someone had stolen up upon him and, quite painlessly and suddenly, bludgeoned him with a sledge hammer. Shortly after (two minutes, five minutes, time had escaped him) he came astonishingly, brilliantly alive, discovering that in some fashion he had acquired a child's rocket gun and that now, with this noisemaker at rightshoulder-arms, he was weaving precariously among the counters, singing at the top of his voice. " 'Gawd . . . bless . . . *A-murrica!* ' " he bellowed. " 'Land . . . 'at I . . . love!' " Sidestepping some khaki arm outstretched to intercept him, he executed a deft marching manual—*wan, hup, reep, faw*—and lurched blindly into a pyramid of Quaker Oats boxes, which flew apart with the impact and came down around his feet in a myriad of separate, puffy explosions. " 'Stand beside her!' " he heard himself roar, tramping on. " 'And guide her . . .' Gangway!" Stark truth seized him even as he marched—he was courting total disaster—and desperate, prayerful words (*Slotkin, old father, old rabbi, what shall I do? Teach me now in my need.*) formed a brief and passionate litany on his lips; but wildly beyond control, he marched steadily through the place, scattering dogs, captains, colonels, children, shoppers, bellowing imperial commands. "Gangway! Out of the way, you Army trash! Make way for a real live foursquare Amurrican!" *Zock!* he went with the rocket gun, taking aim at a cowering Army wife. *Zock!* "That one's to pay back the Founding Fathers!" *Zock!* A portly colonel, quivering, blazing with outrage, came into his line of fire. *Zock!* "That one's to pay for the right honorable lady ambassador!" *Zock!* "That one there's to pay for foreign aid! Globaloney!" *Zock!* It was, he knew numbly, the end of the trail. A shudder ran up his back, and the familiar sour taste, presaging the onslaught of oblivion, rushed up beneath his tongue even as he took sight upon a bespectacled major and his wife, aiming to get two ducks with one blast. "Here's one to comfort the shade of Thomas Jefferson!" he howled. And the rocket gun, expiring, uttered one last feeble and uncertain *Zock!* as he felt strong arms seize him at last, and as the day reeled and heaved and collapsed into darkness. . . .

"You're lucky you didn't end up in the guardhouse, dollbaby," he recalled Mason saying some hours later, as they drove back by way of Sorrento. It was a ride full of lights and darks, strange shifting shadows, and a half-sleep composed of abstruse and perplexing dreams. Totally worn out, he spoke not a word to Mason, even to respond to such singular remarks (though he was careful to store them up in his memory, for future reference and action) as: "You can thank heaven that I got you off the hook, I think you can see how utterly dependent upon me you've become." Even when, somewhere above Positano, he regained strength and sobriety enough to open his eyes drowsily and look at Mason, hearing him say this: "In the complete wreck you've become, dollbaby, I don't think you can fail to understand why I might be determined to get into her pants. Of what earthly use is a *lush* to her? After all, someone's got to give her a good workout—" He kept silent, biding his time. He would have his day. He closed his eyes again and slept all the way to Amalfi, where he was to meet Poppy at the *festa.*

Yet curiously, inexplicably—not to say unforgivably—Mason at last did hold out on him: he did not have the drug in his possession after all. As Cass got out of the car in Amalfi and made a motion to pluck the bottle out of a carton in the back seat, Mason slammed the door abruptly and gazed at him coldly from his place behind the wheel, gunning the motor in savage, sharp bursts. "Hands off, Buster Brown," he said curtly, with venom in his voice. "I'm going to keep that stuff until you *come to your senses.* Look me up tonight." And he stared at Cass with an expression filled with such inchoate, mingled emotions that Cass thought that Mason, too, was about to take leave of his wits. "Look me up tonight," he repeated in a queer choked voice, "maybe we'll be able to strike some sort of bargain." "But for Christ sake, Mason, you said—" Cass began. But suddenly the Cadillac slid away into the dusky afternoon, and vanished up the road toward Sambuco. What sort of bargain had he in mind? Cass never found out, but as he stood there that afternoon on the piazza in Amalfi, swaying slightly, stunned by what Mason had done and by the abruptness of his departure, he was aware that this last look of Mason's, composed in part of such hatred, was made up in at least equal part of something else not quite love but its loathsome resemblance.

I guess now I'll really have to rob the son of a bitch, he thought, as he went into a *drogheria* and bought a bottle of wine. Then after all of this is over I'll sober up. I'll sober up and give him a fat lip.

He was really quite ill. When he met Poppy and the children at the seaside *festa,* she peered at him closely, observed that he looked "gruesome," and insisted that they go up to Sambuco at once. Through the carnival dust he looked at her: her brow was beaded with sweat, and she was quite agitated, and as he listened to her she seemed extraordinarily pretty; what she was saying he barely heard but he knew that every word she spoke was expressing nothing but concern for him. And with sorrow he realized that for a longer time than was morally or humanly reasonable she might as well never have existed.

He was somewhat more sober now—sober enough, at least, to make an accounting of their joint resources, and to discover that they had not enough cash for the bus. "But you bought that bottle of *wine!*" Poppy wailed. "Creepers! So now we'll have to walk *up* five miles!" Indignant, close to tears, she and the three youngest went on ahead, while he and Peggy trailed after. Hand in hand they walked up the shore, up the road among the lemon groves through the closing lavender light. For a while as they scuffed along Peggy was solemn and subdued, glum, chewing noisily on sugar almonds. Then she said: "Daddy, why are you trying to kill yourself? Mummy says she thinks you're trying to kill yourself, drinking so much and everything and going without sleep. She's just been crying and crying. For just days. Are you, Daddy?" There was a distant sound of oars on the water, and from somewhere music, sweet and indistinct, touched with longing. "She told Timmy that you have a sweetheart. Do you have a sweetheart, Daddy?" He paused to light a cigar, saying nothing, thinking: My darling, my dearest little girl, if I could just tell you what— "You know what?" Peggy said. "She told Timmy that you were nothing but an old goat who would never learn. Then she cried again. She just cried and cried." He took her hand and they went up the hill. Jesus, he thought, she knows. Then after this he realized how foolish it was for him to think that she had not known all along, and so he ceased worrying. Peggy chattered about glamour, magic, movie stars. He thought once more of Michele.

It would not be an entirely easy matter, he knew, to wrest that drug from Mason's hands; but suddenly he had such a powerful and mysterious convulsion of joy that it was almost like terror. Then, when Peggy asked him to "invent a movie-star song" he took a gulp of wine and burst out singing:

"Oh, we went to the animal fair,
All the birds and the beasts were there;
Carleton Burns was drunk by turns
And so was Alice Adair. . . ."

And it was not long after this—while talking quite incoherently to a haggard, ill-tempered young American who had somehow smashed up his car—that darkness and oblivion once again began to crowd in around him.

X

So it was that for the longest time after the night itself was done Cass could remember almost nothing. As for all that went on between the time he saw me on the road and the moment, many hours later when, relatively sober, he set out with me down into the valley, his memory was as profound and complete a blank as that of a man who has spent long hours under anesthesia. Yet there often came times when—as he tried to break down the dam which held walled-in all those momentous recollections—he felt he was on the verge of discovering something; the fact, the thing was there, like that infuriating name which remains on the tip of the tongue yet in the end refuses to divulge itself. And this elusive fact was to Cass of raging importance. Because with proof of this fact (which was not so much proof as the final calm certitude that

Mason did rape Francesca) he could take some comfort in the notion that he had acted, at least, out of honest and purposeful motives of revenge. And finally, no less importantly, to get at this single reality would, he knew, lead to some understanding of everything else that took place that night and the next morning and the days that followed. For, as he told me on our riverbank in South Carolina, Francesca's death and his own murder of Mason had the effect on him of obliterating from his mind all but the barest outlines of the events themselves, in the exact manner of shell shock or any other catastrophe which lays memory to rest amnesically, traumatically, mercifully.

Yet Cass did not want this enduring mercy. He wanted to *know,* at no matter what renewed pain. And so it was that—in the same way that Cass, telling me of himself, and of Mason and all the rest, somehow allowed me to view recesses of my own self that I had never known before—I was able with my knowledge of at least part of what went on that night to lead Cass to a place where he could see all those events with new clarity, and together we tore down the walls which had long shut in his recollection.

They must have hitched a ride up the mountain—he and Poppy and the children—for he could never in his condition have made it on foot, but that part would remain hidden forever, because Poppy had simply forgotten and the kids were too young to remember. Then at the palace he had fallen asleep, into a slumber which by all rights should have lasted round the clock, so heavy was his exhaustion, but which instead was tormented by such dreams of stress and urgency (these he remembered: Michele calling to him, Francesca weeping, an appalling foretaste of death in which he felt the precious bottle floating away from his grasp upon the black waters of some storm-swept gulf) that he awoke wailing aloud, sopping in sweat, and while the room circled around him listened to the movie people yawping and cackling in their descent down the stairway toward the pool. It was pitch-dark outside. The air was so humid that it seemed to lap against his skin like a huge tongue. *Don Giovanni* was blaring in his ear, in queer elongated chords and phrases. When had he turned the phonograph on? He did not know, but he did know that it must have been playing for hours, automatically click-clacking its stack of records, and that the distortion was not in the music but in the fever raging in his brain. He turned the music up louder—its very volume seemed to give him confidence, to lend support to the theft he knew he must perform without delay—and then, staggering about and colliding with every accursed object that littered the blacked-out room, he managed to douse his head in a basin full of water, which did not sober him but soothed his headache some and brought momentary coolness to his throbbing brow and face. He heard Poppy talking softly to Peggy in the other bedroom, the rest of the children were asleep. At this point, he recalled, he had forgotten about Francesca, had forgotten about Mason's implied threat against her in the car, or that he might even try to make good that threat this very night; all these things had been pushed to the back of his mind in favor of one single overwhelming thought now which had taken on the quality of a paranoid obsession or a raging runaway lust: *I've got to get those pills down to Michele. I've just got to.* For already there had been the gap of a day and a half in the treatment, and his intuition (which later he discovered was a correct one) told him that too long a lapse between the cessation of one drug and the beginning of another would allow the disease to make savage, renewed, perhaps final inroads upon a system already ruinously weakened and depressed. And he thought: Well at least I won't have to refrigerate these buggers. At least maybe once I get this started I'll be able to get some sleep.

So he padded through the dark upstairs and out into the courtyard and then up the stairway to Mason's balcony. He recalled that at the time it did not bother him *how* he would get the drug. He neither had a prevision of Mason refusing him the bottle, nor, if Mason did refuse him, of how he would deal with the situation and face Mason down. He only knew that by agreement the bottle was his prerogative and his right, and he was out to take it. He was reasonably sure where the bottle was—in the upstairs bathroom where Mason had kept some of the streptomycin for a while, along with the rest of his medications—and not for a second did it cross his mind that anything would intervene to prevent him from getting it; the fixity of drunken obsession at this point governed his every act and impulse. So it was with all the more impotence and desolation that, minutes later, he found himself downstairs again in the dark bedroom, empty-handed. He had gone up, and he had come down, and the miracle drug was still in Mason's bathroom. What had happened? He did not know. He was only dimly aware of having entered Mason's place with a great show of authority and strength—to find the *salone* deserted except for the benevolent director, Cripps, and the pale young American he had encountered hours before on the road. Then as usual, horrid, humiliating, self-defeating things had happened. He had fallen somehow—was it against a piano? Now a great C-major chord strummed in his brain, and his ribs ached mercilessly. He could still hear himself running off at the mouth—though what he had said he no longer knew—and his failure, his inability to cope with the situation brought him to such a pitch of rage that he leaned from the window and began to howl madly into the night. "What's the *matter?*" he remembered Poppy crying, breathless, red-eyed, rushing to him in her nightgown. "Those movie stars, they'll think you're *batty!* Oh, Cass!" she screamed. "What's the matter with you? You're turning into a *maniac!* Be quiet! You're going crazy! You're driving all of us crazy!" But she was off down the hallway on the full blast of his advancing wrath. "God damn you, Poppy, you think I don't know . . . all crazy . . . and furthermore, the bleeding Micks . . . and who was it . . . when Hitler croaked was the only country outside Japan that sent their sympathy . . . who was it, by God . . . the Republic of Ireland or Erah or however the bloody hell you pronounce it!" And then once again he was in the dark prison of the room, trembling, chilled, head in his hands as he listened to some heartless, lost, wailing hillbilly music— "It was only because they hated the English!" he heard Poppy's faint voice in the distance—and forced his reeling brain to work out a new stratagem.

Then he realized he must have dozed off again, drowsing fitfully on the sour bed, only to wake up twenty minutes or half an hour later in the flat harsh light, his heart thumping wildly. He staggered to his feet and went upstairs. For a moment he stood swaying in the dark and odorous living room, hand pressed against his sweating brow, listening to the chatter at the edge of the swimming pool. It had begun to drizzle outside. He saw rainspecks drifting stickily against the windowpanes, at the same time saw the figures around the pool rise and disband and begin to ascend Indian-file back up through the garden toward the palace. Around the pool the floodlights blinked out one by one. He stood in pitchdarkness then, listening to the voices of the movie people approaching nearer, trying to make his brain work, trying frantically to make his head work and figure out a way in which he might steal up to Mason's and take the drug without detection. Suddenly, with maddening belatedness, there occurred to him a way, *the* way—why did these solutions reveal themselves so coyly, after such a perilous long delay? Because, of course, the back stairway was the answer. By the dark back stairway (the same servants' stairs up which he had so often heaved and shouldered boxes of Mason's groceries) he could make a quick entry into the rear of Mason's quarters, creep down the hall past the kitchen and into the bathroom, take off with the bottle and, barring some awkward encounter, escape notice. With Mason and the movie people in the *salone,* only the possibility of encountering old Giorgio or one of the scullery maids would stand in his way—and this would be a simple matter to deal with. The drug, he knew, was all but in the bag. He tightened his belt. There was a ringing in his ears, and now a plunging vertigo, which caused him to wobble dangerously and to propel himself across the black room listing heavily to starboard in a kind of limping, one-sided shuffle, like a man favoring a game leg. He cracked his head against the side of the easel, and was still cursing beneath his breath when at last, with great effort, he located the door and threw it open. Here at the threshold he stood for a moment, regaining his balance, acquainting his eyes with the light. For a long moment he heard nothing, save for the fluttering swoop and patter of a bird which tried to gain exit from the courtyard through a skylight. He had slowly lifted his eyes, trying to catch sight of the bird, when the outer door of the courtyard swung open and in from the street burst Francesca—barefoot, hair atangle, covering her ripped bodice as she scampered across the tiles toward him, and sobbing as if her heart would break. And somehow he knew what had happened even before she told him. Yes, he's done it, he thought, the bastard went and done it like he said.

In the dark living room, holding her close to his breast, stroking her hair as her tears streamed warm against his cheek, he listened and did not say a word as she told him what Mason had done. *"Porco,"* she sobbed, "he is the devil! Oh, Cass, I must kill myself!" He patted her steadily, gently on the arm. "I was ready to go home. So I could meet you like you said this morning. The people had gone to the pool. I was in the pantry. I had some things in a bag for Papa. Some eggs, some tomatoes, a cardboard bottle of American milk, and that is all. He came into the pantry and he turned on the light. I had unbuttoned the top of my dress, you see —to change—and he—he was watching. I mean, he stood there and watched me. And I tried to turn, to cover myself, but before I could do anything he clutched me—grasped hold of my arm. I tried to make him stop, to make him let go. I cried out, and he twisted my arm and hurt me. Then he said to me: 'What have you in the bag?' In English, which I mainly understood. And I said: 'Nothing.' Then he said something else in English, very angry, which I could not understand. He was very angry, very red in the face, and he kept saying these angry words in English that I could not understand. He kept twisting my arm, then finally, he said, *'Dove the earrings?'* Which is something I understood. And I said I did not know where the earrings were, I did not know what he was talking about. Then he said some more in English, very, very angry, and he said the word *thief* over and over, which I understood. Then I started to cry, and I said I was not a *ladra,* that I had not thieved from him anything but the milk and the tomatoes and the eggs. Which were for my Papa. And I tried to give him the bag back, but then he began to shout, and then all of a sudden he became quiet and looked at me in a strange way—here. And then he took his other hand and stroked me—here. And I began to turn away from him but he twisted my arm and then—" She fell silent, weeping softly, terribly, without restraint against Cass' shoulder. "He kept twisting my arm, and oh it hurt so, Cass! I tried to call out—I called for you, 'Cass! Cass!—but there was too much noise, the music in the *salone,* the machines in the kitchen. And then he did a fierce, quick thing. Still twisting my arm, he pushed me down the back hallway. And he took me to his bedroom and pushed me down on the big bed and locked the door. I tried to get up but he pushed me down again and ripped my dress. Then he said in English, 'This is what we do to a thief,' which I understood. Then he came to me on the bed. I scratched him! I scratched his face! But yet he— Oh, Cass, I must kill myself!"

And afterwards, as she lay there dazed and hurting, fastidious Mason (taking the precaution to secrete the door key in the pocket of his dressing gown) had bathed and combed himself, returned, attired in silk, plastering with Band-Aids the gouged-out wounds she had inflicted upon his cheeks. He seemed contrite now, she said, and he tried to put things right as she lay weeping on the bed. For a while he was very sorry, muttering amends. She understood almost none of what he said, though he murmured to her much that hinted of emolument and recompense: the words he said were "dollars," *"molto lire,"* and *"dinero,"* a Spanish word which she comprehended. But his contrition, so honest, so sincere, dwindled with the passing minutes and turned to lust as, once again, slyly removing his dressing gown, he tried to take her. This time, however, she moved too swiftly for him and a universal trick, heard long ago from the lips of one of the loose female gossips of the village, served her in good stead: she rose up on her elbows as he nakedly mounted, lifting one leg sharply and driving her knee with all her force into that place which had caused him so much pleasure and her an extremity of pain. As she told Cass this, and despite her grief, a note of almost joyful vengeance crept into her voice. "I think I broke both of them," she whispered fiercely, and even in his drunk heartbreak Cass verged near gruesome laughter. So, while Mason lay writhing on the bed, Francesca recaptured the key. "I unlocked the door and ran out," she moaned. "And he got up and came after me, shouting. Oh, Cass, he was absolutely *mad!* I understood what he said. He said he was going to kill me. He picked up an ashtray and I thought he was going to hit me with it. *'I kill you!'* he said. But I ran out and down the stairs. And then I ran out on the street. I must have hurt him good, Cass, because he could not catch me. But—oh, Madonna!— what am I going to do? Cass, what will I do?"

That was her story and it was, he knew (turning on the light to see her tear-stained face, shock-ravaged eyes), as close to the bare and bitter truth as modesty would permit her to tell. For a long while he held her in his arms, touched to the heart by a love for her which, curiously deepened by her misery, seemed so sweet and sharp as to be almost insupportable. For minutes she sobbed without letup, as if all the injustice and pain and cruelty in the world had come homing to her breast. Down below, the crashing chords of Mozart thundered without ceasing. At last Cass set her down upon the couch, where she lay crumpled, legs asprawl, still weeping, close to hysteria. Slowly, tenderly, he soothed her, and after a bit she lay still like one asleep. With a half-filled bottle of brandy he went to the window and looked out into the gray and lowering night. Now is the time, he thought, now I'll have to deal with the scum face to face. Now. I can wait no longer. Yet even as he thought this he turned back and saw Francesca lying there and knew again in the midst of his fury that with each ticking of the clock Michele's chance for life diminished and dimmed, and that revenge once more must be briefly postponed. I got to get that P.A.S., he thought, I got to get Michele rolling again. Mason can wait, and the revenge will be sweeter for the waiting. But now it occurred to him that at least he might be able to scare Mason; it seemed to him necessary to make Mason aware that he himself knew what had taken place, and it was for some reason the only honorable course—like a remnant from the dueling code—to prepare his adversary for the showdown to come. For a moment, he thought he was going to vomit. The spasm passed. He sat down at the littered table and with a pen spelled out the note: *Youre in deep trouble, Im going turn you in to bait for buzards.* And as he wrote, barely able to guide the pen with his shaking, intractable fingers, he knew that the skull-splitting pain in his head was the result no longer of booze, or of fatigue, but of a fury he had never thought it possible for one man alone to possess.

He downed the brandy in the bottle to its dregs. After a few minutes Francesca stirred with a small cry; he went to her and helped her to her feet. He gave her the note to deliver to Giorgio for Mason on her way out of the palace. And he was somehow clear-headed enough to ask for Mason's bedroom key. Then he told her to go home to the valley, that later he would join her there. *"Va' "* he said. "Go. Try not to cry any more." Together they went to the door; holding her close, he pressed upon her lips a wild and despairing kiss. And then she was gone. Long after, he thought it strange that, taking leave of him, she whispered *"Addio,"* which means not "good-by" but "good-by forever." Probably, he reasoned, it was only a sad, unconscious way of expressing the loss, so complete and irrevocable, of that part of her which Mason had taken instead of Cass himself. For in no way could she have known—any more than he—that when she pattered across the courtyard, and then vanished into the night, they would never lay eyes on one another again. . . .

"No," Cass said to me, "I never made love to Francesca, ever. I wanted to, God knows. So did she, I know. We would have sooner or later, I know. But we never made love. I don't know what it was that held me back. It wasn't breaking the marriage vows, or anything like that—I was too far gone to worry about a thing like that. No, it was something else, something I find it hard to put my finger on. Maybe it was because she was so young. . . . No, it wasn't that either, really. Maybe just her beauty—this sweetness and radiance she had which made me simply want to contemplate her, to sit in this light of hers, so that the thought of knowing her, of possessing her, of loving her utterly and completely became a kind of daydream which was all the more mad and glorious because of the anticipation. It was somehow as if I knew that if I waited long enough it would just happen, and it would be a thousand times dearer to both of us because of all the hours and days spent brooding and dreaming about it. And you might think it had something to do with some notion of purity or chastity, but it really wasn't that a bit. No, I found some kind of joy in her, you see—not just pleasure—this joy I felt I'd been searching for all my life, and it was almost enough to preserve my sanity all by itself. *Joy,* you see—a kind of serenity and repose that I never really knew existed. I even almost stopped drinking several times there. I reckon I just—I just cared for her, that's all. I loved her. I loved her crazily, it was that simple—the bleeding beginning and end of the matter.

"And—well, she did finally pose for me. In the nude, I mean. Remember I told you how at first she thought I was going to get my hands on her that way? Funny thing, now that I look back on it, about the only two things I did in the way of work there in Sambuco was this dirty painting I turned out for Mason, and these sketches of Francesca, which I've still got. You might say that combination sort of made up the two extremes of the sacred and profane. Anyway, there was a place down in the valley where I'd take her—one marvelous little secluded grove where there were willows and a grassy bank and a stream flowing through. I'd pose her there—she wasn't in the least self-conscious. We'd sit there in the afternoon and I'd sketch away. She'd chatter on about this and that and grab for flowers—I had a hell of a time making her keep still—and finally she'd settle down and grin a bit and then look gravely toward the sea, and we wouldn't say a word, just sit there sketching and posing and listening to the water flowing over the rocks and the crickets in the grass and the cowbells on the slopes. She'd have taken off her clothes and let her hair down—fantastic hair, it came down to her waist. Anyway, we'd sit there and it seemed as if we were under a spell—as if all my madness had been washed away for the moment, clean, and all her toil and misery, too, her sorrow over Michele had vanished into the air, and there we were in the pure sunshine, untouched by anything except this momentary, fabulous, bountiful peace. Then she'd get restless again and start chattering away, and teasing me about this and that, and so I'd have to close up shop, and we'd walk away from the place wrapped around each other, shaking with desire. God knows we should have gone on and done it. But—" He paused. "Anyway, I'll never forget that grove, with the rocks and the cowbells ringing on the hills and the willows, and her in the middle of it, giggling, with her hair like a wild lovely cloud around her, trying to keep still. . . .

"That night in the palace, you see, after she left—I don't know—it was as if dynamite had gone off inside me and exploded me to bits. To think that Mason had done it—in actuality, that is—had taken her, no joke, had made good on this threat of his which I'd thought was only another bit of his blowhard nonsense about sex—it left me shattered right down to my heels. It wasn't just the horror over what he'd done to Francesca, though that was most of it. It was the fact that I just didn't think he was capable of it. I mean I had foolishly let my guard down. You see, after being around him so long, after being exposed each day to this man who had sex in the head like a tumor, I had just finally assumed that he couldn't get it up. I really had. That he just couldn't get it up, and that was that. I mean, it's no secret, really. Forever distrust a man who *celebrates* anything too much. Get a man who's got sex on the brain, one of these types who's always whooping it up about enormous thighs and mystical copulations and frenzied orgasms and such, and then as in Mason's case combine that with an overripe interest in such distractions as dirty pictures, and you've got a man who is without a doubt hard put to be of real service to a woman. He'd probably be much happier if he'd just go on and admit he prefers sailors. And when such a man don't produce any offspring—like Mason—you've got to be especially suspicious; men that claim to get that much in the sack would be bound to slip up once in a while, just out of pure statistics. There's not much difference between this type and a bleeding little prude, really; both of them basically think of a good screw as something as cataclysmic as Judgment Day.

"Well, I had pretty much pegged Mason as this kind of character. I remember Rosemarie, for instance, and something that happened one night. I never got to know her very well. She was always up on the roof sunbathing, or morosely flip-flopping around the palace in her sandals with her nose stuck in the *New Yorker* or *Time* magazine. Lord, I can hear her now: 'Oh, Muffin, I read the most *fascinating* profile on old Ding Dong the Dahlia King!' or, 'Muffin, *Time* magazine has the most *devastating* article on the Italian Communists! I mean, it really makes you see the *incredible* evil of it all!' she'd say. Well, she actually was a good-hearted girl, all right, but her mind seemed to be a bit circumscribed, you might say. So, to come to the point: as I said, I didn't know her too well, but one night he got me to fix a leak in his bathtub—I met her coming down. She was fairly well loaded up on martinis—I smelled the juniper on her breath—and I guess I paused to say hello or something, when before I knew it, there on those dark stairs, she had made a lunge for me and was all over me like glue. One great big shuddering Ingres odalisque, eight feet tall, all pelvis and groin. She could have bent me like a pretzel. Then just as quickly she pulled away from me—she was crying, her daily fight with Mason, I guess—and mumbled that she was fearfully sorry and went on down into the garden. I had both my paws out, but I was clutching at air. Well, you know, I wasn't terribly irresistible in those days. A girl like Rosemarie, unless she was just plain *horny,* she wouldn't make a pass at the bespectacled degenerate who lives in the basement.

"So, Mason the poor bugger can't speak for himself. If you could drag him back from the grave maybe he could say why he did such a thing that night. God knows, I've thought it over and over and it hasn't made much sense. Often I've thought it was bound up with what I've just been trying to get at—with this *difficulty* I always suspected him of having, this failing which must be one of the most agonizing things that can afflict a man, this raging constant desire with no outlet, a starvation with no chance of fulfillment, which must fever and shake and torment a man until he can only find a release in violence. Maybe the only way Mason could be satisfied with a woman was through violence. Who knows?

"Sex meant a lot to Mason—more than any human being I ever laid eyes on. That pornography of his, for instance. What he always was talking about was the new look in morals—that's what he called it—and this business about sex being the last frontier. We had a lot of talks about that; this was along about the time he finally got me to do that picture for him. He wanted all the arts to embrace complete, explicit sexual expression—I'm quoting him. He said that pornography was a liberating force, *épater le bourgeois,* and all that crap—though Mason was deep down the most dyed-in-the-wool bourgeois who ever walked. Anyway, I tried to tell him—without offending him, of course, and losing my liquor supply—how half-cocked all this was. I said naturally pornography excited the glands—that's what it was for. It was fantasy made real. I'd had fantasies like that myself until I broke out into a sweat. Even a Baptist missionary has those kind of daydreams— or something like them—and people who say that they don't have them themselves are simply lying. Hence the prevalence of pornography, which must fill some need—else it wouldn't exist. And there's nothing particularly sinful about getting your desires aroused once in a while. But I asked Mason why, if this was true, pornography had been frowned on and shunned by all cultures since the beginning of time. Why? I asked. It wasn't really a moral issue at all. A dirty book can't corrupt, or a dirty picture either. Anybody who wants to get corrupted is going to get corrupted, even if they have to write or draw their own. Then why had there always been rules against it? It was simple. First, it was to keep sex the seductive and wonderful mystery that it is. And it was to keep the fun in it, too—because most pornographers are so *solemn* about it. But mainly—mainly it was to keep sex from becoming commonplace, cheap, and therefore a merciless, catastrophic, almighty bleeding *bore*.

"Well, Mason pretended to chew over these notions, but it was clear that he thought I was hopelessly naïve. If not a hick and a clodhopper in most ways, with the soul of a licensed embalmer. But all that's aside. He had sex on the brain, and I guess you might say that more than anything else it led to his undoing. He went one step too far. He tried rape and he succeeded.

"But why did Mason do it in this case, right then, that night, right there? He didn't exactly lack resources, you know. There are whorehouses in Naples that specialize in his kind of itch, if itch it was, and for a couple thousand lire he could have bought himself a nice authentic rape, complete with locked unwilling thighs and frantic hands and Neapolitan screams, and he wouldn't have even gotten scratched if he hadn't wanted to. But no, he had something else in mind, I know. So that that night, if you discount the business about the earrings and his rage over Francesca's alleged thievery—which was just a cover-up for something deeper —and put aside for a moment this theory about his impotence— which must be only part of the story—then you come up with one answer: he was raping *me*. No, God knows I don't want to make it look like I'm transferring to myself any of that final and degrading suffering which Francesca endured alone. I just mean this, you see: he must have understood what was happening. He must have seen how things were shaping up. Because for more time than I care to think about I had allowed him to own me—out of spinelessness at first, out of whiskey-greed and desolation of the spirit, but at last out of necessity. And the paradox is that this slavish contact with Mason that I had to preserve in order to save Michele freed me to come into that knowledge of selflessness I had thirsted for like a dying man, and into a state where such a thing as dependence on the likes of Mason would be unheard-of, an impossibility. And Mason must have understood this, too, and not so dimly either. I think he must have understood it a lot more than I did. He knew that for a while he had the pluperfect victim—a man he could own completely, and who lay back and slopped up his food and his drink, and who was so close to total corruption himself that he gloried in being owned. But he sensed, too, that his victim had changed now, had found something—some focus, some strength, some reality—and this was a dangerous situation for a man who wished to keep a firm grip on his property: bum that I still remained, each hour I strove to bring Michele back to health, each day I sweated and strained to regain my sanity by taking on this burden which God alone knows why I accepted—save that to shirk it would have been to die—I moved closer to a condition of freedom, and Mason knew it even if I didn't, and this he couldn't bear.

"So that night he held out on me. I don't think—scoundrel that he was—he had any *conscious* intention of hurting Michele by keeping those pills. But he kept them, no doubt waiting for that moment when, as he told me, I would *'come to my senses'*—which is to say the moment when by some act of fealty, some cheap bargain, through some humiliation, I would repudiate this new independence of mine, renounce any ideas I might have expressed about getting out of Sambuco, leaving him without a lap dog—and so put him into the driver's seat again. Then and only then the bastard planned to give me the pills back, I guess.

"But the pills weren't all. There was Francesca too, and by raping her he raped the two of us: that night I felt he had committed some filthy, unspeakable violation upon life itself. His timing was perfect. At that very moment when through Francesca I had conceived of life as having some vestige of a meaning, he tore that meaning limb from limb. Who knows why he did it? Because her beauty and her innocence drove him crazy? Because he knew she was mine? Because the sodden wreck he owned was struggling out of the mire, out of his grasp? Because in her terrible fright and distraction she called out, 'Cass! Cass!' when if she had stayed quiet, not shouting that name which must have been like anathema in his ears, he might have let her go?

"Who knows why he did it, but he *did* it, and at last I smashed his fucking skull in."

With his head bowed, Cass fell silent, and he remained quiet for a long time. When at last he resumed, he said in a soft and gentle voice: "So I guess now the time has come to tell you how I killed him, and everything else.

"Well, as for the rest of that night, of course, you know almost as much as I do. And for the circus act he made me go through upstairs—about that I still draw a total blank, and perhaps it's a blessing. It seems to me I have a dim memory of having gone through the same thing just a few nights before. Acting the clown, acting out drunkenly, helplessly, any role Mason dreamed up for me. Mason in charge, running me through my paces, and the movie creeps howling—that troglodyte Burns, and those vacant-faced actresses; and Cripps, that director, who sort of took care of me once, he seemed like a good egg, as I remember. But both times I was in the very heart of a coma. But about that night . . . Later, I recall going up the back stairs and lifting those pills from Mason's bathroom. And ah yes—I forgot to tell you: on my way out I got that picture I'd painted for him. I went into the room where I knew he stored all of his beautiful blue art and I found that picture and on the way back down the stairs I ripped it up with my bare hands, frame and all, and stuffed it into an ashcan on the street. It was what, looking back on it, you might call strike one against the house of Flagg. And after that, of course, there was the trip with you to the valley to see Michele. And dragging back up through the valley in the dawn, sober now, but so beaten down with exhaustion that I felt all my nerve ends twitching as if on the verge of some fit or convulsion, and after that—after settling you down to sleep—going upstairs and pacing, and fighting sleep, fighting sleep, consumed even in my half-dead weariness by a fury which I knew would not let me sleep, which I knew would allow me no letup or peace until I had confronted Mason and exacted my just pound of flesh. It was *all* I wished—this you must understand—and it was not much, or so it seemed to me; nothing would right his wrong or restore Francesca's loss, yet stretched to the very limit of all I understood that meant toleration and endurance, and for the sake of my manhood alone, or what was left of it, for the sake of whatever notion of honor I still honored, I knew I had to have some indication—*something,* some token, some mark, some sign—even if it was only a hand bloodied with his blood, or a fist bruised and broken where I had driven it into that smooth, peerless, polished, vainglorious face.

"And that was all, you see. All. Nothing else was in my mind. Had you told me even then, even in the midst of all my foaming, infuriate craze for revenge, that I would be capable of killing him—that indeed, within an hour, I *would* kill him—I would have said that you exaggerated my hatred and rage. Hate him I did, and my rage was like some great snapping mad dog inside me, but no, murder was not in my mind. Only shortly after, when I got that news which turned my blood to water—just then I understood once and for all that it is, in fact, the easiest thing in the world to wish to kill a man, and then to kill him without a qualm, without hesitation or pause or delay. . . ."

Cass fell silent again. Then he said: "But to kill a man, even in hatred, even in revenge, is like an amputation. Though this man may have done you the foulest injustice in the world, when you have killed him you have removed a part of yourself forever. For here was so-and-so. Here was some swine, some blackguard, some devil. But what made him tick? What made him do the things he did? What was his history? What went on in his mind? What, if you had let him live, would he have become? Would he have stayed a swine, unregenerate to the end? Or would he have become a better man? Maybe he could have imparted to you some secrets. You do not know. You have acted the role of God, you have judged him and condemned him. And by condemning him, by killing him, all the answers to those questions pass with him into oblivion. Only *you* remain—shorn of all that knowledge, and with as much pain as if somehow you had been dismembered. It is a pain that will stay with you as long as you live. . . . All the time I spent with Mason, I felt I never knew him, never could put my hands on him. He was like a gorgeous silver fish in a still pond: make a grab for him, and he has slithered away, and there you are with a handful of water. But maybe that was just the thing about him, you see? He was like mercury. Smoke. Wind. It was as if he was hardly a man at all, but a creature from a different race who had taken on the disguise of a man, an imperfect disguise, so that while you saw that he walked and talked and smelled like a man, you were nonetheless aware that here was a creature so strange, so *new*—so remote from the depths of your own experience, your own life, your own past—that there were times when you looked at him with your mouth wide-open, in awe, wondering that you could communicate with each other at all. For him there was no history, or, if there was, it began on the day he was born. Before that there was nothing, and out of that nothing sprang this creature, committed to nothingness because of the nothingness that informed all time before and after the hour of his birth. And it was impossible to understand a creature like this. . . . And so—

"Once early that summer I was drinking with Mason, and I had a reverie—about America—one of those sharp pangs of homesickness that would come over me every now and then, no matter how hard I tried to push them down. It was evening and we were sitting on his terrace, looking over the sea. I listened to Mason talk about his play—about this new look in morals. It seemed to me then that suddenly I was carried back to a time many years before, when I had come up from the South and Poppy and I were starting out in New York, in a drab little apartment on the West Side, where I was trying to be a painter and Poppy would go out each day to work at some damn Catholic youth club or something. Yet, strange, it was not Poppy and me I was dreaming of, but something else—of others, of other young married people of whatever age and time, other young kids I had never known nor would ever know. Before the babies come. Pretty young wives named Cathy or Mary or Barbara, and guys named Tim and Al and Dave, all of them in these sort of cheerless little apartments all over America—and the percolator boiling, and a rainy Sunday morning, and the guy in his underdrawers and the girl in curlers, feeding the goldfish. Or the two of them nibbling each other's ears and then going back to bed, mad with love, or then on the other hand just quarreling, or reading the newspapers while soggy, degrading music comes out of the radio. Why I had this vision I don't know—it was a very sorry vision in many ways—but I had it and I remembered that wet gray light of New York on a winter morning and the butter melting in a dish on the table, but mainly—mainly just these brave and pretty girls, and the brave boys they married, all hurried toward the same weird impossible destiny. Young lovers, stardust—piled up through unimaginable centuries. And suddenly, though I had never known them and never would know them, I loved them— I loved them all—and I wished them well.

"Then I stirred a little and looked up and heard Mason say: 'Let me tell you, dollbaby, do you know what the world's going to be like in a hundred years?' I'd lost track of the conversation but his eyes were gleaming—almost prophetic—as if he really knew. It was one of those moments when he was at his best, when I kind of liked him. He took a big puff out of this cigar he was smoking, and rared back, and for a moment, I swear, he looked so serene and knowing that you would have thought he had just planted his flagstaff on Mars.

"But I was still in that reverie of mine, and I didn't answer. Come to think of it, I wish I *had* asked him to tell me what he thought the world was going to be like in a hundred years because now, you see, I'll never know. It was a mystery he took with him."

That morning Cass remembered hearing the village clock strike five. On the sagging couch, still oozing with the cool damp of the night just passed, he lay with limp arms akimbo, palms upturned, breathing in shallow breaths as his eyes roved the ceiling, the shaded casement windows, the dingy walls carapaced with soot and spiderweb tracings and the wet gray accretions of mildew and time. The clutter of the room thrust up the specter-shapes around him in the graying darkness, the gathering light: the towering walnut wardrobe and the table still littered with indistinct objects (he made out a pipe, five empty wine bottles, a lava ashtray from the slopes of Vesuvius shaped like the head of death) and the ponderous easel with its dangling doll and white rectangular shape of canvas, chaste and untouched. He was a vessel. He sensed his own breathing and a dull throbbing ache along his rib cage and he felt too the slow inward-throbbing of his consciousness, but his thoughts made few connections with each other and, pliant as a strand of weed beneath streaming water, he lay there, inert, drained, exhausted, receiving all. Flies like winged blots, aroused by the heat, spun in eccentric paths somewhere far above him near the ceiling, mindlessly buzzing. And now other sounds of waking fell upon his ears—a bird call, and a girl's sweet drowsy voice singing and, from afar, puttering and somnolent, fishing boats on the gulf, moving languidly to harbor through the dawn. Then these sounds, too, faded and died, and all was still again save for the dim buzzing of the flies in the ghostly space of air above him.

One thing remained supreme: he must not sleep. He must not, could not, sleep, though a horde of unseen forces seemed to impel him toward it. In a moment of total lassitude he allowed his eyes to close; it took the whole of his strength and will to open them again, and his eyelids came apart with an aching flutter, fighting to erase the gray light. He must not sleep, he thought painfully, he could not sleep; and now, as if viewing himself through the eyes of some drowsy stranger he saw himself pushing back sleep, with leaden feet and faltering steps forcing back the door of sleep, that titanic oaken door as lofty and as ponderous as the entry to some medieval keep, which pressed open against all his puny efforts to close it, and behind which, it seemed, all the demons of slumber howled for his soul with a noise like that of a thousand hysteric pipes. Yet now, wonder of wonders, he was closing it. Drowsily he watched himself shouldering back the prodigious door, saw the space of darkness diminish as he filled the breach between the door's edge and the stony jamb, saw the massive hinges quiver with the strain; but then, in an instant, fantasy became dream; sound asleep for what seemed hours, he had indeed forced the door back, forced back sleep (or so a small and treacherous voice murmured in his ear), yet behind the door there was a lovely quattrocento castle—was there not?—and here he strolled amid a crowd of lords and ladies, halberds and masked falcons, wan lovers, and squads of murmuring nuns, in a place where courtyards blossomed with almond trees, and psalteries and lutes played exquisitely and invisibly, and over all was the scent of almond and lemon and balsam. . . . He awoke with a start, choked upon the fragment of a snore. All was quiet. The light was still dim and gray. Only seconds had passed.

Downstairs now he heard a cry—a small high tormented wail which arose in ascending quavering tones and then ceased abruptly, as if garroted—and even as the noise was strangled off he rose up on one elbow, heart pounding and nerves aflame and in a sudden panic of jittery apprehension yet almost simultaneously aware that it was only one of the children, crying out in sleep. For long moments he lay there propped on his elbow, ear cocked, listening, but there was no sound from below. He lay back again. At least I am sober, he thought, at least I will be able to handle the bastard with the calm forbearance and sobriety that he don't deserve but will get. . . . His eyes searched the ceiling. In languid dizzy loopings the flies traced thin black rubbery patterns in the air; one, emboldened by the gathering light, disengaged itself from the swarm, darted out and lit upon the wall, stickily fidgeting. Another removed itself from the mass, and then another; one lit upon his arm. In a half-hour, he thought, the nasty little buggers'll be all over the room, poking their noses in everything. He brushed the fly away. It returned almost instantly, lighting upon his ear, gummily buzzing. He groaned, slapped at it, half-deafening himself. I must do something, he thought. I got to do something about those flies at Michele's. They'll poison everybody in the place, the kids, Ghita, Francesca. . . . He shot erect abruptly on the couch. Francesca! Merciful God, he thought, where was she? The same sweaty and abominable fear he had had two hours before in the valley, when he learned that she had not shown up there at all, engulfed him now: not only had Mason once taken her at some point in the midst of the evening just past, not only had he—the word lay in his mind like something scabrous and diseased—*raped* her, but now at this very moment she was still upstairs with him, wrapped in his unspeakable embrace. Droplets of sweat stood out upon his brow. He found himself trembling violently, and he felt goose pimples break out in a cool rash up and down his arms. Then, almost as quickly as it came, the panic subsided, receded, and passed firmly away: he must not let himself get so out of hand.

No, Michele must have been right, he thought with relief again, as he sank back on the couch. Because though say the slimy bastard had the insolence and swinishness in him to do what he done once, he would neither have the guts or the chance to get her and do it again, so Michele must have been right and she is not up there but staying with that gardener's daughter. . . . He lay there blinking in the somber light, touching his tongue now to a sore cut place on his upper lip, some raw wound acquired God knows when during the chaotic blundering evening that resided in his mind less a space of time possessing even the vaguest semblance of sequence and order than a scrambled collection of tilted, disordered impressions, like a scrapbook pasted together by a baby or an idiot. The piano. Yes, a little—no, it could *not* have been a piano he had fallen over; then if not, how could he still have the dim but certain memory of a keyboard flashing up to meet his jaw and his teeth biting down on ivory? He rubbed the cut again with his tongue, drowsily pondering. I'll swear to Christ right now, he thought, not another bleeding drop of booze ever again. A scrap of music went through his mind like a butterfly, tender, innocent, aching, sweet, somehow bruised, hurt, promising love and assuring repose. *Batti, batti . . . pace o vita mia.* Fair barelegged barefooted Zerlina imploring her country lover *patience, patience,* asking him to forgive. The music returned again, a fragile translucent wing. *Bat . . . ti . . . bat . . . ti . . .* Why did it haunt him now? He closed his eyes, opened them again, listened; far down the slope a bus horn trumpeted faintly, faded out with a sound of perishing mnemonic brass, alloying scattered fragments of hunger and memory and desire. Merciful God, he thought. Sweet bleeding Father of us all, I have come to this. Come to the point where I know I should forgive him for everything, the miserable snake, only to find that there are some things that cannot be forgiven. So now I will simply have to stomp his face in or something, but no . . . I do not know. And he did not know. He did not know what, when he finally gained access to Mason (not long now, he knew, for Giorgio would be unlocking the doors), he would do: he only knew that he would do something, that Mason would be calmly and simply and inflexibly dealt with at last. A sour, corrosive taste came to his mouth, as if he had been sucking on a piece of brass.

So I guess what I will have to do, he thought, is go up there and get him alone somehow and give him a good talking to. Then without much further ado I'll have to kick his teeth out. The bus horn sounded, far and faint in the valley, and he let his eyelids close. The vexation and the rage and the trembling diminished and faded out. And again the horn blew in a tremulous sad alto like the soft decrescendo of dying trombones and once more, stealthily, between sleep and waking, the titanic doors seemed to open and surround him, allowing him brief swift terminable vistas of time past, irretrievable: his uncle's voice, amid the green tobacco heat and stillness of a summer noon, and the smell of goats and somewhere a washpail sloshing, and the green phantom forests, tattered with morning mist, of palmetto and cypress and pine; a rowboat foundered upon the mud of some sluggish southern river, and the scent of dockweed, and a buzzard circling high over smoky swampland, and a Negro voice round soft round, female and chuckling. Then the horn blew again, and he half-awoke, sank back into an instant's dream, like the barest breath of the syllable of a word: swallows wheeled over him in some blue forgotten evening, and there was a swing and a girl—and high, high they went!—and someone's voice was saying, "Son, oh, *son,* it's late, it's time." And at this sound he almost awoke, stirred, flexed his knees and for a second, dreaming of France, dreamed of poplars on a sun-mad hill, blackbirds beneath them as big as hawks, and of Francesca, *his* Francesca there. . . . He felt his eyelids flutter. I've got to wake up, he thought, but now to a parade-ground or drill-field he was beckoned, long ago at dusk in some southern encampment where white barracks stretched in shadeless ranks to the far horizon and men marching shouldered rifles in the twilight and, wild, triumphant, a band tarantaraed beneath a grove of pines—oh how long away!

He awoke to the sound of his heart thudding; the light was still gray in the room, dusty and fugitive. Softly he stirred, feeling the itchy sweat and clinging of his shirt against his back. No, I cannot go to sleep, he thought again, and now pressing his elbows deep into the sagging couch he gradually arose, sat up, blinking, and eased his feet slowly onto the floor. He stood erect then, stroking and massaging his ribs. He yawned, a gulping inspiration of breath that set a sharp pain snapping through his jaws. And he yawned again, helplessly and loudly, with a shuddering roar. And once more he yawned, bawling like a calf, and the silence afterwards was like a sudden noise in his ears. Merciful God, he thought, I'm a bleeding somnambulist. I got to snap out of it. He turned and moved through the clutter of the room.

For a moment he had trouble locating the knobs of the French doors leading onto the balcony. Then he found them, and he pulled the shaded doors open, and the dawn fell on his eyes in an aureole of pearl-gray light. It was cooler now on the balcony, cool and still. Light filled the valley, defining the terraced slopes and the vineyards and the lemon groves and the great hump-backed barren peak, dominating all, that plunged a thousand feet into a sea peach-gold with dawning and as still as glass. Like water bugs, noiseless now, their fish-lure lights extinguished, a fleet of tiny boats scuttled homeward toward Salerno, trailing white scratches of foam. Birds began talking again, tentative at first in soft drowsy solitary chirrups and cheeps, and there was a feathery stir and rustle among the lemon trees. And now he heard the girl's voice once more far down the slope, soft and sleepy and indistinct, singing words he could not understand, and for the briefest instant he had the notion that it was Francesca: he leaned forward over the rail as if to get a glimpse of her, realizing even as he did so that it was not, could not be Francesca at all. He shivered, haunted by a notion bleak, malign, beyond countenance; then this notion vanished as quickly as it had come as, distracted by a sudden flicker of white, he caught sight of the girl, far off, plump, laundry perched upon her head, roundly bobbing among the vines as her sweet cheery voice filled the dawn, diminished, faded against the hills. Then he turned his eyes up toward the end of the valley, knowing that from here he could not see Tramonti, yet half-hoping that something—a wisp of smoke from some hidden chimney—might give evidence of its presence there, secluded behind its sheltering pines. Nothing stirred. Somewhere behind those pines, he knew (or hoped now), Michele slept. Well, let him sleep, he thought. Though it won't do him any good, I guess, at least he will know some kind of foretaste of the ease and oblivion that's going to come. He took a cigar, slightly crumbled, from the breast pocket of his shirt and lit it, and gazed at the valley through a swirling blue cloud of smoke. He puffed on the cigar and gazed once more into the dawning valley. No, he thought, I guess all the wonder drugs on God's green earth would never save him. Never . . . Let him sleep. In the distance, yet closer now, higher up the mountain, the bus horn hooted with its sound of muted perishing brass, its soft dying fall echoing across the hills in fading yellow notes of memory and desire. He champed down on the cigar and for a moment closed his eyes, listening to the falling echo. Who will remember Michele, anyhow? he thought. Slowly he opened his eyes, and gazed at the softly brightening sea, thinking: No, unless dust can feel suffering, there will be no one to remember his death. No one. But if dust can feel suffering maybe he will be blown about a while on the air and maybe this suffering dust will get in the eyes of men who feed too well, and maybe they will weep without knowing why, and maybe this dust will tell them how this man died. A lousy sack of pus . . . He looked away from the sea, smelling the smell of death—smelling Michele and his loathsome disease, hating both. For an instant he was aware that his sudden fury was like that of a child's. That bleeding Michele and his bleeding T.B., he thought. Is it my fault? Is it my fault he's started to piss blood? The whole thing—all—it is a stinking pesthole. . . .

He went back through the French doors into the living room. In the corner there was an old wooden crate, and in it were a dozen phonograph records, their cardboard jackets frayed and smudged and taped against the ravages of his own hands. He pulled one out. There was no need to look at the label; he knew each by its own faded cover, its own peculiar shadow of greasy-fingered stain and grime. He put the record on the battered phonograph, tested the needle with his thumb, set the record spinning along its course, slightly eccentric and wobbling. Then as the needle sputtered and hissed in the first worn gray grooves, he went over to the armchair and sat down. And as he sat there, the music crashed in upon him, aerial and impossible, and with a swift sudden unloosing and opening, as of a thousand magical and lovely windows, consecrating light.

Mozart gives, he thought, giving more in one sweet singing cry than all the politicians since Caesar. A child gives, a shell or a weed that looks like a flower. Michele will die because I have not given. Which now explains a lot, Slotkin. Old father, old rabbi, hell is not giving. . . .

He jerked erect. Because now, through and across the music's swift and sudden ecstasy, above the notched hissing and sputtering of the record itself, he heard—or thought he heard—a voice.

It was familiar—so familiar, indeed, that, knowing just whose it was, he thought his ears were tricking him—and he waited, head cocked, for the voice to call again. For moments he heard nothing. Then once more he heard the voice, faint yet distinct from somewhere out in the courtyard: "Hey, Cass, buddy, come on up and have a drink!" He sat bolt upright in his chair. Mason! he thought. Triple bleeding God! But it couldn't be Mason, at this hour of the morning, inviting him for the ten thousandth time to booze it up. Impossible! It could *not* be Mason, who not only aware that he, Cass, knew what he had done to Francesca, but aware too that he must be, at long last, laying for him—it could not be Mason now, playing right into his hands! He listened. Save for the music, there was no sound. Again he leaned back in the chair, and again the voice floated dimly through the music: "Cass! Dollbaby! A drink!"

Heart pumping, he arose from the chair, stood there facing the courtyard door fuzzily defined, ajar. He went to the phonograph and turned the volume down, stood erect, waiting. Once more no sound. He turned the volume up again: the sweet wailing viola reached its crescendo, the violin joining it, and at that instant of wild junction the voice called from the courtyard again, loud and clear, rather petulant now, and demanding: "Cass!" His eyes moved toward the table, fell upon the Vesuvian skull-shaped ashtray, and he stepped forward and picked it up, waiting again, hefting the smooth lava in his hand. Then he put the ashtray back down on the table, thinking: No, that won't do, that won't do at all. I might hurt the bastard in a way I'll regret. If I take him I'll take him with my two bare hands. And he plunged toward the door, hurled it open with a crash, and stood blinking at the dusky courtyard: there was not a soul in sight. Among the movie equipment—the cameras and the booms and the arc lights—nothing stirred. And high above on Mason's balcony the door—the same door he had tried to force open only minutes before—was still closed, still firmly locked. My God, he thought, I must be going bughouse. I would have swore on a stack of Bibles . . . Cautiously, carefully, he gazed around him, but there was no stir or sound. And in a moment he turned and went back into the living room, sat down. He pounded at his head, as if to dislodge the ringing and the echo in his ears: as he did so he heard the voice again, nattering and querulous and insistent, slyly suggestive now above the flutes and strings, and seeming to emanate not from the outside but from a point much closer, close to his ear.

Let me tell you something Cash, old Cassius my boy . . . He
cautiously turned. His eyes searched the gloom. Nothing moved
there, save the flies, crisscrossing in drowsy flight against the ceiling. And again slowly he turned back. And again the voice came,
with its strange quality of proximity and distance, suggestive,
lewd, and with a soft lubricious lilt: *Let me tell you something,
old Cash, virgin tail can be the very best in* . . . As if on a car
radio tuned to a fading wave length, the voice dimmed and became still. He waited, listening. And as once more he sank back,
the voice returned, abruptly and with raw insulting loudness, as
if the phantom car had emerged from some sound-smothering tunnel: *I've had French stuff and I've had Spanish stuff in fact you
might say I've sampled the whole broad spectrum pole to pole
but they say that until you get yourself between the thighs of one
of the little guinea girls and by guinea I only mean the joking
generic term for* . . . For what? Again the voice disappeared.
He lowered his head and for a moment shut out the dawn, pressing
his knotted fists tightly against his eyelids. *I mean you know my
orientation is essentially liberal* . . . Stars darted here in the
darkness, crumbs and pinpoints of fire, blue whirlpools and globes
white with glistery incandescence, and all seemed touched with
hints of lunacy. Great God almighty, he thought, the bastard's
spooking me.

But then another sound possessed his ears, and he raised his
head to listen. Faint at first, then swiftly louder, it came from the
walls of the town; its initial notes seemed that of a siren or a high-
pitched horn, then quickly redefined themselves as he recognized the noise, knew what it was—a woman's wavering cry of
alarm, hoarse, heedless, wild. Another cry joined the first one,
then another, then another, all crying in unison—then the voices
fell silent at once, as if abruptly gagged and muffled. And for a
long moment there was only dead silence in the town. Then the
cries recommenced, nearer now, and he heard another noise,
strange, which made a pattering, steady, percussive rhythm beneath the cries, and this sound, too, defined itself as it became
louder and closer—footsteps on the cobblestones outside, rowdy,
stumbling, mad with haste. There was a dazzling *cling-clang* as
the feet struck a sewer grating; then the sound was repeated,
quickly, followed by the screams. And another *cling-clang* like a
short sharp collision of iron bars, and now a man's voice which
let out bull-like sounds in a succession of hoarse bellows each of
which terminated in a low, quavering, aspirated moan, curiously

feminine. And then for a moment the cries, which had been bunched together like the calls of a flock of crows in flight, became dispersed and straggled out and again grew fainter, and all he could hear was the frantic patter of feet going downhill past the palace in a skidding slick pandemonium of shoe leather, and one final stray bringing up the rear in a reticent dogtrot, heavily gasping for air.

Gut churning with fear, somehow forewarned as he leaped from the chair and raced outside, Cass reached the street door of the courtyard and had thrown it open before the straggler had passed the palace, calling out *"Aspett'!"* even as he recognized who it was—Windgasser, his face aflame with exertion and with the look in his sleep-swollen eyes of a man who has heard his own death sentence. Dazed, haggard, doomed, he stood plumply gowned in a bathrobe, his hairless shanks trembling in the chill and peach-hued dawn, and as Cass approached him he drew from his pocket an outsized linen handkerchief and passed it miserably and tremulously across his jowls. "Merthiful heaven," he said, "oh, Mr. K.!"

"What happened!" he cried, grasping the little man's sleeve. "What happened? Speak up, Fausto, tell me!"

"That Ricci girl. That peasant girl from Tramonti. Who used to work for *you!* Mr. Flagg's maid! She has been found—" He began to blubber.

"Speak up, dammit!"

"She has been found— She was found on the path to Tramonti! Beaten! Ravished! My dear sir! Dying!"

"Then how is she!" He was faintly aware that, clutching Fausto's sleeve, pinioning beneath his hand a rubbery band of flesh, he was making the hotelkeeper wince, and also now that he was roaring at the top of his voice. "How *is* she!" he repeated, releasing his grip. "How *is* she, for Christ sake? Tell me! Dying you said! *Dying?*"

"Oh, Mr. K.," he wept, and his voice died to a whisper, "she is still alive—but the horror! It was only an hour ago that they found her on the upper path—so they do not know. She is unconscious. But the doctor told me—just now—he told me that she cannot live out the day! But the horror of—"

"Who did it!"

"No one knows. Some *beast* of a person! Someone so totally lacking in any sense of *decency*—" He paused, as if to collect his scattered wits. "I mean— Oh, I just cannot bear to tell you.

I mean, her *skull* fwactured in two places, bones bwoken all over. I ask you, what sort of a murderous beast is it who would do such a vile and abominable thing, in a quiet town like this which for these past years has enjoyed such unpawalleled peace! With the cinema here! Surely they will leave now! Just when—"

"Scum," Cass murmured, in a voice partaking of the grief which had swamped him. "Filthy Swiss little faggot." He raised his arm, saw Windgasser flinch and shrink from him even as he wheeled away from the man and trotted back toward the palace. He felt ice water flowing in his veins. Several more townspeople, rapt, open-mouthed in the hysteria of crisis, rushed past him. A bare-footed woman with a baby in her arms stumbled downhill toward the piazza, uttering between white parted lips a series of frustrated shrieks, bubbling forth in weak gasps. And now as he turned toward the door to Mason's stairs he saw Dr. Caltroni, spectacles reflecting ovals of pink light, astride a rackety motorscooter veering up the hill toward the walls; mounted on the seat behind, a bald young priest swayed, peering with a worried look heavenward while clapping like a chalice to his breast a bottle containing, unmistakably, human blood. Cass turned away, hurried ten short steps down a dark alleyway odorous with garbage, and pulled violently at the doorknob with both hands, nearly collapsing himself back upon the cobblestones as the door—to his vague surprise unlocked—flung itself open with a clatter. Regaining balance, he plunged forward. The stone stairs were slippery with damp, and a musty gray smell as of mice and their excrement hovered over all; he took the steps two at a time, stumbling down once without pain in the half-dark. At the top of the stairs there was another door; this too was now unlocked and he hurled it open, taking a step into Mason's kitchen. The room was deserted. There was no sound here, save for the steady drip from a leaking faucet. For a moment he stood with his ear cocked, peering through the gloom. Noise from the street rose up through the walls, muffled and indistinct. A clock ticked somewhere and now, from far down the hallway where in their rooms the movie people slept, he heard a prodigious snore, tentative and choked, like the faulty initial burst of an outboard motor. He kept listening, heard springs creak once as the sleeper stirred, then again all was silent. He stepped forward, moving with cautious soundless footfall past the sleepers, past closed doors and doors ajar: through one he caught sight of a short, naked, recumbent Jew, the newspaper snoop whose name he had forgotten, with a hairy abdomen and an enormous appendectomy scar, mindlessly scratching his ribs as he slumbered beneath a buzzing electric fan. Cass moved on. In the windowless hallway it was humid—humid and close; he felt himself sweating, and a prickly chill ran up his back and then up his neck, making his scalp feel suddenly as tight as a drumhead. Yet, sweating, he felt parched, juiceless, dehydrated; his eyes were gritty and dry, as was his throat—a gorge full of sand—and abruptly with a hawking noise, loudly, too loudly, he tried to moisten it. He stopped in his tracks, waiting, listening, expecting someone to stir. Across the hall past a half-opened door three clothed male sleepers lay comatose across a double bed, the mouths of each agape, sprawled together like toppled mannequins.

Still he waited. Off in the distance someone groaned. He prowled on, turning at last into a corridor toward Mason's bedroom. With swift silent steps now he reached the door, suddenly drew back, thinking of Rosemarie, thinking that though he might handle Mason easily it would be impossible madness to deal with Mason in combination with his lofty, shrieking consort. But almost at that identical instant, recollecting the numberless times that summer when he had seen Rosemarie, rejected, cast out from Mason's favor, emerge red-eyed in the morning from some separate boudoir, he knew he must now take a chance on her being absent from his side, and once more he approached the door. As he did so, pressing down on the squeaking handle and groping simultaneously into his pocket, he realized with vexation (this he recalled later: his coolness, his calmness, his grief in abeyance—his passion for retribution dominating him so that even such possibly fateful missteps as this one caused him, instead of panic and anxiety, only a flicker of annoyance) that he had forgotten the key. It was on the table downstairs. But it was too late to go back. Inside he heard a stirring, then the voice, already apprehensive, alert, knowing: "Who's there?" Pressing his cheek against the door, he listened. The voice spoke again, louder now: "Who's there?" Still he did not answer, aware now of two lucidly apparent yet baffling and contradictory facts. The first of these was that he was in basic command of the situation, that after months and days of limp and ineffectual bondage when he was unable to break through to prick the cowardice at Mason's core, he was at last on top—he felt Mason's fear of his vengeance now even before grappling with him—and he knew that by that terror alone he could imprison Mason within the room. The door was three inches thick, the walls many times thicker, the long corridor isolated; let Mason squeal for help at the top of his lungs and no-where on the sleeping floor would he be heard. Yet time was run-ning out; the whole accursed palace would soon be astir, and he had no key. The other fact, then, which he calmly and coolly considered, was that though he might be able to trap Mason he could not get at him—he could not, furthermore, risk going down-stairs to retrieve the key—and it was up to him at this moment to find some satisfactory solution to the problem. After a few seconds he spoke in a flat, literal voice through the door: "Mason, you're going to die." He paused, then spoke again: "You might as well open up now, Mason, because I'm going to kill you." And at this point, as if his words substantiated what he did not need to know, he was aware that he was going to kill him. Even as he spoke he was quietly removing his shoes (there was a crack beneath the door; if you were some intended victim, separated from your pur-suer by this door, and, after calling out "Who's there?" and hear-ing only silence, you wished to ascertain if the marauder had gone away, allowing you to flee by the door, would you not bend down and peer through the crack, in order to tell whether you could see his feet? That was Cass' chill immaculate reasoning.) and silently placed them toes foremost against the thin space of light between door and step. He listened. There was only silence in the room. Wheeling without sound, sprinting in his stocking feet up the corridor, he raced through the deserted, party-littered *salone* and out onto the balcony and down the courtyard stairs, conscious of a slight skidding, sideslipping motion in his forward and downward flight but aware too of almost effortless speed as he hit the courtyard on the balls of his feet and bounded in two or three long strides into his living room, where he snatched up the key from the table, lost momentum, reversed motion, wheeled again and traveled noiselessly back across the courtyard and up the marble stairs in swift, choppy, silent steps regaining the cor-ridor and the door—pausing there only to put on his shoes again, which he managed to do with one hand while with the other he turned open the bolt with a soft chunking sound. The whole thing could not have taken more than a minute. He threw back the door, his eyes blinking in the sudden eastward flush of rosy light. No one was in the room. No Mason, no Rosemarie. Nobody. The immense Hollywood bed—sheets an obscene tangle still from Mason's plunder of the night just past—was empty.

He turned to search the closet when, at this instant, something told him where Mason was. And he jerked round then and stood there, waiting. A shout rose up from the distant street, a motor-scooter sputtered in an alleyway. Then for a long moment all was quiet. Did Mason really believe he would overlook his farcical hiding place? Ensconced within the classic refuge of miscreants, Mason had given himself away: the barest patch of a pair of green Bermuda shorts had moved—no more than a centimeter—but it was enough, and Cass slowly crouched low until he was eye to eye with his prey, who was cowering belly-down underneath the bed. For long seconds, like a hound dog in quizzical encounter with a trapped coon, he gazed at Mason, his own nose inches from the floor. No words passed between them; they breathed heavily, simultaneously, and when he blinked, Mason blinked, out of a face leached of blood and misshapen with terror. Then Cass spoke. "Mason," he said again, in a voice soft and even, somewhat tutorial, almost disciplinary. "Mason, you're going to die." Cass heard a shudder, a prolonged expiring breath like wind through a pine tree, and very slowly now he put forth his hand to grasp Mason's wrist, drawing back partly when Mason essayed his first move, whimpered slightly, and shimmied sideways out of reach. "Look here, Mason," he heard himself saying, in those strange level laconic tones, "you might as well just come on out of there. I can't move this here bed. I'm going to kill you, see? Now that's the bleeding fact of the matter. So come on out of there, hear?" There was another whimper, though now, mingled with some different sound—a sob, or a savage gulp for air—and at this point, too late, Cass realized he had made a crucial miscalculation. For in his coon-dog stance—rump upended, nose to the ground, one paw still outstretched in its vain foray beneath the mattress—he was considerably off-balance; dominating the situation from no substantial eminence, attacking weakly from the flank instead of from the center (the foot of the bed, where he could have swiftly extracted him by the heels), he was at a clumsy disadvantage, and it was while he was pondering a new angle that Mason seized the bit and from the other side suddenly rose like a rocket in the narrow space between the bed and the wall. "Buh-WAH!" he cried as Cass heaved to his feet. "WAH!" The sound echoed out of all childhood, a fearful, exacerbated, stricken wail—the cry of a four-year-old, terrified by dragons, thunder, or the dark. And before Cass, lunging across the huge playground of a bed, could get to him, he had bolted through the open door and out into the hallway, speeded by that same terror which had drained all color from his flesh, and which had made all his outcries congeal like faint bird calls in his throat as he scuttled along the corridor past the oblivious sleepers. He ran downstairs and out the back door, away from all help.

Outside in the garden, lumbering far behind Mason, Cass came to a halt and regained his breath. There was not a soul in sight. The town, save for those first few heralds of disaster he had seen on the street, was still sleeping. The garden was empty; beyond it, the valley stretched sleeping and misted in the dawn, devoid of life or motion. Yet as he looked at the wide trampled-down swath cut through the iris and poppies he could tell the direction of Mason's flight as easily as if he had seen it charted, and plunged wetly through the flower banks heedless of the crowd of fat honeybees which stormed up angrily in his path. He reached the end of the garden; here a high, white, wooden picket fence barred his way, and as he mounted it with a single leap, two things occurred almost at once: he saw a bottle-green scrap of cloth where his quarry, moments before, had impaled himself and, dreamily trying to gain altitude in flight so that he might avoid the same mishap, found himself impaled, skewered through the pants upon the identical paling. He struggled for a moment, wriggling loose, saw Mason far up the valley path even as with a ripping noise at the seat of his pants he freed himself and dropped to the stony ground below, hard, sending a shock of pain from his toes to his knees. He was puffing and heaving; not nearly Mason's equal in general vigor, he was dimly conscious that that fact alone might prevent him from doing what he had set out to do, yet even as this occurred to him he felt his legs and thighs moving powerfully beneath him in a resistless gallop, impelled as if by the urgency of some tightly wound clockwork beyond his control. As he ran he sensed the dawn lifting, a new lightness, shadows fading from their cups and hollows on the slopes. Lizards darted near him along the walls, skittering dryly among the dewy vines and lichen. The last dwellings of the town passed above and behind him; along this unpopulated cliffside, in the dust of the path, Mason's footprints were fresh and clear, and now several hundred yards ahead he saw once again the bottle-green flash as Mason, emerging from behind a stretch of wall, slid to a stop at a fork in the path and stood there for an instant, wildly hesitant, elbows working from side to side in indecision. A palace-dweller, he was ignorant of these outskirts; his ignorance was costing him seconds, and it was the right-hand path he must take, Cass knew, *the right-hand path,* the one which went lazily down then up—up the cliff toward the Villa Cardassi—not the left one sloping formidably but briefly up then down again to the safety of the town. He would take the right-hand path, because it looked easier. Sweating, sighing, heart thundering, Cass stumbled and sprawled out against the wall, canceling out his second's gain. As he found his balance and recaptured momentum he saw the green of Mason's shorts receding off to the right, into the deceptive, the proper path.

And now it was getting lighter, the peach and rose glow fading from the sky, and as he himself reached the fork and plunged to the right onto the path with its general disuse and its weedy outcropping of mustard and sow thistle and stunted daisies and crumbled litter underfoot of fallen rock and goat droppings and dust, he knew that Mason was sealed up, bottled, fleeing into a cul-de-sac not only unpeopled but decisively confined and bounded—a long slope with a fixed terminal at the summit's edge where the one choice short of suicide must be to turn and give battle. And as Cass galloped on, the slope getting steeper now, he heard the breath again coming from his lungs in long, amazingly delicate sighs, like the sighs of a man in the embrace of love, and it occurred to him with brief surprise how soft and glowing and gentle was the morning, how serene were these heights and the blue and shining sea below, and how deeply curious was his own fury—so free of passion, of delirium—which could yet push him on toward slaughter with the urgency and certitude of something already destined, preordained, inscribed in time. Yet even as this flashed through his mind, he thought of Francesca, and a swift, infernal vision of her mutilated beauty rose up before his eyes; blood and horror streamed against the sky, gushed heavenward, vanished in a sucking vortex, and for the briefest particle of an instant all went black as his pace slackened, and he let out a single brutish and inhuman roar, his soul transfigured, one and the same with that of his remotest ancestor. Light broke again, instantly; he saw Mason, nearer now—near the summit—pounding up the cliffside. For a second the figure paused, winded, hands on his knees as he bent low, gulping for breath, then stood erect and in a precipitate burst of speed, hair bouncing crazily like a wig askew, ran forward a dozen yards, hurled himself off the path and began to scramble up the slanting face of the cliff. Cass reached the place where Mason had begun his ascent half a minute after the ascent began; hand on his hips, regaining wind, he stood looking up at the pink patch of buttock protruding from the shorts, tanned legs flailing at the rocky slope. It was a distinct advantage thus to pause and watch him; it allowed his own lungs to rest while Mason scrambled up a nonexistent short cut: no matter how he reached the summit, he was imprisoned there, with a drop on the other side of a quarter of a mile, straight down. He may as well have taken the path.

As Cass turned then and galloped on up the path, he removed his glasses in mid-stride, thought better of it, replaced them, cast a glance over his shoulder and saw that Mason, sending down an avalanche of rubble and dust, had nearly gained the promontory. And as he increased his pace once more the breath began to tear itself from his lungs in racking gasps; he stumbled again, righted himself, plunged on up past the abandoned villa with its sagging façade and blasted columns, the marble portico inscription in the morning shade sweeping backward across his vision like the hallucinated glimpse of some impenetrable alphabet—SPERO, SPIRO DUM—vanishing, the smell of damp and fern and rotted stone enveloping him as now, near the summit, short-cutting too, he vaulted a low wall, hurtled forward without breaking stride across darkened spongy ground where an arena of tiny white-faced mushrooms scattered and exploded like people beneath his feet. He gained the peak. Sunshine like a scream; below, the blue sea suddenly came up to meet his eyes, half-blinding him as he leaped up from the ground to the encircling wall and stood balanced there, looking for his victim. Trapped, hemmed in, Mason was fifty yards opposite in the bramble-choked field, head down as he sat propped against a withered, wind-bent olive tree, shuddering for breath. Unable to see his face, Cass could see his neck, which was the scarlet hue of blood itself, and he jumped down from the wall, prepared to hurl himself forward again and upon his prey when at this instant something in his lungs gave a harsh involuntary whooping noise, and fingers of pain encircling his heart caused him to sink to earth like a stricken deer, gasping, helpless, puking, and nearly blind.

For a long while he crouched in the weeds on his knees. His retching stopped. Sight came slowly back. Far off on the still sea a dark cruise ship plowed through the dawn, past a smaller, lighter craft moving south toward Sicily. From the black-hulled ship a plume of smoke went up in salute against the blue; Cass watched, blinked his eyes, heard the roar of the whistle, deep-throated, drowsy, sonorous, floating up faint but clear through light like a pearl. Presently he saw Mason lie down in the weeds, one leg up, one arm thrown over his eyes; Cass lay down too, on his side, drinking the air. The dark ship surged westward, high-prowed, majestic, silent, its slumbering voyagers oblivious of all, its running lights still aglow, but now, even as he watched, winking out one by one. At last he saw Mason draw himself half-erect. With guarded movements he too raised himself partly up, and now Mason seemed to be trying to say something to him, calling out across the field—but what was he saying, what were the words he was forming with his lips? *I didn't? I don't? I'd die?* He seemed to be weeping. Again Mason tried to speak. *It wasn't? It was?* Why didn't he come out with it? Why did he mouth those words, as if imploring him to understand? Foolish Mason flopped back in the weeds once more, Cass flopped back, too, for one brief and final rest, and though he has no recollection of how long they lay there—perhaps five minutes, perhaps less, perhaps more—he does recall that a thirst such as he had never known before swelled in his throat, and that as he lay in his doze, half-conscious, with the noise of cool, delectable waters rushing through his brain, he was carried swift as memory back to the very light of his own beginning, and there in some slumberous southern noon heard his first baby-squall in the cradle, and knew it to be the sound of history itself, all error, dream, and madness.

But he rose, with a stone in his hand, and Mason rose with a knobby club, pale, to confront him, and at that instant, as if from nowhere, one single pigeon shot toward them, then veered aslant in fright with the faintest snapping of its wings. But even as Cass saw the pigeon skim away seaward he had charged, roaring, and he fell upon Mason, who fought savagely, furiously, for the few seconds allotted him. Cass would remember that moment's bravery—the club and the ruthless solid blows it landed on his ribs: it gave to that brief meeting a thrill of unexpected triumph and honor. But as Mason's arms boldly struck out, Cass brought the stone across between them in one roundhouse sweep of his shoulder, and Mason dropped like a bag of sand, murmuring, "Dollbaby." "Dollbaby," he whispered again, in a child's voice, but it was the last word he said, for Cass was atop the prostrate form and he drove the stone again, and again, and still once more into the skull which made a curious popping noise and split open on one side like a coconut, extruding a grayish-white membrane slimy with blood.

Perhaps it was then that he drew back, understanding where he was, and what he had done. He does not recall. Perhaps it was only the "Dollbaby," echoing belatedly in his mind, that caused him to halt and look down and see that the pale dead face, which was so soft and boyish, and in death as in life so tormented, might be the face of almost anything, but was not the face of a killer.

Children! he thought, standing erect over the twitching body. *Children! My Christ! All of us!*

Then in his last grief and rage he wrestled Mason's body to the parapet, and wearily heaved it up in his arms and kept it for a moment close to his breast. And then he hurled it into the void.

Except for the doctor and the priest (Luigi later told Cass this), Luigi himself was the first person that morning to hurry to Francesca's side. Sergeant Parrinello, who went off pompously to the valley path, "the scene of the crime," sent him there. . . . She lay on a bed in the house of Ivella the pharmacist, just outside the town walls; the farmers who found her on the valley path had dared not take her any further. She had lost an enormous amount of blood—so much blood, in fact, that the doctor ventured no hope that even the transfusion he might give her would suffice for more than half a day of life. She was unconscious, her breathing slow and shallow. Yes, she might be questioned, Caltroni said, if and when she became aroused; no disturbance or exertion seemed likely to alter the course of her mortal injuries. The doctor and the priest departed (the rite of *Estrema Unzione* had already been administered); they set off in search of more blood, and said they would return. In crisis, Caltroni was performing nobly. The corporal sat by Francesca's side. An hour passed. A terrific clamor arose outside, and Luigi bade the pharmacist to go out on the street and shut the people up. For a long while there was silence, and Luigi sat there as light flooded the clean white room, watching the dying girl. Once she moaned and her eyelids flickered, and a flush came to rouge the pallor of her cheeks. Then again she went pale, and sank back into her coma, barely breathing. A half-hour passed, and another hour. But, still later, at about nine o'clock, her eyes opened and she breathed a great sigh as she looked around her; then, trying to move one of her shattered arms, she cried out in pain, and the tears started from her eyes. Luigi bent forward and placed another cool damp rag against her brow, as the doctor had instructed. He moved his lips close to her ear then, and very softly said: *"Chi è stato?"* For a long while she was unable to reply. She bit her lip in pain, and for a moment he thought she was going to sink back into oblivion. *"Who,* Francesca?" he repeated softly. And the girl whispered, "Cass."

He drew slowly back in his chair, with a sudden mingling of emotions. He was, as he recalled later, shocked but not surprised, if such a combination of feelings can really exist. Because already he was almost certain who had done it. He had not thought of Cass. And yet when she murmured his name he realized she could be speaking the truth.

Bending down over the dying girl, he recalled the walks which even Cass had not been able to hide. Walks hand in hand in the valley, an American and a poor peasant girl—they were not disguisable, any more than the trips in the Cadillac to Naples. Luigi spoke gently to Francesca. *"Chi?"* he said once more. "Tell me again. Who did this to you?" The girl tried to speak. It was not Cass, it must not be Cass, and yet again, it *could* be Cass. Take a borderline mental case (an American at that) and combine this with some unbearable oppression—and finally love—and *anything* might happen. *"Who,* Francesca?" Now she seemed unable to answer.

There was a rap on the door and the pharmacist's distraught wife appeared at the threshold, to tell him that Parrinello was outside and wished to talk to him. He got up from Francesca's side and went into the rose-fragrant garden, where the sergeant was waiting. It was after nine o'clock. Parrinello was beside himself, slapping a glove against his fat thigh, his face shiny with sweat.

"Has she spoken?" the sergeant asked. "Has she said anything?" His expression was solemn, but he seemed visibly to thrill with excitement.

"She has said nothing, Sergeant."

"She must speak. She *must speak.*"

Luigi sensed something. "What now, Sergeant?"

"Flagg. The American from the Palazzo d'Affitto. The man the girl worked for. He has been found *dead* at the bottom of the cliff below the Villa Cardassi. His head a bloody mess."

Luigi felt the tips of his fingers go numb. "So it was—" For a moment he found it impossible to move his lips. "That is—"

"I've called Salerno. It is a clear case of *doppio delitto.* Captain Di Bartolo is on his way with a squad. Now you must—"

"Double murder? But the girl is not dead."

"Yes, I said double murder!" He paused with a shrewd glint in his eye, a look of discovery. A full page spread in *Il Mattino.* And

Luigi, as if in a dream, saw the fat sergeant waddling forward at some regional police parade, chest bloated and extended for the distinguished rosette. "The little wench had a lover. One of those café bums had been taking her into the weeds. A nice piece, too, and he didn't want to let it go. Then this American she worked for began to fuck her, too. She got confused. She told her first boy friend, or he found out. He went really crazy. Flagg had to get her away from the palace to do it, away from his blond girl. So he took her up onto the valley path sometime last night. And he began to fuck her. But he hadn't planned on a crazy lover. The boy friend tracked them there, and found them in the act. He took care of the girl and then went off after Flagg, and chased him up to the Villa. Then he threw him over the wall. You should see his head, it's a bloody mess."

For such, Luigi thought, for such I let myself become a policeman, to listen to a man who two meters from death can talk with a mouth like this. Bees hummed around them, amid the heavy sweet scent of roses. The impulse to punish, to obliterate the gross face was, for an instant, almost unbearable.

"You say she said nothing?" Parrinello said.

"Nothing, Sergeant."

"Well, keep after her. If she says anything, let me know. I'll be down at the station. One of those café bums. The fellow must be a big man—big and husky. If I could just get the name of the man who did it before Di Bartolo comes I'd be—" He paused, made a sullen grimace, as if understanding he'd revealed himself. "You'd better—"

But before he could deliver the order, Luigi had wheeled about, stalking away without a word as he entered the house again, crept quietly into the bedroom, and resumed his vigil at Francesca's side. The girl, white as a bone, had sunk back into her profound repose, so still now that he thought for a moment she must be dead. But she clung if not to consciousness then at least to life, and he watched her, barely breathing himself. At around ten o'clock, the doctor returned, accompanied by the woebegone gray-eyed priest whom Luigi had never seen before. Together they rigged a new jar of blood plasma on the metal hanger above the bed. The doctor—or maybe it was the priest—said that he was sending a nurse. The priest spoke another absolution, and again they were gone—to Amalfi this time, the doctor said—in quest of more blood. It was hot now, and Luigi took his jacket off, his bandolier and belt. Francesca seemed to sleep more peaceably, and faint color had returned to her cheeks, but still she breathed in her soft shallow breaths, and her eyes were closed as if in death, lids chalky white, and she uttered no sound. He kept looking down at the girl. He had never in his life given peasants much thought or consideration, neither despising them nor feeling for them pity, sympathy or anything, but accepting them only as one might accept the nagging presence of bad weather or an eternal headache or a pet dog so old and ugly that one no longer wished to give it food and water yet could not bear to destroy it or turn it away. His parents had been far from rich but not bitterly poor, and out of all that ordinary life from which he had grown in Salerno he had taken with him as little understanding or caring about pure, wicked, despairing poverty as he had the desire to become excessively rich. His schoolteacher father had wanted him to be a lawyer, but the war had come, shattering all; he had become instead a policeman, and life had reduced itself to a space of excruciating gray disappointment through which he drifted half-educated, purposeless, feeling nothing, ready for any easy bribe, and paying lip-service to a political label of which he was, at heart, deeply ashamed. He tried to do his job well, but what was his job? What? He knew that in this country there was little chance of "becoming"; you were what you were, and that was that. Yet now as he looked down at Francesca he saw not the brutalized, defeated, life-corroded face which had existed like a wish in his mind since childhood but a face which was, even in dying, extraordinarily beautiful, and he felt anguish wrench at his heart. Though he had seen this girl before, he had never really looked at her. He realized with something of a shock that it was the first time he had ever looked *directly* into a peasant face. *Felice.* Happy. This is the word he had always heard about peasants. So poor. But really so happy. They have music. And love. Now, looking down at Francesca, he knew differently. No music at all, and very little love. She seemed to wake, and now to try to speak, and he bent forward, listening. She was beautiful. But only the shadow of a word passed across her lips. She sank back into sleep. He looked down at her, feeling sorrow to his depths. The knowledge of human distress, for the first time in years, washed in upon him like light. He thought of Cass and, in deep misery, wondered what demon had possessed him to attack this girl.

Because at this moment he was certain that Cass had done it. It was no café lounger who was the culprit; Cass was the betrayed lover, the double killer whom Parrinello sought. It was a fierce and terrible thing, but it seemed perfectly true. Why question the girl any longer? Go out and find a bespectacled American in dirty khaki with a look in his eyes of the fixity of doom. It should not be too hard, unless he had already added himself to the gruesome list. . . .

Yet now the nursing sister, a horse-faced nun in white from the convent, glided silently and sternly into the room, without even a nod, planted herself between him and Francesca, starched and pleated rump aslant before his face, and as she did so, and as he moved his chair, something suddenly opened in his mind, like a gust of wind and sunlight blowing open a blind. It could *not* be Cass. And if it was not Cass it could only be the one he had thought of at first. . . . He brooded for a long time while the nun fussed silently over the girl, and shortly after this he saw that Francesca had opened her eyes, wide, and was staring up into space. He asked the nun to leave the room. She refused, scowling. He asked her again, irritably, moving his chair toward the bed and feeling queasy with excitement. Again she refused. Again he asked her. And she refused. *"Vada via! Via!"* he snarled. "Out of here, damn you!" And she vanished, scared, in a swirl of pleats.

He bent down to the girl. "Francesca," he said, "tell me now. Carefully. Who was it that hurt you? It was not Cass, was it?"

"No," she said in a faint weak voice. "Not Cass."

"Who was it then?"

"Signor Flagg."

Puzzlement and confusion. This, he knew, simply could not be. The American with the vacant face like a pretty little boy?

"What did Signor Flagg do to you?"

"He took me—" She began to weep, which caused her breath to heave violently, hurting her, and she cried out in pain. Then she ceased crying and her eyes fell shut and he thought that once again she was slipping back into darkness. But she stirred awake and she looked at Luigi with great staring, frightened eyes. "He took me in his room."

"He took you in his room?"

"Yes." She halted. "Oh, am I going to die?"

"What did he do to you?"

"I—" Weakly, she turned her head. "I cannot say." And by not saying, said it.

"He did not take you on the path?"

She was silent, except for the steady, labored breathing.

"He did not take you on the path?" he asked again, gently.

"I don't know," she whispered, after a long wait. "Nothing. All. I don't forget." She was out of touch, speaking stunned opposites.

"Do you *remember* what happened on the path?"

"I don't forget."

"Francesca, do you *remember*? Tell me, do you *remember* someone hurting you on the path?"

"I don't forget."

"Francesca. Tell me this. Was it Saverio?"

The brief space of time before her reply was like a roaring noise in her ears. Then, "Yes! My God, it was Saverio!" she cried in a hoarse tormented voice. "My God, yes! My God! My God! My God!"

He called for the nurse, but it was not necessary, for the sister had barely reached her side when the girl gave a sudden convulsive twist with her neck, sighed, and plunged back into unconsciousness, trailing behind her sobs of heartbreak and horror as if into the darkness of a cave. Luigi rose from the chair.

"You're going to kill her!" the nun hissed.

"Non importa. She's going to die anyway."

"You monstrous policeman! Have you no feeling when—"

"Shut your face, Sister." He paused. "Forgive me."

He went out into the garden, into the high clear light of late morning. He found himself cursing Parrinello more bitterly than ever before. For if the sergeant had acted, would all of this have happened? No. Only Luigi himself had thought it right to put Saverio away. This was Italy for you. A countryside roaming with lunatics. A madhouse with the inmates in charge. He had long ago passed on his feelings to Parrinello, asking him if he too didn't feel it wise to bring Saverio to the attention of the authorities of the *comune,* who in turn might bring pressure on the defective's nearest relative—an aging half-sister—to have him committed. But Parrinello had scoffed, dismissing the idea as quickly as he had any other sign of initiative on the part of his subordinate. He was a wretched jealous man, with no imagination. He was also fat and lazy, and he wanted no part of any scheme or maneuver outside his province, which was to enforce the law, not to complicate it. Besides, he asked Luigi, what proof had he that Saverio was anything other than the harmless simpleton that he seemed to be? Which was to some extent true, and Luigi had conceded to himself the difficulty of the situation. The evidence, the proof, was meager and vague indeed: several middle-aged Nordic ladies, debarking from the tourist buses, had upon various occasions complained of being "rubbed" or "brushed"; three or four times a washed-out and formless visage—which may or may not have been Saverio's—had appeared night-peeping at the Bella Vista's windows, to vanish at the sound of the invariable scream. Once, two or three summers before, a lady visitor from Strasbourg claimed that the demented clod, while carrying her luggage to the hotel, had exposed his private parts to her, in an alleyway behind the church. This, the most serious indication of all, might have developed into a substantial charge against Saverio, had the investigation not been handled by Parrinello, who had fought against the French in the late war and hated them, and who, observing that the woman seemed a parched, hysteric type anyway, was inclined to accept Saverio's blabbered protestations that he had merely been attending to a call of nature. So that was all there was, on the surface at least. Fifteen years before—during the war and long before Luigi had come to Sambuco—a shepherd girl had been found dead, horribly mutilated, among the rocks on the mountain slope in an area even more remote from the town than Tramonti. This was a lax and confused period. The war was on and nobody really seemed to care. Word of the slaying seeped down to the town days after the girl had been buried. Disinterment and an autopsy were ordered, but for some reason neither was carried out. The mountain people, a benighted lot and more superstitious than Africans, murmured darkly of evil spirits. Others talked of wolves. Still others spoke of a deserter from the German army who had been seen lurking in the woods. And the whole incident was fairly well forgotten by everybody. Luigi, who of course learned of all this long after the event, had always been struck by the fact—which he discovered quite accidentally—that not only had Saverio, who was a huge mad boy of seventeen, been living in the same place at the time, but under the same roof. Obviously there was no proof after all these years. But often it is the most bizarre, familial sort of crime which goes for a long time (perhaps forever) unsolved, even in the midst of city sophisticates. It would perhaps have been unusual for those simple peasants to cast an eye of suspicion on the girl's own brother. . . .

But tell me, *Luigino*, he began to ask himself, if now it is true that Saverio attacked the girl, how is it this Flagg is at the bottom of the Cardassi precipice with his head squashed in? Surely it was not stinking Saverio who was a betrayed lover. Nor was it he who avenged himself on the girl and then threw the American over the cliff. The lout might have ambushed the girl, alone, but never would he have been able to manage a twosome. Then could Flagg have committed suicide? Was that it? Possibly. But if so, why? Remorse? Guilt? He had ravished the girl that night, Francesca herself said that. There was no mistaking the force and brutality of his attack; had not Francesca instantly murmured the American's name, rather than Saverio's? A sign in itself of the savage way he must have gone about it. Was it not thinkable that a man might be so bedeviled by such a deed that he would become impelled to end his life? Yes, it was thinkable. But it was not likely, given the shady nature of this particular American. Quite certainly not a suicidal type, in any case not a man to allow a simple ravishment to torment him. Had he done what Saverio had done—most possibly yes. A man who might in frenzy or passion smash a girl's bones, then rise to see that she was dying—this man might out of guilt or fear hurl himself from a cliff. But it was Saverio who had broken the girl's body, not the American.

The American. But of course: there was the *other* American. And now suddenly it became clear to him that the two crimes, though possibly linked together in a fashion beyond his power at the moment to divine, were independent of each other, and that it could only be Cass who had killed Flagg. Cass was the lover Parrinello had suggested, after all. For Cass had been Francesca's lover, plain as the nose on your face. Flagg had ravished her, and Cass had taken his vengeance. And of all the participants—Flagg, who was dead; Francesca, who was dying; Saverio, a blank mindless space beyond reach of pain or punishment; and Cass himself— only Cass remained to endure or suffer more.

It was at that moment, when a clanging at the garden gate aroused him and he turned to see Parrinello trundle forward in company with the august Captain Di Bartolo, that he recalled the tenderness in Francesca's voice as she first murmured "Cass," and that he decided that there had been in Sambuco this day entirely too much suffering. He sucked wind into his lungs, senselessly, trying to rid himself of a feeling of insanity.

Then he saluted. The expression on the investigator's face was businesslike, grim.

"The girl still lives, Corporal?"

"She is still living, Captain. At this moment she is—asleep. The nurse—"

"Has she spoken?" Di Bartolo said, cutting him off. There was something moderately thrilling and auspicious about this attenuated, priestlike man, with his raked-down fedora and belted trench coat. He had doubtless seen many films about Scotland Yard, which accounted for much of his manner; his record, though, had been spectacular, and more than made up for his professional style, which inclined toward an elaborate and stagy casualness. He withdrew a small yellow pack from his pocket, holding it out to his two inferiors.

"Wrigley?" he said.

The sergeant accepted a stick of gum, as did Luigi, and for a moment the three of them stood there in the garden, gratefully yet rather uneasily masticating.

"Well you see, Captain," Luigi temporized, "she started to tell me that—" In desperation, so as to gain command over his galloping thoughts, he tried to stall for time.

But providentially the captain interrupted, slanting an eye skyward as he said with a thin smile: *"È proprio strano.* But you may always expect it. Lombroso had the theory that the most violent of crimes will occur at early morning, in fine weather—spring or early summer. What a day!" He turned to Parrinello. "What did you find at the place where the girl was attacked?"

The sergeant stirred uneasily within his elephantine self, and shrugged, and looked at the investigator. "I beg your pardon, my Captain. But I do not seem to understand what you mean by—"

The investigator's expression became impatient and stern. "Tell me, Parrinello," he said in a voice already icy with censure. "You mean you did not go carefully over the ground where the girl was attacked?"

"No, my Captain," the sergeant began futilely to explain, "you see, I was so concerned by this American when his body was discovered that I—"

"And you posted no *guard* over the place?"

"Why no, Captain, you see—"

"And in other words that means that at this very moment every gawk and hayseed and souvenir hunter in the *comune* is now on the spot, carefully obliterating any footprint the attacker might have left, pocketing any personal item he might have dropped. Eliminating any valuable clue. Had this not occurred to you at all? Did you take the General Course for security officers, Parrinello?"

"Why yes, my Captain, I mean—" The sergeant's face was as red as a rose; his jaw trembled and, like some gargantuan infant, he seemed to verge already on tears. "It had occurred to me—"

"It had occurred to you *nothing*," Di Bartolo snapped. "Overlook a fundamental like that and I can only say that you are demonstrating incompetence."

"Oh, my Captain!" the sergeant began to protest.

"Quiet!" Di Bartolo commanded. "Look. Time is passing. Where is that list you made?"

"*What* list, my Captain?" the sergeant groaned.

"The list of *suspects,* names and addresses. *The list I told you to make.*"

Fumbling in his breast pockets, Parrinello brought forth only his fingers. He seemed close to disintegration. "I left it in the office," he muttered hopelessly.

"Very well," the captain said, removing pencil and notebook from his coat. The inflection in his voice was cool, noncommittal, yet at the same time, for Parrinello, somehow freighted with disaster. "Very well," he repeated, "give me the names."

"The addresses I don't have, Captain," he said with misery in his voice.

"Give me the names!"

Feverishly, the sergeant tried to regain his lost ground. "Well first, my Captain, there is Emilio Giovanelli. He comes from Atrani. A tough character with a record. A big loud-mouth. He has had a lot of woman trouble. I would venture to say that he is the prime suspect. You have his name down, sir? Then these three. Salvatore Marzano. Nicola Cosenza. Vincenzo Torregrossa. All three are bums. Cosenza served time in Avellino for assault upon a woman. The other two are general no-goods. Torregrossa is a wife-beater. Marzano used to procure in Nocera. So, my Captain, I would say those four. Also, there is this fact. The girl Francesca is on what you might call good terms with the other American who lives in the lower part of the palace. She used to work for him before Flagg. I have heard that he has taken great interest in her father, who is dying of consumption in the valley; also, that he and the girl were seen together several times in what *might* be—how would you say it?—a friendly relationship. I do not think this lead could amount to much, my Captain, but it is perhaps worth looking into. His name is Kinsolvin. C-h-i-n-s-o-l-v-i-n—"

Throughout all the interchange between Di Bartolo and the sergeant, Luigi had felt his heart begin to pound madly, and his mouth had gone so dry that the disgusting wad of chewing gum had rattled around inside it like a marble. He had wanted in some way, in any way possible, to divert suspicion from Cass, but until the sergeant had spoken Cass' name he had had no intention of actually lying on his behalf. With Cass' name still unmentioned, a lie would have been purposeless; besides, despite his inner conviction that Cass had slain the American, he could in no way be one hundred percent certain, past all risk, that Cass was connected with the crime. Parrinello's startling gambit, however, changed all this. While the sergeant again spoke Cass' name, Luigi coughed and, as subtly as he was able, intruded upon the conversation. He felt his scalp tighten in fear. Implicating Saverio would still lead to the problem of Flagg, and then to Cass; only an extravaganza would do. He knew that what he was about to say might be—was indeed very probably—the most important thing he ever said to anyone; if it failed, lacking plausibility in the ears of this illustrious detective, or if he betrayed by his manner the quality of fabrication which formed the very texture of this story he had so recklessly invented, he knew that he would not only not save Cass but send him that much more rapidly to prison, besides bringing total ruination, disgrace, and years of jail to himself. He thought of the jails he had seen—the filth and the slop buckets, the bugs in the beds and the weevils in the *pasta,* the sour wine or no wine at all, the gray and crushing years—and his mouth became so dry that he could barely speak. But he forced his lips open and, gagging back a sort of croak, said in a level and intelligent voice: "If it may please the captain, I do not think that it is necessary to go on with this list."

"What do you mean, Corporal?" said Di Bartolo.

"I mean, sir, that the girl herself has told me what happened."

"And why did you not speak up before?" the investigator said impatiently.

Luigi's eyes roved meaningfully to the sergeant. "I tried, Captain, but—"

"Well, go on with it! What did she say?"

"She said this, Captain." He thought a prayer of forgiveness for himself, for the shame he must bring to Francesca. "She implied that for several weeks she had been having an affair with her employer, Flagg. She had wished to break it off, for the disgrace it was causing to her soul. Flagg was insanely jealous of her and refused. They had been having many liaisons up on the valley path, away from Flagg's other mistress. He took her up there last night, and she refused to submit to him. Once again she spoke of her determination to break off the affair. He tried to force her to submit, but she refused. He went insane with fury and hit her with something hard. He beat her repeatedly, her arms and head and legs. She of course lost consciousness but she came briefly to once, and he was standing over her, weeping with guilt and remorse. He must have understood then that she was dying. She told me that she remembered hearing him cry out—in English, of which she understands a little—'*Oh, I will kill myself! I will kill myself!*' And before she lost consciousness again she saw him run up the path toward the Villa Cardassi. . . .

"This is what she told me, Captain, in God's truth. It seems very plainly to be murder and suicide. I would respectfully venture to offer the captain my opinion that a fall from such a height might alone cause the head injuries—"

Parrinello's big mouth began to work. "A fiction!" he said. "A fantasy! It could not be! The girl's in shock!"

"Quiet, Parrinello!" the detective commanded. He turned back to Luigi. "Tell me, Corporal. Tell me. Did the girl appear to be *lucid* when she told you all this."

"She was of course quite weak, sir. But she was lucid. She was telling the truth. On that I would stake my life."

"A preposterous tale!" Parrinello said. "She was only covering up for her other lover. Women do that all the time. And the disgrace it was causing to her soul!" he mocked. "An American millionaire was getting into her little peasant crack, and it was the best thing she ever had in her life. The idea of—"

If Di Bartolo had had at that moment any inclination toward doubts about Luigi's story, certainly the fact that they were dissipated may be hung upon Sergeant Parrinello and the vileness of spirit which emanated from him at the moment like some wet ignoble mist. He would have scandalized a pimp. Di Bartolo wheeled on him savagely, and for an instant Luigi had the impression of some lean wild beast—a wolf, a mink, a weasel—all teeth and claws, unimaginably fierce. "Silence!" he said to the sergeant, in a voice like a whisper. "*Silence!* Not another word from you! Understand? Not another word! When I want your opinion I will ask for it. In the meantime, Parrinello, remember this. While you have done everything possible to be derelict in your duty, this corporal has been doing his job. Now keep your mouth shut!"

Then they were gone, and Luigi sat down next to a camellia bush, head in his hands, trembling, weak as water. . . .

Francesca died at ten o'clock that night. Luigi had other duties to perform during the day, but he kept coming back to her side as often as he could. He wished to be absolutely sure. Several times she roused from her deep sleep, and each time she was more troubled and distant than the last, but he came to understand, finally, exactly what had happened.

For she had indeed encountered Saverio on the path sometime during the early morning, in the brightest part of the valley when the clouds had passed from the moon. She knew him well, and was not in the least afraid of him, but what Mason had done to her just that same evening clung to her flesh like some loathsome disease which she was fated to endure forever. So it was that when she met Saverio in the shadows and he put out his fingers harmlessly—perhaps no more than as a simple greeting—to stroke her, the intense male hand on her arm brought back, like horror made touchable, the touch and the feel and the actuality, and she found herself shrieking. She shrieked, and she scratched madly out at the flat lopsided face which now itself was stricken with panic. He began wailing like an old man bereft. Then he drew back and hit her, and she fell, yet still she heard herself shrieking, unaware now that this was Saverio, or anyone, aware of nothing save that the whole earth's stiff, protuberant and insatiate masculinity had descended upon her in the space of one summer night. Still she screamed, and the frenzied half-wit clouted her again, this time with a rock, or with the weight of all the firmament, and she must have kept screaming then as she lay broken among the weeds, and long after Saverio had gone away, for even in her delirium she screamed, and she gave one last scream which was in truth only the faintest of sighs, when the two farmers happened upon her in the dawn.

Crickets danced about her head among the weeds. She lay next to a bed of wild roses. And that is how Francesca met the light of a new day.

There was the day following the morning that he killed Mason, and then the night after that. Of this time Cass can recall almost nothing. He is certain that (for the last time in his life) he got drunk, and he has the vague recollection of a seedy little *cantina* on the outskirts of town, where he bought two bottles of wine. Now he is certain too that he convinced himself, despite all intuition that told him otherwise, that Mason *had* killed Francesca ("Remember this," he told me, "remember how often you read in the newspaper some such line as *slayer shows no remorse,* or perhaps *feels no regret for his crime,* and you can be sure that this is true. Because something has happened inside, the same thing that must have happened to me that day. He isn't necessarily cold-blooded or callous. Instead the chances are that he has been rocked to his very foundations. And he begins to believe in the lie he must tell himself in order to preserve his sanity or maybe even his life. He convinces himself that he is in the right, and that whoever it was that he did in had it coming to him like no one since Judas Iscariot."), because that night, after a day spent somewhere in the hills where he stalked alone in drunken rage and sorrow, he had a witness. Would I ever forget that moment when he staggered into the palace, ravaged by ten years of age, seized me by the arm as if I were the Wedding Guest, and with holy vengeance in his eye spoke of Mason standing there grinning in the midst of eternity, fatally beyond reach of more and deserved punishment? Madness was skulking after him at that moment, of this he is sure, and now he knows something else. He knows that when he went forth from the palace, past a swooning Poppy (he does not recall even seeing her, though he does remember his tirade to me), he was headed for the pharmacist's house, for it must have occurred to him that Francesca might still be living after all, and that he might see her before she died. But he was half an hour too late. Luigi told him this, standing alone in the shadows of the house. She had already been taken away. Was it then that, turning his eyes from Luigi's dark face, he looked past the house and saw fires burning mysteriously and strangely far down on the surface of the sea? He can no longer be sure. He knows that Luigi, comforting him, was trying to tell him something else, drew him aside secretly into the garden, in his soft melancholy voice fumbled for words to tell him that truth which he had allowed himself to know only at the instant of Mason's death: his victim was not the killer. Then who was it, Luigi? he must have asked. And when Luigi spoke of the idiot, conjuring the image of the harmless flat-faced lout he had seen almost every day—that must have been the instant when, again, gazing down through the sultry night, he saw the fires quicken and blaze up there in the very bosom of the sea, and saw smoke rise toward the stars, as if from some dark titanic pyre, and knew that he was utterly deranged.

He heard Luigi shout, but it was too late; already he had begun to plunge downhill through the streets of town, running not from punishment but as if from the last shred and vestige of the self with which he had been born, and running until the sensation was not that of running at all but of falling feet first through miles of hot black air.

And when he awoke the next morning, sober now, the sea was still boiling. He saw this from the entrance of the cave into which he had stumbled—a large grotto smelling of goats, somewhere not far from the shore. Outside a stream trickled, forming on the ledge of the cave a stagnant pool. In the morning light he stood half-erect from the damp ground upon which he had fitfully slept, and blinked, and saw the sea as if through the filmiest of gauze. A flock of shrieking sea birds, wings windmilling madly as they fled landward from the gulf, announced the first explosions. Headlong up the valley they flew, their frantic shadows streaking across the land; behind them, as if in pursuit, rose a muffled booming. A hot blast of wind passed through the sun-parched vegetation on the slopes. And now upon the surface of the gulf—far out yet, it seemed, all too threatfully close—there was a roiling and a churning; foam flecked the waters and a stormy turbulence seemed to jar the sea from its very depths, as if shivered from some fathomless volcano. More birds squawked overhead, and across the cloudless morning a shadow interposed itself between earth and sun. For a long while all sound died. Then the sea rose up in torment and spasm; a titanic geyser exploded forth from the uttermost bowels of the gulf, and another, and still another, filling the whole sky from Salerno to Capri with a mountainous dark cloudscape. This melted soon and sank away. But again, closer now, more geysers erupted from the depths, without sound, lathery gray-green masses of sea and lava which rose up still higher, mounting unbelievably toward a benign blue sky. Then back into the womb of the gulf the storm sank fitfully and slowly, without a murmur.

Now athwart the place where the waters disappeared, Cass discerned, a sailboat rode placidly upon the blue, untouched, unharmed, striped white and blue spinnaker belling in a stiff wind. . . .

The people in the villa down below seemed unaware of this commotion on the sea or, if they did perceive it, paid it no heed. They came out on the lawn to play badminton. The grass, carefully trimmed, began at the veranda of the villa, a concrete blockhouse around which each vagrant breeze set a six-fold Old Glory fluttering at its peak, and started at every window a brisk plashing of Venetian blinds. The lawn extended to a place fifty yards beneath him, where began the ragged growth of weeds and buckthorn and thistle, and the edge of the valley wilderness upon which he lay, a silent hidden watcher. On the asphalt driveway, partly concealed by the villa, was a glistening black Cadillac limousine. Below this driveway, emblazoned in paint against the restraining wall of the coast road, was the sign:

BEHOLD ABOVE YOU
THE PALACIAL VILLA OF
EMILIO NARDUZZO
OF
WEST ENGLEWOOD, N.J., U.S.A.

As the people played badminton that first morning, he heard them talk about the murder. Sometimes, to be sure, he could not hear them, or if he heard them at all it was in fragments of words that became harder to understand because of their ceaseless muffled laughter. But when the wind had become stilled or, more often, when the breeze shifted and blew past them toward him from the sea, their words rang out as clearly as chimes from a bell buoy borne across still water. "He was nuts over the kid," he heard the boy named Kenny say, in plainest English. "He was just nuts over the kid and when she said she was going to leave he gave her a good licking. Only he killed her by accident. And that's why he jumped off the cliff." But, "No," he heard one of the older ones say. This was a bald, hawk-nosed man in tennis shorts, who looked like a gangster. His legs were very hairy. The girl named Linda called him Daddy; to the others he was known as Bruno. "No, Kenny, if you look at it realistically. She was cheating on him. That's why he took it out on her. Only you might say he went a bit too far." There was laughter then and a gust of wind blew their words away and all Cass could hear was a high humorous shriek of dismay as the feathered cork bounded high over the net and the girl named Linda brought her lovely sunburned arm back against her bouncing breasts, too late, and swung her racket into the morning's empty air.

That is funny, Cass thought. It is very funny indeed. For if I have killed a man, why and how is it understood that he killed himself. Very curious . . . Beyond the villa now, pacified, the sea lay as still as glass. He dozed off. When he awoke again it was high noon, and the people had vanished from the lawn. The limousine had disappeared, too. A large collie prowled the shadowy veranda, muttering to itself. Cass saw one of the servants come out from the kitchen and pretend to offer the dog something to eat, then rap it sharply across the nose. He heard the two servants talking softly to one another in the noon stillness. They had stolen a wrist watch from one of the family, and were worried. The man's name was Guido, hers was Assunta. After a moment they went back into the kitchen and the collie, still nursing its insult, slouched away into the lee of the villa and out of sight. Cass touched his brow, drew his hand back from the wet skin, aware that he was boiling with fever. Crabwise on his side, he inched toward the stagnant pool and drank from his cupped hand. He shivered as the fever raged within. A horned toad skittered down the sandy bank, paused, gazing at him with beady malevolent eyes.

He slept. When he awoke, he knew that the sun had passed its zenith. The light of full afternoon blazed down, yet the shadow of the rocky outcropping against which he reclined enveloped him, and into the shadows the mosquitoes were swarming, chewing his face and arms. He moved slowly out closer to the stream where there were no mosquitoes. Recumbent, he propped his head against his hand, gazing again at the sea. And sluggishly now, the gulf once more began its upheaval. He watched intently, without blinking, watched the geysers heave up in soundless convulsion, yet now farther out, poised against the horizon, lacking quite the same imminent threat as before. Bells had begun clanging far off up the mountain, in the town, raising an antiphony of peril and alarm. People seemed to be shouting somewhere, in terror. Was it for this? For this weird, silent, volcanic upheaval, presaging the world's end? Or was what he heard only the echo of something which had assailed his ears before? Watching the sea in its mute cataclysm, he dozed off again, shot stiffly erect even as his head plunged earthward from his hand. *Cassio.* His eyes roved upward along the cliffside, searching for the owner of that miraculous, familiar voice. But there. There only feet away beside the pool, perched on a rock above it with an air of timid curiosity, Francesca knelt, gazing not at him but into the shadowy waters. And why was she looking into the pool in such a fashion? Why should she call to him, and then only dream away, peering down with such a diffident, hesitant, even mournful expression, as if searching in the water for some drowned shadow of her former self? He half-rose, in an agony of longing calling out to her with lips and tongue which, strive as they might, could utter not even the whisper of a sound; now, even as he tried to speak to her, she sprouted gossamer wings, faded utterly from sight, no more substantial than that fatuous "September Morn" which had been summoned up, God knew why, out of that drumming household of his childhood, and for which he had mistaken her.

Consumed by fever, he fell back once more and slept. Sorrow prowled through his dreams like an enormous beast, allowing him no rest or ease. When he awoke again it was midafternoon; the sea, now calm again, was dotted with boats, birds, sails. How dared they venture forth on such treacherous waters?

The limousine nosed its way slowly up the drive, came to a halt in its asphalt berth at the side of the house. "Uncle Frank," he heard the girl say, "did you eat up all the *panettone?*" Beyond, the gulf was still and serene. The people got out of the car with empty picnic baskets and went into the house. Presently the boy named Kenny came out onto the veranda, stretching himself. He felt the muscles of his arms and yawned. Over his breast, inscribed in blue on a white T-shirt, were the words IONA COLLEGE. In a moment the man they called Bruno emerged from the house, carrying a bag of golf clubs, and soon he began chipping white balls across the lawn in Cass' direction. Some of the balls went too far, burying themselves among the weeds below the ledge upon which Cass was lying; when he came to retrieve the balls he was puffing, short of breath, and Cass could see the hair in long bristles on his legs and the sweat in blue half-moons plastering his blue shirt against his armpits.

The sun had long since passed its summit, but the day had grown hotter. Cass gazed up at the sun, focusing his eyes at a point near the periphery of its blaze. It was definitely, unnaturally hotter and larger; it seemed nearly twice the size it should be, a burgeoning super-nova. He turned his eyes away, for the first time that day touched with the presentiments of an enormity of fear. The people at the villa seemed faintly to sense this too. They did not look up at the sun, but now Kenny returned to the veranda, followed by the woman Bruno had called Shirley, who seemed to be Bruno's wife; she loosened her halter and Cass heard her say: "It's like an oven." She sat down on a chrome and canvas glider, fanning her face; she was a small woman in beach shorts, and her thighs had gone to fat. Kenny took off his T-shirt and began to chin himself on a bar separating two pillars of the veranda. He was smoothly and strongly muscled and he must have risen to the bar thirty times before dropping gracefully on his toes to the porch floor. With his fingertips on his hips then, he walked around the veranda, eying the floor. He scratched the collie behind its ears. He began walking again, paused, ran a comb through his hair. Then he looked out toward the sea and yawned. The bald fat man whom Cass had heard Linda call Uncle Frank came out on the veranda, a portable radio dangling from a thick fist. "Anybody want a pizza?" he said. But there was no answer. The woman called Shirley had gone to sleep. Now Cass heard the sound of a saxophone, borne away instantly on a gust of wind; caught by this same gust, a golf ball soared sideways, floated downwind before his vision and was lost among the weeds.

The sea was placid, held in momentary abeyance, but the sun had grown hotter still, hung in the sky fiery, huge and, like some dead weight, oppressively heavy and near. The bugger is exploding, Cass thought as he edged back into a shadowed place, it's going to swell up and shrivel us like a bunch of gnats in a flame. He mopped his brow. It must be the reason for the sea boiling up like that. Then why hadn't the people seemed to notice the sun? The sea. He gazed toward the man named Bruno, who had sat down, with an air of tedium, in an aluminum chair. The man surveyed the lawn strewn with golf balls and he leaned forward slightly with his lips moving, as if reproaching himself. Then he too lay back and went to sleep. Faint from inside the house came Linda's voice: "Kenny!" And Kenny turned and said: "What?" "Do you think just Gerda Rumbaugh, Lodi, New Jersey will get there? I'm writing her about the murder!" And Kenny said: "I can't hear you!" "Kenneth Falco, if you don't—" But the words were blown away, and he saw the boy stroll sullenly into the house as Bruno and his wife, supine and motionless in their metal chairs, lay beneath the blazing sun, and Uncle Frank twiddled the dials of the radio. The sea was still. . . .

A smell of cooking meat, blown up toward the cliff upon an evening breeze, aroused him when, several hours later, he lay in his last siege of delirium. It was very late in the afternoon. The sun, sunk to the west over Capri, was like a flaming discus, enormous, threatening, crimson. And again the sea had begun to heave and tremble, casting up silently from the depths of the gulf fountains of itself, mountainous and terrible. Far out, black tornadoes criss-crossed the horizon beneath a lowering rack of black cloud; closer, white combers of oceanic surf crashed without ceasing against the shore, in their noiselessness producing an effect of strange delicacy. The only sound was from below, on the lawn, where the people had gathered in the early evening light. Cass stirred, drenched and aflame. There were steaks cooking on a half-moon-shaped outdoor barbecue. The boy and the girl were again playing badminton; he heard the faint guitar-plunk as shuttlecock met racket, saw the rise and fall of the girl's breasts, the plump bounce of buttock and thigh. From the veranda, lost in shadows now, came a muted tropical rhythm of maracas, marimbas, castanets, while at the edge of the veranda sat the old man of the villa, the patriarch Emilio—it could be no other—swarthy and gray-haired, in a magenta beach gown, benignly smiling as he watched the family at play. Bruno approached the old man with deference, said something that Cass was unable to hear. Cass raised his eyes toward the heavens: the sun blazed intolerably near. A gust of wind pitched a scrap of newspaper high over the villa; pinwheeling madly, it skidded across the roof's edge, bounded in and out among the denuded flagpoles and whirled away from the exploding, tormented sea. A cloud of paper napkins swept across the lawn, and someone cried out: "Oh my God! Oh!" The Venetian blinds clashed and clattered in the upper rooms. From somewhere came the tremendous slamming of a wind-blown door; the swarthy old man turned his head in the fading light, still benignly smiling, and the smell of burning meat was suddenly sweet in the air like a pestilence. Then the breeze died out, Linda retrieved the shuttlecock from the place where it had blown and all was silent, save for the soft tropical rattle and scratch of maracas, and all was still, except for the storm, nearer now, convulsing the black waters of the gulf.

It was then that Cass, sick with terror to the bottom of his soul, arose from the mouth of the cave and fled back along the cliffside path toward the town. He does not know whether he was seen by Narduzzo and his clan; possibly, for when he got up he remembers that his feet dislodged from the ledge a shower of rattling stones. He would have been, at any rate, a barbarous apparition with wild disheveled hair and blazing skin, and perhaps in West Englewood they still wonder at the sick and terrified face of this compatriot rising in the fading light above their lawn.

Nor does Cass know now whether, had he not met that priest on the way back up through the valley, and somewhere near the town, he might not have slaughtered Poppy and the children and himself, just as he had intended but failed to do in Paris long before. For that was what—to save them from this storm, this exploding sun of his own guilt—he was planning to accomplish. To remove from this earth (as once he said) all mark and sign and stain of himself, his love and his vain hopes and his pathetic creations and his guilt. . . .

But not far from the town the path upon which he hastened home converged with another, and it was at this junction that he fell into procession with the priest, a runty, graying, big-nosed little man in cassock and yellowing white chasuble. Upon his face there was a look of profound and mortal worry. Behind him, leaning forward in the long-limbed and awkward gait of adolescence, trailed a hulking acolyte with a pimply face and underslung jaw, who carried the vessels of the mass against his breast with an air of great gravity and concern, as if he had let them slip from his hands in the past and had suffered for his clumsiness. Because there was no choice Cass fell in beside the priest as they walked up the slope toward Sambuco.

"La pace sia con voi," said the priest. "It is hot, is it not? I should not be surprised if we had a thunderstorm." The priest smelled unwashed and the breath escaped from his lips in small whispery gasps as he labored up the hill. Cass did not answer, for the sun seemed to hover nearer, immeasurable and blazing.

"It has been a very tragic time for Sambuco," the priest went on, creating conversation. "You are American, are you not? I think I have seen you before. Were you not acquainted with the American *suicida,* the man who killed himself?"

Still Cass made no reply and the priest, as if to fill up the breach, spoke over his shoulder to the acolyte, who had begun to fall behind. "Don't lag so, Pasquale! Gracious, a big boy like you—" He paused for a moment, then continued: "Many times during these past few hours I have wished to say a *maledizione* against that American. But I have suffered myself to remain calm. Immoral as he was, his torment must have been deep to have caused him to take his own life like that. God will judge him." He was silent for a moment, then repeated with an air of magnitude: "Yes, God will judge him."

Suddenly Cass was forced to sit down at the side of the path. He felt his limbs tremble and a shudder, icy cold, passed through him as he thrust his face into his hands, shutting out from sight the terrible impending sun.

"You look ill," he heard the priest say. "You're shivering. Do you suffer from malaria? These parts are often very bad—"

"Non è niente," Cass replied, getting up. "It is the heat. I have come a long way."

485

"You must be careful with malaria," said the priest. "It is rarely any longer a fatal disease, but it must be treated with care. There is the bark of a certain wild juniper bush that grows on the high slopes which certain people use—"

"*Atabrino,*" Cass said, wondering why he spoke. "Atabrine. Atabrine takes care of it."

"I have never heard of that bark. Do you use it? Is it like quinine?"

"It is the heat, Father," Cass replied, "with me it's the heat. I have come a long way."

Now as they resumed their way toward town the dry little priest, lighting up a cigarette, said: *"Dico davvero.* You may be sure that God will judge him. But what sins he must account for before the Lord! What sorrow he brought to so many people! What pain and anguish! *Che devastatore era!"*

"What a despoiler he was," Cass murmured in echo. "Yes, but —" Yes, but what?

"And you must understand," the priest added hastily, "I do not say that because he was an American. I am deeply fond of Americans. When I was a seminarian we had a friendship correspondence club with other seminarians in all parts of the world. It was my great pleasure to correspond with a young seminarian in the town of, I think it is pronounced, Milwaukee, America. And when he was a priest—his name was Father Switzer; are you from Milwaukee? Perhaps you have encountered him—he paid me a visit in Sorrento, just after the war. A fine jolly man, immensely fat, and very generous too. He gave me a canned ham. Even now we send cards to each other at Eastertime." Behind them the altar boy stumbled, pitched forward against the wall of the path, then righted himself, mumbling apologies. *"Guarda quel ragazzo!* Pasquale, what a colt you are! No, my dear sir, I am extremely fond of Americans. It does not matter what country this man was from. But the things he must account for before the seat of the Lord! His own life—to take it was a mortal, and I might say cowardly, sin. But to have taken the life of that innocent girl, that virgin! And that is not all. For wickedness begets an infinity of sorrow. The girl's father, for example. Who knows? To be sure, he must have been desperately ill. But who knows? Without having had to suffer the extreme shock of his daughter's death he might still be alive. I do not know. None of us here below knows enough about such matters to truly say. But I ask you, my dear sir, would it be un-Christian to judge that he was responsible for that death, too?"

He paused and, when Cass made no reply, said: "Yes, I suspect that it is. Un-Christian I mean."

They had reached a rise in the path, and from this place the town could be seen above them, timeless and golden in the evening light, riding like an old ship ravaged but serene above all in the benign twilit glow of its antiquity, and a bell from the church tower rang out even as they gained the rise, one single silver chime descending upon the lemon groves and the terraced vineyards and the walled paths zigzagging like the brown blasted trails of lightning toward the sea. Smoke from the priest's cigarette fumed about them; the acolyte, sidling up beside Cass, made an unspeakable sound in the back of his throat, spat against the wall, and clapped the holy vessels to his breast. "What is that?" said Cass, halting. "What is that, Father? What did you say?"

"Un-Christian," the priest replied, looking up with curiosity into Cass' eyes. "I only said that it is doubtless un-Christian to judge a man when he is only *indirectly* the cause of—"

"No," Cass said, "the man himself. The other one. Her father. You say he is dead."

"Indeed, he died only a few hours ago. I have just come from his side."

"Michele—"

"Yes, that was his given name. His patronymic was Ricci, a strange irony considering his circumstances. I do not know who told him of his daughter's death. I suspect it was his wife, who seems very stupid, like most peasant women. A shame. He might have lived. But this afternoon when I arrived his will to live was quite obviously gone. Oh, what sorrow in our town!"

Cass sat down on the edge of the wall. "And so he is dead," he said to the priest.

"Yes, my dear sir, and saved from damnation by the closest margin. Because when I came to him he was in a frenzy, shrieking curses at me like a madman. A demon! But as I say, his will to live was over and so finally he settled down and I administered to him the last rites. He slept for a while and then I thought he was gone. But after a bit he woke up, grinding his teeth and weeping. Mistaught wretch. He kept cursing our Saviour, and he called out over and over again for his daughter. You seem to have an interest in this man. Can you tell me what it was he was suffering from? Was it some form of cancer? I have never seen anything like it before, and I have watched so many people die. Because he lay there for a while and he stopped weeping and he closed his eyes again and he became weaker and weaker, and this time I thought surely he was gone. Believe me, I have watched so many people die. But my dear sir, listen to this. Presently he awoke again and I observed that he had both hands grasped around his root. Though he was not in the virile state, of course. I thought for a moment that this was only some childish peasant gesture that he had gone back to in his extremity. But now his eyes opened and I heard him cry out: *'Animo! Animo!* Courage!' he cried. And then, as God is my witness, from that root of his burst forth the most stupendous fountain of blood I have ever seen! And in the midst of this terrible stream of blood I heard him cry out again: *'Animo!* Courage!' Such blood! It was everywhere! And then his hands fell limp, and then his eyes closed. And he lay back and died. Do you suppose this was some form of—"

Cass rose to his feet, fever-swept by the sun, storm-hunted, amid the flood of ancient groaning seas.

"Tutto!" he whispered. "All, then? *All?"* He stepped toward the priest. *"Help me."*

But the priest, who was helpless, took one step away as Cass took another step forward and then collapsed unconscious in the dust.

"But I came back," Cass said to me, "I came back home. Not that night or the next day or even the next night, but early in the morning of the day after that, before the dawn came up. I was not alone. Luigi walked me from the police station; I had been there all that time. He shook hands with me at the palace door, and then he said good-by to me. I remember how still and dark the streets were. And I stood there for a minute in the chill of the morning, watching Luigi as he walked back up the deserted street with that slow, ambling, flat-footed policeman's gait of his and then disappear into the darkness. The madness was not quite over. . . .

"I went into the courtyard. There was a light burning and I could see where the movie people had wrecked the tiles, the long streaks gouged out in the floor. The place was a mess and I remember pausing, looking up at Mason's balcony as if I half-expected some sound, some stir, perhaps good old Rosemarie to come mincing out as she used to do, primping, stroking that hair of hers and puckering up her mouth in boredom as she waited for Mason, and indeed for an instant I somehow thought I heard Mason's voice far-off and muffled in that tired and peevish vibrato, but it was only some other voice I heard, close by the town, calling out in sleep. So I turned and walked across the courtyard until I came to the door; it was ajar as usual, and I walked in. I could barely see, but I could tell that someone had cleaned up the place. The table was cleared, the easel was upright, and there was a chemical smell in the air, as if the place had been sprayed for mosquitoes. I went on downstairs in the dark. I could hear that familiar trickling night-sound, the toilet leaking, and I passed the bedrooms where I could hear breathing and I knew the kids were sound asleep. Finally I came to the last room and I softly opened the door. Again I could hear breathing, this time that gentle sibilance which had been part of my nights for so many years, and I knew that Poppy was asleep, too. I went close to the bed and looked down at her, and she stirred, still asleep, and then buried her head in the pillow with one hand crumpled beneath her like a child's. I pulled the sheet over her shoulder and then I walked over to the window and sat down and gazed out at the gulf. There was not a sound anywhere. I could smell that warm rose-fragrance from the garden below, and beyond was the sea, blacker than the night. There were fishing boats far out toward Paestum, and on each boat a globe of clear twinkling light, grouped together like stars. For a moment I had a dizzy feeling as if I were looking straight downward into the belly of some new and marvelous constellation.

"I felt drained of strength and will, past thought of grief, past thought of anything except for that old vast gnawing hunger which began to grow and grow in me like a flower. And as I sat there, with the hunger growing and blossoming inside me, I knew that I had come to the end of the road and had found there nothing at all. There was nothing. There was a nullity in the universe so great as to encompass and drown the universe itself. The value of a man's life was nothing, and his destiny nothingness. What more proof did I need than that I had traveled halfway across the earth in search of some kind of salvation, and had found it, only to have it shattered in my fingertips? What more proof did I need than that in the bargain I had slain a man wrongly, had taken a man's life for a crime he did not commit? The hunger persisted. I looked out at the sea, almost expecting to see the terrible storm and the boiling and churning again, the fire and the tornadoes, but my brain was clear and the hallucinations were gone. I thought of being. I thought of nothingness. I put my head into my hands, and for a moment the sharp horror of *being* seemed so enormous as to make the horror of nothingness less than nothing by its side, and I began to tremble, and for long minutes I sat there, wondering if now at last wasn't the moment to take Poppy and the kids in a single swift hell of blood and butchery, and be done with it all forever. It began to prey on me, this thought, obsess me, and it must have gotten me so worked up that I made a noise in my throat, because I heard Poppy stir and give a sigh, and I turned in the chair and gazed toward the bed. She was still sleeping. It would be easy. But right then I heard Luigi's voice, adamant and outraged as it had been not more than an hour before: *'Tu pecchi nell'avere tanto senso di colpa!* You sin in this guilt of yours! You *sin* in your guilt!' And suddenly I ceased trembling and became calm as if like some small boy on the verge of a tantrum I had been halted, the childish fit arrested by some almighty parental voice. I sat back again and gazed out at the dark gulf, and the spell of anxiety vanished, as quickly as it had come.

"Because that is just what Luigi had told me, you see, when I woke up in the police station. Gentle, kindly, lost Luigi—he raised the roof, he shackled me with handcuffs to the leg of a cot, and he gave me bloody hell. And as I sat there in the room with Poppy I began to know that what he said was true.

"Because when I woke up in the police station I had one single thought left in my mind. And that was that I should be punished for what I had done as swiftly as possible. That I should be taken away and clapped in irons and made to serve out the years in retribution for this monstrous thing that I had done. Yet when I woke up I could not understand this calm of Luigi's, this benign tolerance—as if I were a friendly guest instead of a murderer apprehended and done for. I was lying on a cot. The strength was all drained out of me, but the fever was gone and I was so hungry that I was chewing at the air. It must have been some time around midnight—there was a clock on the wall—though of what day I had no idea. There was just the two of us in this tiny little room. The place was badly lit and it had that dry musty smell about it of rat shit behind the walls and plain dirt and old crumbling plaster, a real Italian police station. And the first thing I saw was that face, not so much smiling down at me—Luigi almost never smiled—as radiating a sort of enormous and godawful solicitude which somehow always had the effect of a tender and wistful smile even when the face was as solemn as the face on a hanging judge. I asked him how long I had slept, and he told me a night and a day and part of another night. Then I asked him if Poppy and the kids were

O.K., and he said yes, they were O.K., and he mentioned you and how you had watched out after them, and he told me to lie back and take it easy. So I did. Then he gave me some bread and cheese to eat and some *mortadella* and a bottle of that greasy orange soda they make in Naples which tastes like rancid butter. Right then, right after I'd finished gulping all this down, I asked him. I said: 'Well, when do I go? When do you take me to Salerno?' But he didn't answer. He got up from the chair with his bandolier clicking and clacking and he walked over to the window. The night was still and dark, and I could hear a dog barking way off toward Scala, and it reminded me not of the midsummer that it was but of cold autumn nights at home, long ago. I asked him again and still he didn't answer. Then I noticed something odd. I saw that on one of his sleeves the corporal's chevron had been torn off and that in its place hung the chevron of a sergeant, dangling by a thread. And I said: 'Why the sergeant's stripes, Luigi?' And he said: 'I *am* a sergeant.' Then I said: 'Parrinello?' And he said: '*Finito. I* am in charge of the *carabinieri* in Sambuco. In other words, I am in charge of myself.' Then I said: 'You really mean Parrinello is gone?' And he said: 'Transferred. Transferred I believe to Eboli.' And he added: 'They will remove some kilos off his gut there.' To which I said: '*Auguri.*' But he said: 'I need no congratulations. What is a couple of thousand more lire a month? *Poco o nulla.* But soon I'll get a subordinate and I'll be able to browbeat him. To dominate him. I'll become a Parrinello. I'll grow fat and surly, and the cycle will be complete.'

"I asked him again when he was going to take me to Salerno and deliver me to the authorities. I can't tell you my anguish to get this thing over and done with, now that I fully knew what I had done. There was nothing left. I felt as empty and as crushed as an old tin can at the dump and all I wanted was to be buried, covered up, entombed forever. I said: '*Vieni*, Luigi. Let us get started.' And it was then that he turned and came back and sat down in the most grave and meticulous way and told me what he had done— his lie and his cover-up for me, and all the rest. And he had even done more than that. Because at some time during the next day, after Francesca died, that detective, Di Bartolo, had begun to have his doubts about Francesca's story. Not that he doubted Luigi—by then Luigi was his fair-haired boy—but it had occurred to him, as well it might, that the whole tale Luigi reported to him had been only a kind of wild fantasy in the head of a dying girl. But Luigi, mind you, had already counted on this, and late the night before

491

what he had done to bolster his own lie was to locate and spirit away the shoes that the funeral people had taken off Mason's body and he took these and with a flashlight he went up to the Villa Cardassi and there, by God, he erased every footprint he could find near the parapet, mine and Mason's, and then carefully traced a line of Mason's footprints from the brink straight backward to the villa and the path, erasing his own as he went. And for good measure, stumbling across the bloody stone I'd used on Mason, he heaved this away off into the brush where it wouldn't ever be found. So that the next day when Luigi and Di Bartolo went up to the villa there was a perfect *single* running track of footprints leading right up to the exact spot where Mason went over. The track of a man bent on suicide. And the shoes from Mason's body fit these tracks to the exact centimeter, right on down to the embossed design in the crepe soles. And as Luigi went through all this, telling me how Di Bartolo had finally closed the case off as murder and suicide, it occurred to me in the most desolate and creepy way that by these lies of his, all this mad deception, what he had done was to simultaneously allow me to escape into freedom and to trap himself as securely as if he had been a bug caught in the sticky gut of a pitcher plant. For now of course he couldn't recant, he couldn't alter his story; he was in as deep as he could get. Nor could I go to Salerno and give myself up, prove that I was the culprit without implicating Luigi and impaling him on a hook he'd never be able to wriggle off of. Yet as he told me these things and it dawned upon me the position we were both in, sheer crazy panic came over me: it was the idea of liberty. For here my only idea had been to give myself up, immure myself, entomb myself for my crime. And the notion of this awful and imminent liberty was as frightening to me as that terror that must overcome people who dread open spaces. The feeling was the same. Yearning for enclosure, for confinement, I was faced with nothing but the vista of freedom like a wide and empty plain. I shot up on that cot and I said: 'Why did you lie for me, Luigi? *Why,* in the name of God?'

"He said nothing. He turned again and went to the window. I kept raving at him. I called him names. I called him a swine and a dog and a bleeding sentimentalist. I asked him what had possessed him to do such an idiotic thing. But he was silent, and presently I asked him about Saverio. I asked him how, again, in the name of God, he pretended to carry out this incredible, enormous deception with Saverio still at large. Surely the cretin in one way or another would tip his hand, I said, and the true story would be out. '*Eccolo là!*' I said. 'The cop goes to jail. One peep out of the half-wit and they'll *bury* you, Luigi!' But Luigi was forbearing, considering this treatment I was handing him. 'Nonsense,' he said. 'Even if he were to talk, do you think they would believe the half-wit instead of me?' Beyond that, Saverio would be dealt with in the way he should have been fifteen years before. It would be the simplest thing in the world, he said, for the new *sergente* to make the appropriate move, subtly and in good time, toward placing the poor fool in the Salerno madhouse, where by all rights he should have lived these many years. As for Saverio himself, Luigi had seen him not twenty-four hours before in the house of this relative of his near the Villa Costanza. He was babbling happily and didn't seem to have any knowledge or recollection of what he had done. And Luigi fell silent again and looked at me with that grave earnest expression, and then turned away.

"I was monstrous. I don't know how he put up with me. I kept baiting him, you see. 'So it is to save your own skin,' I said. 'You lied for me and now you are afraid that by that lie you may hang yourself. Isn't that true, Luigi? Isn't that true?' I kept at him like this, and finally he said: 'Put it any way you wish.' I couldn't get a rise out of him. And I seemed to be halfway out of my head with fury at the fact that he had put me in this position, put me in a place where I couldn't give myself up. Suddenly he seemed to be just as guilty as I was in every way. And I said again: 'Why did you lie for me, Luigi? I did not ask that favor of you. Why did you do it, in the name of God?' And he was quiet for a while, and then he turned and said: 'I have given some thought to that, Cass, and still I do not exactly know. At first I thought it was because of my liking for you, and that I pitied you. I thought that perhaps I was performing an act of compassion by delivering you from a prison sentence. But now I am not so sure. My liking for you has not changed but I do not think any longer that it was an act of pity.' Then he paused for a bit and said: 'I think it was an act of correction. It was to keep you from the luxury of any more guilt. *Capito?*' And I said, '*Non capisco,*' and I think it was then that I must have gotten up from that cot, raging and cursing, hurling myself toward the door and saying that by God, he could hang, he could rot in jail until the end of time, but that I was catching the first bus to Salerno. A crime was a crime, I shouted, and I would suffer for it! I would suffer for it even if it meant I would have to drag him down in the bargain.

"And it was then that this own rage of his came on him—the first time I ever saw him explode. He leaped toward the door, too, and he fetched me a solid blow across the chest with his fist. I couldn't struggle, I was too weak and worn-out. And before I knew it I was flat down on my back again with one wrist manacled to the leg of the cot and he was standing over me, red-faced, just beside himself with outrage, shouting those words at me: *'Tu pecchi nell'avere tanto senso di colpa!* You *sin* in your guilt!' And he raised general hell.

"We calmed down, both of us. Neither of us said anything for a while. Then Luigi sat down beside the cot. He was silent for a long time, then he looked into my eyes and said: 'I would like to tell you a story.' And I said, calm now: 'A story about what, Luigi?' And he said: 'A story about how it is that I am a grown man and how I have only wept three times since I was a child. An Italian who has wept only three times since he was a child is neither much of an Italian nor much of a man. But I must tell you this story.' And I told him to go ahead. And he said this to me. He said: 'The first time was in Salerno during the war. I was only a boy then, and I had two baby brothers and three sisters. We lived in the back of the city, up near the hills, and when the British and the Americans made their landings on the beach my father thought we would be safe. We did not leave. The battle went on for several days, and presently the Germans withdrew. They withdrew through our part of the city and the Allies pursued them. A building near our house was used by the Germans as a command post. Only then, with the battle very near us, did my father decide to leave. He left first with my mother and four of my brothers and sisters. We had a dog which my mother loved very much and this dog had become lost, and I stayed behind with one of my baby brothers to search for the dog. We could not find the dog and the battle was coming nearer and so I decided to leave quickly. As we ran through the streets my baby brother, who was six, thought he saw the dog in a vacant lot and he called out to it and then ran back to fetch it. This was several blocks away from the German command post. Just as my brother ran into the vacant lot a British plane came over and dropped a bomb which must have been intended for the command post. I ducked, I could see the British target mark on the side of the plane. The bomb fell far short, into a building next to the vacant lot. There was some sort of fuel, oil or gasoline, stored in that building, for when the bomb hit it I saw a tremendous sheet of flame. I was knocked to the pavement by the concussion, but I was not hurt, and when I got up I heard a screaming. I looked into the lot and I saw my little brother running toward me, clothed in flame. He was *on fire!* He ran toward me, all ablaze, screaming in a way that I never knew a child to scream. It seemed as if the whole city were filled with the sound of his screams. It was like *angels* screaming. And then he fell to the street in front of me, blazing like a torch. He died right away. He was no more than a blackened little cinder. I wept.

" 'For a long time after that I never wept again. I grew older and I became what I am, a policeman, cold and impersonal, with few emotions. I never married, mistrusting and hating my own emotions, and their coldness. I never could escape the memory of my little brother, burning, nor did I believe in a God who could create a universe in which it would be possible for a single innocent child to suffer like that. Neither did I forget the British, who had dropped that bomb. Once you asked me why I became a Fascist, and I think I must have evaded your question, for it could not have been simple expediency that led to this choice. Rather I believe that part of it was my hatred of the British, if anything, though I possibly didn't realize it. Deep down I think I knew it was not rational of me to hate the British so. It had been an accident, no worse than a thousand others in the war, but often I could not help but think of that pilot and what he looked like, and after the war when the tourists came again I would see some young Englishman with his gray eyes and his casual arrogant manner and I would say to myself that it was he who had flown over Salerno and cremated my brother. I hated them, their arrogance and their smugness and their affected good manners, and I often vowed that in some way I would avenge myself on some Englishman for what he and his country had done to my brother.

" 'Then once not too long ago after I was stationed up here in Sambuco, there came a certain Englishwoman to the Bella Vista. She lived there for a whole spring and summer. She seemed to personify all that was mean and despicable in the Anglo-Saxon race. She was a hysteric little virgin in the menopause—stupid, ugly, rude, demanding, and parsimonious. She was the terror of the help at the hotel. She never tipped. There was something small and bitter about her that made people actually shy away from her in the streets. Her voice was harsh and strident. She was also very religious—an abstainer—and her tongue never once tasted Sambuco wine. She demanded much and gave nothing. I think she must have been slightly crazy. The people in the town despised her. What she was doing in this sunlight I shall never know. I always will remember her in the piazza, screeching in loud English, accusing some poor devil of a taxi driver of cheating her. Well, one morning when Parrinello was off duty, I was called to the hotel by Windgasser. He was terrified. He thought the Englishwoman was dead. After several days with the door locked one of the maids had gone in and had tried to rouse her from her bed, but she had not moved. Windgasser was afraid to look. I went upstairs and found her in her bed. She was dead, all right, cold as stone. I thought at first it was probably a heart attack. I sent one of the maids for the doctor, and while she was gone I looked around the room and after a bit I found a small empty bottle with its cap off. It was a bottle of sleeping pills, and so quite correctly I assumed she had committed suicide. It served her right, I thought. I remember looking down at her as she lay there, at the pinched, mean little face which even death had not softened, and I was filled with hatred and loathing. She had been a menace and a nuisance in life, and in death she was still, at least, a nuisance. She disgusted me. She had lain in that hot room for three days. She had begun to stink. And she was British. I hated her. Then I looked down and I saw a piece of paper crumpled up in her hand. I unclenched her fingers and removed the paper, and I saw that there were some words in English written on it that I could not understand. I called to Windgasser and he came, and I asked him to read the words to me. And he read them. And can you guess what they said? Can you guess what they said, Cass?' he said again.

"I looked up at Luigi and I said, 'No, I could not ever guess, Luigi.' And he said, in a sort of transliterated Italian which I didn't recognize at first: *'Certamente la bontà e la misericordia mi seguiranno per il resto della mia vita. . . .'* And I suddenly understood and said to Luigi, breaking in in English: 'Surely goodness and mercy shall follow me all the rest of the days of my life, and I will dwell in the house of the Lord forever.'

"And Luigi said: 'Yes, those were the words that were written on the paper. And I asked Windgasser to go away and when he had left I turned around and gazed down at the Englishwoman again. She still looked the same, ugly and ill-natured. But for some reason that I will never be able to explain I found myself weeping. I found myself weeping helplessly, and this was the first time since that day long ago when I saw my brother burning. I do not know why I wept. Perhaps it was because of the terrible loneliness that seemed to hover over that little room. Perhaps it was because

I knew that goodness and mercy had never followed this woman, ever, and there was something in this awful faith of hers that moved me, shabby as she was. Anyway, I suddenly thought of my baby brother and all the Englishmen I had hated for so many years and, still hating them, I sat down beside the body of this miserable little woman and I wept until I could weep no longer.'

"Luigi stopped talking for a moment. Then he said: 'I am not a sentimental man, you must know that. I accuse myself constantly of being stiff and cold, of failing to engage myself in the same kind of life that engages others. It is not natural, really. Sometimes I think I must have the blood of a Dutchman or a Scotchman in me. I do not know. But you ask me why it is that I lied for you in the way I did, and I can only tell you this. I can just tell you that the only other time I wept since I was a child was sometime during that day when Francesca died, and when I realized what you had done, and what would be the consequences for you if you were caught and tried. And would you believe something, Cass? It was not for you that I wept, nor for Francesca, but without self-pity for *myself*—because I understood something. When I wept in this extraordinary way, which is so rare for me, I could not help but think again of my brother and the Englishwoman and then all that had happened here in Sambuco, and I wept out of my own understanding. And that understanding was that this existence itself is an imprisonment. Like that Englishwoman we are serving our sentences in solitary confinement, unable to speak. All of us. Once we were at least able to talk with our Jailer, but now even He has gone away, leaving us alone with the knowledge of insufferable loss. Like that woman, we can only leave notes to Him—unread notes, notes that mean nothing. I do not know why this has happened, but it has happened, that is our condition. In the meantime we do what we can. Some day perhaps the jails will be empty. Until then to confine any but the mad dogs among us is to compound that knowledge of insufferable loss with a blackness like the blackness of eternal night. I have seen prisons, they are the closest thing to hell on earth. And you are not a mad dog. I suppose I lied to try to save you from this kind of banishment. But I suspect that that is not all. I know you and your hideous sense of guilt too well. You are a damnable romantic from the north, the very worst kind. In jail you would wallow in your guilt. As I say, I did not wish to allow you that luxury. Do you see now why I lied for you, my friend?'

"I lay there with that handcuff chewing at my wrist. He was wrenching at my very guts. I felt like I was being suffocated. I looked at him and finally I said: 'Luigi, you are a very singular Fascist policeman.' He got up and went to the window again and stood there, gazing out into the night. 'Suppose I don't go along with you?' I said. 'Suppose I go to Salerno anyway and hang us both? What would happen to you? And what would I get?' He didn't say anything for a while, then he said: 'I would get the limit —many years. I would get more than you. I don't know what you would get. Three years. Five. Maybe more, maybe nothing. After all, it might be said you had some provocation for what you did. But the jails are crowded. The bureaucracy. It would be months, years, before you even came to trial. Then who knows what you would get? You might get off with only the time you spent in detention—crime of passion. You might get twenty years. Justice in this country is insane as it is everywhere else. I read of a railway mail clerk in Verona, I think it was, who for defrauding the government of ten thousand lire received a sentence of fifteen years. On the other hand, in the south there was a man who killed his father-in-law with an ax and got twenty-one months. Possibly the father-in-law deserved it, and the railway clerk was a scoundrel, but it shows you how far we are from an idea of justice.'

"He turned around and faced me and after a second he said: 'For the sake of my own skin I do not think I would ever be so foolish as to do again what I have done. But now that I have done it, I believe that what I did was right. Is not my notion of justice as good as that of some judge who might not like your face and sentence you to five years? Ten years? I think true justice must always somehow live in the heart, locked away from politics and governments and even the law. Maybe it is a good thing I did not succeed in becoming a lawyer. I would have made a poor one. But now I have done what I think was right. And this is what I'm going to do. I'm going to unlock that manacle. Then you will be free to go. You may go to Salerno and implicate yourself—both of us. Or you may go free; you may leave here and go back to America, where you really belong. So I am going to strike off that manacle. Go to Salerno if you wish. Short of killing you, there is no way that I can stop you. But before you do, consider this. Consider a number of years in jail. It is more than a possibility. Think whether these years in jail, away from your family, will satisfy your guilt and your remorse in a way that is not satisfied by the remorse you will have to live with for the rest of your life. Then consider this, too, my friend. Simply consider your guilt itself—your other guilt, the abominable guilt you have carried with you so long, this sinful guilt which has made you a drunkard, and caused you to wallow in your self-pity, and made you fail in your art. Consider this guilt which has poisoned you to your roots. Ask what it was. Ask yourself whether it is not better to go free now, if only so that you may be able to strike down this other guilt of yours and learn to enjoy whatever there is left in life to enjoy. Because if by now, through what you have endured, you have not learned *something,* then five years, ten years, fifty years in jail will teach you nothing.' He came close to me. His face was shining with sweat. 'For the love of God, Cass,' he said. 'Consider the *good* in yourself! Consider hope! Consider joy!' Then he stopped. 'That is all I have to say. Now I am going to strike off that manacle.' And he struck it off. . . .''

"So as I told you, I came home in the dark with Luigi and I left him at the door of the palace and I went downstairs and sat there in the bedroom, looking out at the sea. Poppy was still asleep. It was close to dawn. On the gulf the fishing boats were coming in, these lights moving across the water like a crowd of stars adrift, and a pale glow the color of smoke came into the sky above Salerno and the coast sloping down toward Sicily. I could hear a dog barking, far off, and a cowbell clanking faintly somewhere against the hills. I thought of Francesca and Michele, and all that I had lost, and the grief came back in a wave, then it went away.

"I thought of Mason, too, but nothing happened. I was past all rage now, and grief. If I had been branded by fire I wouldn't have stirred, wouldn't have moved.

"Then you know, something as I sat there—something about the dawn made me think of America and how the light would come up slowly over the eastern coast, miles and miles of it, the Atlantic, and the inlets and bays and slow tideland rivers with houses on the shore, all shuttered and sleeping, and this stealthy light coming up over it all, the fish stakes at low tide and the ducks winging through the dawn and a kind of apple-green glow over the swamplands and the white beaches and the bays. I don't believe it was just because of this at all, but all of a sudden I realized that the anxiety and the anguish—most of it, anyway—had passed. And I kept thinking of the new sun coming up over the coast of Virginia and the Carolinas, and how it must have looked from those galleons, centuries ago, when after black night, dawn broke like a trumpet blast, and there it was, immense and green and glistening against the crashing seas. And suddenly I wanted more than anything in my life to go back there. And I knew I *would* go. . . .

"After a while I heard the two older kids whispering in the other room. Presently I heard them creep down the stairs and outdoors into the garden, and I heard Poppy stir in the bed behind me, and now in this rising morning light I heard the children call out to each other, and I could see them playing some game which was more like a dance. I didn't know what it was but there they were sort of strutting face to face and soundlessly clapping their hands together, like some vision of Papageno and Papagena, or something even more sweet, paradisaic, as if they were children not really of this earth but of some other, delectable morning before time and history. I watched them as if I were watching them for the first time in my life, or as in a dream.

"Then I heard Poppy stir again and she rose up in bed and I heard her say, 'Oh, Cass, you've come back!' And I went over to her and sat down beside her and took her in my arms. I tried to say something apologetic, but I just couldn't—then, at least. 'I thought you would never come back!' she said. 'I was worried frantic! Where have you been?' Well, I told her some sort of lie, figuring that there'd be time enough to tell her later where I *had* been. I calmed her down. And we talked for a while and she asked me a lot of questions, then after a bit she got to yawning and she asked me what time it was, and she lay back against the pillow. 'Well, as usual I don't understand about you,' she murmured as she drifted off, 'but I'm very glad you've come back.' So again I went over to the window and sat down.

"Now I suppose I should tell you that through some sort of suffering I had reached grace, and how at that moment I knew it, but this would not be true, because at that moment I didn't really know what I had reached or found. I wish I could tell you that I had found some belief, some rock, and that here on this rock anything might prevail—that here madness might become reason, and grief joy, and no yes. And even death itself death no longer, but a resurrection.

"But to be truthful, you see, I can only tell you this: that as for being and nothingness, the one thing I did know was that to choose between them was simply to choose being, not for the sake of being, or even the love of being, much less the desire to be forever—but in the hope of being what I could be for a time. This would be an ecstasy. God knows, it would.

"As for the rest, I had come back. And that for a while would do, that would suffice."

EPILOGUE

Dear Peter,

 Enjoyed your letter. Please excuse this card but am harried &
overloaded. Charleston will never become the Florence of the New
World Im afraid but the Sunday amateurs are keeping me busy &
Im up to my ears in work. Also, another trauma. Overpopulation.
Race-suicide. Poppy is having another baby next June & Ive been
walking around Charleston like a wounded elephant, staggering
with the usual pride & despair. Kinsey was distinctly wrong. A man
doesnt even get started until he moves in toward il mezzo del cam-
min. Anyway will write more later but wanted to tell you how glad
I am that N.Y. goes O.K. for you now. You didnt tell me her

name but hope you will bring her down here some day. Who was it in Lear who said ripeness is all. I forget, but he was right.

Buona fortuna,
Cass

THE INTERNATIONAL HOSPITAL OF THE
BLESSED REDEEMER
Order of the Daughters of Wisdom
Via Alessandro Manzoni, 38
NAPLES

16 December 195–

Mr. P. C. Leverett
30 West Eleventh Street
New York 11, N.Y., U.S.A.
Dear Mr. Leverett:

Returning from a visit to my home in France, I found on my desk your nice letter with its customary cheque. I am sending this cheque back to you. We are, as usual, grateful for your kindness, but this time I must inform you that we are declining your gift, and for the most extraordinary and wonderful reason! God has been most merciful to Luciano di Lieto! In my absence, I was told, Luciano made an amazing recovery from the state of coma in which he has been languishing these many, many months. Sister Véronique, who was attending him at the time, tells me that at one moment Luciano was in the profoundest slumber when, like the Phoenix risen from the ashes of his own affliction, he sprang up in bed complaining loudly of a violent hunger. Upon examination it was discovered that the pressure upon his brain had alleviated itself. Luciano was pronounced well by Dr. Cipolla the examining physician. After two weeks of convalescence (during which he ate like a pig and cheerfully berated our Sisters for their inattention) he was sent home to Pompei fully recovered. I knew that this would be joyous news to you, and am hastening to send this message off to you so that you may share in the knowledge of such a wondrous miracle! God's mercy is great!

Thanking you again for all your help, I beg to remain, as ever,
Sincerely Yours in Mary's Immaculate Heart,
Sister Marie-Joseph, D.W.
Director of Nursing Care

P.S.   Since writing the above, I was informed by Sister Véronique that Luciano was readmitted to the hospital this very morning, suffering from a broken collar bone. He incurred the injury by falling down a flight of stairs in his home in Pompei. The durability of this young man is truly remarkable! I have just now come from seeing him, where he is sitting up in bed, cheerfully smiling and eating like a pig. He sends his felicitations to you, and tells me that he has become affianced. I do somewhat pity the girl but I do not doubt that, if she is at all like Luciano, it will be a match of long duration. He will live to bury us all.

A B O U T   T H E   A U T H O R

WILLIAM STYRON was born in Newport News, Virginia, in 1925. He served three years in the United States Marine Corps, and after the war returned to complete his studies at Duke University.

Lie Down in Darkness, William Styron's first novel, appeared in 1951. For that initial work, he was awarded the Prix de Rome of the American Academy of Arts and Letters. Two years later his short novel, *The Long March,* was published. *The Confessions of Nat Turner,* published in 1967, received the Pulitzer Prize.

Mr. Styron, his wife and three children live in Roxbury, Connecticut.